FAMILY CODED

FAMILY CODED

J.H. Warrington

Print information available on the last page.

Rev. date: 10/12/2020

To order additional copies of this book, contact:
Xlibris
844-714-8691
www.Xlibris.com
Orders@Xlibris.com
814173

CHAPTER 1

"Quentin"

RING. RING! "Come on, what you doin'?" I bluntly asked. "I'm pausing the game, so you can answer your phone!" Dame said, attempting to be considerate. "Let me worry about that. You worry 'bout this comeback I'm putting together!" I responded, determined to win this game. RING. RING! "Comeback? You betta comeback off that high, and answer that phone. Before ya girl get in that ass!" Dame logically recommended. "Aw shit! Look at the phone and see who it is. Hurry Up!" I anxiously demanded, remembering that I was expecting an important call this morning. "Nigga don't rush me!" he responded, extending his head to glance over at my cell phone which was on the table next to him. "I was right, *it's Mani.*" he said casually, after looking at the phone screen. "Answer the phone!" I shouted realizing he may be right, in her anger at me.

RING. RING! "What?" he said after I disrupted his attempt to refocus his attention to the television screen. "Hurry up, damn!" I said watching him confusedly shuffle his head around as if he was confused of what was going on. "Aw, shit. Here, she don't want to talk to me, you get that shit." he said before picking up the phone and flinging at my feet in an attempt to get it to me. RIN! "Nigga, you coulda answered the fucking phone!" I irritably stated as I picked the phone from the floor. "Damn, my bad. And we was that close." he mocked, extending only his pointer finger and thumb together to illustrate his point. "Whatever, c'mon let's finish the game." I said as I looked down at the missed call screen and tossed it onto the couch.

"Call her back!" he logically suggested as he placed his controller onto the table. "It's cool, just c'mon." I said grasping the notion that I'd just hear about it later. "Well, at least check your messages, because I don't want no excuses when I bust ya ass and take ya change." he said, noticing the frustrated expression on my face. "Fuck it, c'mon." I uttered hopelessly. "Alright, I don't wanna hear that, *I was mad or depressed* shit when this game's over." he avowed as he picked his game controller back up. "Whatever." I said, trying to get my head back into the game.

A feeling of disappointment and regret began to creep up my spine as I looked at the television screen. "Shit, I'm down by four with a minute, nine seconds left. Why the fuck did I bet him forty dollars?" I asked myself as I resumed playing. "Wha'chu doin?" I asked him, impatiently awaiting the outcome of this game. "Gregs man, the game is over. It's a minute, nine left and I'm on your twenty-yard line. I score here, it just stretches it." he said, expressing the inevitable. "Then run your play!" I said, confident that I could still pull out a win. "Alright, but just remember, you are a linebacker, not a coach." he said in reference allocating a limit to my football knowledge. "Fumble, that's a fumble!" I said unreservedly jumping up and down. "That ain't no fumble!" Dame said as he was skeptical of the result. "It's a fumble. I'm a linebacker, remember? So, I knew you was goin' to the right." I sarcastically asked determined to still win the game. "In thirty-six seconds, I'm leaving here with forty dollars more in my pocket than I came with. Stop me if you can!" he confidently uttered while standing beside. "Can and will, junior! I got thirty seconds. You only up four. I score, I win." I calmly retorted, realizing his concentration breaking tactics. "Then, stop talking and play the game." he said with eager anticipation.

"NO!" I yelled as I exhausted my game-winning play attempt. RING. RING! "Interception!" he yelled excited by his triumph. "Shit!" I yelled bitterly disappointed. "And that's game! Run that change, boss." he said to me nonchalantly. I looked at him, then the television screen and tossed the controller onto the table. "Hand me that phone, I just want to see who it is." I said, walking past, him towards my bedroom. "I'll check the phone, you go find that coinage." he said, anxious to accept his winnings. "Alright, hurry up." I said, continuing to my bedroom to get him his money. RING. RING! "You hurry up." he said reaching for my phone. "We both know he can't beat me, and this *is* my *last* forty dollars." I whispered as the thought of snubbing him crossed my mind. "I can't do that, that's my homie. Besides, that shit fuck up your creditability." I thought as I collected the money from atop my dresser. RING. RING!

"Man, hurry up! It's somebody from ESPN!" Dame passionately yelled from the other room. "Don't answer it!" I promptly said trying to keep up with my avoidance of their calls. "You ghosting, ESPN?" Dame asked sounding both impressed and confused. RING... "Yeah, it's about the draft and my decision whether or not to enter. Here!" I confessed while hesitantly allocating him his money. "What the hell is this?" he mockingly questioned as he stared into his hand. "Nigga, it's your money. You don't want it, give it back." I willingly divulged as I watched him prepare to count the money. "Five fives and fifteen ones? What I look Puerto Rican?" he sarcastically asked after counting the multitude of bills. "You can always give it back!" I genuinely reiterated, extending my hand. "No, I'm good!" he mumbled jamming my last forty dollars into his pocket. "You running it back or what? We can play for ten like we usually do, if that's what you want. Forty was your idea." he asked. "Wait a minute let me check these messages first."

WELCOME TO VERIZON'S VOICE MESSAGING
SERVICE. PLEASE ENTER YOUR PASS CODE…
YOU HAVE 2 NEW MESSAGES AND 4 SAVED MESSAGES…
FIRST NEW MESSAGE, TODAY, 8:46AM…

(Hey Babe, I hope you're not still asleep, you have a ten thirty appointment with your new physical therapist, Mr. Nathaniel. How was last night's awards ceremony? I tried to stay up for your call afterwards, but my mom made turkey and I couldn't keep my eyes open. What is it about turkey that makes you sleepy? Anyway, I gotta go get ready for homeroom. The whole school is waiting to find out if your entering the draft, it's hard for them to believe that I don't even know. I'll talk to you later, I love you, bye-bye. Oh yeah, Danny Graham said hi.)

SECOND NEW MESSAGE, TODAY 8:58AM…

(Good morning Mr. Gregory, this is the personal assistant of Meredith Clary calling to remind you that College Gameday will be being broadcasted from Penn State University on the eleventh. And of your verbal arrangement to speak with them. Thank you for your time and attention and please be assured that we're looking forward to seeing you.)

FIRST SAVED MESSAGE… click!

"Damn, Dame." I sighed frustrated by my morning to this point. "What?!" Dame blankly answered as he continued to wait for my response to playing again. "Nothing." I crossly said before tossing my phone onto the end table. "That girl must got some good pussy." Dame murmured assuming he knew why I was upset. "What you say?" I harshly inquired as I stared at my friend with displeasure. "I'm just saying, for her to be two hundred some odd miles away, and you still have you jump the way you do, damn!" Dame tensely explained. "If you ever refer to my girl pussy again, we goin' at it." I calmly vowed. "You trying to run another game or what?" he regretfully asked trying to distract the topic. "I can't. I gotta get dressed and get to the physical therapist." I said opening the ironing board. "Alright then. I'mma go back to my spot and count this money again. Make sure you ain't short me. Till the next time." he mockingly said while opening the door to exit. "Til the next time, Dame." I scoffed as he closed the door. "Damn, I needed that forty dollars." I regretfully stated as I pulled the ironing board into my bedroom.

Ring. Ring!

> **Omar Gregory**
> **302-555-8974**

"Right on time." I uttered looking at his name on the phone screen. "Yo dad! What's up?" I said happy about the possibility of getting some money back. "Good morning Quentin. How's my tuition money going? I mean... how's school?" he sarcastically asked. "Aww shit." I thought to myself, realizing that it was going to be one of those conversations. "You say that like you pay full tuition. I got a scholarship, member." I said reminding him that I wasn't as deep into his pockets as he pretended it was. I activated the speakerphone and placed my phone on the dresser so I could freely dispose of the iron and board. "It's re-member, and you *re*member it's a partial scholarship. Which means, they pay part of the money, and I pay part of the money. Nowhere in that equation did you hear Quentin pays part of the money." he said sardonically. "I pay with my sweat!" I sternly articulated while closing the ironing board. "Are you sweating now?" he calmly asked. "No." I stated unenthusiastically, anticipating his response. "Well, I just wrote a check." he sarcastically disclosed. "Dad, we gonna go through this every time you call?" I sorrowfully asked realizing that me actually getting to borrow some money was steadily becoming more fragile.

"No. You're right, son. I'm sorry. I called to find out how you're doing?" he sincerely questioned. "I'm alright." I genuinely replied loud enough for him to hear while I stepped out of the room. "You need anything?" he condescendingly asked. "I could use some money." I admitted curiously throwing out to see how it'd land. "Quentin you just got a hundred dollars from me on Friday. You trying to tell me you broke already?" he disappointedly asked. "Yes sir. I had a tutorial this morning that costed me forty dollars." I disappointedly unveiled while I leaned in close to the bathroom mirror. "What kind of course loads are you taking, that's costing you forty additional dollars a class?" he asked bewildered by the particulars of this morning's lesson. "Don't worry 'bout it, dad. I'll be alright. But I do have to go. I have a ten thirty appointment." I hopelessly divulged as I applied my toothbrush with paste. "Yeah, I heard. With a, Mr. Nathaniel?" he intuitively asked. "Yup." I said, before shoving the toothbrush into my mouth. "And who's Mr. Nathaniel?" he curiously probed. "A physical therapist that coach recommended." I indistinctly explained as I continued to brush my teeth. "I see." he said calmly. "Can I ask you a question?" he continued to ask. "Here we go. Here comes the bullshit!" I thought to myself before I answered. "What am I gonna tell you, no? Shoot." I said spitting toothpaste into the sink. "Why is it that I have to hear about the things you have going on, from Emily? And even she has to wait to hear it from Imani." he judgmentally asked. "I don't know dad. But honestly, we really don't talk like that." I realistically admitted while dowsing my washcloth warm water. "Wha'chu don't think I want to know?" he pathetically asked. "Nah, I ain't say that." I sympathetically stated. "You don't remember my number?" he continued just as pathetic. "Yes dad, I remember the number." I guiltily replied as I wiped my washcloth across my face. "Then why?" he asked genuinely inquired. "I don't... Where's Ma?" I asked exhausted by the interrogation. "She's at work. I'm at my office, but I get the idea. I'll talk to you later?" he asked recognizing my irritation. "I'll call you after practice." I said as I tossed the cloth on the towel rack and exited the bathroom. "Alright. I love you Quentin." he said in an almost whisper. "Love you too, dad." I said sincerely as I ended the call.

CHAPTER 2

"Omar"

BUZZ... "MR. GREGORY, YOU HAVE A CALL ON LINE TWO."

"Who is it, Toni?" I politely asked while staring at my computer monitor.

"IT'S GWENDOLYN LEWIS, FROM THE DEPARTMENT OF NATURAL RESOURCES & ENVIRONMENTAL CONTROL."

"Thank you, Toni. And if Tracey calls put her right through." I firmly insisted while half-heartedly considering answering line two.

"UMM... SHE CALLED EARLIER WHILE YOU WERE ON THE LINE."

"Okay, I need you to get her back on the line! And tell Ms. Lewis I'll return her call later." I resolutely requested while waiting for an email response from Elliot.

"YOU GOT IT."

CHAPTER 3

"Tracey"

"A reminder, the research outline for your second quarter reports are due Thursday. And let's not forget, ladies & gentlemen, these reports are one eighth of your grade, each! Which means all four reports..." I started before pausing in astonishment at the timing of my phone's chime. RING. RING! "...combine for half your grade point average. Please excuse me, class." I beseeched as I quickly scooped my cell phone from my desk and looked down at the display screen.

> **Hubbie's Work**
> **302-555-9001**

"Hello." I said after answering the call. I moved swiftly toward a corner in the rear of the room. "Good morning, Mrs. Gregory" Toni formally greeted as if we weren't friends. "Hey Toni, what's up. And what's with the, Mrs. Gregory?" I responded trying to relax her mood. "Well, I am, at work. The reason why I'm calling is to find out why you let your husband out of the house, in shoes and tube socks?" Toni said with a grin so big, I could hear it through the phone. "Not my husband!" I said, pretending to be in shock while knowing what Toni was saying, wasn't true. "Yes, your husband!" she said laughing. "Mr. GQ Magazine?!" I asked playing along with her foolishness. "Yeah, girl. I'm goin' put him through so you can say something, to him." she said continuing to laugh at her prank. "Alright, Toni. See you, Sunday." I said to my husband's assistant. "Sunday?" she asked bewildered by my comment. "Toni, I know you didn't forget" I asked concerned that she forgot and made other plans. "Oh no, I didn't forget! I didn't forget, see you Sunday." Toni said, still a little confused, hoping to figure it out before Sunday.

CHAPTER 4

"Omar"

BUZZ... "MR. GREGORY, YOUR WIFE IS ON LINE 1"

"Thank you, Toni" I gratefully acknowledged before pushing away my keyboard. "Tracey!" I happily exclaimed while picking up my pen to tap on the desk. "Hello Omar." she delightfully replied. "Have you talked to your son lately?" I enviously asked. "Hello, Omar!" she said again, now with a little bit of an attitude. "I'm sorry. Good morning Tracey." I said as the bell to end her 3rd period class loudly exploded behind her.

"Okay you guys, I'll see you all tomorrow and don't forget about tonight's assignments. Alysha, take this thing and don't bring it into my class again!" Tracey barked at her student while trying her best to sound threatening. "Good morning Omar. And to answer your question, no I haven't talked to him. Not since, Saturday." Tracey replied, after returning her attention to me. "He called you?" I asked slightly offended. "Yeah. What's wrong?" she asked seemingly concerned with my tone. "He doesn't call me!" I aggressively admitted. "And this worries you?" she replied at a loss. "Yeah, it does." I genuinely admitted. "He doesn't call you, because the two of you are constantly bumping heads. You push each other's buttons and he's not always in the mood for it." she credibly acknowledged. "That's not true, is it?" I defensively asked. "Yes, Omar it is. But that has always been your relationship. When he's home, he's either in his room, or out of the house. That clingy, talk about everything relationship you have, that's you and Emily. Not you and Quentin!" I said trying to bring Omar to reality. "You mean to tell me that my son, avoids me?" I asked now back to being offended. "About as much as you avoid him!" she said in defense of Quentin. "So, what do I do?" I asked confusingly. "What do you mean, what do you do? This has been your relationship with him since... forever." she calmly answered. "Tracey, this is scary." I worriedly confessed. "Omar, what do you see when you look in the mirror?" she formally asked now sounding like a teacher. "Where are you headed with this?" I frightfully asked while scribbling circles on a file folder. "I want you, to see you as I see you. As everyone else sees you. Confident, intelligent, strong willed, funny, stubborn, caring, honest, and even sometimes cocky." she encouragingly stated to prove her point. "Don't forget cute." I said with a kind of man-like blush. "And of course, handsome. Cute is for bunnies and Easter dresses!" she said with a smile I could hear through the phone.

"My point is, these are all of the things Quentin aspires to be. If you don't see you in Quentin and vice versa, then you are right to question your relationship with him. But if you do, and I know you do, just continue to be there when he needs you and he'll do the same." Tracey wisely advised as she always does. "I love you Tracey!" I sincerely said hoping it was as powerful to her as it was to me. "I love you, too Omar." she whispered before ending the call.

Buzz... "Toni." I called out into the intercom.

"Yes, Mr. Gregory."

"I need you to get that woman from DNREC back on the phone." I insisted after being refreshed by my wife.

"Yes sir. Anything else?"

"Yeah. Have a potted orchid sent to Tracey at work. Pay whatever you must, to get it sent there before the end of the school day. Then have a bouquet of lilies sent to my house this afternoon preferably after four." I happily requested.

"Yes, sir!"

"Toni, are you smiling?" I intuitively asked of my assistant.

"Yes, sir. I like to see men pay that much attention to the people who keep them sane. Keep them happy."

"You're right, if you appreciate someone you should show it. And with that being said, I now need you to send a dozen long stemmed red roses to your house, as well." I appreciatively insisted.

"Aww, Thank you."

"No, thank you Toni." I charmingly countered before reluctantly trying to redirect my attention to my work. "I really don't know what I would do, without that woman!" I genuinely admitted while still staring vainly at the screen. "Alright Omar, get focused. You have a lot of work in front of you and if you want to get out of here at a decent time, you need to get cracking." I said to motivate myself and get my mind off my wife.

DEPARTMENT OF HEALTH AND SOCIAL SERVICES

"DMS - Serving Those Who Serve Delaware"

Division of Management Services

A proposal to modify Delaware State reservoirs' minimum health code standards is required to adhere to new federal health code sta|

Buzz... "Mr. Gregory, Ms. Lewis from DNREC is on line 1."

"Thank you, Toni." I graciously stated. "Good morning Ms. Lewis, how may I help you this morning." I curiously asked in regards to the email she sent. "Well Mr. Gregory, it's in regard to your interest in employment with our company." she confidently stated. "Employment with your company? DNREC?" I asked bewildered by her inaccuracy. "Mr. Gregory, you sound as confused as I was, when I heard of your interest. Of course, my confusion was overwhelmed with excitement with the possibility of a person of your stature, joining our team. But none the less, there was some confusion." she said full of enthusiasm. "Ms. Lewis I'm sorry, but I don't have a clue what you're talking about." I confusedly aggressed while pondering how this oversight could've possibly have happened. "Mr. Gregory, I have here in front of me, an e-mail stating your interest of employment in our company. An interest, in our recently opened Senior Application Support Specialist position. Which we thought was peculiar, because it would be a very significant demotion in pay, responsibility & status, when compared to the position you already hold with the State department." she uttered further confused with each passing word. "I'm glad you guys over there thought that was abnormal. Or, peculiar as you called it. Ms. Lewis, I never sent that e-mail. And at this time, I have an extreme lack of interest in working for DNREC. Thank you for the consideration, though." I condescendingly acknowledged while still bewildered at how this error was created. "Guess Tracey was right." I conceitedly admitted to myself.

"I see, well thank you for your time Mr. Gregory." she disappointedly voiced. "Ms. Lewis, do you mind my asking the sender from which the e-mail was received?" I determinedly questioned wanting to get to the bottom of this. "No, not at all. It was T underscore Blackwell at yahoo dot com. And just so you know, the return telephone number posted to the e-mail was not your number either. At least that's what the person who answered the phone stated." she irritably divulged, upset with the fact that someone was toying with her.

"Phone number? You mind giving me that too." I curiously questioned about this threat to my identity. "Not at all, it's area code two, one, five, five, five, five, nine, seven, one, one." she said welcoming me to the information. "Thank you very much, Ms. Lewis." I gracefully stated. "Thank you, Mr. Gregory. And you have a nice day." she mournfully replied. "You do the same." I promptly declared anxious to find out who's meddling in my life.

To: t_blackwell@aol.com

Subject: Identity Inquiry

Good afternoon.

My name is Omar Gregory and the basis of my inquiry is an explanation of the connection between my employment status and this e-mail address. I have been recently informed that the Department of Natural Resources & Environmental Control has received false information from me via this address. I would appreciate it if I received an immediate reply, as this situation needs to be remedied as soon as possible. Thank you for your time and attention

---

"Toni" I said sternly into the intercom.

"YES, MR. GREGORY"

"Did you send the flowers?" I anxiously asked while I carefully examined my computer monitor.

"ALL TAKEN CARE OF."

"Thank you" I gratefully replied.

"MR. GREGS, YOU SOUND FUNNY. IS THERE SOMETHING WRONG?"

"No, I'm fine. Can you come in here for a second before you go to lunch?" I courteously requested.

"Sure thing"

Tap. Tap. Tap! "Come in, Toni." I cordially called out towards the door. "What's up?" Toni pronounced with a small tone of excitement. "I need you to do me a favor." I delightfully appealed. "What's that?" Toni replied seeming slightly disappointed. "Don't say it like that. It's really not that bad, and it comes with a perk." I said trying to psyche her into it. "Ok. What's the favor?" she adorably inquired smiling after hearing the word perk. "I need you to take this money to a Western Union, to send to Quentin. You do this for me, and I'll allow you an extra thirty minutes for lunch. My Western Union thing should only take you ten of those. Which gives you twenty more minutes to put on make-up, or try on an extra pair of shoes, or have another latte, or whatever it is that you do during your lunch break. What do you do during your lunch break?" I curiously asked pretending to be interested.

"Nothing really." she said in an almost whisper, trying not to show her blushing. "What was that?" I questioned, bewildered by her. "What was, what?" Toni whispered, pretending to be oblivious to what I was referencing. "Are you alright, Toni?" I awkwardly questioned as she headed towards the door. "I'm fine." she quietly responded standing behind the door, just out of sight of onlookers. "You know… you have a way of looking at a woman that's inviting. And the thoughts that I had for a brief second, are somewhat inappropriate. I'll be back in an hour." she said, looking like she was now in a hurry. "Inappropriate?! All I asked was, what do you do during your lunch…" I uncomprehendingly uttered as she scurried out of the office.

Knock. Knock! "Yo, Omar. Where dat fine ass secretary? Whoa!" Hassan interrupted pouring thru the open door of my office. "Maybe when you are feeling better, we can do the lunch thing together. Then, I can find out for myself." I suggested while giving a sharp eye to Hassan for barging into my office. Toni responded with a smile. "If you can keep up. I get a lot done in 30 minutes." she responded before giving me a wink and walking out of my office. "What, man?!" I harshly questioned while watching Toni seductively walk to the elevator. "Nigga, I came……" Hassan defensively started "Close the door!" I sternly interrupted. "…. I came to find out what you were doing? And to see if you wanted to run down Donatello's to get a calzone." he continued now less willingly as he stood to close the door.

"Nah. I'm cool, I got a lot of work to do." I honestly stated while gesturing to the monitor. "You say the same shit every time I come pass here." he uttered pretending to be disappointed. "That's cause I'm at work." I replied with a sarcastic smile. "Whatever nigga! I just heard you ask Toni out." he skeptically acknowledged. I couldn't respond, I looked at him like he was stupid. He must've got the message, because he started laughing at himself. "I get it, though! As bad as she is, I would have hit that her third day here. She been here for what, five, six, months?" he arrogantly exclaimed. "It ain't like somebody goin' tell on you." he quietly added with a proud smile. "You're right, because there's nothing to tell. I asked her to lunch. A friendly outing, like the one that she's having with Tracey on Sunday. Open that!" I clarified loud enough to get my point across, while pointing to the window. "She going out with Tracey?!" he asked surprised. "Yeah." I nonchalantly responded. "No." he yelled, excitedly disappointed. "She goin fuck it up!" he anxiously continued to verbalize. "Fuck what up? What are you talking about?" I asked like I didn't already know his intentions. "I want Toni! That's why you don't want Toni." he seriously conceded. "Toni's not interested in you." I said while punching keys on the keyboard, trying to finish up my work.

"How you know that?" he shockingly asked. "She came pass the house about two weeks ago. We were outside barbequing, you called, and she started waiving her hands so I didn't tell you she was there. Then, when we hung up, she mentioned to me that you came at her. Then she asked me how to basically, let you down easily. She said the two of you wouldn't fit, or something like that." I said with my head down into my keyboard, mockingly grinning. "What she mean, we don't fit? The Radisson got queen size beds! Why didn't you tell me, she shot me down?" he asked smiling abundantly. "For the same reason you didn't tell me you cracked on her, I ain't got nothing to do with that. Now, do me a favor and go head to lunch, so I can get some work done." I said trying to end this conversation directly. "Well since you not going with me, let me use your truck?" he promptly asked after effortlessly brushing off the Toni debacle. "For What!" I asked hoping it was for a different reason than usual. "Because I don't feel like going back to the office, so I might as well see who or what I can get into." he said nonchalantly. "Well, I don't have my truck! I got Tracey car, and you know she not for that." I falsely disclosed with my head down to prevent him from being able to look into my eyes. "Stop lying!" he demanded, doubtful of my explanation. "C'mon man!" he continued. "Here, and don't leave SHIT in my truck!" I demanded as I hesitantly handed him the key. "Good looking" he said before snatching the key as he heading towards the door. "Where your keys at?" I asked remembering the last time we switched he forgot to give me his keys. "Here. My bad!" he said tossing them out of his pocket before exiting the office. "Close the door, man." I said before Hassan could get too far out of the office. "Finally! Ok Omar, let's get started." I said trying to motivate myself.

BUZZ.... "EXCUSE ME MR. GREGORY. IS IT OKAY IF I
BRING YOUR TRUCK BY YOUR HOUSE THIS EVENING?

"Go find something to do man, damn!" I barked becoming snickering at his ill-timed prank.

"SEVEN THIRTY."

"Yeah alright, whatever man. Seven thirty!" I barked confirming his concept so that I could resume concentrating on the job at hand.

CHAPTER 5

"Quentin"

"Like a sprained ankle, ain't nothing to play with." I resonated aloud as I approached a red light. I smiled noticing the sizeable assembly of people at the bus stop. "Thank God I ain't gotta do that." I thought as I observed the collection of familiar faces that I pass every day on campus. "If they don't recognize you Pam, they don't know me well enough to ask for a ride." I said to my car as I brushed my hand across the top of her dashboard. I turn and faced forward to give a check to the red light, making sure it hasn't turned green yet. There was a small crowd of people crossing the street in front of me. Just more familiar faces, but one more familiar than the rest, Tasha. "Damn, I hope she don't see me!" I said aloud while turning the music down, to reduce the draw of attention. "Damn, she fine though!" I whispered, surprising myself by the statement. "Stop looking at her ass, Que!" I scolded as my eyes redirected themselves to her laughing smile and luminous eyes.

HONK. HONK! "I know I didn't just do, what I think I did!" I said disgustingly confused. "Just wave and keep it moving." I mumbled to myself in an attempt to correct my stupidity. "Where you going?" I yelled out of the window as she stepped onto the sidewalk. "Hey Gregs, I'm going to the mall!" she yelled back, smiling from ear to ear. "C'mon. Meet me across the street." I said before crossing the green light and pulling over as not to hold up traffic. I swept my hand across my shirt and pants to knock off any dust or crumbs. I then picked up my brush from the passenger seat, and grabbed the bottle of cologne I keep in the glove compartment to freshen up. "What the hell are you doing?" I asked myself as I changed my music from rap to the first soothing melody that I could find.

"Hey you." she pleasantly said standing outside of the passenger door. "Hey Gregs." a female's voice immediately resonated from behind her. I look past her for the person waiting behind her for her to open the door, so she could climb into the back seat. It was Jax, the sister of J.T., who just happened to be Tasha's man. "Thank, God!" I thought with a smile.

"What's up Jax?" I said excitedly surprised at her presence. She was the obstacle I could use to hide what I was thinking about Tasha. "Where you going?" Tasha asked as she closed the door. "I gotta go to Dicks to get these shoulder weights recommended by my physical therapist." I openly disclosed before pulling off. "Oh, okay." Tasha said seeming interested. "You guys just going to hang out at the mall?" I asked pretending to really care. "No, we'll be in and out." Jax said from the back seat, reminding us that she was back there. "What you listening to? This is not, what was playing when you stopped us!" Tasha said with a smile, like she believed I had intentions. "What you got plans?" Jax added from the back seat smiling profusely. It was no secret that Jax wanted me, as she was very pronounce about it. But it was also no secret that I had a girl, and even if I didn't, I did not want her.

"Is that better?" I embarrassingly asked as I changed the music to something a little more up tempo. "I didn't say change it, I asked what it was all about. I liked the song to be honest." Tasha replied with a comforting smile. "I didn't think that loud, curse filled rap music would be appropriate for riding with women." I said thinking as quick as possible. "You mean with a woman. You mean with Tasha! I saw your face when I got in the car, Gregs. You had no idea that we were together at that bus stop. And you know it!" Jax interjected from the back seat. "What do one thing, got to do with the other? No, I didn't know you were with her. But I'm doing the same thing I would've done if you weren't here. Giving her a ride to a mall, that I was already on my way to!" I sternly stated upset by having to be on the defensive, in my own car! "Stop that shit, Jax! Excuse my language, Gregs." Tasha said as she saw my eyebrow raised by her choice of words.

"I know what you're getting at, and that ain't cool. He's being nice by giving us a ride and you insulting him in his car. If he opened the door and put us both out, you couldn't blame him, could you?" Tasha said giving me a wink as she came to my defense. "God damn!" I thought as that may possibly have been the sexiest wink I've ever seen.

RING. RING! "Where's my cell phone" I thought while searching the floor between my legs and the center console for my phone. "Can you sit up a little? I think you sitting on my phone." I embarrassingly asked of Tasha while inadvertently looking at her ass. "Sorry." she softly said while following my eyes behind her. "Don't be sorry, unless you broke it." I said jokingly, smiling to comfort her. I waited impatiently for Tasha to lean forward so I could get to my phone. I felt Jax's eyes pressed on us as I continued to look behind Tasha for the glow of my phone.

RING. RING! I looked back at Jax, who was still staring at me to be sure I was looking for my phone, and not at Tasha's ass which was a little exposed in a half shirt and low-cut jeans. I'd be lying if I said I wasn't tempted. But I'm Imani's man. That was my reason, my only reason for not looking! "Fuck Jax, and anything she was thinking in that backseat. Whether she know it or not, her brother can't beat me!" I thought to myself confidently. "Here. It was on the floor back here." Jax said as she handed me my phone. RING. RING!

Moms
302-555-8972

"Hey Ma! What's up?" I said glad it was her and not Imani or even worse, big mouth Storm. "Hey baby, you alright?" she said as concerned as always. "Yeah mom, I'm fine." I said to let my present company know, that it was not my girl on the phone. "That's good. I talked to your father, he's upset 'cause you two don't talk." she openly acknowledged. "I told him I would call him, after practice. I don't know what he wants me to do." I said concerned but bewildered by my father's aspirations. "Okay. What time is practice?" she quickly asked to know what time to expect me. "Six, forty-five, we should be done about nine." I said anxious to get her off the phone. "Good. That way Emily and I can both talk to you. Well, I'm going to let you go, and I'll talk to you later. I love you, Quentin" she sincerely divulged. "Love you too, Ma." I said as before ending the call. "Awww, ain't that sweet. You a momma's boy!" Tasha said with a snicker as she took off her earrings. "I think it's attractive, it's valiant!" Jax uttered trying to get back on my good side. I looked at Tasha, then Jax and I chuckled. "Y'all got jokes." I scoffed before turning my attention to the road.

They began to talk amongst themselves and I lost myself in the music until we reached the mall. "Thanks, Gregs." Jax said nonchalantly while squeezing out the backseat to exit the car. "No problem." I replied just as nonchalantly. "Thank you, Que." Tasha seductively said as she gave me another wink before she put her shades back on and turned to catch up with her friend. RING. RING!

Moms
302-555-8972

"Hey, babe!" I said watching Tasha walk away. Her seductive walk enhanced by her high heeled sandals. Throwing her ass from side to side, like she was purposely doing it to tease me. "Hey, Sexy! I missed you this morning. You overslept?" Imani lovingly interrogated in the same concerned voice I've grown so custom to. "No, I got caught up in this football game with Dame." I hesitantly admitted while walking through the parking lot. "I thought practice wasn't 'til tonight?" she confusedly uttered. "No. It wasn't practice, it was Madden." I reluctantly confessed while holding the door for an elderly couple walking behind me. "I guess they got to wherever they had to get to, fast." I thought while glancing around for Tasha and Jax. "Huh?" I said not paying attention to whatever Imani just said. "I said… was it for money? What are you doing?!" Imani irritably inquired because she was being ignored. "Babe, I'm in Dicks. Let me call you when I get back in the car?" I requested rushing her off the phone so I can get everything I have to do, done. "Don't forget to call me. I love you Baby." she whispered disappointed. "Love you, too! But you know that already." I confidently answered. I smiled after hearing her remind me that I was loved, by the most important fragment of my life.

"Fuck these other broads out here. What the hell was I thinking? One night with Tasha, compared to a lifetime with Mani, that's dickhead logic. You know what, I'm going home this weekend to see my girl!" I mumbled to myself as I searched the store. "This shit better work, for eighty-nine dollars!" I thought as I read the box while walking back to the car.

3-0-2-5-5-5-2-1-1-2 "Hey babe." Imani enticingly whispered. "Don't talk like that, you make me want to come home right now!" I requested while pulling out of my parking space. "If you got it like that, come home to me, right now!" she insisted pulling off an attempt to be sexy and sarcastic simultaneously. "I wish I did have it like that." I sorrowfully responded. "How much money did you lose today playing that game?!" she disappointedly asked. "Forty." I shamefully admitted while lowering the music volume. "I need you to start being more responsible, Que." she said seeming more nervous than angry. "What's wrong?" I nervously asked. "Talk to you about it tomorrow. I'm about to lay down, I got a headache." she sullenly divulged. "Imani, it's three fifteen in the afternoon! Why will this be the last time we speak today?!" I asked as I noticed Jax and Tasha at the bus stop outside the mall entrance. I hit my horn and gestured for them to get in the car. "I'm tired and you have a late practice which by the time it's over, I'll probably have woken up, ate and went back to sleep for the night." she apprehensively clarified. "So, I'll talk to you in the morning, okay?" she hopelessly requested as I unlocked the door for Tasha and Jax. "Yeah, alright then." I pathetically responded before ending the call and turning back up my music volume.

"Awww Jax, he missed us!" Tasha said she held the chair forward so Jax could climb in. "That was fast!" I honestly acknowledged, referring to their time spent shopping. Tasha got in, closed the door and I pulled off. "In all honesty, we were trying to shop fast." Jax admitted while organizing the bags, creating more room to stretch out. "So, we could possibly catch a ride back... with you." Tasha interrupted as she kept her eyes on Jax, to be sure she didn't notice her flirting looks at me.

"Brooklyn's bad boy back again... and my back's to the wind." Tasha sang along with the rap. "What?" she confusedly asked after noticing me stare at her. "Nothing." I uttered both shocked and impressed by her knowledge of the song lyrics. "I like this song. I like almost all Lenny Kravitz's music." Tasha admitted trying to solve the puzzled look on my face. "I'm not too fond of rap. But the little bit of rap I do like, is usually something from either Jay Z or Outkast. But I like Kravitz, a lot." she confessed purposely promoting her music preferences. "What else do you like?" I curiously asked seizing after we both noticed Jax falling asleep. "Are you trying to get to know me, Quentin?" she flirtatiously asked. "Just making conversation." I said trying to be nonchalant. "Well, in that case. I don't know. I don't know what I like." she said being sarcastically honest. "Huh? You, don't know what Tasha likes? Favorite pastime? Animal? Nothing?" I asked trying not to seem too obvious.

"I don't know what I like." she answered honestly. "I like to shop." she continued lifting her bags from the floor beneath her feet to show proof. "Earlier, you called me Quentin. No one here calls me Quentin, not since the first two weeks of my freshman year. You know, this's my second year and some of my closest friends don't use my first name. Some of them don't even know it." I added, before she could answer. "Last year, I found your ID on a table in Joegies. I had it for about 3 days, before I turned it in to Nittany Hall." she hoping to seem heroic. "I remember that! I didn't know who turned it in. I guess I should thank you." I voiced, surprised she remembered my name for such a long time. "You're welcome, Quentin Hassan Gregory."

We talked the entire ride back to campus, with an interruption or two from Jax's snoring, which we laughed over. I told her about Imani. She told me about her boyfriend at home in Philly, and some details about her relationship with J.T. here at school. I found a parking space on the street in front of Nittany Hall. Tasha turned to wake up Jax, which gave me the perfect opportunity to get look at her ass. She turned back toward me with a wink which led me to believe, she exposed it on purpose. "Bye, Gregs. Thanks, again." Jax said as she climbed out of the car, leaving the bags behind. Tasha rolled her eyes at Jax before she reached into the backseat to retrieve their property. "You going to be busy later?" Tasha curiously asked as she collected her bags and the bags left by Jax. "I got practice. But you know that already, 'cause J.T. has practice." I composedly conceded exiting the car. "Yeah, I know. I also know, it's over at nine. So again... will you be busy later?" she asked handing me my Dicks bag which she snatched out of the backseat with her things. "I got practice 'til nine, and an eleven o'clock curfew. So, my night is pretty much null and void. Why, you got plans?" I nonchalantly asked while trying to read her body language. "Don't know... maybe." she intriguingly whispered before turning to walk away with her bags in hand. "Damn, she got a fat ass." I said to myself while watching that walk for the second time today. RING. RING!

Emily Gregory
302-555-8973

CHAPTER 6

"Emily"

"What's wrong, Storm?" Quentin said dismally like I was already getting on his nerves. "Why it gotta be something wrong?" I asked harshly, upset by the way he answered the phone. "Cause that's usually when you call me."

I opened the door to London's car and got in. I was just glad that the school day was over and was ready to get from near it. "I was calling to find out if you talked to Imani?" I stated sarcastically. Earlier, for a hot second. Why?" he asked concerned something was wrong. "No reason." I answered pretending to be nonchalant. "Then why you call me, Storm? If there's no reason." he asked continuing to sound annoyed by my call. "Where you at?" I asked hearing the clang of his keys in the background. "Walking into my room!! Again, then why are you calling me?" he said with an attitude. "Why you gotta act like that?!" I asked knowing that I was starting to frustrate him. "Because you called me for no reason, Storm!" he continued with frustration. "I called you to find out if you talked to your girl. 'Cause I talked to your girl. And you, need to talk to your girl!" she forcefully insisted.

"What's going on? Y'all together now? he asked with frustration and desolation. "No, we're not together, she's home as far as I know. I'm on my way to this studio with London. Her cousin met this producer in Wilming...." I attempted to say before he interrupted. "Okay, we need to speed this conversation up, I got practice soon!" he said harshly. "Just call your girl man!" I retorted sharply. "Somebody needs to tell me something!" he snapped more frustrated than he originally sounded. "If you called your girl like I said, then you would know something!" I yelled offended by his anger. "You called me to tell me to call her? This the shit I'm talking about, Em!" he yelled desperately frustrated. "First of all, pump your brakes. Then call your girl and find out if you have a reason to be upset! Then, you can call me later if you need to." I said softly with an early feeling of remorse. I hung up the phone before he had any chance to respond.

"What you stopping for? I'm trying to get to this producer that you keep telling me about!" I declared as London pulled into the handicap parking spot at the Seven-Eleven. "I need cigarettes. Calm down girl, damn." she said as she opened the car door. "You need to hurry up." I yelled out of the car window as she walked into the store. I pulled my auxiliary cord out of my bag, plugged it into the stereo, and got out of London's car. "Ya'll bitches is bitch made, I pop out the cut like a switch blade. While riding this beat, that Swizz made." I recited to the music while standing outside of London's car. "You watching me clappin' like a game show. Let the lames know, it's the main hoe, with that same flow and it's a shame though, cause when I die it'll be with Spit like, Ramo!" I harmoniously voiced while going over the lyrics that I planned to record at the studio.

"Female Pat Reilly of the streets/Used to push Knicks/Now I carry Heat". I intently rehearsed in such a zone that I almost didn't notice the group of guys walking out of the store. I also noticed London's gestures from inside the store, as she noticed them too. Five guys. Two white guys, three black guys and they were all attractive. I looked up, but I didn't stop rapping. I ultimately wanted one of them to criticize, hopefully, even challenge. But none of them said anything, at least not loud enough for me to hear. They just stood there watching me.

The bell which hung from the door of the convenient market that rang every time the door is opened broke me out of my zone. I raised my head just in time to see London coming out of the store with a Slurpee in one hand and a bag in the other. "C'mon girl, damn! I'm trying to get to the studio!" I said aloud with the hope that those guys were paying attention to me. We got into the car, London pulled my auxiliary cord out of the radio, paired it back to her phone and lit a cigarette. We sat there waiting to see what direction my audience was headed. The guys stood there for a couple of seconds watching us pretend not to watch them. They separated into two cars. Two of them got into a burgundy Lincoln with black and burgundy rims. The other three vanished into a white suburban with some huge, chrome rims. We sat there waiting for London to make a move as London played with her phone, trying to find a song. "Find a song and leave it there!" I demanded. "What the hell is wrong with you?" she asked as she started the car. "We look stupid just sitting here." I said with my mind back to getting to the studio. "Did you see the one in the yellow and black jersey?" she asked anxiously. "They all got on yellow and black jerseys, London. They're Newark High jerseys." I answered proudly. "How you know?" she asked in wonder of what I knew. "Because I got that jersey at home. I sleep in it." I said now more arrogant. We both looked back as the Lincoln pulled out of its parking spot and sped off.

"I was talking about number five. The one driving the truck." she said as she began to back out of the parking space. The suburban started to pull out of its spot as well. London paused to let the truck out first, so she could get one last look at its driver. The driver of the suburban saw noticed London's pause and continued to back out. "What the hell are they doing?" London asked in a whisper as the suburban came to a stop behind her car, impeding our way out.

I opened the car door and leaned out. "C'mon! Move!!" I yelled as I held on to the door hoping not to fall out of the car. Nobody responded except London who whispered "What'chu doin'?" as she reached across me to close the car door. She then smiled as she threw the car in park, opened the door and got out of the car. She gracefully walked up to the suburban. The window lowered, and the driver summoned her to come around to his side of the car. The backdoor opened and one of the guys slid out of the truck and hastily walked towards the car door. "Can I help you?" I asked obnoxiously. "Yeah, you can give me someone to talk to." he said sarcastically. "Don't y'all got practice or something?" I asked with a smile. I turned to look at London who was standing in front of the truck with her arms crossed, staring in every direction but toward the driver. "Practice not til six" the guy said as he approached the car door. He leaned on the car next to the window. "Storm, right?" he asked with a look of certainty. "Huh?" I said in awe and confusion. I looked over to check on London who was slowly approaching the car, with the suburban driver at her side. "Storm. They call you Storm, right?" he asked again, diligently. I tried my best to avoid looking excited at the fact that he knew my name. "How he know your name, Em?" London asked viciously from across the car. "I don't know, London. How 'bout you let us talk, so I can find out?" I asked sardonically.

"So how do you know my name?" I asked redirecting my attention to this stranger who knew my name. "I've seen you around." he uttered in an almost whisper. "Around where?!" I said assertively. "Just around." he timidly responded replied starting to look unsure. "You from Newark?" I asked while beginning lose interest. I don't like guys that are not self-assured. "Nope. I'm from, Smyrna." he said cracking a smile. "That's what's up." I mumbled, now completely uninterested in anything that he had to say. I started to nod my head to the music and began looking around. "I hear your brother may enter the draft next year." he said making conversation as he noticed my lack of interest. "For real? You probably know more about it than I do." I said now weary of this conversation. "This girl at my school that he mess with, is telling everybody that he's going." he pronounced with a slight smile. "Well, if that's what she told y'all." I said in an uncaring disbelief. "She didn't tell me. I don't know who she told, but everyone seems to know." he said passionately. "I see." I said completely fed up with this guy and conversation. "You ready?" I said to London as I turned towards the car door. "Alright then. It was nice meeting you." I said as I opened the door and got into the car.

I closed the door and sat there smiling cynically, realizing that I never even got his name. I kind of felt sorry for the guy as he slowly walked back to the truck with his head down. London got into the car and tossed her phone into the center console with huge grin on her face. "That was wrong." she disclosed as she waved goodbye to the white suburban leaving the parking lot. The driver hit his horn to say goodbye as they sped onto Dupont Highway. "Damn, he was fine!" she whispered as she picked up her phone again to look at his name and number. "C'mon. You can look at that at the studio." I said anxious to get to the studio and upset that I didn't meet a new friend too. We pulled back onto the highway, and we resumed our trip to this producer and his studio in Wilmington.

RING. RING! "Hello!" London said enthusiastically after seeing the name on her cell phone screen. "No, it's cool. We still own our way to Wilmington." London said with a smile. "It's Kareem." she whispered pulling the phone away from her face. "Who?" I said pretending to care. "Kareem! The guy, we just met at Seven-Eleven. Number Five!" she whispered excited as a kid with a new toy. "A white boy, named Kareem?" I asked surprisingly confused. "He mixed!" she whispered in his defense.

They talked for the remainder of the ride to Wilmington. She repeated everything that they talked about to me in a whisper, trying to get me as excited as she was. She also told me the name of the guy who approached me. "The guy you shot down, name is Dixon. But everyone calls him, Dirty." she mentioned loud enough for him to hear her tell me. "Hey what's up, Dirty?" I said loud enough for him to hear me. London looked at me and began to laugh. "Kareem said, that Dirty said, that he don't usually come that weak. But your looks, and you brother's reputation for being protective of you, kinda intimidated him." London exclaimed in a sad tone, so they would think she was sincere. "He a punk." she whispered while pressing the phone to her chest and snickering. I just shook my head in a disbelief that he would even admit to such a thing. "Ask dude who this chick is that my brother's messing with?" I asked suspiciously. London repeated my question into the phone. "Chaewon!" she said repeating their reply to me. "Who?" I curiously asked becoming a little annoyed. London could tell that there something beginning to brew inside of me. "Who's Chaewon?" London asked pleasantly into the phone. "Chaewon Hargrove" she said to me with her eyebrows raised. "Who the fuck is Chaewon Hargrove?" I asked snatching the phone out of London's hand. "Kareem, this is Storm! Who is Chaewon Hargrove?!" I unyieldingly asked London's new friend. "She's a junior at our school. Rather well known. Rather attractive. And very, *very* high maintenance." he said confidently. "You don't know her?" he added before I could respond. "No! Why would I know that bitch?" I asked agitated. "She says she's been with your brother for a while. She's even brought your name up a few times." he said bewildered. "Who is this bitch?!" I asked London as I dropped her phone back into her hand. "Why? You wanna go up to her school?" she asked anxiously. "I just might." I answered pounding the numbers of my phone. 3-0-2-5-5-5-8-9-7-4.

"Dad." I said casually. "Hello Emmy. Everything's alright? Did your mom get home yet?" he asked as he did every day. "No. I don't know. I don't think so. I haven't talked to her and I'm not home yet." I said tensely. "You're out in the streets?" he worriedly asked as he always does when he knows I'm not in the house. "Yeah kinda. I've been invited to a studio by London's cousin..." "What's Management's real name?" I quickly whispered to London with my hand over the phone mouth piece. "Joey" she whispered back almost before I could finish my question. "... Joey. Me, London and Joey have an appointment at this music studio. I told you already, remember?" I reminded in my soft and innocent voice. "Don't come creeping in all hours of the night." he said in good spirits. "Okay daddy. See you when I get in. Love you." I said being as honest and sincere as I've ever been. "I love you too, Emmy." he responded as I ended the call. "Where the hell are, we?" I asked London as she giggled into her phone. "I don't know. This is where Joey told us to meet him." she said as she backed into a parking spot. "You and your connections." I disappointedly mumbled.

3-0-2-5-5-5-8-9-7-5. "Yo!" I said quickly. "Yo." Quentin responded just as fast. "Who's Chaewon?" I asked getting right to the point of the call. London turned and looked at me, realizing by my conversation who I called and probably why. "Who?" he asked again bluntly. "Chae-won Hargrove!" I repeated, louder this time. "Just some young girl with a crush." he said defensively. "Why?" he continued. "So, there was never a thing?"

I asked investigating. "Hell no! Mani would kick my ass." my brother said firmly. "That's what I thought" I said knowing that my brother wouldn't lie to me. "Again why, Em?" he sternly asked again. "Don't worry about it, I'll take care of it." I stated, looking up at London who knew by my look that we'd be at Newark High soon. "Storm, stop playing and tell me why?!" Quentin agitatedly insisted. "That bitch going around telling everybody that y'all fucking" I said bluntly.

"Is that what's wrong with my baby?" he laughingly asked. "She told you?" I asked confused, not sure of what I just heard. "Told me what?" he asked just as confused as I was. "Nothing." I said afraid that I may have given away Imani's secret. I could tell that Quentin didn't catch it, luckily. "Storm!" he asked panicky. "What?!" I answered as animated. "Is that what Imani is upset about?" he asked again spirited. "Nah., I don't even think she even heard of this bitch." I said reassuring him that he was okay. "Good. Keep it that way for me, until I get it handled." he said knowing I'd have his back. "Oh, it'll get handled!" I said now anxious to get to Newark High School. "I don't even wanna know what you're going to do. Just keep in touch so I'll know you're alright." he said knowing I'm as protective of him as he is of me.

London tapped me on my lap, pointing out her cousin, Management. He was sticking his head out of the door of one of the apartments, gesturing for us to come to him. "Yup." I said ending the call before Quentin could respond.

CHAPTER 7

"Quentin"

"Yeah, I got it. Tell him I said thank you." I asked genuinely. "Tell him yourself. We just finished working out." she said sounding giddy. "Y'all are nasty. And I don't need to be hearing things like that. I'm your child." I said laughing at myself. "Nasty?" she said bewildered. I just continued to laugh as mom gasped. I guess she finally got my little joke. "Boy! I'm your mother, not your friend. You don't assume stuff like that about your father and I. Now the fact that you thought about it, that's nasty!" she said snickering while pretending to still be serious.

I could hear Storm talking in the background. "Emmy. Do you want to talk to your brother?" mom asked her. "I talked to him already." she openly replied. "Is that a no?" mom continued to ask. "Yes mom, that's a no. But ask him did he talk to Imani yet?" Storm answered. "Quentin, Emmy wants to know if you…" mom began. "I heard her ma. Tell her no, not yet." I interrupted. "Did dad come down yet?" I asked anxious to get off the phone. "Hold on, babe." she said realizing my impatience for my father to arrive. "Omeee, come get my phone! It's Q-Tee!" she yelled.

"Okay, Q-tee. I'll talk to you tomorrow, call me if you need me. I love you baby!" my mom pleasantly said before handing my father the phone. "Love You too, ma." I responded. "Hello Quentin." my dad said sternly. "Hey dad, what's up?" I calmly asked. "Nothing. I'm sitting around here waiting for Hassan to bring me my truck back." he grimly responded. "He got you again huh?" I uttered laughing at my dad's common situation. "I guess. How was practice?" he casually asked. "Practice was practice. I'm sore and tired." I uttered pretending to sound weary. "Well go get some sleep." he concernedly voiced. "I am. As soon as we hang up! Did I tell you, they been playing me at safety?" I arrogantly asked. "Safety, why?" he asked just as proud as I was. "I don't know, but in forty attempts, I only gave up eleven completions and I got two picks," I said anxiously awaiting to tell him this news.

My father and I talked for another 35 minutes before Hassan finally came with his truck. "I'll call you tomorrow, Quentin." my father hastily said while marching to the door to curse out Hassan. "Alright, dad." I said ending the call. 3-0-2-6-7-3-2-1-1-2.

TAP, TAP! "Damn, Juice. If you gonna have company, stay up so you can let 'em in!" I quietly demanded after faintly hearing someone knock at the front door. I lifted from my bed and made my way to Juice's bedroom to notify him of his guest at the door. I walked slowly to give Imani's voice mail time to beep. "I Love you baby. Jus' wanted to let you know! Good night" I said gently before pressing the end button on the phone.

"Juice. Juice! Somebody at the door for you." I yelled through his bedroom door while banging. Juice opened his door and stepped out, scratching himself and upset because I woke him. "Who the fuck is it?" he irritably questioned. "I don't know!" I mumbled going in my bedroom and the door behind me. I stripped down to my boxers, turned on my speakers and dove under my covers.

[QUINCY JONES]
There I go, there I go, there I go, there I go…
Pretty baby you are the soul that snaps my control

It seemed like it took only a couple seconds for me to get to sleep. **TAP, TAP, TAP!** I faintly heard as I just laid there, with my head buried under the pillows. I didn't hear my door creep open, but I faintly heard it close. I figured it was Juice trying to go into his condom stash which he kept in my room, in case one of his many female friends decided to poke around his. I settled back into sleep as the room went quiet again. I felt someone sit on the edge of my bed. I left it as just my imagination because, for some reason I was inadvertently thinking about Tasha.

I felt someone grab my left foot and begin to massage it. It was just what I needed and it way too coincidental to be real, so I let this imaginary foot massage continue. Then I heard the softest, sweetest most wonderful laugh, I've ever heard. Thinking that my imagination was on overdrive, I let it go on for almost a minute before I realized, it felt too good to be my imagination. I lifted my head from under my pillows. I could barely open my eyes, but I opened them enough to see the bright red time on the clock. "Twelve, ten. Good, I got eight more hours." I thought before noticing the silhouette of someone sitting on the edge of my bed. I sat up quickly, rubbing my eyes to get complete focus.

It was Tasha, she was sitting on the edge of my bed lighting the third of the three candles that she'd apparently brought with her. The room was now dimly lit by the two flickering candles, she'd already placed. My music playlist was now playing my favorite Quincy Jones song, adding to the sensual atmosphere. "Hi" she said softly. "Hey" I whispered as I looked her up and down. I hesitantly sat up after she slid up the bed to sit next to me. "You smell good as shit, what do you have on?" she uttered in an almost whisper as she leaned in to engagingly sniff my neck. "You wear cologne to bed?" she bewilderedly asked. "Not really. But I put it on after I shower, and I shower after practice, so…" I sensibly clarified as I slowly backed away from her. "What's it called?" she quietly inquired after noticing me retreat some. "It's nothing special. It's Hugo, by Hugo Boss." I nonchalantly replied. "It's enticing." she whispered. "Don't hear that word often." I scoffed at her overexaggerated attempt. She rose from the bed and watching me watch her. She stood posing with poise. Her reddish-brown, micro braided hair falling from her head and resting on her long black t-shirt with white lettering which read, "*I taught your boyfriend that thing you like*". And her shorts, so short I wasn't even sure if she had any on. All I saw were legs coming from under a shirt. I didn't know what to think. But asking her what she was doing in my room, never crossed my mind. It was like she was supposed to be here.

I dropped back down onto my bed and just laid there staring at her with my hands behind my head. I couldn't stop thinking about how beautiful she was. I smiled watching her admire herself in the mirror. "What?" she asked blushing as she noticed me watching her sway back and forth to the music. "Is this how you go to sleep every night?" she interrupted before I could answer her previous question. "Yeah. Most nights." I replied. "How many songs do you on this playlist?" she asked picking up my iPod. "I don't know. a couple hundred." I continued proudly. "You're so old." she said smiling as she marveled at my speakers which resembled an old school boom box. "All R&B?" she continued to curiously ask. "Mostly." I answered, hoping she would pause long enough for me to get a question in. "You got early classes tomorrow?" she intriguingly asked. "No." I replied taking notice of her purposely not letting me talk. "What time is your first class?" she quickly resumed. "One fifteen. Why?" I said jamming a question of my own in. "I just wanted to know. I wouldn't want to keep you up too late. Especially if you have an early class. But since you said one fifteen, you can stay up all night." she said comfortably. "I control how late I stay up. Thank you." I said full of swagger. "Now, I gotta question." I quickly squeezed in as I continued to lay back on the bed and watch her. "You can ask me whatever you like. Did you know that your clock is six minutes fast?" she asked smiling hard at herself in the mirror. "Yeah I did. Why do you keep doing that?" I asked quickly before she could ask another question. "Doing what?" she asked pushing through my iPod for a song that she preferred. "Manipulate the conversation, so I can't ask a question." I said stretching to look at her ass in the dimly lit room. "Cause I already know what you're going to ask." she said turning her head to me smiling. "Please, do tell." I charmingly stated. "You wanna know what I'm doing here." she asked confidently. "Obviously." I positively assured. "I don't even know. I'm curious to why I'm here too, honestly." she genuinely admitted. "Okay." I said smiling at her sincerity. "What're you smiling at?" she delightfully asked after finding a song she liked.

"Nothing. Continue." I said wondering about her thought of my next question. "Ooh. I haven't heard this in a looong time." she enthusiastically confessed while gyrating to the music. "Next. You probably thinking about J.T." she said smiling cynically. "Not so much as J.T. in particular. But your plans for me? Me and you, rather." I asked not worrying about her boyfriend in the least bit. "Me and you. I like how that sounds" Tasha blissfully disclosed as her smile glistened in the moon's light through the window. "Come dance with me." she continued while extending her hands gesturing for me to come to her. "You got it." I uttered as I scoffed at her gesture. "I'll dance by myself, then!" she said pretending to be offended by my denial.

She slowly danced for what seemed like forever, while talking occasionally. "Question. Where did the name J.T. come from? His first name is don't start with a J. Nor does his last name start with a T." I obviously stated. "You been calling him J.T. for a year and a half and you never thought to ask where it came from?" she asked laughing with her head in my chest. "When I got here that's what everyone was calling him, so I just followed suit. Besides, me and your man aren't the best of friends." I divulged feeling a little silly. "In high school people use to tell him that he looked like the singer, Justin Timberlake. Since a lot of people from Souderton High came here, the name came with him." she said reluctantly. "You serious?!" I asked with a snicker. "Yeah." she said laughing at my laughter.

"Don't think I didn't notice that you danced around my question about your plans?" I asked now more fascinated than ever. "I don't know. I really don't have any plans further than spending the night with you." Tasha replied casually. "And when did you come up with that plan?" I asked her attempting to hide all signs of my excitement. "I planned on seeing you again tonight, the moment I got out of your car, this afternoon. That's why I asked what you were doing later. Was trying to be sure that you weren't expecting company." she softly admitted. "As for spending the night with you, I didn't plan that until sometime during your practice." she arrogantly confessed. "Speaking of which, I saw you trying to show my man up, tonight." she uttered while laughing mockingly. "You flatter me. But we both know that I could never show up J.T., not at safety. He is graded as a top ten prospect heading into the draft." I said slightly envious of all that he had. "That's funny." she said sarcastically. "What's funny?" I asked penetrating. "You played two different positions in practice tonight. Nine tackles, one interception as a linebacker and two tackles, three pass deflections as a safety. But you are trying to give him his props?" she said patronizingly.

"You come off like you'd be a hell of a friend." I honestly acknowledged. "Friend?" Tasha snobbishly queried while powerfully turning to look down at me. "Yeah. Let's be real. You have a man right across campus. A man that we all watch you kiss and cuddle up on, constantly." I sternly reminded. "Not to mention, I have a girl. So, with that... it is, what it is." I resumed sincerely.

"I've been waiting for you to bring her up, since I got here. So, how do you really feel about her? It is, what it is, is not saying much." Tasha asked trying to hide the grin on her face. "I love her." I said quickly. "Then, why are you undressing me with your eyes, while I'm dancing in your room by candlelight?" she asked conqueringly. "Don't make me second guess this Tasha." I said seriously. Tasha laughed at me and put a halt to her sensual gyrating. "I apologize." she condescendingly whispered.

"It's getting late." she said as she walked over and began to stare out of the window. "Do you mind if I reset your alarm?" she asked innocently. "For what?" I asked concerned by her actual intentions. "So that I don't oversleep. My phone doesn't wake me." she softly explained as she began pressing buttons on the clock. "No. Do what you gotta do." I whispered powerlessly while watching her attempt to reset my clock. "You okay?" I continued concerned that she may not be able to see the correct buttons in the dim light. "I got an eleven thirty class, so I should set it for..." Tasha began to question herself. "Eight o'clock, so I can take you to breakfast." she quickly answered herself with a smile, hoping to get one back. She placed the clock back on the dresser and before blew out the candle next to it. She then moved gracefully to the windowsill to blow out that candle.

Leaving only the candle on the desk at the far end of the room. She gracefully sauntered over to the desk to eliminate the finally light. "Hold up. Don't blow that one out yet." I said feeling slightly remorseful.

I vaulted out of the bed, opened my drawer and grabbed a t-shirt. I pulled the shirt over my head and pushed my arms through the sleeves before straightening out the bed so that we could lay comfortably. "How you want to do this? Head to toe?" she said jokingly before bestowing that same sweet laugh I heard when I realized that she was in the room. "Is it alright if I get this light now?" she asked sweetly, bending over to blow out the candle. I looked at Tasha as she blew out the candle. The last thing I saw before the room went dark was Tasha's ass. "Tasha ain't got no shorts on." I thought to myself, hoping I didn't say it aloud. Every part of my body became excited immediately. I drew back the sheets so that she could get into the bed. There was no way that I was going to let her feel my pride. "Thank you" she said as she slinked up the bed between me and the wall behind me.

I plopped down into the bed next to her with my head at the other end. She laughed again. "Get up here, boy." she demanded. I got out of bed and the climbed back in appropriately. "Goodnight Tasha." I whispered. "It is now" she whispered back sensually.

She pulled herself close to me, pressing her breasts against my back and her face against the back of my neck. Her warm breathing made the hairs on the back of my neck stand up. Her arm came across my shoulder and she began to attempt to play with my chest hairs. "Why did you put that shirt on?" Tasha whispered disappointed. "I thought it would be inappropriate, if I didn't have it on." I said attempting to be funny. "Take this shirt off, please?" Tasha pleaded while pulling on the back of the shirt. I arose slightly, just enough to take off my shirt, as requested. "Mani." Tasha whispered, noticing the tattoo on my shoulder blade. I tossed the shirt onto the chair and dropped back down onto the bed. "What'd she do to get you to do this?" she intriguingly asked as she sketched the tattoo with her finger. "Nothing. It was my idea." I awkwardly disclosed as I slightly cringed.

"Quentin, I'm thirsty." she said in a soft, sexy voice. "I got some stuff in the fridge. What you want?" I asked anxious to get back into bed. "Some ice, if you have it?" she asked softly. "I'm sure we do. You sure that that's all you want? Cause, I'm not getting back up!" I assertively acknowledged. "I'm sure." she said confidently. I slid out of the bed and walked across the dark room. I thought I heard Tasha get out of the bed as well, but I ignored it and continued out of the room. I grabbed a plastic cup from atop the refrigerator filled it with ice and headed back to my room. I could hear the rustle of movement from the other side of the bedroom door but when I opened, there was Tasha in the bed pulling the sheets up to her neck. She smiled at me as I handed her the cup of ice. She filled her mouth with a few pieces of ice and handed it back to me. I placed the cup on the nightstand slipped back into the bed.

"? ? ? ?" Tasha uttered incoherently with her mouth full of ice. Tasha continued to chew and swallow some of the ice away before trying to speak again. "Thank you, baby." she said adorably. "You are welcome." I said smiling at the fact that she called me baby. I grabbed my pillow and resumed being curled up with my back to Tasha. I could hear her playing with the ice in her mouth behind me. My toes curled with every sound that she made. Every time I heard her suck and slurp on the ice in her mouth, my body cringed. She finished the ice and moved in close to me again. She pressed her body against mine.

My eyes widened, my mouth went dry and my body went numb as I discovered that Tasha was no longer wearing any clothing. She put her leg up on me, resting her thigh on mine. She then pushed her arm under my body and folded her hands across my chest, so she could pull herself even closer. "Damn, she got some big ass titties!" I thought to myself, feeling Tasha's breasts press against my back as she tried to get close and comfortable.

I flinched as Tasha pressed her cold lips to the back of my neck. "You alright?" she asked seductively laughing. "Uh huh." I said unable to say much else. She continued to run her soft, wet lips across my neck while kneading the palm of her hand into my chest. She worked her lips around to my ear and began to nibble on my earlobe. "Turn over." she whispered before pushing her tongue into my ear. "I can't if we want this to stay blameless." I said certain of my stature. "I'll be good." she said as she reintroduced her tongue to my ear.

"Tasha, stop!" I whispered as I could no longer take her in my ear. I pushed Tasha's leg from mine and turned onto my back, with the hope that it would keep her from being able to put her tongue in my ear. She immediately grabbed my dick, pushed it downward as to not penetrate her and straddled my waist. "We'll stay blameless until we're ready to be blamed." Tasha said as she nestled her head into my chest. "Goodnight" she whispered as she gave a gentle kiss to my nipple.

CHAPTER 8

"Omar"

"Good morning, Toni." I said walking into the lobby of my office approaching Antoinette's desk. "Good morning, Mr. Gregory. How was your weekend?" she asked sarcastically. "Didn't you just spend the night on my couch?" I asked, not realizing she was trying to be funny. "Yeah, I did, didn't I?" she said with a smirk. "Now may I ask, why? Why, when I woke up and went downstairs into my kitchen at three a.m. to get something to drink, you were tossing and turning on my couch?" I straightforwardly asked while watching her laugh. "Me and Tra was out late, and I wasn't feeling too good. She gave me a pillow and blanket and I should sleep over. She also said you'd already be asleep, and when you're asleep you couldn't care less about anything. I guess she was wrong!" she replied with her eyes drooped, trying not to smile. I shook my head in disbelief and continued through the door of my office.

I entered the room, hung my jacket on the hook behind the door, opened the window and turned on my computer. "Toni, when you get the chance, come here for a sec." I said while sticking my head out of my office door. I watched her sigh, now having to stop the shuffle papers that get her ready for the day. "Inadvertently charming, my ass." she mumbled to herself as she pulled away from her desk and entered my office. "I'm glad you realize it was inadvertent." I said to her with a smile as she entered my office. She smiled, realizing that I heard what she said. "What's up?" she asked still smiling. "Close the door Toni." I sternly ordered. Her smile disappeared as she closed the door. A look frightful look covered her face. "Have a seat." I said pointing to one of the chairs which face my desk. She silently sat down as the look of fear quickly turned to despair. "What's wrong with you?" I asked calmly, trying to keep up with her assumption of a problem. "I was getting ready to ask you the same thing." she said softly. I started laughing, I couldn't hold it in any longer. She cracked a little smile, just to follow suit. "What's so funny?" she confusedly said. "You! You're funny." I said smiling. "Why? What I do?" she nervously asked, stepping on eggshells as she spoke. "Why did I call you in here, Toni?" I openly asked as I sat erect in my chair. "I don't know?" she said innocently. "Then why all the anxiety?" I said laughing. "I don't know. I just got that... all good things come to an end feeling." she said beginning to look a little more comfortable.

"So, I'm a good thing?" I said confidently. "This job is a good thing, Mr. Gregory!" she said with a sexy smile. "Alright, now. First of all, what did I tell you about calling me Mr. Gregory?" I sternly asked. "That, Mr. Gregory was your father." she reminded before standing to gracefully walk around my desk towards me. "So, what do I call you?" she asked anxiously. "My wife calls me, Omee. Associates, call me Omar. My friends call me O. But you know all of this already!" I recapped as I pulled my keyboard toward me. "Call me anything, but Mr. Gregory." I mumbled.

She stood behind my chair and put her hands on my shoulders. She leaned over me, pressing her cheek a hair's length from mine. Her long black hair flowed onto my shoulder and down across my chest. "What do your lovers call you?" her sexy, pink glossed, lips parted to whisper. My throat went instantly dry. "The reason..." I croaked in a dry raspy voice as Toni exploded with laughter. "Now who's full of anxiety?" she said chuckling, as she started towards the sofa at the other end of the office. "Uh Um! The reason I called you in here, was to find out where you and Tracey went yesterday. All day, yesterday!" I investigated while still trying to get my head together after her little hoax. "What?!" she asked with a chuckle. "You heard me! What'd y'all do yesterday?" I said starting to smile at the fact that she was laughing at me. "You're serious?!" she said overwhelmed by my audacity. "Yeah, I'm serious! Y'all was out before noon and back... what time did y'all get back? I went to bed after eleven!" I explained as she continued laughing. RING. RING! "Aww, did you miss us?" she asked as she made her way to the door to answer the phone ringing on her desk.

"I'll be right back. You are just too cute." she said smiling as she rushed out. I grabbed the mouse to remove the screensaver and logged on for the day. I figured I'd check my email until Toni came back with the info I needed.

Sender	Subject	Date	Size
Mercedes.com	It's almost time	Mon 09/24	50k
Tiffany Bromwell	**Long Time, No See**	**Sun 09/25**	**11k**
customerservice	**Open Enrollment**	**Fri 09/25**	**34k**

"Who the hell is, Tiffany Bromwell?" I whispered to myself as I opened the email.

> Good morning Omar, long time, no see. How are you? How's Quentin? I hope all is well? I don't know where to begin, I've been planning this moment for several months and now that it's here, I'm petrified. Omar it's me, Tiffany. Your Tiffany, Quentin's Tiffany. I know you've done all you can to push the thought of me out of your mind, but I'm begging you to let me in. If only for a second. I know you think I have some nerve making inquiries about you and your son. But this is real, I'm real, and you two are all I think about. All I've ever thought about! I may have been young, but I wasn't dumb. Omar, I just want to see you, and hopefully one day… see my son. I'm not asking you for anything more than your company, for a minute, an hour a day. Hell, a second or two. I really have an idea of what you're thinking, and I seriously hope that I am wrong. I'm begging you to give me a call when you get the chance. I just would like to know your thoughts (215)555-1179. Please!

"Tiffany?!" I whispered as I glanced around the room for my cell phone. I found it still in the pocket of my suit jacket hanging on the back of the door. 2-1-5-5-5-5-9-7-1-1… click!

"What the hell am I doing?" I clearly asked myself.

3-0-2-5-5-5-1-5-1-0. "Yo." Hassan calmly articulated as he answered the call. "Yo, where you at?!" I animatedly voiced in response. "I'm sleep! One of the perks of making your own hours, you wake up when you feel like it." Hassan murmured in a deep raspy voice. "Wake up man, this is important!" I said anxiously. "You will never guess who I just got an email from." I enthusiastically conveyed. "You right, cause I'm not goin' try. I'm taking my ass back to sleep. Hit me up later with this!" he irritably mumbled. "Tiffany!" I said as Toni came walking back into the room to finish our conversation. "Who the fuck is Tiffany?!" Hassan said while yawning and realizing I wasn't getting off the phone.

I laid the phone on my desk and put both hands in the air with my fingers spread. "Gimme ten minutes" I whispered to Toni. "Tiffany!" I repeated knowing that he'd eventually know who I was referring to. "Tiffany, who? You keep sayin' that shit like I know who you talking 'bout." he crossly said exhibiting that he was now wide awake. "Tiffany Lane!" I said becoming impatient. "Que's mom!" I said giving up, on him. "I ain't got time for his stupidity. If he doesn't have it by now, I'm hanging up." I thought as I rose to walk the room. "Oh shit, I forgot that bitch existed.

What she wants?!" he said in astonishment. "From the looks of this... me! Me and Quentin!" I said confidently.

"What you goin' do?" he asked now focused on my every word. "I don't know. She left me her number. Should I call it? Cause a part of me wants to call this number. A large part of me, wants to call this number." I divulged, hoping to hear the voice of reasoning.

"Yeah, damn right!

Call her, especially if she's trying to give you some pussy." he said returning to his usual sex-driven self. "I don't know, why I called you? I'll call you back. I'm going call Tracey, real quick." I said frustrated with Hassan at times. "You called me 'because I knew and remember, Tiffany. You wanted some validation to call her, so you'd feel better about wanting to do it. And that's what I did. You just didn't like my rationale for telling you to call. Now, you want to call Tracey, which is the dumbest shit I've ever heard you say, in hopes that she'll tell you to call Tiffany for reasons you consider more logical. I held up my end, I was the brother I was supposed to be, now I'm going back to fucking bed. And please don't call me with dumb shit before 10am, anymore this week!" he said profoundly. "Alright then" I agreed before ending the call. "Yo! Omar! Omar!" he yelled into the phone as I pulled it away from my face to hang it up. "What?!" I said, anxious to hang up and call Tracey. "I need your truck." he swiftly confessed. I pulled the phone away from my face and looked at it. "The nerve of this nigga, cussing me out and then asking me for my truck." I mumble while looking down at the phone. "When?" I dismally asked feeling weighed down by the reality that he was right in what he said.

BUZZ... "MR. GREGORY, DO YOU STILL NEED ME IN THERE?"

"That's up to you Toni, but to be honest I kinda forgot what we were talking about." I candidly admitted.

"IS EVERYTHING ALRIGHT?"

"Yeah, I'm fine. Just a little headache, that's all. Thank you for asking though." I gratefully responded to my concerned assistant. "Wednesday." Hassan said indistinctly. "Huh?" I said almost forgetting he was on the phone. "Wednesday!" Hassan said for the second time. "Yeah alright, whatever.

Just don't pull your usual bullshit 'cause Tracey's taking it to work with her on Thursday." I said harshly. "Good-looking out. Alright then." he said sounding a little excited. "Alright then." I said before hanging up the call. I moved the mouse to get rid of the screensaver so I could read the email again. "Good morning Omar, long time, no see. How are you? How's Quentin? I hope all is well? I don't know where to begin, I've been planning this moment for several years and now that it's here, I'm petrif..." I mumbled while skimming through the email.

TAP! TAP! TAP! The door slowly swung open before I could answer. "Here, I thought you could use some of these." Toni said walking into the office with some water and a few aspirins.

I saw Toni and began to crack a smile immediately. "You're are so beautiful!" I said quietly but loud enough for her to hear me. "Thank you." she said, beginning to blush. She placed the water and aspirin on my desk, I gently grabbed her hand as she tried to pull it away and I looked into her eyes. "Why are you single? Seriously?!" I curiously asked. She slid her hand from under mine, turned, and walked towards the door. She closed the door and slowly walked towards the sofa at the other end of the office. I watched her walk, one sexy stride after another, until she reached her destination. She turned and sat down on the couch.

I tossed the aspirin into my mouth, chased it with half a glass of water, and got up from my desk. "I don't know. I really don't know." she sincerely said as I followed over to the couch. "Maybe it's 'cause I'm too ambitious. Or maybe it's 'cause of my independence, or maybe it's 'cause I'm a twenty-nine-year-old divorcee, with a six-year-old son. I don't know what men are afraid of these days." she sincerely detailed as she sat with her eyes lowered. "I can't say that I really care either." she stubbornly added. "I hear that!" I uttered, not knowing what else to say. "Why you ask me that?" she said with a curiously accented sex look. "A woman as beautiful as you are, just doesn't look right, single." I honestly acknowledged. "Is that right?" she chuckled. "I guess. To me it is. What's funny?" I confusedly asked while smiling at her laughter. "Men are from Venus!" she said smiling as she got up. "Wait, wait, wait, slow down. I'm not every man, so it's either I'm from Venus or every other man is from Venus. But we don't all fit in that same boat!" I said defensively. "Okay then, you're from Venus." she laughed. "What do you people from Venus call yourselves?" she asked sarcastically. "We're Venetian." I said, just as sarcastic. "Like the blinds." she mockingly asked. "Yeah, that's where the name comes from. We use them the same way you use, paint and wallpaper. All of the walls on Venus are made of glass, you get the idea." I said as I stood up and headed towards the window.

Toni rose and shadowed. She stood next to me at the window. "Look at this view, it's a postcard picture just waiting to be taken." she pleasantly uttered. "It's downtown, Dover?!" I said confused and shaded from whatever wonder she saw outside my window. "You don't see it?" she asked in amazement. "I don't see it." I replied, gawking intensely. "But I'll tell you what, I'll let you take me to lunch, and you can show me Dover's splendor then. I want to see this, postcard material you speak of. Is that alright with you?" I asked with the hopes of getting her opinion about certain things going on in my world. "Lunch?" she asked hesitantly. "Yeah, lunch! You do eat, don't you? I mean… if that's not allowed, or even just unwanted, you can tell me.

I will not get offended, nor will it change a thing between us. I promise!" I said making sure to not rub her the wrong way. She started laughing "I'm filing sexual harassment charges against you." she said with a smile. I just looked at her while shaking my head and smiling.

"We actually goin' to lunch?" she innocently asked. Her hair fell back into her face, rather than push it to the side like she's done all morning, she let it stay there. I could see her redbone cheeks, actually turning red. And her smile, like a girl's first crush on her older brother's best friend. She was blushing and fighting herself to keep from putting her hand in front of her face to cover it. "Yeah. If you got a problem with this…" I said puzzled by her facial expressions. "No, no. When and where?" she asked pretending to re-establish her composure. I smirked at her trying to hide her anticipation by finally brushing the hair from in front of her face. "I'll be ready at about eleven thirty. And as for where, you're supposed to be showing me your post card, remember? Now if you'll excuse me, I got a couple phone calls to make." I said mocking. "Don't forget to tell Tracey, you're taking me out." Toni giggled on her way out of the door. "I won't! By the way, it's *men are from Mars, women are from Venus!*" I sharply corrected, before she closed the door.

I sat back down behind my desk and picked up the phone. 3-0-2-5-5-5-8-9-7-2. "Good morning, Omie." Tracey said cheerfully. "Tra." I said blissfully after hearing her calming voice. "You Busy?" I asked, hoping that she wasn't. "Well. I am at work." she said sarcastically. "Why?" she added. "Nothing. Go ahead back to work. I'll talk to you about it later." I apologetically said after realizing that I was interrupting her day with my unimportant issue. "What is it? Is everything alright? Omar, please don't tell me something's happened to Quentin or Emily?" Tracey said concerned and excited. "Damn Tra, calm down. It's nothing, really! Quentin's fine, as far as I know. You talk to him more than I do. Just do me a favor and call me during your lunch." I said stalling, trying to figure out a way to tell her about Tiffany. "You sure?" she asked with a lot less fret. "I'm sure I love you!" I said trying to be charmingly reassuring.

CHAPTER 9

"Tracey"

"I guess I was a little eccentric just now, huh?" I asked snickering softly. "Just a little." Omar responded chuckling back. "Omie, you're not supposed to agree with me." I said adorably. "Just being real Tra. That wasn't eccentric, you did a cannonball off the deep end." he said laughing at his little play on words. I have to admit it was cute, I even laughed a little myself. "Okay babe, I'm going get back to work and I'll call you during my lunch." I said as my students started to pour into the classroom. "Speaking of lunch, I told Toni I would take her out to lunch. That's cool with you?" I asked confident in her trust in me. "Yeah that's alright, I'm glad you asked though. Just tell her... I'll call her later." I approved with a slight hint of suspicion of her intentions. "Alright." he said calmly. "Oh, and Omie." I quickly requested before he could end the call. "Yes." he whispered. I froze. It was that, "yes", that sensual, intoxicating, "yes". The one where he holds on to the "s" just long enough to make my eyes close, my head drop and the rest of my body just cringe. "I love you." I confessed after gathering enough composure. "I love you more, Tra." he responded before ending the call.

I stood up and walked to the door to greet the few students who hadn't yet made it into the room. "Good morning, Mrs. Gregory." one of my female students said with a smile, as she walked pass into the room. "Good morning Miss. Hargrove." I responded. "How are you? How's Quentin?" she asked with a smile. "Tracey!" a woman's voice bellowed from the hallway just outside the door. "He's fine and I'll tell him you asked about him. Please excuse me for a second Chaewon? Class?" I cordially asked as the bell rang to start the class. I stepped into the hallway and closed the door behind me. "Hey Rhonda." "Hey Girl. You got a call from someone, from Penn State this morning." she said, sounding concerned. "I knew Omar was hiding something." I whispered to myself. "What'd they say?" I asked trying not to sound panicky. "I wrote the message details down, it's on my desk in the office. You can come get it, whenever you get the chance. They just said they were returning your call, that's all." she said, with a look of confusion. "My call?" I questioned joining Rhonda in her confusion. "Okay, I'll call them during my break. Thank you, Rhonda." I said before turning to advance back into the classroom.

I glanced through my lesson plans and gave the class today's assignment. "I can't do this." I quietly admitted as the thought of unknown information about Quentin become unbearable. I sat down behind my desk and pulled a stack of paper towards me. I figured if I started to mark papers, it would take my mind off my baby. My leg began to shake, and I couldn't keep my eyes off of my cell phone laying on the desk. "Excuse me class." I said as I had reached my limit of endurance. I grabbed my cell phone, stood up, and walked towards the wall intercom.

"MAIN OFFICE."

"Who's this, Dottie?" I asked eagerly.

"NO, THIS IS RHONDA."

"Hey Rhonda, this is Tracey Gregory. That message you were just telling me about, did they happen to have left a number." I asked relieved it was her answering the phone.

"THEY CERTAINLY DID, I HAVE IT RIGHT HERE. COULDN'T MAKE IT TO YOUR BREAK, HUH?"

"Guess not. I have to make sure that my boy is all right." I said pretending to smile. "I'm going to send one of my students down there to pick up the message." I said anxiously. "I'll have it waiting." she said before she hung up the phone.

I turned and looked at my class to see which one, I was going to send to the office. Everyone was pretending to be gripped by the assignment I had given. Completely convinced by their award-winning performances, I decided to go to the office myself. I gave my class another final once over and dipped out of the room. I scampered down to the office. Rhonda was waiting at the office door with a piece of paper in her hand. I grabbed the paper, gave her a smile and hurried back to my class.

CHAPTER 10

"Quentin"

"Gregs! Yo, Gregs!" I heard a man's voice yell. I looked in my side-view mirror to see J.T. and the Shark twins walking towards my car. "I need to holla at you 'bout some things." J.T. harshly barked as he approached my car with his chest poked out. "Things like what?!" I arrogantly asked, already knowing why he was here. "Just some things!" he sternly replied. I looked over at Dame who was sitting in the passenger's seat, determined to hold in his laughter. "How 'bout letting me finish parking my car first." I overconfidently scoffed. I pulled into an empty parking space, slammed the gear shift into park, and reluctantly sighed before attempting to get out of the car. I looked up at the tree gentlemen standing directly outside my door. The began to open just as I reached for the handle. I looked up to see J.T. opening my car door. I forcefully pushed the door open and leaped out of the car. "Don't touch my car." I calmly advised after watching J.T. jump out of the way of the swinging door. "Look, I'm not here for no dumb shit, man. I just would like to know why I keep hearing about you, and Tasha?!" he said looking around for his so-called back up to approach his side.

I watched in astonishment as Tony and Dominic Sharky, both six feet, four inches and close to three hundred pounds each, stood nervously behind him. "So uh, y'all wanna talk about Tasha, too?" I sarcastically asked playing on their concern of any confrontation between us. "Or are you just a safeguard to keep him from getting smashed?" I questioned to goad J.T. "Pussy, who the fu...?" he harshly began after pivoting his head around to be sure his team was ready for any type of engagement. My eyes widened in amazement as he started talking. "We just came to make sure y'all squared this shit away. We don't have no beef with you, mooly." Tone interrupted by placing his hand on J.T.'s chest. Dame took this opportunity to get out of the car, still snickering but ready for whatever was about to go down. He stayed on the other side of the car so that he, nor anyone else could confirm his reputation for being an instigator. I smiled proudly while watching Tony try to protect J.T. from himself. I didn't like watching

Tony squirm, he and I are friends and it was quite disappointing seeing him like that. His brother Dominic and I, now we could use some polishing. I wouldn't mind him hanging around for whatever. But coincidentally, I had things to do with Tasha. So, I had to end this encounter straightaway. "You know what Tone, you right. We ain't got no beef, and we don't want no beef. And I don't need no mediator." I said slightly nodding my head to the right, trying to allow them to leave. By this point, Dame's snickering turned to outright laughter drawing everyone's attention towards him. His laughter at the situation causes me to chuckle as well. "What the fuck you laughing at?" J.T. said before noticing that his means of protection were now both on his right side and about three to four steps further away.

"Who you talking to? Me, or him?! It don't even matter, you..." I calmly began. "Yo, Gregs, you good?" Dame interrupted before reaching into the backseat to grab his things. "Yeah man, I got it. You out?" I asked showing a lack of anxiety in my present situation. "Yeah, I'mma roll." he said becoming bored with us all. "Do me a favor, take Carlito's Way and Big Pussy with you?" I casually asked, before shooting a comforting smile at Tone.

"Aiight! Hey J.T., get your grown man on, buddy! This shit was real high school." Dame calmly criticized after closing the car door. "Raggedy Ann, Andy, y'all should c'mon wit me." he added. Tone practically ran over to Dame, while Dominic walked over slowly staring at me like he really wanted something to happen between us. As they walked away, Dame began to verbally abuse the twins. "Y'all are way too big to be that non-confrontational! It's just sad. Especially for a offensive and defensive lineman. I'm gonna have y'all Coach, or sign y'all asses up for some assertiveness training, or something." Dame said slinging his bags over his shoulder. "Fuck you, Dame." Tone said with a smile. "What was y'all gonna do if Que wasn't in a talking mood?" Dame asked with a look of disappointment.

I looked over at J.T., who was now twice as mad, but only half as bold as he once was. "Ok Brian, what's up? Oh yeah, you were asking about me and Tasha?" I reminded him while closing the car door. I leaned on the car and listened carefully to what J.T. had to say. "Basically, I keep hearing about you and... *my girl*. Everybody's telling me about how she goes into your dorm at night and not coming back out 'til the morning. Now I've tried, but I can't think of any logical explanation for why they would make up shit like that. So, I asked my so-called girl and she chose to be very tight lipped. So, I figured I needed to see you." he explained with a lot less bass in his voice.

"Listen man, it's like this. Your girl and I are friends. If she want to come hang out, she can." I said nonchalantly. "C'mon man, I ain't stupid. Are you fucking her?" he firmly inquired before beginning to lean on my car next to me. I shot him the, "what the fuck you doin', get the hell off my car" look before I began. And since he's not one that I feel I need to shroud from, I told him what he probably didn't want to hear. "She came to the room, like right after practice one night. I didn't call her, never pressed, she just showed up wearing a t-shirt and nothing else. If you want all the details, you gonna have to talk to her. But for future references, intimidation don't really work on me. So, when you finally ready to really come at me... come better than you did today." I calmly recommended before lifting from off the car. "Truth be told, I ain't fuck your girl. But we both know that there's a few out here who can't say that same thing. You share her, you've always shared her and you know it, which makes your actions today all the more comical." I counseled realizing I've been doing my damnedest not to lay his girl, even though her attempts are coming more often.

"You let me know how all this turns out for you, alright." I requested before walking off not knowing or caring for his reactions or facial expressions. "Gregs, so that you know, I didn't beat your ass cause we're teammates and I don't need coach on my back. But as for me, you and Tasha, we're going to finish this!" J.T. uttered before turning to walk away. "You want this ass whooping? Come get it, Brian. Coach ain't never got to know nothing. Don't put your hesitations on nothing but fear." I yelled while strolling through the parking lot.

RING. RING! "Yes." I said sternly. "Where you at?" Imani's soft voice whispered into my ear. "I'm just walking into the apartment. "Where you at?" I asked with a smile. "I'm just leaving school. I had cheerleading practice." Imani divulged. "Did you and Dame make it to the store this afternoon?" Imani asked, always remembering my every move. "Yeah, we just getting back." I openly replied while dropping my bags onto my bed. "Is he still with you?" she asked as I heard a car door close in the background. "No, he dipped out. Who you with?" I asked after hearing a few voices behind her. "Nicole and her dad. I'm hitching a ride with them." she openly admitted. "It better be!" I joked while trying to gather my things for class. "Listen, babe, let me go. I get myself together before class." I insisted as I tossed my class' necessities into my bag. "Okay. Just so you know, my train arrives at one fifty-five on Friday." she added nonchalantly. "You comin' up here?" I asked eagerly. "Yeah, I'm horny as shit." she said sarcastically. "Me too! I'll talk to you after class. Damn, I love you!" I said full of animation. "Ditto" she whispered as she ended the call.

RING. RING! "Yes." I answered after seeing who was calling. "Yo. What happened wit ya boy?" Dame asked with a snicker. "Nothing. He's a clown!" I answered rummaging across my desk for my flash drive. "What was the deal with his entourage?" he asked continuing to laugh at the twins. "The only reason J.T. had them out there was because no one man on earth can take me, and he know it!" I barked playing at being superhuman. "What?!" he asked in disbelief that I would even say such a thing. "I'm fuckin' wit you. I don't know why they were out there. But, did you see Tony? It was pathetic." I said genuinely about my friend and teammate. "Yeah, I think I might've lost all respect for that man." Dame agreed. "We both know, that's your boy. He's your boy, today. He goin' be your boy, tomorrow!

I don't see what you see in that cracker." Dame continued, pretending like Tone wasn't his friend too. "You kinda sound like you blaming me for all of this!" I said defensively. "Ain't nobody say this was your fault, even though it is. I just want to know what are you going to do about it? Cause if you don't handle this the right way, right now, he's going to be a pain in your ass, for a nice couple of minutes!" he logically lectured. "I ain't worried about Brian!" I said confidently. "Wait, hold on. That's my other line." I interrupted before he even got the chance to speak. "Yes." I answered sternly. "Hey, you!" Tasha said enthused. "Hey, what does your schedule look like for the rest of this evening?" I asked seriously. "Why, what's up?" she pleasantly asked. "She must not know he approached me or even had plans on approaching me." I thought. "What you got goin' on later?" I asked relentlessly. "I got a class at five fifteen.

After that, I was coming *home* to you." she said sincerely. "Yeah, do that. Now let me go, I got Dame on the other line." I arrogantly insisted. "Dame... or Imani?" she questioned dismally. "If it was Imani, I would say it's Imani. Now let me go, and I'll see you later." I casually answered. *click* "Oh well, he hung up now." I nonchalantly mentioned. "But let me go anyway and I'll see you later." I charmingly requested before ending the call.

3-0-2-5-5-5-8-9-7-5

WELCOME TO VERIZON'S VOICE MESSAGING SERVICE, PLEASE ENTER YOUR PASS CODE...

YOU HAVE 3 NEW MESSAGES…
FIRST NEW MESSAGE, TODAY, 10:21AM…

"Good morning Mr. Gregory, my name is Rob Leonard, assistant defensive coordinator of the New York Giants. The reason for my call is the inform you that we've been scouting you for some time and we're rather impressed. Iram O'Leary, our most decorated talent scout has given you high praise and has elected to continue his research of you. Pending the result of said research, we are prepared to have you come up here for a visit. Just to look around and answer a couple questions. If you have any questions at this time, Mr. O'Leary will be continuing his visit of your school over the next few weeks. Your coaching staff has his contact information and will release it to you at the permissible time. Thank you for your time, and I hope to see you up here for a visit."

MESSAGE SAVED FOR 30 DAYS.
SECOND NEW MESSAGE…

Click!

CHAPTER 11

"Omar"

Buzz... "Mr. Gregory, it's eleven forty."

"Okay, I'm ready. You got the KY?" sarcastically teased as I glanced down at my watch.

"You're retarded."

"I try to be. Give me two minutes, to shut it down." I requested while still chuckling at my own joke. I took a deep breath, closed out my computer, and walked over to get my coat from behind the door.

Tap. Tap! "Knock, knock." Toni whispered as she slowly crept open the office door. "Here." she continued as she placed a small bottle of KY Jelly on my desk. "What the hell is that?" I asked taken back by her gift. "It's what you asked for." she responded sarcastically. "I know what it is, Antionette. Why do you have it with you at work?" I asked slightly traumatized. "I got it from Monica Lohan, Carson's assistant." she admitted nonchalantly. "You got it from Mon... Carson's assis... why the hell does she have it?" I asked perplexed by the whole situation. "Cause she doing Carson." she answered sharply. She folded her coat across her arm and sat down on my desk to wait for me. "And how do you know this?" I asked curiously. "Everybody knows it. I don't think they're even trying to hide it." she said, despondently. "Not everybody knew it." I said, pretending to feel sad because I was left out. "Maybe if you spend more time with us common folk, you would know some things." Toni said with a sexy smile.

"I'll be damned, Carson's doing his assistant. What else do you know?" I asked pretending to be curious about office affairs. "I know that if you ever get up the nerve to spend some time with me outside of the office, you would know that you wouldn't need this." Toni said, picking the KY Jelly up from the desk and tossing it to me.

"And I thought that Elliott was happy in his marriage." I whispered ignoring the unfitting statement from Toni. "He is. And his time with Monica is one of the reasons for that." she disclosed while staring at me with a smile. "What kinda sense does that make?" I asked with the fear that her answer may make sense. "Even the best husband can be a terrible monogamist. Marriage is a partnership. Did you ever recognize that you go through the exact same channels to start a marriage as you do to start a business?" Toni said confidently. "What does one thing have to do with the other?" I sensibly asked looking for somewhere to put the bottle she tossed me. I started to feel better about her making any sense. "Sometimes you need outside interference to keep shit moving. Marriage is a union of two people who found their happy and want to hold on to it forever, right?" she asked beginning to rise and impatiently head towards the window. "Right." I said, unsure of where she was going with this. "No one person can make someone happy forever. Just like no one thing could make someone happy, forever. If your favorite food was chili, could you live on that and that alone? Happily?! For the rest of your life?!" she interviewed while reaching out for my hand to hold. I gave her my hand as she continued to theorize. "I know I said that you need outside interference, before. But interference, was not the word I meant. It's more like assistance. The trick is to embrace your assistance, not surrender to it. Use it the way it's supposed to be used. If you're struggling to get over a hump, get some help and move on. You see, that's where people make their mistake. The inability to move on." she said magnificently. "You mind my asking who or what caused you to be such an expert on the subject?" I asked as I pulled my hands from her grasp and nodded my head towards the door. "You ready?" I continued as I gestured to help her put on her coat.

I took another deep breath, shook my head, and escorted Toni out of my office with my hand in the small of her back. "Unless you want people to believe that we are the next Monica and Mr. Carson, you need to move your hand, right…!" she whispered bluntly. I moved my hand before she could even complete her sentence.

"So, where are we going?" I asked as Toni escorted me down the hall towards the elevators. "You said you wanted to see downtown Dover, right?" she asked anxiously. "Yeah, I did say that." I said, now skeptical of what I was about to get into. We got off the elevator and exited the building. I raised my hand to hail a cab. "We are walking." Toni quietly informed while quickly reached up and pulled my arm out of air.

"Where are we going? Don't you only get an hour for lunch?" I asked as we seemed to be walking aimlessly. "I was giving you what you asked for. A look at downtown Dover through my eyes. I wanted you to see it without the conference calls in the back of some car. Or the road raging horns. Or the hustle and bustle of the traffic jams. I wanted you to taste the environment. See the people. Smell each shop as we walk by. It's more to it than you know, and it changes every day." Toni said, bowled over with glee. "It's downtown, Dover." I said, bewildered with the amazement that she saw around us. "And again, you expect us to take in all of this wonderment, in sixty minutes?" I asked sarcastically. "No, I don't. But I do know that I'm out with the boss. Lunch is over, when you say it's over. So, if it took sixty-six minutes, I figured that we'd be okay." she said laughing. I shook my head and continued to follow Toni down the street to wherever it was that she was taking me for lunch.

"Here we are." Toni said as she turned and pointed to a gated courtyard behind her. "The Cast Iron Caldron." I said as I stepped back to get a better look at the décor. "You ain't gotta say it like that. They got the world's best soup here." she said defensively. "Soup?" I dynamically asked expecting something more. "I see you're not impressed. We could always go there." Toni said, pointing to another place directly across the street. "Gillespie's Public Jazz House? Sounds interesting. What do they serve? Salad?" I asked sarcastically. "Let's go find out!" she eagerly exclaimed as she enthusiastically grabbed my arm and pulled me across the busy street. "How are you able to move so fast in those heeled shoes?" I curiously asked while trying to keep pace. "I do everything in heels." she said with a seductive wink. "Now come on. We gotta get off the street, before your spotted. Don't want you to get into any trouble." she said, giggling maliciously. "Please know that my wife may not have a fix on my exact whereabouts, but she knows she'll never have to question my loyalty." I said unaffectedly.

We approached the stairway leading down to the entrance of the establishment. "Gillespie's." I said, slightly impressed. "They have an impressive entree selection." I uttered as I read the restaurant's menu which was embedded in glass on the side of the building. I lifted my head and looked around, as if it were no longer possible for me to still be in Dover, Delaware. "Alright now, close your eyes." Toni insisted as she took my arm. "What? Why?" I asked as she began to try and guide me. "Just close 'em!" she commanded as she placed her soft hands over my face. "You're not even covering my eyes. But, if it has to be all that, I'll close them when I get to the bottom of the steps!" I said, fearing she'd have me tumble down the narrow staircase.

As we approached the bottom of the stairway, Toni slammed her hand back across my face to keep me from stealing one last peak. "You think you know me?" I said, laughing at her readiness. "Watch your step." Toni responded as she led me down the last two steps. She opened the door and I was consumed with the sweet fragrance of fresh tobacco and wine. She continued to guide me further into the establishment. She opened another door and the soothing sound of the cello filled the room. It was quickly followed by the rest of the live jazz band instruments. "I knew you would like this" she whispered as she noticed my ear to ear smile.

"Welcome to Gillespie's. May I take you coats?" a man's raspy, voice uttered as Toni guided me through the doorway. "Can I open my eyes now?" I asked excited to see where I was. "No! Leave 'em closed." Toni demanded as she continued to cover my eyes with one hand and helped the gentlemen take off my coat with the other. "Reservation for Antoinette." Toni said softly. "Here you are. We have your requested table waiting. Right this way." a young lady's voice replied. I listened to all the snickering and whispering at the foolish look of Toni leading me through the place with her hands over my eyes. "Here you are." the young lady continued. "Thank you very much." Toni said softly as she helped me locate my chair to sit. "Please, don't open your eyes yet." Toni requested as she removed her hand from my face.

"Now open 'em." Toni said with animation. I opened my eyes to see Toni sitting across from me. We were at a small table in the darkest corner of the room. "Damn." I mouthed while looking around at the impressive décor of the establishment. "Wha'chu think?" Toni said, waving her hand to show off the whole place in one swoop. "This is nice." I said, continuing to look around the room. "Oh wow." I said, noticing the glowing blue light of the entire wall-sized humidor on the other side of the room. "Yes sir. Gillespie's is home to one of the best collection of cigars in all of Delaware." the young lady said, smiling at Toni as if she could empathize with her plotting. "Is that right?" I said as I looked over at Toni, who was smiling proudly. "Here are your menus, your complimentary cigars, and your server's name is Bernard. You guys enjoy time and meal here at Gillespie's." the young lady said as she threw Toni an unsubtle wink and walked away from the table. "I knew you would like it." Toni said, praising herself for her knowledge of my interests. "So, what else do you think you know about me?" I asked continuing to be amazed by my surroundings. "I know enough. Not as much as I'd like to know, but enough." Toni said, noticing that I was still in awe with the place.

"Ok. So, how the hell did you find this place? And what was the wink about?" I said, very impressed and inquisitive of this side of my administrative assistant. "Gillespie's is in downtown Dover. I work, in downtown Dover. One plus one, is two." she said sarcastically. "And as far as the wink, I'm sure I don't know what you're talking about." she said, smiling sinfully. "That's not what I mean. I don't see you, when I see this place." I said, bamboozled by this side of Toni. "What other conclusions have you jumped to, from what little you know about me?" Toni asked acting as if she's offended. "I see you and I see that new guy. The one that's always screaming his name in all the songs. DJ Cali? I think that's it." I said, hoping that she knew who I was referring to. "DJ Khaled?!" she said sternly. "Yes, him." I said, hoping that I didn't sound as stupid as I thought I sounded. "When I see you, I see DJ Khaled, not Quincy Jones." I said absolutely. Toni began to laugh hysterically. "What's so funny?" I asked watching her laugh with her hand covering her mouth. "You! You talk like you're that old. You are what, ten years older than me? If that? What makes you think that I don't know who Quincy Jones is?" she questioned defensively. I scoffed at her attempt to be armor up. "I never said that you didn't know who he was. I just can't picture you as someone who'd listen to him. And this has nothing to do with age, like you said I'm only ten years, your senior. So theoretically, we probably listen to some of the same artists. But when I look around this place, I see Coltrane, Miles, Billie. But when I look at you, I see Beyoncé', Jay Z and somebody Lil or Young." I said to hopefully show that I was more common than I had inadvertently shown.

"Sorry to interrupt. But it's my pleasure to introduce myself, I'm Bernard. And again, I welcome you to Gillespie's. Would you like to start with drinks?" our waiter asked as he placed two, small, ice-filled glasses of water onto our table. "Is there anything that I can help you with? Any questions I can answer?" he continued to interrogate while squatting down to speak to us at eye level. "Um, yes I have a cosmopolitan." Toni said, hiding behind her menu. "A cosmopolitan? You do realize we're still at work?" I asked Toni as I pulled her menu down from in front of her face. Toni looked up at me, then our waiter, back at me, smacked her lips. "He'll have a Manhattan". Bernard looked at me for confirmation as he erected himself from his kneeling position. "The lady has spoken, I'll have..." I started to say. "A Manhattan." Bernard and I said simultaneously. I laughed at our waiter as he continued. "Are you ready to order, or would you like more time?" he politely asked. "Can you give us a few minutes to look over the options?" Toni said, staring at me intently. "Take your time." Bernard said as he completed writing our order, nodded, and then turned to walk away.

"Now, let me tell you what I see when I look at you. I see a man who wants to be a lot more renowned than he is. But there really isn't much complexity to you. You know why you know who Beyoncé, Jay Z and DJ Khaled are? It's because you can't help but like them. You know who Coltrane, Miles and Billie Holliday are because you force yourself to like them." Toni said mockingly. "What makes you think you know me?" I said before I picked up the glass of water. "Almost eleven months of dealing with both your business and personal life." she claimed positively, before following my lead by taking a sip of her water as well. "It's been almost a year, already? Wow." I asked trying to detour her conversation elsewhere. "Yup. In for days, it'll be eleven months. And in that time, I think I've learned enough about you to hold this discussion." she said as she confidently crushed her ice between her teeth. "Oh, do you now?" I asked laughing. "So. What do you think you know about me?" I continued curious in her reply. "I know you work hard because you're scared to play. You're scared someone will see you having a good time. And that can't happen! Can it, Omar?" Toni asked seductively. "What makes you think I'm scared to have a good time?" I asked protectively. "It's not that you're scared to have a good time. You're scared someone will see you, having a good time. That's why you live your life so restricted, so confined. Other people's opinion of you, means a lot. Not to offend but with that mentality, you marrying a white woman doesn't seem to make sense. Or, is that why you married that white woman?!" she inquired putting her menu down.

"Okay, let's get some things straight, right now! One, I married Tracey because I love her, and for no other reason. Two, I work hard because I have a four hundred-thousand-dollar home loan, two hundred and ten thousand dollars in car loans, a son in college, a daughter on her way to college. I could go on. Third, I couldn't care less what anyone thinks of me. Anyone!" I said harshly. "First and foremost, take that bass out of your voice, it's very unattractive. Second. I like Tracey. I can see why you love her. I just can't see why you married her. With your restricted lifestyle, it would seem she would be too much for you." she said aggressively. "The funny thing is, everyone around you, including Tracey knows how to let go. Even Hassan, who's probably the wildest person you know, is your best friend. Which I don't understand at all. Unless. That's why he's your best friend. Are you living vicariously through him, Omar?" she questioned sarcastically.

"You know that life has boundaries, don't you?" I started as the waiter came back with our drinks. "Are you two, ready to order?" he asked as he stared down Toni's blouse at her slightly visible cleavage. He turned and looked at me with a smile as he realized he was caught looking. He then turned his attention back to Antionette as she began speaking. "Yeah, I'll have a house salad with red vinaigrette dressing and an iced tea, please." Toni said, unknowing of the whole staring situation. "And for you sir?" he said while writing Toni's order. I picked up the menu, opened it, and chose the first thing that I saw, "I'll have the shrimp, fettuccini alfredo with garlic toast and a diet Pepsi." I said to the waiter as he concluded writing Toni's order. "Thank you, Bernard." Toni said as he left our table while still writing. "Now, where was I? Oh yeah. Life has boundaries and if we don't live by these boundaries, life will overcome us." I tutored as if she didn't already know. "Yeah, but we make our boundaries. They don't make us. You're pinned in your box of boundaries, because you choose to be. You need to let go every once in a while, loose control, step outta that box. And, you need to do it, now." she said enlivened.

"So, how do I step out of this box you claim I'm trapped in?" I asked curiously. "It's not just me, your wife thinks you're exceptionally confined too. Only she didn't say it in those words." she said teasing. "What'd she say?" I asked, crossing my arms across my chest, pretending to be more defensive than I was. "She said you're neurotic. Unbearably neurotic at times." she said with her hand over her face covering her smile. I held in my laughter and continued with my question. "Again, how do you and my wife suppose I step out of this so-called box I'm allegedly trapped in?" I asked still pretending to be sincere in wanting to know. "I don…" she began as a large piece of ice fell out of her mouth and into her cleavage. "You alright?" I asked passing her a napkin to help. "Ohhh, that's cold!" she said, reaching into her cleavage to retrieve the ice. Toni erupted with hilarity at her current situation. She looked around to see who else was watching as she continued to look for the ice.

RING. RING! "Don't answer it." Toni whispered as she grabbed my hand to keep me from reaching for my phone. "Why wouldn't I answer my phone?" I said, sliding my hand from under hers. I slid my phone from my waist and looked at it to be sure that it's someone that I wanted to talk to.

Emily Gregory
302-555-8973

"Excuse me a second?" I said while watching Toni watch me. "Why is your phone on?" I said callously as I answered the call. "Hey, Daddy." Emily responded softly. "Aren't you supposed to be in school?" I asked uncaringly. "I am in school. It's my lunch period and we walked across the street to the pizza shop." she innocently divulged. "Well, I'm at work. So, what's wrong?" I asked attempting to rush off the phone hence to not be rude to my lunch companion. "I want to record in a real studio, and I need some money to do it.

Now one of the teachers at mommy's school says his son is an engineer at Side B Studios, in Philly. And it takes real money to record there and I was…. thinking… maybe…" she innocently stated in an attempt to win me over. I looked up at Toni who was staring at me with her eyes up and head down while biting her bottom lip. With the thin layer of smoke which covered this section of the room and the soothing sounds of the pianist during a solo, it was one of the sexiest scenes I'd ever see in my life.

"What are you thinking 'bout?" I whispered to Toni with my finger over the phone mouthpiece. "Why?" she answered softly with a sexy smile noticing she got to me. "Cause I wanna know." I whispered back. "Emmy, this couldn't wait until we got home." I said to Emily, excitedly anticipating further banter with Toni. "Yeah but when I talked to my mom, she said to call and ask you." Emmy said childlike. "Your mom told you to call me now? With this?" I said, starting to smile at Tracey's nerve. "Yeah, she said you'd probably be at lunch." Emily naively admitted. "Okay. Get me some information on this studio and we'll go from there." I said genuinely, to my little girl. "Guess!" Toni whispered smiling from ear to ear. "Okay daddy, I'll see you when I get home. Love You!" Emily said, suddenly rushing to end the call. "I love you too, Emmy!" I said, truthfully before ending the call. "Daddy's girl, huh?" Toni said smiling. "Yup!" I openly admitted before tossing my phone onto the table. "Can I call you daddy?" Toni asked smiling cynically. "Maybe under different circumstances. You know you still haven't answered my question, right?" I asked charmingly. "What question?" she asked as she got up and moved her chair next to mine.

"I asked what you were thinking?" I reiterated as I moved slightly away from her. "And I told you, to guess!" she said subtly. "Guess? You're not going to tell me?" I asked smiling with my hands crossed. "No, because it was inappropriate and unprofessional." she embarrassingly admitted before moving her chair back to the other side of the table.

"What are you bi-polar or a Gemini or something?" I asked making myself smile with the pun. "Bi-polar? Who you callin' bi-polar?!" Toni said, with a grimace on her face. "You. First, you were sitting over there talking shit with your panties wet, then you make your way over here, presumably to talk more shit. Now you're sitting back over there like you got in trouble with the principal. So, yeah, bi-polar seems rather fitting." I mockingly clarified as I watched wait patiently for her turn to speak. "Is our little game over, if so…? I didn't get my turn.

And what's that look about?" I asked as her light-skinned complexion began to go red. "That's the problem, that's why I gave up so easily. To you, this is a game. I'm just someone to flirt with, eye candy for your sexual fantasies. I'm not tangible to you and I'm not going to put myself in a position to be fooled into thinking anything otherwise. I honestly want you, Omar. I don't know why but I do. The sad part is… the other night when I laid in my bed, I imagined you next to me. I then realized how much I don't want you. I do… but I don't. I don't want you for real, I just want you for one night. Well maybe not, just one night. Some of the things I want to do to you may require a couple of days. But nothing more. I don't want commitment, I don't want a life with you, I just want… nothing!" Toni said, wiping her hands and mouth with her napkin.

"So, you think about me at night, huh?" I sarcastically mocked trying to lighten her mood. "Is that all you heard?!" Toni asked smacking her teeth. "No, I heard everything else. You want me, you don't want me, yadda yadda. But that wasn't the catcher, the catcher was that you thought about me the other night. That's why you put it out there, right?" I openly asked exhibiting to her that was wiser than she'd thought. "I wasn't putting it out there, I was stating facts and details. And the fact that you were on my mind, was a detail." she said, rolling her neck and eyes. "So why did you stop there with all the details?" I asked teasingly attempting to roll my neck and eyes. "Something is definitely wrong with you!" she laughed as the waitress interrupted to check on our needs. "Would the lovely couple like anything else this afternoon?" the waiter said smiling. "Couple, we ain't…" I began before Antoinette interrupted. "Yes, can you bring him a decaffeinated coffee, with a shot of Bailey's crème, a little sugar and I'll have a toffee nut latte?" she pleasantly asked while looking up at Bernard. "Is there anything else, I can get you?" the waiter said, looking at Toni put her hands atop mine and smile at me.

Toni kept smiling as she realized, not only hadn't I moved my hands from under hers, but I was playing with the charms on her bracelet. "Yeah as a matter of fact there is. Can you run over to the humidor and bring him, a Cohiba Crystal Corona and a Kahlua Robusto Maduro. And bring me…

a box of Cojimar Senoras Almond please?" Toni said with a proud smile across her face. "Very nice selections. I've never been one to smoke cigars, but from what I hear Cohiba and Cojimar are both premium choices." the waiter said as he walked away. I was speechless. This woman was beautiful, smart, sweet, and a cigar connoisseur! Not to mention the fact that, right now I could take her anywhere I wanted to have my way with her. "It's hard being a happily married man with a conscious." I thought as I was overwhelmed by Toni outside of work. "Whoa, I'm impressed. How does a pretty girl like yourself get to know so much about stogies?" I curiously asked while watching her sit self-admiringly. "Well, first of all, I'm not a girl. I'm a grown ass woman, with grown ass desires." Toni replied sternly.

"When I was little, I used to get yelled at a lot for messing up my church clothes. So, to keep out of trouble I would sit out on the porch with my grandfather, father and uncles while they smoke cigars, for hours. It was a sort of their male-bonding thing on Sundays before and after church. I would jump from lap to lap just listening to them as they explained and compared the different cigars. The tastes, the smells, the levels of smoothness, the prices, everything. Eventually, I got curious and wanted to try one. I think I was about 13 when I stole one of my grandfather's, and went into the basement to smoke it. I threw up everywhere!" Antoinette explained as she awaiting Bernard's return. I laughed at Toni's embarrassing little anecdote. "I swore I would never smoke them again. I kept that promise until a couple of years ago, when a friend of mine had a *naughty girl* party at this *gentlemen's club*. The rest is history." Toni continued starting to blush.

"Here you are." the waiter interrupted, as he sat our coffee and cigars on the table. "Will there be anything else for you or the lady?" Bernard continued. "No, that'll be all, thank you." Toni said before eagerly smiling at the waiter. "I took the liberty of bringing your check. I hope that was ok?" Bernard asked as he slid a small cigar box onto the table. I opened the box to find the check, a pen, and a complimentary cigarillo. "This is cool." I said impressed. "I'll be back when you guys are ready." he said, laughing at my enthusiasm. "Woah! Can we get these coffees to go?" I asked glancing down at my phone after lost track of time. Bernard nodded and walked away with our drinks.

CHAPTER 12

"Antoinette"

"A naughty girl party, huh?" he asked unsuccessfully pretending to not be intrigued. "That is a long story, and I doubt you want to hear it. Besides it's probably a little too risqué for you." I stated with the hopes antagonize him into to getting out of character. "So, what's the damage?" I asked nodding toward the check. "Well, not that it's any of your business, but it's about two hundred." he said while pulling out his credit card.

"Okay, well how do you want to do this?" I asked comfortable in the fact that I could cover my half. "Standing up, laying down, old missionary… whatever's comfortable for you." Omar said with a corny smile. "This man really doesn't know that I will do things to him, that his wife doesn't look freaky enough to even consider doing." I thought as I stared at him intensely. "You really need to stop that shit. You call it harmless flirting, I call it, foreplay. If that's what you were going for, then you can have it. Just give me the rest of the afternoon off so I can get ready and find a babysitter." I sincerely requested as we waited for Bernard to return with Omar's card. "I had no idea that you were so ill-behaved." Omar disclosed while chuckling in disbelief. "Cause, you weren't supposed to. Not until I was ready. I'm ready!" I fiercely admitted as I watched Bernard approach.

"Here you go." Bernard stated while handing Omar his receipt. "Thanks." Omar said as he extended his hand for the waiter to shake. "Thank you." I pleasantly said to our waiter while rising to gather my things. "Thank you. Hope to see you guys back here, soon." Bernard enthusiastically said while smiling greatly at Hassan. "how much did you tip him?" I curiously asked based on Bernard's enthusiasm. "Why?" he coyly asked as we headed to the coat check area to collect my jacket. "This is nice!" the young lady uttered as she handed me my half-jacket. "Thank you!" I cordially replied before noticing the mirror on the adjacent wall. I stopped in the mirror to check my face and apply my lip gloss. "You realize that, you never told me about the other night?" Omar revealed apparently wanting to hear more sex talk. "I know. I left it alone, for a reason." I quietly confessed before finishing up in the mirror. "C'mon. We gonna be late." I exclaimed after grabbed him by the hand pulling him out of the door. "You did it again. And if you let me go, I promise I can walk on my own." he said while awkwardly trailing behind me. "Oh, I'm sorry. I'm so used to having to hurry back. What did I do?" I innocently asked after letting go his hand. "You danced around the topic of, the other night." he conveyed as we walked back to work, side by side. "I know. Because you don't really want to know. You just wanna hear me talk dirty." I openly voiced. "Is that what you think?" he asked while pausing his step to bend over to laugh. "I don't think, I know." I arrogantly disclosed as I stopped to watch him buckle. "I don't think you know, either!" he sarcastically responded, playing on my words. "You really think I'm a prude, or something. I'm Philly, born and bred." he sarcastically divulged as he began walking again. "Whatever! You not ready for this." I voiced as we resumed our lover's paced stroll. "No, I'll be honest with you. I haven't told you because once I say it, I can't take it back." I honestly admitted, knowing that this could be the make or break of our relationship. "Just tell the damn story." he said, irritated by my continuous teasing. "Okay. But I need a second to figure out how to clean it up. Can't go full out X rated version." I required of him knowing how sexually explicit the thoughts actually were. "If you're not plucky enough to tell me the real, don't tell me at all." he insisted as he placed his hand gently on my belly to stop my progress after realizing I didn't see the smashed banana peel in my path.

"Okay, big man, if you think you can handle me! It was the other day you were wearing that mint green shirt, and paisley green tie. And you had snuck out to get your haircut, so you could go straight home after work. When you came back, you was looking good as shit. And no matter, I could not stop thinking about you. I imagined it being about one o'clock in the morning, and you calling to tell me you'd be at my house in ten minutes. When you arrived, I opened the door wearing this green, sheer robe that I got. You didn't even make it all the way in the door before you grabbed me, and started kissing me. You backed me out of the door way and closed the door with your foot while still kissing me. You didn't even stop to take off your jacket and stuff. It was then that you realized that I had on just a robe, and you started touching me. That's when you opened my robe and started caressing my waist, massaging my ass and fingering me. Then you lifted me off my feet and backed me against the wall. I wrapped my legs around your waist as you while you sucked on my titties. I put my feet back on the floor so I could turn you around and push you against the wall. I tore off your shirt and began to kiss your neck and chest, working my way down yonder. I unzipped your pants and put your dick in my mouth. I glanced up while giving work, at your closed eyes and your chin raised to the sky. Your lips parted just enough to let you whisper my name, while you palmed the back of my head and began to pump slowly. I finished sucking your dick, stood up, and led you up the stairs to my bedroom. We entered my room and I let my robe fall to my ankles. Then I crawled on my hands and knees from the foot to the head of my bed. I turned on my back, I almost kicked you as I swung my leg around because I didn't realize you were crawling right behind me. You looked at me smiling and without word or warning, you opened my legs and splashed your face down between them. You were kissing and sucking and conquering my clit with your tongue, lewd! I grabbed your head, trying you to push your tongue in further while grinding your face. You..." I said, interrupted by the look of trepidation on Omar's face. "You alright?" I mockingly asked Omar, concerned that my fantasy may have been a little too much for him. "Yeah... wh-why you ask that?" he croaked faintly. "I don't know? Maybe it's the bulge in front of your pants. Or, maybe it's the sweat pouring off your face." I smugly mocked pointing at each respectively. "What?! Girl, I'm fine. That's it?" he asked, misrepresenting his actual posture. "No but I'll stop." I suggested smiling at the amount of quality, alone time we're having. "No. Please continue, I wanna hear how your imagination plays this little fairytale out. Maybe it can keep up with, how I hard really go." he insisted slowly regaining his arrogance.

"Oh ok. Well. you worked your lips, teeth and tongue inside of me. Like I said, conquering the one part of me I thought would never be defeated. I'm cumming, I shouted to let you know how good you felt. Which must have excited you, 'cause you stopped, crawled your way up to me and slowly slid inside me. You tease, I whispered in your ear with my arms wrapped you. You dug your arms under me, to hold me tight enough to roll over on your back, and pull me on top of you. I adjusted my legs so I'd be straddling you comfortably and began to ride your dick. You whispered, God Damn in my ear while you was squeezing my ass. I started kneading my palms into your chest as you pulled on my waist and ass, trying to penetrate me deeper. I started to bang you, gyrating my hips and ass, trying to keep you from getting in to deep. I swear I was really felt that shit! And just like in reality, hurt so good is to be taken in moderation. I was impressing myself, but I wasn't sure if you were impressed. So, I got up and turned around to ride you backwards so that you could see your dick going in and out of me. And... play with my clit. Then I blanked out for a second. The next thing I knew, we were against the dresser with you behind me and my leg up on the drawer. You had one hand squeezing my breast and the other pulling my hair, asking whose is it? And... that was it!" I said as I confidently. "That was it? That was enough! You got a hell of an imagination!" he nonchalantly divulged trying to hide his immersion. "Well, you begged to know." I smugly reminded as we stood abreast waiting for the light to change so that we could cross the street. "Yeah I did." he said, smiling enchantingly.

"Nice suit! It looks good on you." a woman said to Omar as she approached us at the corner to wait for the light to change, as well. "Thank you." Omar responded cordially while nodding his head. "Ohh girl, you got'chu one!" she announced while smiling admiringly at me. I smiled back at her and then at Omar. "Why you don't dress like that?! You see how proud she is to be with him?!" the woman loudly questioned to the man at her other side. "Maybe if I had somebody that look like her I would dress like that." he promptly yelled back as the light changed. "Oh damn!" I whispered before Omar and I looked at each other in amazement and quickly crossed the street. "That was fucked up." Omar said, chuckling after noticing that the coast was clear to react without conflict. "Wow. I don't think I ever heard you drop the f-bomb before. Kinda sexy." I openly admitted, intrigued by Omar possibly showing his street side. He scoffed as he began to straighten his tie after noticing that our building was not too much further ahead. "She didn't have to say that to that man. But she's right though, you do look nice in that suit." I asserted while looking back at the couple continuing to argue across the street. "Thank you." he calmly responded while quickly becoming corporate Omar, again. "Cause you're almost at the job, you not gonna compliment me back?" I sternly asked. "You don't need a compliment, Antoinette. You are a compliment." he charmingly asserted as he grabbed my hand and raised it above my head to pirouette me. I playfully complied as I smiled at him keenly staring at me. He led me in front of him and slowly walked behind me. I continually turned my head back to observe him and each time he was still giving me that look. And damn do I know that look, I've known that look since the sixth grade, when my butt and boobs started getting grown-up. "Just say the word, and I promise to make it twice as good as it sounds." I thought as I turned to walk backwards so I gaze into his brown eyes.

"I don't know about you anymore!" he said with a smile as he recognized the desirous stare, I was giving him. "Why? Cause you want me too?" I blatantly asked while trying to slow down our pace as the building got closer. "I can't even respond to that Toni. And you know it!" he firmly asserted as he inadvertently began to slow down to my pace. "Listen, I'm not trying to ruin home for you. But... I want my night with you. Whether I get it or not, I'm allowed to want it." I honestly confessed. "I don't believe I just put all of me out there, but I did. So, now you know. It really is freeing, though." I uttered feeling slightly liberated from the confinement of those secrets.

"And for the record, no one would ever have to know." I whispered as we approached the revolving doors of our building. "You know what? I do know why I put it out there. I just figured that since you're a hardworking, sexy man, you needed to know that your young, sexy assistant is ready and willing." I confessed before sliding into the spinning door.

"Thank you for the accolade. But Toni, you know you deserve better. You warrant one hundred percent of whoever you're with, and I can't give you that." he whispered escorting me into the building. "I don't want a hundred percent, forever. Because right now, I don't want to *give* one hundred percent, forever. But for one night I *would* take a thousand percent" I said as I pushed the button to summon the elevator. "Toni, listen..." he started. "Just think about it. Let it marinate. If you want it... it's here!" I interrupted as the elevator doors opened and I stepped in. "You cumming?" I said, jokingly. "I think I'mma take the stairs!" he said, smiling with his head down, trying to cover the fact that he was blushing.

CHAPTER 13

"Quentin"

3-0-2-5-5-5-8-9-7-4. "Hello." my dad said sternly. "Dad guess what!" I requested electrified by my exciting news. "Hey Quentin, I was just thinking about you!" my dad calmly uttered apparently disregarding my excitement. "Dad, Patrick Graham is on *my* answering machine." I enthusiastically disclosed as I pulled the deli meat and cheese out of the refrigerator. "Who?" my dad asked curious about my name drop. "Patrick Graham, the assistant defensive coordinator for the Giants!" I said, clarifying my great news. "Oh. Well, he's not the first dc to contact about you. Why so excited?" he ignorantly asked. "Cause it's the Giants. You know I know how bad I want to go to a major market city. Don't get no more major, than New York." I diligently clarified "I never thought, you thought about the economic ramifications of the city you'd be playing for. That's quite uplifting, Quentin. What'd he say?" he receptively asked. "He said that he had a scout down here looking at me and they were impressed by what he saw." I said smiling arrogantly. "They don't usually scout yet. I don't even think they're allowed to scout, yet." he said sounding bewildered. "They not! But he's down here from what Mr. Graham says." I reiterated while spreading mustard onto the bread for my sandwich. "This is not making any sense. I'm hoping for the best, but something about this bothers me." he stated apprehensively. "You would find a way to shoot down my moment of glory. But you're probably right. So, what do I do?" I said as I let out a setback sigh. "Can you contact this scout? Has coach said anything about any of this?" he asked investigating. "No. Coach hasn't said anything about any scouts. At least, not to me. But I don't think they can come out yet. So, I'm thinking this is all *unofficial*." I divulged while methodically placing the lettuce down onto my sandwich. "Okay, you're not to say anything to anyone, not even Coach. Unless, he brings it up first! We're going to ride this out until we can find the source. So, everything is business as usual. You understand?" he sternly asked. "Yeah, that's cool. So, what's up with you?" I asked trying to initiate a bonding moment with my father.

63

"Nothing much. I just pulled into the driveway. I may not be on Tracey's good side right now, but I won't know that until I get in the house." he chuckled. "Damn, what'd you do?" I asked as I closed my sandwich and put my fixings back into the refrigerator. "I had lunch with Toni. Not to mention the fact that an old friend, is trying to contact me. She's really not going to like that one." he disclosed calmly. "And that's why you don't mention it. Either of them. Well, the Toni thing, you might wanna mention that. Just in case, she finds out about it another way." I logically advised while carrying my food to the table. "She knows I went to lunch with Toni. I even called and asked was it okay, before I went." he serenely admitted as the soft music behind him went silent and the opened door alarm began to chime. "Why you do that?" I asked aware that my father was more intelligent than this. "You've never met or seen Antionette, have you? I did it so that she wouldn't think I was involved in the whole boss, secretary stereotype. I did it, so that she knew what it was." he disclosed apparently not realizing how irrational he sounded. "How old are you?" I asked embarrassed that he was this foolish and my dad. "What that got to do with anything?" he perplexedly asked as he closed the car door back to remain in his car to finish our conversation. "You felt you had to have mom sanction your lunch outing with Toni. Why? Does she sanction your lunches with Mr. Carson or Hassan?" I realistically asked before taking a large bite of my sandwich. "No but that's different." he said, still not seeing my point. "What's different about it? You made yourself look guilty when you asked her permission to go." I counseled while disappointed looking for the seltzer water that I forgot to grab. "Guilty of what?!" he questioned quickly. "You made it appear like you were interested in Toni, and you wanted validation from mom to pursue that interest further. So, if it did go awry you can throw her acceptance, right back at her." I unveiled while pulling water from the fridge. "Man, you don't know what you talking 'bout." my dad uttered seemingly impressed. "I can hear you now. Why you mad, you said it was cool to have lunch with her. If you didn't want me to go, you should've said something when I asked you!" I said, doing my best impersonation of him. "Ohhh yeah." I mouthed as a thought of dessert that would go great with my dinner. "You sound like Hassan with all that I tell Tracey too much, shit." my dad calmly defended as I opened the cabinet to look for Juice's stash of snacks. I pushed aside a couple of dusty cans of baked beans and a carton of Quaker oatmeal and confiscated 2 packs out of Juice's hidden box of butterscotch krimpets.

"So, what do I do, Mr. Know-it-all? Mr. Man of the World?" he continued curiously. "Ain't nothin' you can do now. You already laid the track you might as well take that ride, and see where the train stops." I disclosed after happily sitting at my evening meal. "You sound like Hassan!" my dad laughed. "Alright dad, let me go." I said, now ready to concentrate on nothing but my dinner. "Alright Quentin, talk to you later." he cordially uttered. "Let me know how that Toni thing, work out." I requested humorously. "There is no Toni thing." he said sternly. "Alright dad, you keep thinking that! I'll talk to you later." I said to end the call. "Bye, Quentin." he said hastily as he ended the call.

"What the hell…" I whispered as I looked up from my nap squinting with one eye. I scarcely surveyed the room to investigate the noise. "Damn." I whispered to myself as I saw the cup of water which fell from on top of the speaker as the bass vibrated. I ignored the spill and tried to go back to sleep.

"Now what?!" I quietly asserted as a sudden song and volume change caused me to look up again. This time it was Tasha, she was rummaging through my drawers. "What are you doing?" I sharply grumbled with my head pressed deep into the pillow. "Hey baby. I was looking for the blue button-down shirt, that I always put on. I was going to climb in the bed next to you, but I guess that plan is dead now that you're up." Tasha said, with her hands across her chest covering her herself. "The shirt is in the top of the closet and why are you all covered up, you ain't got nothing I never seen before?" I said, confused by her coy. "I don't know." she said as she moved her hands, exposing her breasts. "Sometimes you seem distant. Almost, a stranger." she explained as she turned to look for the shirt. "Is that right?!" I gruffly asked disagreeing with her comment. "Sometimes." she whispered as she began pushing her jeans down over her ass. She finished getting undressed, pushed her hands into the sleeves of my shirt, and slammed down onto the bed. "So, you had plans on getting in bed with, a stranger?" I asked sarcastically. "Wouldn't be the first time. Now, I'm kinda used to it. I always recognize your face but the rest of you, seems to occasionally switch up on me. I sometimes don't know who I'll be spending time with, that day." Tasha painfully whispered as she laid across the bed behind me. "Damn! I really don't know what to say right now." I quietly stated as she rested her head on my back and began playing with a condom she found in my drawer, during her search for my shirt.

"You alright?" Tasha asked apparently accountably concerned. "Pop up for a second." I requested, needing her to lift off of me so I could get up. I stood up and extended my hands to Tasha. "C'mere." I said softly. "And gimme that, it doesn't even fit you!" I joshed as I snatched the condom from out of her hand. "It's cute. I never seen a spiked condom." she said as she smiled and grabbed my hands. I slowly lead her from the bed and into my arms. "Where did you get it from?" she asked curiously. "Juice. He got it from some place in Philly. He hid it in here when Dee came in, 'cause they don't use condoms." I openly replied while pulling her in close. "So. It's unique, why not show it to her?" she asked as we stood there holding each other, swaying back and forth to the music. "Cause, she's a woman" I arrogantly answered while I gradually releasing my hold of her. I pulled back the bed linen and gestured to Tasha to get into the bed. She looked at me with a mischievous grin and anxiously slid under the covers. I walked over to the window and closed the mini blinds before getting into the bed with her.

I crawled into the bed next to Tasha and slid my arms around her, pulling her close to me. I began kissing her cheek then making my way across her face, to her lightly glossed lips. I gently rolled her on her back and resumed kissing her soft, sensuous lips. Then her cheek, around to her ear and down to her neck.

CHAPTER 14

"Tasha"

"Ahhhhhh" I whispered as he worked his tongue across my neck, my spot! I continued to let him play there until I could no longer endure it. I thrusted my arms forward forcefully pushing him up from atop of me. He looked at me awkwardly as I pushed his aside then turned him on his back. I felt him let go a little as I jumped on top of him, to straddle his waist. "He thinks I'm trying to take over and he's backing off." I thought as I felt his opposition regress. "Okay. We can't have that! What to do girl? What to do?!" I continued to think. I started unbuttoning my shirt to let him know, the reason I got on top of him. I began at the bottom and worked my way up slowly, giving him the chance to see more of me with each button. He began to caress my stomach and waist as I continued. I reluctantly continued to slowly unfasten my shirt to avoid the look of serious anticipation. My head fell backward, and my eyes closed as he made his way to my breasts. Palming them, manipulating my nipples between his fingers. He felt so good that I forgot what I was supposed to be doing. All I could think to do was, tease my tongue with my finger.

"You takin' too long!" he said before he grabbed the shirt and snatched it off of me, flinging the last two unfastened buttons in different directions. I jumped a little, as his break of silence and his impulsive movement startled me. "You alright?" he asked smiling at my fret. I helped him get the shirt sleeves from around my wrists. "Shhhhh!" I hissed as I lowered down close to him. Parting his lips with mine, I re-introduced my tongue to the inside of his mouth. I then took a deep breath and let my body limp a little. "Hopefully he'll get the hint and realize he's just been put back into the driver's seat." I thought optimistically. He threw his arms around me and turned me onto my back. "I guess you got my hint." I whispered as he mounted himself atop of me.

RING. RING! "Oh, hell no!" I thought as he stopped to look for the phone. I stared at him with a scowl, waiting to see what dumb shit he was going to follow this stoppage up with. He picked up his phone, looked at the number on the screen, and immediately pushed the button to end the call. "You expecting a call?!" I sternly asked as he tossed the phone aside. He answered me, by softly pecking his lips across my face. Then dragging his tongue down my chin, and onto my breast.

He massaged my breasts with his tongue, giving my nipples sensual pinches with his teeth. "My shit is throbbing." I reflected as I forcefully thrusted my hand into my panties. I began rubbing my index finger across my clitoris. Quentin knew he had me. And to take me even further, he slid off his boxers, moved my hand from between my legs placing it on my breast, and began grinding his pelvis against me. A wall of cotton panties was all that was keeping him from accidentally sliding inside me.

"This shit is actually getting ready to happen. And we both know it. We are not going to let this slip away from us like we did before." I assumed hoping to get my way this time. He continued kneading his dick into my panties covered pussy until I couldn't take it anymore. I grabbed his dick, used it to slide my panties to the side, and began to poke and tease at my clitoris with it. He pushed forward, slowly sliding himself inside me. "Ahhhh, shhhit!" I whispered as I firmly wrapped my arms around him. I pulled him closer to me, trying to have him deeper inside. "You alright?" he asked softly as he continued his long, slow strokes. "Yeah, why?" I asked assuming I did something mysterious. "Just making sure you're comfortable. "Shhh, you talk too much." I whispered trying to smile as he caused me to grimace with every stroke. "Oh, it's like that?" he said, chuckling as he slowly slid out of me.

"Why you stop?!" I anxiously asked while doing my damndest to believe that, that wasn't all he had. I grunted and grumbled with a scowl resembling that of a spoiled child as Quentin peered at me without a sound. "C'mon! Stop playing!" I annoyedly griped after watching him commence a quiet chuckle at my demeanor. "Quentin, you came?" I worriedly asked now becoming more disappointed, than annoyed. He sat up on his knees, straddling me and smiling frantically. "What's so funny?" I asked, back to being annoyed. "You! Now, who's talking too much." he said as he put his hand around my waist. He slid my panties around my ass, and down my legs. "This you or me?" he wittily asked as he held my panties in the air, pointing out the front of them being soaking wet. "If you came, it's a little of both." I answered crossing my arms across my chest while struggling to not smile. He threw the panties across the room and slammed himself back down to me. "Damn boy, that would've hurt if I didn't have my arms crossed. These, are real" I said as I uncrossed my arms and pointed at my breasts. I wrapped my arms back around him, softly walking my fingers up and down his back. "Boy?!" he asked firmly as he tossed the condom wrapper onto the bed beside us. "Yeah, boy! Unless you got something, you want to... *ahhhhh*! *Ohh shit*!" I uttered as he slid back inside me, trying to prove to me that he was not a boy. "No sir, you are right. There is nothing boy about you!!" I appreciated it as I winched while taking him all in.

"Quentin, if you could read my thoughts right now, your head would be as big as you dick is." I continued to think while trying to catch my breath. "*Ahh*!" I released as he continued to push his way in deeper. I grasped his back for security, my nails slightly digging in. "Do not leave nay mark on my back!" he exclaimed after he stopped mid-stroke. "This Imani shit is getting tired." I irritably thought. "Please don't fuck up our first time?!" I selfishly pleaded. He looked into my eyes and smiled. I pretended to smile back. It was enough to make him keep going. I actually wanted to smile, but I couldn't. He took that away from me with his comment, his rules. His restrictions of our relationship, for his protection of theirs.

I think he realized there was something different in my demeanor.

"I guess, he thinks he can make me forget things by playing with my spot." I thought as he began to gently run his tongue across my neck and into my ear, all while continuing to push inside of me. "Damn, I guess he was right!" I whispered as I couldn't remember why I was upset, just a few seconds ago. *KNOCK, KNOCK!* "Ball!", Juice called from outside the door. My eyes opened to Quentin starring at me with a smile. Without a word between us, Quentin and I connected in the thought to ignore Juice and continue on our present path. *KNOCK, KNOCK!* "Ball!", Juice called again. *Bang, Bang, Bang!* "Nigga, I know you in there! Where my krimpets?!" Quentin and I broke into laughter as we looked on the floor at the half glass of milk and an empty box of butterscotch krimpets. "Man, open the door. Ain't nobody in there but Tasha and I know *y'all* ain't fuckin', so open up!", Juice yelled from the other side of the door sounding agitated. "Ahhh! Juice d-*do* me a favor, come back in a... ahhhh! Come back in an hour and I pro-*promise*, I will get you some krimpets!", I said trying to get rid of him the best way I could so that we could finish what we were doing. "Why you do that?", I whispered to Q with a smile.

"Do what?", he answered back in a whisper. "Dig deeper inside me while I'm trying to talk." "Then stop trying to talk!", he said insisted.

I don't know why but the fact that Quentin never stopped stride, was a turn on. "Y'all ain't shit! 'Bout time though. Tasha, I'll be back in thirty five minutes, and you betta have my krimpets. I know Ball and he don't need no hour.", Juice said chuckling aloud. "Fuck you nigga, get away from my door.", Q yelled. "I can't believe y'all. This gone break that man heart, then I'm gone have to break his neck, 'cause he gone come in here trying to break shit, and..." Juice said becoming fainter as he got further from the door.

We laughed at Juice, as Quentin raised my leg resting the back of my knee on his shoulder. "Ahh h h h h h h! Mmm!

Mmmmm! Oh Shit!", I moaned as he began to bang harder. I felt defenseless. Q let my leg go and started to push faster and a lot less deep. "He getting ready to cum.", I thought to myself laughingly.

I felt Q's body lock mid-stroke, "And there it is.", I thought with an unknown excitement. He went limp and fell down onto me, I could feel his heartbeat hysterically as he rested his head on my chest. "I take it you came?", I said soothingly, giving him soft kisses on the forehead and gently running my hands through his hair. He didn't answer, he just laid almost lifeless, as I continued to comfort him.

"This feels good... we feel good.", I said softly as he

continued to lay there. "Yeah, I think we do.", he said as he lifted his head and slid his body up to kiss me. "Now, let me see what I can do, to get you to where I am now.", he said with a smile looking more composed and together. He got out of the bed and went over to his dresser. He reached back into that same drawer, picked his boxers up off of the floor, and began to wipe my vagina with it. "What are you doing?", I asked puzzled. "Minding my business.", he said sarcastically. He threw the underwear back on the floor, opened my legs, and positioned his head between them, lunging in with his tongue.

"Hmmmmmmmm", I released as his tongue probed me, in search of my clitoris. "Ahhh!", I bellowed uncontrollably. I grabbed the edge of the blanket and jammed it into my mouth to silence any more embarrassing sounds. "You

alright?", he paused to ask. "I'm fine. Why you stop!?", I asked ruthlessly. He didn't say anything, he just dove back in. He worked his tongue inside of me, making circles around my clitoris. His tongue had a slight tingle to it, it was strange, but it felt good. "Ooh, wha' chu doin' down there!", I whispered as I felt a cold, light wind brush across my pussy. He didn't respond, he just did it again.

First, there was his warm tongue followed by a cool breeze. It felt like an icy hot does or something similar.

It felt so good that it completely disabled my body. I couldn't move. I couldn't talk. I couldn't even blink! "W- what's in your mouth?", I stuttered.

He ignored me and kept going. I still couldn't move, the cold tingle from him blowing his breath while he worked his tongue inside me, was torture.

I lifted my head from its relaxed state to looked down at Quentin doing his thing. His right knee was on the floor, his left leg on the bed, and his face was hidden between my legs. It was the sexiest sight I've ever seen.

"I love you ", I whispered tight-lipped enough for him not to hear me but hoping he did. RING. RING! Quentin thankfully, ignored the phone this time and we continued on our current journey.

RING. RING! "Can you please do what you did before? That ringing is blowing my concentration." I irritably demanded as the phone began to ring out, again. "Concentration? What the hell you concentrating on, I'm the one in production, remember?" he naively asked as he stopped his thrust to place my leg on his shoulder. RING. RING! "For a woman, cumming is mental. You gotta stroke her mind while your stroking her pussy, for her to cum. Now c'mon and get back to what you were doing, please." I insisted, rushing his return to action. RING. RING! "Calm down, you'll get yours. I promise." he mocked while reaching to search the area of the bed where he tossed the phone. He found his phone, picked it up off the bed, and looked at the screen. "Hey you." he adorably said into the phone after answering the call, while still laying partially between my legs. "What the fuck is you doing?!" I angrily asked as I dynamically swung my leg off of his shoulder. He cut his eyebrows down, put his finger over his lips, and then held a hand out, gesturing for me to give him five minutes.

CHAPTER 15

"Quentin"

"Who is that?" Imani asked after hearing Tasha's voice behind me. "That's some chic Juice had sitting over here watching a movie. She brought the movie School Dance over, and we all just finished watching it." I desperately said, hoping that she'd accept it as truth. I sat up and slid off of the bed moving slightly away from Tasha. I watched Tasha mournfully watch me, hoping she wouldn't purposely try to damage the lie I told Imani. "Oh, … …. ……….!" Imani spoke harshly. I really didn't hear her as I watched Tasha disappointedly harvest her clothes, to put back on. I covered the phone receiver "Gimme five minutes!" I whispered sternly as Tasha began rolling her eyes and smacking her teeth at me. "No, take your time Quentin." she whispered softly appearing more hurt and disappointed than she was supposed to be. "What's wrong?" I mothed as she pulled up the zipper of her jeans. "What's wrong?!" she quietly scoffed while bending to recover her shirt from the floor.

"Quentin. Quentin!" Imani shrieked into the phone. "Yes!" I quickly replied startled by her yelling. "What are you doing?!" Imani asked curiously. "I'm sorry. You and Juice were talking to me at the same time." I deceptively disclosed while watching Tasha continue to get dressed. "I was saying… tell him, hi for me." Imani sternly recapped. "I love you, that's what's wrong!" Tasha confessed with her eyes swelled with tears. She bowed down and gently kissed my forehead, before turning to leave. I grabbed her hand to pull her back to me. She yanked her hand free and walked out of the room, closing the door behind her. "Does he know I'm coming up, on Friday?" Imani naively asked. "Yeah, he said he's leaving for the weekend, too. But he'll hang around long enough to say hi." I bleakly responded, still thinking about Tasha's face as she walked out of the door. "I think they're fighting in the hallway, let me call you back." I abruptly lied to Imani as I jumped up to put on my clothes, to chase Tasha. "If you want to get off the phone Quentin, just say so. You real hectic over there, anyway. So just go ahead." Imani aggressively asserted. "Wha'chu talking about?" I asked worried that she had a hint of what was taking place. "You on a cell phone. And you never had a problem taking me into the hallway before! Just go ahead and do whatever you gotta do! Call me tomorrow if you not too busy!" Imani crossly demanded before ending the call.

"Damn!" I exclaimed as I clumsily hurried to pull up my pants. I stumbled out of my bedroom door, trying to put on my boots and run at the same time. "Where my krimpets?" Juice harshly barked while sitting on the couch focused on the television. I disregarded Juice and ineptly ran towards the door. "You can't go out there." Juice said calmly, without so much as a moderate turn of his head. "I ain't got time right now, Juice." I said sternly as I grabbed the doorknob. "I hear that. You still can't go out that door." he casually demanded. "Why can't I go out the door Juice?!" I bewilderedly asked after letting go of the doorknob. "J.T. walking the building looking for his girl. He was standing outside the door, when I opened it to let Dee in. I told him you weren't here, and that I haven't seen Tasha all day. And if you go out there, you make me a liar!" he explained before stuffing his McDonald's apple pie into his mouth. "Aww shit, Tasha! Was you here when she left?!" I exclaimed prepared to go outside and take on whatever bullshit was being dished out to her.

Juice looked up from his food and cut his eyes towards the kitchen. I followed his eyes to see Tasha, sitting on the counter with her friend Dee, leaning next to her. I walked over slowly towards Tasha and Dee. "Hey, Dee." I said to Tasha's comforter. "Hey Q. Everything alright?" Diyante' sympathetically asked, curiously seeking to find out my side of the story. "Dee, get out of their business. You supposed to be over here, keeping me company!" Juice bellowed from the couch with French fries sticking out of his mouth. Tasha slid off the counter and gave Dee a hug. "Alright girl, you go ahead. I'll be alright." Tasha graciously vowed after releasing her hold of her friend and slowly making her way back into my bedroom.

I stood frozen leaning on the bar style dinette set that Juice's mom bought us last year. With my head down and eyes raised, I watched her open and step into the room. I lifted my head to Dee still leaning on the counter staring at me with a somber look on her face. "Excuse me." I gruffly whispered. Dee stepped aside with her still eyes firmly attached to me as I reached into the cabinet. I grabbed a glass, opened the refrigerator, and poured a large glass of apple juice. Diyante' lifted herself from the counter and made her way over to Juice the couch. "She really does love you." she said softly while lightly tapping me on the top of my back as she passed. "I know. I love her too." I replied before downing the glass of juice. Dee stopped and turned around to look at me with a look of utter shock upon her face. "She good peoples." I continued as I pulled the empty glass away from my mouth. I closed the refrigerator, put the glass in the sink, and started back towards my room.

KNOCK. KNOCK. KNOCK! "Who is it?!" I automatically yelled as I walked towards the door. "Damn, man!" Juice disappointedly voiced with a look of disgust in his eyes. "What?" I said walking past him towards the door, totally oblivious to his concerns. RING. RING! "You answered the door!" he irately stated while rising to get the door after noticing my redirection towards my phone, which was in my room. RING. RING! "Is Q there yet?" a male's voice yelped from the hallway outside the apartment. I ignored the person at the door for the moment and continued to retrieve my ringing telephone. I approached my bedroom door to find it locked. TAP. TAP! "Tasha. Can you at least open the door, so I can get my phone?" I pleaded as I tapped on the door. RING. RING! Tasha opened the door, jammed the phone into my chest, and closed it as suddenly as she opened it.

"Yes." I said, answering the call, neglecting to look at the screen. "Good evening. My name is Tiffany Blackwell. Is Quentin Gregory there?" an unfamiliar woman's voice pleasantly asked. "Yes." I said reluctant to admit who I was, but curious of the caller's identity. "Can I speak to him please?" she pleasantly requested. "Can I ask who's calling?" I asked as I noticed Juice at the door. "Who is it?!" he asked again, following the ill response from when I asked. I redirected my attention back to the woman on the telephone. "My name is Tiffany Blackwell, is this Quentin?" the woman warmly questioned. "Yo Juice! What's going on?

It's J.T., I'm still looking for Que. Did he come back yet?" J.T. exclaimed from the other side of the door. "Yeah, this is Quentin. How can I help you?" I cordially queried the woman on the phone as I sat down on the arm of the couch. "You don't know me, and I would really like to change that." the woman said hesitantly. "Man, open the door!" I said to Juice fiercely, with my hand over the phone receiver. "Who is this? And what this is really about?" I curiously addressed to the woman on the phone.

Juice opened the door and J.T. stepped in, followed by someone I'd never seen before. I held up my finger gesturing for them to wait a minute while I ended the phone call. "I'm an old friend of your father's. He may have told you about me. From what I remember of your father, he probably has." she uncertainly expressed. "No, I don't think so. But who knows, he's spoken of so many of his past friends and acquaintances over the years, you may have been shuffled in that deck somewhere. But what does any of this have to do with me?" I cautiously asked while watching J.T. and his friend grow increasingly impatient. "That's understandable, even though he knew me as Lane and not Blackwell. I hoped I would have been more prominent in his conversations with you." she low-spiritedly revealed.

"Lane? As in, Tiffany Lane?!" I actively inquired. I could hear her smile through the phone. "Yes, God yes! You know me!" she energetically divulged. "Yeah, I know you. Your name used to come up all the time. My grandfather and dad used to argue with my grandmother and my uncle about you. Those arguments used to come up around the holidays and when I had school stuff concerning moms. Then Tracey, my step-mom, used to bring your name up. She used to suggest my dad put forth an effort to find you, when I did good in school and sports. I guess she didn't want you to miss anything. He didn't think it was that important. I guess I didn't either." I said earnestly. "Maybe, this was a bad idea. I'll go, I'm sorry I bothered you." she whispered dismayed. I looked up to see J.T. and his antsy friend whispering amongst themselves, near the door. "Not a bad idea, it's just not a good time. Is there any way that I can call you back? I am curious about a few things." I asked honestly, as I got up to greet my guests. I removed the phone from the side of my face long enough to address J.T. "Do me a favor, close that door?" I said to J.T.'s companion who was standing closest to the open door. "Yeah, anytime! I'd like that very much." she animatedly answered as I got back on the phone just in time to hear. "Is this your number? Two, one, five. Wait! Two, one, five? You live in Philly?" I asked, surprised that she was so close. "I'm just outside of Philadelphia. Ten minutes… if that." she excitedly uttered. I was waiting for her to finish with a why, but she didn't, she left it alone. "Five, five, five, ninety-seven, eleven, is your number?" I amiably asked. "It certainly is." she confidently stated. "Alright, I'll give you a call after a while." I warmly committed. "Okay, I look forward to hearing from you Quentin." she happily agreed. "You have a nice night, Ms. Blackwell." I pleasantly emphasized. "You too Quentin." she whispered solemnly she said before ending the call. I handed the phone to Diyante' who was still sitting on the couch with a look of concern in her eyes from what she thought was about to transpire.

"Do me a favor? Call Tasha and find out where she at, please? Oh, and let her know that her man is here." I said, smiling at Dee, hoping to get a smile back. "Let her do that in another room, so that me and you can talk!" J.T. while wringing his hand together, trying to give the impression of him being tough. I walked over to Juice's bedroom door to open it for Dee who was already walking towards me after hearing J.T. "So, we gonna ask Juice and... I'm sorry I didn't catch your name. Did you catch his name, Juice?" I asked Juice, purposely taunting our visitors. "Nah, I didn't! What's goin' on boss, I'm Juice?" Juice condescendingly asked, extending his hand for this strange man to shake. "Put your fucking hand down!" the stranger ordered Juice in a deep, raspy, voice.

J.T. smiled at the audacity of his friend. Juice looked around to figure out who the stranger was talking to in the manner. "Nigga, you came into my house! Now you can either extend your hand to me, or get it broke!" Juice said, agitated by the same audacity that made J.T. smile. Our strange visitor smiled and took off his hat and jacket and threw it on the back of a chair. "Pussy you don't pay no bills here. You wanna take you clothes off, do that shit in the hallway." Juice said to his strange adversary. "You pick that shit up and take it to the hallway!" the strange visitor dared. "Don't she got a phone call to make?" J.T. said, referring to Dee, who was still standing there watching Juice and this stranger intensify. I moved out of the way so that she can go into Juice's room. "Let her do that in your room Ball, I ain't get the chance to clean up yet." Juice said while gathering the stranger's jacket and hat.

"Go in there, call my girl and tell her to meet me here. We gotta talk!" J.T. aggressively demanded od Dee. "You never answered my question. Are we gonna send Juice and...? I still don't know your name, sir." I sarcastically reminded. "Tell you what, I'mma call you Big Pussy!" I arrogantly stated while staring down J.T.'s so-called protection. "We gonna ask Juice and Big Pussy to step out the apartment? Or, is this a doubles match?" I continued to ask, showing my lack of fear of whatever he and his companion have come to bring. "I ain't going nowhere!" Big Pussy said promptly. "I don't know, you might wanna follow your shit out into the hallway. 'Cause it's a lot of young college men out there, and a jacket and a hat won't last long on the floor unguarded." Juice disclosed with a sarcastic smile after opening the door and tossing out the apparel.

"You talk too much!" Big Pussy expressed as he slowly approached Juice while he closed the door. "An..." Juice began before Big Pussy raised his fist and forcefully smashed against the side of Juice's mouth. Juice fell onto the reclining chair and then rolled onto the floor. I rushed this stranger, pushing him up against the wall. I punched him with my right hand in his left side lower abdomen, as he bent down from the body shot, I followed with a left headshot to his right temple. J.T. grabbed me from behind and tossed me onto the floor. With his momentum and our legs entwined, he fell onto the floor next to me. He rose before I could, dove on top of me, and started throwing punches. I looked over to see Big Pussy still against the wall, he was low and curled up as Juice was punching him on top of his head and kneeing him in his stomach. J.T.'s opportunity was a wasted one, for out of maybe six or seven punches he only landed two. One in my right ear, it rang a little, but nothing serious. The other on my left shoulder where it meets my neck, again nothing serious. I raised my left forearm colliding it with J.T.'s nose. I followed that with my right hand to his left jaw, continuing with my right elbow to the left side of his nose, all in one endless swing. J.T. fell back, giving me just enough leverage to overpower him. With my left hand on the right side of his neck and my right hand on his left shoulder, I lunged him forward tossing him into the back of the couch. He bounced off the couch and hit the floor still holding his nose. I stood up over him, as both he and I noticed my bedroom door swing open to both Dee and Tasha standing there panicking as they watched. "Fuck you doing here!" J.T. hollered while lying on the floor with his hand covering his nose and mouth.

I stepped from over J.T. and began to walk towards my room, and Tasha. Tasha saw me coming and quickly started towards the kitchen. "Tasha, tell your boyfriend don't bleed on my rug!" I said, noticing the blood dripping onto the floor from under J.T.'s hand. "Fuck your rug, man!" J.T. barked as he spits the gathered blood and saliva out of his mouth onto the small piece of area rug just behind the couch. "You just don't know when to stop do you?" I harshly asked as I promptly scurried over and kicked him in his hand covered mouth. "Just shut up!" Dee empathetically advised J.T. while filling a sandwich bag with ice. I made my way over to Juice, with Dee right behind me. "Juice, you good?" I said extending my hand to give my colleague a handshake. "I'm good! Just like freshmen year." Juice said, holding his large McDonald's milkshake up to his eye with one hand, and grasping my hand with the other.

Dee squeezed herself around me and onto Juice's lap. "He got you in the eye, baby?" Dee asked Juice as she took the cup away from his face replacing it with her bag of ice. "Fuck no that pussy ain't hit me in my eye. I hit my eye on the arm of the chair, when he snuck me. Bitch!" Juice confessed before removing the lid of his milkshake and throwing it at our strange new friend. Everyone, including J.T., who was now trying to sit up, watched the milkshake pour down this man's face. "Tasha, I know you mad at me, but I need you to find my phone and call Dame and Willow. Tell them I need them down here, now. Tell I said... not now, but right now!" I assertively requested. "Me and Brian gotta fix this shit, quick!" I continued as I went into my bedroom. I grabbed a t-shirt out of my drawer, checked my face in the mirror, and then grabbed the bottle of cleaner and some rags out of my closet. I was on my way out of the room when Tasha came barging in. She pushed me out of the path of the door and closed it behind her. She snatched the bottle and rags out of my hand and tossed them onto the bed before throwing her arms around me, and her tongue down my throat. I put my arms around her and held her as tight as I could, tighter than I've ever held Imani.

"C'mon, we gotta go." I said as I released my hold of her and opened the door. We came out of the room just as Dee was letting Dame and Willow in. "Your man came back, Dame." I ridiculed while confidently following Tasha out of my bedroom. For some reason being around Dame made me cockier.

"Aww shit! I know y'all ain't dip on 'em!" Dame disappointedly asked. "Fuck no!" Juice asserted while shaking Dame's hand. "Yo, your sister looking for you." Dame said to J.T., who was sitting on the floor with his back against the couch. "Why the fuck you come back?! And by yourself! What kinda dumb ass shit, was that?!" he continued as he and Willow made their way deeper into the apartment. "That mu-fuckah wasn't by his..." I said, attempting to point out J.T.'s ally. "What the fuck?!" Willow uttered after noticing J.T.'s collaborator. "Who the fuck is dude?" he continued to whisper to Tasha loud enough for everyone to hear. "Who the fuck *is* dude?" Dame yelled, in correspondence with Willow as he got close enough to examine our stranger. "Yo. Buddy! Homie!" Dame said as he tapped our stranger on the shoulder. "Yo, he fucked up!" Dame said as our visitor began to vomit wildly on himself and the floor. "Throwing up like that, he might have a concussion, yo." Willow informed as he searched my apartment for snacks. "I don't know about no concussion but I damn sure hope his hand's broke." Juice mumbled to himself, but I heard him and I couldn't help but smile. "Remember when I had that concussion last year, I was fucked up! Where the krimpets at? Y'all always got krimpets." Willow continued as he rummaged through the kitchen cabinets. Juice shook his head in disbelief after looking at me and then Tasha, who had her head down on the table hiding her laughter. "We ain't got no damn krimpets! Now, get out of my kitchen, and help us figured this shit out." I said at the sink, making mop water to clean up with. "Alright man, damn. Whose case of cappuccinos is this?" he asked aloud, ignoring me. J.T. quickly raised his head to see what Willow was referring to.

"Mine." Tasha softly admitted while remorsefully staring at J.T. "Can I get one?" he asked Tasha, with his head still buried in the refrigerator. "Get out of my refrigerator and help us. or get the fuck out!" I yelled at Willow. "Go ahead, Willow. And I already know what you gonna say. Yes, we go back like car seats and time in the fall! Now I know who drank almost my whole case, last week." Tasha said while giving me the evil eye as she dampened a hand full of paper towels for J.T.

I smiled at Tasha, as I at that moment realized that she meant more to me than she was supposed to. "I gotta get the fuck outta here." J.T. acknowledged after seeing Tasha's relationship with me and my friends. "You need to have a seat! You'll be the last one to leave." Juice said, pointing to direct J.T. towards the dining room chair. "Where the hell is Rudy? With all that noise, he should have been here?!" Juice curiously added.

"We took care of Rudy and y'all owe us forty ones for doing it! Cause, *you* wanna sit there and tell us, we not helping!" Willow said to me with a smile. I couldn't help laughing at him. "Yo, what the fuck we gone do wit dude?!" Dame said, enthused as he continued to consider J.T.'s friend. "Y'all shoot his pockets?" he continued before reaching his hand out toward Big Pussy's pocket. "C'mon with that shit, Dame!" J.T. sternly said as he rose from the floor, dabbing his nose with a tissue. "The dead has arisen." Dee entertainingly said. "What's his name so they can stop messing with him?" she continued to compassionately ask. "Roman. His name is Roman. Hey Dame, help me get him up, so I can get outta here." J.T. seriously requested as he began to stretch. "You must be the fuck, retarded. He covered in throw up, with pink shit in his hair and on his face. I ain't touching that mutha-fuckah!" Dame exclaimed as he ultimately backed away from Roman. Everyone but J.T. began laughing hysterically. "I already told you, you ain't going nowhere, so sit down." Juice strictly ordered J.T. as Dee continued to stroke his head. "Willow, what did y'all tell Rudy?" Juice demanded to know, as he was now taking things seriously. "What the fuck *is* that? And how did it get in his hair?!" Dame asked Tasha making her relapse into her side-splittingly laughter.

"It's strawberry milkshake. Juice got mad and threw it on him." Tasha replied while wiping her tears and trying to regain her poise. "Yo, who cares. Dame! Will! Somebody, say something!" Juice barked as he was now thinking of the possible repercussions of what happened. "Dame told him the truth." Willow explained with a bowl of cereal in his hand. "Dame, what'd you tell him!" I asked sternly. "Don't nobody get offended, alright!" Dame requested getting clearance for his story. "Man, just tell us, what the fuck you told him." I said, becoming impatient with Dame and Willow's playfulness. "No, don't nobody get offended... *alright!*" Dame said again to make sure he got his point across. Everyone nodded their heads as he began. "I told him the truth. I told him to imagine, Tasha's ass" he said as he watched Tasha smack her teeth, then start to blush. "Man, stop playing!" Juice harshly demanded. "I'm not playing. You know Rudy a pervert, so you got to start off talking about a chick when you talk to him. Anyway, I told him to imagine Tasha's ass. Then think about the fact that she's J.T.'s girl, but she's always with Que. And sooner or later, y'all was gonna bump heads. And that day, was today. I told him y'all was up here rumbling. Then I asked him if he really wanted to file a report, on the school's top two NFL prospects. I told him a lot of people are going to get into trouble, and when all the smoke clears, he's going to be the one to lose the job that he likes so much. Y'all remember Mr. Jones, that's what happened to him. He dimed on Chris and them last year, and the athletic department went gunning for him. Oh, and I gave him my last forty dollars. So, somebody owes me." Dame explained gradually. "I remember Mr. Jones. He was cool peoples." Dee said cheerfully.

"Alright this is what we gonna do. Me and Dee are going back to her room, I'm going to stay the night there. Dame, you and Willow get this nigga out of here, get Joey and Tyson to help you. *Take him off campus!* Y'all three got shit to work out, some truths need to be told, so sit down and talk." Juice said as he pointed out Tasha, J.T., and I. "None of this leaves this room. *Right ladies?!*" Juice continued, looking at Dee and Tasha, who were helping J.T. wipe the blood off his face and clothes. "Ain't nobody goin' say nothing." Diyante' exclaimed, as she got up and started gathering her things to leave with Juice. "Better not, 'cause if their coach finds out they were fighting, they could lose their spots on the team. And if my coaches find out, I lose my scholarship. And we can't have that!" Juice hard-heartedly clarified.

CHAPTER 16

"Tracey"

"Alright, girl. Omar just came in, which means it's time to spend time with the hubby. I'll text the number of my realtor friend, when I find it. Byyeee." I warmly said while ending the call just as Omar walked in. "No kiss?" I said, pretending to be offended as Omar walked past me, for the second time. "You were on the phone." he said defensively as he leaned down to give me a kiss. "Well I'm not on the phone now." I said, playfully pulling him down on top of me. "Ow, shit!" he cried out while jumping up, and holding his side. "What? What's wrong?" I said, swift and panicky. "Something in the bed poked me in my side." he said, pulling back the linen which covered my naked legs and the school work I was doing before he walked in. I moved the books to the other side of the bed. "I'm sorry babe, come here and let me rub that for you." I said in a seductive whisper. "I'd rather you rub my head, it's killing me." Omar bellyached like an overindulged baby. "Aww, come here." I said sympathetically, while for gesturing him to come lay on the portion of the bed between my legs. "Wait, give me one second. I gotta go get something, to take this Motrin with." he said as he headed towards the door.

"Come in Emmy." I said, pulling the covers back over my legs. "Hey baby." Omar said as he kissed Emily on the forehead and slid past her in the door way. "Hey daddy. Where you goin'? I need to talk to you, too." Emily said to Omar as he continued on his way down to the kitchen. "I'll only be a second, babe. Talk to your mom until I get back." Omar said to Emily as he stroked her hair in passing. "Yeah, come talk to me, until he gets back." I said, recognizing her inclination to talk to her daddy. "What's wrong with him?" she asked always worried about her father's well-being. "He has a headache." I answered quietly. "Oh." she said as she sighed and turned to leave the room. "Where are you going?" I asked nosily disappointed that she felt that she has to exit the room. "There's no point in talking to him, if he already has a headache." she said, stopping at the door. "Why, did you have plans to give him a headache? Come sit down." I said, simultaneously looking after both of their comfort levels. "No, I never plan on giving him a headache, it just happens." Emily replied sitting down on the bed. "Not tonight, okay?" I pleaded calmly. "Yeah, alright." she said solemnly.

"I hear you have a new friend." I said calmly, as to try not to sound meddlesome. "New friend? Who?" she asked curious of what I knew. "Dixon, Dixon Montgomery. And from what I hear, you really like him." I teased while watching her grimace. "What? Where you hear that? Whoever told you that needs to get their facts straight, he wants me!" she said defensively. "Just be careful. Now I don't know if you two are having sex, hopefully you'd tell me if you were." I carefully requested as she started looking around the room trying not to look at me directly. "Just be careful with him. Dixon, only cares about Dixon! Now I know you're not stupid. But I don't think the four young ladies that go to Newark High, that he's gotten pregnant in his three and a half years there, were stupid either." I firmly warned doing my best to not appear overbearing. "I got it mom. I know I'm not always worthy of it, but you can trust me on this one." she reassuringly conveyed. "Okay." I said, feeling a little better about the situation.

"Who is Chaewon Hargrove? Is she in one of your classes?" she asked curiously blunt. "Yes. Why?" I nosily probed in an attempt to find out how she knew, and what she wanted with Chaewon. "No reason. I just keep hearing her name, that's all." she said nonchalantly. "From who, Dixon? You know he, like most of the other guys in school, has a crush on her." I said, making it know that I knew more than she did. "Well then, I'm sure you heard she got a crush on your son, from that same circle that told you, 'bout me and Dixon?" she said as she rose to leave the room. I followed her out of the room with my eyes as she sidestepped, letting Omar make his way in carrying an overflowing napkin of cookies and a large glass of milk. "Oh, and mom, just so you know. Dirty, I mean Dixon, freely admitted he's scared of Quentin. I'm the last person he's thinking about getting pregnant! Goodnight y'all!" she said with a cocky smile as she hijacked a few of Omar's cookies and walked out of the room.

"Get who pregnant?!" Omar barked, slamming his glass of milk onto the nightstand. I looked down at the small spill Omar created when he put his glass down. "Calm down baby, Emily's not pregnant." I said, sliding from under the covers. Omar peered down at his mess and then started towards the bathroom, probably for the same reason as I got out of the bed. "Where are you going?" I asked a few steps closer to the bathroom than he was. "To get some tissue to wipe that up." he affirmed appearing to have something on his mind. "I got it. Go enjoy your milk and cookies." I said warmly. "What's all the talk about Emily getting pregnant and being scared of Quentin, and all the other bullshit." Omar asked as he sat back down on the bed. "It was just that, b, s. Just ignore it. Nobody's pregnant, and Quentin's fine." I said, reassuring Omar that his family name was still unscathed. "That's all it better be is bullshit! To hell with my son, that boy needs to fear me. Especially if he is thinking 'bout getting my daughter pregnant!" Omar mumbled while shoving cookies into his mouth.

"I have to ask. I've been waiting for the last two days, for you to tell me about your lunch date on Monday." I unequivocally admitted, wiping the nightstand. "You already know. I'm sure you talked to her." he said standoffishly. "Yeah, I talk to her. But we don't talk about that. We talk about girl stuff, that's not something I would ask her. That's something, I'd ask you." I said, confident in Omar's word. "It was alright. No, it was better than alright. I had a really nice time. It wasn't the company, so much as the locale. We went to this place called…" he sincerely opened to admit. "Let me guess, Gillespie's?" I intuitively interrupted while dropping the soiled tissue in the waste paper basket. "Yeah!" Omar enthusiastically answered while holding a cookie down inside his glass of milk. "I knew you two talked about it." he indistinctly mumbled while munching on his favorite snack. "Yeah, we did. Three weeks ago, when I mentioned that I wanted to take you there for your birthday. I wanted you to get your Fuente Don Arturo or whatever it's called? That, special anniversary cigar that you want so bad." I calmly disclosed as I lifted the sheets to get back into the bed. "Damn, babe. I'm sorry. I didn't know." he solemnly divulged while continuing cookie eating method. "I'm sure you didn't. How could you have?" I sullenly asked after gathering my schoolwork to complete grading assignments.

CHAPTER 17

"Omar"

"Here. Good looking out." Hassan said as he tossed my keys onto the end table. "Yours are over in my jacket pocket." I informed while trying to finish up a paragraph. "You put gas in the tank?" I asked severely after raising my head from my book. "Don't I always?" he said with a slight swagger. "What's wrong with you?" Hassan nosily asked. "Nothing, I'm good." I said before closing my book and rising from the sofa.

"I been trying to call you since you left the office." I said, following Hassan towards the den. I detoured to the kitchen to grab a few beers, before making my way down the steps. "Here, I don't think the ones down here are cold yet." I explained while handing him one. "Thanks." he stated accepting the beer. "And I saw you called, my bad. I didn't see 'em, until I was on my way here. By then I said fuck it, I'll see what you want when I get here." he said, reaching behind the bar for a bottle opener. "Yo, while you back there, grab those keys." I said to Hassan as I slammed the pool balls into the triangle. "Where'd you tell Jills you were going tonight?" I intuitively asked while clearing the table to play. "Here., I had to bring you your truck back, since I used it to grab some supplies to show the contractors. She's knows if I'm here, we're gonna hang out, bullshit around, shoot some pool, whatever. And now that we're hanging out and shooting pool, I didn't lie." Hassan said sincerely as he tossed the keys from behind the bar, across the room. "You really do believe that bullshit, don't you?" I said as I caught the keys. I opened the door which adjoins the den and the garage. I "Yup!" Hassan said faintly, his voice drowned out but by the sound of the garage door opening. I walked through the garage and across the driveway to my truck.

"What'd you say?" I said to Hassan as I stood in the doorway and watched the garage door close before coming into the house. "I know you didn't go check your truck." Hassan irritably repeated. "No. I went out to grab, this." I said, holding up a piece of paper with a phone number on it. "What's that?" he nosily asked as he bent to shoot. "Tiffany's phone number." I answered watching the ball bang into the corner pocket. "You didn't call that number, yet?" he confusedly asked. "Nope. Should I have?" I asked while watching him continue to shoot. "That's your problem. What's the number, I'll call it!" he said, confidently fetching his cell phone from his pocket. "Hell no. Not in my house! And what's my problem?!" I passionately asked as his shot failed to be successful. "You think too much. But oh well, fuck it. You don't care, I don't care. I'm breaking, right?" he nonchalantly asked as he began to gather the balls back into the triangle.

Hassan took his shot at breaking the triangle, sending the pool balls in 16 different directions. "Nothing fell, right?" I asked mockingly. "Nah, nothing fell. It's still open." he said disappointed in his break. "In that case you might as well sit down and get comfortable, 'cause I'm gonna be a while." I boasted as Hassan sauntered over to the bar to grab his beer. "Is this one mine or yours? It's opened, and I don't remember if I opened mine or not." he said casually. "Yours, they're both yours." I said, studying my next shot. "Nice shot." Hassan quietly uttered after watching my two balls fall simultaneously. "Thank you." I said overconfidently. "I know what I wanted to ask you. How was your date with that fine ass Toni?" he enthusiastically asked while still waiting for his turn. "It wasn't a date, it was lunch! How you know I went out with Toni?" I asked genuinely curious. "I talked to Que yesterday." he openly admitted while gulping down his beer. "That boy calls everybody, but me! What did else he say?" I asked sternly. "We talked for a little while, about a lot of shit. Some things he needed fatherly advice about, but couldn't tell you. The same type of shit I ran to your dad with." he said confidently. "Like what?! Hassan, is my son alright?" I concernedly inquired becoming slightly agitated. "He's fine. He's my nephew, you think I'd let something happen to him? Besides, he didn't call me, I called him. I had to find out what was going on with my young nympho." he said with a devilish grin. "What young nympho?" I asked after finally missing a shot, giving Hassan a turn. "I got this lil 22-year-old Hawaiian girl up there. And on occasion I'll call him and ask him to go make sure she's alright." he said, taking his first shot of the game. "That's just, sad. So, what's going on with my boy, I haven't talked to him in a couple days." I asked after disappointedly shaking my head. "Nigga, you talked to him Monday and today's what, Wednesday!" he said scoffing sarcastically. "Just tell me how he's doing?" I said sternly, trying to keep in the laughter of him noticing my overenthusiasm. "He's doing fine, like I said! Fucking and fighting… college shit." he said unconcerned. "Fucking and fighting? Aww. Hassan, don't tell me he slid out on that little girl." I said, feeling modestly sorry for Imani. "See, that's why he doesn't tell you shit, cause you judge." Hassan disclosed as he continued to take his shot. "I'm his father, I'm supposed to judge! And who the hell was he fighting? And I don't want to hear about it being on campus, or having shit to do with Juice." I said as I sat down to prepare myself for the dumb shit coming my way.

"Juice was in it with him, but this time it was Quentin's fault." he said, taking a swig of his beer. "It was Quentin's fault. Ok, what'd he do?" I fretfully asked before rising to pour something a little more effective than a beer. "He screwed some girl, and her boyfriend didn't appreciate it." Hassan nonchalantly uttered. "So now what?" I asked disgustingly concerned. "Well, as it is, they're both on the football team and..." he said, missing his shot. "Nuff' said." I interrupted while pouring my triple shout of bourbon.

"And the girl?" I disappointedly asked while advancing to the table to take my turn. "I don't know, but who cares. It was a college fuck. Happens all the time." he said, polishing off the last of his first beer. "Oh, I guess I might as well tell you this, too. He talked to Tiffany briefly, Monday night." Hassan reluctantly stated as he watched me bend to prepare to shoot. "That should've been the first thing out your fucking mouth, Hassan! To hell with that fighting and fucking, shit!" I angrily yelled as I erected, neglecting the rest of the game. "Who the fuck, do she think she is?! Now, I gotta call her! Whether I want to, or not." I annoyedly said as gulped down my drink.

"I'll be right back!" I affirmed before hurrying up the steps to change my clothes. I opened my bedroom door to Tracey sitting on the floor with her hair pulled back and her glasses on. "That's all you seem to do, grade papers." I sarcastically murmured while pulling a pair of sweatpants from my drawer. "It would seem that way." she said while focused on her work. "Did I tell you I love you today?" I asked sincerely, as I slid a pair of pants on over my pajama bottoms. "Yes, many times." she whispered as she raised her head slowly. "You're going out?" she continued to ask. "I'll be right back, I gotta go prove Hassan wrong real quick. No more than half an hour, if that." I said as I threw on a sweatshirt and slid back into my bedroom slippers. "You want something from the store?" I asked promptly. "No, but thank you." she said considerately, as I leaned in to give her a kiss. "Hey. When I come back, I need you wearing nothing but a smile. And the smile is important. So, make sure you have it on! I love you, Tracey." I said sincerely. "I love you too" she whispered trying to smile as I exited the room.

"Emily, I'm going to the store. Do you want anything?" I yelled as I walked through the hallway passed Emily's door. "No! But Imani said if you're going past her house can you bring her an ice cream Snickers and a bag of hot cheese popcorn." Emily opened her door and shouted as I reached the bottom of the steps. "What, that girl done lost her mine!" I mumbled to myself as I grabbed my keys off the end table before trotting down to the den. "C'mon take a ride with me." I said to Hassan who was drinking his beer and scrolling through movie selections on Netflix.

I grabbed my empty beer bottle and tossed it into the recycling bin as I passed it in the driveway. I got into my truck as Hassan came running out of the garage behind me. "Where we going?" he said as he got into the truck. "I don't know yet, I just didn't want to make that call from inside my house." I said as I backed out of the driveway. "Then, here." he continued as he handed me the piece of paper with Tiffany's number on it. "Damn, good looking out." I said, seizing the paper from him and tossing it into the center console. "Damn you memorized it, that fast." Hassan said sarcastically. "This shit ain't funny, man. What the hell she want?" I desperately declared while trying to find somewhere to stop and call this number. "You know what, pull into this gas station so I can run in and get me some cigarettes. And you can make your call while you wait." Hassan said, noticing my dilemma.

I pulled into a parking spot and Hassan promptly slid out of the truck. "Yo, grab me a bag of cheese pop-corn and an ice cream Snicker." I hurriedly beseeched before Hassan closed the door behind him. I reached into my pocket for my phone, took a deep breath, and opened the center console for the paper. "Here we go." I said aloud as I took another deep breath. 2-1-5-5-5-5-9-7-1-1, "Hello." a soft voice said, answering the call. "Good evening. Can I speak to Tiffany, please?" I hard-heartedly asked while doing my best to remain cordial. "This is she. So, I guess this means Quentin told you I called?" she said, with a breathy chuckle. "Yes, he did. And that's why I'm calling. I would appreciate it, if you didn't call him anymore. Just until we fathom things through." I strictly insisted while doing my best not to erupt with questions of her intentions. She continued to chuckle. "Fathom things through? Do you always talk like that?" she asked while tauntingly snickering. "No but this is a business call, so my conversation must remain professional." I emotionlessly. "Business call? Is that what this is?" she asked as her laughter ended abruptly. "Well, yes. It can't be a personal call, because we don't know each other personally." I said nonchalantly. "You don't think we know each personally? We know each other, biblically!" she chuckled again while trying to brush off anything offensive that she might have pulled from my last statement. "No, we don't! We *knew* each other biblically." I said, reminding her of the truth. "Okay! I'm gonna respect and honor your request, and contact Quentin until we *fathom things through*. With that being understood, would you be willing to try to get to know me amicably? Just enough to give me the opportunity to try to form a relationship of some kind, with my son." she carefully implored. "He's old enough to make his own decisions. But as far as with me, it somewhat sounds like a good idea." I firmly agreed, believing this to be a great opportunity to recognize her intentions. Her breathing became more hesitant as she began to sniffle softly. "Thank you." she whispered. "Don't worry about it." I nonchalantly stated. "In fact, I have something I may have to home for, very soon. How about, I try to make that a definite, and make it for an upcoming weekend? Would you be alright with a meeting, then?" I asked sympathetically. "Yes. God yes." she softly whimpered.

I looked up to see Hassan making his way out of the store. "So, I'll call you soon with the particulars and you have a good night." I said, calmly trying to hurry and end this call before Hassan got back to the truck. "You too. And may God continue bless you, Omar." she said as she ended the call. I plugged the auxiliary cord into the phone and threw it in the cupholder just as Hassan opened the door.

"Yo, I had no clue it was almost ten o'clock. I betta get my ass home." he said after jumping into the truck and glancing at the clock on the dashboard. He closed the door and I backed out of the parking space and ultimately onto the road. "That only applies when you're out doing dirt. But you told her you were with me and as it is, at this very moment you really are with me. So, don't worry about it. In fact, call her now while you're with me, so that one of your stories finally looks true." I advised as I felt confident about the pending meeting with Quentin's mother. "You're talking like you think Jills may know something. You think, Jills knows something?" he asked with an expression of sheer panic on his face. "I don't know. I know Neema's not stupid!" I honestly answered as I journeyed on my way. "If an inkling of the thought that she knew crept into my head, I'd file for divorce that day!" he sincerely professed as he reached for his phone. "Then why do the dirt!" I asked confused by his sincerity. "I ask myself that same question every time I walk in the door, and I've yet to come up with an answer. The fact is, I got a bad ass wife at home. Smart, funny, sassy, sexy, and waiting and willing to do whatever it takes to make me happy.

And I can't seem to stay out of somebody else's pussy." he admitted as open and honest as he's ever been. I just looked at him and shook my head, he was right and we both knew it. "You wanna know something else? When I come in from doing dirt, I gotta go straight to sleep." he said calmly as he lit his cigarette. "Ain't that what we all do? Bust a nut and go to sleep." I said, laughing sarcastically as I grabbed my phone from the cup holder. "Nah, I'm joking." I continued. "I can't look Neem in the face. I get all disappointed and ashamed of myself. Put it like this, many a night I pull in my driveway and contemplate going to sleep in my car. Just so I don't have to look her." Hassan said sincerely as he called home to his wife.

3-0-2-5-5-5-8-9-7-3 "Hey daddy. You on your way back yet?" Emily said full of enthusiasm. "No. I'm at Imani's house, I think? Are you still on the phone with her?" I calmly asked. "Yeah?" she curiously answered. "Well, tell her to come outside and get her stuff. And I'll see you when I get home." I instructed casually. "O-okay daddy." Emily bewilderedly stammered amazed by the fact that I did her friend the favor. Hassan finished cringing behind the tone of his wife's voice, hung up the phone, and jammed it into his pocket. "Why're we here?" Hassan asked casually as Imani came walking up to the truck with her mother standing in the doorway behind her. "Hey Ebonie, how are you doing?" I yelled to Imani's mother from the driver's seat. "Hey O! I'm good! You?!" Imani's mother yelled back while waving wildly.

"Hey Mani. Is everything all right? You talked to Quentin today?" I asked Imani, as I handed her, her bag. "Yes, everything's fine. I talked to him earlier after practice. We talked until he fell asleep. But that's alright, 'cause I'll see him next Friday, when I go up to his school." she timidly divulged while standing outside of the truck. "I didn't know you were going to visit him next weekend."

"Yeah, me and my cousin are supposed to go. But I'm not sure if she's still going. Either way, I'm going to see my baby. Hi, Unc." Imani said, chuckling as she looked past me at Hassan. "Hey Mani!" Hassan said, giving her a big smile. "Here." I said, handing her the bag of snacks that she requested. She looked at the bag and exploded in a smile. "Thank you." she said softly. "You know what?! Here! This, should make your trip a little easier." I said while struggling to tunnel into my pocket. I pulled out a small ball of crumpled bills and handed it to her. "Thank you, Mr. G. I'll give him this as soon as I get there." she said wholeheartedly, while awkwardly accepting the money. "For what?! That's yours, he gave that to you! To make *your* trip easier, he said. Don't give Que, shit" Hassan reiterated sternly. "He's loud, but he's right. I did give that to you so you could have a nice trip. Just in case *he* doesn't have it." I calmly repeated as she blushingly stood there. "Now you go ahead in the house before you get something stuck in your foot. I just realized you don't have any shoes." I said to the woman my son says he wants to marry. She walked off slowly waving goodbye as she crossed the front of the car. We watched Imani quickly trot back into her house and we pulled off.

"I don't believe you just went through all this bullshit, to bring this little girl some candy and a bag of chips." Hassan said, shocked at the fact that I did the favor as well. "Hell, it was the least I could do after hearing what the guy who tells her he loves her, has just done to her." I strictly defended. "So, you feel guilty, because *he* did dirt?" Hassan asked, not quite understanding my motives. "A little. Shouldn't I, though? I really thought I raised him better than that." I said, gawking at the ass on a woman at the bus stop. "I guess, if that makes sense to you. Now stop the truck, so I can get *her* number." Hassan said as he noticed the same ass that I did. "What happened to all that embarrassed and disappointed shit you were talkin' earlier?" I questioned as I pulled the truck over. "I'll let you know how embarrassing it is, when I bouncing that ass off my dick!" Hassan whispered as he walked past my window making his approach on his next innocent victim

CHAPTER 18

"Emily"

"Where you at?! We gon' be late!" I asked harshly into my cell phone as I poured my father the glass of orange juice he asked for. "I'm almost there, bitch. Just be outside, in 5 minutes!" London strictly answered ending the call. "Here daddy." I said as I handed him his orange juice. "Where's mine?" my mom said enviously while traipsing down the stairs in her housecoat. "You didn't say nothing about wanting no orange juice. And I'm late for school." I said as I grabbed my jacket and headed for the door. "I would correct your grammar but..." my mom said, stepping into the kitchen to pour her usual cup of tea. "...what good would it do" my mother and I continued simultaneously. "Yeah 'cause I got teachers at school, I don't want a teacher at home." my mom mocked impersonating my usual retort to her comment.

HONK. HONK! "That's London. Gotta go!" I uttered about to dash out of the door. "Wait! You're home! You not goin' to work today?" I asked after ultimately realizing she was still at home and in her robe. "I can stay home, too?" I asked while reaching for the door. "I have some appointments to keep. So, I can't do the whole mother, daughter day." she answered favorably. "Tracey, why are you explaining yourself to this girl? Girl get yo ass in that car, and go to school." my dad interrupted as he gave my mom a kiss on the cheek and slid out the door past me. HONK. HONK! "See you later mom." I said, pretending to solemnly I walk out the door. "Bye daddy." I said softly as I followed him across the lawn to my mom's Volvo parked in the driveway. "You taking mom's car today?" I while detouring toward London, awaiting in her car. "Yeah, she gotta go to the doctors." he said laughing. "Why she need your truck, to go to the doctor?" I asked as I threw my bag into the backseat of London's convertible, parked behind my mom's car in the driveway. "Cause it's across the street from the mall." he laughed as he slid into the car.

"C'mon girl!" London said as I climbed over the door and fell into the passenger seat. "Bye Mr. Gregory." London melodiously sang as she backed out of the driveway. HONK. HONK! "Damn girl, ya dad is fine!" London said as my dad responded with a honk of the horn. "I told you before, this ain't American Beauty, bitch. I will fuck you up!" I said ruthlessly. "I said he was fine, I ain't say I wanted to fuck him." London defensively disclosed. "Now, your brother, I would fuck the shit outta him!" London sincerely admitted. "Whatever. You feel like taking a ride?" I asked after disregarding her comment. "Girl, I'm the one driving. You mean, a drive." she said sarcastically. "Whatever! You feel like driving up to Newark High?" I asked, really not in a mood for her sarcasm. "For what?!" she asked curiously excited. "I got a few things to take care of." I said with a smirk. "Like, Chaewon Hargrove?" London instinctively asked, knowing me almost as well as I knew myself. "Don't act like you don't wanna go! You know you wanna see me handle this bitch. Not to mention, see Kareem." I retorted showing I knew her just as well. "I ain't say, I didn't want to go. What about your mom, though?" she asked vigilantly asked while deliberating her decision. "You just heard my dad say she wasn't going to work." I stated reminding her of this perfect opportunity.

"Alright, c'mon." London ultimately agreed after very my logical persuading. "Wait it's just us?" London added after realizing that things could possibly get a little unorthodox. "Yeah, any more than me and you would draw too much attention." I said, thinking strategically. "What they try to jump you? You..." London apprehensively began to suggest. "As long as you don't sit there and watch it happen, I'm good." I said, cutting her off to make sure I didn't have to reconsider taking some else. "I ain't going to let them jump you, but I am way too cute to be out here fighting." she said, impressing herself in the rearview mirror. "Drive the car!" I harshly insisted while nodding my head at her vanity.

Chapter 19

"Omar"

"Toni can you come in here for a minute, please?" I politely asked after waiting for Antoinette to return from the mailroom.

Buzz... "On my way."

"Good morning. I'm not sure if I've said that to you yet this morning." I said as she entered my and office closed the door behind her. "Good morning Mr. Gregory." she said gently with a smile. "What can I do for you?" she continued as she gestured a request to sit down. "Of course." I smoothly said as I stood up to get my cup of coffee which I left on the bookshelf when I came in. "And what did I tell you about that, Mr. Gregory noise. We had sex against the wall in your house remember." I whispered, sarcastically mocking her fantasy of her and me. "So, what can I do for you, Omar." she retorted seductively. "Don't say it like that! I may take you up on it one day." I said as I looked at the door to make sure it was closed. She ignored my remark, smiled as she stood up began to strut her way across the office to the sofa.

"Why do you always do that?" I perplexedly asked while watching her gracefully sit down on the sofa. "Do what?" she asked grinning cynically. "Sit here, then immediately get up to go over there." I intriguingly resumed while gesturing at the two areas in turn. "Cause, I know you like the walk away view." she openly confessed. "See. I can make conceited remarks, too." she arrogantly continued while waiting for the reason I summoned her into the office. "Anyway. I need you to clear my schedule starting tomorrow after lunch." I implored as I sit down on my desk. "Is the reason any of my business?" she nosily asked while staring at me intently with her hands crossed in her lap. "No, not really. But I'll tell you, anyway. I'm going away this weekend. And I don't want to have to worry about anything while I'm gone. Or as soon as I got back. With that being said, clear Monday as well." I described while actively swinging my legs. "Taking the wife out for the weekend?" Toni asked as while apparently struggling to keep her professional smile. "Why do you always say shit like that?" I asked again perplexed by her reasoning. "Shit like what?" Toni argumentatively asked with a perplexed expression on her face.

"You always asking about Tracey. Then you walk off with an attitude, when I tell you. And that's supposed to be your girl." I explained as Toni smiled with the corner of her mouth and shook her head. "She is my girl. And that's the reason I'm not fucking her husband on his desk, right now." she divulged arrogantly and slightly aggressive. "That ain't the only reason!" I mumbled to myself hiding behind the cup of coffee I raised to drink. "Now let us get to the business at hand." I continued, transparently changing conversations. "Yes sir, Mr. Gregory." she sarcastically uttered while staring at me blankly. "Are you alright?" I asked observing her expressionless appearance. "Yes, I'm fine. As you were saying? Clear tomorrow afternoon, through Tuesday morning. Is there anything else?" she sternly requested before rising to prepare to leave. RING. RING! "As a matter of fact, there is." I cold-heartedly answered after returning to an employer, employee stature. "I need you to retrieve the proposal files for the Seaford school district and talk to doctor..." I resumed before standing to open the door for the duration of our meeting. RING. RING! "Answer your phone, Toni." I said sympathetically. "Excuse me for a second, please?" she standoffishly lobbied before dashing out of the office to retrieve her phone from her desk.

"Hello." Toni said harshly at her phone as she stepped back into the office. I opened the windows and stared out, trying to give Toni some privacy. I sipped on my coffee and watched the cars below. "Nobody looks like they knew where they going. I guess that's just life." I whispered to myself as I scoffed at the ones that looked like they didn't know where they were, let alone where they were going.

"Well I'm at work right now, so the best I can do is come down there afterwards!" Toni snarled into the phone. I turned to look at Toni who was now pacing in front of the sofa. Toni noticed she had my attention and quickly sat back down on the sofa. She picked up her PDA to continue with our work. "Okay, well I have to go. Thank you again for the call, and I'll see you at four thirty." she said before folding her phone and dropping it into her lap. "I'm sorry about that Mr. Gregory. I believe you needed me to talk to Dr. Knorr about a meeting, in regards to the Seaford..." Toni restarted before being interrupted again. RING. RING! "I'm so sorry." Toni nervously said while frantically muffling her phone's chiming. "It's your wife." she effortlessly boasted while glancing at the phone screen. "Should I answer it?" she timidly continued. "Yeah, why not?! It's not like we're at work or anything like that." I sarcastically mentioned while portraying the strict boss. RING. RING! Toni laughed, and then answered the phone. "Hello. Girl you try'na get me in trouble. Your husband is staring at me, like this might be my last day." Toni whispered with her head down, trying to conceal her exchange. "Y'all go ahead and talk. You already know everything I need you to do. Just get it done!" I demanded as I gestured to Antoinette that it was alright to leave. "My meeting with Dr. Knorr, make it for some time after Wednesday." I insisted as she rose to leave the office. "Yes sir." Toni complied while sashaying out of the door.

Toni reached back to close the door behind her with a smile. I turned on the small radio on the bookshelf, sat down behind my desk, and pulled the piece of paper with Tiffany's telephone number on it out of my shirt pocket.

(Soft music playing)

2-1-5-5-5-5-9-7-1-1. "Good morning." Tiffany said elegantly after answering the call. "Tiffany?" I cordially asked of the young lady on the phone. "Yes." she melodiously acknowledged. "I'm rather surprised that you don't know my voice, Omar." Tiffany sarcastically stated. "Well, it has been twenty years." I said, trying to sensitively give her a reality check. "I really wasn't sure if I would hear back from you." she skeptically disclosed. "I said I would call you back, and I did. I also said I would clear my schedule, and try and get up there on an upcoming weekend. I plan on doing that, too. My daughter has some things she wants to do up there, this weekend. Would you be available to meet Saturday?" I overbearingly asked. "Is that Keith Washington's Kissing You I hear, behind you?" she asked vibrantly. "Excuse me?! Uh, yeah I guess." I confusedly disclosed after pausing to listen to the music faintly playing on the radio. "I'm sorry, that's one of my favorite songs and I so seldom get to hear it. But as for your request, I'd love to share my world with you this weekend." she tenderly responded. I removed the phone from my ear and bewilderedly stared at it. "Share her world?" I mentally repeated not knowing how to take her last statement. "You sure? Because you seem to be all over the place." I openly indicated as I turned on my computer monitor. "Yes. I'm sure. I'm just overwhelmed by it all, Omar. Saturday would be awesome. Just let me know when your near, and I'll send you the address." she warmly clarified. "Ok. Talk to you,

Saturday." I said while staring aimlessly at the screen. "Can't wait. Enjoy your day, Omar." she said before ending the call before I could respond.

"Why, and why now Tiffany?" I began to again heavily ponder about her sudden resurgence.

TAP! TAP! TAP! "Mr. Gregory. Omar!" Toni yelled as she slowly opened the door and peeked her head in, trying to get my attention. "Huh." I said, awakening from my state of unconsciousness. "Is everything alright?" she awkwardly asked. "Yeah, I'm good." I promptly answered coming back to reality.

CHAPTER 20

"Emily"

"Wha'chu doing?!" London harshly asked as I grabbed her phone from the center console. "I'm looking for what's his name's phone number. Kareem, that's it!" I replied before looking through her cell phone contacts. "You can ask, first!" she harshly notified as she attempted to reached and take the phone away from me. "You ain't got nothing else in here, that I want to see. I ain't fucking you, and I don't want your man!" I informed as I scanned up and down the screen for her friend's number. "This it?" I asked showing her the screen. "Don't it say his name?" she sarcastically questioned while maneuvering through traffic. "What you gonna do?" she nervously asked panicked that I may put a damper in her so-called game. "Call him, and tell him we're outside. And, to meet us in the library." I strictly insisted as we pulled into the parking lot. "You know where the library at?" London asked amazed as she diligently looked for a location to park. "My mom teaches here. I've been coming here before I started Dover High. Now call your man, and tell him to meet us." I demanded as I pointed out an open spot. "He ain't my man, yet!" London said, blushing while she backed into the suggested locale.

I waited for London to put the car in park and promptly leapt out. "Hey what's up, Em'?!" a voice yelled from a car pulling into the empty spot, a couple spaces over. "Hey, Reesey cup." I said after his tinted window lowered just enough to expose his identity. I walked over to the car as he started getting out. "Where you going?" London anxiously asked while vacating her car. "Right here!" I exclaimed while pointing to Reese's car.

"Hey Reese!" I happily stated as I approached his side. "Hey girl!" Reese loudly sang out while enthusiastically throwing his arms around me. "What, y'all up here wit' ya mom?" he colorfully questioned while observing past me at London. "We just came to visit." I deceitfully answered. "You mean, go to the office and get a pass visit? Or one of them, I can't be seen 'cause I'm out here creepin', visits? Cause you know those the ones, I like!" Reese outrageously disclosed as he slid past me to get to his trunk. "The second one. You know me, girl. I like, what you like." I merrily divulged as I followed Reese with London at my side. "You can say that again, girl. whooo!" Reese showily bellowed while holding up his pointer finger on both hands to show extended length. Damn! You got a whole Macy's make-up counter, in here." London said amazed while rubbernecking the assortment of beauty products Reese had in the trunk of his car. "Can I use some of that?" London familiarly asked pointing to a box of lip gloss labeled PANAKAKE BEAUTY by Ayesha. "Fish, I don't know you!" Reese discourteously stated while sucking his teeth. "I'm sorry y'all. Reesey cup, this is my girl and my heart, London. London, this is Reese." I sincerely professed while reaching into London's trunk for a mirror. "How you doin' London? I see you looking and I know I'm a lot to take in. So, pilfer a deep breath and embrace the world of Reese." Reese arrogantly insisted as he scowled at me while rubbing lotion on his hands and up his arm. "Did you just roll your eyes at me Reese?!" I asked as he ogled me holding one of his mirrors.

London just stood there with her eyes roaming and her mouth slightly open. "Probably. What's with the whole... my girl, my heart stuff, and I get... oh this is Resse!" he snapped as he stared into the mirror putting on make-up. "No offense." he openly said to London as he handed her the box of lip glass she had asked for. "Girl, shut up! You know you my baby, too." I reminded Reese as I pushed him aside to utilize the hanging mirror. "I better be! Cause you know I don't usually like tilapia, but I like you." Reese acknowledged blatantly. "And, I hope you know what you doing with that. Don't come over here looking half-way decent, and then walk away from my car, looking like Beetlejuice! I don't need you screwing up my already dirty rep." Reese demanded of London as he snatched the smaller mirror from me and furnished it to her. London accepted the mirror while still a little taken back by Reese's nerve. "Excuse me?! Half-way decent? Child, we both know I look good!" London said, glaring at Reese who had begun to help me apply eye shadow. "Bitch, I saw you when you walked over!" Reese said as he briskly rubbed his thumb under my eye. Reese peeled himself away from me, pivoted to look at London and cracked a smile. "What makes you think you look good?! Not only do you not know how to apply these beauty enhancing products, but to look at you... you don't even know what you need to put on." he said as he snatched the lip glass out of London's hand. "When will y'all bitches learn that make-up is more than that shit that they sell in the Chinese store?" he said as he grabbed London by the chin and turned her head from side to side.

"Okay, you have what I call, "The Adele Givens syndrome" better known as dick-sucking lips. God knows I wish I had 'em!" Reese said, pushing boxes around in the trunk looking for something. "I don't look like no Adele Givens." London defensively stated. "Don't be mad at me Boo-boo, be mad at mommy and daddy. I'm not the one who gave you those lips. I'm just the one who's gonna make 'em look good. Here." Reese said as he handed her two items. "What this?" London asked with a smile. "That's flesh colored lip liner and a nude, matte lipstick." he replied while teaching to London what she thought she already knew. I laughed at London's sudden look of amazement at Reese's knowledge. "Girl, Reese is gonna be the new Bobbi Brown! He's already working on his own line." I said, trying to make London feel secure with accepting her ignorance.

"Bitch please! Bobbi, ain't got shit on me. I'mma wipe her shit off the map, too. The only one that can fuck with a bitch is that Panakake by Ayesha, shit." Reese flamboyantly declared while pointing out the box of lip gloss to display the label. "This the only bitch out here, on my level." he outrageously vowed while clapping his hands in cadence as he spoke. "Lem'me see your cell phone." Reese asked as he retrieved his cell phone from his pocket. London recovered her cell phone from her purse and placed in the passcode to unlock it. Reese handed London his cell phone and took hers. "Put your number in here." he said, programming his number into her phone. "Now let me get out of here, I got classes to cut." Reese colorfully acknowledged before he confiscated his make-up from London, tossed it in and then closed his trunk. "Later, fishes." Reese melodiously squawked as he snatched his hand out of his pocket and flung a handful of confetti into the air before heading off. "I really should hear from you soon 'cause I spotted a couple boo-boos on your face, Boo-boo." Reese yelled from across the parking lot. "I'mma call you. You might even here from me, tonight." London yelled back as she smiled at the new number in her phone.

"He cool as shit! Why I ain't never meet him, before?" London crossly asked with grimace. "You ain't gotta know everybody I know. But he is cool, ain't he? And after he do your make-up, he'll show you how to dress it up. Hair and clothes. And some of the shit, he can get for you, cheap. You just can't ask how he got it." I bragged to London about Reese's credentials. "Damn, it's like that?!" London asked excitedly. "Yeah. Just like that. Now come on, we gotta meet your man in the library." I said as I opened the side door of the school. We crept down the hall somewhat before effortlessly blending in with the students of Newark High. RING. RING!

"Aw shit." I complained as I turned the ringer volume down on my cell phone and jammed it back in my pocket. "Who was that?" London nervously asked shadowing me down the hall. "Nobody, now come on!" I casually relied as I hastily navigated our way through the school. "You goin' have to slow down. Three-inch wedges." London said, pointing down to her feet. "Ain't nobody tell you to wear no damn wedges." I said as we reached the door of the school library. "I, was going to school this morning. I didn't know I'd be sneaking in and out of buildings with, Trinity from the Matrix!" London said, following me into the library.

We found an empty table in the back, grabbed a couple of books to look understated and sat down to wait for Kareem. London pulled a mirror out of her purse and began primping herself. "Same 'ol London Mathews." I proclaimed smiling at her self-absorption. I pushed the books to the middle of the table and laid my head down to rest my eyes before my big unknown.

"Look, we got a couple of trespassers here!" a man's voice whispered aloud while standing over me. I jumped up, startling Kareem and his friend who were standing behind London as she rested across from me. "Damn, you alright? You jumped up like you was gettin' ready t…" Kareem's friend asked while I stretched my head to crack my neck. "To run. I'm not trying to get arrested." I interrupted as I tapped London to awaken her. "Good morning sunshine. Not to rush you or anything like that, but second period just ended. So, if we gonna move, we gotta move now to avoid bullshit security." Kareem said to London making sure he was the first thing she saw when her eyes opened. We collected our things and headed out the door with Kareem and his friend.

"So, who's this?" London asked Kareem with a smile just as big as his. "Oh, my bad. Storm, this is Marc. Marc, this is Storm." Kareem confidently stated as he trailed me through his school. "Storm. That's… cute." Marc uttered while watching me diligently survey the students monopolizing hallways. "What's your real name?" he continued while scurrying to catch up with hurried velocity. "Do I know you?" I asked sternly as I stopped to turn and wait for London and Kareem who were walking at a lover's pace. "You're answering a question with a question." he said as he looked me up and down. "Now let's see if we can do this again, so we can try to win you back some of your allure. Okay, ready, here we go… Hey Storm, I'm Demarco. Demarco Harris, but most people just call me Marc. Now I hear people call you Storm. And that's cool and all, but when I think of a storm, I think of really bad weather or, the black chic from the X-men. And you don't put me in the mind of either, so I'm not going to keep calling you that. I need you to give me, your real name." he requested with a sexy and confident swagger.

"My name is Emily. Emily Gregory." I said with a pout, pretending not to be enticed by his demeanor. "Emily, I like that. So, Emily. What are you guys doing up here, at Nuisance High?" Marc charmingly asked as London and Kareem finally drew near us. "My mom works here, so I'm up here a lot. I know almost as many people here, as I do at my own school." I bragged as I leaned back against the wall, focusing my attention on Marc. "There you go again. You didn't answer my question." he said arrogantly. "You know what?! That self-centered, smart ass attitude is going to get you ignored… or punched in the face!" I sarcastically clarified while pretending to not be interested. He fell onto Kareem's shoulder while laughing frantically. "What is so funny?!" I harshly asked before walking away, feeling slightly disrespected. "You. I heard about how you gave "Dirt" the business. And I'm sitting here watching you try to do the same with me. Just so you know, my name ain't… Dixon. I push back!" Marc said arrogantly as he began following me down the hall.

"What was your question?" I asked still smiling at his arrogance, which was rather cute. "What's the deal for today? Why was today the day you two chose to honor Newark High with your presence?" Marc asked ironically to both London and I. "I'm up here trying to meet a friend of the family. So, she says." I divulged nonchalantly. "Who?" Kareem said, infringing in on our conversation. "She up here looking for that Chaewon, chic." London said, finally taking her eyes off Kareem. "For real?" Kareem asked enthusiastically. "Maybe. Why, have y'all seen her today?" I asked pretending to be less anxious as I actually was to meet her. Kareem turn his head back to look behind him. He then turned back around and looked at his friend Marc. "We just walked past her! I mean not even 30 seconds ago." Marc said as he looked beyond Kareem to see if she was still there. "There she go, right there." he said, noticing she was still standing in the same location. "Where?!" I said, a little over enthused. "Right there." he said, pointing down the hall toward a crowd of females. "Which one? It's about twenty people down there. Let me guess the one with the dark blond hair and green shirt." London asked after observing me anxiously tear down the hall, to get down there before she made her way into the classroom. "How is she a friend of your family, and you don't know what she looks like?" Marc asked while jogging next to me, completely unaware to my intentions. I wanted to ride him for answering a question with a question, but I was too fixed on the bitch at hand. "We don't know that bitch, she just going around telling everybody that she knows us. Now which one did you say she was?" I eagerly asked as we loomed on my prey.

"Do I really want to get involved in this?" Marc questioned after realizing what's going on. "You're not involved in anything, cause there is nothing to be involved in. Now, which one did you say she was?" I asked becoming both antsy and frustrated. "The one that just wrapped her arms around, our school's resident Flame." Kareem said as he and London drew near. "C'mon girl, she's the one hugging Reese." I said as I snatched London up by the arm and dragged her down the hall. "Girl, what are you gonna do? Just go up, and hit her?" London asked trying to keep pace. "And stop pulling me like I ain't got on wedges!" she demanded harshly. "You might want to take those off. Just in case." I said as I let go my grasp of her arm. "Just in case, what?" London nervously asked as we reached Chaewon and her friends. "W'zup, girl? Y'all still here?" Reese enthusiastically asked with his arm resting on Chaewon's shoulder. "Yeah. But we about to leave, since I found who I was looking for." I said as I stepped forward approaching Chaewon.

"Hey Chae?" I gleefully exclaimed turning my full attention to this pseudo friend of my brother. "Do I know you?" she arrogantly said while surveying me and sipping on a juice box. "You must, being as though you fucking my brother and all." I said as I began to size her up as well. I felt her girlfriends start to gather in close as Reese removed his arm from her shoulder. I turned to look for London who was watching Kareem slowly make his way down the hall towards us. "What? Ain't nobody fucking your brother. One, I don't fuck white boys. That's just not my style! Two. If I did, then he'd look like you, he wouldn't be worth my time." she laughed, trying to get a laugh out of her friends and a rise out of me.

It worked! I turned around to see what London was doing, now that it was about to get physical. Chaewon put her bag down, handed her juice box to one of her friends and took a step forward. "Lil girl, I will whoop your white ass. Now I told you, ain't nobody here fucking your little dick brother. So, you need to move on, before I become too much for you!" Chaewon said confidently, looking around at all her friends. "Oh, for real!" I said as I took a step back and began rolling my hair into a bun. Chaewon she took off her sunglasses and shoes and handed them to one of her friends. Reese stepped between us, put his hand on both of our shoulders and began to push us further apart. "Y'all know y'all goin' get locked up, if y'all do this here. Especially you. You could get locked up for just being in the building." Reese said, looking directly at me.

He turned and looked at Chaewon full of confusion. "You really don't know who she is?" he continued to ask Chaewon. "Yeah. She a dirty little white girl who about to get her ass kicked, if she don't get out my face." Chaewon said, reaching and pointing around Reese. "I got your dirty little white girl!" I said as I reached around Reese and grabbed a handful of Chaewon's hair.

Reese jumped out of the way to avoid getting hit, giving me the opportunity to swing with my other hand. I hit her in the face as both of her hands were busy trying to pull my hands out of her hair. I swung again hitting her in her cheek, and again hitting her in the ear. She let go her hold of my hand, which was still grasping her hair and swung for my face, scratching me across my forehead. I felt one of her girlfriends grab me by my side. "Oh, hell no, get the fuck off of her!" London yelled as she grabbed Chaewon's friend and pushed her against the lockers. I continued to swing, hitting Chaewon in her face and arm. I felt a hand grab my wrist squeezing it, causing me to release the hold I had on Chaewon's hair. Then I felt a strong arm around my waist, picking me up off my feet and spinning me away from Chaewon. I looked up to see Reese holding Chaewon back and Kareem separating London and Chaewon's friend. The I noticed Marc holding me in his arms about six inches off the ground.

"Aww shit, here comes Officer Reed." someone in the crowd that formed around us yelled. Everyone scattered in different directions. "Get outta here before they lock yo ass up, and your mom get us all suspended!" Reese yelled as he held Chaewon against the lockers. Marc turned and ran down the hall with me still in his arms, as Kareem followed pulling London. "Bitch I better not ever see you again, I'mma fuck you up." Chaewon bellowed as Reese pushed her into her classroom. "Where y'all park, out back or on the side?" Marc asked as he attempted to decipher which route to go. "The side." I answered pointing in the direction of the door we came in. "You can put me down now!" I sternly said to Marc, recognizing that I could move faster on my own. We made it to the door and through the parking lot, to London's car. The four of us jumped into London's car as a Newark Police squad car came pulling into the school parking lot.

London let the car pass before she made any attempt to move. She quickly pulled out of her parking spot, going in the opposite direction of the squad car. "So, what, y'all going back to school with us?" I turned to ask Kareem and Marc who were sitting in the backseat. "Awww shit." Kareem said as a second squad car slowly pulled into the driveway in front of us.

CHAPTER 21

"Quentin"

"Wake up baby." Tasha whispered softly into my ear as she leaned over me lying in bed. "I didn't know you was here. You weren't in bed when I got in last night, were you?" I asked lifting my head from my pillow. "No. I left before you did last night. I guess you didn't remember, huh? You were too busy on the phone with Imani, ignoring everyone else in the room." Tasha expressed with a scowl. "Don't start Tasha. Not today, please!" I pleaded as I sat up and swung my feet to the floor. I reached down and scooped up the balled-up pair of sweats on the floor, to step out of the room in. "What are you staring at?" I curiously asked. "You! Why? I can't look at you?" she inquired as she continued to grimace. "You staring, like... you know what, forget it. What's up?" I asked as I inspected the pants before putting them on. "Did you know that the first time I had you, was the last time I had you. And even that was... limited." she said as she gazed at my dick while I pulled my pants up. "Yeah I know, I thought about that too." I sincerely acknowledged while quickly putting it away to obscure her view. "What, am I not attractive to you, Que? Cause I'm not a conceited person, but I'm far from ugly. There ain't a man on this campus that'll tell you, that I am." she said superciliously staring at herself in the mirror teasing her hair. "Girl, ain't nobody say you was ugly, nor did I say that I wasn't attracted to you." I disclosed as I grabbed my toothbrush, tooth paste and wash cloth and headed for the door.

"So then what is it Quentin?" Tasha asked concerned. "I know *tough ass* Tasha ain't bitchin' about a piece o' dick! Not, *I'm every woman's envy and every man's fantasy,* Tasha! Not, *this ass impressed you, its incarnation is inescapable,* Tasha! Not..." I said reminding her of the mottos that she has preached to me on numerous occasions. "Okay. Okay, I get it. I'mma go." she said slightly embarrassed. She gave me a melancholy smile, put her head down and headed towards the door. "Tasha sit yo' ass down. Damn. I'm goin' go brush my teeth!" I said as she reached the door. I gave her a slight nudge away from the door and walked pass her out of the room. I looked back just in time to see her smile before closing my bedroom door.

"What's the deal, with the Get Along Gang coming through all early in the morning?!" Juice proclaimed as he twisted and turned on the couch trying to get comfortable. "What Get Along Gang, and how the hell you end up on the couch? You was already in your room when I came in last night?" I said to Juice as I peeked into the other and saw uncomfortably on the sofa. "I'm glad you observed that, so now I can go back to sleep, and you answer the door from now on." he said as he hobbled off of the sofa. "What you talking 'bout? Who came pass this morning?" I asked oblivious to what Juice was talking about. "Man, who didn't come past here this morning!" he bad-temperedly mumbled as he gathered his pillow and bed linen from the couch. "Oh, and let your man Dame know that if he ever knocks on my door before seven again and nobody's dead or dying... I'm in his ass. And I don't care what he got for you." he said stumbling to his bedroom door. "Yo, what's this package on the floor next to the couch?" I yelled to Juice's bedroom door as I snooped around the box looking for a label of some kind. "Don't it got your name on it!" he sarcastically yelled from inside his room. "Oh damn. Yeah, it does." I said excitedly finding the tag with all of the information on it. "So, it ain't none of my business to know what it's about!" he yelled back frustrated from his lack of sleep. "Fuck is you bitchin' for? Don't you got a nine, fifteen class. It's ten of nine, you might as well not even lay down." I said harshly.

"Shit. Ten of nine means I got another ten to twelve minutes to sleep, if you would ever let me get there! Oh, Dame brought your cell phone it's on top of the TV." he gruffly informed as I continued to inspect the package.

CHAPTER 22

"Emily"

"My dad is going to kick my ass, fucking wit chu'! All I had to do was take my black ass to school, like I had planned on doing, this morning. But nooo, I sat there and let you work me into ending up here. I don't even go to this school! So not only am I going to get in trouble for fighting, but I'mma swallow trespassing on this one too." London furiously grumbled as we sat in the main office of Newark High, wearing handcuffs. "London, shut up! First of all, you wasn't fighting, I was! Second, me and you both know you don't have a problem swallowing." I ironically enlightened with a grin, trying to lighten her mood. "Emily, get away from me. Move to the next chair over, cause I'm about to beat ya ass! I don't know if you noticed, but I'm in handcuffs! And that fat white guy up there talking to the old lady behind the counter, is a cop! And if you look at my face, and look at his face, and look at her face and look at everyone else's face in here, you'll notice the only person in here smiling… is you!" she harshly articulated as her rage complimented by the tears of terror which poured from her eyes left a mascara trail going down both sides of her face.

I moved over like she requested. Not because I was scared, she'd beat my ass. Because ain't too much she can do, in handcuffs. But because, she was my best friend, and I didn't mean for any of this to happen to her. Boom! The office door sounded as it was swung open, banging into the wall behind it. Two more police officers and a school security officer came trampling in, escorting both Chaewon and Reese by the arms. "Find somewhere and sit down!" one of the police officers said to Reese as they released their hold of his arm. Reese came over and plopped down into the chair between London and me. They kept their hold of Chaewon and walked her up to the counter. "Why they got you in here Reese?" I quietly questioned. "Cause, I was at the fight and that bitch Ms. Brand told them she saw me in the parking lot talking to you and your girlfriend, this morning." Reese said smiling at the cop sitting across from us. "So what, you in trouble too?" London asked solemnly. "Cheer up, little guppy.

Messing up that pretty face with those tears. No, I'm not in trouble. Cause Mr. Gene, told 'em the truth. When he saw me out there, I was trying to break up the fight." he said to London pulling tissue out of his pocket to wipe her tears.

"You know you talk too much. Now sit yourself down right here, so we can see what we goin' do with y'all." the police officer said as he tossed Chaewon into a chair across from me. "Bitch, what you looking at?!" Chaewon aggressively asked as she stared at me from across the room. I looked at her and then the cop who was sitting in the chair about two feet to her left. The cop noticed Chaewon and slid his chair over towards her. "You almost smashed my fingers!" Chaewon stated as the arms of the heavy wooden chairs slammed together. "You know, you really do talk too much." the cop agreed quietly, leaning over to Chaewon. "Damn, you ain't got to be all up in my face." Chaewon said leaning away from the police officer next to her. "And what the fuck is you looking at!" she continued, redirecting her attention towards me. "Shouldn't she be cuffed too?" London sensibly asked the officer, while nodding her head towards Chaewon.

Chaewon stood up and launched towards me, as the cop grabbed her arm with one hand and his handcuffs with the other. "If I didn't think you needed 'em before, I do now. Turn around." the officer ordered before placing the handcuffs on Chaewon and shoving her back into the chair. "What the fuck is you looking at, faggot?!" Chaewon cried out looking at Reese, who was shaking his head. "Don't bring it here, fish! Cause, even a puppy bitch knows not to bite the hand that feed 'em!" Reese ferociously notified with a scowl and his fingers snapping. Everyone within earshot turned their heads to smile or snicker, including the police officers. "Don't say shit to me Maurice! Sitting in here being all friendly-ed up with this bitch." Chaewon insisted embarrassed by Reese's comment. "Which brings up my next contention. I thought she was a friend of yours? I mean, you said you used to suck on Quentin Gregory, right?" Reese continued skeptically. "I did! I still do… when I feel like it." Chaewon admitted glaring mercilessly at Reese.

"Hold up. My man, did you just say, which brings up my next contention?" the officer said as he stood up to advance towards the door. "Yeah, contention. It means…" Reese flamboyantly started. "I know what it means, but I didn't think you knew what it meant. But I do want to thank you. Because you just proved my contention about inner-city school education, to that other officer over there." he said with a smile as he walked out of the door. "Anywhoo." Reese said returning his concentration on Chaewon. "What?" Chaewon asked confused, still trying to play tough. "So why don't you know her, if you mess with her brother." Reese recapped while waving, opening and closing his hands in the air. "Cause, I didn't say I messed, with her." Chaewon said defensively. "Cause, she lying." I calmly retorted. "Ain't nobody got to lie to you, bitch!" Chaewon harshly yelled. "Hey watch your mouth. In fact, shut up!" the officer roared to Chaewon from the counter.

CHAPTER 23

"Quentin"

"Look at this shit my mom sent..." I excitedly expressed charging through my bedroom door. "Oh Shit!" I whispered, as I was stopped mid-sentence and step, by Tasha. She was comfortably relaxed on my bed, completely naked with the exception of a pair of my sunglasses. "I like these glasses. Can I hold 'em?" she asked with a crooked smile as she slid the glasses off of her face. I dropped the package and remained motionless. "Well, is that a yes?" she said as she began to crawl across the bed towards me. "I didn't say, anything." I quietly uttered. "You didn't have to. Your friend is speaking loud enough, for both of y'all." she said as she reached out and touched my now erected penis with the tip of her finger.

I looked down her arched back, to her perfectly shaped ass. "God damn!" I thought noticing her hands on my waist. "I think you need help taking these off?" Tasha whispered, tugging gently on my sweatpants. She slid my pants off my waist and they fell to my ankles. "Uh, uh, uh." she softly hummed as she put her arms around my waist and pulled me closer to her, slowly sliding my dick into her mouth. I quivered as a chill ran through my body. "I looked down and smiled while she slid my dick out of her mouth and. "Now you know I felt that, right?" she arrogantly questioned as she pulled my dick out of her mouth and smiled. "Felt, what?" I said laughing, pretending as if I had no idea what she was referring to. "Okay, I'll let you have that one. If you let me have this one." Tasha bargained as she pointed to my dick. "And if I don't, you gonna what? Tell on me? You gonna tell everybody that you made e cringe? Had me trembling?" I sarcastically asked while elusively awaiting her return to action. "Yup! I certainly am." she jokingly admitted, smiling as she backed up and sat upon her knees. "Well we can't have you doing that, now can we?" I certainly concurred. "No, we can't. You got that tough guy rep to think about." she said as she went back down to her hands and knees.

"Sheeesh!" I bellowed as she leaned forward, palmed my dick and eased it back in her mouth. I put my hand on atop of her head and began to caress. "Pull it." she mumbled with a mouth full. "Turn around, so I can get a good grip." I suggested so I can get behind her and penetrate.

CHAPTER 24

"Tracey"

Hey, where are you?" I frantically asked Omar. "In my office, waiting for a conference call. Why what's up?" Omar cheerily responded. "Your daughter. She's about to be arrested for assault... and trespassing!" I casually disclosed. He promptly when inaudible as I waited for a response. "Omar!" I yelled making sure that he could still hear me. "Yes." he said nonchalantly. "Did you hear me?" I asked confused by his lack of conversation. "Yeah, I heard you but I'm waiting for a "just kidding" or a "psych" or something." he said calmly. "Well, don't hold your breath while waiting. Because someone's going to need to bail your daughter out of jail." I irritably expressed as I hastily moved through traffic to Emily. "For what! Where is she!" he asked anxiously. "She's at *my* school..." I began before he interrupted. "Hold on, Tracey" he said sternly. "Toni!" Omar yelled with his hand over the phone receiver. "Toni, C'mere! Come here now, please!" he continued to yell. "You on your way up there?" Omar sternly asked. "Tracey!" Omar said excited. "What!" I punitively answered. "Are you going up there?!" he anxiously repeated. "Up where?" I asked confused at which one of us he was talking to. "The school, damn it!" he said hostilely. Doink! "Don't yell at me Omar!" I yelled in return. "Yes, I'm on my way there now!" I continued while looking at my incoming text.

{Monique}
Get here asap. Can't stall much longer.

"I'll meet you there! Do not let them take her to jail!" he demanded before hastily ending the call. "Whew! It's going to be a long day. How do I tell you about this now, Omar?" I sullenly asked myself as I headed to rescue my daughter.
3-0-2-5-4-5-8-9-7-5.

"YO! YOU'VE JUST FOUND YOURSELF COLONIZED IN THE WORLD OF "Q", LEAVE ME A MESSAGE SO I KNOW YOU'RE HERE!" BEEP...

"Hey Q-tee, just calling to tell you that I love you. And to find out if you've you talked to your sister? She's really been acting out far past usual, and I thought maybe you knew something! Just call me when you get this, and don't tell your dad that I asked about Em. He already has enough on his mind. I love you, baby. Bye-bye." I reminded my son before ending my discussion with his voicemail.

CHAPTER 25

"Omar"

"What's wrong, Omar?" Toni worriedly asked while adhering to my harsh request for her to come into my office. "Clear the rest of my day. Re-schedule as many as you can for tomorrow. I'll work as late as I need to. Meet with anyone, at any time!" I conveyed while hastily packing my things to leave for the day. "Okay. Now, what's wrong?" she asked again, sincerely concerned. "I don't know yet, something to do with Emily being stupid." I admitted before rising up to leave. "Please, call me when you know." she pleaded as I brushed past her on my way out of the door. 3-0-2-5-4-5-8-9-7-5.

"Yo! YOU'VE JUST FOUND YOURSELF COLONIZED IN THE WORLD OF "Q", LEAVE ME A MESSAGE SO I KNOW YOU'RE HERE!" BEEP...

"Quentin, this is your father, call me as soon as you have a moment. We need to talk!" I said on Quentin's voicemail. "What the hell am I getting ready to walk into?" I mumbled as I snaked through traffic trying to get to my daughter before the police took her away.

RING. RING!

> **The Misses**
> **302-545-8972**

"Yes." I frustratedly responded as the phone chiming broke my moment of self-reflection. "Did London's father call you?!" Tracey asked harshly. "No, why?" I asked not really caring about London, her father or his situation right now. "Because he just called me cursing and hollering and blaming Emily for getting his damn daughter, in trouble. I kindly reminded him that he is a man, and if he gotta problem, he is to call you with it! If his wife gotta problem, she knows my number!" Tracey passionately explained. "He's not going to call me. But thanks for the heads up." I acknowledged while snickering at my wife, who was trying to sound tough. "There is nothing to feel good about here, Omar." she sternly disclosed. "Alright let me go, I'll be there shortly." I admitted as I turned onto the highway off ramp. "Okay. I'm pulling into the parking lot, now." Tracey crossly disclosed. "I'm about ten minutes behind you"

I pulled up behind one of the squad cars in the Newark High School parking lot. I got out of my car and noticed one of the police officers sitting inside the car on a cell phone. "Can I have a minute of your time?" I asked as I tapped on the window of the car. She hung up the phone, and stepped out of the car. "Can I help you?" she politely asked with a smile. "Yes. My name is Omar Gregory, and my daughter is the reason you're here. I just wanna know, what's going on?" I asked openly while preparing attentively listen. "Is your daughter the one that goes here or is she one of the, visitors?" the officer said pacifying my concerns. "My wife works here, but my daughter goes to Dover High. I'm still trying to figure out, why she was here?" I cluelessly asked while trying to look around the office at computer in her car. "She was here to fight, Mr. Gregory." this woman officer said to me with conviction. "Fight who... why?" I asked becoming more ignorant with every bit of new information. "I think those are questions you need to ask her." she said as she put her hand in the small of my back and escorted me into the school.

"Hey Mr. G!" one of the student office aides bellowed as I walked into the office door. I threw him a head nod and then directed my attention to Emily who was sitting on a bench with London, in handcuffs. "Can someone please explain to me, what's going on?" I pleaded as I approached the counter. "Omar Gregory, it's nice to finally meet you. I'm Monique, the principal here at NHS. I'm just sorry it had to be under these circumstances." the woman behind the counter admitted while exiting an office with her hand extended to greet me. "Nice to meet you." I half-heartedly said as I waited for the issue at hand to surface. "Lil Emily's been coming around here for years. We watched her grow, so this is a bombshell to us, too." Monique sullenly continued as she looked around at the chaos my daughter caused. "Would someone mind taking the handcuffs from my daughter. I promise she's no threat to anyone in this room." I pleaded as I watched my daughter stare at me sorrowfully.

"No! Leave them on!" Tracey roared from across the room as she barged in the main office door. A hush went over the office as Tracey stormed over to Emily, and slapped her across the face. "What the hell are you thinking?" she barked at Emily, motioning her hand to slap her again. "Ma'am, I understand your plight. Believe me, when I would've gotten a lot more than that. But unfortunately, if you hit her like that again, we're going to have to arrest you for assault!" one of the officers said to Tracey, intervening in her dealings with Emily. "C'mere Tracey." Monique called as she headed back toward her office. Tracey turned away from Emily, gave the officer a cold look, and followed the principal into her office. "Alright, how do we deal with this?" I asked the officer leaning on the counter writing something with a phone to his ear. "Well, this young man right here, is actually about to go back to class." he said pointing to the boy sitting between London and Emily. "Okay, I'm happy about that. Yay, for him! What about these two?" I said pointing to my daughter and her friend.

"Well depending on the what the school board says, if they ever get back to the phone. I'll be honest with you. Your daughter will probably be arrested, for trespassing and assault. Her friend will probably just get trespassing, since I got three eye witnesses who say she wasn't in the altercation. Yes sir. Excuse me one second." the officer courteously requested as he redirected his attention to the phone call. I turned and took the empty seat between London and Emily. "What the hell is going on?" I asked rubbing my eyes in frustration. "And I want the truth!" I continued severely. I looked at Emily, who was beginning to show the innocence of a person her age, with her tearing eyes. "I'm sorry daddy. I just..." Emily started. "I'll tell you what happened, Mr. Gregory!" London sternly interrupted while wiping her face with Reese's tissue. "Okay London, what happened?" I said as I turned to listen to my daughter's best friend.

CHAPTER 26

"Tracey"

"Tracey, you really need to calm down. You know I'm going to do everything in my power, to make sure nothing happens to your daughter." Monique reminded as she picked up her desk phone and started dialing numbers. "I know Nikki. It's just knowing my daughter may end up getting arrested, is not easy to muddle through." I said looking out of her office window at the police van parked in front of the school.

"So, does anybody know what actually happened?" I asked the principal of Newark High School as she waited on the phone to hear her orders from downtown. "No not yet we..." Nikki started. "Nikki, I'm pregnant!" I blurted out exhaustingly, relieved to get it out of my system. "What? Congratulations, girl!" she said with a smile as she came from around her desk to hug me.

"Sierra."

"YES, MISS. BLAKE"

"Can you please ask the officer in charge to come into my office?" Nikki requested of her secretary into the intercom.

"HE'S ON THE PHONE WITH SOMEONE DOWN AT THE SCHOOL BOARD"

"Yes, I know. He's on the phone with the same people, that I'm on the phone with. Inform him he can finish his conversation with them, in here." Nikki pleasantly expressed as she pressed the button. "So, tell me what's going on? When did you find out? How far along are you? What did Omar say?! Details girl, I need details!" Nikki excitedly interrogated after her interaction with her assistant. "Nikki look at me. You don't think I'm too old to be starting over?" I asked knowing she would reassure me that I wasn't. "Hell no. Girl, what are you, thirty? Thirty-five?" "I'm thirty-nine. I got one almost outta college, and the other on her way to juvenile hall.

I was almost done!" I whined while plopping down into the chair facing Nikki's desk. Nikki started laughing, which made me smile because I was being serious. "Girl, being a mom don't stop when they graduate... or go to jail!" she said still smiling hard.

Knock. Knock! "It's open!" Nikki said aloud as she ended her call with the superintendent's office. "Come in officer, you can have a seat." Nikki offered gesturing toward the chair next to me. The police officer came in and sat down as Nikki continued. "I've just spoken with the assistant superintendent of the school board and they have given me full dominion over the outcome of today's events. This is what I want to do. Newark high school is not going to press charges on either one of these children for *assault*. But we will continue to preserve the *trespassing* charges. Which as you know makes this a matter for the school police, and not the Newark police department. The people of this school and its community need to realize that we have a no tolerance attitude, for those who are infringe upon rules & regulations. Of this school, or any school in this district." Nikki declared in a strong, clear voice. "Okay, I guess we're done here then. Before I go, would you mind if I talk to the board to get verification of your authority. I don't wanna leave here now, and hear about it later." the police officer explained as he rose to his feet. "Be my guess." Nikki said as she picked up the phone receiver and handed it to the officer. Nikki threw me a wink and I answered it with a smile. "I don't know why I was smiling, my daughter still got *trespassing* charges to deal with." I thought as the officer stepped around Nikki's desk to use the phone.

"Okay, everything seems to be on the up and up. But I have a question before I go, if you don't mind?" the officer requested as he stopped at the door. "No, I don't mind." Nikki politely answered, looking ready for anything. "If you have this quote, unquote, *no tolerance* attitude towards the rules and regs, why drop the *assault* charges? Wouldn't that better get your point across, or at least teach them both a lesson?" he logically asked of the principal and my boss. "It's funny that you used the words *teach them a lesson*. Yes, I'm the principal of this school. But I'm an educator, first. Both of these children have illuminant futures ahead of them. Both are good, college bound, students with great family support and structure. And sadly, we don't see that as often as we should. So, to be honest, I don't want to hinder that, with avoidable *assault* charges. Charges which allocate *criminal* records, and as you would assume, *criminal* records get frowned upon by college boards. Now. Miss Hargrove, I know she's gonna get it because I'm going to be the one to give to her. But the person I feel the sorriest for, is

Ms. Gregory. Not only does she have *trespassing* charges and believe me, I'll make sure that the school district arbitrator gives her a lot more than she can handle. But she also has... her mother and father!" Nikki said pointing to me and towards the door, so the officer could see our involvement. "And that's why I'm trying to avoid those *assault* charges. I want them to learn what they did wrong. Let's call it, my warning shot." Nikki said explaining it to both me and the police officer at the same time. She must have known I had the some of the same questions the cop did.

Knock. Knock! "Come in." Nikki sociably invited. "You guys have a great day." the police officer uttered as Omar almost collided into him while plunging into the office. "You too officer." Nikki and I replied as the police officer exited the office. "What the hell is going on in here? Somebody besides London, needs to tell me something!" Omar said while trying to steady himself. "Oh God, I really feel for her!" Nikki said smiling after watching Omar fall into the room.

I reached out, grabbed Omar, and tightly held him close to me. "Nobody heard me?!" Omar irritably asked, as he looked uncomfortably contorted in my arms. "Yes baby, we heard you. Don't worry about it, it's been taking care of." I said looking at Nikki with a smile. "Nikki, this is my husband, Omar. Omar, this is principal, Monique Barkley. This is the Nikki that calls the house, on occasion." I said to Omar, relieved that this situation was ensuing closure. "Hi, how are you doing? Sorry about all that." Omar said slightly embarrassed with his entrance. "Not a problem. I understand your passion." she said with a smile.

"Now if you'll excuse me, I have to call the school police and have your daughter arrested." Nikki said as she picked up the phone. "What?!" Omar said confused as I pushed him out of the door of her office. "Walk me outside, I'll explain everything." I said as we came from behind the counter. "You ladies have a seat. You're not going, anywhere!" I said to Emily and London as the police officers removed their handcuffs. "In fact, c'mon, let's just go home. Gimme a second to tell Nikki, I'm leaving." I said as I stopped shoving Omar towards the door and back tracked to Nikki's office. "Why are we leaving my child?!" Omar asked severely as I walked away from him heading back behind the counter. As I approached the office, I couldn't help but smile as I read the moniker on the door. "That's my girl." I whispered to myself as I raised my hand to the door. Before I could knock Nikki opened the door, startled by me being that close, "Girl, you scared the death outta me." she said as I looked at her with a smile, because she jumped. "I was coming out to find you." she continued loud enough for all to hear. "Why what's wrong?" "I was coming to tell you that the school police are on their way to take your daughter and her friend down to the school board. And you can pick them up from there, in a couple of hours." she continued audibly while looking past me at Emily. "Good, because I was coming to tell you that Omar and I were about to leave. We got some *things* to talk about." I said with a hopeful smile. "Okay, I'll give you a call this evening?" she said extending her hand.

I could tell she knew I wanted to embrace her, but we were at the workplace. I walked from behind the counter back past Emily and her friend. "Mom! You leaving?" Emily questioned with her eyes terrifyingly widened. "Goodbye Emily." I said trying to look as gloomed as possible. I walked over to Omar and grabbed his hand and pulled him as he stared at Emily. "What the hell is going on Tracey?! Why isn't she leaving with us, if the principal handled it?!" Omar asked confused, as I escorted him arm in arm out of the building.

CHAPTER 27

"Omar"

3-0-2-5-5-5-1-5-1-0. "Omar!", Hassan said cheerfully. "Yo. Why did I have to pick my daughter up, from the police station?" I asked still unable to believe it myself. "Nigga, it was the *school police*." Hassan mocked trying to down play my family problems. "How you know?" I asked mystified that he was consistently three steps further in on everything, than I was. "Ah, you like that don't you?! Messed ya head up, didn't I? I hear it all in your voice." Hassan laughing haughtily. "Nig...! Just tell me how you know!" I said retracting myself from getting upset. "I talked to Que earlier, and I got Toni with me now. And..." he casually began to explain. "Wait! My Toni!" I interrupted as his statement astonished me. "Nigga, wha'chu mean, your Toni." Hassan said laughing in disbelief.

"That's right... *his* Toni!" Toni yelled from behind Hassan. "You know what I meant. You actually pulled that?" I amazingly asked in an almost whisper in case Toni was listening extremely hard. "You didn't think that it would turn out that way?" Hassan replied cryptically. "You poke, yet?" I very curiously whispered. "Have you talk to Que, is the question.", Hassan said trying to change the subject. "Ha, ha, ha! I take that, as a *no!*" I said laughing condescendingly. "No, I haven't talked to him today. I tried to call him but I got his voicemail." I continued still snickering. "Take it as a... *not yet!* And you need to call him because there's some shit going on, that you need to be aware of." Hassan said being the uncle that he had always been. "Like what?" I asked thoughtlessly. "Like, his mom sending him a package." Hassan said boldly. "Tracey?" I asked hoping to hear a yes. "Tiffany!" he said bluntly. "Shit! Did he tell you what it was?" I said now upset and growing more anxious by the second. "Yup. But it was alright. I told him, I thought..." Hassan calmly began. "Nigga, don't tell me what you thought, tell me what it was!" I impatiently interrupted. "This woman sent him a card for every birthday she missed. And each card, had a gift card in it." Hassan replied sensing my urgency. "Awww, that's so sweet!" I heard Toni say in the background. "I'mma call you back!" I said rushing to end the call, so I could call my son. "Not tonight. And if you get a call..." Hassan began to explain the routine. "I know. A, b or c?" I interrupted knowing what he'd say next. "B." he positively replied. "Cool, you're passed out on my couch after one too many." I reassured before ending the call.

3-0-2-5-4-5-8-9-7-5. "Hey dad, I was waitin' for ya call." Quentin answered casually. "With that being said... talk to me." I said trying to remain poised and collected. "Tiffany Lane sent me a package today." Quentin confessed openly. "Okay. What was it?" I said as I flamed my cigar and sat down in my favorite chair. "It was a couple of pictures of her while she was pregnant. I'm assuming, with me. She was pretty lady." Quentin divulged continuing to keep his casual demeanor. "Yeah, I know! What else was in the package, Que?" I asked anxiously. "A couple of ultrasound pictures and a bunch of birthday cards with gifts cards in them!" he said enthusiastically towards the end. "Gift cards?" I asked curiously. "Yeah, a lot of them. Twenty to be exact!" he excitedly disclosed. "What kind of gift cards?" I calmly asked as I rose to pour myself a drink. "Well. The first couple of birthday cards, were actually little kid cards. You know, the ones with age and cartoons on 'em. One of 'em, you could even color the back page. Each one of those had a twenty-five-dollar Walmart, Target or Toys R Us gift card in it. After that, the cards got more mature as the ages went up. Four or five of 'em had hundred-dollar Footlocker cards in 'em." he said eagerly. "Okay. What else?!" I probed gravely while pouring my glass of scotch. "Uhh, let me see. Hand me those?" Quentin requested of whomever was in the room with him. "You want the whole box?" a young lady's voice said from behind Quentin.

"You have *company*?" I asked nervously. "Something like that." Quentin said trying to be discreet to both me and his company. "Yeah Quentin, we need to talk about that too." I said realizing the dangerous path that my son was venturing down. "Anyway." he said as if I was being an annoyance. "There's a couple of Macy's cards in here. Some Best Buy cards in here. Some Apple cards in here. And the rest are those Visa gift cards, that you can use anywhere." he excitedly enlightened. "How much all in total?" I asked now feeling disgusted. "I don't know dad. I didn't add it up. I just opened the box, smiled, and put it back down." he said already apparently growing exhausted by my interrogation. "Okay. Other than that son, how are you?" I said trying not be any more frustrating. "I'm good dad. Just trying to keep my head above water." he said sincerely. "Is it becoming too difficult for you?" I asked concerned. "Nothing I can't handle." I smiled listening to my son be cocky.

"Is there anything else you want me to know before I hang up" I asked hoping for something. "Nah, not really. I'm just waiting for you to tell me to seal the box, and send it back." he legitimately admitted. "Not this time, son. She sent it to you. It's yours to do with, as you wish. Just remember, my shoe size is an eleven and a half." I lightheartedly affirmed as I plucked my cigar ash into the tray. "Alright dad, I got'chu." he happily assured. "Okay son, you take care." I said noticing by his tone that he was about ready to end the call. "You too dad. I love you." he naturally said. "I love you too, Quentin. Goodnight." I said hoping he knew how important he was to me. "Goodnight dad." he said before ending the call. I snatched the tv remote from the end table and turned on the television. My mind raced, and I couldn't help think about Tiffany. Emily's bullshit. Even Toni and Hassan. "What the hell is he doing with *her*? That's *my toy*!" I intriguingly pondered. "Damn. I know I didn't just let that run across my mind!" I whispered to myself whilst both surprised & disappointed.

"Dad!" Emily yelled from the top of the basement stairs. "What!" I answered distressed by her disturbing another moment of solitude. "Mom said are you going out anytime soon!" she continued to yell. "First of all, stop yelling and come down here when you're talking to me. And no, I'm in for the night." I said to my child who should really know better. "I can't come down there, and still hear her. She all the way upstairs, in your room." she said as she stretched half-way down the stairs. "No mom, he said he's not going anywhere!" she yelled as she made her way back up into the kitchen. I took another pull of my stogie and sip of my drink after realizing my three-way shouting match with Emily and Tracey, was over. "What the hell do you want with us, Tiffany?" I sighed as I reclined my chair and closed my eyes.

CHAPTER 28

"Omar 1998"

"Just stay here until my dad leave and then you can go out the back door." Kiana whispered as she pointed under her bed. "What time your dad leavin'? I gotta get down to warm-ups before the relays!" I asked quietly as looked at the small spot she cleared for me under the bed. "Shhh! He gotta be to work at nine, so he leave like eight-fifteen." she whispered as she was tying her shoes. "Kiana! Tamia! If y'all going with me, you need to come on!" Kiana's mom shouted from down at the front door. "Here I come." Tamia responded from outside her bedroom door. "I'm coming!" Kiana shouted pursuing her little sister's reply.

I looked at her grimly and I crawled under her bed. She placed some dirty clothes and other junk around me to disguise my presence and stepped out of the room. "I'm coming right now!" she said before as she came back into the room and reached under the bed. "Okay, just stay down there and you'll be alright. And here take this so you don't get bored. Just make sure you turn it down." she advised while giving me her sister's Gameboy and then leaving the room for good. I heard Kiana gallop down the steps, then open and close the front door with a bang. I inspected the game for the volume control before I turned it on. "What the hell am I doing down here? And what the hell am I going to do with this?!" I whispered irately.

"Aww shit. This ain't too bad." I whispered with a celebratory smile as I reached for my tiny, silver, lining in my dark situation. **RING. RING!** "What time it is?" I wondered while feeling like I'd been playing with this game forever. "I hope I don't miss my ride to the relays." I thought as I waited in hope that the phone would alert me to Kiana's father location. **RING. RING!** "Yeah." I heard Kiana's father hoarsely voice as he answered the phone. "Damn, I know he wasn't sleep, all this time. I coulda been got the fuck outta here!" I whispered as I turned off the game and listened for any opportunity to get out of the house. "What! I told you about calling, what if my daughter was here? *What if my wife was home?!*" he exclaimed as his voice got closer to Kiana's door. "Huh?" he uttered with the acoustics of him being in the bathroom. "What you mean you outside, now?" he asked seeming both surprised and a little eager.

I remained stationary listening for some type of clue to his whereabouts or intentions. "Drive around back and park your car in my neighbor's yard. I'll leave me back door open, for you to come right in." Kiana's father said as he made his way down the stairs. "I know he not getting ready to bring nobody in this house?!" I whispered as I tried to readjust my position, to try to see into the hall at whoever walks pass.

Kiana's father sprinted back up the steps, still holding the phone in his hand. He stopped at the top of the stairs, started to dial a number into the phone and continued while heading into the bathroom. "Fuck this! He not leaving no time soon, and I'm not missing the relays!" I said to as I began to dig myself out from under her bed. I quietly arose to my feet and tip toed across Kiana's room towards her closet.

"Julian. Julian!" a woman's voice moaned, softly from downstairs. "C'mon up." Kiana's father said, sticking his head out of the bathroom door. I made it to Kiana's closet and began to move the large pile of clothing on the floor in front of the door. "Jules." the woman's voice cried out as she gracefully made her way up the stairs. I dove behind the door for cover, praying to not be seen by this mystery woman. I waited in anticipation, looking at my narrow view of the top of the stairs from behind the door. "Damn, her voice is sexy as shit." I whispered intrigued. "Julian, where you want me?" she seemed to sing as the voice started to materialize into view. "Oh my God!" I said almost loud enough for her to hear, as I stared at this woman standing at the top of the stairs.

She was a beautiful, tall, brown skinned woman with long, light brown, braided hair. "In my room. Right there." Kiana's father mumbled as he opened the bathroom door and pointed towards his bedroom with a toothbrush in his mouth. She headed towards the bedroom, pausing at the small mirror on the hallway wall. I continually looked her up and down, from behind the door of my so-called girlfriend's room. Her low-cut, mid-drift, sweater, showed off both her large, breasts and her enticing stomach simultaneously. Her short, skirt hugged her attention-grabbing ass, and displayed just enough leg to capture curiosity. I watched her amuse herself in the mirror, teasing her hair and applying lip stick. She slid her Dolce Gabanna's glasses off of her face and threw me a wink, before putting them on her head.

"Did she just wink at me? Oh shit, she knows I'm here! Please don't tell on me!" I thought to myself as I slid down to the floor while still behind the door. "How long you gonna be?" she asked piercing through the bathroom door as she passed it heading for the bedroom. "I'm coming out now!" Kiana's father replied as he turned off the electric shaver. "Okay." she said as she continued into the bedroom. She turned around to see if I was still watching, then bent over to unlace her sandals, purposely exposing her ass engulfing her thong. She slid her shoes off her feet, dropped them where she stood and turned and smiled at me before going into the room. Kiana's father came out of the bathroom, in a pair of pajama pants and no shirt and followed her into the bedroom closing the door behind them.

"Wait baby, I gotta use the bathroom." Kiana's father's accomplice said as she opened the door and leapt out of the room. She slid down the hallway pass the bathroom, to Kiana's room door. "When I give you the signal, get down the steps." the mystery woman whispered to me through the crack behind the door. She gave me another wink and turned towards Kiana's parent's bedroom, opening and closing the bathroom door as she passed it. She stood in the doorway, unzipped the small zippers on both sides of her skirt and gently peeled it off her body. "Damn!" I thought to myself as I watched the show that she was intentionally putting on for both Kiana's father, and me. I watched her adjust her black, lace, thong, then walk deeper into the room.

I came from behind the door and posted myself in the doorway, ready and waiting for my signal. "What the fuck is my signal?" I thought as I listened to the ruffle of the sheets and the whispered banter coming from the bedroom. "Aww shit." I said quietly to myself as Kiana's father's pajama bottoms went fluttering into the door, sliding to the floor. My imagination became untamed as I wondered what this woman was doing to him. I extended my head out of the room a little, to try and get a peak. Honk. Honk. Hooonnnk! My curiosity was broken by, what I hoped wasn't my ride to the relays. "Damn, I hope that's not my ride! What time is it? C'mon, chick… hurry up please!" I anxiously whispered. "Ahh!" Kiana's father gasped from the bedroom. "Oh shit." he continued to whisper joyfully. I smiled at this woman, who seemed to have all the control in that bedroom.

"Go ahead baby. I did what I said I would, and handled my part. The rest is up to you." she said loud enough for me to hear. "I hope that's my signal cause I'm going." I whispered as I started out of the room. I crept out of Kiana's room and into the hallway towards the top of the stairs. "Daaaamn!" I said in amazement as I got a full view of the event in Kiana's parent's bedroom. I stood unconsciously motionless, watching this woman on top of Kiana's father. She was completely naked sliding up and down on top of him. The tattoo of the "Playboy Bunny" on her left buttock seemed to wink at me as I stared at this woman gradually slide up and down on his dick. I watched her massage her palms into his chest. I examined her hips twirling with each time back down. I poured over her head tipped back, her mouth open gasping for air, as she maneuvered him in deeper.

Hoonnnk. Hooonnnk. Hooooonnnnk! The impatient horn blowing outside the bedroom window broke both her and my concentration. She looked into the hall as I started down the stairs. We threw each other as smile, as she disappeared from my view. I quietly ran through Kiana's living room, glancing out of the front window as I passed it. "Damn, that's them!" I thought to myself, noticing my track team perched around a van, parked across the street. "I shoulda went right out that front door!" I whispered to myself as I headed for the basement. "Damn! I ain't goin' be able to lock it back 'cause, she locked it from the inside!" I thought to myself, as I unlocked the back door. "I hope they didn't knock on my door yet!" I said to myself as I sprinted up Kiana's driveway, towards the awaiting party in front of my house.

"There he is right there!" I heard someone yelp as I came running around the corner. "Gimme 1 minute." I said aloud, as I sprinted directly to my front door. "Where you been? They've been out there waiting for you, for about ten minutes." my mom asked as I came crashing into the house. "Out running!" I answered as I ran up the steps to collect my things. "Out running? You must really take me for a fool, Omar!" my mother mumbled as she returned to the kitchen. "Alright mom, see you at the relays, love you, bye!" I yelled as I leapt down the stairs and out of the door. "Okay, let's go!" I shouted to my teammates as I ran to the van. I jumped in the van and maneuvered towards the back. The rest of the team followed and we pulled off.

"Where the hell were you this morning?!" my coach's son asked from behind the wheel. "I had some relaxation techniques to take care of. Gotta stay loose, right?" I replied with a smile. "So where was you at, for real?" Hassan asked sitting next to me ransack my bag. "Wha'chu doin?" I asked probingly as he rifled through my things. "Looking for my Gatorade gum, I threw it in here the other day." he said seeming disturbed by my question. I just looked at him and shook my head. "So, you finally got Kiana, huh?" he asked quietly. "How you know?" I asked in amazement. "Cause, I know you. And where else would you be coming from this early, on a Saturday morning!" Hassan said sarcastically. "So, did you hit?" he asked again piercingly. "Yup, and she wasn't no virgin either. Wasn't a damn thing tight about her." I openly admitted as I snatched the gum from Hassan. "I told you, she wasn't a virgin." Hassan happily reminded. "Puerto Rican Manny hit that like 3 months ago. He said she wasn't no virgin then." Victor intervened from directly in front of us, as he turned around to show his interest in our conversation.

"Puerto Rican Manny? Where you here that bullshit from?!" I suspiciously questioned. "E'rybody know. And we all tried to tell you! You just couldn't get passed, the right across the street part." Hassan said authenticating Vic's hearsay. "Whatever. He might've had it first, but I had it last." I said to the two of them. "You don't know where she at. She could be bustin' a nut, right now." Hassan ironically divulged. "Mike, turn that up!" I yelled to my coach's son as I noticed the song playing on the radio.

"O! Omar! Man wake up, we there!" Hassan yelled relentlessly. "I'm up!" I said trying to regain focus and familiarity of what was going on around me. "Aww damn." I said as I noticed everyone else lined up on the curb outside the van with my coach pacing back and forth in front of them like a drill sergeant. I grabbed my bag and jumped out of the van. "Wa'sup Coach" I said as I lined up with the others. "Oh, nothing much Omar. How are you? How's your family?" Coach Trufant said cordially. "Everyone's well. They can't wait to come down here…" I started delightfully surprised. "Okay guys, drop your bags on the ground in front of you, go in through that door. Go to your left, and down the steps." coach interrupted abruptly. "You were saying, son." Coach continued to me as we began to follow the rest of the team into the building. "Everyone's doing good. My dad even brought his video camera to…" I cheerfully continued. "Aren't you forgetting something, son?" Coach said as he gestured to bags still resting on the curb.

I let out a sigh of despair as I walked over to the large pile of duffle bags awaiting my claim. I grabbed the bags and headed back to the building as coach held the door open with a smile. "For future reference… be on time!" he said still smiling, as I passed him in the doorway. I caught up with my teammates who were standing in the hall waiting for Coach Trufant and I.

"Yo, come look at this." Victor said to me and Hassan as we stood listening to the directions being given by the assistant coaches. Victor walked us down to the end of the hall to an opening which gave us a view of the field. "God Damn! Look at all these people. I wonder who here?" Victor enthusiastically marveled. "They're here. You're here. I'm here. We're here! What the fuck are you talking about?" Hassan callously questioned

Victor. "He mean famous people. Important people… dumbass!" I said to Hassan just as callous. "Bill Cosby is definitely here, other than that who knows? Oh, Rendell is probably here too. "I said to Victor as we headed to rejoin our teammates. "You think Cosby's here for real?" Victor continued to question in wonderment. "Among others!" Coach Trufant interjected as we approached his side. "Now if you all are finished with the tour, we can go warm up." Coach overruled as he opened the door to a locker room.

"Yo Omar, c'mere!" Hassan yelled from the other side of the track. "Wait hold up." I said as I was still in awe from all of the praise, I was getting for my races that day. "Dad, you got the whole day on tape or just my races?" I eagerly asked, excited to see myself on TV. "No, I didn't get the entire day, but I did get all of your team's events. And of course, all of your and Hassan's individuals." my dad said while holding his new camera proudly. "Hassan's calling you." my dad continued, while pointing out Hassan waiving frantically. "Yo, O… c'mon man!" Hassan insisted as he vigorously gestured for me to come over to him. "Dad, when y'all leavin'? 'Cause me and Has want to hang around a little while longer. And then we can just catch the bus home?" I requested of my father after recognizing that he may cramp my style with attention I was getting. "Right now. And you gotta let your mother know about that. I don't know if she has family plans after this, or what." my dad said pulling any disappointing replies out of his hands. "Mom. Mom! Me and Hassan going to stay here, alright?" I yelled to my mother who was on the other side of the gate talking to Coach and Mrs. Trufant. "You do know that no one is coming back for you. Which means you'll be on the bus!" she replied sternly while walking towards us, after saying her goodbyes to the Coach and his wife. "Yeah, I know." I confirmed as she approached us. "If you understand that, I'm fine. You got bus fare?" my mother inquired as she grabbed my dad's arm. I nodded my head at my mother's inquiry before looking at my dad pitifully. "Teddy give him some money, for the bus." she continued to my father. "Here hold this." my dad instructed my mom as he handed her the small carrying case which held his new camera.

"What about Hassan?" my dad asked as he reached into his pocket for his wallet. "I'll call his mom when we get home and let her know where he is. He'll be alright." my mom replied as she waved to some my other team mates and their parents. "No, does he need bus fare?" my dad queried while exploring through his wallet. "We don't know. So, just give 'em this ten right here and they'll be fine." my mom said delving into my dad's wallet and snatching a ten-dollar bill. "Alright boy, don't come walking into my house at no crazy hour." my dad said calmly as he stuffed his wallet back into his pocket. "Okay baby, y'all be good. And, congratulations. I'm very, *very*, proud of you!" my mom said as she threw her arms around me. "Hey be careful with that case!" my dad said to my mother frantically. "Teddy, ain't nobody gonna break your camera. Give your son a hug, and let's go." my mom ordered. "Alright pops, I'll see you later." I proclaimed as I embraced my father. "Did I tell you I was proud of you?" my dad said with a gratifying smile. "Yeah you did." I said gratefully. "Well, I am. And I'll see you at home, at a decent hour!" my dad reiterated before my mom seized his arm and they walked off.

I turned and ran over to where Hassan was standing. "Damn, finally! Where ya mom and pop goin'?" Hassan asked as I reached his side. "They leaving. We on the bus." I said shoving the ten that my parents gave me, into my sock. "What did you want?" I assertively asked reminding him of his need for me to appear. "You see that girl over there." he said pointing into a crowd of people standing around a booth, eating hot dogs, and drinking soda. "Hassan, it's like twenty, thirty people over there. Which one is *that girl*?" I realistically acknowledged as I threw my hands up admitting defeat. Hassan let out a sigh as he continued. "The one leaning on the guys back putting her sweatpants on. The one in the hoodie!" Hassan terribly clarified. "The one with all the Army people around her?" I asked nonchalantly. "They Marines. But yeah, her." Hassan replied excited that I finally got it correct. "What about her?" I asked casually. "She want me." Hassan said enthusiastically.

"Okay, congratulations." I said nonchalantly. "See that's why I don't be wanting to tell you stuff!" Hassan said disappointed that I wasn't as excited as he was. "Tell me what? That she want you!" I retorted defensively as we continued to stare in their direction. "Tell me you got her, not that she want you! How you even know?" I blatantly questioned as I began surveying the field for someone for me. "Cause, I talked to her already." he conceded aggressively while watching me scout the field for prospects. Her and her cousin came up to me asking about you, and we started up. But fuck it, you right. C'mon, let's go find Vic and them." Hassan strategically disclosed as he pretended to walk away to find our teammates. "What about me?" I asked now slightly interested by his mentioning of my name. "Nothing really. Her cousin liked your run." he said cynically while falsifying a nonchalant conduct. "Who's her cousin?" I asked also pretending to be nonchalant. Hassan came over and placed his arm around my shoulders while scoffing at my obvious interest. "Let's go see." he insisted as he began pushing me towards his newest admirer. "Stop. I'm good, I can walk." I asserted after recognizing the multitude of people who could be watching him push me along.

I followed behind Hassan as he excitedly meandered over to the stands. "Yo, slow down. What the hell you running for?", I asked disappointed by his seemingly desperate actions. "Yo, stop!" I demanded of him as I grabbed him by the shoulder. "What?!" he said disturbed by my interference with his hurried pace. "Nothing. You got it, go 'head." I said pulling myself out of his embarrassment. Hassan turned around and continued pace towards his friend. "Just so you know, I'm reporting this shit in school on Monday!" I yelled to Hassan who practically running to the stands. He turned around and looked at me with a smile and slowed down pace. "Yo man, c'mon." he said laughingly as he stopped to wait for me. "Was I just running, to this chick?" he ashamedly asked. "Yeah, you was. And I'm going to be the one to tell people about it. Even though she is a nice, little grip." I said as I could now see a close view of Hassan's next applicant. "So, which one is her cousin?" I asked as we were about to approached the small crowd of people surrounding Hassan's friend. "The old head chick over there, with her. The one in the black jeans and the fatigue hat." Hassan whispered as we reached his friend. "Where? It's like 20 pair of black jeans up there! And I don't see no fatigue hat either." I discreetly mumbled to Hassan as we approached.

"Asia…. Omar. Omar, this is… Asia." Hassan said as his enthusiasm began to rise again. "Hey what's up?" I said calmly. "Hey." she serenely replied. "You alright?" I scornfully asked Hassan, hoping that maybe a little embarrassment would bring him back down to reality. "What? Yeah, I'm fine." Hassan said defensively. "Okay." I expressed in a sarcastic disbelief.

"So, I hear y'all was talking about me?" I asked immodestly. "Yeah, we…" Asia whispered blushing. "No, I was talking about you." a woman's voice interrupted gallantly from behind Asia. I leaned over to look pass Asia to see who was speaking. "I really enjoyed your race. You remind me a lot of my husband, Ronald. Your style of running is just like the one he had, when we were in school. He just he wasn't as fast as you." a woman said as she emerged from the small group of people behind Asia. The woman approached the three of us and put her arm around Asia's shoulders. She pulled Asia close, whispered something in her ear and they both started giggling. I looked over at Hassan who was trying to laugh at whatever they were laughing at, and just shook my head in disappointment. "Aunt Tiff you remember…" Asia began. "I met him already, I don't know Omar yet." the woman intervened as she was reluctant to be introduced to Hassan for the second time. I cut her a peculiar eye for knowing my name, before turning to look at Hassan. "What?" Hassan obliviously murmured as everyone starred at him for some type of introduction. "What? Y'all need to grow up and stop playin', y'all already know each other." Hassan said condescendingly. "Wha'chu doing the rest of the day?" he boldly asked Asia, seemingly unconscious to her dissatisfied viewpoint. Asia and her cousin just continued to disappointedly stare at Hassan. I could do nothing but shake my head and scoff in disbelief.

"Y'all serious? Okay, Omar this is..." Hassan sarcastically began, with the expectation of me finishing with her name. "C'mon man. I know you know it, because Asia just said it." Hassan said with a cynical smile. "You know what Hassan never mind! Go find something to do man... speed-on somewhere!" I said callously, trying redeem myself from the scar Hassan left in my process. I looked at Asia who was fighting her smile at Hassan's arrogance, then her cousin who was far from smiling at the same thing.

"Hi you doin' sweetheart, I'm Omar?" I said welcomingly as I extended my hand. "Hello Omar, I'm Tiffany." the woman responded smiling greatly as she extended her hand to meet mine. "For real, can you hang out with us for a little while?" Hassan straightforwardly questioned Asia. "I don't know. I gotta see what my mom got going on, after this." Asia admitted pretending to not be as excited as she was. "I got your mom, don't worry about it. But don't you think you may wanna go home and shower first?" Tiffany said sardonically. "Yeah maybe I should." Asia said naively. "Nah, she fine. We all smell like sweat. It's the fragrance of champions... *eau de Penn Relays*." Hassan said smiling at his own corny jokes. "She a female, dumbass! Why would she want to go somewhere smelling like sweat? Why would you want her around you smelling like sweat?" I asked Hassan mercilessly as payback for the harsh introduction. "C'mon Omar. I want you to meet my husband, Ronald." Tiffany said as she grabbed my arm, not giving me a choice. I followed her back to through crowd of people she emerged from.

"Ronald. Ronald." she said as she tapped on the shoulder of a very large man. She turned and smiled at me, slightly embarrassed at his ignorance of her presence. "Ron!" she shrieked. "Hey babe." he said as he turned and threw an arm around her. He kissed her on the cheek, and continued his conversation, completely ignoring her want. Tiffany turned around, looked at me and shrugged her shoulders. "Ronald, I want you to meet somebody." Tiffany got in his and asserted. "Anybody, babe." he arrogantly said. "Ronald, this is Omar. Omar, this is my husband, Ronald." Tiffany said, seemingly proud to know me. "Hey what's up, little man. I saw you doin' ya thing out there. You gonna mess around and be the next big thing!" Ronald said, outwardly routine while extending to shake my hand. "Thanks man. Yeah starting to hear that a… lot." I mumbled to myself as he was no longer paying attention to me. His attention was now to his wife, whom he had already started another conversation with. "Here, you take the jeep back to the hotel. I'm going to go hang out with Darryl, for a little while." he said as he handed her a set of keys and went directly into another conversation before, she could even reply. I turned and began walking back to Hassan and Asia who were now on the other side of the field, sitting on a bench, enjoying each other's company.

"Hey Omar, wait up." Tiffany bellowed from behind me, trying to move as fast as she could while lugging a large duffle bag on her shoulder. I stopped to wait for her. "So where are y'all planning on taking my niece?" she asked as I gently slid the duffle bag off her shoulder. "Thank you, you're such a man." she flatteringly confessed with an adorable smile. "Not a problem. I'm not taking her nowhere. And if everybody's going back home to change first, then I'll just stay there." I said as I threw her bag over my shoulder and continued walking. "I wanna apologize for Ronald's behavior. He gets like that when we come back home for visits. He becomes so wrapped up in his friends and family, that he becomes kind of an ass. But he really is a teddy bear. But again, I'm sorry." she stated sorrowfully. "You need to stop apologizin' for 'em, and go get an apology from 'em." I mumbled to myself quietly. "Huh?" Tiffany asked with a surprised expression on her face, as if she'd heard me. "I didn't say nothing. And no apology needed." I said as I smiled back.

"Yo, you ready?" I asked Hassan as I put the duffle bag down on the bench next to him and Asia. "Yeah, I'm ready." Hassan said as he stood up. "Y'all on the bus?" Asia asked reluctantly wanting Hassan to leave her. "Yup." Hassan replied as tucked his t-shirt in, and straightened out the rest of his clothes. "You gonna walk us out?" he said as he continued to fix his appearance. "Can I, real quick?" Asia asked Tiffany anxiously. "Wha'chu askin' me for?" Tiffany asked unaware of Asia's reasoning. "Ain't I riding back with you and Ron?" Asia asked unknowingly. "Ron is going out with your uncle Darryl, so it's just me and you." Tiffany said sounding discouraged. I watched at Tiffany regretfully look down at the duffle bag. "Excuse me." I said as I nudged her aside and grabbed the bag. Tiffany and I followed Asia and Hassan out of the stadium at their lover's pace.

"So, you like Northeast." Tiffany asked trying to make conversation. "How do you know I go to Northeast?" She smiled pointing to my shirt front. "Not to mention the fact that I watched you and your *team* run." she said pleasantly. "Oh yeah." I said feeling a little dim. "It's alright. It's school, I don't think that there is anything better or worst about it than any other school I've ever been to." I continued after her smile seemed to be reassuring. "You don't seem excited, to have just run in the *Penn Relays*, not to mention winning most of your races." she said surprisingly. "Not try'na' sound cocky but I've been here before. None of this is new to me. Now my first time, I couldn't sleep for days after that." I said trying to keep her attention. "You don't come off as a fifteen-year-old." she said with poise. "That's because I'll be sixteen in two months." I said charmingly.

"Yo, Has!" I yelled to my friend. "Gimme one second." I said to Asia before speeding up pace to catch up with Hassan. "What's up?" he said happily as he stopped to wait for my approach. "Instead of them walking us to the bus, let's walk them to their car, so I can dump this bag for them." Hassan looked at Asia, who had begun to smile because of the gentlemanly gesture. "Alright." Hassan said adherently. I turned to wait for Tiffany, who was admiring her surroundings, with a substantial smile on her face. "Everything all right?" Tiffany asked merrily. "Yeah! We gonna walk y'all to the car, instead of walking us to the bus-stop, since this bag's kinda heavy." I said charitably. "That's sweet of you, thank you." she said with genuine gratitude.

"You want this in the back seat or the very back?" I asked as she opened the door to unlock the rest of the doors. "Put it all the way in the back." she said as she closed the door to help me put the bag in the back of the jeep. "This is nice." I said to Tiffany as I admired her vehicle. "Yes, it was." she said with a smile. I looked at her full of confusion, not that I was unaware of those type of thoughts, but they were impossible from her... about me. "Oh, you meant the jeep? Yeah it is nice isn't it." she said in a seemingly disheartened tone.

"You ready?" Hassan asked as he walked to the back of the jeep after making sure Asia got in alright. "Yeah, I'm ready." I said to Hassan as he continued to saunter past us. "Sorry about Hassan, he can be a little rude until he gets to know a person." I apologized before glaring at Hassan. "And then let me guess, he becomes a lot rude?" Tiffany said cynically. I laughed at her joke which was a lot more on point than she'd ever know. "Nice meeting you, Tiffany. I enjoyed your company." I said genuinely. "Likewise, Omar. Now get in, so I can take y'all home. I don't think Asia's done with your friend, yet." Tiffany said with a cunning smile. "No, that's alright. Thank you anyway, though." I said self-importantly. "C'mon, I insist!" Tiffany said unyieldingly. "Yeah man, she insists." Hassan said as he was already closing the door from inside the backseat of the car. "I guess, I'm out voted." I said as I walked Tiffany to the car door. "Thank you." Tiffany said as I opened the door for her.

I closed the door and walked around the back of the car to get in next to Hassan. "You can get in the front." Asia said as she jumped out of the car, racing me to the door handle. I opened and closed the back door for her before made my way to the front seat.

"So, where am I going?" Tiffany asked as she backed out of the parking spot. "I live up West Mt. Airy, close to Chestnut Hill. And if that's too far up, you can jus' drop us off up Broad & Erie. Or Broad & Olney. Or anywhere on Broad Street." I said trying not to be intrusive. Tiffany smacked her teeth and reached for the power button on the radio.

"You live in West Mt. Airy? I used to live up that way. My first apartment was up there, you know where the Forrest Village Apartments are?" she said turning the music down to conversation levels. "Yeah, on Wadsworth Ave? Hassan live right across the street from there." I said confidently. "I used to love that apartment. I moved there straight from home. No furniture. No nothing." she said laughingly. "Where was home?" I asked curiously. "My mom's house, sixteenth and Lindley. That's still home, no matter where I live." she said with a smile. "Where do you live now?" I asked pryingly. "My husband and I just moved from Norway to Montreal, about two months ago." she admitted grimly. "Norway? Montreal?" I asked inquisitively. "Yeah, when you're in the Marines, sometimes you gotta move like that." she said disheartened.

"You're a Marine? You don't look like a Marine." I said narrow-mindedly. "What does a Marine look like?" she said pretending to be defensive. "Well the men look a lot like your husband. Yeah, he looks like a Marine!" she said naturally. "And the women?" she asked as she smiled ironically. "They look like... the men." I said hesitantly. "Like men? Nigga, Marine chicks look like, Alice the Goon!" Hassan said abrasively from the backseat. Tiffany rolled her eyes toward the backseat then started to laugh. "Honestly. He's not that far off." I said still laughing. "If that's the case, you really don't look like a Marine!" I continued certainly. "Aww! That's sweet." Asia said melodiously from the backseat. Tiffany started to laugh, "Yeah, that is sweet, thank you." she said covering her blushing face. "The funny part is, Hassan may be on to something. As I think about the female friends I have on base, they do all fit the same... what's the word...?" Tiffany stated trying to find the right descriptive word for her friends. "He-man!" Hassan interrupted abruptly. "That ain't right. Lucky, I'm not a Marine or I'd really take offense." Tiffany said with a sardonic smile.

"How long have you been a Marine's wife?" I asked nosily. "Six years. I went to college for two years. And while I was there, Ronald decided to join the military." Tiffany explained attentively. "All that moving don't make it hard to call a place home?" I asked sympathetically. "No, not at all. Philly is my home, always will be!" she said proudly. "Your parents, they still live in the same house?" I asked keeping pace with the conversation. "Look at you, with all the questions." Tiffany said seemingly flattered by the attention. "Just trying to get to know you. Sorry, if I'm being too personal." I genuinely apologized. "Oh no, not at all. The house still belongs to my family, but none of us live there. My brother Darryl rents it out to some pregnant woman. My dad died when I was three and my mom lives with my brother David and his family in West Chester." she said solemnly. "You know my mom thinks that lady, is having uncle Darryl's baby. And that's why she don't always have to pay rent." Asia interjected from behind us. "Tell your mom to mind her business. Never mind I'll tell her!" Tiffany said taken aback. "So that's it, two brothers?" I asked intently. "You mean all of us?" she asked in awe that I was being so attentive. "Yeah, it's just you three?" I answered swiftly. "No there's one more, my sister Ayanna, Asia's mom." she said looking back at her first and only niece with a smile. "Wait. Asia is your niece?" I asked awe-struck. "Yeah, why?" she asked ignorant to my presumption. "I don't know. For some reason, I thought I heard someone say she was your cousin." I answered sarcastically looking back at Hassan. "Cousin, niece, same difference." Hassan said uncaringly.

"Okay, where am I going?" Tiffany asked as we cruised through my neighborhood. "Make a left at the light, then another right down the second street on your right-hand side, and that's my block." I said a little apprehensive of having them drop us off on my street. "And what about you Hassan?" Tiffany said hesitantly. "Omar's house is good. Thank you." Hassan said warmly. "Hey, wha'chu doin' tomorrow?" Hassan said charmingly to Asia. "I don't know? Call me." Asia answered sweetly as we turned onto my street. "When?" Hassan asked smoothly. "Gimme an hour to get home and get cleaned up." Asia said with a smile as Hassan got out of the car. "Thank you very much, Tiffany. I really appreciated the ride, and your company." I calmly said in an attempt to be charming. "You are not fifteen years old!" Tiffany said with an illuminating smile. "I told you, I'll be *sixteen* in two months." I said as I opened the door to exit. "You getting up front?" I asked Asia as I held the door open. Asia got in the car and I closed it behind her. "Goodnight Tiffany." I said intriguingly sincere. "Good night, Omar. I'm going home to get that apology that you said I'm owed." she said with an enticing smile. "Good night Asia" I said as I backed away from the car giving them room to pull away.

"Damn. If she was our age…!" Hassan said as we walked up the lawn to the house. "Yeah, I know. She was giving up crazy vibes. And for a minute, it didn't seem like our ages meant shit!" I said wholeheartedly. "I just realized, we're home and it's only seven thirty. We shoulda just caught the bus, and found something else to do." Hassan said realizing how early it was. "That's what I was trying to do. But you the one, *she insists*, and jumped ya dumbass in the car!" I said recapping the situation. "Yo, that girl had me trippin', didn't she?" Hassan said self-consciously. "Yup… sure did!" I said as I opened the door and stepped into the house.

"Yo, pass me the phone." Hassan said anxiously. "Man, you were just with her, what… two hours ago." I said as I passed Hassan the telephone. I got up off of the sofa and headed to the kitchen to give Hassan some privacy and to get another soda.

"You want a soda?" I yelled to Hassan from the kitchen. "Yeah, a grape." he yelled from the living room. I walked back into the living room and placed Hassan's soda on the end table next to him. "Hold on. Yo, what we doin' tomorrow?" Hassan asked calmly. "I don't know. Nothing, why?" I asked nonchalantly as I turned from channel to channel trying to find something to watch on television. "I don't know yet. She talking to Tiffany about what they doin' tomorrow, and she asked if we had plans." he said relaxed. "Oh. Alright then. Ain't nothing on, so I'm goin' to bed. You got it." I said as I tossed Hassan the remote and a head nod.

"You going to bed?" my mom said as she stopped me at the base of the steps. "Yeah, I'm tired." I yawned as I stepped aside so that my mom could come down the stairs. "You should be, you had a long day. Where's Hassan? I know he didn't go home." my mom said gently. "No, I'm in here ma." Hassan yelled from the living room. "On the phone, I bet." my mom said tenderly. "You need it?" Hassan asked intently. "No Hassan, go ahead and talk." my mom said uninterested in the phone. "I'm so proud of y'all." my mom said as she ran her hands through my hair. "I know. Good night mom." I said as I gave my mom a kiss on the cheek and hurdled up the steps.

"Good Morning Omar, I take it you're not going to church, being as though you aren't dressed yet." my father said as he stood at the bathroom sink shedding magic shave off his face with a butter knife. "Nah, not today dad. I'll be there next Sunday." I murmured as I stood in the bathroom doorway watching flakes of magic shave fall into the sink. "You need to get in here?" my dad said noticing me still watching him. "Yeah, kinda." I said standing there admiring my father. My dad put the knife down on the sink edge and walked out of the bathroom.

"Dad, I'm out." I said as I stepped out of the bathroom. "Good morning baby." my mom said as I passed her in the hall. "Hey ma." I replied with a smile. "What, no church this morning?" she said as I started down the stairs. "No, but I'll be there next Sunday." I answered quickly. "You said that last Sunday." she said loud enough for me to hear at the bottom of the steps. I shook my head and smiled.

"Yo, you still on the phone! Did y'all ever hang up?" I said as I entered the living room to see Hassan still in the same spot, I left him in, the night before. "Yeah, we hung up." Hassan said defensively. "Nah, that's Omar." Hassan said into the phone as I turned on the TV and left the room. "Yo, Asia said, good morning. And bring me some apple juice, so I ain't gotta get off the phone." Hassan yelled as I opened the refrigerator. "How you know I was getting apple juice?" I yelled back as I sorted through the refrigerator for my favorite drink. "Cause I know you?" Hassan yelled confidently.

"Here!" I said as I handed Hassan his glass of juice. "How long y'all been on the phone? Did Kiana call?" I asked as I sat down to watch TV. "Nah. But Tiffany said, good morning." Hassan said sarcastically. "Tell her I said, hello." I said trying to be nonchalant about the fact that she referred to me. Hassan smiled at me and repeated what I said into the phone. "Yo, Asia said Dorney Park opened up on Friday and do we wanna go with them. *So, do we?*" Hassan asked with his hand over the telephone receiver. "You got money? It cost like twenty dollars to get in there and all I got is that ten my dad gave me yesterday." I said practically. "I take that as a no." Hassan said in agreement.

"Quincy, you leaving." I said to my brother as he came fumbling down the stairs with a suitcase and three huge laundry bags. "Yup, so go throw some shoes on and help me carry these bags out to the car." he demanded. I jumped up, ran to the hallway closet and grabbed a pair of sneakers. "Damn Omar, next time I'm home we gotta hang out." Quincy said as I grabbed two of the laundry bags out of his hands. "That's your fault Que, you the one who was hardly here!" I said disappointed. "I'm an important man, lil brother. And a man as important as I am, has a lotta people lookin' to see him when he stops through for a visit." Quincy said arrogantly. "Whatever." I said skeptically as I closed the door behind us.

I waived back at his girlfriend who was waiving frantically from inside the car. "Hey Omar!" she yelled as the window rolled down slowly. "Hey Jillian." I yelled back less enthused. "You know she wants you to ride with her to take me back, so that she doesn't have to ride back home by herself." Quincy declared, mindful of his girlfriend's anxieties. "Yeah I know. But who knew y'all was leavin' this early? And Hassan in there, unless you want him to come too." I responded sarcastically. "Hell no. Two hours in a car with Hassan, nope! Yeah, you stay home with him, maybe next time." he replied as he gestured for his girlfriend to push the button which opens the trunk. "And on the subject of Hassan, how long has he been sleepin' in my room?" Quincy asked defensive of his property. "Mommy told him he can sleep in there, right after you left." I answered directing all blame towards my mother. "Well, you and mommy need to make sure that my shit remain the way I leave it." he said critically as he threw his bags into the back seat of the car. "What?! A wreck? A mess?? Real fucked up?" I countered as I tossed the bags into the trunk of the car. "You know Hassan ain't gonna do nuttin' to your stuff." I continued, slightly offended by his strife. "Yeah I know but accidents happen." he said with a smile, noticing my disposition. "You are living proof of that. Mom told me the story about her and dad and why they got married." I joked as I closed the trunk. "Whatever! Alright Omar, I'm outta here. And the next time I'm home, it's me and you. I'll even let you buy me lunch or somethin'." he lobbied with a smile while opening the door to get into the car. "You actually gettin' in that car without sayin' bye to mommy?" I said before pivoting back towards the house. "Aw shit! I be right back, babe." Quincy announced to his girlfriend as he closed the car door and scurried to catch up with me.

"Mom! Mom, I'm leavin'!" Quincy yelled as he squeezed passed me in the doorway. "You got everything?" my mom asked as she came sauntering out of the kitchen, gnawing on a piece of bacon. "Yeah mom, I'm good." Quincy replied as he tore a piece of my mom's bacon and jammed it into his mouth. "Okay baby, you have a safe trip. I love you, always have, always will." my mom said as she always did to my brother. "I love you too mom, always have, always will." Quincy responded as he slid into my mother's open arms, slightly picking her up as he hugged her.

"And boy, I don't wanna see no more D's. I promise you, I won't pay for 'em. You hear me?" my dad declared profoundly as he marched down the steps to see my brother off. "Yeah dad, I hear you." my brother said directly. "With that said, you have a good trip. Drive safe, and call me when you get there." my dad said as he opened his arms to hug my brother.

"Alright lil bro, I'm outta here. You be you." Quincy said as he extended his hand. I brushed his hand away, "I'mma walk you to the car." I exclaimed as I opened the door. "Alright Hassan, you be you." Quincy yelled into the house as he walked out of the door. "Alright Que. Yo, tell Jillian to call me when she gets back." Hassan bellowed from the top of the steps. "Whatever nigga!" Quincy hollered from the porch. "Quincy, I told you I don't wanna hear that word!" my mom's decree faded as I closed the door behind us.

"What you want Omar?" Quincy asked aware of my intentions for walking him out to the car. "I need some money" I replied confidently. "I thought so. What makes you think I got money?" he asked naively. "C'mon man, you got money. Daddy just gave you some." I said bluntly. "How you know?" he said surprisingly animated. "Daddy give you money every time you go back." I said expressing I knew one of his secrets. "How you know? Do, mommy know?" he asked unsurely. "Yeah, she know. E'rybody know. Shit, he gonna bitch about it for the next two, three days." I explained harshly. "Then why he always being all secretive about it?" he asked confused, as he got into the car. "Same reason why mommy acted so secretive when she just slid you some. You gonna give it to me?" I asked in a hurry to catch Hassan while he was still on the phone.

"Here., I didn't know y'all saw that." Quincy replied as he dug in his wallet and pulled out a ten-dollar bill. I looked down at the money and then cut my eye at him. He was sitting there with a smile on his face as he extended his hand out of the window of his girlfriend's car. "C'mon man. That's all? I'm trying to go to Dorney Park." I said trying not to sound too ungrateful. "What?" he said pulling the ten-dollar bill back. He looked at me and then at Jillian, who was sitting in the car next to him with a widespread smile. "Stop." I heard her whisper as he started to put the ten back into his pocket. He handed her the ten and continued into his pocket, pulling out another bill. "Here man." he said somberly as he grabbed the ten from her and handed both bills to me. I took the money out of his hand. "Good looking out, Que." I said as I jammed the money into my pocket. "Alright man. You be you, O." he said as he put the car into gear. "You be you, Que." I said as I tapped the roof of the car and backed away so he could pull off.

I reached into my pocket to see exactly how much my brother had given me. "Hassan! Yo, where you at?" I yelled as I walked into the house.

"Right here. Why are you yelling?" Hassan said standing about ten feet to my left. "You still on the phone?" I asked enthused. "Nah, she said she goin' call me when they get back from the park. Why, what's up?" he asked as he jammed another piece of bacon into his mouth. "I'mma go talk to my dad, real quick. Call 'em back and see if they left yet." I said as I turned to run up the steps. "I know they didn't leave, we just hung up." Hassan mumbled with a mouthful.

"Dad." I said as I knocked on the door to his bedroom. "Come in." my dad said casually. I opened the door and plopped down on the bed. "How can I help you, Omar?" my dad said casually, as he faced the mirror tying his tie. "I was wondering if I could go to Dorney Park, today?" I asked eagerly as I stood to help him with his tie. "Dorney Park? With who?" my dad said curiously. "Just some friends." I answered nonchalantly. "Oh, just some friends huh?" my dad said with a proud smile. "Who's driving?" he continued, still smiling. "They are. All I need is your permission." I said hopeful that he'd offer money as well. "And some money?" he said beginning to chuckle. "What so funny?" I asked bewildered while patting his chest after completing his tie. "You. You're growing up on me. Now you're asking me for money to go on dates. Getting old!" my dad said gratified with my maturation. "Who, me or you?" I teasingly asked. "Well son, every year you age, I do too. You do know that, don't you? I won't be around forever." my dad said as he gave himself a once over in the mirror. "Yeah, dad. But you know, you're not old." I said as I left his room. "Don't forget to ask your mom. I'm just the bank." my dad said aloud from behind me.

I ran downstairs to find my mom. "Mom!" I yelled as I searched the first floor of the house. "Yes Omar." I heard my mom say faintly from the top of the stairs. "Mom!" I said as I darted back up the steps to greet her. "Yes Omar." she said again softly. "Can me and Haas go to Dorney Park, with some friends of mine?" I asked calmly trying my best to look like her innocent, little boy. "Dorney Park? With who? What friends? Do I know them?" she grilled as she gestured for me to step aside so that she can come down the steps. "No mom, you don't know 'em. They're just some friends of me, and Hassan." I said as I followed her down. "Okay, well who are they? Can I at least meet them?" she asked with a hint of concern in her voice. "Valerie, let it go. You can't meet 'em, you're his mom." my dad said as he marched down directly behind us. "No dad, it's cool. Mom, you can meet 'em as soon as we get back. I would say before we go, but you'll be in church." I said to comfort my mom and save my dad from a bad day.

"You mean, where you need to be?" my dad sternly asked to get back in on my mom's good side. "What time will you be back?" my mom asked as she opened the closet to grab her jacket. I slid passed her and snatched the jacket off the hanger. "I don't know. When they close, I guess." I said trying to help my mom put jacket on. "And you're alright with this?" she asked my father as she took her jacket from me and threw it across her arm. "I'm fine, if you are. They've yet to show me they can't be trusted. So, why not? Hell, I wanna go." my dad said as he handed my mom her umbrella. "Ok. Give 'em some money then." my mom demanded.

"Yeah, he clearing it with his folks now." I could hear Hassan say as I closed the door behind my parents. I ran into the living room waiving the money my dad just gave me. "How much you got?" Hassan asked as I started counting the money. "Twenty from Que, ten from yesterday at the relays and he just gave me another fifty!" I said excitedly dancing across the floor. "We set?" Hassan asked sounding a little off balance. "We set!" I said reassuringly. "Tell 'em we can go. I'm gonna go get dressed." I continued as I sprinted up the stairs.

"You mind?" I asked Tiffany as I gestured to hit the horn on her steering wheel. "Be my guest." she said as she leaned back giving me room. Honk. Honk. "C'mon man!" I yelled to Hassan succeeding the horn blasts. "I'm coming!" he pouted back as he came rushing out of the house. "And lock the door behind you!" I yelled from the jeep before he could make it off the porch. "Y'all relationship is cute. How long y'all known each other?" Tiffany said after laughing at me and Hassan yell at one another. "Too long, sometimes. They tell us we were preordained to be this close. His father and my mom and dad grew up together, in the same foster home. And then our dads were adopted by people from the same neighborhood. So, they just continued to hang together, they even ended up in the same schools. And since my mom and dad were boyfriend and girlfriend, and she wasn't too far away they kept her in the loop, too. We been a team since before we were even born. They deny it, but I swear they purposely got pregnant at the same time. You can't tell me they didn't." I disclosed as Hassan opened the car door. "Hey Tiffany. Hey beautiful." Hassan said staring at Asia as if he'd look away for a second and she'd disappear. "Hey Hassan. You happy, now? You got him near you, again." Tiffany said smiling at the cute couple in the back seat.

"Two adults, please." Tiffany said as she slid three twenties under the glass. She grabbed her change and stepped aside so I could pay for Hassan and I. "Can I get two adults?" I said as I reached into my pocket for my money. "That'll be thirty-nine, sixty-four please?" the woman in the Dorney Park shirt said from behind the booth glass. I counted out forty dollars and handed it to the woman. "Thank you." I said as she slid my change under the glass. "Uh oh. Look at you, with all the money. If I would've known that, I would've got you to buy my ticket." Tiffany said with a big grin. "And I would have, if this was different." I said seriously. "You mean you're not my date for the day?" she said pretending to be upset. "I told you." Hassan turned and mouthed to me with his arm around Asia. He discreetly extended his hand for the ticket. I took the ticket out of Tiffany's hand and handed them to Hassan. "Now I bought your tickets." I said to Tiffany as I playfully extended my arm for her to grasp. She surprisingly took the suggestion and we walked into the park, arm in arm.

"Alright we're gone." Hassan said with his hand out for some spending money. "What time is y'all curfew?" Tiffany asked laughing sarcastically. "Curfew? We don't have a curfew!" Hassan said harshly, trying to impress Asia. "What about school tomorrow?" Tiffany asked bewildered "As long as I get up without a problem, I'm good." I disclosed as I handed Hassan half of the remaining money. "Well in that case, you two can meet us back at this fountain at... let's say seven-thirty." Tiffany said as she handed Asia a ten-dollar bill. "Seven-thirty. Cool." Hassan said as he extended his hand for me to embrace. "You be you." he said releasing my hand to turn and escort Asia away. I watched Tiffany's face as she smiled watching them disappear into the crowd. "Look at my niece." she said proudly to herself.

"Hey, what time is it?" Tiffany asked as she pinched off another piece of her funnel cake. "Uhhh. Seven-eleven." I said struggling to see my watch around Tiffany's giant, blue, panda bear. "I wonder if they're at the fountain, yet?" she continued. "I doubt it. Hassan's not good with time." I proclaimed distrustfully. "You wanna go now anyway, and just wait for 'em?" Tiffany asked pleasantly. "I don't care." I said casually.

"You got a girlfriend, Omar?" Tiffany courteously asked with a smile as we sat down on the wall of the fountain. "Sorta." I said referring to Kiana. "Sorta?" she asked skeptical of my response. "What's that supposed to mean?" she nosily continued. "I got, Kiana. And I'm not really all that sure how faithful she is. But I can't really get too mad at that, because... I'm not really into her." I admitted after placing the huge bear on the fountain ledge next to me "Then why is she your girlfriend?" she disappointedly asked. "Uhh." I said trying not to answer. "I don't know." I continued while shrugging my shoulders. "You don't know?" she probed continuing with her disappointment. "Why don't you know, Omar?" she probed with a mischievous smile. "I know. It's just kinda weird talking to you, about it." I awkwardly confessed. "I already knew, that you knew. I probably know. It was just funny that you couldn't, tell me. It's not like I'm your mother, or something." Tiffany said as abruptly rose. She promptly looked down at the ledge and then turned her head to attempt to check her back. "Am I wet?!" she frantically asked as she turned her back to me so I could confirm that she was not being splashed by the fountain. "Your fine." I said as I attempt to steal an extended stare at her butt. "I'm sorry. I thought I felt wet. Now, what were you saying?" she said remorsefully as she reluctantly sat back down. "Nothing really. Just you're a woman, I'm a man, and we think different." I divulged as I watched her begin to happily holding her bear. "I don't know about, a man. But I really don't see fifteen, when I look at you." she genuinely divulged. "I told you before, I'll be sixteen in two months." I said with a smile, relieved that the subject was changed.

"Aww, that's so cute." Asia said as she and Hassan slowly advanced up behind Tiffany, the bear and me. "What's cute?" I asked thinking she was talking about Tiffany and I. "That!" Asia said as she shoved her small teddy bear into Tiffany's arm and snatched the giant panda from out of her lap. "Damn, O. How much that cost?! My bad, Tiffany." Hassan said remembering that Tiffany was an adult. "I'm not your mother either, Hassan." Tiffany said as we stood up to leave.

"Sex." Tiffany said softly as we walked back to the car. "Huh?" I said excited, confused and surprised all at the same time. "Your *sorta* girlfriend. You only liked her cause she was giving it up, right?" Tiffany said consciously. "Why you think that?" I asked with a smile ineffectively trying suppress my uneasiness. "You don't have to make that face. I'm not judging you. I just know that you're a teenager and with y'all, it's always about sex." Tiffany sensibly clarified. "I guess." I said trying to be nonchalant. "So how was it? Was she your first?" Tiffany asked intrusively. She laughed as I cut my eye at her. "Why you look at me, like that?" she continued. "Just wondering, why you wanna know?" I asked curiously. "I told you… I'm not your mom. I'm a friend, almost like an older sister." Tiffany said unable to contain her smile. "If had an older sister, and she damn sure wouldn't look like you." I straightforwardly stated. Tiffany turned away from me to hide her facial expression. "Look at you, got me all blushing." she said after confiscating the bear and holding it up to block my view of her face. "That's a good thing?" I asked pretending to be naive. "It would be, if I wasn't married and you were ten, twelve years older." she confessed as she slowly lowered the bear. "I can see where your problem lies" I said charmingly. "Where were guys like you when I was fifteen?" she sincerely asked. "We were there, you were probably just one of the girls that took a guy for face value." I said intuitively. "You're right. I was pretty vain back then." Tiffany said with a smile as we approached her jeep. She opened the back of the jeep and tossed in the panda.

"Well here you are." Tiffany said softly as we pulled into the driveway of my parents' home. "Yeah, here we are." I responded while I looking into Tiffany's eyes. "Hey, wake up man!" I said harshly as I tapped Hassan on the leg. "I'm up." Hassan barked before waking up Asia to say his goodbyes. "Good night. Call me when you get in." Hassan said as he kissed Asia and opened the door to get out. "Okay. Goodnight, Hassan." Asia voiced melodiously. "Alright Tiffany, you have a good night." I said smoothly. "You too Omar. And thank you for the bear." Tiffany said wholeheartedly. "Wait." Tiffany said as I turned to get out of the jeep. "What's wrong?" I asked concerned as I turned and noticed the peculiar look on Tiffany face. "Nothing's wrong. I just been wanting to give you this." Tiffany said as she leaned in with a soft, kiss to my cheek. "Good night Tiffany." I whispered as I got out of the car.

I caught up to Hassan as he was waiting at the door for me and my keys. "Damn. She really feelin' you!" Hassan excitedly said as he closed the door behind us. "Yeah, I know right. What about you, and Asia? How was Dorney Park?" I asked nosily. "It was alright. She don't like getting on real rides, so we spent the whole day doing bumper cars and the ferrous wheel." he sorrowfully "Aww damn, that's a waste of a Dorney Park trip. Me and Tiff got on everything." I gloated calmly. "I'm happy for you." Hassan said sarcastically. "At least you got to spend the day with, 'ol girl." I said trying to comfort as I started up the stairs. "Spend the day, doing what? Riding rides?", Hassan said confidently. "Just a matter of time, homie. Just a matter of time. You get in there. I'm going to bed. You be you, Haas." I said as I moved sluggishly up the stairs. "You be you, O." Hassan said as he disappeared into the living room.

"That's why she was always in his face, man." Victor said jammed his book into his bag. "C'mon man, we gonna miss the bus." I said as we hurried out of the classroom. "Alright man." I said as I shook Lenny's hand while passing him in the hall. "Bye beautiful." I said to Cassandra as I kissed her on the cheek before setting my sights towards the door. "Wait up man, damn!" Victor yelled from a few feet behind me. I shook a few more hands and kissed a few more cheeks before making my way out of the door. "Where is Haas?" I said as I made my way down the crowded staircase outside of the school.

"Yo Manny. Manny!" I yelled as I noticed Puerto Rican Manny standing in the parking lot looking lost as usual. "You see Haas?" I continued as I approached his side. "Nope. Why, what's up?" Manny said staring at the girl getting into the passenger side of the car in front of us. "Nothing. I'm trying to go home." I said noticing the young lady as well. "I ain't seen him, all day. But if I do, I'll tell him you looking for 'em." Manny said as he rocked back and forth to the music, which filled the air when the car started. "Tell 'em I left." I said as I shook Manny's hand and departed. "Yo Vic!" I yelled to Victor who was just coming out of the doors. "You coming?!" I continued to yell as I headed for the bus stop. "You go 'head, I'm gonna go 'cross to the pizza shop and hang there for a minute." he said pointing across the street. "Alright then. You be you!" I said as I hastily made my way towards the bus stop.

Honk. Honk! "Yo, Omar. O!" I distinguished as Hassan's voice, through the noisy crowd of students who were waiting to get on the bus behind me. I turned around to look for Hassan. Honk. Honk! My concentration was broken by the coarse explosion of a car horn, trying to get someone's attention. I turned to get back off the bus, shifting and maneuvering through the crowd which was now disgruntle with me for holding up the line. "C'mon man!" I heard Hassan yell as I cleared the crowd. I looked up to see Hassan across the parking lot, waiving frantically from the back seat of Tiffany's jeep. I ran over to the jeep, greeted Tiffany and Asia with a smile and shook Hassan's extended hand.

"What y'all doing here?" I said as I jumped into the front seat and closed the door. "Well, hello to you too, Omar." Tiffany said with a smile. "I'm sorry. Hey Asia. Hello Tiffany." I said adorably. "So, why are y'all up this far north?" I asked forthright. Tiffany smiled. "We came to get y'all?" Tiffany said cheerfully. "Asia wanted to see Hassan." Tiffany whispered with a big grin. "Oh, like you didn't want to talk to Omar, again?" Asia energetically disclosed from the back seat. Tiffany began to blush, noticing my smile to Asia's statement. "Y'all hungry, I'm hungry." Hassan said trying to change the subject, for Tiffany's sake. "Can we stop at Roy Rogers or something?" he continued eagerly. "Yeah, that do sound good. Can we stop, Tiff?" Asia asked in agreement. "I don't care. I gotta find one though." Tiffany said casually.

"What time is it?" I asked as we pulled into my parents' driveway. "Three, fifty-five. Why, you in trouble for being late?" Tiffany said with a cynical grin. "In trouble, for what? I told you, we don't have a curfew." Hassan said proudly. "I was just asking?" I said nonchalantly. "Then, why are we here?" Tiffany asked quietly. "Cause, I live here?" I perplexedly asked just as quiet. "Besides, you the one that's driving!" I continued plainly. "Why, where you wanna go?" Hassan asked keenly. "If I would've known all that, I wouldn't have rushed back." Tiffany said obliviously. "You had somewhere to go?" I asked concerned. "Not really. Was thinking about going to Strawbridge's. Why? You wanna go?" Tiffany casually asked. "Nooo!" Hassan and Asia said simultaneously from the back seat. "Too bad, y'all going! We all going!" I said sneeringly with a smile. "Y'all don't wanna go?" Tiffany asked heartbreaking. "Not really." Asia said shamefaced. "Alright, I'll go another time." Tiffany surrendered. "No. Why? Cause they don't wanna go? Leave 'em here! That ain't fair." I said interjecting. "Yeah, leave us here." Hassan enthusiastically agreed. "You wanna stay here for a little while, Asia?" Tiffany asked, ready and willing to leave without her. "I don't care." Asia said pretending to not be excited. "Alright then, y'all stay here." I said to Hassan as I handed him my keys. "If we staying, can y'all drop us off at my house. Cause Ma Val'll be home soon, and she gonna have a buncha questions." Hassan asked as he refused to take the keys from my hand. "You gonna ride, with me?" Tiffany asked eagerly. "Yeah, I thought I was." I said reserved.

"Where we going?" I said as we pulled into the parking lot at the Adam's Mark Hotel. "I just gotta run up and get my debit card." Tiffany said as she as she slammed into a parking spot. She quickly opened the door and hurried out of the car. "You coming up, or you gonna wait here?" she continued as she hesitantly took the keys out of the ignition. "Uhh." I said thinking of the size of her husband who may be up in the hotel room. "C'mon." she said as she snatched the keys and vaulted out of the car. I slowly got out of the car and followed a few steps behind her. "C'mon. Why you walking so slow?" Tiffany said as she held the door of the building open for me.

DING! "What's wrong with you?" Tiffany turned and asked noticing my skepticism with getting off the elevator. "C'mon, before the doors closes." Tiffany nagged as she clutched my hand and pulled me off the elevator. "What's wrong with you?" Tiffany said seriously concerned. "Ain't Ronald in there?" I said as she stopped at her room and reached for her key card. "I dropped him off at my brother's house, before I went to pick up Asia from school." she said with a cunning smile. "Now c'mon." she said as she opened the door to her hotel room. I cautiously walked in behind her. "Boy, if you don't chill out." Tiffany said as she tried to tidy up the room, by quickly grabbing something and palming it. She went into another room and came back empty handed. "You forgot a pair." I said to Tiffany referring to a pair of ladies' underwear laying across the arm of the couch. "That is… what you snuck outta the room, ain't it?" I observantly asked with a smile. Tiffany laughed. "What you smiling at? They're clean. They're brand new. See!" she said as she picked up the underwear and flaunted the tags. "Why was you trying to hide 'em, then?" I asked tauntingly. "Just trying to be modest. Don't want you to see my mess." Tiffany said blushing as she carted her underwear off into the other room. "It's just underwear. It's not like, I saw you in 'em." I said loud enough for to hear from the other room. "Even though I'd love to see that." I mumbled to myself as I crashed down onto the couch. "What you say?" Tiffany said aloud from the other room. "Nothing, talking to myself." I said relieved that she didn't hear me. I sat on the couch and read the hotel brochure, while waiting for Tiffany to come back out of the other room.

"Omar." Tiffany called aloud. "Yo." I responded as I peeked around the Visit Pennsylvania magazine. "Omar." Tiffany summoned again. "Yes." I said as I tossed the magazine and arose from the couch to see what she wanted. "Omar, c'mere." Tiffany beckoned as I approached the closed room door.

"I'm coming in." I said as I turned the knob and slowly pushed on the door. The door swayed open to reveal an unmade bed slightly covered in discarded clothing. "Tiffany?" I whispered as I slowly stepped into the room. "Tiffany." I said again as I walked towards the bed. "Yes Omar." she said pulling my attention towards the opposite corner of the room. I looked up to see Tiffany, standing in front of a mirror, wearing nothing but the panties she just brought into the room and its matching brassiere.

I stood staring at Tiffany's well shaped body. "Well, you do like? You did say you'd love to see 'em on me, right?" Tiffany said with a smile as she began to model her underwear for the both of us. I chuckled charmingly and walked over to the bed. I sat down and watched her continue to parade in front of the mirror. "You're not acting like a fifteen-year-old, standing in front of a half-naked woman. You're not even acting like an adult man, standing in front of a half-naked woman. What am I, ugly or something?" Tiffany said as she began to become sluggish in her movement. I looked at Tiffany and started to laugh which caused her to laugh. "I ain't think you believed that last part." I said with a charming smile.

"I take it, this isn't the first time seeing a naked woman." Tiffany asked as she admired her own body in her new underwear. "I told you, I'm no virgin." I said proudly. "I said… woman." Tiffany said conceitedly. I laughed at Tiffany's arrogance. "No. This isn't my first time seeing a naked woman." I said with a grin as I thought about the woman that came to visit Kiana's father Saturday morning. "Now, where would a little man like you, have seen a naked woman? Let me guess… on tv? Online?" Tiffany said with big grin. "Yeah on tv." I responded sardonically. I rose to my feet and began to walk towards the window. "How high up are we?" I asked nonchalantly, pretending not to be enthralled that she was still in her underwear. "We're on the eighteenth floor." Tiffany said with a hint of disappointment in her voice. "You alright?" I said noticing her distress. "I'm fine." she said with a pseudo smile as she walked past me to get to the chair her clothes were on. "Damn, look how high up we are?" I said as I pretended to be in awe at the view. I started laughing before noticing the beauty of Tiffany's body as she bent over slightly to pick up her pants. "What you laughing at?" Tiffany said as she walked back in front of me attempting to duck to not obstruct my view. I grabbed her by the arm as she passed, stopping her from continuing. "You." I said as I pulled her in front of me.

"What are you doing, Omar?" she asked softly with no resistance to my touch. "Looking outta the window." I said as I put my right hand around her waist and pulled her close to me. I took another step towards the big, bay window. I forced Tiffany to walk with me, by pushing her body with mine. "Look." I said as I grabbed her left hand with mine and pressed it against the window. "Look at what? All I see is you, having me stand in this window, in my underwear." Tiffany said contemptuously. "We on the eighteenth floor. It ain't like anybody can see you." I said sarcastically smiling. I stood there behind her, pointing out the satellites behind the CBS 10 building across the street. "Damn, you smell good." I said as leaned in to take an intense whiff of the back of her neck. "Thank you. Now, can I put my clothes on?" Tiffany assertively asked. "Yeah. I'm sorry, go ahead." I said as I released my hold from around her waist. I took a step back giving her the space and opportunity to move in whatever direction she needed. Tiffany didn't move to either side, she just slid her hand down onto the railing in front of the window.

I put my hand on atop hers, and returned to my up-close position. "I thought you said I could get dressed." she said softly. "You didn't move fast enough, so I changed my mind." I said charmingly. "What are you trying to do, Omar?" she said in a soft, tense sounding voice. "I'm just admiring the view." I said as I looked her up and down. "You really don't sound like a lil fifteen-year-old, young man. But you are starting to feel like... a man." Tiffany said as she backed up, grinding her ass into me. "Don't do that." I warned brazenly. "I feel you growing." Tiffany said patronizingly. "That's why you need to stop." I genuinely warned again. "Boy. I'm only teasing you, calm down." she said blatantly as she stopped grinding. "That's the thing, I don't do teasing too well. If I see something I want, I take it." I said confidently. "Listen to you. Who you think you are?" Tiffany asked grinning as she was impressed by my arrogance. "And if I wanna do this, I will." Tiffany continued as she resumed swaying her waist back and forth, brushing her butt against my fully erect penis. "Alright, keep playing!" I strictly cautioned. "What you gonna do, lil man?" she asked giggling. "Nothing. Nothing, at all." I said passively. "I sorry." she adorably said resembling a heartbroken child.

I parted the hair that cascaded down her back, exposing her neck and shoulder blades. "Damn, you smell good!" I said again as I leaned in for another whiff. I gently ran my nose dragging my bottom lip across the back of her neck. "What are you doing?" she whispered as she twitched and squirmed to get from in front of me. But my hands holding on to the railing on each side of her were like a cage. "Nothing. Just standing here, like I've been doing." I said as I softly licked my lips. I leaned in and began to delicately press my lips to her neck. "I said... I was sorry." she stammered as she deeply exhaled. "You have nothing to be sorry about." I said continuing to entice.

I continued to kiss on Tiffany's neck, slowly making my way down the middle of her back. I was on my knees by the time my tongue made it to her top of her panty line. "I said, I was sorry. Please, stop." she quietly whispered as she breathlessly cringed. "You really want me to stop?" I quietly questioned after pausing the process of running my tongue across her waist. "Yes please, before we get in trouble." Tiffany sighed, begging me to stop. "What happened to... if I wanna do this, I will." I said as I slowly slid her panties off of her waist, down her legs, to the floor. I looked up from the floor at her perfectly shaped ass. "That's a line we can't cross, Omar." Tiffany said as she bent over to pull up her panties. "Wha'chu doing?" I said as I quickly got down onto my knees, placing one on the carpet and the other on top of her panties. "C'mon Omar. Gimme my panties." she whined as she realized she couldn't pull them up.

"Girl, I'm only teasing you, calm down." I ironically mocked as I gently kissed on the back of her knee. I continued to kiss the back of her leg, slowly making my way towards her ass. "Sound familiar?" I asked teasing. "I said... I was sorry. Now can I have my panties back, please?" Tiffany asked resolutely. I lifted my head away from her leg and raised my knee off of her panties. "Thank you." she said softly as she bent over to retrieve her underwear.

I looked at her ass bent directly in front of my face. I watched her panties gradually climb her legs, slowly rising passed her knees, towards her that ass. I quickly wrapped my arms around her thighs preventing her from pulling them any higher. "What are you doing?" she asked while continuing to tug on her underwear. "Nothing." I said smiling with reference to what I was planning to do next.

I spread apart her soft, plush cheeks and began to probe the inside of her ass with my tongue. "O-oh God!" Tiffany moaned while tripping over her tongue as she convulsed in bliss. "Oh my God." Tiffany continued to whisper while uncontrollably grinding her ass into my face. I wrapped my arms around her thighs and began to pull and push her, influencing her movement in unison with mine.

I moved my hands from her thighs after realizing she was swaying in harmony with me, on her own accord. Tiffany reached back and grabbed the top of my head, vigorously massaging my scalp. I unfastened my pants and slowly slid them down to my knees, covering my actions by digging in deeper with my tongue. "Oh my God! You need to stop!" Tiffany yelled rebelliously. "I can't." I said crediting that I was no longer in control of my actions. "I can't." I whispered while slowly rising to my feet with my kisses, climbing gradually up her back. "I can't." I persistently whispered while gently kissing across her shoulder blades.

I returned to the back of her neck, slightly skimming my tongue across. She bent over promptly, using her body to push me away in an attempt to keep me from her "spot". I grabbed my dick and took advantage of her bent over position, by using it to find and rub against her clitoris. She quickly stood upright, trying to hinder me from harassing her any further. "Oh no, you can't do that." she said quickly as she viciously pushed me back and bent down to grab her panties.

"Whew" she said following an exhausting exhale. "Tiffany, you alright?" I asked as she scurried out of the door, panties in hand. I fixed my clothes and started towards the door to follow Tiffany. By the time I reached the door Tiffany was hastily making her way back into the room. "You alright?" I asked again softly. "Yeah. Wait out there while I throw my clothes back on, so we can get outta here." she said harshly as she pushed me out of the room and slammed the door. I picked up the hotel brochure and walked over to the window.

"C'mon, you ready?!" Tiffany said as she came rushing out of the room. She picked up her purse from the end table and marched towards the exit door. "Are you gonna say something?" I asked as she brushed pass me to unlock the passenger side door. "Something like what, Omar? What do you want me to say?" she responded as she walked around the jeep. "Anything" I said concerned about how she was feeling. We got into the car and pulled both of our doors closed, simultaneously. "Anything like what?! Anything like, the person who's supposed to want me, is out somewhere doing who knows what, with who knows who. While the person who wants me, is a fifteen-year-old child." Tiffany maliciously expressed before she forcefully turned the ignition key. "And I don't even know what I want. Anything like, that!" Tiffany continued as we pulled out of the parking spot.

"You get your credit card, or we not doing Wanamaker's?" I asked trying to change the subject. Tiffany smirked as she bobbed & weaved through the traffic on Lincoln Drive. "It was Strawbridge's. And no, I don't think I can do it today, maybe another time." Tiffany said with a false smile. I sat there quietly with my eyes closed and my head back, hoping to really fall asleep while pretending to.

"Omar... Omar!" Tiffany yelled as she pulled in front of Hassan's house. "Can you tell Asia to c'mon?" she asked as she looked passed me towards the door. "Uh huh." I said as I slowly slid out of this truly uncomfortable situation.

"I told you I was gonna hit." Hassan reminded Manny as we crossed the street. "What? Who?!" Manny asked confused. "The jawn from the Relays." Hassan announced proudly. "Little, light skin?" Manny said slightly amazed. "Yes, sirrr." Hassan said as he opened and held the door for Victor, Manny and I. "And, I heard you spent the night at Kiana's, Friday night." Manny said to me with a crooked smile. "How you know that?" I asked him as we all huddled around his locker. He nodded his head towards Victor. "Figures. You can't hold water!" I said to Victor harshly. "I ain't know it was a big secret." Victor said in his own defense.

"Where you going?" I yelled to Hassan as he continued down the crowded hall without us. "I'll be back." he yelled as he disappeared into the multitude. "I also heard that you almost fucked some old head jawn." Manny said as he slammed his locker shut. "What?! Where you hear that?!" I said trying to pretend like I didn't know what he was talking about. "You know where I heard it." he sarcastically. "Ya boy Hassan, run his mouth like a female." Manny said as the three of us walked down the hall towards where we last saw Hassan standing. "See, I ain't the only one that can't hold water." Victor said pompously. "And that's what you're proud of?" Manny asked as he shamefully shook his head at the ignorance of Victor's statement. "What happened? Why you ain't get it?" Manny continued to nosily interview. "What? Hassan ain't tell you the whole story?" I asked slightly surprised that he didn't already know. "Nah, the chick from Penn called on his other line. And that was the last I heard about it. So, what happened?" he asked again pryingly. RING!

"Damn, saved by the bell." Manny said with a mocking smile as the bell to start first period rang. "Yeah, I guess. Where Hassan go?" I asked as time began to become an issue. "I dunno. But you lookin' for 'em by yourself. I'm going to class. If I'm late again, Mr. Worley calling my crib." Manny said before hurrying down the hall. "Yeah me too." Victor said as he scrambled to catch up with Manny.

"Oh well." I sighed as I discarded the idea of looking for Hassan and headed to class. "You betta hurry up, you goin' be late!" a voice announced as it quickly scuffled passed me. I looked up to see Hassan almost running and trying to dodge the traffic that impeded his way to class. "Hold up!" I yelled as he continued his sprint pace. "Can't, I'll come find you after class!" Hassan said squeezing into the door of his classroom as his teacher began to shut it.

"Ladies and gentlemen, I need you all to realize that you are not to just jump up when the bell rings. I may be a substitute but until Ms. Purple returns, this is my classroom. And with that said, you are not to leave until I dismiss you." this stranger said as he stood in front of the door, still trying to establish his authority over the class. "If I miss my bus, you taking me home!" a young lady's voice pierced from the back of the room. "Then if I were you, once dismissed, I'd hurry." he responded sarcastically calm. RING! Everyone jumped at the sound of the last bell of the day, but no one left their seats. "Ok ladies and germs, class dismissed." he said with a proud smile as he opened the door. The entire class stood up almost simultaneously. "I heard that and thank you to whoever said it. That just means I doing a good job." the tall red headed substitute teacher said referring to the mumbling and murmuring as the herd of students stampeded out of the room.

"What took you so long?" Hassan said as I approached him and Victor in the parking lot outside of the school. "Last period, I had a sub. He was feeling himself." I said as we walked across the street towards the gas station, convenience store. "Literally?" Hassan joked as we approached the entrance of the store. I just shook my head and opened the door for the three of us. "You want something?" I said turning to Hassan. "Has!" I yelled looking around for Hassan. "He outside, talking to some girls in a jeep." Victor said promptly as he waited in line to pay for his snacks. "A white jeep?" I asked curiously excited. "Yeah. Why? Who is it?" he asked curiously. "I don't know. Here, pay for these." I falsely told pretending be as out of the loop as he was. "That'll be two-fifteen, please." the young lady behind the counter said to Victor before he reached into his wallet. "Thank you." I said for him as we exited the store.

"Heeeyy Omar!" Asia said melodiously as Victor and I stepped out of the door of the convenient store. "I thought you didn't know 'em!" Victor said sarcastically. "Hey what's up Asia!" I said as we walked up to Hassan who was leaning into the window of the jeep. "Hey O." Tiffany casually said while looking up from the steering wheel. "Hey." I meekly responded. "What's wrong with y'all?" Asia said noticing the conduct of both Tiffany and I. "I'm alright. Oh, my bad. Asia, Tiffany, this Vic." I said trying to change the subject by introducing my friend. "How y'all doing?" Victor said trying to look and sound cool. "Hey/Hello," the ladies said simultaneously. "Would y'all like a ride home?" Tiffany asked softly. "Yup!" Hassan said as he bolted to the back door of the jeep. "Nah. No, thank you. I think I'mma jump on the bus with, Vic." I resentfully replied while closing the back door for Hassan. "What?!" Hassan said surprisingly. "You sure?" Tiffany said nonchalantly. "I'm sure." I said as I reached into the window to shake Hassan's hand. "Ok." Tiffany said as she started to pull off. "How you know I didn't want a ride home?" Victor asked as we walked to the bus stop. "Cause, she wasn't talking to you." I said informally as I opened my bag of Doritos.

RING. RING! "I got it." I said as I passed my mom in the dining room, stealing a piece of her granola bar. RING. RING! "Hello." I said muffled by chewing, after snatching the phone from the kitchen wall. "Yo, wha'chu doing? Wha'chu eatin'?! Wha'cha mom cook?" Hassan probed quickly. "What?! Man, what did you call for?" I irritably asked while continuing to gnaw on my granola bar. "Damn, what's wrong with you! I ain't want nothing. I was calling to make sure you was home, before I came over." he said defensively. "Yeah, I'm here. How you getting here?" I asked apprehensively. "Walking. Unless your pop let you drive his car, to come get me." he replied sarcastically. I smiled as I became a little curious to what my dad would actually say. "Hold on!" I said as I dropped the phone and darted towards the stairs. "Dad, dad!" I yelled as I approached the top of the steps. "What?!" he yelled back as he opened the door of his bedroom. "Can I drive your car, to pick up Hassan?" I self-assuredly asked. "Boy are you crazy?!" my dad asked sternly as he closed his door back as quickly as he'd opened it. "He said, no." I said after picking up the phone. "I just found a ride, get dressed!" Hassan said quickly as he promptly hung up the phone.

HONK. HONK! "Hey Omar." Kiana said as she rode by in the passenger seat of her father's car. I waved to the car as they cruised by with loud music playing. "If she only knew." I said laughing as I approached the corner of my block. "Who car is that?" I said to myself as I noticed an unfamiliar car in my driveway. I continued to walk towards the house while crunching on the second bag Doritos that Vic bought for me from the store. "Who is that?" I said again noticing that there were people inside the car.

"C'mon man!" Hassan yelled as he came storming out of the house with a handful of pretzels that he just grabbed from the bag in my mom's hand. He gave my mom a kiss on the cheek and then turned to run to me. "Yo!" Hassan yelled as he trotted across the lawn to get to me. "Yo. I got Asia, Tiffany and your mom's permission to go to hang out. Let's go!" he said as he pulled me towards the car. "Hold, wait. Hang out where?" I said as I attempted to pull away from his grasp of my arm. "Do it matter?!" he asked eagerly. "Yeah. I'm trying to see Kiana later." I said indisputably. "Kiana?! Where that come from?! What's wrong with you?" he asked anxiously. "Nothing." I said trying to convince myself of that answer. "So, you not going?" he asked disappointed. "Nah, you go 'head." I insisted, not completely sure how I even felt about going. "Alright then, you be you. He ain't going." Hassan unhappily disclosed as he walked towards the car. I stood and watched them back out of my driveway, onto the street and pull off.

DING. DONG! "I got it." I yelled before leaping out of my room. I passed my mom at the top of the stairs, and took a bite of her banana. "I thought you were going out with Hassan, and your friends." my mom said delayed in protecting her food. "Nope, staying here, with you." I delightedly said while galloping down the stairs with a mouthful of banana.

"Who is it?" I yelled as I approached the door. "Man, open the door!" Hassan yelled back from the other side. I opened the door and Hassan immediately grabbed me and pulled me out. "Ma. We leaving, love you!" Hassan yelled before closing the door behind me.

"What'chu doing?!" I asked as Hassan pulled me towards the car idling in the driveway. "We out! That's all you need to know." he firmly asserted while continuing to pull me across the lawn against my will. I snatched my arm out of Hassan's hold and stopped walking towards the car. "You don't wanna hang out wit us?" Asia asked from the back seat of the car. "I'm just tired, that's all." I answered solemnly. "That ain't why." Tiffany said as she looked up with a grin. "How you know?" I asked bewildered by the fact that she even spoke. "I just do." she said confidently. "C'mon man! You can sleep in the car. I'm trying to go." Hassan interrupted as he hurried towards the rear door of the car. "Then go!" I said sternly as I turned back towards the house. Hassan looked up at me with a hopeless look, sighed and stepped away from the car.

"Go where, HASSAN?!" I asked turning away from Tiffany's view to finish our discussion as I felt slightly sorry for my best friend. "Do it matter?" Tiffany shouted enthusiastically. "That right there means, y'all don't know." I said confidently while admitting to myself that I was now excitedly curious about spending time with Tiffany. I sighed after realizing that I was about to surrender to my best friend, again. "Alright." I misleadingly sighed while pretending to reluctantly drudge myself to the car.

"Y'all wanna go to the movies?" Tiffany asked turning down the radio. "That's what you came up with, after riding around for an hour?" I asked sarcastically. "Yeah, let's go see Suicide Kings, I heard it was real good." Asia eagerly responded. "That'll work." Hassan nonchalantly followed. "What about you?" Tiffany softly asked with a smile. "Do I have a choice?" I asked smiling back at her. "No, I already made the decision for you. I was just letting you think that, you had a say in the matter." she said pretending to be aggressive. Asia let out a little snicker at her aunt's audacity. I looked back at Hassan who was beginning to laugh himself. I shook my head and turned to look out of the window to hide my smile. "Aww, baby it will be alright." Tiffany said with a smile as she placed her hand on my lap.

"Go see what time the show starts." Tiffany ordered as she pulled up to the building entrance. "Y'all sure y'all wanna see, Suicide Kings?" I asked skeptically. "Yeah." Asia said swiftly. "Why? What else is playing?" Tiffany asked as she leaned across me to see the movie billboard. "It's it that, or Déjà vu." I said to Tiffany to prevent her need to lean across my lap. "Just get 'em for, Suicide Kings." Tiffany said while handing me two ten-dollar bills. I jumped out of the vehicle and sauntered to the ticket booth as Tiffany continued to find a parking spot.

"Six, twenty. So, we got like eleven minutes." I said as the three of them came around the corner of the building, laughing. "How've you been?" Tiffany asked quietly as we sat waiting for the movie to begin. "Alright, I guess." I quietly responded. "I know I left things awkward between us. I'm sorry for that." she continued apologetically. "I understood why you stopped. I even agreed with you and, wanted to apologize for starting the whole thing. If you would've gave me the chance, you would've known that." I whispered frankly while pretending to keep my attention on the movie screen. "That's why I'm apologizing now." she leaned in to whisper in my ear, purposely brushing her soft lips against my earlobes.

"So, now where we going?" I casually asked as we pulled out of the parking lot. "Why? You gotta curfew, now?" Asia asked trying to be funny. "Didn't I tell you before, we don't get a curfew!" Hassan answered quickly. "How are you, gonna answer for him?" Asia high-spiritedly asked. "I'm good, Asia. I can stay out later than you and your aunt, if need be. So, if you got somewhere else to go, then go." I confidently said to Asia and Tiffany, respectively. "Y'all are so cute. But I don't have anywhere else in mind. I just needed to get out for a minute." Tiffany admitted. "So, how'd you like the movie?" she continued seemingly changing the subject. "It was ok. Now, why the need to get out? What's on your mind?" I asked genuinely concerned. She looked at me and smiled. "You really are... nothing. If you really wanna know, we can talk later." she said as she looked back at the ears around us. Now concentrating more on her need for segregation, I smiled, shook my head and then turned up the radio.

[Usher]
You make me wanna leave the one I'm with;
Start a new relationship with you

"Yeah, no. Hell no!" Tiffany said before quickly turning down the radio. "You don't like Usher?" I asked surprised by her abrupt response to the song. "Oh, I love Usher, and I like the song. Just, not right now." she said while searching the radio stations for a song more tolerable. "Whatever." she mumbled before giving up on the radio altogether. "Look at these two." I said referring to Asia and Hassan in the backseat, kissing. "That's just why I'm taking them home." she asserted as she glanced into the backseat. "Taking who home?" Hassan said abruptly pulling away from Asia. "C'mon Tiff, we wanna go where ever y'all going." Asia complained while pulling herself up onto the back of Tiffany's chair. "We ain't going nowhere! I was taking him home, too." Tiffany enlightened inhospitably. I looked at all the excitement in the backseat of the car and began to laugh. "What time is it? You feel like going down to the water?" I softly asked Tiffany trying to bring everyone down to a calm. "Yeah, let's do Kelley Drive!" Hassan said excitedly co-signing with my suggestion.

Tiffany looked in the rearview mirror at Hassan and then over at me and smirked. "What's funny?" I asked nosily. "I haven't parked down on the drive, in years. Not sense, I was y'all age." she said continuing to smile. "There you go. Trying to say we young, again." I said sarcastically. "No one said anything about you being, young. Besides, age is just a number, remember?" she responded just as sarcastic.

We pulled into one of the small parking spaces along the Schukyll River. Hassan and Asia jumped out immediately. "I'm not trying to be here long y'all." Tiffany yelled to them as they hastily made their way further from the jeep.

"So, how are you? How've you been?" she reservedly interviewed while staring vacantly at the water. "No. That's not how this's gonna go. You said we'll talk later. It's later, so talk!" I demanded as I watched her stare off into naught. "I am, oh so sorry, sir. What do you want to know?" she said pretending to be intimidated. "You can start with why you felt the need to get out." I pryingly suggested. "Because my husband is more in love with himself than he is with me, and he's finally coming to terms with that." she said solemnly. "Oh wow." I whispered at a total loss for words.

"You wanna get out, and walk a little? Get some air?" I queried assuming outside would be more comfortable than the dense air in the car. "No, I'm alright" she replied softly. "Why you think that about your husband?" I asked hoping to get some clarity as to what's really on her mind.

"At nineteen years old, I married the prettiest guy in Mt. Airy. We were the perfect couple. Young, gorgeous and very, very vain." Tiffany chuckled while admitting. "It was cool, back in the day. But at some point, we were supposed to grow up. And Ronald, hasn't seemed to grasp that yet. He's still that seventeen-year-old that I used to go see on the basketball court. I guess that's why I was the only one excited when he said he was going to the Marines. I thought, it would grow him. Grow us." she solemnly continued. "Well for him to be so child-like, he has made a lot of grown up decisions. Going to the Marines, was a grown-up decision. Marrying you, was a grown-up decision. He can't be all bad." I said trying to reassure her that she's where she is supposed to be. "He's not. And don't get me wrong, I do love him. I just feel like he..." she revealed prior to stopping and taking a long deep breath. "When you're young and don't get me wrong, I'm not old in the least bit." Tiffany said doing a little hip winding dance in the car seat to show that she can still move her body. "But when you're young, it's always *all* about you. As you get older, responsibilities hit and you start becoming the least of your priorities. As you get older, you take grasp of the decisions that make you the person you are trying to become. Ronald hasn't seemed to begin to do any of that." she passionately proclaimed. "And waiting for him is starting to wear on me. I actually think he only joined the Marines, so that he could continue to have someone tell him when to wake up. Tell 'em, what to wear. When to eat... what to eat!" she continued smirking and shaking her head in disbelief. "C'mon let's walk" I suggested, now needing some fresh air, myself.

"Where y'all going? We was on our way back to, the car." Asia said as we approached them walking along the jogging trail. "Here we come now. We'll meet y'all at the car in ten minutes" Tiffany said lifting her head from my shoulder. "Tiffany, you said that the last time we passed y'all, forty-five minutes ago." Hassan said sarcastically. We looked at one another and laugh hysterically. "C'mon let's go." I said pulling her arm towards the direction of the car. "Yeah. They sound anxious to get home." Tiffany said sarcastically. "Don't act like you don't know why" I replied to her pretending not to know they're current desires. "That's my niece boy!" Tiffany said with a smirk and widened eyes. "And, my homie." I said as we walked slowly behind Hassan and Asia.

"Goodnight, Omar." Tiffany whispered after paring the jeep in front of my house. "Goodnight, Omar." Hassan and Asia sarcastically sang in unison as I got out of the car. I walked around the front of the jeep and headed across the lawn to my front door. I stopped and turned to watch the jeep back out of my driveway. "You alright?" Tiffany asked stopping the jeep when she noticed I was watching them. "I'm fine" I mouthed to not alert my parents or anyone else peacefully sleeping. "Ok. Goodnight Omar." Tiffany mouthed back before resuming her departure.

"Ohh, apple crisp!" I said aloud as I foraged through the refrigerator for tonight's dinner. RING. RING! "That ain't nobody but, Quincy or Hassan." I thought as I scurried to the phone to keep it from ringing again at such a late hour. RING. RIN! "Hello!" I answered abrasively. "Yo, wha'chu doing?" Hassan asked anxiously. "About to go to bed!" I harshly whispered while returning to the refrigerator. "Yeah. Can you come out for a minute?" he asked disregarding my fierce tone. "For what? No!" I answered showing my irritation of his call. "Just answer the door, in 10 minutes." he replied continuing to completely disregard my irritation. "Come to the back door. I'm unlocking it now." I said quickly surrendering to Hassan's normal pushy demeanor.

I turned off the television and tossed the remote onto the sofa after hearing the back door open and close. "Omar." a female's voice whispered from the kitchen. I hurried through the house to find Tiffany standing in the kitchen, by the back door. "Hey." she softly uttered. "Hey" I confusedly replied. "Don't look so glad to see me." she whispered sarcastically. "I'm always glad to see you. Now, wha'chu doing here?" I asked worried of what my mom would say if she came downstairs. "Everything alright?" I asked after rotating to inspect for my parents. "Nothing's wrong. I just didn't want to go back there, yet." Tiffany said smiling. "What about Asia?" I asked confused at how she was able to go so any places so quickly. "I just dropped her off at Hassan's. His mom is never there!" she continued enthusiastically. "I know. That's why he's always here. She's always at work." I agreed still cautiously looking around. "So, now I have to find something to do til she's *finished*. I mean until it's time to pick her up." she said cynically. I laughed at her intentional mistake. "You were right the first time" I scoffed. "Where'd you wanna go?" I asked anxious to get out of a common area of the house. "I don't care. I just didn't wanna sit in a hotel room all night, by myself. That's as far as I thought it through. Then Hassan said that you weren't doing anything, and would keep me company. So, he called for me." she excitedly said with her voice climbing a bit louder than a whisper. I slid passed her and locked the back door. "C'mon" I said as I gestured for her to follow me up to my room.

"Now we don't have to whisper. Just let me throw some clothes on, and we can go wherever you want." I said escorting her to the reclining chair next to my bed. I looked around the room for something laying around to throw on. "Are you in the dirty clothes?" she asked smiling as she watched me rummage through the clothes hamper. I shook my head, sighed and walked over to the closet for something to wear. She stood and walked over to the closet next to me. "We can't just stay, here?" Tiffany asked curiously rummaging through my closet. "If that's what you want." I responded thankful that I didn't have to find anything to wear. "So, what time do you have to pick Asia up?" I asked grabbing my plate of apple crisp and sitting on the bed. "Whenever I get there. I'm assuming the longer I take, the better." she responded pulling my grey, dress shirt out of the closet. She tossed the shirt across the back of the chair and continued to explore the room. "Yeah you may be right." I said as I reached for the remote control and turned on the television.

"Shit! what time is it?" I whispered to myself as I looked around the room. "It's only eleven thirty. You were only sleep for about half hour, forty-five minutes." Tiffany said looking at me peculiar after her presence somewhat startled me. "Oh." I said remembering my current situation. "You plan staying the night in that chair?" I asked charmingly. "And is that my shirt?" I continued to interrogate, forgetting that she removed the shirt from my closet. "Yeah." she replied quietly. "To which one? The night? The shirt? Or the chair?" I asked sitting up noticing the half-eaten apple crisp left on the night stand. "The shirt. I changed while you were asleep. I hope you don't mind." Tiffany said with a flirty smile. "The only thing I mind, is that you waited for me to doze off before you undressed." I joked revisiting my plate of apple crisp. "You should've stayed up. It was a hell of a show." she said laughing. "I'm sure it was." I said as I put the empty dish on the nightstand. "Well, I'm about to go back to sleep. You alright?" I asked as I began to strip down to my underwear and get under the covers. "I'm fine. Make sure you leave enough room for me under there." she stated softly.

"I'm sorry." I said insincerely realizing that I was poking Tiffany with my erection. "It's ok. You gotta get a bigger bed, so that the next time I'm over we won't have this problem." she teased. "This is going to be a long night." I thought as I held my penis between my legs to keep from poking Tiffany's back. I wasn't going to let what happened in her hotel room happen again. It was a ridiculous tease for both of us, and left me still feeling a little uncomfortable. Tiffany realized my predicament and decided to show her acceptance of this new instance. She slid her body back and began to grind her soft ass into my pelvis. "Thank God she got on panties" I thought to myself, while doing my best to abstain. When she figured out that she couldn't find my penis with her body motions, Tiffany opted to use her hand. She discovered my dick being squeezed tightly between my legs. "This can't be comfortable." she whispered as she snatched my dick from between my legs. She slid it down her panties and placed it between her ample ass cheeks. "Now, ain't that better?" she intuitively asked. I did my best to remain still but it was altogether impossible.

I grabbed my dick and began to rub it slowly up and down between her cheeks. Before long, I realized that she was harmoniously grinding with me. She pulled my dick out of her panties and ascended out of the bed. "You mind if I take some of this off, it's a little warm under those covers." Tiffany said as she began to slide her panties to the floor. "No. Get comfortable." I eagerly advised. I lifted to my head and reached into the pillowcase for a condom, trying to be as inconspicuous as possible. "You can't hide that!" Tiffany said referring to erection lifting the covers like a pitched tent. "Guess not." I replied watching her walk around to the bottom of the bed. "Remember the hotel. Cause, I do. Now it's my turn to tease." she forewarned as she slid under the covers head first.

Tiffany began to softly kiss my ankle. She then slowly worked her way up my leg and paused at the bottom of my boxers. "These are in the way" she said as she snatched off my underwear and tossed them behind her. "I-I told you that I don't do teasing, w-well." I stuttered trying to whisper my warning. Tiffany laughed and replied "Boy, calm down. If this is what I wanna do, this is what I gonna do". She slid over to my other leg and maneuvered her way back down to my ankle. "I'm calm. You finished with the teasing?" I casually asked while pretending not to be enthralled. "Not yet" she said as she scurried up the bed to my dick. She lifted her head over my dick and slowly came down guiding it into her mouth with her tongue. She continued to suck and pull on my manhood while gently rising her head up and down. "Oh shit" I said as my body clenched each time, she ran her tongue across the head.

"Now, I'm done teasing." she said as she slowly kissed her way up my chest to my neck. "You sure, that's how you wanna play?" I asked looking for the opportunity to put on the condom which was still in my hand.

Tiffany continued to kiss my neck, slowly migrating to my cheek and eventually my ear. "Yeah I'm sure." she confidently replied after finally stopping what she was doing. I leaned and pressed my face to her neck. "Damn, you smell good." I recapped as I began to gently kiss her neck. "Thank you. Now, what are you doing?" she asked softly as she inadvertently tilted toward my kisses. "Paying you back for all of that teasing, you were just doing." I openly admitted. "But I was just paying you back, for the hotel. You had your tongue, in my ass." she continued, maneuvering so that I can continue kissing. "Oh. So, you want me to stop?" I asked confidently. "Well, since you already started, you can keep going." she whispered anxiously.

She slid back down my body and settled her head on my chest. I could hear her exhaling heavily as she nestled in. I began softly run my fingers through her hair. "Damn, her hair is soft as shit. This bitch is perfect." I thought with an uncompromisingly smile. I secured the remote control to turn off the television to linger to in this serene moment that we fashioned. I felt her cheeks began to rise to a grin as I softly moved her hair from her face. "You're smiling, I feel it." I whispered as we lay in the dark room. "Yeah, I am." she said as she lifted her head to display it. She followed her head lift with her body, and crawled back up until she was straddling across my waist. I grabbed my dick and held it down to keep it from touching her while in this position. I continued to just look at her.

Tiffany was smiling from ear to ear. And I couldn't help but smile, in unison. "What are you smiling at?" she asked while looking profoundly into my eyes. "You. You're, so beautiful. And you're glowing. And, you're smiling. You're beautiful, glowing, smiling and in my bed, with me." I chaotically answered as I tried to gather a solid thought. She started to blush, covered it with a laugh and continued to stare into my eyes.

"What are you thinking? Honestly. Cause you have a cute, almost devious look about you, right now." I asked curious of why she had that cunning smile. "I was just thinking 'bout how I had just finished teasing and was straddling you naked and you didn't make a move. Someone out there would say, that's because you *are* sixteen." she said still smiling. "She's trying to get to me." I thought, chuckling at her audacity. "I didn't do anything because it wasn't the time." I said confidently. "And why not?" she whispered curiously. "A couple of reasons. One, you weren't sure if you were ready. I had to give you the chance to think about what could happen, if that happened. Then, you had to decide whether or not you wanted to keep going. I like you, Tasha. And I don't want to miss out on another day and a half, if this fucks our heads up, again. I only have you for 4 more days. Two, I still have the condom in my hand. Can't be inside you without that, right? Three…" I started to whisper before she bluntly interjected.

She grabbed my hand which was holding both the condom and my dick, and pulled it. My dick sprung out of my hand and struck her on butt. Her eyes raised when she discovered that I did have a condom, ready, in hand. "Look at you." she said smiling and slowly shaking her head awestruck by my nerve. "I was just being ready for whatever, you was bringing." I openly replied. "And, you thought of all of that while I was teasing you?" she continued seemingly impressed. "Yeah, there was more but you rudely interrupted me." I said boldly. "That's because you were right and I didn't want to hear anymore. Didn't like being reminded of our lost time. I missed you." she honestly whispered. "So, what was three?" she continued asking. "Three was just a reminder that you were still on top of me, and hadn't gone anywhere. Which meant that there was still opportunity." I arrogantly informed. "Oh really?" she asked scheming. "Really." I said calmly. She began to suspiciously laugh at my nonchalant demeanor. I snickered at her expressed amusement at my obvious act. My laughter caused my body to move slightly and I felt my penis start to slide off her ample cheek, down into the crevice of her ass. Her subtle jolt showed that she noticed it as well. "You better get that." she said as she slightly lifted her waist to direct my attention to where my dick was. Her slight readjustment put my penis at the tip of her moist vagina. "Get what? It's fine." I whispered recognizing that as fact, as long as neither of us moved. "That!" she said as she lifted her waist hastily, and returned down slowly pushing me inside of her.

"Tiffany. Tiffany!" I whispered as I gently shook her shoulder. She lifted her head from the pillow and looked up at me. She was both still glowing, and smiling. "What time do you have to get Asia?" I continued to whisper. "Call Hassan, and see what they wanna do." she said softly. I picked up my phone and dialed Hassan's number. "Yo." he answered raspingly. "What's up?" I asked as I did every day. "Same shit." he replied as he did every day. "So, what we doing?" I asked looking for some kind of signal to his intentions. "I'm about to get dressed. Meet you on the *real* late eighteen." he said casually. "Alright" I said before he hung up the phone. "Y'all didn't say anything about me, and Asia" Tiffany said in an almost laugh. "Yeah, we did." I replied confused at her statement. "So, what's the plan then?" she said confident that she was right in her previous statement. "Well, I'm gonna go back to sleep for an hour, then get dress, then head out to the bus which comes at eight, forty-two. Hassan is goin' back to sleep, or finish doing whatever he's doing. Then he's gonna get dress and jump on the same bus which gets to him, at eight forty-six." I said confident that I knew that I had this handled. "You are really something else." she said laughing at my confidence. "Ok, Mr. *No Sweat*, I gotta go to the bathroom. How you gonna figure that one out?" I arrogantly scrutinized, shook my head and opened the door, unshaken. "Straight across the hall." I said poised and self-assured. Tiffany grabbed the shirt that she started out in, and slowly crept towards me at the door. "No one's here." I said laughing at her attempt to be stealth. She looked befuddled as she slid past me in the doorway and headed towards the bathroom.

"Okay, where is everybody." Tiffany said as she entered the room. "My dad drops my mom off at work before he go in. She has to be there by six, so they leave at like five fifteen." I said running to reset my alarm clock to give myself the extra time, Hassan and I agreed upon.

"So, how much time do you got, now?" Tiffany asked while fixing her hair in the mirror. "I got about an hour and fifteen minutes before my alarm goes off." I said firmly, as I jumped back into bed. "A whole seventy-five minutes, huh?" Tiffany said as she climbed back into bed with a twinkle in her eye.

RING. RING! "Don't answer it." Tiffany whispered as she swept her hand across my forehead, catching the sweat before it poured off my face onto her. "It's Hassan. He gonna miss second period too, if I don't tell him to go ahead." I replied while feeble and out of breath. RING. RING! I fell onto Tiffany and fumbled around on the night stand, for the ringing phone. RING. RING! "Yo O. I'mma be late, late. So, go 'head." Hassan said abruptly before I could say a word. "I was about to call you with the, same thing." I blissfully mumbled with Tiffany's legs wrapped around my waist, still slowly pushing in and out of her.

CHAPTER 29

"Quentin"

"Daddy is trippin'!" Emily unreservedly stated with concern for my father's well-being. "Dad? I heard you was the one, trippin'." I retorted competently anticipating her explanation of what happened. "Not really. Me and London, went looking for that girl Chaewon. The one with all the mouth." she admitted, her tone an apparent finger point at me. "We see how well that worked out for you, didn't we? I told you not to do shit like that, when I'm not around." I sternly scolding. "I'm fine!" she said assuring. "You fine?" I asked curious to what she was referring to. "Yeah. Not only did nobody press charges, but I didn't even get punished. I even heard mom on the phone saying that she couldn't believe that dad said I can still go to Philly, tomorrow." she said astonished. "What's in Philly?" I asked curiously. "I'm going to studio this weekend. Lil' Drummaboy Recording! I told you this already." she strictly said, upset that I didn't remember. "And dad said you can still go?" I asked skeptically. "Yeah, I told you... dad is trippin'." she said sounding both concerned and excited simultaneously. "Why wouldn't dad cancel that?" I curiously questioned. "I don't know. I thought he was going to. But I am so, so glad he didn't." she acknowledged anxious to go. "Yeah I don't know either. What did ma say?" I asked baffled by the situation. "She said I can't go. Then he said that they'll talk about it, when they home from work." she said bewildered. "Yeah, you ain't going." I said realizing how the battle would play out. "Shut up." she said realizing that I may be right. "So, I got a few minutes. Tell me what happened yesterday." I informally insisted.

"Where the hell is Rudy?" I asked myself as I approached my apartment to find J.T. and Dominic Sharky in front of my door. "Fuck y'all want?" I offhandedly asked as I pushed past the two of them to unlock my door. I put my key into the lock as the door snatched open. "Y'all still out here?" Juice said as he held the door open for me to enter. "Come in." I insisted as I slid past the three of them. "You becoming a real stalker, you know that?" Juice continued to J.T. as he came in behind me. "Yo, this little friendship shit with you and Tasha need to stop! I'm not going to continue to be disrespected." J.T. exclaimed as I headed to the kitchen counter. "You remember the last time that you came in here, all loud? I'm still trying to get'cha blood out my carpet. You might wanna calm down." I said to J.T. as he followed me across the room. "You trying to take it there, again? Well, I'm here. I'm ready!" J.T. said as he tossed his bag to the floor. "You don't want that, man. What you wanna do… is play ball, finish the year, and go pro." Juice said from the couch.

KNOCK. KNOCK! "I thought I saw you two come in up on this floor." Rudy said as he pushed the door open after a marginal knock. "We not going to have another problem here, are we?" Rudy asked as he reached for his two-way radio. "Nah, we good." Juice said halfheartedly looking for the remote. "Yeah, we're good. Just had to talk, really quick." J.T. followed. "Don't play me, white boy." Rudy said as he brushed past J.T. and me, to reach into the refrigerator. "I know what you're here, to talk about. I got eyes! And some consequential knowledge for all you youngin's, that young lady, is doing her. What you need to do white boy, is go do you! And stop taking everything so seriously. Reality check, this is college, man! Shit happens! The only thing y'all need to take serious here, is your leanings." Rudy preached while moving things around in the refrigerator to make a decision on his snack. "It's sad, cause none of y'all seem to have come here for that. This is just your doorway to the league. You need to take advantage of this opportunity. This is once in a lifetime shit! But somebody already told y'all this, I'm sure." Rudy earnestly resumed as he tucked a soda under his arm and opened a pack of Juice's krimpets. "If I leave here and some shit jump off, I'm not calling nobody. I'm not contacting the A.D. I'mma handle y'all my damn self! You heard… what you heard!" Rudy affirmed as he opened the door to leave. "Like I won't whoop his old ass." Dominic mumbled as he closed the door behind Rudy.

"So, let me see if I got this straight. You feel disrespected by me, cause your girl didn't wanna fuck you no more, and started fucking me?" I asked sarcastically. "What makes you think she stopped fucking me?" he asked cynically. "And yeah, to me that's rather disrespectful." he continued. "So, you come here to me? I didn't chase her. She came, at me. She showed up in my apartment, half naked. What makes you think, I would ever turn that down?" I said defensively as I put away the groceries I had come home with. "You can't be mad at him for that, man. What guy would turn that down?" Dominic said, resting his hand on J.T.'s shoulder. "I don't need you to co-sign right now, Dom. What I need, is for the shit to stop. My whole future is on the line here." J.T. exclaimed while tossing Dominic's hand from his shoulder. "What the hell you talking 'bout?" Juice said from the couch. "Ya boy. He in here fucking my girl and I can't do shit about it, cause it'll affect my status on the team. Now everybody's looking at me, like I ain't shit for letting it happen. You got 'em staring, while I'm eating lunch. They mumbling, while I'm in class. They even talking shit, on the practice field." he said sincerely. "Damn, I never even thought about all that. If I was fucking her, and I'm not saying I am. But, if I was… I guess I could empathize with your situation." I said honestly while smirking at his pathetic bellyaching. RING. RING!

Imani Chance
302-555-2112

RING. RING! "I gotta take this call, so I'm going to say we're done here." I arrogantly said as I answered my phone. "Hey babe." I said enthusiastically. "Hey, I'll be there to-morrow!" Imani sang. "I know babe." I replied trying to sound as excited as she was. "I'll be waiting at the train station for you at one, fifty-five." I continued as I gathered J.T.'s attention and pointed to the door. "Good, cause I'm supposed to be there at two and want to be in your arms by two, ten." Imani said motivated by her readiness to see me. "Yeah, you need to go handle that." I heard Juice responding to J.T., as he and Dominic headed towards to door. "So, what the fuck we gonna do about this?" J.T. yelled across the room as he grabbed the door. "Hold on babe. I said we're done here! There is nothing else to talk about." I yelled back with my hand over the phone. "You know what, you right." J.T. said has he held the door for Dominic. "Juice, you're right too. I gotta handle it myself." he continued before stepping out of the apartment and closing the door.

CHAPTER 30

"Imani"

"No girl, I'm almost there. So, you better say everything you need to now. Cause I'll be unreachable, for the next 3 days." I proudly bragged. "Damn. The dick is like that?!" she asked appalled by my tone. "And then some! Why you think I'm in the predicament I'm in now?" I said with a broad smile. "Girl, you know it ain't really about that. I just miss him." I said sincerely. "Yeah, I know. I don't know why though, my brother is a real asshole." Storm said genuinely. "Yeah, but he's my asshole." I said proudly. BEEP!

Deanna Harriston
667-555-1070

"That's my cousin on the other line. She probably got more excuses why she couldn't come. Let me talk to her real quick. I'll call you before I get settled." I ensured. BEEP! "Alright." she said before ending the call.

"Hello" I said after switching lines. "Why wasn't you answering my calls?" she bellowed into the phone. "Cause, I was on the other line." I answered reasonably justifying. "I was talking to Storm about something important me and her brother, going through. Why, what's wrong?" I asked while trying to remain consistent with my discretion. "Nothing! My mom wanted me to make sure you was alright. So, I was calling you before you got there and went m.i.a." she directly explained. "Well I'm almost there now, so you better talk while you got me. Cause once I get there, I'm all his." I declared while laughing proudly.

I looked out the window as we pulled into the terminal. People were starting to stand and gather their things but it was mainly to stretch after the long ride. I watched all the people outside waiting at their cars as the bus rolled to a stop. At this point, all I could feel was excitement maneuver its way up my body. I loved coming up here to see my baby. Everyone in the parking lot looked to be as cooped up and restless, as we were on the bus. I snickered as they too, looked like they were rising and stretching in preparation for our arrival.

"Look at that man, right there!" I whispered with an uncontrollable smile noticing Quentin appear from inside of the terminal building. I quickly grabbed my bag and charged my way up the aisle, to the door. I slowed down when stepping off the bus, as not to show my excitement. "Look at you, always eating." I said as Quentin approached the bus. "What? It's only, an Icee." Quentin said trying to hide the small piece of soft pretzel that he had left in his hand. "You're such a liar." I said as I ran and jumped into his arms. "God, I missed you." Quentin whispered into my ear as he squeezed me so tight, that he almost seemed to forget that I was human.

"So where are we going? And don't say back to your dorm to do it! We got all night for that." I said smiling at his always dirty mind. "I wasn't!" Quentin said laughing pretending to be on the defensive. "But, you don't wanna go unpack. At least put your stuff down?" he continued while trying to look as harmless as possible. "I can do that later. Thanks for your concern, though" I replied sarcastically. "So where do you wanna go?" he asked genuinely. "I don't know. You really didn't have anything planned?" I asked becoming slightly bothered. "No. I was just living off it, moment to moment. I'm still euphoric just seeing you." he said reluctantly. "What am I going to do with you?" I said shaking my head with a smirk. "Can we at least go out to eat?" I continued to inquire. "Of course. Meals and stuff like that, I got handled. I'm ready for that. It's the other things, I'm always clueless about." he said genuinely. "Well let's get something to eat and go from there." I said reassuring him that all was well.

CHAPTER 31

"Omar"

"What I tell you Emily? Stop touching my music!" I said sternly while snatching the auxiliary cord out of her phone. "But dad, don't nobody wanna hear that." Emily complained as she twitched and flapped in the passenger seat. "I don't care what y'all wanna hear. Wish I could say that we're at a crossroad. But we're not! Now plug my phone back in!!" I demanded as I turned the volume down in the meantime. "I don't mind your music Mr. G." Joey said from directly behind me. Emily turned and gave her friend a resentful look, before plugging the cord back into my phone. "Thank you, Joey. And I'll thank you too Emily. Thank you not to touch it again." I said as I turned the volume back up.

"Taking off my coat, clearing my throat." I yelled excitingly as the music returned to my liking. RING. RING! "About how long before we get there?" Emily asked solemnly disappointed. I held up my finger gesturing for her to wait a minute. RING. RING!

The Misses
302-555-8972

"Hey Babe! You okay?" I asked casually. "I'm not sure. I woke up to an empty bed this morning, and no goodbye from my husband. Would you be okay, if you were me?" Tracey questioned dubiously. "No babe, any scenario where I have a husband, would leave me really not okay!" I sarcastically mocked. "I take it, you have yet to make it downstairs?" I resumed before she could counter. "No, why?" she asked obliviously. "Because, I've never once left you without saying goodbye." I said with poise. "What time did you pull out?" she asked curiously. "After you finished." I said looking around to make sure that no one else was paying attention to my conversation. "You so nasty." Tracey said getting my pun immediately. "I'm not talking about last night." she continued with a slight

170

chuckle. "Wait. Aren't you in a car full of children?" she asked both quickly and nervously. "They can't hear my conversation." I said attempting to speak not as loudly. "Dad! I know you not over there talking all nasty!" Emily interrupted boldly. "Girl, mind your business. I'm talking to your mom, about grown up stuff!" I said to Emily as far from serious as I could. "So dear, we left about forty-five minutes ago! I didn't want to wake you." I said so everyone could here. Tracey erupted with laughter. "That's what you get." she scolded humorously. "Babe, let me call you back. Cause with me on the phone, she's reaching for my aux cord and I'm not trying to hear that mumble shit." I said earnestly. "Okay babe. Love you" Tracey said still laughing. "Love you too babe." I said honestly.

"Engine, engine, number nine." I resumed singing as I maneuvered up interstate 95 to my city of birth. "Pick it up. Pick it up. Pick it up." Emily's friends joined in from the backseat. I laughed at the fact that they actually knew the song lyrics. "How do you know this song?" I asked in awe to her friend London. "My mom listens to the same music you do. I hear these songs all the time." she dispiritedly disclosed. "Don't sound so sad, London. This is good music!" I said encouragingly. "Yeah, this is Black Sheep. I actually tried to sample one of their songs for a track I had for you. But I couldn't make it play with the song concept." Joey added as he rocked back and forth to the music. "Whatever! Y'all just trying to impress my dad." she sneeringly said feeling betrayed by her friends.

"What are you gonna do, while we're at the studio?" Emily asked curiously. I laughed at her trying to make sure that I wouldn't be there to hamper her good time. "Not sure. Probably hang out with your grandmother all day." I said uncertain by the plethora of possibilities with me being back home. "Ooh, I wanna see Grandma Val." Emily squealed enthusiastically. "Maybe. If it's not too late when you're done." I said encouraging.

I gradually toured down South Street to see if I saw a sign or something saying the word "studio". "What's the address to this place?" I asked quickly tiring of looking and driving slowly. "It's on South Street." Emily barked quickly. "I'm on South Street!" I countered. "Eight one eight South Street" Joey said after looking into his phone. I stopped in the middle of the street in front of the address Joey announced. "Alright people, get out and go have some fun." I said as I unlocked the doors and hurried them out of the car, as to not impede traffic for too long. "Dad, you going far? Can I have some money to get something to eat?" Emily asked as she slid out of the truck. "Why you wait 'til now to ask me? I asked noticing the line of cars behind me becoming impatient. "Here!" I continued while reaching into my center console for the few dollars I keep laying around the truck for emergency. "Thanks. Don't forget nine o'clock. Love you." she reminded quickly as she hurried to close the door.

"Hey mom!" I said startled as I opened the door to see her standing there. "Hey baby!" she said as she rushed over to hold me. "How are you? Wat'chu doing here?" she asked after lifting her head from my chest. "Just came up for a quick visit. Thought I'd surprise you, since I haven't seen you in a while." I replied vibrantly. I couldn't help smiling in my mother's presence. "That's nice. Now what are you really doing here?" she skeptically asked, suspecting the worst as she usually did. "I came to see you. Why it gotta be something else? Did I interrupt you, or something?" I said pretending to be offended by her accusation. "No. Never, baby. It's just, you just only come to Philly for funerals, or business reasons. And you're not dressed for a funeral." she said defending her line of questioning. "No. No funeral, no business." I said reassuring her that all was well. "It doesn't even matter. I got my baby. Come, sit down and talk to me. How's Tracey and Emily? Better yet, how's Quentin?! Have you talked to him?" she asked enthusiastically. "Everyone's fine. Quentin's doing good. I spoke to him a day or two ago." I said rising to head for the kitchen.

"What's that I smell? Apples?" I asked eager to hear her response. "I made a caramel, apple crisp for my... friend." she said restraining. "What friend?!" I said sternly surprised at what she said. She disregarded my tone, by giving me a dirty look. "Boy, please." she said taking no notice of my hostile stance. "Your dad's been gone seven years, Omar. I will always love your father, but I think I mourned him long enough! I'm allowed to have a friend!" she retorted sharply. "Now, do you want some of this crisp or not?!" she continued harshly. "Why wouldn't you be allowed to have a friend, mom? I just didn't know that you had a friend. And yes, I'd like some crisp, please. That is, if your friend wouldn't mind." I sarcastically said trying to lighten her demeanor. "I'm sorry Omar. I've been playing this conversation out in my head for weeks. I thought you'd be closed minded about this, as you are with a lot of other things." she said wholeheartedly. "And what do you mean, if my friend wouldn't mind? You're my boy!" she continued as she brought me some crisp. "You want some ice-cream?" she asked sweetly. "Nah, no thank you mom. This is enough at eleven forty-five in the morning." I said thankfully. My mother pulled out a chair, and sat down next to me at the table. I set down my fork, and grasped her hand. She gently placed her hand atop of mine, and I did the same. "What's wrong mom?" I asked genuinely. "I miss my family. I miss your dad. I miss you guys, loving my cooking." she said as she removed her hand from under mine and returned my fork to me. I didn't know what to say. I procured the fork from her hand and slowly resumed eating. "So, tell me about this friend." I requested as I gestured for another helping of his desert.

"Hey babe. What's up?" I asked Tracey. "Nothing. I love how that sounds. Nothing." she said exhaling slowly. I laughed at her moans of tranquility during her time alone. "You sound nice and relaxed." I said happy that she was able to take advantage of her deserved opportunity. "I am." she peacefully. "Good!" I said with a smile. "You at your mom's?" she asked pleasantly. "Yeah. She's upstairs getting dressed to go out." I answered casually. "Y'all going out?" she continued to ask. "Yeah, we going to the mall. Then she's going on a date, with her friend. Did you know she had a *friend*?" I asked still captivated by the news. "Wow! Your mom has a boyfriend?!" she asked amazed by the discovery. "Yup. Some retire business owner. He apparently loves my mom's deserts." I said explaining all I knew about my mom's suitor. "I bet he does." Tracey said roaring with laughter. I shook my head and did my best to hold back my smile at her joke. "Let me go." I said still smiling. "I'll call you later to make sure you are still okay. Continue to relax, cause when we get there, we're just going to ruin it." I said hopelessly. "Babe, you are my relax. You should know that. You relaxed me, with this call. You unquestionably relaxed me, last night. I love you, Omar." she said trying to set my mind at ease. "I love you too, babe. I'll call you later." I said sincerely before ending the call.

"Alright mom. I'm about to get outta here." I said reaching the top of the stairs looking around. "Your leaving?" she asked from her bedroom at the end of the hall. "Yeah, I just spoke to Victor. I'm gonna head over there, and hang out with him for a little while." I said as I followed her voice down the hall. "How is Victor these days?" she asked as she sat at her vanity, applying make-up. "He's good, as far as I know. I just hope he's not broke cause I not loaning him money, nor fronting any bills." I said compellingly. I stood behind my mom pretending to primp her hair. "Same 'ol, Victor." she said handing me a hairbrush. "Yeah. Some things never change." I said while brushing her hair gently. I placed the hairbrush back onto the vanity and leaned in close to my mother's cheek. "I'll be in Philly all day, so if you're not busy later, I'll stop back with Emily." I divulged softly as I kissed her cheek and made my way out of the room. "Ok baby. I'll call you when I get back." she replied affectionately. "Alright mom. I love you." I bellowed as I journeyed down the hall. I smiled as I passed the closed door to my childhood bedroom. I could hear my dad calling me from his room as I started down the stairs. "This house brings back so many memories" I thought to myself as I opened the door to leave.

"Vic!" I bawled as he opened the door. "Look at the American dream!" Victor said thunderously in return. Vic was always trying to both insult and praise me simultaneously. "Here you go, talking shit already!" I said extending my hand for him to shake. "I'm just messing with you, man. But you do got the nice job, nice cars, nice house, and the white wife." he said stating the obvious as he grasped my hand. "Yeah. But I also have the college degrees, nice car notes, nice mortgage and nice sized bills. But if you wanna play hard, you gotta work hard, *first*." I logically advised. "I hear you." he said while chuckling at my lecturing. "You wanna beer, or something?" he continued. "Nah man, I'm good." I responded comfortably. "So. What brings you up this way?" he asked prying for any gossip he could get his hands on. "Emily wanted to go to some music studio on South Street, and I had to meet up with some folks face to face, so…" I openly answered after sitting down on his oversized sofa. "Meet folks face to face? What the hell, you a drug kingpin now?" he asked sarcastically. I laughed at Vic's roast of my vague explanation. "You got all the jokes today, huh?" I asked while moving pillows across the sofa to get more comfortable. "I'm just fucking with you. So, what's good homie?!" he asked enthusiastically. With two beers in hand, he tossed the loveseat pillows onto the other end of the sofa and plopped down. "Here." he said handing one to me. "You always say no, and then get up ten minutes later." he continued. I laughed at how well he knew me. He picked up the remote from the end table and turned on the television. "I got a call from Tiffany, not too long ago." I said seriously. "Que mom?" he asked dumbfounded. "Yup!" I answered nonchalantly. "Fuck her. Man, she walked off with our whole senior year. What she want?" he asked antagonized by just her name. "That's what I'm here to find out." I replied casually. "Apparently, she's back in Philly and wants to talk. She even reached out to Quentin?" I relentlessly continued. "Wow. What'd she say to him?" he asked taking a large swig of beer. "As far as I know, nothing really. According to Quentin, she just introduced herself. Oh, and sent him a bunch of birthday cards." I said venting to my childhood friend. "So, that's why you up here? Where Haas? He feeds on this kinda shit?" he asked inquisitively. "That's why I didn't even tell him, I was coming today. He thinks it's next Friday. I don't need his bad advice, not today." I said smiling. "Yeah. You can get enough of that shit, from me." he said chuckling at his self-berating comment.

"All right man. Let me get outta here." I said standing up to stretch my legs. I looked over to see Vic asleep, with his legs draped over the arm of the loveseat. "Oh, you're up?" Vic's wife Tamia whispered as she crept down the stairs behind me. "Hi, Omar." she sang quietly with a smile as she crept over to me. "Hey Cricket!" I said quietly, assuming she didn't want to wake Vic. She put down the laundry basket that she was carrying and opened her arms to embrace me. "How are you?" she whispered. I snickered as I grabbed her wrists and closed them back across her body. "Now you know we don't hug, Cricket. Stop that." I quietly reminded her. "Why not? And what I tell you about calling me Cricket?" she threatened. The faint sound of the clothes dryer alarm interrupted both my answering her, and her continuing her pseudo threats. She picked up the laundry basket and headed for the basement door. "All right, Tamia. That doesn't even sound right coming out of my mouth. Tell sleeping beauty here, I'll stop back by before I leave." I testified as I fastened my coat. "Ok. Bye Omar. And the name is, Cricket." she said with a smile as she opened the basement door. DOINK!

> **{Vic}**
> O. Need u cone check out my braker box. Mia
> said she smell smoke in the basemet.

"Need you to come check out my breaker box. Mia said she smells smoke in the basement. If it ain't one thing it's another with Vic." I mumbled to myself as I read and responded to his text.

> **OMW. Still in front of your door.**

3-0-2-5-5-5-8-9-7-3. "Hey Mister G." London yelled as she answered Emily's phone. "Hello London. I'm just calling to make sure that everything is okay." I yelled back trying to be heard over the music behind her. "I know. Storm said that you'd call, and just to answer the phone if you did." she said apparently expecting my call. I listened as the music was becoming faint. "So, is everything okay?" I asked hesitantly. DOINK! "Yeah. Everything is fine. You're gonna win parent of the year, for this one. She in heaven right now." London said excited for her best friend.

"Glad y'all are having a good time. I'll be there at eight thirty. But call me, if you need me before then." I said genuinely. "Ok. Anything else you want me to tell Storm when she come back out of the booth?" she asked harmlessly. "No London, I'm good." I replied attempting to sound as harmless. "Ok, bye Mister G." she said as the music started to build behind her again. "Bye, London" I said loud enough for her to hear me.

I opened the door to Victor's basement and stepped in. Cricket was loading the dryer without any sense of worry. "Where Vic?" I asked puzzled by him not being present. "Shhhhh. He's upstairs, asleep." she whispered. "He just texted me, Cricket!" I said trying not to become frustrated. "No. I just texted you, from his phone. I figured that would be the only way to get you to come back. Sorry. I got excited." Cricket said with a sinister smile. I looked at her up and down and shook my head skeptically. "Point me to the breaker box." I said feeling disturbed by this unexpected interruption. She placed the laundry basket atop the dryer. "It's in the garage." she said as she grabbed my hand. I followed Cricket's lead to a door that I had passed when entering the basement. She opened the door and pointed across the room. I stepped in with the expectation of the smell of smoke. I didn't smell anything as I made my way to the breaker box. I approached the box and slowly opened it. "I don't smell, a damn thing" I uttered to myself as I flicked the breakers looking for a discrepancy. I inspected the box, the connecting wires and then the box again, just to be sure.

"I don't smell anything." I said as I headed back to the basement. "You heard me?" I asked Cricket who was sorting through the piles of clothes on Victor's pool table. "No dear, what'd you say?" she asked softly. "I said I didn't smell anything. You sure, you smelled smoke?" I asked concerned that I'd be called back once given the opportunity to leave again. "Maybe I was wrong. Or maybe, I just wanted you to come back." she confessed pleasantly. "C'mon Cricket. Wha'sup? I got things to do." I said realizing there was more to this than I'd previously recognized. "I just wanted to finish talking. Just wanted to see you a little longer. Remember, we were friends once, too. In fact, we were friends first. But everyone gets a minute, but me." she sincerely disclosed. I snickered at Cricket's attempt to be reserved. "Wait! You're serious?" I inquired, shocked by her unfamiliar behavior. "Yes." she replied hoisting herself up onto the pool table. I walked over to the pool table and leaned on it next to her. "What do you want to talk about?" I asked ironically.

We spent the next twenty minutes catching up with the present and reminiscing of old times. I laughed at her hopes of catching me looking at her hour glass figure as she paraded around the room, flaunting. "What are you laughing at?" she asked with a big smile. "Nothing. Just thinking about something." I responded casually. "Whatever, Omar." she retorted, just as casual. "So, you felt you had to go through all that extra, just for us to talk?" I inquired pretending to be upset. "I think I should be offended." I continued. "Yes, I did feel that way. You mean to tell me that you would've stayed, and had this conversation with just me, if I didn't corner you? According to you, we can't even hug." she said adjusting the washing machine settings. "Corner me? Wha'chu mean, you cornered me? I could've left, right out of the garage. And we can't hug cause the last time we got close enough to touch, you ended up bent over in the bushes at your family cookout, remember?" I accurately reminded. "Omar, grow up." she said tossing clothing into the washer. "Nothing is going to happen that we don't want to happen. We're not animals." she informed firmly. I chuckled at Cricket's theories, acknowledging that she was right. She looked at me laughing and shaking her head.

My eyes widened, as without word or warning Cricket's bra covered breasts came bursting out of her jacket. "What the hell?" I asked astonished. "These my gym clothes. I have to wash them." she said nonchalantly as she continued to unzip and remove her jacket. She took a step back and shot it into the washing machine as if playing basketball.

"I guess that's my cue." I said as I turned to head for the door. "Always on the go! That's our, Omar." she said nodding her head and snickering. "Wha'chu want me to do? You down here getting naked." I said struggling to not sound like a coward. "One, I'm not getting naked. And two, if I was, you've seen me naked! Again, grow up Omar." Cricket said so nonchalantly it caused skepticism. "You going to keep using that?" I said becoming exhausted with even trying to battle her. I turned and headed back into the room. Cricket stopped me as I crossed her path to the washing machine. "C'mon. Try and block my shot." she said as she grabbed more clothes to shoot. I stood motionless and smiling while her shirts, bras and balled socks flew passed me into the machine. "When did you become so serious?" Cricket asked earnestly. "Don't know. I guess, I grew up." I said sarcastically. I couldn't tell her the truth. That, I was staring and hoping that her nipple would slip out, with all of her moving and hopping. It'd would be inappropriate. I looked down at my watch, to take my eyes and mind off her partially exposed breasts.

"I better get outta here for real, though. I do have something important to do." I said noticing that it was after four. "Well, if you have something to do, I won't continue to keep you. Just let me get my hug and then you can go." Cricket said as she turned to lean on the stairs railing for balance, as she pulled off her socks. While continuing to face the railing she provocatively bent over and gradually started to peel her tight yoga pants from around her plump backside.

"What the fuck you doing, Cricket?" I asked amazingly impressed by Cricket's ass. "My laundry!" she insisted as she slowly reached around me to place her pants into the washing machine. "Now gimme my hug, so you can get going." she whispered comfortably. She slid her arms around me to close and start the machine before snugly embracing my waist. I was still in shock that I was holding her almost naked. I mean, I've had her before as Tracey's husband and Victor's wife, but not since we promised to abstain for the benefit of our marriages.

I rested my arms atop her shoulders and embraced around her neck as to prevent my hands slipping elsewhere. "Oh wait, can't forget this." she said as she released her clinch of me. She unfastened her bra and tossed it in. "C'mon Cricket. You're killing me." I said feebly. "Now, come back here." she said returning her arms around me. She pushed me against the washing machine and pressed her head into my chest. "How am I killing you? I'm just giving you a hug?" Cricket confirmed sarcastically. I smiled at her sarcasm and leaned down to kiss her forehead. "I'm not going to let you do this to me again, Cricket." I said becoming more defenseless. "Remember when you use to call me, your addiction? I used to love hearing you say that." Cricket whispered enthusiastically. "Yeah. That's because no matter who you or I were with, I always ended up back inside you. And that includes your sister! But all of that is over. We can't go there, anymore. We made promises. So, please let me get the hell out of here, before I give in to that addiction again." I pleaded as I disconnected my arms from around her neck and gently placed them at my sides. "That ended 'cause you went to Delaware, not because we said words. Promises are nothing more than words." she seriously professed while continuing her hold. "If you still lived here, we'd be still at it. And as far as my sister, you were just some dick for Kiana. Some dick, that lived across the street. She didn't ever want you. You were, convenient." she sternly explained as she lifted her head from my chest. "And I'm not holding you hostage, you can leave whenever you're good 'n ready. The question is, are you ready?" she continued after loosening her clinch of my waist. "Yeah. I think, I am." I unconvincingly said as I grasped her arms and used them to turn her around.

I put my hand in the small of her back to escort her forward a step so I could escape from behind her. "Well, that dick right there is telling me, you're not ready to go at all." Cricket whispered as she thrusted her butt back into me. I slightly nudged her forward and slipped from behind her. "Cricket, what hell you doing?! We can't fuck. You belong to Vic. And that's my guy. Not to mention he's right upstairs." I said uneasily. Cricket stood up straight and turned to face me. "I belong to me! You might want to talk to *your guy* about what he's been doing, before you ask me what I'm doing. And as far as him being upstairs, he's sleep. And if he do wake up, your truck is gone, so he won't be looking for you. And I'm no longer his type, he won't be looking for me either." she uttered woefully.

I didn't know what to say, as her words confused me. And I didn't want to turn this into another hour-long conversation. "Excuse me." she continued softly as she brushed me aside to lean on the washing machine. She put her hands on her hip and pushed her panties to the floor. She then ran her middle finger over her clitoris and brushed it across her tongue. I smiled at her continuing to bend over to pick up her panties. "What are you smiling at?" she asked as I stood in shock over what I just witnessed. "What was that about? You over there testing the merchandise?" I inquired as I pretended not to be intrigued. I walked over to the pool table to grab my jacket. "Something like that. I do that every time they come off." she said twirling her underwear around her finger. She lifted the washing machine lid and tossed them in. "I need to be sure my nectar tastes good, before I serve it. If I don't like it, how can I expect you to." she said self-assuredly.

I reluctantly reached blindly for my jacket as I couldn't take my eyes off Cricket standing there completely naked. "You gonna put that on?" Cricket asked as she nodded her head to me reaching for her robe and not my jacket. I looked down at my hand lingering over a white Kimono robe. "Pass that to me, please?" Cricket asked extending her hand out for the robe. I tossed the robe into her hand. "Oh, now that I'm leaving, you want to put clothes on." I said with a smirk while tucking my jacket under my arm. "Yeah. I got tired of all the rejection." she said laughing as she slid into the robe. "Nobody's rejecting you! I'm just trying to save you from yourself. And God knows this ain't easy, with you looking the way you do. Some places you go, you can't come back from." I said indisputably.

"I don't need you to save me, Omar" Cricket said as she snatched my jacket from under my arm and tossed it back onto the table. "And not every trip needs a round trip ticket. Sometimes, you don't wanna come back!" she said profoundly as she slowly unzipped my pants front. She reached her hand into my pants and clutched my solid erection. "Whoa. Whoa. Whoa!" I said as I quickly gripped her hand and backed up to release her hold. She smacked her lips and reluctantly let go, partially exposing my pride. "Now, I feel rejected." she said as she turned to look for my jacket. I shook my head and smiled at her show of disappointment.

I tipped my head to catch another look at her ass under her flowing robe, as she bent over the table to reach for my jacket. Impressed by the glistening of her skin, caused by all of the moisture between her thighs, I could no longer resist her. "Fuck it." I mumbled as I stood behind her, grabbed my partially exposed dick and pushed it inside of her awaiting vagina. "D-damn!" she whispered shocked by my actions. "I told you, nobody was rejecting you." I said sternly as I unfastened my pants.

"Bout time you came to your senses!" she exhaled as she spread further onto the table. I continued my thrust inside of her as my pants fell to the floor. "Oh, we goin' there?" she said as she dug her feet into the floor to establish more command of the situation. I ignored her motion of authority and began to massage her soft, thick ass. I continued thrusting in and out of her, while my hands roamed along her back and ass. She reached back and ran her hands through her hair. "Here. You need something to do with your hand." she said handing me a handful. I accepted her proposal of hair and began to pull. "Ooohh" she moaned as she began gyrating her hips to reciprocate.

CHAPTER 32

"Quentin"

"Hey Juice!" I heard Imani say enthusiastically from the other room. I walked out of my bedroom to see Juice and Imani embracing near the door. "Damn babe. Give the man a chance to come in." I teased. "Shut up, Que." she countered with a large smile. "He's just jealous 'cause nobody ever wants to hug him." Juice said sarcastically. "What's good with you? How's Dee? Is she around?" Imani asked enthusiastically. "I'm alright. I can't complain. Except, when it comes to sharing space with this dude." Juice said pointing at me and smiling. "Yeah, I know." Imani agreed giggling.

"I see you got your grown man shoes on there, son. Where y'all headed?" Juice asked mockingly. "Deon Cole is at the Side Split tonight, so we going there. But first, we're heading over to Carmine's in Grove Park." I said smiling from ear to ear. "You finally making it over to Carmine's, huh?" Juice said smiling with me. "He finally got a reason to." Imani said as she sashayed back into my bedroom. "Good looking out, on the recommend. Don't forget to tell Dee she's here for the weekend." I whispered to Juice as I shook his hand. "Already took care of that. But I'll make sure to keep reminding her." he said loyally. "Cool." I said free from worry.

"Come on Mani, we gonna be late!" I said aloud. "I'm coming!" she yelled back as she came stumbling out of the room attempting to fix her heels while walking. I grabbed Imani's jacket and walked over to her, to give her my body to lean on while putting on her shoes. "Alright man, we outta here." I said to Juice as I helped Imani into her jacket. "Alright, see y'all later." Juice said from the kitchen. "Bye Juice." Imani said as we stepped out of the door. I extended my arm for Imani to hold as we journeyed down the hallway. "I so miss this." Imani said as we approached the vestibule staircase. "Me too." I said genuinely as I looked at her with pride while escorting her down the steps.

"Ooh girl, that jacket is fierce!" an approaching woman's voice said. I looked around Imani to see Tasha quickly walking towards us, as we approached the exit doors. "Thank you, my baby bought it for me." Imani said proudly as she released her hold of me and began to somewhat model her wrapping. "He has good taste." Tasha said as she quickly passed us in the doorway.

I looked at Tasha full of trepidation as she hastily made her way to the parking lot. "Oh, hey Que." Tasha said as she turned back to again glance at us. Unable to speak, I continued to walk slowly with Imani. "She said hi to you. Why you gotta be so rude?" Imani asked nudging me in Tasha's direction. "Oh." I said to Imani, coming out of my trance. "Hey." I yelled to Tasha as she was no longer close enough to hear. "You're just, sad." Imani said snickering. I pulled my keys out of my pocket as we approached the car. "I'm driving! I haven't driven this car in a while." Imani stated eagerly running to the driver's side. "That works." I said as excited as she was.

CHAPTER 33

"Omar"

"I don't believe I just did that." I thought to myself in a disappointing awe as I pulled out of Victor's driveway. 2-1-5-5-5-5-9-7-1-1. "Good afternoon, Omar." Tiffany said pleasantly. "Good afternoon, Tiffany. Did I catch you, at a bad time?" I asked calmly. "No, not at all. I was actually just sitting around, awaiting your call. I was just expecting it, a little earlier." she continued warmly. "I was expected?" I questioned curiously. "Well, you said that you'd be here today. By here, I mean in Philly. And that you may even come to talk." she said sounding hopeful. "Oh. Well, I have to pick up my daughter off South Street at nine. So, I have a few hours. Where am I going?" I asked nonchalantly. "My house." Tiffany responded promptly. "One, five, one, Wesley Way. It's in Glenside." she continued. "Alright. I'm on my way there now." I responded.

I pulled into the driveway of the house with the numbers 151 on the mailbox. I immediately took notice of a women's silhouette in the window. "Here we go." I whispered to myself as I slid out of the truck. I gathered my things and closed the door before slowly pressing forward towards the house. The curtains were still swaying even though the figure was no longer in the window, as I approached the front of the house. I took a deep breath and raised my hand to the doorbell. I was cut short by the door slowly opening, before I could bear down on the door bell. "Come in." a voice said faintly from behind the door. I opened the screen door and stepped in delicately. I turned as the door slowly closed behind me, gradually revealing Tiffany Lane. She was standing there trembling, with her hands partially covering her nose and mouth.

She was as beautiful as ever, even with her eyes full of water and tears streaming down her cheeks. "I don't believe this." she whispered wiping the tears from her face. I inadvertently smirked at the awkward in the room. "You laughing at me?" she said as she continued to switch hands to wipe her tears. "No. Not directly." I said nonchalantly. I continued to stand there, assessing her little by little as she attempted to compose herself. "I'm so sorry, Omar." she whimpered. "It's okay, take your time." I said looking around the room. "Excuse me for second?" she requested before hurriedly stepping around me to get into the next room. "Please, have a seat?" she continued, pointing to the sofa as she passed it. I made my way over to the sofa and sat down. "Would you like something to drink?" Tiffany asked from the other room in a now clear and pleasant voice. "No, thank you." I replied as I fumbled through the magazines on the table next to me.

"I'm good, now. Let's start again. Hello, Omar." Tiffany said affectionately after barging through the door, into the room. She smiled and extended her hand for me to grasp. I rose to my feet and embraced her extended hand. "Hey Tiffany. How you doing?" I sarcastically replied to her greeting. Tiffany cut her eyes towards the sofa, gesturing for me to sit back down. "I know you're trying to be facetious. But I'm doing good. A lot better now, even though I'm nervous as hell." she honestly conceded while standing uncomfortably. "Nervous? Why nervous?" I asked pretending to more collected than I actually was. "You're still Omar. Always the coolest somebody, in the room." she laughed as the tea kettle began to shriek from the behind the door. "I'm having tea. You sure you don't want anything?" she continued before she sprang back towards the kitchen to cease the kettle's squeal. "Nah, I'm alright. Thanks." I said still smirking at her previous comment.

"Soooooo, I'm just going to come out, and address it. You show up outta nowhere. And what?!" I straightforwardly asked loud enough for her to hear from the other room. "You wouldn't understand, Omar." she solemnly stated as she entered the room with a saucer in hand. "You want us to be a family or something? You want us to split Quentin, on the holidays? Both give him away, at his wedding? I mean, you gave up that family shit twenty years ago. You chose your family over *our* family, and I've always understood that choice. Eventually, I even grew to respect it. It couldn't have been easy for you, it damn sure wasn't easy for us. But you endured, as did we. So…" I said captivated by what answers she could possibly give. "Yeah, I did. I persevered through it! I died every day." she interrupted mercilessly. She stationed her cup of tea on an awaiting table coaster and sat down on the chair adjacent from me. "So, why am I here Tiffany? You died every day? You like death?!" I asked continuing to be unsympathetic.

"No Omar, the exact opposite. I've spent every day of the last twenty years dying slow. And I just would like that to stop." she said softly as she slowly raised her tea. "The day I lost my son, was a day of total enlightenment. It was the day I realized, that it was the beginning of the end for me. It was the day I realized I'd never have family, where I was. I'd never want a family, with who I was with. It was the day that I realized, that I didn't just lay with some boy to make myself feel better about my adulterous husband. I was actually very happy in that young man's arms. It was the day I realized, I let myself become ashamed of my greatest creation. I carried that boy for nine months and then with help, convinced myself that life would be better without him. Both his life, and mine. And, what did I do with this enlightenment? I pushed it deep down and ignored it. When I couldn't ignore it, I wiped my tears and pretended to." she continued as she leaned back deep into the chair with her tea in hand.

"Here." I said handing Tiffany my phone in an attempt to break up the monotony of her prolonged stories of self-illumination. "What's this?" she asked oddly. "Take a look." I said designating the picture of Quentin on the screen. She grasped the phone and quickly glanced at the picture. She snickered and then handed the phone back. "I remember that picture. That was, uhh… around this time last year." she said with a grin. "How you know that?" I asked bewildered and slightly impressed. "Well, for one, his hair. He still has that blond tint in it. He cut that out at the beginning of this year. Right around the time he started to let his goatee grow. Two, he has put on weight since he took that picture. Not much but it's noticeable, especially in his arms and chest." she said grabbing a laptop from under the end table shelf. She opened the laptop and handed it to me. With my eyebrows still raised, I slowly reached my hands out to accept the laptop. "How do you know that?" I asked completely dumbfounded by what she knew. "The password is QHG1999." she said with arrogant smile. I typed the password and a picture of my son immediately appeared on the screen. I looked up at her, surprised by her possession of the picture. "Where did you get this picture? How'd you get this picture?" I asked still in awe. "We live in the age of information, Omar." she laughed at my suspicion. She rose from her chair, stepped around the table and slowly walked behind the chair that I was resting in. She courteously leaned over me, to get closer to her computer. Her breasts rested on my shoulder, softly grazing my cheek. I smiled impressed by her choice of perfume. "That's Chanel." I whispered to myself. "You smell good." I scoffed before beginning to search for files on the laptop. "Thank you." she said softly. "You know you said that same thing, twenty years ago." she lingered on slightly laughing. "You remember that? So, how did you respond then?" I asked as she opened a file. "I said thank you, it's Chanel number five and then continued to kiss your ear." she said softly next to my ear.

"Here." Tiffany whispered as she lifted herself and gestured to the screen. "Wow" I mouthed, recognizing dozens of pictures of Quentin. "There's at least a hundred, here." I said continuing to be wondered but what I saw. "A hundred and nine to be exact." Tiffany said proudly. She gracefully maneuvered her way back over to her chair and sat down. I continued to look at the pictures as Tiffany proudly sipped her tea. "My mind is blown right now. I never even seen, half these pictures. How'd you get them?" I asked intriguingly. "Honestly, I pretty much... stalk him." she boasted with a smile. "Stalk him?" I asked anxiously after hearing that word. "I follow him, on all social media. I'm a member of the parent association, at Penn State. Just like I was, at Dover High School. I am subscribed to any newspaper, that may cover him... the Dover Post, the Daily Collegian, even the Centre Daily Times. Anywhere he could possibly be, I'm there." she said as softly.

CHAPTER 34

"Imani"

"I haven't been chauffeured around like this in a long time." Quentin said as he comfortably reclined in the passenger seat. "So, did you like Carmine's. Was it worth the wait?" I asked mocking his conversation with Juice. "It was suitable, for where we are. Can't expect much from a country ass town, in the *middle* of Pennsylvania. But I'm full, so I guess it was worth it. I loved the company, if that means anything." he said nonchalantly as he nestled deeper into his reclined position. I smiled at his inadvertent compliment. Quentin never tries to impress, he just speaks his mind. But that in itself is impressive. He always knows what to say, without even knowing what he said. "It means everything." I said as I leaned down to kiss him.

"Que, you gotta wake up, cause I don't know where I'm going." I yelled as I rode back passed the school campus. "I'm up babe. Just laying here relaxing." he said as sat up to take notice of where we were. "You're going the right way." he continued as he grabbed the previously opened Powerade from the center cup holder. "You need me to drive?" he continued as he gulped down his drink. "No, I'm fine. I just need you to point me in the right direction. You know these people? He's waving at you!" I said as I noticed the guy in the car next to us, gesturing. "You gotta get used to that, babe. Your man is famous. Especially up here, in State College." he said confidently. With a huge smile, he turned to look out his window to see as to whom I was referring.

"What the fuck they...?" he said shaking his head as if disturbed when recognizing the car. "What's wrong?" I asked looking harder at the individuals in the car. "Ain't that the girl, that liked my jacket?" I asked observing the woman in the passenger seat. "It sure is. Her, and her dumb ass boyfriend." he mumbled as he turned away from the window. "Oh? Well as long as you know 'em. I really did think they were some kinda paparazzi, or some real weirdos." I said nervously. "They are weirdos. That's J.T. and his girl, Tasha." he said laughing. "The J.T. you're always talking about?"

I asked remembering how Quentin really didn't care too much for him. "Yup, one and the lame." he replied quickly without thought. I smiled proudly, reminded how impressive Quentin was with his wordplay. "I can only assume they're going to the show too." he sighed with a dampened tone. "So! Let 'em go. It's enough comedy, for everybody. Why do we care what they're doing?" I asked perplexed by his tone. "I really don't care, but J.T. can be real joe. And I'm just not for it, tonight." he countered seeming to notice my confusion at his demeanor. "I don't think he'll bother as much, with me on your arm. What man would?" I asked reassuring our good time.

We continued to follow them down the small streets of the college town. "Follow them into the parking lot just after the next light." he said trying his best to disguise his slightly somber façade.

I turned into the parking lot and immediately saw a car backing out of a parking spot directly in front of the building entrance. I raced across the lot and slammed into the parking spot before anyone else. I looked over at Quentin who smiled with pride. I smiled at his smile, turn the car off and grabbed our jackets from the backseat. "C'mon babe. Let's go laugh." I said as I tossed his jacket across the car.

"What's up Q?! You always get everything! You even got the parking spot I wanted." J.T. yelled as they passed us headed towards the entrance. I put my jacket on, as Quentin waited for me in front of the car. I slid my arm into his and we headed to the door, which was surprisingly still being held by Quentin's teammate, J.T. "You can go 'head man, thanks." Quentin said as we approached the door. "I got it. Just c'mon, or we gonna miss the opening act." he said as we stepped into the door pass him. His girlfriend was standing in the vestibule with her arms crossed and a scowl on her face. Quentin smirked as we passed her and headed into the auditorium. "I'd be mad too. That's just bizarre." I whispered while holding tight to my man's arm. We maneuvered about the room looking for a table with a great view of the stage. We found one near the stage, with just enough room to move around and close enough that we can quickly make our exit at the show's end.

"Are you guys ready now, or would you like me to come back again?" the waitress asked as she came over for the second time. "No, we're ready." Quentin said nonchalantly. "Can I have an order of chicken nachos and a lemonade, please?" I asked as I handed her my menu. "And for you sir?" she asked courteously as she penned the order. "I'll have the molted lava brownie and a coffee." Quentin said determined. She pleasantly thanked us both, tucked the menus under her arm and disappeared from sight. "I'm so glad you're here, babe. I really missed you." Quentin said as he extended his hands for me to take hold. I ignored his hand and slid my chair over closer to him. He immediately lifted his arm and embraced me. That warm feeling of home quickly consumed my entire body.

The lights dimmed to signal the start of the show. I was still nestled up under Quentin as the waitress came back with our order. "Thank you." Quentin said as she passed him his coffee. "Is there anything else I can help you with?" the waitress said cordially. "No thank you." I said before she slowly began to disappear again.

"There you go!" J.T. bellowed in excitement as he seemed to dance his way over to our table. "Look at you! You even got a great spot in the club! Is there anything you can't get?!" he continued animated. I embarrassingly looked over at Quentin in fear of him becoming twitchy. Quentin just looked up and laughed disapprovingly. "Maybe you should pay more attention the stage. I mean, you came here to see a show, not be a show." he said to J.T. nonchalantly. "I'm just paying homage to the man, with it all." J.T. said cynically. Quentin stood up to be face to face with his so-called teammate. "And you have." he said staring J.T. in the eyes. J.T. released his focus of Quentin, smiled and turned towards the exit. "Excuse me beautiful. I apologize if my behavior came off disrespectful. I may have had one drink too many. I'd never intentionally disrespect your relationship." J.T. said softly as he passed me. Quentin slowly sat back down, continuing to stare at J.T. as he exited the auditorium. "What's his deal?" I asked softly. "I don't know. But I'm gonna find out!" Quentin said seriously.

CHAPTER 35

"Omar"

"I'm hungry. Guess I can't assume the same about you. With you sitting there eating cookies for the last hour and a half." I said as I glanced down at my watch for the umpteenth time. "Well you the one that keep saying you don't want anything. I could've fixed something a long time ago. And are you trying to call me fat?" she inquired condescendingly. "I didn't call you anything. Look in the mirror, would you call you fat?" I said pointing to the wall sized mirror across the room. "Forget I asked that, cause no matter how slim, all women call themselves, fat." I continued shaking my head.

She stood up and paraded slowly over to the mirror. "I'm not fat at all, I look good for my age! And I only snack like that when I'm nervous." she said modeling to herself in the mirror.

"We're dancing around the fact, that I'm hungry." I brazenly disclosed. "Alright, so what do you want to do about it?" Tiffany tauntingly asked while still flaunting in the mirror. "I would say let's finish this over dinner but, I gotta be on South Philly in like two hours. I can't chance being late for that. I'll just wait and get a slice from Ishkabibbles." I said resolving my own dilemma. "What about me? I don't get to eat?" she said desirously. "Thought you wasn't hungry?" I asked perplexed at her question. "I never said that." Tiffany said defensively. "But pizza sounds good. How 'bout we go grab us a pizza, now?" she proposed as she jammed another cookie into her mouth. "I'll call it in, and it'll be ready by the time we get there." she continued as she snatched her phone from the arm of the chair.

I looked up at her giddily swaying back and forth while on the phone. "What kind of pizza would you like?" she whispered. "Doesn't matter, as long as it's no mushrooms on it." I replied setting her mind at rest that whatever she picked would be fine. "Ok. Can I have a sausage and pepperoni Sicilian, please?" she said into the phone. I stood up and made my way over to my coat which was hanging on a hook by the door. "That'll be fine. Thank you." Tiffany said as she ended her call "Here, let me help you with that." she said softly as she began to attempt help me put on my coat. "I got it. Thank you anyway." I said as I slipped into my coat.

With keys jingling in my hand I held the screen door for Tiffany as she locked her door. We stepped off of her porch and walked in sync towards her driveway. "Vrrroooom" my truck roared as Tiffany I approached the vehicles. HONK! CLICK! "Where you going?" I asked watching Tiffany unlock her car. "I thought I'd drive, since I *am* the host." she said charitably. "What? You don't gotta tell me twice." I said overjoyed. I jumped into my truck and quickly backed out of Tiffany's driveway, so she could pull out. I left my truck in front of her house and joined her in her car as she pulled up next to me.

I shook my head and smiled at her music choice. "What are you smiling at?" she inquired curiously. "Not sure why, but I expected Teena Marie to be on in here. And, there it is." I responded with a chuckle. "Maybe you know me better than you think." she said with a red-faced smile. "After twenty years. I don't think so." I said quickly trying to re-establish legitimacy. Suddenly saddened, she lowered her eyes and turned to face forward. "Let me ask you a question. I've been holding this in all night and if I don't ask it now, I won't ever." I said anxiously. "Ok. I guess it's time for the meat and potatoes portion of the visit." she said somberly with a smirk. "I guess so." I responded just as somber. "You mind?" I continued, extending my hand to turn down the radio. "Not at all." she whispered timidly as she turned the radio down from the steering wheel. I sat up, brushed my hands across my lap and took a deep breath. "Why? And why now?" I asked seriously.

"That's two questions." she said with a lighthearted laugh trying to diminish the density in the small area of the car. "Well, answer them one at a time." I responded casually. "I'm guessing what you're looking for is an answer in regard to my intentions. And if that's your question, you don't have to worry Omar. I am not out to lay claim to his soon to come, fame and fortune. I'm not looking for any credit, or anything like that. I don't want anything more, than to get to know my lost son." she sincerely avowed. "You keep you using the word *lost*. The word lost is fitting, when you put up a fight. You give it your all to the finale, but you are just not up to task. That's not what you did. You gave up! You walked away from the situation *you created* and left it for someone else to deal with. Granted, you left it with the co-creator. You still, took the easy way out." I said with conviction. Tiffany shook her head and smiled, "You been waiting twenty years, to say that to me." she said confidently. She pulled in front of the pizza shop and slammed the car into park. "Yeah, I guess I have." I said as I opened the door and stepped out of the vehicle.

"Can I help you?" the young lady asked from across the counter. "Good evening. I'm here to pick up the order, for Tiffany." I said amiably. She looked down at her computer monitor as I reached into my pocket, for my wallet. "One moment." she said before turning to retrieve the food. "Here you go." she said returning to the counter with the pizza in hand. I opened my wallet and pulled out a twenty. She looked at me puzzled. "Uhhh, sir. This pie, has already been paid for." she said surely. I thanked the young lady, grabbed the pizza and walked out of the shop.

"Why'd you pay for the pizza? You didn't have to do that." I asked immediately upon entering the vehicle. "Cause like I said before, I'm the host." she replied just as quickly as I asked. "I appreciate that, but I always pay for mine." I said as I handed her the twenty still in my hand from the pizza shop. Tiffany laughed. "That sounds all well 'n good, but I'm not accepting that. Thank you, anyway." she stubbornly announced. I rolled the bill up into a ball, and tossed it into the center cup holder.

"Would you like a beer, with your pizza?" Tiffany asked as we waited for the traffic light to change. "Why, you wanna pay for that too? No thank you, I'm good." I said noticing the cold beer sign on the store up ahead, which must've prompted her to ask the question. "Yeah. I would've, if you had said yes." she replied catching my quickly thrown sarcasm. I didn't take notice of her last comment as my attention was on the almost collision behind us. "Whoa! He almost lost it all!" I said to myself as I stared out the back window.

"Be careful of this car coming up on your right. He just pulled out of that beer spot and he's feeling it." I said as a white and black sports car quickly zoomed up to us. "I see him." she said as we approached the up-coming intersection. We sat in silence, anticipating the car's move, when the light changed. The light flashed green and the car tires screeched as the apparently drunk driver rocketed his left turn, narrowly escaping the oncoming traffic.

"Watch out!" I yelled as a truck rapidly advanced towards us subsequently avoiding the reckless move. A loud bang followed by the sound of grinding metal and plastic filled the air. Sparks and debris from both vehicles tossed about, as we were slightly pushed around inside the car.

"You okay?" I asked Tiffany as soon as I was able to gather my thoughts. Tiffany remained motionless with head resting on the airbag deployed from her door. I maneuvered my head lower, to get a look into her eyes, then tapped her shoulder. "Tiffany! Are you alright?!" I asked again. She lifted her head and slowly turned to me. "Yes, Omar. By the grace of God, I'm fine. You?" she responded after a deep breath. "I'm good." I said nonchalantly. "You sure you're alright?" I asked as to confirm as I glanced around inside the car. "Yes Omar. I'm fine. Just a little shaken up and slightly embarrassed." she gently decreed while rubbing her palms progressively sown her face. "Embarrassed?!" I asked perplexed. "Well, you can explain that later. I'm gonna go check on dude. Stay there, and try not to move." I instructed Tiffany as I opened the car door. I stepped out of the car and looked around. The white, Camaro with the black, soft top was nowhere to be found. But the consequences of his actions were surely present. "Hey buddy. You alright?" a young man said as he approached. "I'm fine." I replied as I turned to greet him. I wanna check on the other guy." I said as I slowly walked over to the truck we collided with. People began to emerge from their vehicles. Soon there was an immense crowd of people blocking the intersection. "You shouldn't be moving." a lady yelled. "Are you okay" I heard a man say faintly. "Wait for the ambulance!" someone else demanded. I approached the truck and observed another accident. I rushed around the truck to see it entirely. "Oh damn!" I whispered as there was a car plunged against the light pole and another stationed in the middle of the street.

I hustled back around to check on the driver of the truck. "Hey. You alright." I said as I approached. The door window was cracked, and the door was too damaged to open. I sprinted around to the other side to make sure the driver was okay. I opened the passenger side door to see the driver sitting there, with his head in his hand. "Hey Buddy. Are you okay?" I asked vigorously.

"Is he okay?" a young lady asked as she moved towards me followed by three others. "How's he doing?" the young man trailing her quickly ensued. "No response." I said as I turned to reply. "I'm here." the driver tenaciously responded to us all. I leaned into the truck to get a closer look at him. "Are you sure okay?" I probed again for assurance. "I'm fine!" the driver responded in a raspy voice. "Enough for me." I said as I backed out the truck. I headed back over to Tiffany who was now attempting to climb out of the car.

"So, you don't want an ambulance ma'am?" the police offer asked as he tore the top page off of his writing pad and jammed it into his jacket pocket. "No. I'm fine, officer. Thank you." she said pleasantly to the police officer. "Ok. You know you best. How about you, sir? You want me to call the EMT over?" the officer asked courteously. "Nah. I'm good man. But thanks a lot." I responded promptly.

"It's twenty after eight, Omar. You gotta go get your daughter." Tiffany said warmly as she paced back and forth with her phone in hand. "She'll be fine. I have to make sure you're alright." I said charmingly. "I'm fine. At least I will be as soon as *Flo* gets back on the phone." she said laughing her own joke. "Flo is taking care of you personally?" I asked to assist her with lightening the mood. "Yeah. I'll tell her, you said hello. Now, go get your daughter and get home to your wife." she said comically. "With your consent." I said as I rose slowly from her sofa.

Chapter 36

"Quentin"

"Morning." I said as I stumbled out of my room. "Wha'sup." Juice said as he slumped past me in a robe and Roger Rabbit slippers. "Good morning guys." Imani sang spirited from the couch. "Morning babe" I grumbled as I walked over to kiss her. "Mmm hmm." Juice grumbled. "You two look like zombies marching through here." she laughed as she turned to face us with her knees in the couch. "I forgot how much I hate mornings, when you're here." Juice continued to mumble. "I got you guys breakfast." she said pointing to the large array of food on the counter. "Damn, thanks babe!" I said excitedly seeing the food. "Thank you." Juice said with already a mouthful. "How much I owe you?" he continued picking up one of the cups of coffee. "You don't owe me, nothing. This is all on Mr. Gregory." Imani bragged quickly. I looked up from the food, cut my eye at Juice and then shook my head at Imani. "In that case good fella, you owe me whatever half that receipt says." I said earnestly as I grabbed the paper plates from the cabinet. "Eat up." I said sarcastically as I handed him a plate.

"Whatever nigga." Juice mumbled as he pushed past me to pile onto his plate. "Not you, your dad." Imani said as she hopped up from the sofa. "My dad?" I asked as she snatched a plate from my hand. "Yeah. He gave me seventy dollars to bring with me." she said casually. "My dad, gave you seventy dollars?" I asked again completely bewildered. "Yes, your dad! He gave me the money, and said to make sure we have good time." she snapped as she shoved me aside to get to the counter of food. "My man, mister gee!" Juice enthusiastically declared as he gathered his food and strutted into his room.

CHAPTER 37

"Hassan"

"Good morning Teach" I said as I slid the glass door open and stepped into the kitchen. "Hey Haas. You want some coffee?" Tracey said as she stood over the stove pouring hot water from the kettle. "No thank you. I'd love some of that bacon, though." I said cunningly. "What bacon?" Tracey asked puzzled. "Exactly!" I said sarcastically. "Hey Drizzle." I said to Emily as she crossed my path while coming down the steps. "Hey Unc." Emily answered. "Why you always come in the back door? Who you hiding from?" she continued as she plopped into a chair. Tracey laughed in agreement. "Hiding? Now you know better than that. Where ya dad?" I said both impressed and slightly offended by her wit. "He's upstairs. I'll go get him." Emily said as she put her phone on the counter and sprinted up the stairs. "Teach look, a teenage phone. You know how many secrets, are in that phone? I mean like area fifty-one & the meaning of life. Hell, the script to Bad Boys four, is probably in there!" I said pointing to Emily's phone. "Let's look! You know the code?" I asked as I picked up the phone to examine it. "Put her phone down. My daughter is a good girl. She has to be. Have you met her father?" she said arrogantly. I laughed at her pride in her husband. "So, I guess it's a no to that bacon?' I asked sarcastically serious. Tracey laughed as she took another sip of her coffee.

"Hassan, I'm pregnant." Tracey openly disclosed as she hid behind sipping her coffee. "Cause of bacon?!" I asked completely caught off guard. "What I meant to say was, it's Omar's right?" I said still dazed by the news. "Of course, it's Omar's, Hassan! I need you to be serious, I'm frightened enough, as it is." she whispered genuinely. I slowly walked over to Tracey to give her my shoulder in case she needed it. "Scared about, what?" I asked perplexed by what her concern could be. I seized her cup of coffee for myself. "Scared of what? Hassan, I'm almost forty. I got one, already in college. Another, about to start college. And I gotta figure out how to tell *my husband*, that we're starting over. You don't think I have a reason to be a little *apprehensive*?" she said as she began to lower her head. "No, I really

196

don't. This was a threat to happen every time y'all did it. He knows that, he took biology." I said as I took a large mouthful of coffee. "I swear Hassan, you have no empathy." she said softly. "Sorry dear, fresh out. And speaking of fresh out, was y'all outta sugar when you made this cup of coffee? I swear boy, I will never get white taste buds. No salt. No sugar. Y'all just eat air, and drink water." I said cynically. "And as far as telling him, you'll be fine." I said as we could hear Omar slumping down the stairs. "Brother." Omar said nonchalantly in a raspy voice as he passed me heading for Tracey. "Brother." I responded lowering my eyebrows because the greeting "brother" between us, always meant we were not alone but need to talk as soon as we were.

"Good morning babe." Omar continued as he approached Tracey with a kiss. "Good morning, baby? You want some tea?" she responded pleasantly. "You know, I watch her make you tea every day. And now that I know what her tea tastes like, I understand why you're bitter." I said playfully. "Yes, babe. I'd love some tea. Do we have any Danish? Can I have a cheese Danish, with it?" he asked politely. "Don't worry about no Danish, she was about to make us some bacon. And waffles!" I said enthusiastically. "I thought we didn't have any bacon." Emily said floating down the steps. "Don't pay Hassan, any attention." Tracey said approving Emily's notion. "We're going downstairs. Call me when it's done, and I'll come get it, babe." Omar said as he headed down to his favorite room of his home. "You might as well, wait for it. What the hell she got to stir? It's not like, she puts sugar in it." I said starting to follow Omar. "Hey. Pssst. Congratulations." I turned and mouthed to Tracey with a smile before trotting downstairs.

"You look like shit." I genuinely said to Omar. "I feel like shit." he responded just as genuine. "So, why didn't you tell me you was going home." I asked curious of the answer he could possibly give. "I did tell you!" he said guarded. "No, you didn't. And I'm not saying, you had to. I was just wondering, why you didn't." I said casually. "If I didn't tell you, how you know?" he asked seemingly baffled. "I called Vic yesterday, I had to hear his side of the story. Damn, I wish I went with you. I woulda loved to seen his face, on that one. But anyway, he said you stopped by his crib for a few after you left your mom's. I figured it had to be something else. I know you ain't ride all the way up there, just to confront Vic." I replied. Omar slowly tipped his head and squinted his eyes as if he was completely lost to what I was talking about. "You do know what happened to Vic? Don't you?" I questioned seeing his look of cluelessness. "No! What happened?" he asked more interested in hearing my story, than telling his own. "He looked fine when I saw him." he continued. "First, tell me what happened when you went up there." I demanded quickly.

"Dad!" Emily interrupted by yelling, before she started down the steps. She handed Omar his tea and a Danish on a small plate. "Thank you, baby." he said as she quickly darted back upstairs. "Remember the other night when I talked to Tiffany Lane?" he whispered calmly. "Yeah." I answered promptly. "Well, she asked me to come up to Philly, to talk. And I wasn't going agree to it. But at the same time Emily got invited to a studio up there, and wanted me to take her. So, I went." he started. "You saw Tiffany?" I asked astonished as I grabbed the nerf football from the sofa and plopped down. "Yeah. And I swear to God, she looks just like she did twenty years ago." he dramatically answered as he sat down next to me.

"Oh damn." I said as the conversation had just become significant. "Yeah." he responded gravely. "So, what happened?" I asked considerately. He looked me in the eyes with a grimace and then shook his head. "It was crazy seeing her again. I mean I knew I'd see her again one day. If for no other reason than just, how small the world is. But I didn't think it'd be like that, and not any time soon." he said gravely.

"So... what happened?! Did y'all talk? Fuck? Fight? Don't tell me, you punched her in the face." I said seriously. Omar looked at me as if my last statement had disappointed him. "I only said that cause that's what you been saying you was going to do, for the last twenty years." I continued, explaining my reasoning for the comment. He chuckled. "No man, I didn't punch her in the face. We just sat at her crib and talked, for hours. That was before she tried to kill me, in a car accident." he said as he sincerely. "What? You was in a car accident?! Do Tracey know, any of this?" I asked anxiously. "No." he said as began to look and feel around for the television remote.

I looked up at the time and realized that it was almost time, for Quentin's game to come on. I found the remote in sofa cushion next to me. "Here." I said as I tossed it to Omar. He used it to turn on the television and placed it on the coffee table in front of us. "Now, tell me what happened yesterday. From the beginning!" I demanded as I leaned forward to give him my attention.

CHAPTER 38

"Quentin"

"Hey." I said as I slid into the car. "Hi baby." Imani said as she leaned in to kiss me. "How you feel?" she continued after pulling her tongue out of my mouth. "I didn't think I could feel better than I did, but I do." I said awestruck by her kiss. "No pain, or nothing? You want me to rub you down?" she asked genuinely. "No, I am good, right now. You know I never feel anything after a win. But can I have a rub down raincheck, for later?" I asked trying to sound endearing. "If you're good." Imani said adorably. I laughed at Imani and reclined in the chair. "Where we going?" I asked pretending to really care. Anywhere she took me would be acceptable, as long as she was with me. "I was going back home. My baby likes sex after a game." she said seductively. "And what a game, that was! Oh my God! I forgot how exciting watching you play was! Your sideline to sideline, has gotten so much better! Babe, you didn't whiff on one tackle! And you got a pick!" Imani said proudly. I sat back and listened to Imani boast about my feats on the field today. I shook my head, smiling at her animation and enthusiasm.

"C'mon." Imani said seductively as she opened my door and escorted me out of the car. "I never drove across campus before." I chuckled as we entered the building that I call home. "I didn't know what kinda shape you'd be in after the game, and I didn't want you to have to walk if you didn't feel good." she said as we walked arm in arm up the stairs.

I could feel Imani's body droop as we walked into the room to Juice sitting on the sofa still watching football. "Hi Juice." Imani said surprised he was there. "Hey Imani." he responded amicably. "Good game, Junior." Juice said animated as he extended his hand to me. "Thanks." I said modestly. "They about to interview your boy." he continued vigorously. "Well, he did have a good game." I admitted as Imani began to pull on my sleeve and gesture towards my bedroom. "Looks like you about to put in work." Juice laughed, noticing Imani's slight impatience.

"What are you thinking?" I asked as I rested my head on her naked bosom. She slowly brushed her hand across my head, as she had constantly done when I laid there after sex. It was always our time of clarity and absolute honesty. "Please God, don't let her ask me anything about another woman." I prayed to myself as I listened to her heartbeat's tempo diminish. "Have I told you how much I love you?" she sniffled quietly. I immediately raised my head after hearing what sounded like her crying. "What's wrong babe?" I asked as I climbed up her body to face her eye to eye. "Nothing. I just love you so much." she sniveled as she tried to wipe her tears. "What's wrong, Mani?" I demanded as I moved her hand and wiped the tears from her eyes. "Come here." I whispered as I positioned on the bed next to her and gestured for her to lay on me. Imani leaned over the bed to reach for her clothes, exposing that beautiful ass and those sexy legs. She pulled some tissue from the pocket of her jeans and tossed them back to the floor. She then slid her way back over to me and laid her head on my chest. I took the tissue from her hands and continued to wipe her face with it. "Yes, baby. I know how much you love me." I said answering her previous question. "And, I love you. Now, you already told me *nothing's wrong*. But what you didn't tell me, was what you were thinking." I uttered softly as I began to maneuver my fingers through her hair. "I felt you looking at my butt. Would you love me if I was fat?" she asked as she laid their comfortably. "Yeah! My love for you doesn't have conditions. You should know that." I continued soothing. She reached forward and seized her tissue which I placed on the bed next to us. "What if I became really fat?" she continued. "Yes, Imani! Am I really that vain?" I asked honestly concerned. I felt Imani smile, reacting to the tone of my last question.

CHAPTER 39

"Imani"

"What if I became *fat and annoying*?" I asked nervously, thinking he already knew what I was about to say. Quentin slowly stopped everything to ponder my question. "You hear me?" I asked to make sure he was ok. "Yeah, I heard you. Just trying to figure out where the silly questions, and the tears, are coming from?" he asked earnestly. "Quentin, I'm pregnant." I abruptly interrupted, confirming his thought before he had the opportunity to ask the question.

Quentin lifted me off of him, and raise up out of the bed. He walked to the end of the bed, and stopped. He remained motionless with the exception of his slight tremble. I stared at Quentin's naked body silently, for as long as I could. "Please say something." I whispered as I gripped the tissue and tried to prepare myself for the worst.

"Were you pregnant when you just came here bending over my dresser or had me lifting you against this door?!" he said pointing out the places we had just had sex. "How about when you were just jumping and diving around, doing your best WWE impression? W-were you pregnant then?" he continued with his lips pressed against his praying hands.

"Quentin, I am seven weeks." I responded softly. "Then why the hell are you trying to kill, my little girl." he said unpleasantly. "So, you not mad?" I asked cautiously. "Hell yeah, I'm mad. You jumping around here like you Gabby Davis and you are carrying, my little girl." he said sternly. I jumped to my feet and ran across the bed to embrace him. I threw my arms around him and squeezed as tight as I could. "I love you so much." I sniveled in his ear as tears poured down my face. "See, that's what I'm talking about. You're jumping around like that, with my little girl inside you!" he said sternly while refusing to put his arms around me. "Your *little girl* is fine. She's not even the size of a dime yet." I sobbingly reassured him. "You sure?" he asked anxiously. "I'm sure. I'm also sure her name is Gabby Douglas, not Gabby *Davis*." I said sarcastically. I slammed back down onto the bed and pulled him down next to me.

"What are you really thinking?" I asked as he sat there starring into my eyes. "You're having my little girl." he said starting to smile. "Stop saying that. It could be a boy. But yes, I'm having your baby." I said following his smile with one of my own. "You're having my baby?" he repeated as his eyes livened. "I'm having your baby." I echoed smiling harder as I could see his excitement starting to build.

CHAPTER 40

"Antoinette"

"Y'all really get into the game around here." I uttered while helping myself to another glass of wine from Tracey's bar. "Yeah, it can get a little unruly, when Quentin's team is playing." Tracey replied as she began clearing our clutter from the table. "I can tell. With the shouting coming from upstairs, downstairs and next door, this is fan club central." I said as I collected the last of our things to help. "Yeah, my baby has a lot of supporters." she said as made her way back into the room to continue to clean.

"I couldn't ask you before, 'cause you were into the game. But now that it's over... what did he say?" I whispered as I quickly followed her back into the kitchen. She held up her finger, signaling for me to wait one second. "Babe, how many tackles did Quentin have?!" Omar barked as he erupted through the door. "You almost hit Toni." Tracey declared softly as she began laughing and motioned towards me. He pulled the door towards himself and looked behind it. "Hi Omar." I whispered adorably. "Oh. My apologies, Antionette. I didn't see you there." he said lightheartedly. "I know." I said as I stepped around from behind the door.

"What'd she say?" a man's voice bellowed from behind Omar. "He had seven solo and assisted on four." Tracey said proudly. "Told you he didn't have thirteen tackles!" Omar turned and yelled down the stairs. "Hassan is always trying to boost Quentin's game stats." Omar said as he placed his dishes into the sink. "And you often diminish them." Tracey responded as she began to wash the dishes he just placed.

"How many was it, Teach?!" Hassan asked as he raced up the stairs. "And you better not say some damn five and two half tackles, like your retarded husband!" he continued sternly. Tracey and I both began to chuckle at Hassan who didn't notice me standing behind the kitchen island. "Oh shit, hey Toni." Hassan turned to me after hearing me laugh. "Here we go. I'm going to get dressed." Omar said discouraged as he started up the stairs. "Hey Hassan." I said to Omar's friend. I watched Omar swagger up the steps until Emily appeared. "No Hassan. He had seven tackles, he assisted on four tackles, he had one interception and three pass break-ups." Tracey said seeming suspicious. "Dang mom, you sound like Imani with that." Emily said as she floated down past Omar on the steps. "Hey Storm." I said as Emily approached me for a hug. "Hey Toni." she responded as we embraced. "C'mon Toni. Let's proceed to the patio, it's nice out." Tracey said as she slid open the patio door. I grabbed the bottle of wine and paraded behind her.

"To answer your question, no, I haven't told him yet. My plan was to tell him last night, but he and Emily came home after I had already gone to sleep. And as you can see, Sunday morning here at my house is quite distracting." Tracey said as she opened the table umbrella. "Yeah, I see that." I said thinking of Omar in his pajama pants and t-shirt. "But, I'm almost there. I told Hassan." she continued genuinely. "You told Hassan, before you told Omar?!" I asked taken aback by the audacity. "Yeah, but they're one and the same. Sometimes I feel like I married them both." she said casually. "Lucky you." I inadvertently uttered loud enough for her to hear me. "If you say so." she sighed sarcastically. "You don't think you're lucky, to have Omar by your side." I asked honestly. "No! I know I have a prize, and I work hard to keep it. But luck has nothing to do with it. You don't think I see other, *more talented* women out there, with their eyes on that. C'mon Toni. I'm not blind, nor am I stupid." Tracey said as she looked deep into my eyes. "I don't have those same *talents* that you have, so I gotta work for mine." she said genuinely. "What talents? Evidently you have some type of talents Tracey, you have him!" I said obviously.

"Hey Jills." Tracey shouted as she stood up to greet the woman exiting out onto the patio. "Hey Tra." the woman sang as she advanced towards us. "How you doing, girl?" she continued as they embraced one another. "I'm good. Still secretly pregnant, but good." Tracey said as she sat back down. "Toni, this is Jillian. Jillian, Toni." Tracey said as she slid out a chair for her to sit in. "Hi." I said reserved. "Toni? Omar's assistant, Toni?" she asked seemingly intrigued. "Umm, yeah?" I replied uncertainly. "Nice to finally meet you, Toni. I've heard your name, more than once." she said judgmentally. "All good, I hope." I said suspecting her thoughts of insecurity. "Of course." she said methodically. "Good. I would hate for a false representation, to make a bad impression." I said as I stood up to greet her. I looked her up and down confidently and refilled my glass with wine. "No one told me to bring a glass out with me." Jillian said trying to lighten the vibe. "Allow me." Tracey said as she rose to go back inside the house. "Girl, sit down. I know where the glasses are." Jillian said quickly standing up to intercept Tracey. "No, you sit and get comfortable. I have to go inside anyway, I'll get it." Tracey said as she squeezed passed her friend and headed for the house.

Tracey closed the door and Jillian immediately turned her attention to me, as I knew she would. "So, Jillian. How do you know Tracey and Omar?" I promptly asked, initiating conversation before she could. "My husband Hassan, and Omar, have been like brothers for their entire lives. You've met Hassan, right?" she asked obviously already knowing the answer. "You're Mrs. Hassan? Aww, girl c'mere, you need a hug." I said as I extended across the table to hug Jillian. "Yeah, you've met Hassan." she said as she hesitantly sat back into her chair. "That man is a piece of work." I said as I fell back into my chair. "Speaking of pieces of work, look at you!" she said vigorously with her eyes widened. "What?" I asked looking around for a problem.

"Stand up again." she insisted as she stood back up and extended her hand to escort me. "What?" I said again, confused as I stood. "Oh my God, look at you girl." she said as she ushered me into a pirouette, so she could admire me entirely. "No wonder Tracey has been bringing up her talent, lately. I mean, I saw the top when I came over but I didn't know there was all that, with it." she said as she released my hand and continued to admire my body. "Aww, stop it." I said as I quickly sat back down. "She was talking about her *talents*, before you came out. What does that mean?" I continued to whisper, looking over at the door for Tracey.

"She actually spoke about that, to you?" she asked seeming concerned. "Yeah, what *talents*?" I asked again waiting for some kind of answer. "Talent, is a reference to your shape. It's one of term we've picked up, from the boys over the years." she explained casually. "Ohhh." I said softly finally understanding her meaning. "Tracey sometimes gets discouraged by her shape, with her being a white girl, with no extraordinary curves." she continued quietly. "I don't understand her rational. I mean, she got Omar, and he ain't going nowhere. His eyes don't wander, at all. Believe me!" I said genuinely. "You know firsthand, huh?" she said with a chuckle. "What I meant was…" I started to explain. "It's alright. I get it. He's a very attractive man. They both are." she said softly. "Just so you know… this may last her entire pregnancy." Jillian continued as the sound of the door interjected.

The door slowly slid open and Tracey streamed out with a glass and another bottle of wine. "Here. I'll be back. I'm finally about to tell

Omar. Even though I think Hassan may've already told him. He knows something." she said as she sat the glass and bottle on the table.

"You want us to leave?" I asked solemnly. "No, no, no. You guys sit and enjoy the wine. I may need you after." she said nervously as she turned and headed back to the house.

CHAPTER 41

"Omar"

"Hey dad. I was just about to call you." Quentin said enthusiastically. "Why? Is everything ok? Are you ok?!" I promptly questioned, concerned about his willingness to call. "Don't mind him Que. He's just being over anxious as usual." Tracey said as she searched the bed for her bra. "Hey Ma. I'm glad you're there, I need to tell you too. Am I on speakerphone? Where's Storm?" he asked excessively. "Yeah, you're on speakerphone. We actually called, to tell you something." I said impatiently ready to continue the conversation. "I bet'cha our news is bigger than yours." Tracey added excited to express her news. "I bet'chu it's not." Quentin said proudly. "But we'll see. What's your news?" Quentin said tranquilly. I looked over at Tracey who was trying to slither back into her pants. "Are you going to tell him?" I asked her as I aggressively put my shirt on. "I thought you were." she replied as she fastened her pants. "Well, is someone going to, tell me something?" Quentin asked fearlessly. I extended my hand to give Tracey the floor, to make the announcement. "Well first, we have to say bravo on your performance today. Seven solos and a pick. That's so great, baby. And second, you're finally going to have that little, grey baby to pick on." Tracey said smiling from ear to ear. "What the fuck?!" Quentin voiced in astonishment. I looked around to find the person that Quentin thought he was on the phone with. "My bad, dad. But, you gotta admit, that phrase fits!" he admitted elatedly. "My mom and dad, are having a baby?" Quentin said to someone on his end of the phone. "Congratulations Mr. and Mrs. G!" a woman's voice bellowed from behind Quentin. "Who's that?" I asked curious of what female he'd feed our family business to. "It's Mani. Who else would it be?" Quentin said assuredly. "Hey Imani! Thank you." Tracey sang jubilantly.

"Congrats y'all. I couldn't be happier for you. For us!" Quentin reiterated. "Thank you, baby" Tracey said as she pulled her Penn State jersey over her head. "Thank you, Quentin. So, what's you're big news?" I said now putting the focus on him and his news. "You were right, Tracey.

Your news was a lot bigger than mine." he said sounding slightly dismal. "You sure? What was it, baby?" Tracey said losing her zeal with thoughts of Quentin's feelings. "Yo man, are you okay?" I asked noticing changes in his conduct. "Yeah dad, I'm fine. I just wanted to tell y'all that Imani is here, so I finally made it to Carmine's." he said contented.

I looked over at Tracey, who shook her head at me in disbelief. "I know." I mouthed to her. "You sure that's it?" Tracey asked skeptically. "Yeah ma, that's it." Quentin said trying to reassure us of his good news. "Well that is good news. You've wanted to go there, since we dropped you off." I said attempting to sound satisfied for him. "Alright dad, I only got Mani here for another twenty-four hours. So, let me get as much time in as possible. We might even go back to Carmine's. I'll call you guys tomorrow. Congrats again." Quentin said suddenly. "Ok baby, I'll call you tomorrow. I love you." Tracey said sincerely. "Love you too mom, later dad." Quentin said honestly. "Talk to you tomorrow, Quentin." I said as I picked my phone up from the bed to end the call.

I slid open the door and watched Tracey dance her way out. Hassan was sitting next to Jillian, who still trying to feel out Antoinette. "An hour? It took you an hour to see what she had to say?" Hassan barked as we approached the table. Tracey's evident glow showed that she was eager to tell her friends her situation. "Oh, they weren't just talking!" Toni answered Hassan flamboyantly. Tracey began to giggle. "I'm sorry, girls. It got a little hot up there after I gave him the news." Tracey said with a mischievous smile. "So...???" Jillian asked enthusiastically.

"We're having a baby!" Tracey squealed as she threw her arms around me. "Congratulations!" Jillian shrieked as she jumped up to embrace Tracey. Antoinette followed behind Jillian with a hug of her own. "I'm so happy for you two." Jillian continued as she tossed her arms around me. "Thanks sis." I said as I attempted to end her hug quickly. I let go of my hold of Jillian and rapidly stepped around the women to greet Hassan. "You left me down here with these two, while you up there getting some? I'd have been pissed, if your bar wasn't stocked. But seriously, congrats man." Hassan said as he grabbed my hand for a gentleman's embrace. "I see you opened my personal bottle. But thanks man." I said as I nodded my head towards the half empty bottle of 1800, next to the full glass on the table where he was sitting. "We gotta go get a cigar." Hassan demanded proudly as he pulled his keys from his pocket. "I know the perfect place." I chuckled as I looked at Antoinette. "We'll be back." I said as Hassan and I started towards his car in the driveway.

"I called you and you didn't answer or call back, young lady. Where have you been?" Tracey criticized as Emily came bouncing into the house. "I did call you back and when I didn't get you, I called dad! He said you were good and wanted to talk when I came home." Emily said in her defense as she squeezed into the small place on the sofa between us. Tracey looked at me while I slowly shook my head confirming Emily's story. "So, what're we talking about?" Emily asked as she grabbed the remote from my lap. I snatched the remote from Emily and turned off the television.

"The floor is all yours." I said to Tracey proudly. She looked at me with an unsettled sigh and began to speak. "Emily, our family is having a baby." Tracey said softly. "What?!" Emily said surprised at the news. "Yeah." I said proudly confirming. "Oh wow! I don't believe she told y'all. Does Que know yet?! What'd he say? How did he take it?! I gotta call him!" Emily dynamically probed while bouncing wildly. I looked at Tracey, who was just as bewildered as I was. "Yeah Quentin knows. And he was applauding. But now, we want to know how you feel. Your opinion, is just as important." I acknowledged as she enthusiastically looked for her phone. "I've been happy since I first found out. We was worried about what you, and Quentin was going to say." she said as she stood up to continue to look for her phone.

"Wait. Emily, have a seat. What are you talking about? How could you have known?" Tracey asked more confused as ever. "Imani told me a while ago." Emily said condescendingly. I leaned back and perplexedly eyeballed Emily. "Imani told you, what?" Tracey asked curiously. "That… she's pregnant. Y'all just said our family's having a baby." Emily recapped sternly. "Emily, I'm having a baby." Tracey confessed keenly. "You?" Emily asked comprehending all the confusion. "Wait! Imani is pregnant?!" I snapped intensely. "Does Quentin know?" I continued harshly. "I don't know. Mom, how are you pregnant?!" Emily snapped, as she tried to come to terms with all that's going on.

CHAPTER 42

"Quentin"

"Congrats, big dog." a man's voice bellowed from behind me. "Congratulations Quentin." a young lady sang as she walked pass us. "Thanks man." I yelled back. "Thank you, sweetheart." I said to the young lady as I held the door open for Imani.

"I only wanted to drive that one time. You had me driving since I been here." Imani said as she started the car. "I'll drive, get up." I insisted quickly. "I'm already over here, now." she said with a cynical smile. RING. RING! "That's Storm again, ain't it?" she asked as I looked down at my phone. "Yup." I said as I turned off the ringer and tossed it into the cup holder. "You're gonna have to talk to them sooner or later." she said reminding me of the inevitable. "I know." I just don't feel like being judged right now. Approve, disapprove, it's still a judgement. That's why I didn't tell him earlier. I just want to enjoy it for a while." I sighed while holding the button and watching the window gradually lower. "Ok." she whispered as she massaged my head with her non driving hand. "So, what are you in the mood for? And don't say Italian cause we had that last night." I asked as we pulled from campus. "Then, I don't know. You know, I always want Italian." Imani said disclosing the obvious. "Yeah, I know babe. I figured since you're pregnant, you may want something else. Just don't start craving weird shit." I pleaded honestly. Imani snatched her hand from my head and chuckled. "I don't think, that starts yet." she said still laughing. "But I could go for a meatball, from Jimmy Johns." she continued gingerly. "Yeah, it's started. You've never asked for anything from Jimmy Johns, before. But if that's what you want, it's one not far from here." I said smirking at her meal choice. "You sure you don't want to go out to eat?" I asked getting assurance before I get excited. "Yeah. My mom got me liking those damn sandwiches." she said sanctioning her choice. "Ok, then it's just up the street." I said relieved about the financial savings with the meal change.

"You so stupid. You had that whole store, in there laughing at you."

Imani laughed as we exited Jimmy Johns arm in arm. "Uh oh. There's your boy." she continued as she noticed J.T. before I did. "What's up mister and misses Que?" J.T. yelled as he stepped out of his car. "You left before I can praise you on your game. Oh, I heard the good news. Congratulations! You really do got it all, don't you?" he continued brazenly. I nodded my head at J.T. and continued towards the car with Imani. "Hey Que! Have you seen Tasha? We got into a little disagreement last night and I hear she spends a lot of time in your building. Thinking, maybe you seen her?" J.T. called out as we approached the car. "Nah man. I haven't seen your girl, been too busy with my girl." I calmly said after opening the door for Imani.

"I don't know babe. He got something on his mind. He can't be that throwed off." Imani said softly while half-heartedly attempting to ponder J.T.'s dilemma. "Whatever it is, it don't have shit to do with me! I ain't seen his girl." I said casually making sure to not show any type of annoyance. "Did he really misplace his girlfriend?" Imani asked joking while still confused by his conduct.

RING. RING! "You're gonna have to answer her, sooner or later." Imani said as she played with my earlobe. "Here, I'll answer it." she said as she nudged my head from her naked chest to reach for my phone. RING. RING! "Make sure it's her before I answer it. Don't wanna mess nothing up for you." she said sarcastically as she showed me the phone screen. "Just answer it! Anyone who'd call me, knows you're you." I said quickly seeing that it was my mother. RING. RING! "Hi Ms. G." Imani said gently. "Omar, come here. He finally answered the phone!" I could faintly hear my mom yell. "You might as well put it on speaker. I can hear her yelling." I said calmly to Imani. "Hello Imani. How are you? Everything's okay?" my mom pleasantly asked. "I should be asking you that Mrs. G." Imani said softly. "Hey ma." I interjected to make my presence known. "Hey *baby*. How's my *baby*?" my mom asked with a little more enthusiasm. "Where are they? They on the phone now?" my dad said as he emerged into the speakerphone range. "Yeah mom, I'm fine, just tired. Hey dad." I said casually. "Put some clothes on. You talking to my parents, naked!" I mouthed to Imani as I pulled up my boxers. "So, we ended our call abruptly, earlier. You never told us how you really feel about the pregnancy. You okay?" my mom said calmly. "You ready for all this?" my dad added harshly. "Yeah, I'm ready. But I really got no choice, right? It's happening, whether I'm ready or not." I said earnestly to my father. I looked over at Imani who was confused at my exchange of ideas. "I couldn't have said it better myself, son." my father said proudly.

"Babe, look! I just got this from your sister." Imani whispered as she showed me a text Storm sent to her phone.

> **{Storm}**
> **Mom and dad kno u preg. Call me!!**

"I know." I whispered as I shook my head to Imani. "So, do we say something?" Imani asked nervously. "No, they will." I whispered surely. "So, Imani, you never told me how you were. Are you taking care of yourself?" my mother asked casually. I looked at Imani with a smirk. "Yes Mrs. G, I'm doing real good." Imani answered quickly. "So, does your mom know?" my dad asked extremely transparent. I smiled at Imani's facial expression of my father's blatant questioning. "Huh?" Imani uttered in amazement. "No not yet. I was going to come home, and we were going to tell all of you at the same time. Face to face." I said quickly to save my drowning girlfriend. "But I guess that's null and void, now." I continued, with the knowledge that everyone but my father believed me. The indistinct banter of my mother and father slightly bothered Imani. She looked at me with a look of terror in her face. "Don't worry about it." I whispered calmly. "That's just my mom talking my dad off a ledge, like only she can." I continued as I fell back onto the bed. "You sure, cause I gotta go back home to them. You don't!" she whispered sternly. "I'm sure." I whispered as I picked the phone from the bed and removed the speakerphone feature. "Speaking of that. Dad, I want Imani to take my car home, since I'm not there. This way she can get around reliably. That's cool?" I asked with hopes that he would for all intents and purposes agree. I pulled the phone away from my ear in anticipation of the bombardment of the loud opinion from my father. "Yeah. I didn't think of that, but it very much makes sense. Not to mention, it's both responsible and commendable." my dad said bowled over at my generosity. I looked up at Imani who was also astonished by the idea of her taking my car home. "Alright dad, if you don't mind, it's been a long day. Can we finish this conversation tomorrow?" I said drained from the day. "Yes baby. I think we all need to get some rest. Today, was really a roller coaster of emotions." Tracey said softly. "Yeah, that's a good idea. Quentin, I'll call you tomorrow. We have a lot to discuss." my dad said hardheartedly.

CHAPTER 43

"Hassan"

RING. RING!

Omar Gregory
302-555-8974

"Damn, O. Seriously?!" I mumbled with a mouthful of Pringle chips. "We was together all day yesterday and you never told me what happened with Vic." he declared firmly. "Nothing that I know of, other than the thing with the dude in the truck." I said ignorant to what he was referring to. "What thing, with dude in a truck? What happened?!" Omar demanded. "How do you not know this stuff? You know everyone, I know." I asked curiously. "Cause, I don't go home like that. I only know stuff about up there, when you tell me. I only know that something even happened with Vic, cause Cricket used it as an excuse to give me some." I said casually. "You ain't tell me that you saw, *Mia*." I said surprised that he harbored that information. "I said I stopped by Vic's place!" he aggressively declared. "You didn't say you fucked his wife. I know that was your first, and your *go-to*, but damn, it's been like ten years. Are you ever going to give that up?" I honestly questioned while pulling up in front of the barbershop. "Are you ever going to tell me what happened to Vic?" he inquired sarcastically.

"Vic got caught in his work truck giving his foreman a hand-job." I said as calmly as I could while doing my best to restrain my laughter. "What?!" he said astounded by the news. "Yeah, you heard me. One of his co-workers recorded him kissing and jerking this nigga off, in the trash truck. He showed it to the bosses, and they both got fired. I heard homie that told, is the foreman now. That's why he was home when you went over there, he not working. I thought you knew all this." I said truly amazed that he was ignorant to something of this magnitude. "Don't you think if I'd have known about it, we'd have talked about it already!" he said roused

213

and distressed. "So, Vic is gay?!" he continued to ask. "I would assume so." I scoffed as I entered the barbershop. "If he not, his boyfriend is." I continued, making a mockery of the situation. I waved to the barbers and other patrons before attempting to sit down in the waiting area. "C'mon." my barber signaled before I could get positioned. "This shit not funny man." Omar insisted while trying to hold in his laughter. "Damn, no wonder Cricket was so pushy." Omar said finally finding justification. "Yeah, that's why!" I said condescendingly. "Now, I got news for you." Omar said casually. "Alright wait. Gimme twenty minutes to get my cut. I'll call you right back." I said as my barber dramatically fanned the cape over me.

3-0-2-5-5-5-8-9-7-4. "What's the big news?" I said curiously as soon as he answered the call. "The son you claim, is having a baby!" Omar said nonchalantly. "What?! That shit was true?! I thought she had it mixed up, with Tracey being pregnant! Oh shit!" I said in complete awe. "Yeah, *oh shit* is about right. Wait! Who'd you hear it from?" Omar asked calmly perplexed. "I told you I have a young thing, up there on campus. She told me last night. But I didn't think she knew what she was talking about. So, I brushed her off. But the bigger question, what he gonna do? This is big in regards to that going to the league, finishing school, stalemate." I confirmed, amazed at the news about the boy I helped raise. "He's going to be a father!" Omar said unsympathetically. "But let me go. I gotta call him to find out more about that, and to tell him about Friday." Omar said humorlessly. "You didn't tell him about that, yet? Let me know how that goes." I genuinely requested. "Alright then." he said before I ended the call.

CHAPTER 44

"Omar"

3-0-2-5-5-5-8-9-7-5. "Hey Dad." Quentin said cheerfully. "Hey. How are you doing, today?" I asked subtly while searching the garage for my gas can. "I'm good. I'm a standing in the parking lot, watching Imani drive away in my car." Quentin pitifully admitted. I laughed as I imagined Quentin's face as his car rolled down the street without him. "You sure you're alright son?" I asked laughing derisively. "Yeah, I'm good. I know you probably got your hand over the phone, cracking up. But I really am, okay with this." he said honestly. "Wow Quentin, you've really grown. And, you're actually having a baby. I'll be a pop-pop." I uttered still euphoric about the whole thing. "Yeah. But dad, you're forgetting something, you are having a baby as well? You'll be a da-da too." he happily reminded me. "I haven't forgotten. Oh, son believe me, I haven't forgotten!" I said sincerely as I discovered the can under a pile of leaf bags.

"Before recently, have you ever *really* wondered about your mother? Who she was? What she was like? Anything? And I'm talking serious here, son. Brutal honesty, no feeling spared. I love you, and know that you love me. With that knowledge, we can speak freely and nothing changes." I said reassuring him that all was well. I emptied the gasoline into the lawnmower, which I had waiting in the middle of the driveway. "Honestly dad, I never really thought about her, til recently. I've always had a mom. Between Grammy and Tracey, I never once remember going without." he said genuinely. "You have no idea how it feels, to hear you say that." I said sincerely while pushing the lawnmower down the driveway to the front of the house. "Would ask where this is coming from, but I'm guessing you talked to Tiffany Blackwell." he assumed confidently.

"That's an understatement." I mumbled quietly. "Not only did I talk to her, I saw her. We were even in a car accident, together." I hesitantly confessed. "What?! When did all this happen?! I thought you said to keep away from her." he reiterated aggressively. "I told you, to keep away from her. I had things I needed to find out. One specifically, her intentions." I said unsympathetically as stood next to the lawnmower after realizing that it was pointless to bring it out, while on the phone. "So how did this all come about? How'd you end up seeing her?" Quentin inquired remaining in his aggressive tone.

"Well, I was in Philly with Emily and she invited me over to talk." I said defending against his aggression. "That's why you still let Em go, even after she almost got arrested. You had that whole thing, already set-up! Does ma know you saw her?" he asked accusing. "No." I answered shamefaced. "Yo dad. Speaking freely, that's fucked up. You spent the whole day with her? Cause I know you didn't sit in the music studio, with Em. Did you even find out *what's up?*" he asked dynamically. "Ok Quentin, I'm going to let that go cause we're speaking freely and your clearly upset. But let me tell you something and hopefully it'll stay with you, because you're going to be a dad soon. My *only* priorities are to protect, provide and develop, you, Emily and Tracey. With those priorities, I do things that you may not like. Things that, I may not like. Some things you see, most you don't. But it all, gets done! So, to protect my son… yes, I made that trip. To protect my wife and marriage, no I won't tell her about it. At least, not now. Hopefully one day, you'll understand. I don't expect you to today, though." I lectured to my son as I pulled the lawnmower back up the driveway.

"So, how'd the talk go?" Quentin asked calmly. "It went well. At least, until the accident. But I think, I did the day backwards. I went and saw mom, before I saw her. I should have done it, the other way around. Would've loved my mom's advice on that one." I said casually.

"What'd you guys talk about? I know it was about me, but what'd you talk about?" he asked keenly. "It was all about you. Your exploits and achievements. Hell, she knew more, than I did. She was showing me pictures and articles of accomplishments, that I didn't even know existed. She truly is, a fan." I said approvingly before leaping onto the bed of my truck. "Wow, how'd she get all that?" he inquired intriguingly. "She's on everything you've ever been on. The Dover Post, the Daily Collegian, the Centre Daily Times, if you were in it, she was on it. I mean all the way down to your high school newspaper. Sounds kinda stalker-ish, don't it?" I said cynically while sitting in my truck bed bitterly staring at the grass, that I no longer feel like cutting. "Yeah, dad should I be worried, seriously?" Quentin said suspiciously.

"And that right there, is why I went to Philly. Why, I had to talk to her first!" I declared dominantly as I slid out of the truck and sluggishly pushed the mower back into the garage. "You can calm down. You have nothing to worry about. She's just a lonely woman, who regrets her biggest mistake. As far as I can see, she's harmless. Just wants the chance, to one day get to know you." I said confidently as I treaded through the garage. "What should I do?" he asked intently. "Nothing. Continue living the way you've been. You gotta baby to prepare for." I said absolutely.

"Dad, I'm having a little girl." he said enthusiastically. "I know." I said proudly. "Wait a minute. How do you know it's a *little girl*? How far along is she?" I asked becoming slightly nervous. "She's only seven weeks. But I know she's a girl." he said confidently. "I hope so, for your sake." I said encouraging his fantasies as I stepped into the house.

"Dad. Baby girl coming, has me thinking. Maybe I should enter the draft, and finish school down the road." Quentin said uneasily. "I was waiting for *this* conversation." I said expecting to hear him speak about finances. "That's certainly an option. A practical one. A lucrative one! I mean, the CBA put the rookie contract at what, four-eighty a year? And if you decided to go in that direction, I would not condemn you in any way." I said authentically. "Yeah but that four hundred eighty thousand, is if I'm drafted in the top three rounds. What if I don't make it dad? What if I'm not good enough?" Quentin said sincerely. "Then you'll become the sports broadcaster that you were educated to be. You have put yourself in a position where you have options. And all of them, every single one of them, is a path to success." I said genuinely.

CHAPTER 45

"Quentin"

"Yeah. I am set-up alright, aren't I? Thanks dad." I said sincerely to my father. "Yes. You've truly become the man, I hoped you be. I couldn't be more proud of you." I said as candid as I could possibly be. "I just hope my little girl will be proud of me, too" I said quietly as I sat on the bench playing in the dirt with a stick I found. "He, or she, will be." my dad said supportively. "Ok dad, thanks for everything. I gotta go now. I gotta get in here and cram, since I couldn't study with Imani here." I admitted honestly to my father. "You go do that. I'm going to go sit, and watch football until I pass out. I'll cut the grass another time. Love you, son." he said ending the conversation. "Love you too, dad." I responded before ending the call. I rose to my feet, tossed the small stick into the bushes and headed into my building. "Congrats Que." a woman's voice sang from behind me. I turned to reply and noticed Tasha stomping across the parking lot in the distance. "Thank you." I said quickly to the woman coming into the building behind me. I held the door for the young lady and ran pass her up the stairs. I quickly opened my apartment door, stepped in and swiftly closed it behind me. "Juice. Juice!" I called out, upon entering the room. Ecstatic that he was not home, I danced across the apartment to my bedroom door.

KNOCK. KNOCK. KNOCK! Knowing that it was Tasha, I continued to remain in my bedroom. "Only Tasha would still knock on my door after seeing my car gone." I whispered to myself as I sat on the edge of the bed waiting for her to vanish.

KNOCK. KNOCK. KNOCK! "Que, you in there?" Juice asked as he beat on my bedroom door. "Yeah, hold up." I said as staggered up to the door. I opened the door to Juice standing with a handful of cigars in one hand and the tv remote in the other. Behind him was Dame, Willow and Willow's visiting little brother Nasil. "Congratulations Nigga!" he yelled enthusiastically as he pushed the cigars into my chest. "You know we can't smoke these." I said as I smelled and examined the cigars. "I know. I thought you can just keep them and remember uncle Juice, when you one day can." my friend said genuinely. "Thanks man. But I promise, we'll light these together." I said as I shook his hand.

"Why you in there napping, on a no class Monday afternoon? Wha'chu hiding, or something?" Dame asked aloud from the sofa. "Man, I'm just not in the mood for, Tasha." I said as I followed Juice into the living room. "That means Imani's gone." Juice said as he turned on the television and plopped down on his favorite couch cushion. "I guess everything's back to *normal*, huh?" Willow said sarcastically. Everyone began to snicker and chuckle at Willow's little joke. "Whatever?" I said unappreciative of the laughter at my expense. "I'm only fucking wit'chu. But you do have to admit, you got some exceptional shit going on." Willow said with his head in the refrigerator. "Whatever, man. Move!" I said as I pushed Willow out of the way, to get into the fridge. I grabbed the smoothie Imani purchased for me and headed toward the couch. "Hey before you go get comfortable, I need you to run me to take my brother to the Greyhound." Willow said as I crossed the room.

KNOCK. KNOCK. KNOCK! "Man go 'head. First you talk shit. Then you ask me to run you somewhere? Explain to me why, you thought that was gonna work out." I said while unconsciously opening the door. I turned to see Tasha standing in the doorway. I stood there with my mind racing, staring almost through her. "Well, can I come in? Is the coast clear?" she asked cynically as she strutted pass me into the apartment. "Hey y'all." she said as she swayed across the room towards my bedroom door. "Heyyee!" Willow's brother, Nasil sang, star struck by Tasha's appearance. "Wa'sup Tasha." Dame said nonchalantly. "It's still light outside, you by yourself? Were you followed?" Juice mocked staring at the door. "No Juice box, I was not followed." she said before she stepped into my bedroom and closed the door behind her. "I guess you can't hide now." Juice mocked. The entire room again felt the need to laugh at my predicament's ridicule.

"Girl, I missed it by about two minutes." Tasha said as she poured out of the bedroom in my high school jersey. "Damn, I forgot she was here." Dame whispered. "That's why she came out the room. It's been hours, and no one's paying attention to her." I said bluntly as I watched Tasha stroll across the room to the kitchen. "I came out 'cause I wanted something to snack on, mind you! I just hope nobody ate my flan, while I was *gone*!" Tasha loudly proclaimed before opening the refrigerator door. "Girl, let me call you back." she continued bitterly while searching the fridge. "No, it's in there. I saw it earlier." Willow said awkwardly. "Thank you Willow." Tasha said remorsefully as she found her dessert. "I know Quentin couldn't take you, to take your brother. Did he tell you why?" Tasha said sharply as she spooned her dessert into her mouth. "No, but it's alright. Juice took us in Rudy's van." Willow said timidly. "He didn't tell y'all that he gave his car to his girlfriend?" Tasha asked harshly. Sighs and groans quietly erupted throughout the room. "Did he at least tell y'all that she was having a baby? Hope it's his." Tasha snapped as she turned her attention towards the sofa and its occupants. "Time for us to go." Dame said as he stood, looked at Willow and then Juice. "Nigga sit down, I live here!" Juice chuckled as he turned back towards the television. "Dame sit down, and enjoy the game." I said sincerely as I stood up to approach Tasha. "Tasha, just like I'd never let Imani or anyone else ever disrespect you, you will *not* disrespect her! Now, if you got some things on your chest that you want to get off, spit it out." I asserted intensely.

"Goodnight y'all." Tasha said softly as she drifted back into the bedroom and closed the door. "Let me go handle this. I'll holla at y'all later." I said as I extended my hand to Dame. I walk over to Willow still sitting at the table at the far end of the room. "Alright Will, til the am." I said as I gave Will a soldier's salute. "Til the am, Que." Juice said as he raised his cup. "Til the am, Juice." I said as I opened my bedroom door.

I stepped into the room to see Tasha sitting on the bed with her head in her hands. I slowly closed the door as she lifted her head, her eyes full of tears. I reached onto the closet shelf and grabbed a roll of toilet tissue. I gently slithered over and sat down next to Tasha. "Here." I whispered as I rolled the tissue in my hand and offered it to her. "What do you want me to say, Tasha?" I asked quietly. "I don't know. I knew who you were when we started this. I knew what you had, when I gave you me. I knew where your heart was, when I gave you mine." she said somberly while wiping away her tears with the tissue.

"That's not fair to you. You didn't go into this, by yourself. And you're not the only one hurt by it. You think I like seeing you like this?" I said trying to conjure solemn and somber within myself to show compassion. "I don't know. What I do know, is I'm not going to even pretend like you're a victim of this. You're the only one who has benefit from all of this." she said as she dabbed her eyes with the handful of tissue. "At least I know how you feel, now. Took you long enough to tell me." I said attempting to wrap my head around the entire situation. "Do you Quentin? How do I feel about all of this?!" she asked aggressively as she stood up. "The guy that you're seeing, still has someone at home. And it's upsetting when she makes her presence known." I said giving my best interpretation of her situation.

"*Upsetting when she makes her presence known?* Are you serious?! Do you think we're still there?! That was thirty-four days, twenty-one fucks, sixteen study dates, nine dinners, four lunches, ten brunches, five breakfasts, twenty-eight secrets, six sunsets, fourteen back rubs, ten front rubs, thirteen movie nights, three sick nights, four pair of panties, three bras, one toothbrush, one deodorant, one loofa sponge and a personal drawer in the God damn refrigerator, ago! So no, it's not the guy that I'm seeing. The man that I'm in love with, is in love with someone else. That's it in a nutshell!" she said as she pulled personal items out of an Adidas shoe box blended in with the multitude of other shoe boxes in my closet. I sat there in awe and completely speechless. "I don't know what to say, Tasha. You love me? That's big." I said as I tried to gather my thoughts to say or do something, anything to temporarily charm my way out this. Like, I've always done.

"You don't need to say anything Quentin. Yes, I love you. And I can see she does too, why wouldn't we. Just consider yourself lucky. You have three people in your life, who are completely in love with you." Tasha said as she pulled the jersey over her head exposing her partially naked body. She tossed the jersey on the back of the chair, stuffed her personals back into the box and crawled into the bed. DOINK! I turned to look at her as she snuggled to get comfortable under the quilt. "Three people?" I asked after finally catching up to what she'd said. I stood up to get my phone from atop the desk. "Yes. Me, Imani and you." she completed after a long pause. Continuing to have nothing to say I reluctantly looked at my phone text message.

> **{Mani}**
> **I kno ur probly nodding off watching football**
> **but WE wanted u 2 kno... WE Luv U.**

CHAPTER 46

"Omar"

"Good morning ladies." I said to the assembly of women on the elevator as I stepped on. "Good morning, Mr. Gregory." two of the women said simultaneously. "Good morning." another said quickly lifting and returning her head to her phone. "Congratulations, Omar." an unseen male voice pierced from behind the women. I turned around and sifted through the assemblage to see Elliot Carson. "Elliot, didn't see you there. Good morning." I said surprised by his presence. "I bet you didn't." he chuckled referring to the congregation of young women on the elevator. Now APPROACHING THE SEVENTH FLOOR. WATCH YOUR STEP WHEN EXITING. The elevator announced interrupting Elliot's fantastic notions. "How's everything going?" I asked making conversation. "Excuse us." one of the ladies said as two of them stepped off the elevator. "Everything's going well." Elliot said just as uninterested. "How's Renee?" I continued to ask. "She's doing well. Not as well as Tracey. I hear she's expecting. I know I'm a week late, but congrats again." he said casually. "Thanks." I said genuinely. Now APPROACHING THE TENTH FLOOR. WATCH YOUR STEP WHEN EXITING. The elevator again announced as doors parted slowly. "Good morning, Mr. Gregory, Mr. Carson." Elliot's assistant Monica said as she stepped onto the elevator. "Good morning, Monica." I said joyfully mocking. "Good morning." Elliot responded self-consciously. "Congratulations. I hear your gonna be a father, again." she said slightly enthused. "Yeah, thank you. I guess I'm not as old, as I thought." I said jokingly. Now APPROACHING THE FOURTEENTH FLOOR. WATCH YOUR STEP EXITING. "I guess not." she said with a smile as she stepped off of the elevator. "I'll see you in the meeting, Gregory." Elliot said as he followed Monica off of the elevator. "Until then, Carson." I said as the door slowly closed. "Wow, she really is a bad one. I wonder how much he's paying for that?" I mumbled as I got one last look at Carson's assistant.

Now APPROACHING THE EIGHTEENTH FLOOR. WATCH YOUR STEP EXITING. "Congratulations." erupted from every direction as I stepped off the elevator. "Thank you. Thank you, all" I said as I waved my briefcase and paraded towards my office. "Good morning, Daddy." Antoinette said as I approached her desk. I shook my head and nervously reached in my pocket for my office door key.

"Took a whole week, for it to get out. That's a lot longer, than I thought it would. And why do you say shit like that? You of all people, know there are always ears." I said as Toni followed me into my office. "I can get away with it now. Everyone now knows you going to be a daddy. They don't have to know, you're my *daddy*." she said cynically. "And how does, everyone know?" I asked curiously. "I may have told it to Tish, in the mailroom. But in my defense, I've been announcing it all week. How was I to know that it'd make though the whole building, ten minutes after I told her?" she uttered in an attempt to pretend to be naïve.

"Now, I have a question for you. Why did everyone get a hug when y'all told us on Saturday, but me? What, you don't trust me? Or am I too, talented?" Toni asked as she closed my office door. I hung my jacket on the coat rack and went over to open the windows. "Huh? That was six days ago. That's been festering inside you since then? And I gave you a hug, didn't I?" I said as I lifted the window. "Now, you know you didn't give me a hug! You even looked at me, to see if I was paying attention. I was, I just haven't said anything. I'm very, very observant, Omar." she said as she slowly approached me. "Yeah, I believe you've said that before." I said nonchalantly as I sat at my desk and turned on my computer.

"There it go, right there." I said as I spotted my favorite red tie, hanging on a hook on the back of the door. I jumped up to switch my ties. "Can I help you?" I said as I noticed Toni following behind me. "I thought you were getting up to finally give me my hug. You gave everyone else, a hug." she said sweetly. I stepped back and continued to untie my tie. I examined Antoinette up and down, confused by her immediate objectives. "I saw that. You just stopped at my breasts." she said sensually. "What?!" I said completely unaware of my actions.

I tossed my tie onto my desk and retrieved the one from the door. "I told you, I am very observant. And I *observed* you staring at my breasts." she continued. "Whatever. If anything, I stopped to look at that button, struggling to survive. He's about to have a cardiac, trying to hold that shirt together." I said as I advanced back behind my desk. Toni looked down at the button. "It's not that bad." she declared animated. "I'm not really supposed to even button this shirt up, that high. But I am, at work. Maybe, I should unbutton it. Then you can see first-hand, how *talented* I really am." Toni teased as she played with the sole button holding her shirt together. "How you know about *talent*? I don't talk like that, around here." I inquired as she progressed around my desk to me. "And, where are you going?" I continued as she was almost to me. "Told you, I'm coming to get my hug, then I'm... ooops." Antoinette said as she unbuttoned her shirt. "Whew, that do feel better though. Maybe, I should just keep going." she said as she continued to unbutton her shirt. "Maybe... you should go to work. And remember, I'm the boss." I said genuinely. "Your right. I'm sorry. Just gimme my hug, and I'm gone." she insisted as she stood over with me with her large breasts cupped in her lace bra slightly exposed. "If that's what it'll take." I said as I rose from my chair. "C'mere" she said as she gestured for me to come to her. "Congratulations, Mr. Gregory." Toni sighed as she clinched me firmly. "Damn!" I thought as her firm breasts pressed against me. "Umm. Excited, are we?" Toni asked cynically. "Huh? What are you talking about?" I asked ignorantly as I backed away from her.

"This is what I'm... *oh-oh damn!*" she said as she grasped the front of my pants for my erect penis. "What the hell are you doing?!" I inquired unwelcomingly as I jumped back quickly. "You're so right! I really don't know what I was thinking. This is not the time, nor place. I-I am truly sorry." Toni said sincerely. "Just fix yourself and go back to work, Antoinette." I said severely. "Yes sir." Antoinette said obediently. She turned towards the corner of the room to fasten her blouse semi-privately.

Knock. Knock! "Hey Omar, did you get the..." Elliot Carson said as he crashed into my office. "Yeah Elliot, just ignore the closed door. Did I get what?" I said irritated as I followed his eyes over to Antoinette, who was nervously trying to button her shirt. "Is everything alright? Did I interrupt?" Elliot voiced sneeringly. "What do you want, Carson?" I said exasperated by his presence. I tapped my chest, looking for my tie to Windsor, while never taking my eyes from Elliot. "I came for a print out of Clancy's memo, I accidentally erased it. But if, it's a bad time?" Elliot said sternly. "Excuse me gentlemen." Toni murmured as she quickly side stepped out of the room. Elliot peered at Antoinette as she left the room with her back to us. I quickly pulled up the file that Elliot requested and sent it to him. "I just emailed it to you. You can print it down there." I said hastening him out of my office. "Thanks. And congrats again." he said as he threw me a wink and strolled out of the office.

"Girl, I got a whole new respect for that white woman. She, a real bitch. How the hell she takin' all that shit, every night? *And* she getting' the whole thing, cause she ain't got no ass to keep him from diggin' all the way in.

He could *never* put my legs up." Antoinette uttered covertly with her head in her computer screen. I stood in the doorway listening to Toni's phone conversation. I laughingly crept back into the office, with the hopes to not interrupt her conversing. I grabbed my keys and hurried back to the door, to continue listening to Toni brag on me. "I must've looked so thirsty, this morning. I hope I still gotta job, after today." Toni continued to whisper.

"Ahem. Toni, about this morning." I discreetly uttered, interrupting her exchange on her personal call. "Let me call you..." Toni started before I interrupted. "You don't have to hang up. I just wanted to reassure you, that we're fine. You got a little excited this morning, and I enabled it. It's now water under the bridge. So, if you're worried, don't be. Not about me, and especially not about Elliot. Alright?" I asked sincerely as I extended my fist to give her a pound. Antoinette looked up at me, smiled comfortably and bumped her fist to mine.

"Let me call you back." she said quickly into the phone before hanging up. "Did you know Mr. Carson doesn't like you?" she whispered as she pulled close to my ear. "You don't have to whisper, dear." I said confidently. "And yes, I knew that. I'm not too fond of him, either. Him being a weasel is actually common knowledge, but we're at work and must play professionally." I continued surely. "Well, he not playing professionally. He came in there trying to catch us doing something! Sydney told me that as soon as that door closed, Felicia called down to Monica, and then he came running up here." she continued to murmur while looking around for anyone watching. I couldn't help but laugh at the whole, high school whisper game here at work. "This really goes on?" I chuckled into a cough. "Did you hear me?" she asked apprehensively. "I heard you. And I'm sure, that's what he did. His name is mud with the whole *Monica thing*, and he doesn't want to sink alone. But I'm not worried about it and you shouldn't either." I said reassuring her of my authority in the building. "I'm going on an extended lunch, so defer everything that comes along until after 2pm. I'll see you when I return" I continued as I tossed my sport coat over my arm and walked away.

CHAPTER 47

"Hassan"

"Lisa, Angela, Pamela, Renee, I love you. You're from around the way." I sang as the loud music drowned out my voice. 3-0-2-5-5-5-8-9-7-5. "Hello." Quentin voice casually resonated throughout the car. "Number twenty. How are you? It's been a while, everything alright?" I asked in wonder of the excuse he'd use this time. "Yeah, everything's okay. My bad that I haven't touched base in a while, I've just been busy." he admitted instinctively. "I understand that, student athlete, and all. But you're, okay?" I asked truly concerned about my nephew. "Yeah, I'm good." he responded honestly. "How're the fellas? How's PS two?" I inquired probingly. "I don't know, Unc. She came over talking love and other shit, and then just dropped the whole subject." he said baffled. "Love?" I asked unsure if I heard him correctly. "Yeah, she said she loves me, and has an account of everything we've ever done. I really think, she meant it." he said nonchalantly. "If she loves you, we may want to involve your father. He's the one that's good with, the *long game*." I advised quickly. "I thought, about it. But we'll see. I'm going into practice, so I'll hit you later." he said hastily. "Make sure you do." I said as I ended the call.

> **Omar Gregory**
> **302-555-8974**

"I was just about to call you!" I testified answering the call. "Why? What's up?" he inquired curiously. "You're what's up! I hear you had Toni bent over in your office, and one of the top dogs walked in on it." I said proudly. "Huh? How?" he uttered quickly. "How do you always know everything?" he continued in bewilderment. "You been asking that same question, for thirty something years. When are you going to realize that I got eyes everywhere, and ears everywhere else?" I asked confidently. "I guess, right now." he faintly acknowledged.

"You know I didn't do that shit, right?" he asked tensely. "Yeah, I know. I'm probably the only one who knows. I'm definitely the only one, who believes that shit. But I know *you*, you ain't built like that." I said genuinely. "I just hope Tracey know, how *I'm built*." he said apprehensively. I laughed at Omar's hope for his wife's gullibility. "You can forget that. No matter how hard she tries to convince herself that you didn't do it. This one… she's going to believe went down. Did you see how she was looking at Toni, on Saturday?" I asked surprised that he wasn't more observant of his wife, around other women. "No, how did she look at her?" he asked naively. "I don't know. You know that look that women give to other women. Envy, admiration, like, dislike, jealousy and a bunch of other shit, all rolled into one." I said secure that he knew what I was referring to. "Yeah." he said confidently. "That look! Hell, she was staring at her ass more than I was." I said sarcastically. "Shit! You think she heard?" Omar asked nervously. "Oh, she heard about it. Jill called me just before I called you. And she was my third call! And we both know, that I was the second call she made. I'm actually surprised, that Tracey hasn't called you yet." I said with concern. "She's probably trying to process it all. Let me call her and defuse this, before it explodes." he said gullibly. "No, no, no, don't do that! What are you approaching or apologizing for, if it's nothing? You didn't call and explain spilling your coffee on Kevin, last week. Why? Because, it wasn't conversation worthy, it wasn't important. You're too old for me to still be teaching you, these things." I said rescuing him from himself. "You right. About calling her, not about teaching me. You don't know enough to teach me shit." he said nonchalantly.

I chuckled at his audacity. "But my pile of shit is getting higher, and sooner or later it's gonna spill over. Between this shit with Toni, and seeing Tiffany, I gotta say something." he said anxiously. "No, you don't. You didn't do nothing. You didn't push the button, in either one of those situations. Which personally, I think was dumb. I'd have paid homage to both of them. Especially Toni, I'd have folded her in half!" I said honestly. "So, I should just let it go?" he asked sincerely. "Yes! Why bring up something, when there's nothing to bring up? You're creating controversy where there is none." I cleverly coached. "I don't want this shit to come up behind me, and bite me in the ass. I figured I'll get in front of it, and face it head on." he said grimly. "With that logic, why aren't you thinking about telling her about you and Cricket? You actually did something there." I asked harshly as I pulled into my office parking lot. "C'mon Haas, that doesn't even make sense. Why would I bring that up? Why would I give that issue... life?" he asked slowly, realizing his lapse of judgement. "You're right!" he continued surrendering on his own accord.

CHAPTER 48

"Tracey"

"Hey Tracey, you okay?" Arman asked as he approached me in the hall. "Hey Arman. Yeah, I'm well. Why? Do I not look, okay?" I asked curious to his line of questioning. "Yeah, you look fine. Just greeting, that's all." he said as he kept pace down the hall. "Oh. Well, in that case, how are you?" I asked accompanying his demeanor. "I'm great. Just had two students in my class try to kill each other over an open window, but other than that everything's good." he admitted humorously. "That's good. I mean the, you're great part, not the students fighting." I said attempting to break open a smile. "I knew what you meant. Oh, and I am told congratulations are in order." he said enthusiastically. "Yeah, I guess congratulations, is what you're supposed to say. Thank you, Arman." I said chuckling before speeding up pace to get to my class before the bell sounded. "No problem, Tracey. I'll see you around?" Arman asked as he stopped in front of his classroom door. "You will." I replied as I turned back to wave. I hurried to my room so I could close the door, once the bell sounded.

"Good afternoon, ladies." I said greeting the last few students to enter the room as I approached the door. "I said, good afternoon ladies." I repeated to the small group of young women entering as the bell rang. "Good afternoon, Ms. Gregory." Samarah said as she slid passed me. "Hi, Ms. Gregory. Congratulations!" Harley followed vigorously as she too came into the room. "Whatever!" Chaewon uttered as she pushed pass the other two.

"Alright people, settle down. We're going to do something different today. This is a one-time thing, so don't get too excited. Does everyone have their phone? If so, I want you to take them out and get onto YouTube. You are to look up, and watch *Adam ruins the first Thanksgiving* and we will discuss it momentarily. Chaewon, can I see you outside the room, for a second?" I said aloud as the class began to quietly celebrate. "Ugh. Man, damn." Chaewon whispered as she reluctantly trudged to the room door.

"You called me out here to thank you, cause I didn't get locked up? Thank you." Chaewon said before I could even get the door closed. "No, I don't want or need that. I deserve it, but didn't expect it. What I did expect, was respect. Whatever you have going on with my daughter, is between you two and has nothing to do with school. And I'd like it, to stay that way." I said sternly to my former class favorite. "You're right, I'm sorry." Chaewon said as she reached for the doorknob to open the door. I moved her hand away from the knob and pushed the door back closed. "Chaewon, look at me. You and I, are better than this. So, with that said, I have a question. Your relationship with my daughter, is neither here nor there. I really don't care about that. I would like to know about your relationship, with my son." I asked quietly. Chaewon looked up at me as tears began to swell in her eyes. "Don't move." I uttered as I opened the door and quickly paced to grab some tissue from the box on my desk. "Jonathan, I promise to quiz you all on this, before today's class is over." I said noticing a student with his head in his hand and eyes closed. I hurried back with the tissue, to Chaewon in the hall. "Here." I said as I handed her the tissue. "Thank you" she whispered as she wiped her running tear. "You okay?" I asked holding the second tissue in case needed. "I'm fine. I just really thought, that he liked me." Chaewon whimpered softly. "Who? Quentin?" I asked as I slowly ran my arm across her back. "Yeah. We *hooked up*, after last year's homecoming game. And then a few times after that. Then, I heard he had a girlfriend so I approached him about it. And that was the last time we spoke. I didn't want nobody here to know I got played, so I tell them we still kickin' it." she said as she gestured for the tissue in my hand. "Let me guess, that's what the fight with my daughter was about. She was defending her brother?" I asked enlightened by her profession.

"Ok. And both situations, are over and done with?" I asked curiously. "Quentin, yeah. I honestly don't know what I'll do, if I see your daughter in the street." she said earnestly. "Then I guess I have to make sure you never see my daughter *in the street*. I'll handle Emily." I said as I opened the door to escort her back into the room. "Ok. Everyone but Chaewon, put your phones away!" I barked as I walked over to my desk and picked up my phone.

3 Missed Calls
Toni {2}; Hubby {1}

"Call Toni." I commanded softly into my phone. "Hello." Toni said softly. "Hey Toni. You know I can't answer my phone in front of those kids. I have to set an example. What's up?" I asked attempting to sound as nonchalant as I possibly could. "I was calling to see if you had a chance to talk to your husband about what happened earlier." she uttered nervously. I pushed open the doors and stepped out, taking a deep breath of the smell of freshly cut grass. "Good night, Ms. Gregory." a man's voice sang from behind me. "What happened earlier? Good night, Samuel." I said dividing my attention between the two. "The whole thing with me, and Omar. I'm sure you heard about it." she confessed with confidence. "Yeah, I didn't give it much thought though. I'm sure, it was nothing." I said as I marched across the parking lot. "Well, so that you know, nothing happened. I was just fixing my shirt buttons with my back turned." Antoinette explained eagerly. "I didn't think anything happened, Toni. I trust *Omar*! He's too conservative for what you two are being faulted." I said continuing to convince myself of his innocence. "Good, cause I don't want nothing hanging between you and me. I like our friendship." she said obviously attempting to be sincere. "No worries, Toni. Not of you, or anyone else. Like I said, I trust my husband. He may glimpse and glare. But he's too much of a proud prude, to do anything. His reputation, means everything to him. He can't have that tainted." I declared indisputably. "Damn girl. You sound like you trust his need, to just be him more than his love, for you." Toni said observantly. "Is that how that sounded?" I asked sarcastically as I pulled out of the school parking lot.

"Hey dad." Emily said faintly from the hall. "Hey baby. Where's your mom?" Omar responded as his voice grew. "I'm in here." I bellowed from behind the bathroom door. "Hey babe." he said as he peeked into the bathroom. "Hi, Honeybear." I replied softly as I massaged my arm with the oil infused bath water. "Damn. I thought this day would never end." Omar said as he stepped into the bathroom. He advanced over and sat on the edge of the bath tub. "You okay?" I asked while gingerly unfolding my washcloth. "Other than having to deal with the downpour of immaturity in that building, I'm fine." he openly divulged. "Mmmm, yeah. We gotta talk about that." I expressed as he confiscated the washcloth from my hand. "Yeah, I know. We will, later. Right now, I wanna know, how your day was?" he queried while caressing my back with the soaked cloth. "It was okay, nothing adventurous. Nothing like your day. I found ten dollars near the copy machine." I uttered as he massaged his way up to my shoulders. "You're real funny." he said in reference to my remark about his day. "Oh, and I spoke to the young lady that was in the altercation with Emily." I mentioned as he dropped the cloth into the water and began to knead his hands into my shoulders. "What did was her side of the story, sound like?" Omar asked before dipping his cupped hand into the water, to pour onto my shoulders.

I gestured for Omar to pass me the loofa behind me. He dipped it into the water, covered it with a small amount of soap and placed it into my hand. I brushed the sponge across my breasts and began to maneuver them to clean thoroughly. Omar stopped massaging and slowly moved his head into position to watch me. "You mind?" I asked as I covered my nipples with my forearm. "I was getting close so, you could tell me what the girl said." Omar joked defensively. I smiled and slowly shook my head at his charm. "I see why Toni wants a run at you." I whispered after he resumed his massage of my shoulders. "Huh?" he murmured as he pressed his thumbs into the back of my neck. "Nothing." I said knowing that he caught my comment. "Oh, ok. So, what'd the girl say happened?" he asked promptly. His way of showing me that he was pardoning and moving on from my smart remark. "In a nutshell. She and Quentin had a brief encounter and Emily apparently went to defend her big brother's *good name*." I stated in between excessive moans. My way of accepting his so-called pardon.

I pointed to the towel folded on the toilet seat. "I wonder where Em gets that barbaric way of thinking from?" he asked sarcastically as he opened the towel for me to step into. "You believe this, Chaewon?" he continued to ask as I stepped into the towel. "I don't know. She did say that he ended it, once she questioned him in regards to Imani. So, I'm under the impression that if he did that, he let her think he was available. And when he was exposed, he ran." I said as I wrapped myself in the towel. "That's exactly what he did!" Omar said harshly as he disappointedly stepped out of the room.

CHAPTER 49

"Omar"

"Babe, you down here?" Tracey asked as she seemed to float down the stairs holding her bathrobe closed. "I'm right here." I said popping up from behind the bar. "You ok? You took that information about Que kind of hard." she said as she came over to sit at the bar.

"Quentin is better than that!" I said sternly as I reached under the bar and pulled a flute from the shelf. "Omar." Tracey said quickly. "Huh?" I answered unconsciously while turning to grab the chardonnay from the small refrigerator. Tracey began to laugh as I continued to automatically cater to her. "Omar!" she said again as I filled the flute with wine. "Yes babe." I quickly responded as all of the thoughts swirling in my head came to a halt, and I seemed to snap out of my trance. "Are you going to drink that, because I can't?" she asked, rubbing her belly to remind me of her current state. "Oh, I'm sorry babe. I completely forgot for a second." I said before gulping down the glass of wine. "Is this about *just* Quentin? Or a combination of his alleged actions, and your predicament this morning?" Tracey inquired intuitively. "I've always taught that boy the qualities of man-hood, the value of his name. Not only his first, but his last name as well. When people speak his name, he wants it to be about something powerful and prideful. When people speak the name Gregory, I want it to be with admiration." I preached as I stepped from behind the bar and stood in front of Tracey.

"Omar, you're making it more than it is, baby. I mean, we're talking about horny, young adults here, nothing more." she said as she pulled me close enough to wrap her arms around my waist and bury her head in my chest.

"I wish it was nothing more." I said sorrowfully. "I need to talk to you about something. It's nothing I'd stress over. But you know my biggest flaw, is thinking everyone thinks as I do." I admitted as I sat on the stool next to her. "Yeah, no one is as *unconcerned* as you are." she said gently. "Does that honestly bother you?" I asked sincerely concerned. "I sometimes wonder if you'll ever put your true feeling out there for someone else to recognize. But I ultimately come to doubt it, that's not you. You care, just in your own little way." she said softly as she rested her hand atop mine. "Now. This *something* you have to talk to me about, will I need to call my lawyer?" she mocked as she stared into my eyes. "I hope not." I responded as I slowly averted looking in her direction. I slowly slid my hand from under her hand. She immediately grabbed my hand and pulled it back down. I compliantly let her continue to hold my hand down and awkwardly reached for my drink with my other hand. "Oh." Tracey said realizing why I was moving my hand. "Tell me your news, so can decide whether or not to give Azrael a call." she authentically insisted.

"I saw Tiffany Lane." I muttered as I gulped down my drink. Tracey gracefully removed her hand. "Quentin's mother?" she asked with a bewildered grimace upon her face. "Yeah." I uttered while rising to go refill my glass. "Details!" she hissed sternly.

"And, that was my whole night." I said at my confession's conclusion. "It's not that I didn't want to tell you, I didn't know how to yell you." I continued, cowering at her focused gaze. "According to your story, you didn't do anything. Why wouldn't you know how to tell me? Have I not been approachable to you, in the past?" she asked softly. "I wouldn't know. I've never had anything this to approach you about. Kind of felt like I cheated." I said as I gulped down my drink.

I lifted the bottle of 10yr old Copper and Kings brandy and quickly refilled my glass. "I'm a little disappointed, but I not mad." she said as she stood, clutching her bathrobe closed. She slowly moved behind me and put her hand on my shoulder. I sluggishly lifted my head turned toward her comforting hand.

"Took you a little longer, than I thought." Tracey softly conceded while she began to lightly massage my shoulder. "What are you talking about?" I bewilderedly asked as I attention towards her relaxing hand. "I already knew that you saw Tiffany. I've known since, Saturday." she openly admitted while placing her other hand on the bar, atop mine. "How'd you know?" I asked amazingly impressed by her sharp comprehension. "I took the call that you received from Progressive insurance company about the car accident, that you *two* were in. That was almost, a week ago." she divulged candidly. I slid my hand from under hers and poured another glass of brandy. "I'm sorry. I just didn't know how to tell you, without saving face." I honestly confessed as quickly gulped down the glassful. She softly kissed the back of my neck and continued to tenderly massage my shoulder to distract from her to covert pilfer of the Copper and Kings bottle. "That's enough." she mouthed as she placed it back on the shelf behind the bar. "I mean it." she said softly while stepping pass me heading towards the stairs. "I really thought there was nothing, that you could not tell me. I didn't think I made you feel like you had to save face around me. I feel slightly foolish." she sighed as she clutched her bathrobe and glided up the steps just as graceful as she had come down.

I opened the door slowly to see Tracey sitting on the bed, sensually massaging lotion onto her legs. Her exposed back and petite ass seemed to call me as I closed the door. I gradually made my way over to where she was sitting and sat down next to her. "I'm so sorry." I said with my head down. Tracey looked at me and smiled. "For what? What are you sorry for, Omar?" she asked as she pointed to my hand with the bottle of lotion. I opened my hand and she gently filled my palm with lotion. I rubbed my hands together and softly began to massage the lotion onto her shoulders and upper back.

"I really don't know what, I'm sorry for. Just have a feeling of grief, like I really did something wrong. Can't explain it." I said as I pulled into the parking garage. "Baby that's called, guilt. You kept a secret from your wife, and now you feel guilty about it." my mother advised strictly.

"Well she know, now! So, why do I still feel guilty?" I asked while aimlessly punching the keys on the keyboard. "Because you made it seem like you only told her, cause you were backed in a corner. Now you feel bad cause you think, that's what she thinks." Hassan said unsympathetically. "You said the same thing my mom said earlier, in so many words." I responded pitifully. "You spoke to ma Val? How is she? How's uhhh, Shelby?" he inquired curiously. "Wait! I didn't tell you about Shelby." I stated perplexed with how he knew. "No, ma did, like a month ago." he said nonchalantly. "How the hell do you always know everything, before I do?!" I asked a little bit upset that he has information that should be mine. "Two reasons. One, I keep in touch with people. And two, you're and asshole and everybody don't want to deal with that all the time. So, they give the information to me, to tell you, because they know I don't give a fuck about your fucked-up way of thinking." he responded ruthlessly. "Damn Haas, am I really that bad?" I inquired modestly concerned. "Yeah." he answered without a second thought.

CHAPTER 50

"Quentin"

WELCOME TO VERIZON'S VOICE MAIL MESSAGING SERVICE,
YOU HAVE 1 NEW MESSAGE AND 4 SAVED MESSAGES…
FIRST NEW MESSAGE, TODAY, 9:51AM…

"Hey Babe, just dropped your mom off. We went to breakfast after our appointments. Both appointments went good. Everybody's healthy. I'll call you when I think you're up. I'll talk to you later, I love you, bye-bye. Oh yeah, Ms. Turner, the one you had a crush on, she said hello."

I smiled at Imani's message as I normally did when she left one. KNOCK. KNOCK. KNOCK! "Come in." I ordered calmly as I continued to search through my drawers for my grey Polo sweater. "Wha'chu smiling all hard about?" Tasha said as she slowly stepped into the room with her hands full of shopping bags. "Nothing. Just thinking about something Dame said last night." I said burying my thoughts of Imani and the baby. "Must've been hilarious for you to still be laughing. What are you doing?" she asked as she tossed her bags on the bed. "Looking for my sweater." I answered crossly. "Well, can you stop long enough, to give me a kiss?" she requested as she tossed her arms around my waist. I kissed Tasha, and immediately went back to my search. She smirked at her lack of attention and hastily stepped out of the room. "Here." she said as she promptly returned with a garment on a hanger, wrapped in plastic. I caught the piece of clothing out of the air and scanned it, briefly. "I had it cleaned." she said boorishly as my eyes widened after recognizing that it was, my grey sweater. I smiled at Tasha as she sashayed over to the bags, that she threw onto the bed. "You didn't have to do that." I said modestly as I examined the sweater, humbled. I placed the sweater on the bed and began to comb through my closet for the jeans I intended to accompany it. "They're on the end, behind the black slacks." she said while inspecting the items she seized from the bags. I adhered to her suggestion and checked behind the slacks. "How'd you know what I was looking for, and where they were?" I asked as I snatched the pants off of the hanger. "Cause, I put them there." she said sternly. "I put those away just like I do all of your clothes, after I clean them or get them cleaned." she continued painfully as she resumed sorting through her bags.

"Can you pass me that?" I asked as I pointed to my sweater on the bed next to Tasha. "Here." she said as she flung my sweater to me. "I bought these, for you." she said as she pulled a pack of underwear from one of her bags. I joyfully grasped the donation from Tasha's hand, tossed it back onto the bed.

I extended my hand, requesting her to come to me. Tasha stood and reluctantly progressed toward me. "What's wrong?" I asked as I pushed my arms into my sweater. "Nothing." she mumbled as she grabbed my sweater and assisted in pulling it over my head. "For real, Tash. What's wrong?" I asked again, as I placed my hands on her waist. "You are always quick to presume that you know me, but ask the dumbest questions." she said as she continued to help me dress. She pulled my shirt collar through the neck of my sweater, fastened the next button on my shirt, and ran her hand across my shoulders. "You have no idea, do you?" she continued as she gently brushed my hands from her waist and squirmed just out of my grasp's reach. "Of what?" I inquired as I stared into her eyes, completely dumbfounded. "Of anything, Quentin. I hate this sweater. It's old and Polo is played out. But I must say, you do look good wearing it." she said making an effort to change the atmosphere. "What?! Polo ain't played out! I don't even think Polo can, play out!" I said going along with her subject change. Tasha shook her head and headed towards the door. "Knock on Juice's door and make sure he's up, please?" I requested as she disappeared from the room.

"He's not in there." Tasha said as I stepped out of my bedroom. "He's gonna make us late, my train leaves in an hour!" she continued to pace through the room. "You'll be alright. It's not like you have bags to check-in. Let's go find Rudy and get his van keys. Maybe he's seen or heard from Juice.

"Rudy!" I yelled across the vestibule from atop the steps. "Hey young'n. Heyyy Miss Tasha, I see you still breakin' hearts." Rudy said as we approached him. "Hi Rudy." Tasha giggled as she usually did when Rudy complimented her. "Sup' old head. You heard from Juice?" I asked as I greeted Rudy with a fist bump. "Yeah, he slid through here 'bout twenty, thirty minutes ago to get my keys." he said as he continued to smile at Tasha. "You see which way he headed?" I asked quickly. "Yeah, he went outside." Rudy said, pointing to the door. I ran to the door to look out to see if Rudy's van was in its usual parking spot. "There he go, right there. C'mon Tasha!" I said quickly as I opened the door. "Hey boy you tell Juice, that I know he's my sister's husband's nephew, or some shit like that. I know we family in there somewhere, but if he thinking about bringing my van back here dirty or dented, think twice." Rudy said harshly. "We'll be careful, man. Besides, we probably paid for the last car wash that thing had, anyway." I responded as I gestured for Tasha to hurry along. "I'll not repeat myself, young'n. Good day Miss Lady." he continued as he resumed his stare at Tasha's ass as she hurried out. "Jive ass kids, always want something for nothing." he mumbled as I let go of the door behind Tasha.

"Yo Juice!" I yelled as I tapped on the window of the running van. "Why the hell are you out here sleep, in his van?" I asked as I helped Tasha in and handed her, her bag. I closed the door behind Tasha and climbed into the front seat of the van. "Because I was tired, and knew y'all had a schedule. I didn't want to be the one that made her late." Juice said as he put the van in gear and checked his rear-view mirrors. "Aww, that's so sweet." Tasha said as she nestled into the plush seat.

"Damn, there goes my morning. Y'all got company." Juice said, suddenly disappointed while unenthusiastically slamming the van back into park. "What?" I inquired, quickly looking at Juice and then the rear-view mirror. "Damn." I said noticing J.T. gradually walk up the side of the van. "What's wrong?" Tasha asked just as her boyfriend approached the door.

I slowly lowered the window to speak to J.T. "What's up Juice? Hey Tasha. 'Sup Que? Where y'all headed?" he asked calmly as he peeked his head into the van to see if anyone else was inside. I looked over at Juice and noticed J.T.'s friend standing outside the driver's side of the van. "I don't want to have to fuck you up this early in the morning, man. Can't this wait, til later?" Juice questioned nonchalantly as he continued to watch J.T.'s friend pace back and forth. "This is between me and them, Juice. If you got something to do, go do it." J.T. responded sternly. I looked over at Juice and we both looked perplexedly at J.T.'s audacity. "Here, let me out, I'll just go with him. This shit is getting old." Tasha said exhausted by it all.

Tasha grabbed her bag, slid the van door open, and reluctantly trampled out with a sigh. J.T. immediately grasped Tasha's arm with one hand and slammed the van door with the other. I opened the door in an attempt to get to J.T. Tasha immediately pushed my door back closed and looked up with a fabricated smile. "No. This is needed." she whispered as she tossed her bag over her shoulder and slowly walked away adhering to J.T.'s lead.

"Her train comes in an hour. She better make it!" I yelled out the window to J.T. as he led Tasha to his car.

"What the fuck just happened?" I asked Juice as he sat quietly in bewilderment. "Karma, man. Karma." he said solemnly as he turned the van off. I opened the door and stepped out the van as J.T.'s car pulled off with he and Tasha in it. I walked around the van to Juice and we quietly walked back into the building. "I'm glad y'all didn't get into nothin' out there, young'n. Especially in my van." Rudy said as he snatched the key from Juice's hand. "Y'all young'ns need to stop all that foolishness over that girl. She ain't goin' be nuttin but trouble, til she figure it out." Rudy continued as Juice and I started up the stairs. I took Rudy's advice to heart as I climbed the stairs.

"I don't know why I paid for her ticket home! We go on break in two weeks. Whatever she had to do, couldn't wait until then?" I mumbled as I opened the refrigerator. "Apparently not. But you did your job, as her man." Juice said as he fell onto the couch. "Her man?! She left with her man!" I said defensively. "C'mon man, are you really that dense? Cause I don't remember you having had, that many concussions." he asked sternly as he searched the couch for the remote. "Tash and I are just having a good time." I reiterated to Juice as I tore open a container of grapes. "Yeah ok, Mr. Good Time. Well, just so you know she got out the van to finally hip J.T., to what's really going on." he made known as he smiled after locating the remote. He signaled for me to give him some of my grapes. "How you know what she went to do?" I asked handing him the grapes. "Cause, I've pissed off enough women to know when they're fed up." he said before sloppily smashing a handful of grapes into his mouth.

"You think she told him?" I asked intrigued by his revelation. "I think she went to confirm it. He already knew, hell e'rybody knows. I just hope she don't fuck up, what we have." he said while tossing grapes in the air and capturing them between his teeth. "Wha'chu mean we?" I said catching Juice's mockery. "I got dogs in this fight too, nigga. I ain't gonna lie and say that I don't like coming home, to a clean apartment. I like, not doing laundry. And I love, not shopping. But most of all, I like the peace she brings. You not all over the place, now that she's around." he said as he gestured for more grapes. "That's a little much, Juice. You really think she does all of that?" I asked tossing him the container of grapes. "Nigga, when's the last time you washed your own drawers. Cause I know I haven't washed my clothes in at a month and a half. Yet they're always magically cleaned, and left folded on my bed. Yes, I do think she does it's that much.

Que, she's trying to show you that she's more than just some ass on the side." he said continuing to toss grapes into his mouth.

"Alright whatever Juice, I'm going to steal some more sleep before practice." I said as I treaded towards my room. "Yo. These grapes, are good as shit. Where you get 'em from?" Juice sarcastically asked before I closed my room door behind me. I quickly re-opened the door after realizing that Juice's final comments expected an answer. "Tah... point taken!" I yelled as I slammed my door closed again.

CHAPTER 51

"Tracey"

"What would you say, if I asked you to invite Tiffany Lane to have Thanksgiving dinner with us?" I asked slowly brushing my hair. "Huh?" Omar uttered peeking up from his tablet. "Quentin's mother. We should invite her over for the holiday." I echoed casually. "That's what I thought you said." Omar stated as he calmly disregarded my suggestion and submerged back into his reading. "I'm serious. I see no reason, why not." I continued to recommend as I placed the hair brush on the vanity and advanced towards the bed. Omar shook his head, turned off his tablet and placed it on the nightstand. "Do you really want me to acknowledge this suggestion?" he asked dumbfounded. "Yes, I want to know what you think about it?" I asked as I slid into bed next to him.

"I think you're losing your fucking mind. Why the hell would we invite her over here for dinner? What sense does that make?" Omar peculiarly inquired. "How would you feel if your life's situation, took Quentin away from you?" I sincerely asked my husband as I laid down on the bed next to him. "That's where the misconception seems to dwell. No one, or nothing *took* Quentin away from that woman. She gave him up willing, and never once looked back!" he said as he leisurely removed his glasses from his face. "Never looked back? From what you've told me, she's never stopped looking back. I can't help but think about how woeful her life must've been, without her child." I said as I nestled up against his shoulder. "I was in the middle of my junior year of high school, when she handed Quentin to me. I was very, very young, I had plans and I was completely unprepared to be a father. But, I did it! I persevered for the son, I created. And, I did it with Theodore and Valerie on my back, every minute of every day! I gave up *my* plans, for *her* son. I gave up being a kid, for her son. So, I really don't give a shit about how depressing her life was... is." he said intensely. "So, that's a *no* to inviting her?" I asked again to let him know I was just as adamant about this, as he was. "Yes, that's a no!" he said as he reached to pick up his drink from the nightstand. I lightly smiled awaiting his next suggestion.

"I'll tell you what, ask my mom if she'd mind her here for the holiday. If she says yes, I'll consider it." he said confidently as he sipped his tea.

"I planned to. I plan to ask Quentin as well. I mean, he does have the main say in this affair." I said gently as not to agitate him again. Omar chuckled, gulped the last of his tea and turned off his lamp.

"Uhh, what are you doing?" I asked faintly as Omar began softly kissing on my neck. "I'm about to see if you can get pregnant… again." he said charmingly as he continued on his present course. "I don't think that it works that way. But it's worth a try." I breathed as he began to slowly work his way up to my ear. He soothingly coursed his hand through my hair, while his lips searched across my face and neck. "C'mere." he said as he usually did to lure me to ascend onto him. I smirked while bestowing him my hand to escort me atop of him.

I brushed my hair from my face and gradually lowered, to kiss him. "I love this man, so much." I thought to myself while continually pecking him lightly throughout his face. After momentarily teasing I deferred to him, and celebrated the bliss of his embrace.

3-0-2-5-5-5-8-9-7-5. "Good morning Q-tee!" I said enthusiastically. "Good morning Ma." he said in his raspy, morning voice. "I'm sorry baby. I thought you'd be up by now." I said honestly. "It's okay. What's up?" he said as his voice began to clear. "I want to talk to you about, Tiffany Lane." I proceeded gingerly. "What about her? Haven't talked to her since that one time. Dad told me not to, said he'd handle it." he said now fully awake and alert. I laughed at Quentin's failed attempt to mislead me. "C'mon Que, you've spent your whole life looking for times and opportunities where it'd be understandable, for you to overlook your dad's opinion. And this, is one of those times." I reminded, trying to stimulate his need to transcend his father. "Why haven't you talked to her *really*?" I continued to ask smiling mischievously. "Don't know. She's tried to call, since I last spoke to her. I just had no urge to answer. For what?" he carelessly explained. "You really are your father's child. You're not in the least bit curious about… anything?!" I asked, puzzled why I was the only inquisitive one in all of this. "No, not really." he said apathetically. "You never wondered what she looks like? If you have any siblings? Aunts, uncles… cousins?" I asked genuinely. "Never thought about it. Can't miss what you never had. Besides, I already know what my mom looks like. And, I know I have one uncle, two aunts and three cousins." he confessed absolutely. "Why, this sudden fascination with *the biological*?" he maintained probingly.

"I wanted your consent to inviting her, to Thanksgiving dinner." I answered nervously as I stood to go into the bathroom. "Why?" he asked as bewildered by my rationale as his father was. "At first… it was to see where the little boy that I fell love with and claimed for myself, actually came from. But now it's just as much that, as it is to prove Mr. Know-It-All wrong. He needs to learn, that everyone doesn't always think the way he does." I whispered as I closed the bathroom door behind me. "I take it Mr. Know-It-All, is home with you?" he asked laughing at my whispered confession. "Yeah, he's still asleep. Expecting him to wake up any minute now, since he does have to work today." I stated quietly. "Oh ok. Well then, I'll call him later. And as far as dinner, let me think about it, ma. Proving my dad wrong really helped your argument, though." he said cynically. "I'm sure it does." I said laughing at my son's mischief. "Okay baby, you go ahead back to sleep. I'm going to start getting ready for work." I said sincerely as I began my morning bathroom routine. "I'm up now ma, but you go ahead and get your day started. I'm about to do the same." Quentin said calmly. "Alright baby. I love you Q-tee." I said sincerely as I began to lather my face.

CHAPTER 52

"Tasha"

"I love you too." Que said softly as I stepped into the room. He ended the call and pushed the phone under the pillow next to him. I took off my jacket, hung it on the back of the door, and began to position the items in my bag neatly onto his dresser.

Quentin looked exhausted as he laid his head back down onto his pillow "Good morning, babe." he said faintly as I slowly lowered to sit next to him. "Good morning, baby." I said leaning in to kiss his cheek. "Who you could you possibly love, at six, thirty-sixteen in the morning?" I asked starting to massage his shoulders. "Never mind. I don't wanna know, not sure my heart can take it." I sincerely proclaimed. He reached under his pillow for his phone. "Here." he uttered handing me his phone. I took his phone and pushed it back under his pillow. "It was, my mom." he said quietly. "I said, I didn't want to know." I reiterated while continuing to massage. "Wait! You talked to your mom?!" I continued enthusiastically after gathering his response. "Yeah. Why wouldn't I talk to her?" he asked inquisitively. I smiled, relieved that they were continuing to speak oblivious to my knowledge. "I didn't know that you kept in touch with her, that's all. I'm glad that wasn't just a one and done experience, on your birthday." I replied cheerfully. "Huh?" he uttered as he sat up looking perplexed.

He smiled as his look of confusion, cleared from his face. "Ohhh, you thought I was talking about my biological." he said in a dismissed revelation. "No babe, I don't speak to her, at all." he continued casually. "Oh. I thought that you decided to give her a chance." I revealed solemnly. "You sound like my step-mom. Can you believe, she wants to invite her to Thanksgiving dinner?" he asked still dumbfounded by even the suggestion. "I actually like that idea. Damn. Ya step-mother, is a boss! It don't get no more secure, than that." I said amazed by the news. "You would, like that idea. Forever the Saint." he said as he rose up to kiss me. "Believe me, I'm no Saint. I just really believe in love and family. I don't think there's anything more important, than the power of those two influences." I said sincerely. "No, a Saint you are not. You are way too much of a freak to be that." he said as he bounced up, smiling. "Whatever boy!" I said animated, attempting to hit him as he fled.

I rolled over onto my stomach and laid there, staring at him. "Now that I got'chu flappin' ya gums, I got a question for you. Why'd you go home, two weekends before break? What was so major, that it couldn't wait? I wasn't going to ask, but I been thinking about it. And since I paid for the train, I figured fuck it." he asked obnoxiously while putting on his football warm-ups. "It's about time. I've been waiting all week for you to ask me that. That, and what happened when I got into J.T.'s car." I pompously replied as I continued to watch him get ready for practice.

"Well, I already have an idea of what happened in J.T. car. The whole campus know that you broke it off with him. They also think that you did it, to be with me. I know he didn't hit you, cause you didn't come back with any bruises. Besides, he's not dumb enough to do that. I also know he took it hard, because he played like shit last week. And then he almost got his ass handed to him, when he came at coach wrong during practice. I also know that you made your train, because I had Juice look into that for me." he said sitting on the bed to put on his sneakers. "So... that's why Dee called me, while I was on the train!" I said laughing at his guile. "Yeah, I guess. So, are you gonna tell me, or what? You in some kinda trouble? Family emergency?" he asked casually while lacing his shoes. "Both, and neither." I honestly admitted after sitting up from my laying position. Quentin smirked and then shook his head in disappointment when he didn't receive the information that he anticipated. "With all my heart, I promise I will tell you when the time's right. Right now, just know that I'm yours and I love you." I revealed standing up to disrobe. Quentin smirked again before kissing me on the forehead. "Okay." he said as he grabbed his coat and headed out the door. "That's all I get?" I mumbled as I kicked my pants and panties from around my ankles.

RING. RING!

> **Grandma T**
> **215-555-9711**

"Hey." I said trying to sound as enthusiastic as I possibly could in a raspy voice. "I am sorry, Honey. Did I wake you?" she asked softly. "Yeah, but I shouldn't have slept this long. I have psych class in 30 minutes. So, thank you." I pleasantly assured. "Your welcome, glad I can help. I was just calling to make sure you're okay, and that you have everything you need." she said with kindhearted concern. "I do, and thank you. But you don't have to do all of that, I'll be fine." I said earnestly as I rose to dress for class. "I'm sure you will. Just always remember, I'm here. Tasha, you have no idea how much I appreciate you including me in this." she said with genuine gratitude. I smiled at how appreciative she was. It made me feel good knowing that I could make someone else, feel this good. "Yes, I do Ms. Blackwell. You haven't stopped telling me, since I saw you. I promise this will be a joy we'll all share." I comforted as I slid into my boots. "Ok dear, well I hear you getting ready for class. so, I won't continue to bother you." she said softly. "You're no bother Ms. Blackwell. But I do have to get going. I'll call you later?" I requested while staring down at the clock on the phone screen. I grabbed my coat from aback the chair and dashed out of the room. "Yes, I'd like that." she said softly. "Then that's what I'll do. Bye-bye, Ms. Blackwell." I said looking up at Juice in the refrigerator pouring himself something dark and carbonated to drink. "Bye-bye Tasha." she said before ending the call. "Ms. Blackwell? That wasn't...?" Juice asked meddlesomely. "No Juice. Bye Juice. See you later Juice." I responded quickly as I grabbed the beverage from his hand before he could drink any, and scurried out the door with it.

CHAPTER 53

"Quentin"

"C'mere." Tasha insisted tugging on the waist of my shorts. I reluctantly adhered to Tasha's directives and allowed her to pull me in her direction. "You're just not going to let me finish packing, are you?" I said as Tasha pulled me up against her. She shook her head, threw her hands around my waist, and gave a slight pinch to my butt. "What are you doing?" I asked peculiarly. "Don't act like you don't like it. You do it to me, all the time." she chuckled. With her leaning against the dresser, I had no freedom to do it back. She smiled watching me look for an opening to get my hands onto her ass. "Here." she whispered, marginally lifting from the dresser. I took advantage of her assistance and placed my hands where we both wanted them. "I do it to you because you like it." I said as she redirected her hand's embrace to the back of my neck and leaned back, wedging my hands between the dresser and her ass. I looked down at Tasha as she was looking up at me with doe eyes. "I love it." she said as she slowly drew me in for a kiss.

"This is not helping me pack! You said you were going to help me pack. Just like, I helped you pack yesterday." I said pilfering an intermission in her kissing. "I know. It's just not easy to watch, let alone help, you pack. Packing, means you're leaving. And leaving means, going home. And we both know, what home is. Who, home is." Tasha said solemnly as she released her hold of me and slightly lifted from the dresser so I could slide my hands behind her. "I don't know what you want me to do, Tasha. I can't leave now, even if I wanted to. She's carrying my baby." I said earnestly as I turned to continue packing. "So, you honestly promise me that we can revisit this conversation, once the baby's born?" Tasha asked hopefully. "Yes. I can promise that, without a second thought. I probably think about it, more than you do." I said to ease Tasha's concerns. Tasha grinned, shook her head, and then began to collect the things from atop my dresser. I reached into the closet, looking for a shoebox that felt too light to have anything in it. I found an empty Timberland box and pulled it from the collection. "Here, put that stuff in here." I said tossing her the empty box. Tasha laughed and continued to gather my hygienic necessities. "You want this green cologne in here with the bra and thongs too?" Tasha said still snickering. "Bra and thongs? What the hell you talkin' bout?" I said turning to see what Tasha was referring to. "I was asking which cologne you wanted in the box with my panties and bra?" Tasha grinned holding the Timberland box I passed her. "You know you can't go home, with panties like this. How you gonna explain, the ass these belong to?" she smirked, pulling a pair of her underwear out of the box. "What the hell?" I asked amazed at her revelation. "You the one that threw me the box without looking in it. I told you I claimed some of them boxes. Since I don't have a drawer and had to keep it outta sight, I had to improvise." she said condescendingly. "Can you take your clothes outta that box for now, please?" I pleaded earnestly while continuing to lob clothes into my duffle bag. "Ok. I'll just dump it into a drawer for now. But I want my box back!" Tasha said with a smile as she stuffed her panties into my underwear drawer.

I waved from my window down to Imani as she looked up from the passenger seat of my father's truck. She waved back enthusiastically, opened the door, and eagerly slid out of the truck. I saw her mouth something to my father before he too looked up towards my room window. My father gave me a soldier's salute before leading Imani into the building. I turned and grabbed the bags and boxes that I'd packed with Tasha earlier. I quickly surveyed the room to make sure no evidence of Tasha's existence was anywhere on display. "Mr. G!" Juice said aloud as he opened the door for my father. "Good afternoon, Juice." I could faintly hear my father say from the other room. "Hey Juice! Hey Juice! Hey Juice!" Imani rhythmically chanted as she danced into the room behind my father. "Hey Mani! Hey Mani!" Juice recited attempting to catch Imani's rhythmic timing. I opened my bedroom to Imani just releasing her embrace of Juice. "There go my baby!" Imani shouted as she tore in my direction in an almost sprint. I quickly released all I was holding as Imani intensely leaped into the air towards me. She landed into my arms with a crash, causing me to fall backward. "What are you doing?!" I said sternly after we slammed down onto the bed. "I missed you so much." she uttered sandwiched by peck kisses on my face and neck. I harshly pulled away from her and stood, before helping her up off of the bed. "C'mon! You can't do, shit like this! It ain't good for the baby. Fuck around and come out retarded, or something!" I said rushing to escort her up off of the sheets that I was on with Tasha, just 3 hours before. "I do more than this exercising every morning. I'm fine. I promise. The doctor's words, not mine." she comforted as I checked her up and down and brushed her clothing straight. "You're my heart, carrying my soul. You can't do stuff like that. At least not in front of me." I pleaded while she stared at me in awe.

I stood there, staring at Imani gaze at me with a tiny sparkle in her eye. She always had a way of making me feel like I'm extraordinary. There was something about that sparkle that made me feel like a God amongst men. "God, I missed you." she said as she slowly advanced to kiss me. "I missed you, too." I whispered just as her soft lips parted mine.

"C'mon. Y'all got eight whole days to do this. I wanna get back before the game." my father said as he picked up some of the bags I'd dropped in the doorway when Imani barged in. I reluctantly pulled myself away from Imani, to greet my father. "Hey pop." I said as I approached to embrace my dad. "Hey Que." he responded calmly as he pats my back, during our half hug. I picked up the rest of the bags and followed my father out of the bedroom. "Grab that Timberland box for me." I lobbied to Juice as I passed him. "I'll get it." Imani announced as she followed me, following my father. "No, no, no! He can get it!" I declared quickly turning back to protect the box from Imani's grasp. "Here babe. I need you to get our food out of the fridge." I continued, swiftly escorting Imani to the kitchen.

I observed Imani watch me point the box out to Juice, with a look of serious curiosity. "Just this bag?" she asked with a suspicious demeanor while she pretended to bury her face into the refrigerator. "And the case of water." I said timidly as I redirected behind my father. "A case of water? She can't carry that! Give her the box and let Juice carry that!" my father intervened unsuspectingly. "It's ok paw-paw. It's only a six pack of water. Quentin wouldn't do anything to purposely hurt me, he loves me too much." Imani softly responded trying to protect me from anyone's ill thoughts. I looked back at Imani with a smile, and then at Juice who was wildly flipping the box in the air behind me. "Yeah, let's switch." Juice said adhering to my father's demands in an attempt to appease everyone. I turned to look at Juice with a subtle, disappointing shake of my head. He extended the box out towards Imani, and she collected it with a big smile. Juice turned to look at me, placed his hand on his neck as if choking himself, and subtly scratched his neck with his thumb. I smiled knowing all was well and continued to follow my dad's lead without worry.

"So, Mr. Hiller, when are you leaving?" my father asked Juice as we passed him the bags to arrange in the back seat of the truck. "My sister sent me a plane ticket, for Monday morning." Juice uttered half-heartedly. "I take it, you don't want to go?" my dad asked observing Juice's tone. "Don't get me wrong Mr. G, it's not my family. It's that down South, small, town shit. Ohhh, my bad Mr. G!" Juice quickly atoned. "It's alright, Juice. I told you, you could've come home with us." my dad reminded while laughing as he inspected the other side of the back seat to reassure that Imani had more than enough room. "And I told you, you should have! You a city boy, now. And Dover ain't Pittsburgh, but it's faster than Sweetwater." I added on my father's coat tail. "I can't tell my family *no*, not on Thanksgiving. But thanks anyway." Juice replied. "Besides, the Thanksgiving Dinner conversation at your house, is gonna be a *real barn-burner.* Not sure if I'd want to be there for that." Juice said sarcastically animated. "Yeah me either." my dad mumbled. "You're from a town called, *Sweetwater?*" Imani asked as she waited on the other side of the truck for confirmation to get in. "Yup. Sweetwater, Tennessee. I thought you knew that." Juice said as he leaned on the side of the truck's bed to see and hear Imani clearly. "No. I did know you was from Tennessee, though. I always wondered why you didn't have that strong accent." Imani uttered softly. "I chucked that accent long time ago. I think it was before they were even calling me, Juice." he said proudly. "C'mon. Don't hate on Sweetwater." I laughed walking around to escort Imani into the truck.

"How did you get the name, Juice." Imani asked curiously while trying as slow as possible to get into the car so she could hear Juice's anecdote. "I hope this ain't a long story, cause we gotta go. Remember the game. The game!" my dad interrupted as he tapped his finger on his watch. Juice walked around the truck to greet us and finish his story. "I went to do my last two years of high school in Pittsburgh, with my dad. And when I got there, it was already two other Barry's at the school. To not confuse us, they started calling me Barry Sweetwater. Then that became, just Sweetwater. Then some broad who didn't like me said that my name was stupid, and sweet water, was nothing but juice. It stuck." Juice said quickly. "How was that Mr. G? Fast enough?" Juice said to my father who was coming around the truck to where we were. "That, that was certainly brief, Juice. Uninteresting, but to the point." my dad chuckled as he opened the passenger door. I laughed at my dad's critique of Juice's story. "You're driving." my dad demanded as he pulled himself into the truck and slammed the door. I nodded my head at my father and then made my way to the driver's side of the truck. "See you later Mr. G." Juice said as he extended his hand into the passenger window for my father to shake. "I sure hope so, Juice." my dad responded, grasping Juice's hand. I stood outside the driver's side door waiting for Juice to make his way around the truck. I glanced at Imani, who as staring back at me, gleaming with pride. "Til the next time, Barry." I said sincerely as I turned, noticing Juice's approach. "Til the next time, little brother." he responded genuinely, extending his hand for me to clutch.

"Bye Juice." Imani sang melodiously as we began to pull out of the parking spot. "Bye Imani." Juice responded melodiously. "And Juice…" my father meddled suddenly. "Yes sir?" Juice answered courteously. "The next time I see you, have a better backstory as to why they call you Juice. Sometimes the truth, just isn't captivating." my father recommended sarcastically. "Yes sir!" Juice chuckled as he turned towards the building

CHAPTER 54

"Omar"

"Hey baby!" Quentin yelled, startling me. "What the hell are you hollering about?" I asked, sitting up quickly. "Her right there! Look at her, she is so beautiful." Quentin whispered as we slowly traveled down our street. "Who?" I asked sharply as I gathered myself. "His car." Imani answered, as Quentin continued to be dumbfounded. "His face lit up, as soon as we turned the corner." she continued to explain. "Are you serious?" It's a damn car. You woke me up, for a car. A car I see, every day?!" I said slightly rubbed up the wrong way as with reason to why I was awakened.

"I must admit, I forgot how nice it is to be chauffeured." I said as we slowly pulled into the driveway. "How would you know how nice it was? You was asleep, the whole ride." Imani asked sarcastically. "I know! But we made it home before the game start and I got a nap in, don't get any nicer than that." I responded equally sarcastic. Quentin quickly turned off the engine and jumped out of the truck. He ran around to the other side of the truck to his car, parked parallel to us in the driveway. "God, I missed you. You miss me?" he asked before embracing his car with a big hug. "Boy, stop being extra and get out the way so I can get out." I insisted to Quentin, who was standing between my truck and his car, blocking my ability to open the door. He relocated his hold of his car just enough for me to get out of the truck. I opened the door for Imani, who was staring at Quentin in bewilderment. She quickly grabbed the box she was carrying and slid out the truck. "When you done molesting your car, get the rest of your stuff out my truck. I'm going to watch the game." I demanded as I grabbed a duffle bag and headed for the house. "Thanks for coming to get me, dad." Quentin said sincerely as he lifted up from his car. "That's my job, son. Just wait, your time's coming." I responded grinning cynically.

"Hey dad. You alright?" Quentin said as I opened the door and stepped into the kitchen. "Hey Quentin. Yeah, I'm fine. Those damn Sixers need help, but I'm fine. Come to get some ice. Tracey get home yet?" I asked as I stood at the refrigerator door, filling my ice bucket. "Nope." he said waiting for the microwave to stop. "So, what was you hiding from that young lady earlier? I saw Juice checking out that box of yours, pretending to toss it around." I inquired consciously. Quentin looked up at me bewildered and then smirked, seemingly impressed by my spot of his misleading endeavor. "What you talking about?" Quentin grinned pretending to be as naïve as he thought I was. "So that's the answer you're going to give me?" I asked, hinting a reminder of how sharp I was. "It was nothing dad. Just a gift for her and the baby, that I didn't want her to see yet, that's all." he said as he pulled his plate from the microwave. "Oh ok. I understand that, I guess." I said calmly as I snatched one of the nuggets from his plate. "Let me know when your mom gets here. I'm hungry and I'm down here filling up, on chips and dip." I said as I jammed the nugget into my mouth. "Dad, you really don't feel any way about my biological coming here?" he asked as he sat down at the island to eat. "Of course, I do. But you're going to learn something, that only few men know. Your opinion, really doesn't matter. As man's man, you're not expected to even have feelings. So why would anyone ever consider them. But good woman, will always make you feel like a king, and make you believe you had the final say so. Even though whatever decision was made, was made way before you were brought into it. Your biological was coming here, no matter how I feel about it." I said as headed towards my den. "So, what do I do? How am I supposed to act?" he asked sincerely. "Do what you do best, son. You, act like… you. And we'll just try and figure out the rest, together. Deal?" I said as I grasped the door knob. He nodded his head slowly in agreement. "Deal, pop." he uttered as he chomped on his chicken nuggets. I smiled proudly at my son before pulling on the door knob. "Oh, and don't forget to ask your mom for some money to go buy that gift for Imani and the baby, that you just lied about." I said as I headed down the stairs.

Chapter 55

"Emily"

"Somebody better tell'em, he don't want it this week, my brother home!" I responded as we pulled into the garage. "Who are you using Quentin's name to threaten, now?" my mom asked as she shut off the car engine. "I'll call you back. My mom's about to start up again." I said despairingly as I opened the car door. "We're trying to send Que back to school, and then to the pros. If that's what he still wants. Not to prison!" she said sternly as she got out of the car. I walked around the car and waited as she reached into the backseat for the bags. "You hear me, Emily?!" she continued sternly as I hadn't responded to her previous comment. "Yes mom, dag!" a voice squealed faintly. I quickly did a moderate glance with the hopes that it was my imagination. "Good." my mom said as she handed me some of the bags. "So, you did hear that?" I asked frightfully. "Hear what?" my mother responded obliviously. "Mom, I didn't answer you." I said as I waited for her to grab the remainder of the bags. "What're you talking about?" my mom said as she closed the car door. "Mom if you heard that *yes mom dag*, that wasn't me." I said as I slowly reached in my pocket for my basement door key. "Girl, that's your imagination. There's no one in here with us. You probably hear your father yelling at the tv. I'm sure that he's in his man cave watching the basketball game. Now reach over and hit the switch to close the garage door." she directed calmly. "I don't know why dad would be yelling *yes mom dag*, to a basketball game. But I'm telling you now, if something happens, I hope you can run with that baby." I said honestly as the garage door slowly closed. "You'd leave your pregnant mother?" she asked dumbfounded by my comment. "Don't worry mom I got you!" Que said jumping out from aside the car. "Daddy!" I screamed, dropping the bags as I partially fell back. "Omar!" my mother shrieked as she hysterically pulled on the door knob.

Quentin quickly leapt over the front of the car to pacify me as I was trying to stand and come to terms with what was happening. "I'm sorry Em. I didn't know you was going to freak out like that." Quentin said

254

riotously laughing as he pretended to comfort me. "What the hell are y'all doing in here?" my dad yelled as he snatched the door open. "Oh my God, dad. Quentin almost scared us to death." I cried out as Quentin and I collected the dropped bags from the floor. "He almost scared *you* to death. I knew he was there." my mother said self-assuredly as she handed her bags to my father. "Hi honey." she continued as she reached up to kiss him. "Yeah whatever mom. You was screaming, too." I said as I began to find it all funny as well. "Y'all play entirely too much!" my dad said as he turned to get back to his game. "My Qu-tee!" my mom shrieked as she enthusiastically turned to squeeze Que. "Hey ma." he responded as he snuggled into my mother's hold. "Sup Em." Quentin said as I pushed pass the two of them to follow my father into the house.

"For a second, I thought you was going to give me up." Quentin said to my mother as they finally entered the den from the basement. I handed my bags to Quentin as he passed, heading for the stairs. "Not this time, your sister deserved that one." my mother chuckled. "Baby, dinner in ten." she continued as she followed Quentin up the stairs. I continued to sit on the arm of the chair next to my father as he watched the game. "It's okay babe. He'll be here for a whole week and, payback is a bitch." my dad comforted as he laid his head back on my arm, which I had behind his neck.

"It's been longer than ten minutes, hasn't it?" my dad bleakly uttered. "I'll go check." I said sincerely to my father. "I don't know mom. I'm trying to see all of the wonder and beauty that y'all talking about. All I keep thinking about, is fear and worry. I mean, I don't know how to be a father." Quentin stated as I entered the kitchen. "No one does. No matter how many children you have." she said genuinely as she scooped Chinese food from its container onto a plate. "Let me guess, it's been longer than ten minutes, and he's hungry?" she continued now looking in my direction. "Yeah." I said with a smile as she always seemed to know my father's thoughts and actions. "Omee, come and eat!" she yelled as she placed a large plate of food on the table.

"You should've seen your face Storm. Damn, I wish I had my phone on me." Que bragged as he stood in mom and dad's bedroom doorway waiting. I stuck my head out of the bathroom to catch mom's reaction to Quentin's use of foul language. "You didn't hear that?!" I asked my mom sternly when she showed no reaction to it at all. "Huh? No, what'd I miss?" my mother asked while sitting on her bed, daydreaming and rubbing her belly. I looked over at Quentin who was smiling after he realized that he messed up, but got away with it. "Nevermind." I said stepping back into the bathroom to continue grooming. "Storm, c'mon. We only going to the garage, and I'm not trying to be out all night." Quentin complained as he came into the room and sat on the bed at mom's feet. "You know your sister, she has to make it so that she is noticed, no matter where she is." I heard my mom attempt to whisper. "Mom, you really knew he was in garage with us?" I asked as I stepped out of the bathroom. Both she and Quentin began to smirk about it again. "Yeah baby. Quentin and I caught eyes while he was crawling on the floor, and I was getting the bags from the backseat." she said trying to dismiss my feeling of irrationality.

"Alright, I'm ready." I stated as I flaunted my way out of the bedroom. "Alright ma. We'll see you in the morning." Quentin said as he jumped up from the bed. "Ok. You two take care of each other. And that doesn't mean get into trouble, Emily." my mom said firmly. I smirked at my mom's skepticism of me. "Goodnight, mom." I said as I began to follow Quentin, who was already out of the room. "Good night, you guys." she said softly before blowing me a kiss. "Oh. Someone please wake your father and send him up here, before he claims that we left him down there on purpose." my mom yelled as we headed down the stairs.

Mani
302-555-2112

"Hey, we about to pull up now." I said as we turned onto Imani's street. "I was looking for your brother. But since you said *we*, that means he's with you. Why y'all coming here? Should I be throwing something on?" she said securely. "Nah, he bringing you, your dinner." I answered perplexed. "I love that man." Imani whispered proudly. "She didn't know we was coming?" I peculiarly asked Quentin. "No. I just figured she'd be hungry. Ask her what's wrong. She was looking for me, for a reason." Que demanded as he parked the car. "Que said, What's wrong?" I asked anxiously into the phone. "Nothing. I just haven't heard from him since earlier, and we're hungry." she declared softly. "What is it?" Que asked reluctantly. "Nothin'. She missed you." I responded reassuring. "Tell her, I'm outside." Que continued to demand as he exited the car. DOINK! "He's at your door, now. So, I'll talk to you tomorrow." I said quickly, anxious to get to my incoming text message. "Alright girl." she said before ending the call.

> **{London}**
> **U won't guess who's at the garage...**

"London and her games," I mumbled to myself as I sat in the car waiting for Que to return.

> **{Me}**
> **Who?**

I carelessly responded, while pairing his radio to my phone's Bluetooth.

DOINK!

> **{London}**
> **That bitch Chaewon from Newark**

"Oh shit!" I whispered with a big smile.

> **{Me}**
> **Im done wit that bitch. I said what I had to say**

I retorted looking up to see if Quentin was coming out yet.

> **{Me}**
> **Now if she got sumtin to say or want sum mor work thats dif**

I turned up the radio and enthusiastically began to do my best Kendrick Lamar impression. "I got millions. I got riches buildin'... in my DNA!" I shouted excitedly with the music.

DOINK!

"I know you ain't have me out here waitin' while you was in there, gettin' some!" I said aloud as Quentin got back into the car. "Wha'chu talkin' bout?!" he responded while turning down the radio. "You was in there, forever!" I said discouraged that I may have lost the chance to see Chaewon again. "I was in there for eleven minutes. We counted! And for your information, I was in there talking to her mom and watching her perform to this loud ass music you was out here playing." he said pompously. With a scowl on my face, I picked up my phone which fell to the floor during my performance.

{London}
Where u at?!

"Now where we going" I asked sarcastically. "To the garage! Why?" he asked, ignorant to the situation at hand. "Just wonderin' if you was gonna leave me in the car, again?" I smirked sarcastically as we sped onto North State street.

{Me}
omw!

"I might as well tell you, you about to find out anyway." I said to Que as he got back into the car. "What?" he answered handing me the pack of gum that he just purchased. "Chaewon Hargrove is back there." I said twisting open the gum package. "How you know? Let me guess London texted you while I was in the gas station?" he said smiling at my fake reconnaissance. "No, while you was at Imani's." I said sternly defending my street savvy. "Oh. But yeah, I know she here." he said pointing to the group of people walking out of the gas station towards the back of the building. I threw a piece of gum into my mouth as we rode the rocky, gravel driveway, looking for a place to park.

"So. wha'chu wanna do?" I asked in regards to his intent to handling Chaewon. "Stay outta trouble, like mom said." he said certainly as he exited the car. "Huh? That ain't you. What, you getting old?" I asked seriously as I followed him toward the garage entrance. "No! I'm getting, to the league. And one dumb nigga with a phone and Facebook, can change all that. So, I'm cool on that one." he answered as we approached the door. "And, so are you!" he commanded harshly as he banged on the door. "I hear you. But if it's self-defense?" I asked cynically as the door swung open. "If you prove self-defense, hey you had to do what you had to do." he smirked as I stepped in behind. I immediately scanned the entire room looking for London. "Alright then, Que." I said as I started off to walk the room. "Alright then." he said as he headed towards the crowd of people shouting his name.

CHAPTER 56

"Quentin"

"Quentin!" my dad shouted from the bottom of the stairs. I opened my bedroom door and gradually made my way to the top of the staircase. "I need you to help me with this table leaf." he continued calmly. "Alright, here I come." I said before heading back to my room to retrieve my shoes. DOINK!

"So dramatic." I uttered to myself before texting back.

"Thanks." my dad said as I climbed from under the table. "Your welcome." I said as I stood to my feet and brushed myself off. "You plan on staying in your room, texting all day? You know your girl will be here soon." my dad said with a cynical smirk. I grinned at my dad and headed up the stairs. "Always think he know everything." I mumbled to myself as I reached the top of the stairs. I trudged backed into my room, thinking about my dad and his thoughts. "Always think he know everything." I continued to think as I rummaged through my bag for something to wear, for the day. "How does he always know everything?" I complained aloud as I snatched my purple sweater from my bag.

"You got some black dress pants hanging in your closet, that would nice with that." my father uttered as he stuck his head into the door. I continued to display the sweater in the air, contemplating what to wear with it. "I got the grey jeans that I usually wear with it in my bag." I said insistently as I put the sweater down to dig for the jeans. "Ok. That sounds nice." my dad said as he stepped into the room. I found the jeans and placed them on the bed. My dad slowly crossed the room and sat down next to the jeans. I grabbed the sweater and precisely positioned it atop the jeans to imitate how it would look. My dad smiled and tipped his head in approval. "I know that all this is a little, extraordinary. Just came up to find out, how you're doing?" he asked delicately. "I'm ok. I'm hungry. Can't wait to eat. That's about it." I said as I uncaringly shrugged my shoulder. "Ok. I just needed to be sure that you knew how to handle, what's going on in your head? I see that you found a way." he proclaimed now wringing his hands, with his head down. He slowly stood, gave me a smile and headed for the door. "You're a stronger man than me, Quentin." he sighed as he pulled the open to leave.

"How do you always know everything?" I asked before he could step out of the room. "I don't. I wish I did, though. Maybe then, I wouldn't make so many mistakes." he said as he stopped his stride through the door. "Some mistakes, are subject to interpretation. I mean, I was a mistake and I turned out pretty good." I comforted as he continued to hold the door. "Pretty good? I thought you were sharper than that." he said peculiarly as he quickly pushed the door closed. "Don't ever in your life refer to my son, as *pretty good*, you understand?!" he said harshly as he moved in close to me. I took a step back, bowled over by my father's ferociousness. I tripped over the dumbbell I left on the floor after my morning workout, landing between the wall and the nightstand. "Yeah." I uttered as he was now standing over me, extending his hand. I grasped his hand and he pulled me up from the floor with seemingly no effort. "Damn dad, I ain't know you was that strong." I said trying to ease some of his tension. "Yes, you did." he said grinning at my pathetic attempt to make him feel better. "Listen, I take my son very seriously. He's the most important man, that I know. The man I admire most in the world. So, for you to call him *pretty good*, offends us both. And no, you were not a mistake. I knew what I was doing, when I did it. I also knew what it could lead to. And if given the opportunity to change what happened, the only thing I'd change is… I wouldn't have fell asleep. Cause, I think she ate some of my apple crisp." he said comically while walking back towards the door. "I didn't mean mistake, like that.

I just meant that, I wasn't planned." I explained as I gathered my things preparing for my shower. DOINK! He laughed as he grasped the doorknob and began to pull the door. "Oh, you were planned! From the moment I saw her, I planned to hit that." he chuckled as he stepped out of the room. DOINK! "Oh, and that young lady whose attention you have. I hope you know what you're doing. Remember, Imani is carrying *your* baby. She now holds all the cards." he reminded sticking his head back into the room before closing the door. "I got it handled, pop." I said confidently as I moved towards the door with my robe in one hand and soap in the other. I stopped at my dresser to take a look at my phone.

> {Tasha}
> **Hey. Did she get there yet?!**
> {Tasha}
> **I wont keep bothering you about it. Just want u 2 know that I love u and 2 see if u were still coming up 2 Philly tomorrow?**

I read the texts Tasha sent and became even more confident that I was in control of the situation. "If you say so. And as far as dinner later? You sure *you* good with that? If not, we have about an hour to come to terms with it, or run." he genuinely said as I approached the door. I pulled the door opened and followed my father out of the room. "Yeah, I think I'm good. But just in case I'm not, keep your truck keys in your pocket and park on the street." I said as I passed my dad and stepped into the bathroom.

CHAPTER 57

"Tiffany"

"Hey Missy, you were looking for me?" I asked as I peeked my head into her office. "Yes, Tiffany. I know you had planned on leaving early for the holiday dinner with your son. But I think I need you to hang around to reassess the finals on the Merkham account." she said uncertainly. "Missy, I have to be on the road by twelve. That's gonna take hours. You can't do this to me." I pleaded as I opened her door wide enough to squeeze through. "I can, but I wouldn't. You just have to come in on Saturday, *your day off*, and sign off on it. Because corporate loves you so much, they want you to do it personally. But, I'm gonna do it for you, cause I'm that kind of boss. Now don't forget I did this when you do your corporate eval." she said confidently. "Thank you, Missy. I won't!" I said quickly as I blew her a kiss and dashed out of her office. I scampered to my desk to shut down my computer and gather my personal effects.

"I'm so happy for you." Alicia said as she dabbed her eye with a tissue. "Thank you, girl. Now stop, before you make me cry again." I said softly trying not to become emotional. "God has really shown, that He controls all things." Raina said as she slid up behind me, placing her hand on my shoulder. "Prayer works. All you have to do is ask." I said as I caressed her hand. "Won't He do it?" she asked aloud tossing her hands into the air. "Yes, He will!" I responded softly as I rose to reach my coat. "Won't He will!" Alicia shouted, banging her hand on her desk. "Ladies, I love the Lord too, but we're at work, let's try to keep the volume down." Missy shouted from her office. "What she grumbling about? We're the only ones here!" Raina whispered obnoxiously.

"Alright ladies, here goes nothing." I said zipping up my coat as I pressed the elevator button. "Wrong. Here goes, everything." Missy shouted from her office. "That's right!" Eric agreed from behind his cubicle. "I'm so, so happy for you Tiffany." Alicia said again as the elevator doors opened. "Me too. God Bless your journey." Raina followed. "Bye, everybody." I said tunefully as I stepped onto the elevator. "Bye Tiffany." everyone serenaded just as harmoniously while the elevator doors closed.

"Call Asia." I said aloud. "Calling Asia." the car's computer responded respectively. "Hey. You outside?" Asia's voice quickly resounded throughout the car. "Yeah, so hurry up! We're already going to be running into traffic. I don't want to combine that, with leaving late. I'm nervous enough, as is." I said sternly. "We on our way out, now." she responded promptly. "Ok." I said before she ended the call. "We? What she mean, we?" I uttered to myself as I stared at the front of her house.

"What now?" I sighed as Asia's son came stumbling out of her front door with his mom pushing him from behind. "C'mon Kris, hurry up before we leave you." she turned back towards the house to yell. "I'm coming!" Asia's daughter Krystal yelled back as she fumbled with locking the door. "Hey auntie! Happy Thanksgiving!" Asia said delightfully as she approached the car with her hands full of bagged entre pans. "Can you open the back for me?" she asked as she pointed her son towards the back door, then continued her way to the rear of the car. "Hey Aunt Tiff!" Krystal shouted while walking across the lawn towards the car. "Hey Kris." I said calmly.

"My mom told me where y'all going, for Thanksgiving. You not excited?" Kristal asked as we turned the corner at the end of Asia's street. I disappointedly looked over at Asia before answering her daughter. "Yeah Kris, I'm excited." I answered still glaring at over at Asia. "She just don't wanna look, too excited. She try'na play it cool." Asia interrupted with a smile. "Oh ok, I get it!" Krystal responded nodding her head in approval. "No offense kids." I apologetically said to the children before I starting in on their mother. "Why are they here? I didn't say I was bringing the whole family, when I accepted this invitation." I asked harshly. "You didn't say you was bringing the whole meal with you either, but you are." Asia answered sarcastically. "We going to my daddy's." Asia's son Tyson enthusiastically answered, lifting his head from his tablet. I looked around with my eyes raised, for some type of explanation. "Taking them to their father's, Asia?! That's in the opposite direction, of where I'm going. I really don't have that kinda time. I can't believe you're gonna make me late!" I sighed as I looked at Asia for clarity. "One, it's twelve-thirty. We only have an hour and a half, maybe two, hour drive. And dinner doesn't start til four. I promise you won't be late. Two, we taking them to their grandmother's house. She lives right off ninety-five. So, it's on the way. You're really going to have to calm down, Tiff." Asia said as she rummaged through her bag. "You don't understand Asia." I said disheartened. "Mom, she's going to see her son for the first time, ever! You don't think she has a right to be nervous, scared, excited, confused?" Krystal interjected from the back seat. "No one was talking to you, little girl. Stay in a child's place! This is an adult conversation!" Asia said strictly as she continued to search through her bag. I peeked at Krystal through the rearview mirror as she grimaced at her mother and slammed her headphones into her ears. I turned and smiled at Krystal as she seemed to have a better understanding of what I was going through than her mother. "Aunt Tiff, you have a son?" Tyson asked as he looked up from his tablet for a second time.

"Bye mom. Bye Aunt Tiff. Happy Thanksgiving!" Tyson yelled as he ran towards his father's open arms. "Bye auntie. Have fun and take pictures." Krystal said enthusiastically as she reached back into the car for her backpack. "Bye baby, I will." I responded pleasantly. "Bye mom." she quickly, disgruntledly, continued as she closed the door. "Bye mom? Girl where's my hug and kiss?" Asia said slightly offended. Krystal reluctantly reached her arm and face into the window to address her mother. "I love you. Tell your brother, I love him too." Asia said as she wrapped her arm around her daughter's neck and kissed her cheek.

"Here." Asia announced as we gradually pulled onto the crowded onramp of interstate 95. I extended my hand as Asia placed in it a small, foil-wrapped object. "What is this?" I asked before inspecting the object. "Just eat it." she replied as she opened the foil and popped one into her mouth. I lifted my hand to open the foil as the faint smell of sugar and candy-filled the car. "Bitch, is this an edible?" I yelled before quickly raising the foil to my nose. "Eat it. It's a gummy bear." she said nonchalantly beginning to unwrap another one. "Don't eat another one of those things!" I demanded as she continued to unwrap her second piece of candy. I shook my head at her unbelievable endeavor. "You really don't get it. Even your teenage daughter, gets it. I don't see why you can't?" I said callously as she lowered her candy from her mouth. "Why would you eat that, Asia? Why would you think, I would eat that? Asia, I going to see my son. My son, Asia! For the first time, ever! Why would I show up there, high?! What sense does that make?!" I continued to yell ruthlessly. "First of all. Don't yell at me, I'm grown. Second, I promise you... *high* is a whole lot better than how you're planning on showing up there right now, all tense and neurotic!" Asia responded calmly. "I really wish you could understand." I said as tears began to fill in my eyes. "What the hell makes you think, I don't *get it*? You're scared, I'd have to be simple-minded not to get that."

she said snatching the candy and replacing it with a handful of seemingly used tissue. "I'm not scared. I'm horrified!" I uttered accepting the tissue. I looked at the tissue, then at Asia, and then again at the tissue. "It's clean! It was just balled up in my pocketbook. See!" she said exposing the old tissue pack from her purse. "You have to be heartless not to be afraid, right now. I just don't want them to see you whimpering, and cowering, in the fetal position. I want them to see you strong. I want them to see you independent. I want them to see your usual fearless, self. I want them to see that sexy, cocky, bitch that Omar wanted to fuck, twenty years ago. Not that homely, lonely bitch that he intimidated to the point where she crashed her car, a month ago! They need to see you as the bad bitch, that you are. I want you to go in there… and intimidate them. Let your son know where he got, half that excellence." Asia preached as she tossed the candy back in her bag. I smiled at how Asia's pathetic attempt at motivating me, actually worked a little.

CHAPTER 58

"Omar"

"Stop trying to look like you're hurrying up, and hurry up! I'm missing the Lions game!" I yelled to Jillian as she pretended to scamper across her driveway with a multitude of bags. "Why am I even coming to pick you up? Your car's, right there!" I said pointing out Jillian's car as she plopped into the front seat. "Cause your wife told you to! And her reason, is because my husband's already on his way there, with your mother I might add. And there's no point of us having two cars there." she answered sarcastically as she situated the bags in her lap. I shook my head and immediately sped from in front of her door.

"You ready for this?" Jillian asked sincerely as we pulled into the driveway. "It's not like I got a choice, right? But I'll tell you and my mom, the same thing I told Tracey. Y'all got yourselves into this, if it goes bad, get yourselves out. I'll be eating, drinking and watching football." I assured as I snatched the bags from her lap and exited the truck.

"Where's Jills?" Tracey asked as I came through the patio doors. "She's back there somewhere. It's not like she had bags to carry." I said as I dropped the bags on the counter. Tracey opened the refrigerator, grasped a beer, opened it and took a small swill. "What the hell are you doing?!" Jillian yelled as she entered the kitchen. "Here baby, I already got the game on for you." Tracey winked as she handed me the beer and patted my ass. "I'm blessing my husband's beer. Hell, I took less than a sip." Tracey answered defensively.

"Hey mom!" I voiced excitedly as I stood to greet my mother. "Hey baby." she answered just as animated. "How are you? Why're you limping?" I asked enthusiastically concerned for my mother's well-being. "I'm ok, baby. Where my grandbabies?" she asked as Hassan helped slide her coat from her back. "Quentin! Em! Come down and say hi to your grandmother." I yelled as Jillian and Tracey came into the room. "Hi mom." Tracey said as she came over to embrace my mother. "H-hey ma." Jillian stammered as she was relieved of her wine glass, whilst leaning in to give a kiss to my mother. I looked up at the booming Quentin caused as he crashed down the steps. "Hey old lady!" he yelled as he reached the bottom. "There's my baby boy!" she declared as she dashed to Quentin's arms. "Boy, put my mother down! And why can't you come down the steps like a human being?" I yelled as Quentin lifted her from her feet. "Now Omar, you know you ruined a banister or two when you were a kid." my mom said softly in Quentin's defense. "You tell 'em grandma Val." Emily said as she sauntered down the stairs to greet her grandmother. "The difference is, he's not a kid, mom. You know what, forget it. I'll let them have their grandma." I said hopelessly.

"Sup lil brother?" I asked Hassan as he re-entered the room. "Sup. That was a long ass ride, man." he replied as he collapsed onto the sofa adjacent to me. "And don't ask me. She wouldn't tell me, why she limping either. Nor do I know how long she staying. Or, if she made more than one sock-it-to-me cake." Hassan continued as he opened the beer he brought from the kitchen. "Damn, man. Can you give me a chance to ask the questions?!" I asked sternly.

DING DONG! I turned around nervously as the doorbell sounded a second time. "No boys, don't get up. I'll get it. That twenty feet from the sofa to the door, looks treacherous." Jillian said before answering the door. "Hey, Mrs. Jillian." Imani said as she stepped into the house. "Hey Unc. Hey, Paw-paw." she continued as she took off her coat. "Hey Imani." I said cordially. "Hey." Hassan followed nonchalantly. "Oh damn. Girl, you really starting to show." Jillian said to Imani as she escorted her into the kitchen.

"Yeah, that really was, a close one. The Lions pulled it out, though. You go rack 'em. I'm going to the kitchen, real quick." Hassan snickered knowing that I'd rather be out of sight when Tiffany arrived. "Y'all just gonna leave me up here?" Quentin cried as I headed for the den and Hassan the kitchen. "Nothing wrong with ya feet. C'mon." I said as I opened the door to the den. "It's been a long time, since we played. Care to partake?" I asked Quentin, tapping him with a cue stick. "You don't want this, dad." Quentin said confiscating the stick from my hand. I laughed at my son's arrogance. "This ain't football, boy. Now, you on my playing field! I'll rack 'em now, cause this'll be the last time I do it." I stated conceitedly as I reached for the triangle.

"Where is it? You didn't get none?" I said as Hassan came dancing down the stairs empty handed. "Nope!" Hassan replied condescendingly. He continued to dance across the room to his imaginary music with a patronizing smile on his face. "No, she didn't!" I pronounced aloud, missing as easy shot for the win. "Yup!" he responded as he plopped down in my dad's favorite chair to watch the game. "Mom!" I yelled up from the bottom of the stairs. "Stop crying. It's upstairs." Hassan admitted to keep from getting into any trouble. "You know everybody hates it when y'all do that, right?" Quentin queried as he slammed a ball into the pocket. "Do what?" I asked now smiling at the good news. "Talk without speaking. Y'all just had a whole conversation and nothing was said." Quentin said missing his follow up shot. "Well, Hassan went to the kitchen to get a piece of grandma's cake. He didn't get any. But he found out that she made one, just for him. He came down here bragging, then admitted that she made me one, too." I explained as Quentin looked more perplex with every word.

"I didn't say she made you one." Hassan said sarcastically. "I said, it's upstairs. Didn't say she made you a *cake*. Whoa, nice catch!" Hassan continued as he stared at the television. "Now, I'm confused." I said as I tried to figure what Hassan was referring to. "Now you see how we feel." Quentin said as he turned to look at the television replay of the catch. "She didn't make you a cake, she made you one of those apple crisps, that you like so much." Hassan confessed, relieving my dad of his excessive stress. "Oh, that's even better." my dad whispered excitedly.

CHAPTER 59

"Imani"

DING DONG! "You rung the bell already?" a woman's voice faintly asked from the other side of the door. "Yeah. What're we supposed to do, just stay out here? It's cold!" another woman's voice responded. "You could've at least given me a chance to get ready!" the woman said as I opened the door. "Too late, now! Hi, the Gregory residence, right?" one of the women questioned now directing her attention to me. "Yes. Come in." I nervously answered while moving aside so they could enter. "Thank you. I'm Asia. And behind me, is Tiffany." she said as they stepped inside. "How you doing? I'm Imani." I said trying not to look overzealous. "Hello Imani." the woman introduced as Tiffany said gently. "Hey, how're you doing?" I asked as I closed the door behind them.

"They're just trying to play it cool. I'm sure they're down there just as nervous as you are." Ms. Jillian said as she filled Ms. Tiffany's goblet with wine. "I wish you'd let me call them up here. It's bordering on being embarrassingly rude." Ms. G said sternly in an attempt to be loud enough for them to hear. "Like Jillian said, they're nervous. You know men are cowards." Grandma Val advised before gulping down the last of her wine. I laughed with the women at the cowardice of men.

"Here Grandma Val, let me refill that for you." I asked following her into the other room. I claimed her glass from her and headed over to the bar. "Thank you dear. How's your mom? She's not coming this year?" Grandma Val asked pleasantly. "No, she's not coming this year, but she's good. She's actually at my grandpop house, cooking. I told her I'd be there, when I left here." I replied as I poured wine into her glass. "Oh ok. Well, tell her I asked about her." she requested genuinely. "I sure will." I promised as I handed her back her glass. "Hey grandma. You ok?" Emily asked as she bounced down the stairs. "Oh baby, I'm fine. I'm just sitting in here resting. Not sure how I feel about that woman in there, and I don't wanna be rude. In fact, baby come here."

she said to Emily seriously. I took this time to excuse myself to leave them to their conversation.

"It's ok, really. I've only been here ten minutes or so. Besides, I'm not sure if I'm ready either." Ms. Tiffany said as I entered the room. "Knowing them, they're not nervous. They're down there waiting for a break in the game." Ms. G said consciously as she reached into the oven. "I didn't even think of that." Ms. Jillian said as she poured gravy into a serving boat. "Anything, I can do?" Ms. Asia asked finally putting down her wine glass. "No Asia. We got it, keep doing what you were doing." Ms. Tiffany replied sarcastically. "What's that supposed to mean?" Ms. Asia responded defensively. "It means, what it means." Ms. Tiffany continues as she walked her tray of sweet potatoes into the dining room. Ms. Asia ignored her demeanor and went to Ms. Jillian. "Hey girl, you need help?" she asked right away. "Yeah, I can use your hands." Ms. Jillian said to comfort.

"So, you're the brave woman that made Hassan Worth, your husband?" Ms. Asia asked as she filled each place setting's glass with cold water. "Excuse me one second, girl. Imani, go tell your man that he's going to have to come up here. Because he has to bring up some ice. Thank you." Ms. Jillian said quickly directing her attention to me. "Now you were saying, Asia?" she said immediately redirecting her attention. "I was just saying how good of a woman you had to be to marry, Hassan." Ms. Asia reiterated. "Girl, you don't know the half of it!" Ms. Jillian replied as I dashed to the door of the den. I took a deep breath and then proceeded downstairs excited about what was going to happen when he came up. "Que." I said pleasantly as I made my way down. "Yes babe." he said looking up at me midway down the stairway. "You alright?" I mouthed rushing to Quentin who was sitting at the bar with his head down. "You alright?" I whispered again as I got close. "Yeah. You?" he responded appearing misplaced and unsure. "I'm fine. Your aunt wants you to bring up some ice." I whispered as I leaned in and rested my head on his shoulder. "Ok. Here I come." he whispered back trying not to move enough to disturb my comfort. I kissed his cheek and made my way back up the stairs. "Hey. What's the vibe up there?" Quentin uncle Hassan asked as I started on the stairs. "It's not as bad as you'd think. Everyone's drinking and laughing. Grammy's in the living room, with Em. Ms. Tiffany and Ms. G are in the kitchen, getting the food together. And Ms. Asia and Ms. Jillian are finishing up arranging the dining room. Everyone's basically waiting on y'all to come up." I confessed before going up the stairs.

CHAPTER 60

"Quentin"

"I got'chu. I'm right behind you." my dad reassured as I hesitantly staggered up the steps. I could hear the giggles get louder as I reached the door atop the stairs. I took a deep breath and slowly turned the doorknob. "Here they go right here, grandma." Emily shouted as she stood in front of the door.

I stepped through the door and with my head down I hurriedly carried the bag of ice across the kitchen and out to the patio. "Quentin. Quentin!" Tracey shouted as I approached the patio doors. "Babe, he's coming right, right back. Let him get a quick breath of fresh air." my dad interrupted as I stepped onto the patio.

"Wheeew" I exhaled deeply as stood outside of the doors. I look up through the glass and noticed my dad was still watching me. "Damn. No matter what, he really does always have my back." I said to myself kneeling to empty the bag of ice into the designated cooler. "That he does. Always has." a woman's voice said faintly behind the sound of the leaves rustling in the wind. I quickly raised my head to survey my immediate area. There, leaning against the house, attempting to light a cigar was a woman, watching me. "Whoa!" I yelled, startled by her presence. "I scared you. I'm sorry." she laughed pacifyingly. "I just didn't want to disturb your conversation." she continued sarcastically. I smiled at her not so subtle sarcasm. "No bother. You're good." I responded as I realized that I poured too much ice into the cooler. "Quentin, right?" she intuitively asked after deeply pulling on her cigar. "Yeah." I answered inquisitively. "No, I'm not your mother. If that's what you were thinking." she declared resuming her intuitive rationale. "I didn't think you were. You don't look old enough." I said confident in my known description. "What, they told you she was old?" she snickered cynically exhaling a fragrant puff of smoke. "Not old. Just, significantly older than my dad. And you, look like you could be around his age. So, I'm guessing you're Asia." I divulged as I scooped ice back into the almost empty bag. "Why, Asia? I could be anyone." she asked curiously. "Why would she bring, just anyone? She's pretty much a stranger here, herself. Would make since to bring someone as familiar, as she is." I explained as I examined the bag to see if I had put back enough ice. "In that case, yeah I'm Asia. They told you about me?" she asked not seeming shocked that I knew her name. "My dad and Hassan told me, everything." I said looking into the house to see my mom now watching me, along with my father. I confidently smiled knowing, that I was always under my parent's protective umbrella. "So, where is she?" I asked scanning inside the house for a glimpse of Tiffany. Asia walked over and kneeled next to me. "There! Sitting in the chair behind... that's Hassan?!" she asked in awe. "Yeah. He's the one standing at the counter, cutting the turkey. Which makes my dad, the one leaning on the counter next to him." I clarified trying to get a peek around Hassan. "Hmph. He's aged well. You all have." she mumbled staring at Hassan with an expression of appeal in her eyes. "Yeah. Twenty years'll do that to you." I thought to myself as I stood up, continuing to get a glance of Tiffany. She extinguished her cigar against the concrete ground, erected herself next to me and then gave me a brief eyeball inspection. "Wow, look at you! You look like your dad... and your mom." she said overwhelmed by my face and stature in clear view. "I look like her?" I asked while holding in my enthusiasm. I continued to attempt to look through the door glass, around Hassan. I finally became disgruntled and tapped on the glass to get their attention. This caused both my father and Hassan to turn toward me and Asia, standing at the door. I waved to Hassan to stand aside as my father came and opened the door. "You alright?" he asked curiously. "I'm good." I replied as I snatched the door from him, sliding it back closed. I continued to tap and direct Hassan to move a little to his right. And my father, who was now standing next to him, I waved for him to shift to his left. "Damn, I still can't really see her." I said growing more anxious and frustrated. Asia laughed. "This is just sad. It's obvious you're intrigued. How about, instead of standing out here, we go in and introduce?" she asked stirred by my dissatisfaction. "Oh, by the way, I'm your cousin Asia." she said extending her hand for me to shake. "Quentin." I said as I clasped her hand.

I released her hand and she pulled the door open. I stepped in, in front of her and handed my father the small bag of ice that I'd been influencing. "Hi, Omar." Asia enthusiastically voiced after shadowing me inside. "Hey Asia, been a long time. I see you've met, Quentin." my dad said cordially. "You okay?" my dad asked as he accepted the bag from me. "Yeah, I'm good." I said looking into my father's eyes. "Why wouldn't he be ok? I'm a great cousin." Asia declared animatedly. "Hey Hassan!" she continued. "Good. Just what I've been waiting on!" Aunt Jillian interrupted as she quickly stalked into the kitchen and confiscated the bag of ice from my dad. "We can eat now, y'all." Aunt Jillian yelled as she sashayed back into the other room after giving Hassan a uncomplimentary look. I looked at my dad, then Asia and we all chuckled at Hassan. "C'mon. Before we eat, let's go meet your mom." Asia said as she clinched my hand and pulled me toward the other room. "Yeah. Let's go meet *Tiffany*." my dad uttered hurriedly following Asia and I.

"Aunt Tiff..." Asia started gently as we stood over her sitting in the love seat. "Wait. Wait, wait!" my mom loudly interrupted as she rushed to the end table to retrieve her phone. "Tra. Everything doesn't have to be a media production!" my dad declared while standing behind Asia and I. I surveyed the room as all eyes were on me and Tiffany. I looked back at my father and Hassan, then my grandmother sitting on the adjacent sofa, followed by Emily and Imani, who were standing by the front door. I looked in every direction but down at the woman sitting in the chair in front of me.

"Ok, is everyone ready?" Asia asked sarcastically before she began. "Aunt Tiffany, I'd like you to meet... Quentin Gregory." she continued. "Hello." I wanted to say as I looked down at this woman staring up at me. But I couldn't speak. I couldn't move. I could hardly breathe. All I could do was stare back at this woman staring at me with her eyes swelling with tears.

"Let's give them a minute alone." my Aunt Jillian murmured as she reached down over my shoulder with a tissue. "Thank you." Tiffany breathed, reaching up to claim the tissue from my aunt's hand. "Yeah, y'all go 'head and start without us." my dad grumbled as everyone else began to disperse.

"I don't need a minute, Aunt Jills. I'm fine." I uttered as I wiped my hand across my eye to catch the gathering tears. "You can go ahead dad. I'm right behind you." I sniffled observing everyone except my father heading towards the dinner table. "Only, if you're sure." he confirmed as he firmly rubbed my shoulder before heading for the table himself. "I'm sure. I'm coming, now." I said as I began pivot to follow him. "Wait. I've been holding on to this apology for twenty years. I've recited and rehearsed it, countlessly. And now that the time's here for me to say it, I refuse to just freeze up." Tiffany said as she reached up to attempt to embrace my hand. I continued to stand there speechless, waiting to brushoff whatever she had to say. "And as many times as you rehearsed apologizing, I'm sure I've rehearsed how I'd give you my ass to kiss." I thought as she cupped my hand inside of hers.

Ignoring the tears now streaming down her cheeks, she took a deep breath and began. "I've been going over this moment in my mind for, forever. And now that it's here, I don't know what to say. I know, no matter what, I'll never for one second think that I'm forgiven. I don't think, I'd forgive me either. I understood and accepted that, a long time ago. I also know that I can't point the finger at anyone for this, but me. Believe me, I've tried. I thought of everyone, and everything. So, I accepted that a long time ago too." she chuckled, trying to console herself. Seeing, that she wasn't done, I kneeled down next to her in the chair so that she no longer had to look up. "I just, more than anything, want you to know that I'm sorry. I'm sorry, I was selfish. I'm sorry, I was irresponsible. I'm sorry, if you thought for one second that you got a bum ride." she confessed as she dabbed the tissue that she had crushed in hands, on her eyes. "The only thing that I'm not sorry about, is making Omar Gregory your father." she acknowledged as she began to stare into my eyes again. "Yeah, me too." I agreed as I stretched to reach the box of tissue on the end table, at the other side of the sofa. "I never, not for one minute, had a bum ride. I was showered with the things I needed, and spoiled with the things I didn't. My life was great. I never had to look for my mother, and never once couldn't find my father. I had it all." I said reassuringly as I looked over at my dad. He was sitting at the table staring at us, while forcefully stabbing his fork down into the wooden surface. "Yeah, he is an amazing man, isn't he? He even married amazing." she said as she followed my sight line to my father. "Yeah, she's the shit too." I said about my mother as she threw me a wink when she saw me focus on her. I pulled another sheet of tissue from the box, before standing to restore it. "Alright c'mon, we gotta go eat with the rest of the family." I said extending my hand for her to hold as she erected to her feet. "I can't go over there like this. I look a mess." she sniffled uncomfortably. I handed her the tissue I had proclaimed from the box. "You look like a woman who just saw her son for the second time, in his twenty-year life. I'm sure they'll understand." I comforted while staring at the watermarked trail of make-up running down her cheeks. "No, I have to go to fix this." she said as she dashed towards the bathroom.

CHAPTER 61

"Hassan"

"I would like to make a toast." I declared after rising to my feet and extending my glass to the center of the table. "I was just about to do that." Omar said as he quickly stood and elevated his glass to mine. Everyone followed until all glasses were outstretched across the table. "Family. It's where life begins, and love and dedication never end. To my family." Hassan wholeheartedly expressed. "To family." everyone followed in unison.

"If my Teddy was alive to see this." mama Val said softly as she slowly surveyed the table, smiling. "See what, ma?" I asked curiously. "His family. His pain in the ass son. His best friend's pain in the ass son, who became his son's pain in the ass best friend. Their success. Their wives. His grandchildren. One's gonna to be in NFL and the other, a famous rap star. And who knows what the new one, will be? He would be so proud of you two. Of all of you. You guys have all exceeded his plan." she expressed as she smiled proudly. "Yeah, I miss Papa Ted. I don't think any of us would be where we are, without his guide and influence. I know, we wouldn't still be married." Tracey added behind my mama Val. "Wha'chu saying?! Y'all almost broke up?!" Emily asked, shocked by Tracey's last statement. "No!" Omar jumped in quickly. "Don't lie to the child now, Omar!" mama Val said as she raised her wine glass to her mouth. "Yes baby. Your dad and mom had their problems too, way back. They only seem perfect now, because they were both willing to transform and mature." Jillian answered contemptuously looking at Hassan. "I used to have to call Papa Ted on your father, all the time. If it wasn't for him straightening your dad out, we wouldn't be here." Tracey said as she gently slid her chair closer to Omar. "Damn, O. I'm glad you got your shit together. You outta have known better." I laughed hoping to get some of Jillian's tension off of me. "Now Hassan. Don't act like Teddy didn't have to get on you, too." mama Val sternly reminded. "We've gotten calls from your wife, as well. You're sitting there rather quietly Jill, tell'em." she demanded of my wife as she gestured for Quentin to refill her wine glass. "Whatever mama. That's the wine talking." I laughed, hoping there was some truth to my skepticism. "No, it's really not! Every time I put you out. It was mama Val or papa Ted that talked you back into the house, not you." Jillian admitted as she too raised her glass for Quentin to fill. "Oh damn." Asia giggled as she continued to observe. "You say *every time* like it was a lot. It was three damn times in nineteen years!" I declared in an attempt to defend my nobility. "It's fine Hassan. We all make mistakes. As long as we learn from them. Wish I had a Papa Ted, when I was married." Tiffany sincerely acknowledged. "For real!" Asia genuinely agreed. "To Papa Ted, may his roots stay firmly planted." Asia declared as she picked up her wine glass and stretched to the center of the table. "To Papa Ted" everyone said happily as we nimbly collided our glasses to one another's. "To my, Teddy Bear." my mother followed pleasantly. "So, now that we've given respect to papa Ted, is this a good time to ask you about this so-called boyfriend, grandma Val?" Emily asked in the most cordial way she knew how. "I'm glad you said it, 'cause I was thinking the same thing." Quentin trailed immediately. I shook my head in disbelief and quietly continued to eat my food, while waiting for an answer.

"Well everybody, this has been, special. And, I'm not sure how I'm gonna do it. But now, I gotta go have dinner with my family." Imani cried out as she reluctantly rose from the table. Quentin rose with her, to escort her out. "Good night, Imani." Omar mumbled with a mouthful of mom's "sock-it-to-me" cake. "Goodnight Mani." Jillian yelled from the kitchen. "Night Mani." Tracey sang as she happily sat and sipped her only allowed, small glass of wine. "Goodnight honey, it was so nice meeting you." Tiffany said gently. "It was nice to meet you too. I hope to see you again." Imani responded genuinely. "Night, night." Asia said as she shuttled dirty dishes from the table to Jillian, in the kitchen. "Uhh… night, night to you too?" Imani uttered back awkwardly. "Night, night." I mocked inadvertently slamming down my beer to pick up my fork. "Goodnight baby. You take care now." mama Val said softly. "Goodnight, Grammy." she whispered as she leaned in to kissed mama Val's cheek.

"Ok, what I miss?" Quentin inquired as he returned from accompanying Imani out to the car. "You missed your uncle over here stealing slices of cake, but other than that, nothing." Tracey said nonchalantly. "What? C'mon, man!" Omar barked in offense. "Ain't nobody stealing no cake?" I snapped back staggered by the accusation. "Damn man, you got a whole cake in the car!" he continued as he stretched his neck to see where I was hiding the cake slices. "First of all, ain't nobody stealing cake. And b, that cake in the car is my personal cake. Moms made that for me. Whereas *this* cake, she made for everybody. So, if I want some, I'll feel free!" I explained sternly as I gently sliced into the cake. "Baby, I was just joking. I don't believe you really getting that excited, over cake." Tracey admitted as she embarrassingly slid her chair slightly away from him.

"Y'all are too cute." Tiffany chuckled as she circled the top of her wine goblet with her finger. "You really do have a wonderful family, Tracey. I really don't know how to thank you for inviting me to this." she continued admiringly. "No thanks needed." Tracey responded softly. "Well, I can think of something. Can you teach her how to make that cabbage?" Emily abruptly asked while pushing her chair into the table. "Yeah, they were good!" I complied before cramming the entire slice of cake into my mouth. "If that's what you want, I can do that. I can do that with no problem, dear." Tiffany responded as we all watched Emily walk across the room. "Thank you. See mom, it wasn't that hard at all." she said before exiting the room. "Please don't head her." Tracey said timidly turning red. "I really, don't mind. That is, if you really want it?" Tiffany pledged kindly. "Take the deal." I mumbled to Tracey as I pushed my chair back to stand. "I guess y'all going back downstairs, now?" Jillian asked condescendingly. "Yup. That's where the bigger bar is." I replied mockingly as I grabbed another slice of cake to travel with. "Bigger bar?" Asia asked intensely, lifting her head from her phone. "Can I come too, or is it like the he-man woman haters club down there?" Asia eagerly continued. I looked at Omar, then Jillian, then back at Omar. "No, it's not like that at all. You can come down." Omar accommodatingly answered. "Be careful darling. There's a lot of belching, scratching and cigar smoke down there." Tracey uttered as I started down the stairs.

"We pull no punches, down here. You lost woman, rack 'em!" Omar commanded as Asia stood pouting. "I know!" she replied sternly as she reluctantly headed to grab the triangle. "I guess it's me and you?" I said to Omar as I grabbed the stick and rose from the sofa, to play against him. "It's always me, and you." I responded regretfully. "So, Ms. Asia. What's up? How you been? How's life?" I interrogated while waiting for Omar to break. "Well Mr. Hassan, I'm doing good. I…" Asia started alluringly. "Who got next? Can, can I play?" Jillian said slurring outstandingly while trailing Quentin down the stairs. I looked at Asia, then Omar who were both laughing outlandishly. "Yeah, of course you can, after I beat your husband. In fact, I didn't break yet, you can play your husband." Omar said graciously. "No, you go head. I'll sit over here with Quentin and… Asia."

she responded shadily. "No. Believe me, it's cool. We was just whining about the monotony, before you came down. This'll break it up, some." Omar explained as he handed Jillian his cue stick. "Well, if you insist." Jillian said as she claimed the stick from Omar. "You break." I said smiling at my wife as she pretended to be interested in shooting pool.

"Come show me how. I forget how to do this." Jillian insisted as she bent over in her shooting stance. "What do you want me to do?" I asked becoming frustrated with her behavior. "Get behind me, and show me how to do it! Pretend I not your wife. I'm just a pretty face, down at the lounge." she uttered barely coherent. "How 'bout I pretend you are my wife, and do this!" I suggested as I bent over her, pressing my body tightly against her butt. "Umm!" she uttered as she felt my presence. "We may have to end this night early." she expressed as pushed back into me. "Let's at least finish, this game." I proposed as I backed up to give her room to shoot. "Aww, no more help?" she said before thrusting the stick forward. The colorful balls went propelling from corner to corner, side to side, across the table. "I sometimes forget you can shoot." I said surprised by her break.

"Next!" Omar shouted after beating Jillian with an eight ball to the side pocket, trick, bank shot. I smiled with pride as I watched my wife take Omar to the brink of a loss. "C'mon Asia, your turn!" Jillian called out as she collected the balls into the triangle to reset the table. "You mind if I take this one, Asia?" Tiffany inquired as she came sashaying down the stairs. "Damn, I was just about to light the stogie." I mumbled, noticing Tracey behind Tiffany on the steps.

"Don't worry Hassan, I'm not staying. I just came to check on your wife. You can smoke your funky cigar." Tracey announced aloud while she headed towards Jillian standing at the bar. "Damn Tra, you heard him? I'm closer to him than you are, and I hardly heard him." Tiffany asked amazed that she heard my low tone under all of the room noise. "I raised Quentin and Emily Gregory. Mumbling is a second language, in this house." Tracey said arrogantly as she approached Jillian. Omar and I both quickly looked up at each other in astonishment at Tracey and Tiffany's verbal to and fro.

"Honey Jack?" I asked Omar as he circled the table, corkscrewing his cue stick in the chalk cube. "Honey Jack." he responded as he prepared to shoot. I maneuvered my way around the ladies standing at the bar to get behind it for the bottle. "Hey. You alright?" Tracey said softly to her best friend. "I'm fine. Why?" Jillian answered just as gentle. "Because, you're playing pool down here in the den. You never come down here. You hate it, down here." Tracey reminded quietly. I poured Omar and my drinks while pretending not to listen. "I don't hate it, down here. I just don't come down here, often." Jillian explained softly. I shook my head subtly at Jillian's tall tale. "So, why are you down here?" Tracey asked recognizing Jillian's concealed truth. "While you're back there pouring, can I get a taste?" Asia asked from across the room. "Yeah, sure. But I'm not bringing it over there, you gotta come get it." I replied sensibly staying within eye and ear shot of Jillian. "That's why!" Jillian leaned and sternly whispered into Tracey's ear. "Bro!" I yelled to Omar from behind the bar. "Here, can you pass this to him." I said to Tracey, handing her Omar's glass and a cigar. "Quentin, turn on the air filter for your mom." Omar demanded, seeing the cigar in Tracey's hand. "It's okay babe. We're going upstairs." Tracey insisted while distributing to Omar, his drink and cigar. "Come with me." she continued to demand as she led Jillian to the steps by the arm.

"Is she shooting at the eight?" I asked as I looked up at the table. "Yeah. If he don't end it now, it's over!" Tiffany said arrogantly. I rose and stood next to Quentin, who was diligently watching the game. RING. RING! "I shoulda recorded this." Quentin eagerly disclosed, excited at his dad's pending, embarrassing defeat. RING. RING! "Hey babe. You missing it. Tiffany is whoopin' my dad, in pool." Quentin laughed as he enthusiastically answered his phone. "In fact." he continued as he snatched his phone from his ear, pressed a button and aimed it at the table. "Can you see it babe?" he asked animatedly. "Y'all acting like I never lost before!" Omar said confidently. "Not like that. It's a lot of babies on that table, you gotta a whole daycare going on there." I said as I watched Omar prepare for his shot. "Babies? Daycare? Wha'chu talking 'bout?" Asia said as she slinked up next me and posed, resting her elbow on my shoulder. "He's talking about all the low numbered balls, on the table. Pool shooters, call them babies." Tiffany explained as she confiscated Asia's glass, sipped some of her drink and handed it back to her.

"So, how you been Hassan. I haven't been given too many opportunities to ask you. You looking as good as ever." Asia said discreetly. "I'm doing well. Healthy. Happy. As you can see, I'm married. No children. And you know, just living life. Staying outta the way." I whispered back as I continued to watch their game. "Damn good shot, O!" I yelled as Omar attempted to mount his comeback. "So, how 'bout you?" I asked Asia while she continued to rest on my shoulder. "Welllll... I'm divorced. But not looking for anything, serious. I have two children. Krystal's fourteen, and Tyson is six. I still live in the same house, we did it in. And like you, I'm healthy, as you can see!" Asia said amputating her arm from my shoulder to model her figure to me. I looked at Asia demonstrate and then quickly gave my attention back to Omar's game. "Damn!" Omar whispered as he grazed the six ball on a bad angle. "Ohh. he missed! She about to take him out!" Quentin said into the phone pressed against his ear. "That's ya ass." Tiffany uttered as she lined up her final shot.

CHAPTER 62

"Omar"

"Your husband taught you to shoot, like that?" I asked Tiffany as she slid down onto the sofa next to Quentin. "No, he didn't play. I learned from my brother, and then honed my craft on the base." she said arrogantly. "Well you did a damn good job. I don't learn, often." I admitted as I sipped my drink. "You mean lose?" Asia boasted, with a smile. 'No, he meant learn! He says every loss, is a learning experience." Hassan interjected from behind his beer can. "I can speak for myself, lil brother. But thank you." I said quickly. "Yeah, I learn from defeat so that, it doesn't happen again!" I said arrogantly. "Whenever you ready for another *lesson*, just let me know!" Tiffany snickered.

"Babe, let me call you back. This is getting good." Quentin chuckled, derailing his phone conversation. "No. Seriously, you should be proud. No one beats my dad on his table except Hassan, on occasion." Quentin continued proudly as he looked over at me with a smile. "I am. I've been proud since I walked into the door, Quentin. I was proud when I used to read the Dover Post, especially when they posted the honor students. Now I'm proud when I read the Daily Collegian, or watch SportsCenter. As the woman who carried you, I'm proud of you. As just a woman, I'm proud of you. As a black woman, proud of you. As a football fan, I'm proud of you. If I'm not anything else, I'm proud. You… are amazing." Tiffany said submissively. "Thank you." Quentin whispered modestly. "She ain't lying! You are all, she talks about. Your grades, your football stuff, your hair, when you gain weight, when you lose weight… everything." Asia roughly interrupted. I sat back proudly feeling just as accountable for his accolades as he is. "I see you over there, Omar. Yes, you deserve more recognition than I could ever give." Tiffany mentioned as she looked at me admirably. "He's a man, and you did that. And a lot of his life, in terms of age, you were a boy yourself. I'm sorry you had to go through that." Tiffany solemnly continued. "Yeah, we missed out on a lot. But we got a lot out of it too, so…" Hassan said calmly as he nodded his head to Quentin. "Yeah, you two were inseparable. So, you'd have to assume whatever Omar missed, you probably missed too." Asia admitted comically. "They still are inseparable." Quentin incorporated nonchalantly.

"You talking like you wasn't the third musketeer your whole life. If it wasn't for football and Imani, you'd still be hanging around his office or following me around." Hassan barked sarcastically. "You right, so let's toast to Mani and football." Quentin replied as he raised his glass. "To Mani, and football." I shouted, elevating my glass to his. Asia and Tiffany followed in on the humor, by raising their glasses as well.

"This Imani sounds really special. Didn't really get too much time with her, during dinner. Tell me about her." Tiffany quietly requested of Quentin. "What's there to tell? She's smart. She's funny. You saw what she looks like. And we've been together, for going on six years." Quentin replied obliviously. "Wow, six years? You were fourteen?" Tiffany asked perplexed by how young we were. "You were fast like your dad, huh?" Asia responded with a chuckle. "I wouldn't say that. She's a good girl. She made him wait three, four years, before letting him take advantage." Hassan said bluntly. Tiffany looked at Hassan and slowly shook her head. "I just meant that for her to be so understanding and forgiving about an impending baby, she has to really love you." Tiffany said in awe of Imani. "Oh, that she does!" I responded in support of Quentin. "But give her some credit for the baby too, it is half her fault." Quentin joked before jaggedly standing. "If you as lazy with that as you are with everything else, gotta give her all the credit!" Hassan cynically mocked. "Whatever man. Does anyone want anything from upstairs?" Quentin inquired as he sidestepped between Tiffany and the coffee table. "No thank you." Asia said pleasantly. "No honey, I'm fine." Tiffany tailed, looking at Quentin in downright bewilderment. "Nah. I'm good." Hassan joined in quickly. "I don't want anything, but check on your mom for me." I requested as he reached the bottom of the stairs. "And your aunt Jill. I probably ain't been shit, since she got pulled up there." Hassan added. "I'm sure you weren't shit, while she was down here." Asia sarcastically replied. Quentin smiled and darted up the stairs. "Wait, I'm confused." Tiffany said softly. "Yeah, you look confused." Asia declared raising her glass to her lips. "I'm glad you said it." Hassan agreed. I snickered communally with the others. "What is it? What's wrong?" I asked curiously.

"I don't know. This new generation is just... goofy. How can he put any of the blame of this pregnancy, on Imani? And how can she be so accepting of such?" Tiffany asked almost dazed. I looked at Hassan, who was just as baffled as I was by Tiffany's questions. "I don't know how long it's been for you. But you do remember how fucking works, right? You have to, because you're here tonight because of the outcome of you... fucking." Hassan asked sardonically before guzzling down the last of his beer. "Yes Hassan, I remember sex and its consequences. I also remember that what you do with one, has nothing to do with the other." Tiffany responded bluntly. "What are you talking about?!" I asked just as Quentin hopped down the stairs with Emily shadowing him. "How is it Imani's fault, that Quentin and Tasha are having a baby?" Tiffany asked obliviously. "What? Who the fuck is Tasha?!" Emily yelped before anyone else could respond. "Oh shit!" Hassan whispered smacking himself across the eye and forehead with the palm of his hand. "Daaammn!" Asia testified melodiously, her hand covering her mouth.

"What? What's wrong?" Tiffany unsuspectingly asked at everyone's responses.

CHAPTER 63

"Quentin"

I just stood there dumbfounded at the bomb my biological mother had just dropped. I slowly looked over at my father who seemed to have steam gradually ascending from his head. "Two!" he yelled once he noticed me looking at him. "Two women!" he continued to yell as he jumped to his feet, took the last large mouthful of his drink, and then launched his glass into the television.

I continued to stand there motionless as my breaths decreased and heartbeats increased, between them. "What was that?!" my aunt Jillian asked aloud as she, my mother, and grandmother came crashing downstairs as fast as they could. "What's wrong?! Is everything alright?!" my mom asked zealously as she reached the bottom of the stairs. "Nope." Emily said as she gestured for them to look at the television. "Two fucking women!" my dad uttered maniacally, as he fell back into his chair. "What happened down here?!" my grandmother asked alarmingly after seeing the television. "You guys got a broom around here, somewhere?" Asia asked Emily as my grandmother's question seemed to fall on deaf ears. "Omar baby, what happened?" my mother asked my father, who was sitting with his head in his hands. "It's one right over here." Emily said as she escorted Asia to the garage door. "Baby, what is it?" my mother repeated as she approached my father, slowly. "Quentin?" she said as she turned her attention towards me. "Y'all hear us talking. One of you niggas, better say something!" my grandmother snapped vigorously. "This mutha-fuckah here, has both Imani and some other girl name Tasha pregnant at the same damn time!" Hassan said furiously as he lifted his hand from his face. "Completely fucking over his life, and career." my father piggybacked immediately. "Nooo, Quentin." my mother said softly as she stood over my father with his head pressed into her stomach. "You kids never heard of, protection?" Grammy asked sternly. "Wait a minute y'all. How do we even know this Tasha, or whatever her name is, thing is true?" Aunt Jillian asked aggressively. "The young lady came to me a few weeks back, and told me she was pregnant with Quentin's child. She said she really believes in family. And really wanted me to get to know Quentin, and the baby. When you all were talking about Quentin's baby at dinner, I just assumed you were referring to her. I had no idea Imani, was pregnant too." Tiffany said solemnly. "I'm so sorry." she continued to whisper as tears began to fall from her eyes. "Why are you sorry? It was that dickhead, that fucked up!" Hassan said bluntly. "What the fuck were you thinking?" Emily asked, coming back into the room with the snow shovel in her hand. Emily always found a way to take advantage of the opportunity to drop some permissible profanity. "Alright, everyone. We're not going to all just sit here, and dump on Quentin like this." my mom said disheartened. "Yeah, especially since we don't know if any of this shit is true!" my Aunt Jillian said blatantly. Asia stopped sweeping and let go of the broom. "Are you calling my aunt, a liar?!" she responded belligerently after the broom hit the ground with a loud crack. "Why would she come here, and lie about something like that?!" she continued to ask impolitely. "She wasn't calling your aunt, a liar. I think she was referring to this, *Tasha's* story." my Grammy intervened as she went to pick up the broom. "Mama, please don't touch that broom. She dropped it, she'll pick it up. And yes, I was talking about this other girl, and her story!" Aunt Jillian said violently staring at Asia. "You dropped your broom, sweetie." she aggressively informed, pointing to the broom for Asia to recognize. "All I'm saying is, how do we know if any of this is true? It could all be bullshit." Aunt Jills continued to declare as she stood behind Hassan's chair and began to knead his shoulders. "It's true." my dad uttered as he stared at me mournfully. "Jillian has a point. How do we know this to be fact?" my grandmother asked, joining my aunt's contradiction. "Look at his face, mama. We've seen that look before." Hassan reminded solemnly. Everyone's head turned to look at me. "It's true. I mean, I didn't know anything about it until, just now. But I can't deny, it's likelihood." I hopelessly admitted, releasing my ambitions that if I remained catatonic, this nightmare would end.

"Goodnight. It was so nice meeting you! You have my number, so I expect to hear from you quite often." my mother stated pleasantly as she and I escorted our guests to the door. I quietly helped my grandmother put on her coat as she continued to look at me disheartened. "Don't worry baby. We're going to find a way to come out of this, okay." she comfortingly whispered as she tossed her scarf around her neck. "Where you going mom?!" my dad said noticing everyone heading to the door. "I thought I'd catch a ride back, with the ladies. As to not put you or Hassan, out your way." my Grammy said as my father scurried to remorsefully send her off. "I thought you was spending the night." Hassan said rising from the sofa. "Yeah, me too! And it's never out of our way." my dad said unhappily. "No, I think I'll get home while the getting's good." she responded with regret. "Look at you. Two big 'ol mama's boys." Asia said as she stood by, waiting to leave. "Here boy. Take your grandmama's bags to the car!" my dad commanded, handing me her purse and a large shopping bag. "I'm sure he was already going to do that Omar!" my mom said sharply. I grabbed the bags from my father and headed out the door.

"Goodnight everyone." Asia called out as she immediately rushed out behind me, to catch a few pulls of her cigar before getting into the car. "It was that good, huh?" Asia asked cynically as she lit her cigar. I pretended to smile at Asia's remark while I stood there shivering. "You'll be alright. It could be worst. You could have *three* women pregnant." she exclaimed as she exhaled the cigar smoke into the air. "You don't have three women pregnant, do you?" she swiftly continued to inquire. I sniggered at Asia as the door came flying open again. "Alright, lil cousin. Hope to see you again, soon." Asia quickly divulged with a half hug after noticing them come out of the house. "Yeah, you too." I uttered sincerely while slightly embracing my new cousin. "Goodnight Tracey, thanks again. Bye Omar." Tiffany bellowed as she stepped out of the door behind my grandmother. I rushed up to my grandmother's side to accompany her down the pathway. "I told your father not to bring it back up, until tomorrow. By then, he'll have calmed down. You'll let me know, if he doesn't follow those orders?" she asked as we approached the car. "Yes ma'am." I mumbled as she opened her arms to hug me. "Goodnight baby. Grammy, loves you." she said squeezing me tightly. "I love you too, Grammy." I said softly as I opened the door for her. "Here." my grandmother said gesturing for me to hand over the bags my father gave me. I gave her the bags and closed the door.

"Well Quentin, even though it didn't end as joyous as it began, this was still the happiest experience of my life. I'll never forget this day. It was a real dream come true." Tiffany announced earnestly while extending her hand for me to shake. "Yeah. Experience and dream, are two words that come to mind." I countered, grasping her hand. "I feel like, I ruined your holiday. I'm sorry." she pleaded softly while still slowly shaking my hand. "Don't be, it's not your fault. When did she tell *you*, she was pregnant? And how did she even get your number?" I pryingly asked as stood outside of the car. "Oh, she didn't call me. She came to my door." she confessed still fascinated by Tasha's determination and courage. "Came to your door?

When? How?" I asked becoming frustrated with Tasha's investigation. "About two Saturday's ago she came to my house, and told me who she was and that she was carrying my grandchild. I asked her how she knew who I was, and how to find me. She then showed me a picture of the birthday package, that I sent you. Turns out, she doesn't live too far from us. She's a very nice young lady. We ended up spending half the day together." she admitted genuinely. "Did she tell anybody else about it?" I asked anxiously while stepping behind her to grasp the car door handle. "Yeah." she whispered apologetically. "From what she told me, she told everybody... but you." she answered, unfortunately. "I'm guessing that was your job." I declared woefully whilst pulling the door open. "Yeah, now that I think about it, you may be right. Which makes it hurt, that much more." she said sorrowfully as she slid into the car. "You have nothing to be upset about." I whispered softly. "Goodnight y'all. Goodnight Grammy!" I said aloud before pushing the door closed and turning back toward the house. "Goodnight, Quentin." Tiffany mouthed from inside the car before blowing me a kiss and pulling away.

CHAPTER 64

"Tiffany"

"You ok back there, Ms. Valerie?" I asked peeking into the rearview mirror. "I'm fine baby. A little sleepy, but ok." she replied pleasantly. "Ok. Just let me know if you need anything." I requested sincerely. "Some co-pilot." I mumbled to Asia, who had her head resting on her hands, asleep. "Why you say that?" she vaguely uttered, proving that she wasn't asleep. "Well Tiffany, since you asked, there is one thing." Ms. Valerie interjected softly. "Anything." I said genuinely, while looking at Asia who was now shaking her head slowly. "I need to know, how you did it? How'd you carry and then walk away, from that little boy?" she queried intensely. "I was waiting for that question. I actually expected it hours ago." I responded actually caught off guard. "Yeah, I thought Tracey woulda asked that. At the very least, Quentin." Asia added as she woozily erected to attend to the conversation. "You wouldn't have gotten that question from them, it's too confrontational. My son's family is only hard-hitting when he's not around. They respect him. So, around him, they're as soft as a cloud." she justified gently. "I can see that." Asia said in agreement. "You were saying." Miss Valerie questioned determinedly. "Well Miss Valerie..." I started disgracefully.

CHAPTER 65

"Tiffany 1998"

"Ronald, we gotta talk." I said following him as he frantically paced back and forth, from room to room. "What is it, babe? I'm kinda in a rush." he responded rapidly. "In a rush? Now where you going?!" I snapped watching him finally find his preferred shirt. "We discussed this earlier. I'm going to club, with the twins." he exclaimed as if I'd sanctioned before now. "Another night out with your friends? Really?!" I asked frustrated by his lack of attention. "You been in the streets with your friends since we been back!" I snapped as I dug through the pile of loose clothing for the remote. "It ain't like I been out doing anything! I'm with your brother, half the time!" he said harshly as he stormed into the bathroom and closed the door. "That ain't saying much. He a fucking whore, too!" I yelled into the bathroom door. "Call me what you want, I ain't out doing nothing I ain't supposed to be." he mumbled aloud before turning on the shower. "Shit, that's hot." he yelled as he stepped into the shower. "When you gonna take a second, and even act like you married? If you didn't want to get married, you shouldn't have fuckin' asked!" I continued to yell as I made my way to the sofa, remote in hand. "Don't go there!" he yelled partially opening the door to be sure I heard him. "Don't go where! I'll go wherever the hell I want! I'm not the one, that can't be trusted!" I said as he again closed the door shut. "Well go then! And stop bitchin' about old shit!" he yelled from the other side of the door.

Hey Babe. I realize that since we been back home we haven't spent much time together. I promise to change that. Just trying to catch up with a few people and take care of a few things. After that I'm all yours. I promise. You know I love you babe, so just chillax and stop trippin.

Love Alwayz;

Sgt. Ron

"Hey Babe. I realize that since we been back home… yadda, yadda… just chillax and stop trippin'. What the hell he gotta take care of? And, chillax and stop trippin?" I indistinctly mumbled while reading the note left, on my husband's pillow. "Stop trippin'?!" I began to yell as I gradually became irate at the audacity of his note.

"Wow. He's always been arrogant, but I'd have never thought he was that callous with it." Ayanna said, astonished at the details of the note. "Well, if he think he the only one that can come back home and show off, he's definitely misguided." I divulged as I sat on the bed trying to figure my course of action. "In fact. Asia there?" I asked, sorting through my suitcases and piles of clothing for something to wear. "No, she's still in school." my older sister pleasantly confirmed. "Oh ok, I guess I gotta venture out by lonesome then." I said unaware of where to go, or what to do. "Unless, my older sis wanna go hang-out with me. If you go, I can be adult with it." I hopefully suggested. "I can't, I'll have Darryl's baby, remember?" she uttered seemingly relieved to have an excuse not to go. "Oh yeah, I forgot." I dismally said, realizing I was doomed to be alone.

RING. RING! "Hello." I roughly moaned as I lifted my head from the pillow for the second time today. "Hey Auntie, you sleep?" Asia energetically asked. "Why Asia, what's up?" I asked hoping there was no reason for concern. "If you not sleep, can you come get me?" she confidently asked. "Yeah alright, if I ain't still sleep." I indifferently answered as I slammed my head back onto the pillow. "Thank you. I get out at two-twenty. That's three hours from now." she enthusiastically reminded. "Ok Asia!" I harshly mumbled before hanging up.

2-1-5-5-5-5-3-3-4-3. "Hello." Ayanna pleasantly uttered. "Yanna, your child called me, asking me to pick her up from school. And my half sleep ass, I told her I would." I said contemplating abandoning Asia, and just apologizing later. "Ok. There you go, you were looking for her earlier. Now you two can hang out. Did you run those errands, you had?" Ayanna asked reminding me of my responsibilities. "No. I'm gonna just go, after I get her. So, she'll be late, but she'll be with me." I mentioned as I vigorously attempted to put on my jeans. "Ok, thanks for letting me know. I'll see y'all, whenever y'all get here." Ayanna agreeably replied. "Ok." I calmly said before hanging up the phone.

"What's so bad, that I had to come pick you up? Somebody after you, or somethin'?" I asked eagerly as Asia arrived at the window. "No! I just didn't want to catch the bus." she replied as she enthusiastically opened the door. "Girl, you had me all worried. I'm thinking, you in some kinda trouble." I declared passionately. "Why? I didn't say nothing like that, when I called you. I just asked you to come get me." she accurately acknowledged. "Whatever! I got running around to do. So now, you do too." I stated sardonically. "I don't care. As long as Ayanna knows, I'll be home late. Cause she been on my back a lot lately." she said willingly.

"You ok? I heard, you and Ronald been arguing." she asked sympathetically. "How you hear that?" I asked just to confirm what I already knew. "Ronald told uncle Darryl, and uncle Darryl tried to tell my mom. But she told him, to mind his business." Asia said spectacularly. "Me and your uncle always arguing, it's just what we do. Yeah, I'm fine." I said shamefully.

"Ohh. Is that the right time?" she asked vigorously roused. "Why would it be set to the wrong time, Asia? Yes, it's the right time." I replied sarcastically. "We should go get Hassan, since we already up this way. That'll make you feel better." she stated enthusiastically. "That'll make *you* feel better!" I repeated while smiling at her suspicious tactic. "Is Omar with him?" I asked uncertain about whether or not I wanted to see him. "You know they always together. So yeah, probably." she naively answered. "Why?" she continued quickly. "Just asking." I replied just as fast. "You blushing? Oh my God! You like Omar?!" Asia probed while trying to reposition to get a better look at my face. "Girl, ain't nobody blushing! That's somebody's little boy, I'm grown!" I said while grimacing to guard my thoughts. "Whatever! I think you like him." she continued persistently. "Here girl, sing!" I instructed while turning on the radio.

"Back here, thinking 'bout you. I must confess I'm a mess for you." we sang in unison with the radio. "There they go, right there! Up there, near the gas station!" Asia interrupted after noticing them crossing the street up ahead.

"Hey boo." Asia yelled melodiously to Hassan as we pulled into the gas station. "Boo? When we get to being boo?" Hassan stated sternly before smiling enormously. "Boy, I'm only playing with you. I ain't thinking about you and ya lil girlfriends, up here. We just wanted to see if y'all wanted a ride home, that's all! And why you standing outside, what you stole something?" Asia asked in tone just as stern as his. "Whatever! Hey Tiffany, wha'sup? What y'all really doing up this way?" Hassan asked casually as he approached the driver side window. "Just like she said. We were up this way and we saw you coming outta school, and thought to ask if you wanted a ride. Nothing more." I falsely recapped. "You were just coincidentally, up this way?" Hassan asked skeptically. "You do know that me and Omar together, right?" he suspiciously asked, looking at me and then Asia. "Yeah, so. Y'all always together!" Asia answered obliviously. Hassan snickered, realizing that Asia didn't know what he knew. "Yeah, so!" I repeated, staring into Hassan's eyes, hoping he had known to not speak of what happened between me and Omar.

"Hey Omar!" Asia said melodiously as he stepped out of the door with his friend. "Hey what's up Asia!" he responded while walking up to Hassan. "Hi, O." I said as calmly, trying my hardest to hide my allure. "Hey." he responded nonchalantly. "What's wrong with y'all?" Asia asked, noticing both Omar and my demeanor. "Who me? I'm good." Omar stated turning from side to side, pretending to search for who Asia was referring to. "Oh, my bad... Asia, Tiffany, this Vic." he continued unmistakably trying to change the subject. "How y'all doing?" his friend said with in an obvious attempt to look cool stance. "Hey." Asia said keenly. "Hello. Would y'all like a ride home?" I asked staring at Omar. "Yup!" Hassan yelped before he kangarooing to the back door. "Nah. No, thank you. I think I'mma jump on the bus with Vic" Omar replied while closing the back door for Hassan. "What?!" Hassan shrieked unexpectedly. "You sure?" I doubtfully asked. "I'm sure." Omar answered, reaching into the window to shake his friend's hand. "Ok." I said before slowly pulling off. "Why didn't he want a ride home? What y'all two love birds arguing?" Asia asked cluelessly. "No. Why you say that?!" I unconsciously answered thinking that she was referring to Quentin and me. "How you know?!" Asia answered looking at me full of confusion. Hassan's snicker turned into outright laughter.

"Rookie." I chuckled at Hassan as he seemed to feel slightly guilty at Asia's ignorance at the whole situation. "Nah, we not arguing. I think he just needed, some time to himself." he said seriously to us both.

"So, where else we going?" Hassan asked curiously as we vacated the bank's parking lot. "Home. Unless you want me to drop you off, somewhere else." I responded cynically. "Somewhere, like where?" Hassan mockingly probed. "I don't know, anywhere." I replied, pretending to not know where this was going. "You can say it. You want to take me, to Omar's house. I wasn't planning on going there, but if that's where you want to go..." he taunted, smiling cynically from the back seat. "She know she want to go over there, she frontin'." Asia jokingly mocked. "I know. That's why I said, if that's where you want to take me. I'm alright with that." Hassan swiftly added. "Now why would I wanna go over there, if that's not where you going?" I inquired without conviction. "You tell us!" Asia demanded smiling immensely.

"There he go right there." Asia disclosed, pointing at Omar slowly walking up the street. I looked down the street to see Omar casually walking towards us, eating a bag of chips. I began to smile at the thought of being in his presence again. "Hit the horn!" Asia excitedly requested. "No. He'll see him when he come back out." I said as we sat waiting in the driveway of Omar's family's home. "C'mon man!" Hassan yelled before darting across the lawn towards Omar.

"Why he acting like he don't wanna go?" Asia asked anxiously after noticing Hassan pulling Omar's arm. "I don't know. But, if he don't want to go then fine, we leave him here." I asserted aggressively as we watched Hassan and Omar stand in the lawn and discreetly bicker. "Nah, you go 'head." Omar casually maintained as Hassan slowly began to step away from the exchange. "He ain't going." Hassan said as he walked towards the car. "Ok." I confirmed nonchalantly as he approached my open window. "You still coming, right?" Asia asked frenzied. "Yeah, I'm going. That's him being a dick, not me." he said as he opened the door behind me.

"The other day, he couldn't wait to get lost with us. Now all of a sudden he not trying to be bothered?" Asia mumbled while primping her hair in the vanity mirror. "What you do Tiff?!" Asia indistinctly snapped, with a bobby pin in her teeth. "Wha'chu mean, *wha'chu do Tiff*? I ain't do nothing, to that boy!" I retorted sharply while pulling up in front Asia's house. "For real Hassan, why don't he wanna hang with us?" Asia asked again as I turned the ignition key. I gazed through the rearview mirror back at Hassan, who immediately threw a wink when he noticed my staring at him. "Cause, y'all gave him a choice." Hassan insisted sternly as he reached to open his door. "Wha'chu mean, we *gave* him a choice? What was we supposed to do? Force him to go?!" Asia asked unconsciously whilst pushing away the sun visor. "Don't answer her, til I get back. I gotta hear this one! I'll be right back." I requested promptly as I quickly exited the vehicle.

"I wanna see this." I anxiously stated as we stopped at a traffic light not far from Omar's house. "You just want to see, him. Stop acting like you don't, like him. You're allowed to have feelings. You're married, not dead." Asia happily reminded. "You just can't do nothing with 'em!" Hassan laughingly advised from the backseat. "Hahaha." I sarcastically pretended to laugh as I pulled back into the driveway of Omar's house. Hassan laughed again and swiftly jumped out of the van. "How's he gonna to pull this off. Just drag him out the house?" I wondered aloud as Haas leapt up onto the porch.

"Man, open the door!" Hassan yelled into the door. In compliance to Hassan, the door aggressively swung open to Omar standing in wonder. Hassan clutched his friend and lugged him out the house. "Mom, we leaving, love you!" Hassan bawled before closing the door.

I followed Asia's giggles with my own, as we watched Hassan pull Omar across the lawn. "We out! That's all you need to know." Hassan said as he approached the car. "You don't wanna hang out, wit us?" Asia pleasantly asked from the back seat of the car. "I'm just tired, that's all." Omar softly answered as he looked at me in despair. "That ain't why." I interjected smiling at Omar's made-up look of pity. "How you know?" he asked curiously. "I just do." I responded confidently continuing to smile. "C'mon man! You can sleep in the car. I'm trying to go." Hassan desperately suggested before walking towards the back door of the car. "Then go!" Omar asserted before hesitantly turning back towards his house. Hassan looked up at Omar and bleakly let go of the car door handle.

"Go where, Hassan?!" Omar faintly asked before turning away from me to discreetly talk to Hassan. "Do it matter?" I interjected enthusiastically. "That right there, means y'all don't know." Omar deduced confidently. I looked at Omar and smiled after observing that every time I glanced at him, he was already staring at me. "Alright." Omar uttered to Hassan before he half-heartedly walked to the car.

"So, how've you been?" I softly enquired, as we sat in the theater pretending to be interested in the movie. "Alright, I guess." he answered nonchalantly. "I know I left things awkward between us. I'm sorry for that." I continued pleasantly. "I actually understood why you stopped me. I even agreed with you, and wanted to apologize for starting the whole thing. If you would've gave me the chance, you would've known that." he whispered bluntly. I leaned in close to his ear as to not disturb anyone, with our conversing. "That's why I'm apologizing now." I admitted accidentally brushing my lip against his ear while whispering.

"Soooo, how'd you like the movie?" I asked Omar, to liven the car with a new topic. "It was ok. Now, why the need to get out? What's on your mind?" Omar responded with a concerned façade. I looked over at him and just smiled, "You really are... nothing. If you really wanna know, we can talk later" I disclosed, remembering that we weren't alone in the car. Omar seemed focused on whatever was on his mind and turned on the radio to hide it.

"What's funny?" Omar inquisitively asked. "I haven't parked down on the drive, in years. Not sense I was y'all age." I confessed with a smile. "There you go. Trying to say we young, again." Omar stated feeling personally insulted. "No one said anything about you being, young. Besides, age is just a number, remember?" I sarcastically reminded. "I'm not trying to be here long y'all." Tiffany yelled to Hassan and Asia as they were already out and rapidly scurrying away from the jeep.

"So, how are you? How've you been?" I tenderly questioned as I gazed at the moonlight reflect off of the water. "It's later, so let's talk!" he charmingly demanded. "I am, oh so sorry, sir. What do you want to know?" I asked in awe. "You can start with why you felt the need to get out, tonight." he asserted curiously. "Because my husband is more in love with himself than he is with me, and he's finally coming to terms with that." I somberly admitted. "Oh wow." he whispered awe-struck.

"When you're young, it's always *all* about you. As you get older, responsibilities hit and you start becoming the least of your priorities. As you get older, you take grasp of the decisions that make you the person you are trying to become. Ronald hasn't seemed to begin to do any of that." I honestly declared. "And waiting for him is starting to wear on me. I actually think he only joined the Marines, so that he could continue to have someone tell him when to wake up. Tell 'em, what to wear. When to eat... what to eat!" she continued smiling at what my world has become. "It's after eleven. The cops are going to come clear this out soon." I sadly thought. "C'mon let's walk." he suggested punctually.

"Where y'all going? We was on our way back to, the car." Asia stated before I looked up to see her and Hassan advancing toward us. "Here we come now. We'll meet y'all at the car in ten minutes" I said lifting her head completely from his shoulder. "Tiffany, you said that the last time we passed y'all, forty-five minutes ago." Hassan barked sardonically. I started to laugh and seeing Omar laugh, cause me to laugh even harder. We looked at one another and chuckled. "C'mon let's go." I said pulling her arm towards the direction of the car.

"Goodnight Omar." Hassan and Asia said harmoniously from the backseat. "You alright?" I asked noticing him come to a standstill after stepping onto the porch. "I'm fine" he quietly whispered before opening the door. "Ok. Goodnight Omar." I whispered in return before pulling away.

"Goodnight Hassan." I chuckled, in awe that my thoughts were still with Omar. "Ahh, goodnight." he replied while disappointingly pulling himself away from Asia. "Aright Asia. Call me, so I know you got in good." he continued to whisper as we gradually pulled to a halt in front of his home. He opened the door, stepped out and slowly walked across the path to the building entrance. "Hey Aunt Tiff, you picking me up in the morning?" Asia quickly asked. "Yeah, that's the plan. Why?" I asked suspiciously. "Just wondering, if you can pick me up from here? And tell my mom I stayed with you?" Asia timidly implored while staring out of the window at Hassan. "What?! Girl, you done lost your mind! I mean, I'm cool. But, not that damn cool!" I harshly retorted as I too watched and waited for Hassan to enter the building. "Ok. I was just asking." she said calmly. "He's inside." she updated as she gently raised her window shut. "What, you too upset to get up front?" I asked sarcastically as I turned from off of Hassan's street. "No. I'm good Aunt Tiff." she confidently answered. "That's the problem. You're too good. This is going way too easy, compared to what I'm used to with you. No whining? No complaining?" I inquired dubiously. "No, none of that, Aunt Tiff." she snickered as she tranquilly leaned her head back. "You're acting way too grown, right now. Too mature, to be you. What're you up to?" "Nothing. I'm gonna act just like you said and do what a grown-up would do. Go home, throw some clothes in a bag, and catch a cab back up here." she nonchalantly revealed. "What?! No, the hell, you not! You gonna take ya ass in the house and go to bed, like a regular sixteen-year-old does on a Thursday night." I demanded sternly. "Don't worry, I won't tell nobody that you know what I did, if you don't tell nobody you knew where I went." she innocently bargained. "Come on Asia, don't do this to me! Have you ever done this dumb shit before?" I pleaded, hoping this wasn't something new. "Not before the other night." she naively confessed. "I'm going to fucking kill, Hassan." I uttered with my foot steadily pressed against the accelerator. "It's not him, Tiff. I promise you, it's me. And you can't say nothing to him, cause he think you dropped me off up there the other night. He don't know, I caught a cab." Asia desperately admitted. "Are you crazy, Asia? What are you thinking?! Oh shit!" I exclaimed as I hurriedly slamming on the brake before practically going through a red traffic light. "You okay?!" I continued to ask nervously. "Yeah, I'm fine. If that was my fault, I'm sorry." she replied unhappily. "You don't understand, there's finally something exciting going on, something heart pumping. And not to mention, *he*'s a lot more fun than sitting in the house watching tv, by myself." Asia continued genuinely. "Believe me, I understand a lot more than you think I do. But you gotta understand, it'd be against the *responsible adult code* for me to go along with this." I sincerely educated. "You don't have to go along with it. Just don't tell on me." Asia laughingly requested. "I don't fucking believe this." I said as I abruptly whacked on the left turn signal.

"Asia, I'll be here first thing. And I won't be in the mood for your spoiled, bratty bullshit. Just get in the car and shut the hell up." I warned as we pulled back in front of Hassan's building. "Dag, all that? I really give you that much trouble?" she asked authentically. "Not usually. But, right now, yeah!" I answered harshly. "How he gonna know you even here?" I continued to bark. "I just gotta go to the door and buzz him. I hope he didn't go to sleep that fast." she enthusiastically promoted before jumping out of the vehicle. "Hurry up!" I shouted as she gradually walked towards the building. "I am." she turned to mumble back. She turned back towards the building, proceeding her walk to the door as it came flying open. It was Hassan, who without hesitation exceedingly embraced Asia. They stood in front of the building in one another's arms talking quietly. "Tiff!" Asia said aloud as she eagerly ran towards the vehicle while pulling Hassan's hand. "Where you going this late?" I curiously inquired. "He *was* about to walk down to Omar's." Asia hastily interjected. "Were you?" I asked pretending to not be fascinated. "Yeah. To hell with that, now!" Hassan enthusiastically declared. "I just gotta call him and tell him I'm not coming, so he can go lock the door back." he casually continued. "You sure? I can drop you off over there. It's not like I have anywhere to go." I inadvertently admitted. "No. We gonna stay here!" Asia eagerly disclosed. "But that don't have to stop you, from going over there. He left the back door open, cause he waiting for Hassan. I don't think he'll be mad, if he sees it's you." she keenly continued. "What?! Girl, sometimes you don't think. What reason would I have, to go over there?!" I asked struggling to simulate a lack of appeal. "How 'bout to finish up." Hassan teasingly mumbled. I looked at him with misrepresented malcontent, before smiling slightly. "Wha'chu say babe?" Asia pleasantly asked. "I just said, for her to just walk right in the back door. She'll be alright. And at least it'll give you *something* to do, somewhere to go." Hassan informed candidly.

"I don't believe I'm doing this." I said to myself as I parked in front of Omar's neighbor's house. "The boy is only sixteen, you are twenty-five, and married!" I continued as I hesitantly began to pull the key from the ignition. "But when he's around, I don't feel him as being sixteen. And he's more attentive and mature, than Ron has ever been." I debated as I snatched out the keys and lowered the vanity mirror. "If you go through with this, it is making you the villain in your marriage. Not to mention, he's somebody's baby." I continued to contend pushing away the mirror. "I'm not the one that started all of this. And I refuse to go back to the hotel to sleep alone, or wake up to another fucking note. Fuck dat! Not to mention, the fact that I don't gotta fuck 'em." I remembered as I forcibly pulled the mirror back down and continued to check my face and hair. "But you want to, 'cause he felt good and, he made you feel good. He even made you cum and he didn't put shit inside you." I continued disputing with myself. "That right there should be enough in itself, to make you go." I snickered merrily. "But the bottom line, he's sixteen and you're married!" I quickly opposed again. I slowly pushed the visor closed, grabbed my keys and opened the car. "Fuck the bottom line!" I said as I vigorously exited the jeep.

"What the Fuck, Tiffany?" I asked myself as I crept along the side of the house. "Somebody downstairs, watching tv. I hope it's him." I whispered noticing the glare of a television light through the window curtains. "I'm too old, to be doing this shit. And way too old, to like it." I snickered, excitedly slithering under the window towards the backyard gate. "It'd be just my luck that was his dad in there, watching tv." I whispered as I approached the back door. "At least then, I'd feel better about the age factor." I laughed as I turned the door knob.

"Omar". I whispered as I tip toed into the kitchen, with my heart pounding incredibly. A sigh of relief fell over me as the television light flashed off, and Omar's silhouette came marching from the dark room. "Hey" I whispered smiling from ear to ear. "Hey" he replied with a look of total perplexity across his face. "Don't look so glad to see me." I whispered sarcastically. "I'm always glad to see you. Now, wha'chu doing here?" he whispered. "Everything alright?" he asked frantically turning to look around. asked after rotating to inspect for my parents. "Nothing's wrong. I just didn't to go back there, yet." I explained smiling greatly.

"Shit! what time is it?" he quietly uttered after springing awake and looking around the room. "It's only eleven thirty. You were only sleep for about half hour, forty-five minutes." I confessed as he gawked at me awkwardly.

"Well, I'm about to go back to sleep. You alright?" Omar candidly asked before stripping down to get into bed. "I'm fine. Make sure you leave enough room for me under there." I said softly realizing that I had just reached the beginning of the end.

"I can't let tonight get out of hand like last time. Can't cum, and run, like I did last time. Wouldn't be able to live with myself. Running from this kid, twice." I thought, realizing I needed to show him who was boss this time. "Where is he?" I pondered as I continued to back up with the intent of feeling him dig into my ass. The actuality of not finding him with subtle movement, caused me to think to use a more aggressive method. I squeezed my hand back between us to search for his dick. "What the hell?" I questioned to myself, realizing why I couldn't feel it while grinding my ass into him. "This can't be comfortable." I whispered while grasping and pulling his dick from between his legs. "Now, ain't that better?" I said after pulling my panties down just enough to put his dick against my ass.

"Remember the hotel, because I do. Now it's my turn to tease." I avowed, slithering under the covers to start my troublemaking.

"I-I told you that I don't do teasing w-well." he stuttered. "Boy, calm down. If this is what I wanna do, this is what I gonna do" I laughed sliding my lips up and down his legs. "I'm calm. You finished with the teasing?" he asked sternly, pretending to be unaffected. "Not yet" I answered crawling my way back up his almost naked body. I stopped at his dick and began to gently rotated my tongue across the top of it. I ran my tongue down the shaft and returned back up, ending with a gently peck on its head. I slowly lowered my myself down onto his dick, using my tongue to direct it into my mouth.

I pulled him out of my mouth and began to kiss my way up his body. "Now, I'm done teasing." I confessed slowly kissing across his body.

"Damn, you smell good." he alleged as while reintroducing his lips to my neck. "Thank you. Now, what are you doing?" I asked powerlessly welcoming his kisses. "Paying you back, for all of that teasing, you were just doing." he conveyed. "But I was just paying you back, for the hotel. You had your tongue, in my ass." I reminded, moving so that he could easily get across my neck.

"You're smiling, I feel it." Omar whispered as we laid embraced. "Yeah, I am." I admitted, smiling harder at the fact that he was so attentive. I lifted so he could see the size of my smile before crawling up his body and straddling his waist. Omar, always the gentleman, used his hand to uncomfortably bend his erection to keep it from touching me. "I wanna say wow, Quentin. But this ain't the time for that." I thought, referring to how advanced he was. "What are you smiling at?" I whispered looking down into his eyes. "You. You're so beautiful. And you're glowing. And you're smiling. You're beautiful, glowing, smiling and in my bed with me." he charmingly answered. I smiled at his refinement. His maturity and sophistication is so alluring. I started to blush and quickly tried to cover it with a laugh as he continued to stare into my eyes.

"Three..." he began, before I hastily seized his hand and pilfering it from his dick. It sprung out of my hand and heavily smacked me on my ass.

"You better get that." I advised while raising my waist to point out the potential danger of where his dick was. "Get what?! It's fine." he answered naïve to my next course of action. "That!" I answered slowly shepherding his dick inside of me.

"Tiffany!" he said tenderly moving my shoulder. "What time do you have to get Asia?" he asked quietly. "Call Hassan, and see what they wanna do." I insisted. "So, what's the plan then?" I asked sternly after he spoke cryptically to Hassan. "Well, I'm gonna go back to sleep for an hour, then get dress, then head out to the bus which comes at eight, forty-two." he declared arrogantly.

"So, how much time do you got, now?" I connivingly asked while pretending to be preoccupied with myself in the mirror. "I got about an hour and fifteen minutes before my alarm goes off." he resolutely confessed, before jumping into the bed. "A whole seventy-five minutes, huh?" I mumbled as I crept back into bed with him.

CHAPTER 66

"Asia"

"Tiff. Tiff!" I yelled in an attempt to get her Tiffany's attention. "Girl, what's wrong with you?! You can't be going somewhere else in your head, while you driving! Especially, with me in the car!" I continued severely. "Girl, I'm fine. I was just thinking!" she declared dynamically. "Why don't you *think* about answering Ms. Valerie question." I strongly reminded after looking back at Ms. Valerie impatiently awaiting an answer. "Oh, I'm sorry Ms. Val. I'm still a little overwhelmed, by today. And I must admit, talking to you is kinda unnerving. I can't even imagine, what you think of me." Tiffany disclosed. "What I think of you isn't important, I'm just an old lady." Miss Valerie advised from behind me. "That's not true at all, Mis. Val. You, raised Quentin. You, were his first mother. The one that shaped his smile and imagination." Tiffany stated genuinely. "All the more reason for my question." Miss Valerie reiterated. "Well Ms. Val, I was married when I was with your son." Aunt Tiffany started. "And twice his age." Miss Valerie contemptuously interjected. "Yeah. But when I was with him, it didn't feel like it. He was so sophisticated, so mature and charming. For a minute, I didn't see seventeen." Aunt Tiffany confessed quietly enchanted. "That's because, he was about to turn sixteen." she sneeringly criticized. "But I can understand. His father was the same way, and he definitely has always been his father's child." Miss Valerie explicitly explained. "Well, like I said, I was married. Even though it wasn't a great marriage, at the time. I wanted to, needed to… make it work. If for nothing more, than to prove I at least tried. And that son of yours. Well, he came along when I my marriage was at a really low point. Just when I needed him *least*. When I was at my most desolate, and vulnerable. And he was so pleasing, Ms. Val. Even without trying, he was pleasing. I mean, it was at a point where just his presence made me feel good. He came in and created what was, and is still, one of the most incomparable moments of my life. In turn producing, *the*, most incomparable moment of my life. And even though I'd caught my husband cheating multiple times up to that point, mine was worse. Even when he admitted not three months into my pregnancy, that he was the father of a two-year-old girl. I still thought, mine was worse. Because I was taken over, by a fifteen-year-old boy." Aunt Tiffany piercingly divulged. I tipped my head back as my eyes uncontrollably widened after hearing that my now deceased uncle, fathered a child. "That pain! That embarrassment! How could I do that to my husband?! How could I do that to the man, I vowed for better or for worst to? I couldn't! So, for rest of my marriage, I set out to fix my mess. Through all of the backlash, and accusations. Through all of the slander, and anguish. Even amongst his continuing infidelity and disloyalty, I was determined to fulfill my marriage vows. By the time Quentin was born, I was no longer me. So, releasing him to his father was not even a second thought. In order for me to configure the life I set out to when I said *I do,* that boy's baby had to go." Tiffany continued to irreversibly admit. I felt a sense of empathy, watching my favorite aunt, my Marine tough aunt, become so vulnerable, so fast.

"I know that was cleansing. But I know, the why. I've always known, the *why.* What I couldn't understand was, the *how.* There was nothing you could do or threaten, to get my boys away from me for even a second. You chose to give yours up, for a lifetime. How, could you choose to walk away from that baby? I imagine, that had to take great strength. Which always made me believe that you were also strong enough, to stick it out." Miss Valerie unsympathetically specified. "Where were you when I was making the decision, to put me before my baby?" Tiffany sniffled gesturing at my pocketbook. "Wasn't in God's plan for me to be there." Miss Valerie prudently answered.

"Here we are, Ms. Val." Tiffany said as we pulled into her driveway. "If today has been nothing else, it's been a long time coming. Thank you, and good night to you Ms. Lane. Ms. McDeyess." Ms. Valerie said as she slid out of the car. "I'll get those for you. Ms. Val." Tiffany said as Ms. Valerie reached back in the car, to grab her bags. "Thank you, honey." Ms. Valerie said as she waited outside the car for Tiffany. She waved goodbye to me, before turning to lead Tiffany slowly up the driveway and across the porch, to the front door.

"I miss my mom." Tiffany dismally sighed as she abruptly plopped back into the car. "I knew, you were thinking that. I could tell when you asked, why wasn't she around." I confessed to my aunt. "I'm sure she could, too." Tiffany said as she backed out of the driveway. "You think?" I asked remiss to Tiffany's evidence of Miss Valerie's insight. "Oh, I know! I believe she knew Quentin wasn't my last pregnancy, too. And I think she knew, why." she passionately announced. "What do you mean, why? You did get pregnant, once. But you had a miscarriage, right?!" I asked astonished that she had secrets that she couldn't tell me. "No, I only told y'all that. It was actually, three times. Your uncle was persistent." she whispered with a dispirited chuckle. "Three times?" I uttered in absolute empathy. "You don't have to sound so regretful. One of them wasn't a miscarriage, I just couldn't do it." she explained, gratified in her decision. "You couldn't do it? Wha'chu mean, you couldn't do it?! Was this before or after, your meltdown." I interrogated harshly. "After. It was two years, before Ron died." she comfortably replied. "So, I'm not understanding why you didn't have it? It was your husband's baby." I asked perplexed at her decision. "Because I recognized, it wouldn't be another Quentin. Another Quentin, wasn't possible without Omar. Ron couldn't cook up anything that perfect." she said confidently. "You do know, neither could Omar?" I sarcastically inquired. "Yeah, I know. But he'd be the closest I could possibly get to it." she rationally divulged.

CHAPTER 67

"Quentin"

"... the night go?" Imani softly whispered before gently kissing my cheek. "You never called. And when I called looking for you, Storm said you was already sleep." she continued while sliding onto the bed behind me. I gradually lifted and turn to face Imani. "Hey babe." I said groggily, before dropping my head back onto the pillow. I cringed slightly as the thought of last night's news, quickly stampeded back into my mind. "She'll never forgive me!" I dreaded as I stared at this woman. I quickly covered my mouth to suppress any odor while talking. "It's ok. I've smelled you worse than this." she smirked pulling my hand away from my mouth. "Well, c'mon. How'd it go?" she impatiently repeated as she nimbly laid her head on the adjacent pillow. "I wish I woulda stayed. My family is so dry, and boring." she continued genuinely regretful. "I should've just stayed, and let my mom bitch." she remorsefully admitted while staring into my eyes. "So, tell me about your mom. Your cousin was cool as shit." she continued to impatiently question. "They were... eventful." I uttered before abruptly sitting up and slamming my back against the head of the bed. "Eventful? That's all you got?" she disappointingly asked, before following me into the sitting position. "I know something happened! Stories? Family drama? Anything?!" she eagerly continued to probe. I took in all of her questions with the intent to answer them, but the thought of Tasha being pregnant remained resolute in my mind. "She didn't mention anything extraordinary about her family. Just started naming people. But you were there for most of it, believe it or not." I reservedly uttered. "Quentin. What's wrong? Something happened, after I left. Her visit ended up bad, didn't it?" Imani sweetly asked, noticing my lack of involvement in the conversation. "How do I tell this woman that loves me, about Tasha? Let alone her being pregnant." I thought intensely as I rested my head against the headboard and stared into her eyes. "Yes, and no." I responded impartially. "Well to make it easier on you, I'll only ask about the *yes* part." she kidded as she pulled my head down to rest it on her chest.

"Good morning, Paw-Paw." Imani said melodiously, as she reached the bottom of the stairs. "Good morning Imani. How are you this morning?" I faintly heard him answer as I reluctantly followed her down the steps. "I'm good. I'm about to make Que and Ms. G., some breakfast. You want some?" she asked cheerfully. "No, I'm fine. Thank you." he answered somberly after noticing I was behind her. I glanced over at my father sitting in his chair. "Excuse me." I sullenly requested before treading around Imani into the kitchen. "Ok. Well, I'm here if you change your mind." she said frolicking behind me.

"What's wrong with y'all?" Imani intuitively asked while watching me stare out of the window at the multitude of cars and people. "Huh? Who?" I uneasily responded, quickly turning to face her. "Y'all. You. Your dad. Your mom. Even Storm is acting funny, but not like y'all." she thoroughly disclosed. "What happened last night, that has everybody acting so funny?" she curiously questioned as she continued to maneuver through downtown Dover traffic. "Nobody acting funny. They probably just tired, and as for me I'm fine. I'm thinking about this doctor's appointment." I answered, unsuccessfully trying to conceal any characteristic of anything wrong in my demeanor. "They're tired, and you're fine? C'mon Que. You barely talking to me. You and your mom only said two words to each other, during breakfast. And your dad hasn't gotten up or said a word to anyone but me, since I been there! What's wrong?" Imani sincerely asked reaching across the center console to seize my hand from my lap. "Not right now, babe. I promise I'll tell you, because I have to. But, just gimme a few." I asked genuinely as I gently massaged her hand with my thumb. DOINK! "That's nobody but Tasha!" I thought, hearing my phone's text notification. "Now that you said that, I really wanna know! It has nothing to do with the baby though, right?" she anxiously asked before pulling my hand to place on her belly. "Oh noooo, baby girl will be fine." I confidently reassured while rubbing my hand across her stomach. "I'm only saying okay, cause we're here, and I trust you." she said pretending to feel better about the whole thing.

We pulled behind a line of cars waiting to enter a parking garage. "You might want to answer your phone, now. The doctor gets upset, when you not paying attention to him. I'm leaving mine, in the car." Imani warned as we inched closer to the garage entrance booth. "I don't care, if he get upset." I responded feeling slighted by the warning. I pulled out my phone only to appease Imani. "Please God, please make it acceptable, in case she's watching." I thought as I put in my pin to open the phone.

> **{Juice}**
> **W'sup lil bro? You good?**

"Tell him I said hi." Imani said blatantly confirming that she saw it too. "Stay outta my personal business." I joked, relieved that it was no other message. "What personal business?" she mocked as we approached the booth. "Thank you." she said as she grabbed a ticket from the machine. "You do know that that's a machine you're talking to?" I inquired as I texted Juice back.

> **{Me}**
> **Nothin much big guy. Stuffed and hungover. Wasup wit u?!**

"Thanks doc." I said extending my hand to the doctor. "My pleasure, and it was nice to finally meet you, dad." the doctor said as he firmly grasped my hand. "He was cool as shit." I whispered, catching up to Imani in the hall. "I told you! Now, if only we could get your dad to come up here." she said, enthusiastically grabbing my hand to hold. "He won't come here?" I promptly asked. "Nope." she answered joyfully escorting me back to the car. "Why not?" I bewilderedly continued as we stepped onto the elevator. "Cause your mom told him she thinks the doctor, has a crush on her." Imani giggled, playfully pressing all of the elevator floor buttons. "I am so glad you came here with me." she gleefully continued, pushing me against the back wall of the elevator. "Is this our floor?" she quietly asked while staring into my eyes. "No." I answered modestly. "Good!" she whispered before abruptly pushing her tongue into my mouth.

"Hey, how'd you like Dr. Hurschwin? Cool, isn't he?" my mom pleasantly asked as I stepped into the kitchen behind Imani. "Yeah, he is." I answered honestly, relieved that she was even talking to me again. "Too bad Mr. G won't go to see, for his self. Some men just can't help, being men." Imani sarcastically smiled. "One day, I'll get him there." my mom insisted as she pulled a bottle opener from the drawer. "Now, speaking of Omar, we've been speaking extensively about what was discovered last night. And the only thing we've agreed upon, is that you and he have to talk." she cordially continued before opening the refrigerator. She reached in and pulled two beers from the refrigerator. "Here." she said handing me the opener and beverages. "Is anyone going to tell me about last night? I mean, you did say it's something I have to know." Imani reminded as I hesitantly seized the bottles from my mother. "Yeah, it really is. Would you like to talk to Imani, first and I just tell your dad to wait?" my mother cordially asked. "No. Let me handle this, first. One's going to be a lot worse, than the other." I confessed. "Gimme a few, babe." I requested as I headed into the other room. "C'mon Imani. You can tell me about your appointment." my mother said as I left the room.

"Hey." I uttered as I entered the room. "Hey." she responded, looking up from her phone. "You okay?" I asked slowly looking around the room for a place to sit. "I'm fine Quentin. And I hope you up here to tell me what the hell is going on? I don't like not knowing, when it has something to do with me!" she insisted as she moved over to give me room on the bed to sit. "I'm ok here. Get back to your comfortable." I said sitting on the chair on the far side of the room. "I don't even know how to start." I nervously admitted as I intertwined my fingers and rested my head atop my closed hands. "How about, at the beginning!" Imani demanded as she slid across the bed to sit on the edge closest to my chair. "Ok." I sighed before taking a deep breath.

"I cheated on you." I swiftly confessed. "I know I was wrong and I, uh... I deserve whatever you decide. All I can say is I'm sorry, and *beg* your forgiveness." I continued before pausing to wait for a response from Imani. I opened my hands, let my head fall back and my eyes close. "What do you mean that's *all* you can say! That's not the beginning! Now, start from the beginning like I said. I wanna know it all!" Imani growled. I opened my eyes and looked over at Imani. She was rocking back and forth at a snail's pace, with her teeth grit and her eyes swelled with tears. I was in awe witnessing Imani like this. I continued to stare at the tears pour from her eyes as she seemed not to blink or breathe or move in any way other than the swaying. "Wha'chu staring at?! Don't you got a story to tell!" Imani barked as she reached for the framed picture of us on the nightstand next to the bed.

"So, everybody knew I was getting fucking played for a fool, but me?" Imani angrily asked while squeezing her hand, with my blood covered shirt. "No. They all found out last night when my biological told us that Tasha came to her house, and told her about the baby." I shamefully answered while looking down to see if there was anything more on the sock, that I was using to stop my bleeding. "And, you're not a fool. You were in love." I genuinely reassured. "*Am* in love. That's *why* I'm the fucking fool. I really thought you loved me, too." she divulged as her wrath progressively withdrew back to grief. "I do. God knows, I do!" I pleaded, staring at the woman who was an hour ago, elated to be carrying my child. "Wow! Guess

I should be glad you don't hate me. Imagine what you'd do to me then."
Imani sarcastically uttered. "So, this girl Tasha was why that white boy
CJ was acting all funny, while I was up there?" she asked trying to put it
all together. "Wait! The girl, that liked my jacket? That was her?!" Imani
asked disappointedly in awe. "Yeah, that was her. Oh shit, your hand!" I
stated, reminding her about her wound. "I knew I shoulda followed my
gut, and questioned you then. What, the white boy found out about y'all?"
she probed as she removed the shirt to observe her cut hand. "He thought
he did, we did our best to convince him otherwise." I replied, extending
towards her to try and get a look at her hand. "Aww, she wasn't as good at
hiding it as you were?" she scathingly scoffed while continuing to examine
her hand. I quickly jumped up and hurried to the door. "Dad!" I yelled as
I slightly cracked the door open. I swiftly closed the door back and began
to pick up the shards of glass and other debris from the floor. "What
about Juice, Dame and your other friends? They know?" Imani continued
to interrogate as I kneeled beneath her cleaning. "Nobody knows about,
this her being pregnant shit. But yeah, they know the rest." I nervously
admitted, being this close to her.

Knock. Knock! "Come in!" I yelled while picking up the confetti
made from pictures of Imani and me. "I really don't fucking believe this!
Y'all was just one big happy fucking family over there, huh?" Imani said
as my father entered the room. "What's wrong?" my dad asked before
observing the room.

"Damn, she got you good!" my dad scoffed, noticing the large, blood
centered bump over my eye, my split lip and blood in my hair. "But you
deserved it." he continued surveying the all of the destruction caused by
our little quarrel. "Look at her hand. Does she need a doctor, or stitches
or something?" I asked pointing out Imani's hand. "What? Where?!" my
dad asked nervously taking hold of Imani's hand. "I don't think so, but
we're going anyway." my dad said helping Imani up and escorting her out
of the room.

CHAPTER 68

"Tasha"

"I know you're not even formed yet, but just your foundation is enough right now." I whispered to the small stack of paperwork from the doctor's office, gathered on the bed. "Before anything else, I want you to know that you're here for a reason. You're proof of how much I love, your daddy. I know in the past I've been somewhat cavalier, with my life. Especially my love life. I know I've used that word love selfishly and even deceptively, but I can I honestly say that I really love that man. Yes, I did. Scratch that… do, in some aspect have love for Brian. But I was never, in love with him. He was never going to be, your dad. He was, the best thing available. I grew to love him, like you would a close friend. I just wish I could make him want to leave me, so it'd be over and done with." I genuinely declared. "Baby, please don't look at mommy as immoral or uninhibited. I'm not perfect, I just look it." I joked, looking over the papers as I transferred them from the bed to the desk. "I've never been here before. This… this is the first thing that you and I are going through, together. So, please don't expect mommy to know much about it. Ok? I'm learning too." I said as I grabbed my phone from the desk and plopped down onto the bed.

"I'm texting your daddy. Cause he has yet to call me today. Even though he knows I'm dying to hear about how it went with, Grandma T." I condescendingly narrated before texting.

> **{Me}**
> **Good evening baby.**

"Oh God. What if she told him about the baby, over dinner?" I thought, realizing his excitement could go either direction. "Please don't hate me, Quentin." I uttered as I lie there anxiously awaiting his response.

RING. RING! "Here goes nothing." I uttered as I rummaged my hand around for the phone ringing somewhere on the bed behind me. RING. RING!

I impatiently turned around to look, after being unable to find the phone, blindly. "Hey!" I hastily said hurrying to answer as not lose the call. "Hey." Brian calmly responded. I pulled the phone from my ear and looked at the screen. "Damn!" I whispered after seeing Brian's name on the screen. "Hello" he faintly reiterated as I continued to regret answering his call. "Hey." I replied grimly. "What's up?" he calmly inquired. "Nothing. What's up with you?" I asked indifferently, with hopes that he'd notice my lack of interest. "Nothing. I didn't see you at the Souderton Game. Everything alright?" he asked apparently reaching for a topic to converse about. "That's because I knew you'd be there, and just didn't feel like it with you. Why did I answer this call?!" I quietly questioned myself before replying. "Yeah, no, I didn't make it this year. But I'm fine. Thanks for checking up on me." I half-heartedly replied. "You don't gotta thank me. But you can answer a question for me." he requested calmly. "Ok. What's the question?" I curiously asked. "What's going on here? What are we doing?" he asked bluntly. "What do you mean?" I asked, hoping to be wrong in what I assumed he was questioning. "You know what I mean. Please don't play at being dumb." he required sternly. "I ain't playing, at anything. I don't know what you're talking about when you ask questions like, *what are we doing.*" I said severely. "I'm talking about, us being together. Then not together. Then you're not sure. Then let's fix it. Then you don't know. And now I'm hearing that you may be pregnant! So, now that you know what I'm talking about, I'll ask again. What's going on here?" he furiously asked. "Oh wow. He may be just mad enough, to leave me this time." I stated, scoffing at his frustration. "You didn't mention his name like you usually do, when we have this argument." I acknowledged surprised that Quentin wasn't specified. "That because it's exhausting." he said disheartened. "Yeah, I was thinking that too." I agreed nonchalantly. "Why do you want me, Brian?" I calmly asked curious to what he seems to be relentlessly holding to. "Why do I want you?" he repeated marveling at my unawareness. "Yeah. What do you see in me?" I candidly recapped, showing my comprehension of my question. "Eleven years. That's what I see, in you. All of my firsts. My first day of middle school. My braces. My first kiss. My first fight. My first football game. The prom. My parent's divorce. My virginity. You were by my side, for all of that." he passionately disclosed. "I remember all of those." I conceded, smiling from the nostalgic thoughts. "Believe me, I wanna let you go." he genuinely admitted. "You do?" I asked surprised at his confession. "Yeah. I know I'm not perfect, but I don't deserve this. I just don't think I know how to do life, without you." Brian continued to openly confess. "You'll be alright. You're about to be drafted to the NFL. You'll get to live that, *lifestyle of the rich and famous*. And hopefully get on Cribs, if they bring it back." I encouragingly reminded. "You remember that?!" he asked surprised that I haven't totally disregarded him and our past together. "Yeah! Why wouldn't I?! We used to watch that show every week, fantasizing about that being us on there one day." I confirmed enthusiastically. "Yeah. Everything back then was *we* or *us*." he sorrowfully acknowledged. "How were you able to let that go so effortlessly. Especially for broke ass, second team Gregory?!" he asked, astonished at my ability to do it. "I didn't say it was easy, it just had to be done. It was time. And I didn't do it for Quentin. I landed in his arms, after I had already fell out of yours. Believe me, it wasn't my intent to be malicious. Selfish, yes. but not cruel. I'm sorry for that." I authentically apologized as I began to skim through my phone for pics of Quentin. More specifically, Quentin and I. "Hey, that's life, right?" he said playacting a nonchalant demeanor. "Don't say that, it comes off bitter." I genuinely advised while smiling intensely at a pic Juice took of Quentin and I making love. "Bitter? Nooo, not me. You pregnant for real this time?" Brian sourly asked. "This time?" I asked confused by the implied accusation. "Yeah. You told me that you were pregnant once before, you don't remember?" he confidently divulged. "No! You got me confused with someone else. Something you wanna tell me?" I sternly asked, assuming that his previous cheating was more significant than I had known. "No Tasha, it was you! It was right after the first time you stuck your tongue in my mouth. Remember?" he evoked strategically trying to raise sentiment. "Yeah. Yeah! I remember, that's when you gave me mono and I thought I was having morning sickness." I said dynamically. "I didn't give you mono, because I never had it. I just pretended to have it, so I can stay home from school at the same time you were." he said haughtily. "Aww, that's sweet." I genuinely admitted. "So, are you really expecting?" he tenaciously recapped. "Yes. This time, I really am pregnant." I said sneeringly. "I'm assuming you're certain, it's not mine." he promptly patronized. "Yeah. I still don't think it's possible for you to get me pregnant, from kissing." I said just as condescending as was. "Damn. That's fucked up, Tasha!" Brian severely asserted. "I told you, none of this was intended." I said reiterated calmly. "I guess I shoulda fucked Kristie Lee, when I had the chance." he admitted casually. "Eww. You want Kristie Krabs?" I flamboyantly asked, before laughing at his revelation. "Stop that! We both know that you started that rumor, when you found out she kissed me at the Delta party. You know she never had, anything."

he reminded bitterly. "If you say so. I myself, think you can do better than that." I honestly confessed. "And what makes you think that you can't still have her. Believe me, she hasn't gone anywhere." I instinctively continued. KNOCK. KNOCK. KNOCK!

"Come in." I said gently. "Hey girl!" Erica spiritedly said as she and K'lynne crashed into the room. "Hey y'all." I said with composure, gesturing for them to relax as I was on the phone. "Every time we see you now, you on the phone! Tell him you gotta hang up, ya girls are here!" Erica unreservedly continued. I waved my hand again gesturing for her to bring down her enthusiasm a little. "Who that? Que?" K'lynne quietly queried, tapping my arm to get my attention. "Yeah, it's Que! Hey Que!" Erica vivaciously blurted, following K'lynne's question. "No! It's not, Que!" I mouthed to them with my hand over the phone. "Brian, I gotta go. I guess, I'll see you back at school." I calmly informed, anxious to reprimand Erica. "Not if, I see you first." Brian pleasantly joked. "Bye. And good luck with Kristie Krabs." I laughingly wished him. "Bye Tasha. Congrats on the baby. And tell ya boy, I still owe him one." he countered solemnly before ending the call. I smirked at the remark, recalling the last time Brian attempted to fight Quentin.

"What is wrong with you? You got no panache." I said to Erica sternly. "I was just saying hi. It ain't my fault you cheating on him too, hoe!" Erica responded while exploring through my closet. "I'm not cheating on Que. I was actually saying goodbye to Brian, if you must know." I eagerly retorted. "I thought you did that weeks ago." K'lynne asked in a state of bewilderment. "She did, until she remembered that Que still had his pregnant girlfriend, at home! You know Tasha ain't giving her all, especially if he not giving his!" Erica swiftly answered. "Anyway. I tried to, but me and Brian got so much history. It was hard to just, walk away from that." I answered honestly. DOINK! "But you're done now?" K'lynne realistically asked. "Yeah, I am." I replied, eagerly grasping my phone to expose the text.

{Bae}
Hey.

"Oh, I absolutely am!" I genuinely reiterated as I eagerly responded to Quentin's text.

> **{Me}**
> **Where u been all day? Y havn't u called/txt me?**

"Look at you, Tasha, nose all open. You really do love him. Look at her K'lynne, she glowing!" Erica said while pulling a dress from my closet. "I see." K'lynne said skeptically. "I already know what you thinking. And before, you probably would've been right to think it. But's different, this time. So, don't take this the wrong way. But I don't care if you don't accept it as true, not this time." I said profoundly as I awaited Quentin's response.

DOINK!

> **{Bae}**
> **U know I gotta play the role when she around**

"Play the role? He the one that's always saying that we aren't to bring up home." I mumbled uncertainly. "Huh?" K'lynne said as she stared at me trying to deem my thoughts while texting.

> **{Me}**
> **What happened 2 our relationship limits?**
> **Nothing about home remember?**
> **{Bae}**
> **Relationship? We was jus fuckin that's all!**

"Just fucking?" I repeated dynamically. "What the hell you mean we was just fucking?" I repeated again with even more enthusiasm. "What? He said that? Lemme see!" Erica demanded as she pulled another item from my closet and tossed it on the bed. "Yeah, it's alright. Don't worry about it. He's just talking shit. I got this!" I said masking Quentin's unexpected anger, to my two oldest friends.

> **{Me}**
> **Just fucking?! You funny! I bet I bought the drawers u got**
> **on right now. I know for a fact u bought my panties.**

"Damn. I really thought he'd be at least civil about the baby." I thought as my eyes closed and face grimaced. "See and you trying to get serious with him! Ohhhh, this jacket would look nice with my retro Air Max's and that choker, I gave you. I hope it's here, and not up at school." Erica said sternly as she tossed the jacket on the bed and headed over to my dresser to find the neckless. "Seriously, what's wrong Tash? You don't look as happy, as you did a few seconds ago." K'lynne quietly inquired, noticing the change in my facial expression. "Nothing." I whispered, pretending to brush off the text messages. DOINK!

> **{Bae}**
> **That was $20 I had left on a gift card. It was nothin!**

"What?! I know you mad, but what you not gonna do is lie." I quietly grumbled so to not further alert my friends.

> **{Me}**
> **$20? The panties I got on are the ones you got when you spent that $350 on my outfit, just to go out on your arm for the nite. That same outfit you tore off me that nite after the show… remember?**

"You not gonna act like I don't mean nothing, cause you there with that bitch. Let me set this straight, right now!" I thought as I responded to Quentin's text. "Hey. Why you ain't tell us you went to the hospital?" Erica inquired before picking up the papers with the hospital logo on them. "You were in the hospital? Are you alright?" K'lynne said rising from the bed to commandeer the papers from Erica. I quickly jumped up to try and intercept the papers from Erica, before K'lynne could get to them. "Oh, this is important then." Erica enthusiastically said as she moved to the other side of the room to avoid seizure of the papers. "It's nothing. I'm fine. Seriously. I just went in there for a check-up." I declared as Erica began to read the papers. DOINK! "Don't you got something you're dealing with on your phone?" K'lynne said as she gathered close to Erica to read the papers as well.

"Oh my God. Tasha, you're pregnant!" Erica said quietly, placing her hand over her mouth in awe. "What?! Let me see!" K'lynne insisted, before snatching the papers from Erica. "You bitch! When were you gonna tell us?" K'lynne whispered as she discovered the staggering news for herself. "I don't know." I said as I hopelessly stopped attempting to claim the paperwork. "Are you ok? Are you excited?" Erica asked concerned for my well-being. "I was." I mournfully admitted as I turned back to look at my phone, lying on the bed. "Is it Quentin's?" K'lynne nervously asked. "What kinda question, is that?" Erica interjected before I could answer. "Yes, it's Quentin's." I answered nonetheless. "I was just trying to picture what my little niece or nephew, gonna look like." K'lynne said, blatantly pretending to encourage. I plopped back down on the bed, and reluctantly grasped my phone. "We're gonna be aunties!" Erica said eagerly as she confiscated the papers from K'lynne.

> **{Bae}**
> **Well u hold on to those memories babe, I'm gonna focus on my REAL family from now on.**

"Yeah, looks like they're gonna need y'all. Cause according to this, I'm gonna be a single mom." I uttered as I read and re-read Quentin's text. "Wha'chu mean?" K'lynne said sitting down next to me. I lifted the phone to show her the text.

"He's apparently pissed about my being pregnant. Or maybe it's the way he found out. I don't know!" I said as I downheartedly rested my head on K'lynne's shoulder. "When'd you find out? How'd you tell him?" Erica asked while looking across the papers for a date. "I found out a few weeks ago and I didn't tell him. I told his mom, who he met yesterday, for the first time." I solemnly admitted. "So, his mom, who he never met, comes to him for their first meeting, on Thanksgiving, with a message saying I'm pregnant, from the girlfriend he's not supposed to have." K'lynne divulged, slowly reiterating the gathered facts. "Basically." I embarrassingly conceded. "Wow. You hear how messed up that sounds, right?" Erica said splashing down on my other side. "Yup." I regretfully acknowledged. "So, I understand why he's mad. But he must be fuming. Cause he not even talking. like himself." I declared as I showed Erica the text. "Wha'chu mean?" Erica responded, pulling the phone from my hand. "He not being charming or charismatic or none of that. I mean, even when he mad, he make you wanna fuck him! I'm not getting that, from these texts." I willingly confessed as I wiped my eye to eliminate the tears beginning to fall. "Damn. I gotta meet this guy." K'lynne said tapping my arm to gesture for me to lift up from her shoulder. She reached onto the nightstand next to the bed, and claimed a tissue from the box. "Yeah, I wanted you to." I said, while wiping my hand across my cheek. "What do he mean *real family?* He trying to say, he gonna disregard my niece?!" Erica asked intensely. "That's what I mean. He's not even the type to ever even think about, abandoning his child. Not his m.o. at all. Not even mad is that in his disposition. But then again, neither is going for the jugular. And he's doing that, so. Maybe I don't know him, like I think I do." I quickly disclosed, exposing the truth in Quentin's character. "Well going back in these texts, you're not being yourself, either." Erica said reading the texts. "So, lets push the envelope. Didn't you tell me that he seemed to not even care who walked in the morning he left for vacation?" K'lynne said, snatching the phone from Erica. "Yeah." I responded as I took the tissue from K'lynne's hand and stood to go to the window. "Ok. Let's remind him of that!" K'lynne deviously said as she began to text. "No don't send that." I said as I raised the window for some fresh air. "Why not? It's the truth, ain't it. I'm just, reminding." K'lynne continued. "Girl, he's only acting like that cause she's in his face, and you're up here. But we can ride down Delaware, if you want to. Ohh, put that in the text!" Erica demanded as she pulled the phone away from K'lynne. "I like how you started this K'lynne." Erica continued as she read K'lynne's text. "Hey y'all, don't send that text! I'm serious!" I demanded as I dabbed the tissue under my eye while staring at a squirrel in the tree, just outside of the window. "Too late, I hit send already" Erica said as she dropped the phone onto the bed.

> **{Me}**
> You wasn't tryna focus on your "REAL FAMILY" when you woke up in my arms and tried to make love one more time before your dad and that ugly little girl came to get you! So why now? Cause she there and I'm not? Cause I can come down there if you want.

"Now, why you call his girlfriend ugly? She not ugly, at all. Y'all just trying to start shit." I irritably voiced from the window. "There you go defending him." K'lynne disappointedly expressed. "Tash, looking back, I don't think that's him sending these texts." she intuitively continued. "Just like we just sent that last one, I think someone else is sending his texts, to you. That's why I put ugly little girl in there, a man will just brush that off. A woman won't." K'lynne admitted as she held up the phone to show me. "I really think that's his girlfriend with his phone." K'lynne confidently disclosed. "Makes sense. You did say, he doesn't seem like his self." Erica agreed as she rose to come over to me. "I can't stop thinking about Que." I said to Erica as she leaned on the window sill next to me. "I still can't believe, you pregnant." Erica gently admitted. "Yeah I know, me either." I matched as I continued to wipe my eyes. DOINK!

"Look. I told you! That's his girl!" K'lynne excitedly yelled after reading Quentin's last text. Erica scurried over to grab the phone. "Yeah that ugly shit, really did set her off." Erica admitted while watching K'Lynne enthusiastically bounce on the bed. I pulled my head out of the window and gradually pushed it shut. "Here." I said walking toward Erica while gesturing for the phone.

{Bae}
Ugly? Whore u know ain't shit ugly bout my girl! You jus mad cause she my home and u jus a homeless bitch. And u can come down here if u want. U might not like how it turns out for u.

I scoffed reading the last two texts. "You three are so immature." I said slightly relieved. "If she was the one doing all the talking, you don't know how he really feels about it." K'lynne pleasantly confirmed. "Yeah, I was just thinking that." I acknowledged before I collapsed down onto the bed next to K'lynne. "C'mere." I said to Erica as I grabbed her hand and pulled her down beside me. "I love y'all." I confessed to my two close friends. "I know it sounds weird. But I actually feel better, not knowing how he feels. At least I don't know for a fact, that he hates me and the whole idea of us having a child." I genuinely proclaimed as I grabbed K'lynne's hand as well.

"This girl is funny." Erica said while re-reading the final text. "You want me to text something back to her." she charitably asked, eager to continue. "No. That's not necessary, now that I know it's not him." I said alleviated that I was still ill-informed of his mindset. "You can't fault her, Tasha. She has every right to be mad." K'lynne openly voiced. "You're right, and every right to hate me." I pleasantly agreed. "Yeah. But disrespect, is disrespect. You don't owe her any loyalty, and you didn't rape her man! Did you?" Erica mockingly asked. "I did once. He woke up, and I was sucking him off." I overtly admitted. "You nasty bitch." Erica flamboyantly chuckled. "We've all done that, that's not rape." K'lynne lightheartedly disclosed. "And you'll have him back to get to do it again, in what two days?" Erica suggestively reminded. "Yeah, that's true. In fact…" I deviously uttered as I seized my phone and began to reply to Imani.

{Me}
Imani, I'm not going to continue going back and forth
with you. Yes I know its you. You go ahead and deal with
Que now and I'll handle him when he gets home.

CHAPTER 69

"Quentin"

"So?" Imani aggressively questioned. "So, what?" I sullenly asked exhausted from all of the turmoil over the last few days. "What do you mean *so what*? So, are you ready to tell me you not going back?!" she asked harshly. "No. I'm not going to tell you that, at all. That doesn't make sense. That's my entire life. My entire future. The baby's… entire future!" I stated rationally. "Don't bring my baby into this. I'll get a job, and he or she'll be just fine!" she scornfully retorted. "Your job possibility or my career in the NFL, which do you think will make more money, right off?" I sensibly challenged. "You try'na say, I ain't gon' be shit? I may be a single mom, but I promise my child will not ever be hungry!" Imani stated harshly, feeling insulted by her twist of my remark. "I'd never let that happen, that's my child too." I said confidently. "Maybe, maybe not. That's just, what I told you!" Imani coldly uttered. "I'm gonna ignore that, and… you believing, that I said you ain't gonna be shit. I'll take them as you being as cruel to me, as I was to you." I said remorsefully. "You haven't seen cruel yet, nigga." Imani sternly disclosed. I chuckled slightly at Imani's unsuccessful attempt to threaten me. "I'm sure I haven't, babe." I patronizingly retorted. "Don't mock me, Que." Imani whispered. I smiled at her use of my nickname. "I really can't believe you're actually going back, to her!" she continued to solemnly express. "I'm not going back, to her. I'm going, to school. I don't know, how else to tell you that." I sincerely declared. "You don't even plan on finishing school! You can't just call'em and tell'em to come scout you, from here?" Imani pleaded pretending to be unfamiliar with procedure. "From where? Dover? It doesn't work like that, and you know it." I reiterated as I snatched the covers from over me. I left the phone on the bed, swung my legs to the floor and stood to stretch.

"Quentin, I know you hear me!" Imani barked as I retrieved the phone again. "No, I didn't hear you, sorry." I half-heartedly apologized. "So, you're choosing her and that baby over us, is what I said." Imani repeated as I staggered to the door. "No. But I did make a mistake, and if that child turns out to be mine, I won't abandon it. I just can't do that, sorry." I sincerely answered while making my way down the hall. "I don't know if I could handle being next to you, for all of that. I know it's not the baby's fault, but I can't say I wouldn't resent that baby. I wouldn't want to put him or her through that." Imani earnestly admitted. "So, wha'chu saying?" I asked, closing the bathroom door behind me. "I don't know. I can't stand being near you, but I don't wanna lose you. I don't want you to touch me, but I miss you holding me to let me know everything will be alright. I hate you, almost as much as I loved you. I need sign of what to do!" Imani somberly confessed.

"C'mon Que!" Hassan yelled up from the bottom of the stairs. "He's coming, can we have a minute?" my mom arrogantly yelled back before raising her arms to embrace me. "C'mon Tra. You had all morning, to say your goodbyes. He's going back to school, he's not dying." my dad pitifully retorted. "They'll be alright." she said as she wrapped her arms around me. I chuckled at my mother's arrogance. "I would give you the *stay out of trouble* lecture, but I guess it's too late for that, huh?" she asked continuing to squeeze me. "It's never too late for you to give that, ma. Sometimes, I listen for it and when I don't hear it, I miss it." I responded wholeheartedly. "In that case, don't get into any *more* trouble, Q-tee. And continue to make us proud." my mom demanded before kissing my cheek. "Do my best." I said somberly as she released her hold of me, letting me slowly make my way to the stairs. "He's going to do a lot of barking but it's because he cares, you know that." she assured as she followed me. "Yeah, I know." I whispered. "Also, don't forget to check your account tomorrow afternoon. You'll have money in there, by then." she whispered as she sashayed down the steps behind me. I shook my head in response, before stepping into my father's view. "So, don't think of asking him for any money." she continued loud enough for my father to hear. "I won't." I answered turning to her with a cynical grin. "Have you said goodbye to Emily? Imani?" she asked as she followed me to the door. "I saw Em earlier, before she left out with London. Not expecting to see, Imani. I spoke to her this morning, though. She's still mad that I'm going back." I said despairingly. "That's on her. You got things to accomplish. You leaving school to start your career, is one thing. You leaving for a girl and a baby, is a whole different animal." my dad said as he fastened his coat. I turned to my mother for comfort, as the melee began. She slowly nodded her head, and headed in the opposite direction. "She ain't so mad that she brought that car back, is she?!" Hassan harshly asked, convoying with my father. "She'll be alright, just give her some time to heal. You just get things straightened at school. We'll deal with home." my mom compassionately agreed as she came out of the kitchen with two bags and a food container in her hand. "Quentin, you do know that we're going to eventually have to meet this young lady, right?" she continued to ask as she transferred the items from her hands into mine. "Yeah, I know." I said reluctant to even the notion. "Damn Teach, more bags? You do know we taking my car, right?" Hassan said avidly. "And what does that mean, Hassan?" my mother dryly asked. "He doesn't allow eating or drinking in his car." I interjected as I handed her back the items to put on my coat. "That's not what I was saying. I'm saying, I don't have the same room that Omar has, with his truck." Hassan retorted to defend his reasoning. "These two little bags won't cause the need to rework much. You can even hold 'em in your lap." my mother stated sarcastically, handing the container and bags to Hassan. "C'mon y'all. I wanna get there, and get back." my father said while opening the door. "Love you, babe." he continued as he reached to kiss my mom. "Later Teach." Hassan said as he stepped out of the door. "You have everything?" she asked as she approached to hug me once more. "Yeah. I'm good." I said as I unequivocally embraced the mother who raised me. "Ok babe, try to get a nap in on the road. I know you were up late last night, not to mention it'll be a way to avoid being alone with Thing One and Thing Two during this tense time. I love you Q-tee." she said as she released her hold. "I love you too, mom." I said into her eyes before following my father out of the door.

"Has, can we swing pass Imani's, real quick? I promise, I won't be long. I just can't leave without saying goodbye." I pleaded sincerely as I tried to get comfortable in the backseat of Hassan's car. My dad turned to me, slowly shook his head, then quickly turned his attention to Hassan, who was now pairing his phone to his car radio. "Sorry son, there's no time for extra stops. We're trying to keep schedule." my dad solemnly said after an extended pause. "Yup." I replied softly as I attempted to gather room to retrieve my phone from my pocket.

"Yo." Hassan calmly said, waving his hand trying to get my attention. I looked up from my phone at Hassan as he pointed out of the window. I smiled, appreciating that we were turning onto Imani's street. My dad peered over at Hassan, with a look of both disbelief and disappointment. "C'mon O. Don't act like we haven't gone through shit before, too." Hassan stated responding to my father's expression as we pulled in front of Imani's house. My dad nodded in agreement, opened his door and lifted his chair for me to contort out of the backseat.

"How you doing Miss Ebonie?" I said as Imani's mom answered the door. "I'm a lot better, than you are." she said aggressively as she stepped aside for me to enter. She waved to my father and uncle in the car and then closed the door. "Imani!" she yelled as she gazed at me with disgust. "Here I come." Imani yelled back from upstairs. I waited by the door as Imani reluctantly came down the stairs with her hand still bandaged for our last encounter. "Hey" I said pitifully as she approached. "Hey." she nonchalantly responded. "On your way back to your side chick, or main chick? I'm still not sure which one I was." she calmly continued to ask. "Neither am I." I genuinely thought to myself. "On my way back to *school*, yes. Just came by to make sure you didn't need anything, before I left." I desperately uttered. "I'm fine. We're fine." Imani continued to nonchalantly respond. "Ok. Well, I'm going to head out then." I said observing her mother watching our encounter from the other room. "Tell her, I said hi." Imani miserably whispered as her eyes began to swell with tears. "I wish I knew how to show you that I'm only going back to build a life for you, and baby girl." I sincerely beseeched as I opened the door to leave. "I used to think that." she replied as she stepped behind the door to close it. "I know." I whispered as she slowly closed the door. I looked over at my car, which seemed to stare back at me. "You take care of them like you did me, Ms. Grier." I uttered to my most prized possession as I approached Hassan's car. "How'd it go?" my dad asked, seeming genuinely concerned. "I really don't know." I said as I squeezed into the backseat of Hassan's car. "We'll make sure they're alright, while you're away." my dad vowed as we pulled off.

"Que!" my dad startlingly yelled. "Huh?" I mumbled, opening my eyes to us slowly coasting through the parking lot of my campus home. "That was fast." I continued to utter, still unaware of anything. "If you say so. Felt like four hours to me." Hassan said as he slid into the first available parking space. "Me too." my dad agreed as he impatiently removed his seatbelt. "Lord have mercy! Haas, they didn't look like *this*, when we were in school!" my dad said gawking at the women buzzing through the parking lot. I slid out of the car behind my dad. "You say the same thing, *every* single time you come here!" I reminded my dad as I slid pass him while he held the chair forward. "And that's your response to it, every time." Hassan mockingly reminded me. "Just pop the trunk, so we can get started and get back." my dad said shaking his legs to stretch.

"Hey, you at the white car, can I have a minute or two?!" a female's voice alluringly asked from behind us as we stood over the trunk gathering the pieces to commandeer. I watched my father swiftly pivot to observe the face attached to the voice. I reluctantly turned to see who it was. Assuming that it wasn't Tasha, knowing she'd be considerably more modest given the circumstances. "Soooo, this's the young lady possibly carrying my grandchild?" my dad asked, admiring the woman slowly approaching us. "No sir, that's mine." Hassan interjected quickly. "Y'all go ahead and unpack. I'll be back in forty-five." he continued as he eagerly stuffed his car keys into my hand and walked towards the young lady. We watched Hassan charismatically walk up to this voluptuous woman, and then continued to eyeball them until they were out of sight. "God damn. That may be a little too much for ol' Haas. Did you see her titties, trying to pop out that shirt?" my dad favorably asked. "Sorry dad, didn't really notice. I became more focused on the walk away. I'm an ass man. "Damn. That's a comment I'd have shared with my dad, had the status quo been different." I mumbled quietly to myself. "I hope one day, we get us back." I thought as I turned to gather my luggage. "Where's yours? She looks like that?" my dad asked in an attempt to set free some of our strain. "I don't know. She may not even be back yet. I haven't talked to her since, Thanksgiving Day." I answered closing the trunk. "Well, when we get upstairs, call her and find out. I want to meet her, especially now that I got time to kill." my dad said as we stepped through the door of my building.

2-1-5-5-5-5-9-4-4-9 "Hello" Tasha weakly whimpered. "Where are you?" I calmly asked as I placed the phone on speaker and positioned it on the counter. "Why? You haven't cared for the last three days, why care now?" she said as her voice began to gradually strengthen. "Tasha, neither of us going to play the victim, right now. I'm just wondering if you made it back to State College, yet?" I asked intolerant for her dramatics after dealing with Imani's for the last few days. "Yeah, why?" she bitterly asked. "Would you mind company for a few minutes?" my father charmingly intervened from across the room. "Who is this?" Tasha callously snapped. "Oh, I'm sorry. This is Que's father, Omar Gregory." my dad serenely disclosed, attempting to soothe Tasha. "Oh. Hi, Mr. Gregory." Tasha swiftly and softly responded. "Hello. Tasha, right?" my dad asked, continuing to soothe. "Yeah." she answered softly. "How are you, Tasha?" he inquired while gesturing for me to help him lift a tote. "I'm ok." Tasha said beginning to sound more bewildered than anything else. "I heard your news, congratulations." my dad calmly acknowledged. "Thank you." Tasha timidly replied. My dad tossed me an arrogant wink as we carried the tote into my bedroom. "So, do you have a second? I promise not to keep you long, and to keep my son a gentleman." my dad tranquilly continued to beseech. "Yeah, I'm not really doing anything, right now. And Quentin, doesn't scare me." Tasha pompously responded. "Damn. I think I like her." my dad mouthed as we went into the other room to grab the last of the bags. "How far away are you?" Tasha asked, apparently trying to gather a thrust of energy. "We're at the apartment." I answered undeniably. "You're already up here?!" she fretfully replied. "Yeah. We'll be over there, in a few." I said nonchalantly. "Ok." she acknowledged, prominently expressing her anxiety.

KNOCK. KNOCK. KNOCK! "Here I come." Tasha faintly stated in response to my father's knock on her door. "Bet that's a phrase you've heard before, isn't it son?" my dad whispered still trying to eliminate the uneasiness between us. After struggling to hold it in, I exploded with laughter, just as Tasha opened the door. My dad's eyes widened as Tasha stood in the door. She was standing as statuesque as I'd left her, wearing her favorite form fitting pair of jeans and the burgundy hoodie Hassan bought me the past Christmas. "Hey." Tasha uttered perplexed at my hilarity. "Hey." I responded, attempting to compose my laughter. Tasha continued to stand stationary, staring into my face while unending her look of confusion. "Can we come in?" I asked, surveying into the room around her to be sure all was ok. "Yeah, I'm sorry. Please, come in." Tasha pleasantly invited after realizing her inactivity. "Tasha Langley, this is my father, Omar Gregory." I said as we stepped into Tasha's apartment. "Hello, Tasha. It's nice to meet you." my father good-naturedly stated, extending his hand for Tasha to place her hand into his. "It's nice to finally meet you too, Mr. Gregory." Tasha cordially responded while gently placing her hand onto his. "How are you? Is everything, ok? And before you lie to me, find a mirror." my dad charmingly advised while showing authentic concern for Tasha. "I'm ok, really." Tasha falsely proclaimed after exhaling deeply. "Ok, Tasha. I'll take your word for it, and not the word of the bags under your eyes from crying." he continued as put his hand atop hers. He released his hold of her hand and she immediately pressed her fingers under her eyes to attempt to depress the swelling. "Please, sit down. I need something to drink. I just got back this morning, so I don't have much in there. But I can offer, what I have. Would you like something to drink?" Tasha cordially asked before she sauntered into the kitchen retrieve herself a drink. "God damn, Que!" my dad mouthed while approvingly shaking his head. "I thought you'd never ask. You got some Courvoisier or some E and J, in there?" my dad wittily asked, as he quickly sat in the single chair that he saw my eyes on. I stood there, disapprovingly looking down at my dad after his humorless joke. "I'm just joking, dear." my father admitted aloud as we could hear Tasha open her soda. "And, no thank you. But thanks for the offer." he continued as Tasha peeked back at us for a legitimate answer before coming back. "I think I'd understand if you weren't, just joking." Tasha sarcastically said, eyeballing me while she promenaded her way back over to us. "Would you like something to drink, son?" my dad suspiciously asked with an unrevealed purpose. Tasha grimaced with an expression of disgust, rolling her eyes up into her head. "No. I'm good." I answered casually as I leaned on the wall staring out of the window. "Well, go get it anyway." he sternly replied gesturing for me to leave the room. Both Tasha and I turned to survey each other and then my father, in bewilderment. "Better yet, you can go find Hassan for me. I don't wanna get back too late and knowing him, he'll try to go again." he earnestly broadcasted, while attempting to remain discreet. Tasha covered her mouth with her hand to hide her condescending grin as she sat down adjacent from my father. I looked at my father in disbelief of the task he just demanded. "You serious?" I questioned him, in awe. "Yes. Why wouldn't I be serious?" he responded, seemingly as shocked as I was that I'd question his stubbornness. "I don't even know where *to start* to look." I criticized as I looked out of the window at the vastness of the campus. "You go to this school. He's around here somewhere." my dad unsympathetically insisted. "The Loft on Bellaire Avenue. Her name is Kierra or Kiki. And any woman out there will point her place out, to you." Tasha confidently intervened, as she looked up at me as if she was my savior. My father ogled Tasha absolutely dumbfounded by her complete recognition of everything that we were referring to. "How the hell did you know who, and what we were talking about?" my dad inquired still flabbergasted by her insight of the how things stood. "I know my title doesn't usually call for it, but Quentin and I do a *whole* lot more than just have sex." Tasha stated passionately. "Well, there you go. Kiki, on Bellaire Ave. When you find him, call me and I'll meet y'all at the car." he reiterated attempting to discreetly nod his head towards the door. "Alright, whatever!" I uttered as my dad inadvertently reminded me that I had Hassan's car key in my pocket. "I'll be damned if I'm walking to Bellaire Avenue, not right now." I thought as I turned towards the door. "Hey, call me later, we have to talk as well." I said as I opened the door. "Oh, I'll do better than that. I'll come over when I think you're settled." Tasha delicately retorted as I opened the door. "Yup" I casually said stepping out of the apartment. DOINK!

> **{Dad}**
> Hey. Just go to your place and wait for Hassan there.
> Don't go looking for him. Needed an excuse.

KNOCK, KNOCK, KNOCK! "It's open." I hollered from my bedroom at whoever was at the front door. "Fellas! We good?" Hassan asked as he strutted in. "Nope." I said aloud as I ran my hand across the bed to smooth out the bed sheet. "Where ya dad? Don't tell me he left me. I wasn't that long." he laughed as he surveyed around for my father. "Damn. Y'all got a lot done. I must've been gone longer than I thought. Where ya dad?" he repeated, stepping on the empty trash bags to enter into my bedroom. "He at Tasha's." I casually admitted while attempting to fan my blanket onto the bed. "Tasha who?" Hassan worriedly asked as he grabbed the other end of the blanket. "Your baby mom, Tasha?" he quickly continued. "Yeah. He needed to talk to her, alone." I reluctantly answered after hearing her classed put that way. "What the hell, is he doing? C'mon!" he insisted as he stopped with his semi help and dropped the blanket. I stood there bewildered still holding the blanket as he charged out of the room. "C'mon. Before he does, or says something stupid." Hassan called from the other room. "Wha'chu mean, something stupid? What could he possibly do?" I obliviously asked as I pulled my bedroom door closed. I grabbed my coat from the back of the chair and followed Hassan to the door. "You haven't talked to her, right?" he sharply asked. "No." I moderately answered as I fastened my coat. "So, we ain't know her plans. We ain't know what she was thinking. Your dad could say something to change her mind, and fuck things up." Hasan said as we stepped out of the apartment. "We gotta make sure you, stay on top of this. You, control how this plays out!" he instructed as we gradually made our way down the stairs of the lobby.

I tapped Hassan on his shoulder and gestured toward the main door to point out my father, holding the door for Tasha as they came in together laughing hysterically. Hassan immediately advanced my father, standing between he and Tasha. "Oh, you already here. You ready to roll?" my dad calmly asked Hassan. "In a minute. Let me talk to you for a second." Hassan answered as I turned to go back up the stairs. "Hey." Imani softly said as she slowly arrived at my side. "Wha'sup." I informally responded while curiously looking back at my father and Hassan, who had yet step away from the entrance door. "You don't mind me coming now, do you? Since we were both coming over here at some point, I figured I'd just come now and have someone to walk with." Tasha hesitantly explained. "No, it's cool. Go ahead to up, let me see what's going on with these two." I replied giving her my keys. Tasha gently seized the keys from my hand and slowly made her way up the stairs. I watched Tasha's ass as she gradually trekked up the steps. She reached the top of the landing, turned and grinned as if she knew I was watching. I smiled back at Tasha before starting towards my father. "What the hell are you talking about?" my dad asked as I reached earshot of their conversation. "You! You all curled up, boo lovin' with this girl? What the hell are you doing?" Hassan sternly whispered back. "You don't think we need to get on top of things? We don't know this girl. We need to control, how this shit plays out." he calmly answered. "*We* don't need to do shit. That's his job, he's the one that's fucking her! Not you!" Hassan answered harshly, while pointing at me. "Can we take this upstairs, to my room?" I said noticing a large group of people carrying luggage approaching the other side of the door. "No, we can't. Wonder why?" Hassan sarcastically answered referencing Tasha already situated in the apartment. "Stop being a child." my father said before turning and heading for the stairs. "And I know who did the fucking up, but they're kids. Sometimes shit sounds better, coming from an adult." my dad continued as the three of us marched up to my apartment. "They in their twenties, they are adults! And you… you had this nigga when you was sixteen years old! You the last nigga, to be giving advise!" Hassan discreetly stated as we reached the busy hallway of my apartment. "No, I'm the first nigga to be giving advice. I went through, what I'm preaching. A nigga like you, would be the last nigga to give advice." my dad retorted modestly. I looked around at the hustle and bustle of my neighbors passing by as my father and uncle bickered just outside my room door. "Can we take this inside, so the world doesn't know my business? I gotta live and go to school, with these folks?" I asked as I notice a few of them starting to stare. They both simultaneously looked at me with "You customizing it, O. I been there since day one. You ain't go through shit that I didn't go through, with you. Not one fucking thing. I missed prom too, nigga!" Hassan quietly rectified while stepping into the apartment. I followed my father as he slowly walked in behind Hassan. "You're right. Across the board, you are absolutely right." my dad openly admitted. "That's all I needed to hear." Hassan proudly boasted. "Where ol' girl?" Hassan continued noticing Tasha was not in the room. "Tasha!" I called out before opening my bedroom door. "She not here." I disclosed when I couldn't find her after peeking into Juice's room. "She had to have been here, we walked into an unlocked door." I reassured as I now began to look around for my keys.

"Alright nephew, we gotta go. Cause, if I gotta hang around here any longer, I'm going back over baby girl room. Handle your business. We'll call you, when we get back to Dover." Hassan said looking at his watch. "Yeah. We gotta long ride ahead of us, and I promised your Aunt Jill that I wouldn't get him home too late." my father said as he advanced toward the kitchen counter to collect his things to leave. "Alright y'all. Thanks again." I said I hugged my father and then uncle.

"Que! You here?" Tasha faintly inquired from the other room. "Where else would I be? Can't go anywhere, you have my keys!" I reminded Tasha as I slowly traipsed out of my bedroom toward the kitchen. "You alright?" she asked, following blankly behind me. "I'm tired. Both mentally and physically, but I'm sound." I answered as I opened the bag that my mom sent with me. I smiled at the large portion of my father's crisp in the container tucked away at the bottom of the bag. I gleefully tossed it into the microwave and opened the fridge with hopes of something cold to drink. "I'm guessing now isn't a good time to talk, then huh?" she pleasantly asked while leaning on the refrigerator door. "I said I was fine. Talking was my idea, remember?" I replied with my head in the refrigerator. I pulled out one of the two apple juices in the fridge and signaled at her to lift up, so I could close the door. "Yeah, but if you're tired. We can always do it, later. Neither of us is going anywhere. For real, for real." she said tossing the rest of the perishables from the bag into the refrigerator before slowly closing the door. "Tasha, if you got something else to do, or somewhere else you'd rather be, please don't let me stop you." I said as I turned to stare into the microwave at the spinning dish. "Damn, it's like that?! You changed a lot in a week." she sternly suggested from behind me. "Yeah. Apparently, so have you. Ow, shit!" I uttered being burned while removing the hot desert. "We haven't seen each other in a week, haven't spoken in days, and this is how you want to start it?" she detailed while handing me my cold apple juice bottle to soothe the burning feeling. She confiscated the dish with her hand pulled into her sleeve so she could carry it and gestured for me to follow her into my room. "How you want me to sound? I had to hear about you being pregnant, from someone that's damn near a stranger." I pointed out as I slowly meandered behind her. "I know, and I'm sorry you had to hear about it that way. I really am. But honestly Quentin, that's all I'm sorry about." she dismally admitted as she placed the dish on the dresser. "What do you mean that's all you're sorry about?" I asked ignorant to her subject's course. I schlepped over to the bed and plopped down in preparation for another extended and possibly combative conversation. "Just what I said. I'm having the baby of the guy I'm in love with, that just makes sense to me." Tasha said as she inspected the shoe boxes in my closet, looking for hers. "And that's as far as you women think it. No financial future? No extended living? No pre-arranged set-up? Just have the baby, and everything will hopefully work itself out?" I harshly asked, maybe giving her some of my frustration build-up from Imani. "What the hell makes you believe we don't think about those things? Even more than you?! But what's done is done. Life is written in pen, not pencil! Hell, sometimes, like now, it's written in magic marker. So, you adapt. You pull out a different color and decorate it, cause it's not going anywhere." Tasha sternly retorted as she stopped her search and turned to give me her undivided attention. "I'm not saying that I don't agree with you. I understand life, and having to deal with the real. I'm just saying that having a plan makes life more productive, and a lot easier. And if you do stray from the path, and have the chance to get back on track before the train derails." I logically testified. "It's still in there." I continued while pointing out the drawer which she dumped her things into, before I left for break. "Wow, you left it in there? I thought reclaiming your drawer, would've been the first thing you did when you got back." she sarcastically disclosed. "But what I'm looking for, is not in there. It was in a different box." she appreciatively continued as she sat down next to me. "So, let me ask you what you were getting at, before I take my clothes off. It's been a week, so I had every intention of raping you. But, if you saying what I think you saying, I'll go back to my toys." she sternly divulged. "If I wasn't trying to prove my point, this would be where I'd back track and fix the rails, so the train stays on course. But I guess I gotta take this one for the cause, and let it continue to derail." I willingly asserted. I opened my apple juice and took a large gulp to recharge for the next wave of conversation. "Well, let me help you out… for the cause. I'm not getting rid of my child, if that's what you're proposing. It's coming out, the same way it was put in… by God's hand. Is the train now steady enough for you?" she passionately conveyed before heading over to the mirror. "I didn't ask you to get rid of the baby. I'm just asking if you've established a plan or even considered the need for one?" I pleaded while watching her display of narcissism in the mirror.

CHAPTER 70

"Tasha"

"Of course, I've considered the need, and how much I stand to lose without one. I had three semesters left before I walked away with a BBA from Penn State. Now, you know what I'm walking away with?" I resentfully asked while moving in close to the mirror to inspect my face. "Imani's man's baby." I gravely replied suddenly feeling dismayed after yet again recognizing my current horror. I continued to lean into the mirror, but now condemning the beautiful young lady staring back at me. "Funny. I've heard this confession before, but the last time it was *Tasha's man's baby.*" he solemnly uttered as he laid back on the bed with his palm of his hands pressed against his eyes. "I'm sure you have. Cause that's her reality. Just like, this is mine." I proclaimed, curbing my enthusiasm after hearing that Imani has surrendered him to me. I turned from the mirror and stood over the bed, looking down at Quentin scoffing, with his hands over his face. "What's funny?" I curiously asked beginning to subtly unclothe. "Reality! Yours is, you're having a baby. Hers, is the same. Mine… is me, having children with two different women. That's at least four headaches, for the rest of my life." he disconsolately expressed with his hands still covering his face. "Quentin, you did that to yourself. I didn't pull that condom off you. Oh wait. Yes, I did." I cynically owned while propping on the edge of the dresser to pull my jeans around my ankles. "Well, I didn't tell you to push back in. You could've stopped right then, and there." I cynically continued to mock. He continued to scoff as he removed his hands from his face. "You right! I did it to myself, and I gotta live with it." he unfavorably forfeited with his head tipped back and eyes still closed. "For the rest, of your life." I stated as I gradually climbed back onto the bed to straddle across his chest. "Lift up." he insisted. I adhered to his bidding so that he could slide up to have his legs completely on the bed and me straddling his pelvis. "That's better. Now c'mere." I whispered while slowly lowering to kiss him. "What happened to you being all mad, and unforgiving?" he perplexedly inquired mildly retreating from my kisses. "For what? I accepted what I was getting myself into, a long time ago. You could say, I kinda had a plan." I sarcastically joshed as I lifted to unfasten his belt and pants. "So, you planned for all this to happen?" he probingly interrogated as he conformed to my stimulating behavior. "No. But, I'm happily adapting to what's in front of me." I seductively answered as I reached into his pants to fill my hands with his rock, hard dick. I pulled it out of his pants and began to sensually pull up and down on it.

"You like this plan? I'm calling it plan D" I enticingly whispered as I used his dick to push my thong slightly aside, mildly brushing it against my wet pussy to tease. "You're insatiable." he whispered as he attempted to propel forward to push inside of me. DOINK! "I'm yours, is what I am!" I insisted before submitting, plunging myself down onto his dick to prevent him from checking his phone. I wasn't going to let a text ruin what we started. Not this time!

"Que!" I scarcely heard Juice yell from the other room. "Babe. Babe!" I startlingly grumbled as I lethargically nudged Quentin. "Huh?" he mumbled, slightly lifting his head from the pillow. "Juice is out there calling you." I uttered as anxiously tried to get comfortable again. "Yo!" he audibly responded back. "Oh, he is here." I faintly overheard him continue. "Hold up. Don't open the door. I'll be out." Quentin swiftly yelled as he struggled to cover my nudity with a blanket. "Hmph." he grunted as he reluctantly slid down to the bottom of the bed. "You wouldn't have to do that if you moved the bed from against the wall. I'm just saying." I reiterated as I tried to re-position the blanket that he tossed over me. "Nobody asked you." he wittily retorted as he scooped his pants from the floor. "Tell Juice, I said hi. I'm going back to sleep. And don't forget to check your phone. You got a few texts, while we were doing it." I cynically divulged while snuggling under the blanket. DOINK!

"She still ain't got no clothes on!" Quentin whispered as he tried to unnoticeably climb into the bed behind me. "Why would I get up for that? I can sleep naked, it's not like you've never seen it." I softly uttered from under the covers. "Now, you gonna be up all night." he mockingly advised. "I'll be alright, I got you to pick with. What time is it, anyway?" I asked lifting to try and see the clock on his dresser. "It's ten-thirty." he answered swiftly. "You let me sleep all that time. I could've helped y'all. How's Juice? He ok??" I affectionately asked stunned by the time lost. "He's good. All unpacked and settled in. We even went food shopping." he disclosed as he situated himself under the covers. "I would've gone. I need some things, too. How'd y'all get there?" I probed as I turned to face him. "Look at you, all bruised up." I whispered before gently massaging my thumb across the bump over his left eye. He smiled and gradually closed his eyes. "He got his truck back, so we're good again." he yawned before tardily covering his mouth. I chuckled at how delayed he was, at hiding his yawn. "Good for him. Or should I say, y'all. You'll benefit from that too. You tell him, I said hi?" I softly asked as I progressively moved the massage to his ear. "Yeah, among other things." he admitted as he tranquilly moaned and swayed to my manipulation of his earlobe. "Other things? You told him?!" I shockingly asked stopping with the massage. He stopped swaying and swiftly opened his eyes. "You told him?" I nervously repeated. "Of course, I told him. He's like my brother. But I actually just gave him the details, he already knew." he said as he placed his hand atop mine, assisting me in resuming his ear massage. "Who told him?" I asked attempting to conceal my trepidation. "Dee, but you had to know that was gonna to happen, when you told her. And even if it wasn't her, he'd have heard it sooner or later. I'm sure it's already swirling, through the rumor mill." he condescendingly responded while holding my hand pressed against his cheek.

I pulled my hand from under his, and cringed slightly at the thought of my name negatively circulating across campus again. Quentin noticed my standoffish temperament and gently slid his arms in to soothingly embrace me. DOINK! "You'll be alright, babe." he charmingly said, reminding me why I love him. "Oh shit, I forgot all about my phone!" he said climbing over me to get to his phone. "I could've gotten that for you." I uncomfortably uttered as he lay on me reaching onto the floor for his phone. "It's cool, I got it." he said as he crawled back over me onto the bed. I scoffed at my own assumption of his skepticism of me with his phone. "You don't trust me with it? Afraid I'm going to text certain people, like they texted me?" I sarcastically asked. "No. You got too much class, for that. And I'm sorry that went down, that way. You didn't deserve any of that. I did, but you didn't." he pledged before turning on his back, to look into his phone. "Yeah your dad told me that she hit you with a trophy and tried to stab you with a picture frame. That news didn't go over too well with me. Especially, all of you thinking that you deserved that, too. Lucky for her, your dad's as charming as he is." I sincerely divulged as he stared into his phone.

Chapter 71

"Quentin"

{Grammy}
Hi baby. Just checking to make sure you made it back to school ok. Call me when you can. Grammy loves you.
{Mani}
Cum bck ovr lets talk
{Mani}
I kno u aint leave!
{Mani}
With nothing being answered u still left?
{Mani}
U that busy that u cant text me bck? REALLY?!
{Storm}
Call ur girl. Tell her to stop calling me evry 5 min. b4 she get cuss the fuck out.
{Mani}
I kno u went back to her. Wat yall fucking now? That's why u can't text me back?
{Mani}
Wats Juice number? I need 2 ask him sumthin
{Mani}
Its that good that u can't text me bck?

{Dad}
Hey son. Just letting you know that we made it back safely. Love you. Goodnight.
{Mani}
Fuck u Quentin. Don't call me bck.

"What's wrong?" Tasha softly asked noticing my sudden loss of life energy. "Nothing!" I falsely responded pushing my phone under the pillow. "Goodnight, babe." I uttered before turning to get comfortable enough to fall asleep. "Goodnight, Love." Tasha responded before kissing me upon the forehead.

"Mmmmm hmmmmm!" I moaned aloud as I extended my arms out to stretch. "Oh shit, my bad." I immediately whispered quickly lowering my arms, remembering that Tasha was next to me. I didn't want to awake her with my morning antics. I regained focus and glanced over at the empty space, that I expected Tasha to still be occupying. "She left? It's that late?" I thought as I surveyed the room. "She must've had an early class." I mumbled realizing that I no longer had to be reserved with how I conduct my morning. I ascended to my feet and walked across to my bed before energetically jumping to the floor. I trotted over to my dresser to retrieve some clean underwear and inspect myself in the mirror. "Damn. I really do feel good today and I don't know why." I said while merrily rocking side to side in the mirror. "Something smells, good." I said extending my face over towards the door. "Somebody's making coffee?" I enthusiastically pronounced as I assembled the things I needed to shower and stepped out of the door. "They're making way more than just coffee." I whispered as I recognized the other odors of breakfast. "But, mmm the coffee!" I melodiously crooned. "Mmm, bacon." Juice simultaneously resonated after being hit with the smell when stepping out of his room. "Yo." I said seeing Juice across the room standing in front of his door. "Yo." he replied as he smiled at me and headed for the kitchen. I deferred following behind him and headed straight to the shower. "Guess she decided to look out, and make breakfast before class." I said turning to head into the bathroom. "Good morning Juice." I heard her faint voice seem to sing before I closed the bathroom door.

"Is that coffee still hot? Save me some, please?" I loudly asked while trekking from the bathroom to my bedroom. I stepped into my room and closed the door before getting an answer from either Tasha or Juice.

"Can you pour a cup of coffee in my big, to-go mug, so I can take it with me, please? I got class in twenty-five minutes." I yelled after re-opening my bedroom door. I finished tying my boots and hurried out of my room. I could faintly hear the clang of dishes and conversation as I opened the hall closet to grab my coat and bag for class. RING. RING! "Shit!" I said hearing the muffled ring of my phone from under my pillow. "Can one of y'all throw that coffee in the microwave for a second, please." I beseeched as

I dashed back to get my phone. RING. RIN…! The phone ringing abruptly stopped just as I dove onto the bed to retrieve it. I unlocked the phone and glanced at the screen as I slid off of the bed.

> **Missed Call**
> **Tasha {1}**

"What the hell?" I mouthed as I gradually made my way to the kitchen. "Tasha and them tight ass jeans!" I considered to myself as I stuffed my phone into my pocket. "I told you, you can't put your phone in your pocket with those tight ass pants on." I sarcastically reminded as I approached the kitchen. "Ok." Imani scoffed as she turned around from the sink with her hands covered in suds. "Imani?!" I loudly said in awe of her presence. "Good morning to you too, Quentin." she pleasantly maintained with a smile as she snatched a sheet of paper towel to wipe her hands. "Wha'chu doing here?" I asked nervously thinking about Tasha being somewhere near. "You not happy to see me?" she continued to inquire. "I told you Juice. He don't love me, no more." Imani chuckled as she refilled Juice's mug. "I'm always happy to see you. You just haven't been happy to see me, lately. And we won't discuss, how much I love you. I'm just surprised to see you." I explained as I stood, stunned by her being there. "Well I got the car, and it's only a four-hour drive. I can do this every day. This way you won't get lonely." Imani replied. "Come on Imani. You got school, doctor's visits, shit like that. How you gonna do those things, if you up here every day? Not to mention, the wear on the car. I mean, I know you're upset but you still have to be sensible." I sternly advised as I started becoming noticeably irritated, with the immaturity behind her anger. "You gonna be late, man. Your coffee in the microwave, get it and get outta here." Juice demanded sitting at the table holding a cup of tea. "You right. I'll see y'all, when I get back." I agreed as I tossed my bag over my shoulder and motioned towards the microwave. Still nervous, I gradually surveyed the room for Tasha or any evidence of her presence as I made my way out.

2-1-5-5-5-5-9-4-4-9. "Please answer your phone." I mumbled to myself as I paused slightly after noticing my car standing out in the parking lot in front of my building. "Hey babe." Tasha said as I turned to see if Imani was in the window watching me talk on the phone. "Hey." I said scurrying to quickly get out of my apartment window's line of sight. "I called you a few minutes back, but I thought you were already in class and hung up." Tasha pleasantly acknowledged. "I saw that. I'm just on my way to class, now." I declared as I continued to hurry across campus. "Aww, Quentin! I knew I shoulda hung around there for a little while longer, this morning." she disappointedly responded. "Yeah, I was about to ask you, what happened this morning?" I stated, wondering if she crossed any type of paths with Imani. "I had a counseling meeting with student services, at eight-fifteen. I didn't want to wake you up, you having such a long night. So, I snuck out, went home to change my clothes, and went to my meeting." she efficiently explained "Damn, you was outta here early, then." I said, slightly relieved at the unlikelihood of them seeing each other. "I left at about, six-thirty. But I planned on making it back, by the time you were outta classes." she sweetly confirmed. "Well, hold up with that plan. I may be busy later." I fretfully pronounced, approaching the entrance door of my destination. "Too busy, for me?" she asked, pretending to be in low spirits. "You ain't gotta put it like that. Something just came up, that's all. I promise to tell you about it, as soon as I can. But let me go, 'cause I just walked into class." I said as I maneuvered through the horde of students, to the group of empty seats on the rear row of the lecture hall. "Ok babe. Just call me later. Love you." Tasha openly admitted. "Love you too." I said before ending the call.

"Wow. I left headquarters annoyed and disturbed, by Imani just popping up on me. I'd have loved that, just a few weeks ago. And Tasha's now the one, getting my concern and I love you's." I thought as I shamefacedly texted Imani.

> **{Me}**
> **I really was happy to see you. You just surprised me.**

"Still no answer." I thought as I checked my phone one last time, before class ended. "And that's a wrap, ladies and gentlemen. I bid you all adieu, until we meet again." Professor Mariston said as he re-opened the door to the room. "Why come all the way up here, just to show you still mad?" I mumbled as I exited the building. "This is some, real bullshit." I said as I headed to my mass communications class.

"I need to go check things in the apartment. Make sure Imani's okay, before I head up there to class." I reasonably deemed before opening the door of the building. "I got time to kill, I don't always have to be there thirty minutes early." I mumbled before jogging back to my apartment. "Miss Grier, how could you do this to me?" I griped as I swiftly approached my car still in the same spot as before class. "I thought we were better than that. You couldn't have run outta gas, or nothing?" I continued as I slowed to inspect my former most prized possession. "I miss you too." I said before resuming my hastened effort to check on Imani.

"Hey." I said as I opened the door to Imani stretched across the sofa. "Why you back so early? It's Monday. I thought you went to class at ten-thirty, and didn't get done til four. Or was that a lie, too?" she aggressively asked lifting her head from the couch cushion. "So now, you gonna take everything I've ever told you as a lie?" I belligerently asked as I trotted passed her to my bedroom. "Yeah." she honestly replied raising the remote to turn off the television. "Then what the fuck is the point, of us even talking then. If that's the case, leave and don't come back. There's no point in us conversing, if it's not going to be believed or accepted." I harshly stated before closing the door behind me. I reached into my bag and unloaded everything associated with my earlier class. "I understand her plight, but damn! At some point this shit gotta be tiresome of her own bullshit, too. Why can't she deal with it, the way Tasha is?" I mumbled as I tossed my bag over my shoulder and reluctantly stepped out of the room. Imani was now sitting up on the sofa crying, with her hands over her face in an attempt to cover her tears. "Damn." I thought as I gradually walked pass her towards the kitchen. "Here." I said returning to her with Juice's container of wet wipes from atop the refrigerator. She looked up at me standing over her and ignored my gesture of kindness. "It's here when you need it." I disclosed before dropping the container on the sofa next to her. "We weren't supposed to end like this." Imani whimpered while wiping her flowing tears with her hands. "I know. We weren't supposed to end, at all." I softly agreed as I retrieved the container of wet wipes and removed a few. "Here" I insisted while stuffing them into her hand. "If we wasn't supposed to end, why'd you end us?" she genuinely asked whilst dabbing her cheeks with the wipes. "I can't answer that, now." I considerately responded. "I didn't think you, would." she swiftly retorted. "I didn't say wouldn't. I said, can't. I have to get to class, and that question's too serious for a bullshit answer." I responsibly explained. "We can talk about it, when I get back." I pledged as I started to make my way towards the door. "You won't be able to then, either. You'll be on your way to practice. And after that it's studying… then sleep." Imani desolately scoffed. "I'll make time." I sympathetically maintained before reaching to open the door. "Don't worry 'bout it, Quentin. That's not what I really wanted when I came up here, anyway." Imani earnestly disclosed. "Well, what did you really come up here for then?" I asked holding the door knob, truly intrigued and awaiting whatever answer she'd give. "I honestly wanted to catch you with, your family. So, I can see it for myself and know that this book of ours is closed for good." she softly admitted while reaching down onto the floor for her cup of tea. "I thought that's why you came. Well again, we'll talk about it all when I come back." I confirmed before stepping out of the room.

{Me}
You in class?

"Let me put Juice on alert. Even though he can handle himself, he may not feel like that shit tonight. I know I don't." I said as I texted Juice to forewarn him that Imani was still there.

"Damn, this really is the end of me and Imani." I solemnly mumbled to myself as I realized that Imani and I were for all intents and purposes, over.

"Wow, I wasn't even driving yet." I scoffed recalling life before Imani. I turned back to look for my window of the towering apartment building, I called home. With hopes that Imani, was standing there. "Damn Que. You've loved that woman for what seems like forever. And now that she's giving you what you wanted more than anything, you've found a way to forsake her? Smart man!" Doink!

{Juice}
Jus leavin. Omw 2 lab. Wats up?

"Good." I mumbled to myself before deciding to call Juice rather than text him back. 4-1-2-5-5-5-2-6-2-9. "Yo." Juice calmly pronounced. "Yo. Just wanted to let you know that Imani still up in HQ, acting the fool. My bad about your morning. I ain't expect that at all." I embarrassingly confessed as I continued to trek to class. "My morning was good. I woke up, to breakfast! And you ain't gotta apologize, for the other shit. Sometimes, shit happens" Juice honestly reassured. "Where you at?" Juice curiously continued. "Walking to *Mass Com*." I confidently replied. "So, you still ain't talk to her?" Juice intriguingly asked. "Not really." I nonchalantly replied. "You know she expected you to skip classes, to talk to her?" he asked seemingly amazed at my lackadaisical demeanor. "I'm sure. But that don't even make sense. One. It's me! I'm not skipping class, for no *dumb shit*. Two. *It's me*! *I'm* not, skipping class for no dumb shit." I reiterated, reminding Juice to whom he was speaking. "I know. But to *her*, this is ain't *dumb shit*." Juice retorted, reminding me of a woman's perspective. "And, I agree. I also gave her multiple opportunities, to talk. She wanted to fight, and pout." I said defending my position and actions. "She's a woman, fam! Fighting and pouting, is what they do. And please don't tell me, you stopped back pass the room." he disappointingly pleaded. "Yeah. I was trying to be courteous and make sure she was ok, before my next class." I rationalized hoping he'd understand my purpose. "Well, that's not what you did! You just showed her that you had another opportunity to talk, and again you chose otherwise!" he scoffed while enlightening me on my blunder. "Her fault! Again, I tried to talk to her! Now she gotta wait until, I'm available!" I demanded still hoping he'd comprehend my viewpoint of it all. "God damn." he said as his light scoffing became absolute laughter. "What?" I asked fascinated to understand what he seemed to have already acknowledged. "You digging that hole deeper, and deeper. Let's hope Tasha is the life line, you making her out to be." Juice expressed seemingly trying to understand my point of view. "I'm not making Tasha out to be, my life line." I beseeched hopelessly while walking into class. "Right now, is just not the time to have this conversation, with Imani. Especially while she crying, we'd just talk in circles." I desperately upheld as I stood over my desk sluggishly slipping off my coat and bag. "You gonna talk in circles anyway, she's a woman! I hear you're in class, so go learn as much as you can. In fact, you may wanna hang around after class, for some extra tutoring. I'm glad you can play ball. Cause you're not gonna do well in communicating it to others, thinking the way you do." he joked, referencing my being in a communication class and not communicating well with Imani. "Til, the next time." he continued to laugh. "Til the, next time." I responded before ending the call.

DOINK!

> **{Juice}**
> **Yo leave wherever u r and get home now!**

"What the hell is wrong with him?" I thought to myself as I re-read Juice's text.

> ### {Me}
> ### Wats up?! You alright?

I gathered my things while waiting for Juice's response. DOINK!

> ### {Juice}
> ### It ain't me. It's you! Tasha is here w/ Imani!

"Oh shit!" I said as I jumped out of my seat and clumsily dashed out of the room. 4-1-2-5-5-5-2-6-2-9. "Yo." Juice excitedly voiced. "What the fuck?! They in there fighting?!" I vigorously asked as I hurried down the aisle, while trying to pack and close my bag. "Is that Que?" I could hear Imani harshly ask, in the surrounds behind him. "Yeah, it's him." Juice answered sternly. "Yo, you need to get here now." he quietly said, redirecting his attention back to me. "Let him finish his class. We're not in a rush." I could hear Tasha faintly articulate. "He's already on his way. I'll be right back. Please don't disrespect my headquarters." he firmly pleaded. "Where'd you go?" I naively asked as I tossed on my coat before reaching the building exit. "In my room. It's crazy tense out there." Juice relentlessly responded. "Yo, what the fuck happened?!" I frantically asked as I pushed through the doors of the communications building. "What you mean, what happened? You was fucking them both, and got them both pregnant! You didn't think it was going to ever, come to this?" Juice sternly asked. "I mean right now, man! How Tasha know she was there? Why she even, show up?" I asked curious to why Tasha would switch her judgment and come over. "I already spoke to Tasha, and she knew I was in class. Why the fuck, would she even bother to come over?" I continued to babble flustered and oblivious as I trotted across campus. "J.T." Juice revealingly emitted in a low tone. "Say that again?!" I shockingly asked I stopped all movement to hear him clearly. "Yeah. He saw Pam Grier parked outside, and decided to start some shit by steering Tasha over here." Juice continued to clarify. "And you keep telling me, to leave it alone." I harshly reminded before resuming my race across campus. "I promise you Juice, if I see him…" I strongly announced as I jumped over the bench on the lawn of my apartment building. "J.T. ain't the problem, right now. You got this shit, to deal with." Juice unsympathetically encouraged. "What? They started fighting, or something?" I caringly asked as I hastily entered the building. "Stop all that running, young'n. You damn kids, always in rush. Ain't gonna be happy, until you need one of dem pros-pros… y-you know what I'm talkin' 'bout. Dem fake legs. Like that white man who ride dem bikes." Rudy urged as I darted through the vestibule. I ignored Rudy's demands and vaulted up the stairs. "Juice, they fighting?" I repeated as I reached the hall outside my apartment. "Nah. Right now they both playing it cool. But that, ain't gonna last too much longer." he answered calmly. "Alright, I'm here." I said as I finally approached the door of my apartment.

CHAPTER 72

"Hassan"

"I got some things to take care of first. But I 'll definitely swing pass there, before I leave from up this way." I vowed as I knocked my signature cadence on the door. "Don't forget man." Victor unwaveringly pleaded. "I said I'll be there." I hastily reminded, attempting to end the call before the door opened. "I got it." a young lady's voiced bellowed from the inside the house. "Alright then." Victor said closing the call. "Alright then." I responded before ending the call and thrusting my phone into my pocket.

"Hey. You must be Krystal." I pronounced, pretending to smile at Asia's daughter as she fiercely pulled the door open. "Yeah. And you are?" she inhospitably asked, standing at the door shielding all behind her from my eyesight. "I'm Haas, your mom's expecting me. Being as though we hung up the phone just five minutes ago, you'd think she'd have been the one to answer the door." I replied countering her antagonism with some of my own. "You'd think that." she standoffishly uttered. "Mom, I'm leaving. And your company's here!" she called out as she stepped aside, showing an unwilling submission to my arrival. I stepped in and held the door for Asia's daughter to depart. "Mm, mm, mm. You actually showed up? Same 'ol Haas." Asia disappointedly uttered as she appeared at the door. "You say that like, we weren't just on the phone. You knew I was coming." I brazenly clarified as Asia gestured for my coat, after securing the door. "And what's same old Haas, supposed to mean?" I continued to ask while staring at her ass as she escorted me through her home. "The first little hint of some pussy, and you moving heaven and earth. Any other time, it's your ass to kiss." she confirmed as she repeatedly turned to watch me, watch her. "Is that right?" I skeptically asked as surveyed Asia's home in passing. "If our experiences have shown me nothing else, it's shown me that." she said finally settling in the kitchen. "Our experiences were twenty years ago. I was a horny teenager." I sensibly enlightened as I leaned on the counter adjacent to where Asia established herself. "Then why are you here now? You not, still a horny teenager. Well you not, still a teenager." Asia

342

sarcastically asked leaning down to, in all appearances, purposely expose her cleavage through the top of her low-cut dress. "I came, 'cause I was in the area and an old friend asked me to come by. Just like when I leave here, I'm going by Victor's house. As far as me being horny, I don't do horny. Nor do I do hints, I'm straight up with everything." I sternly replied. "The real question is, why you asked me to come by? You offering pussy? Is that why you brought it up?" I cynically asked as I pointed out to her, my view of her breasts. "The only thing I'm offering right now, is tea. Would you like some?" she maintained as she half-heartedly erected herself to impede my view. "No, I'm good." I promptly replied.

"It's damn near December, Vic. Why do you still have a fan in the window?" I said as I noticed Victor's bedroom window while parking in front of his house. Knock. Knock. Knock! "Mia!" I enthusiastically responded after she opened the door melodiously yelling my name. "What's good?" she enthusiastically asked as she stepped aside keenly granting me passage into her home. "Nothing and everything, Mia. Nothing and everything." I self-importantly broadcasted as I danced my way into Victor's house. "What about you? You good?" I asked as I turned to hug Victor's wife. "I'm good. I'm, real good! I'm pregnant! At least, I hope I am." she enthusiastically revealed. "Oh shit! Congratulations!" I said as I continued to embrace Tamia, rocking side to side in merriment. "Shh! Victor doesn't know. And don't congratulate me yet, I won't know officially til tomorrow." she whispered as I released my of her. "What do you mean, he doesn't know? And what is it with you women telling me, before you tell your fucking man? Tracey did the same shit." I quietly asked as I removed my coat and dropped it on the bench by the door. "She's pregnant too? Lucky her." Tamia said with a great smile. "Where's Vic?" I said as I sauntered through the house to the kitchen. "He upstairs. Probably on the phone, with his boyfriend." she painfully expressed as she followed me into the kitchen. "Don't start that shit, Mia. We know what happened and y'all apparently dealing with it, since you may be pregnant. Ain't no need, to bring it back up." I insisted as I opened the refrigerator. "Wait. I thought Vic couldn't have kids." I asked as I searched for something cold to drink. "Well, look who finally decided to join the party. He can't!" she deviously admitted as she pointed to the crisper drawer. I opened the drawer to find a Victor's supply of Nesquik Strawberry Milks. "Yeah, Vic!" I whispered as I snatched up a bottle. "What the hell?" Vic said as he walked into the kitchen, pulling his shirt over his head. "Wa'sup man?" I said opening the milk. "How you just gonna go in my stash?" he said surprised of my overconfidence. "That's my cue." Mia said disappointed by Victor's arrival timing. "Excuse me." she said dismally as she squeezed pass Victor to leave. I peculiarly scrutinized Mia reaction to Vic's entrance. "What's up with that? Thought y'all fixed it." I awkwardly asked as I jumped up to sit on the counter. "Nah, it's bad, man. She turned her office back into a bedroom, so she can sleep in there. We don't talk to each other. If I come into a room, she jets right out!" Victor remorsefully confessed as he too reached into the fridge for a Nesquik. "Damn man, I'm sorry to hear that." I sincerely announced as I continued to gulp down the milk. "I brought it on myself. If I woulda just ignored that curiosity, I'd still have a home." Victor regretfully said as sulked on an adjacent counter. "And a job. Wha'chu doing, about that?" I asked unsympathetically reintroducing his, here and now. "I interviewed at a few waste management companies, over the last week or two. My hope is, one of them will come through." he uttered with his head down, facing the counter. "Well, that's good, I guess." I said unsuccessfully attempting to reassure him. "You brought all this shit, on yourself." I thought as I watched him try to look pitiful. "So, what's up? Why'd you need me, to come through?" I asked ready to go take care of the business that I came up here for and then head back home. "Damn, I can't just want your company?" he sincerely asked as he raised from the counter. "Nigga. Don't say shit like that, out loud. Niggas might hear you, and get the wrong idea." I chuckled as I slid down from the counter. "Damn it's like that? You branding me as a gay, too?" he inquired disappointed by my judging statement. "Cut that pity me shit, out! You had your hands on another nigga's dick, and was enjoying it. That's gay! You're gay, and that's fine. What's fucked up is, that you didn't tell Mia. She deserved a choice, in all of this." I sternly informed. "Hmph." Tamia said as she sauntered into the kitchen carrying a saucer and spoon. "I'm not gay, man. I just lost my head, for a second." Victor solemnly mumbled as we watched Tamia cross the kitchen. "Where'd you lose it, in his pants?" I sarcastically asked. "Victor you were kissing another man's neck. You're gay! Conversation done!" I harshly barked as Tamia loudly placed her glass bowl and spoon into the sink. "But don't worry, you're not the only one who keeps secrets." I contemptuously continued as I watched Mia watch me. She rolled her eyes and slowly attempted to slide pass me, to exit the room. "Hold up, before you go." I insisted while grabbing her arm. "You two are clearly over and done with. What y'all gonna do, keep living like this?" I seriously asked of both of them. "Ask him, he knows my terms." Mia answered looking down at my clinch of her arm, then up at me. "That's why, I reached out. I'm looking for a place, and wanted to talk to you about any openings in your building." Victor disgracefully acknowledged. I slowly released my grip of Mia's arm, in awe of their decision. "Jills handles the leases, but I'll sink it and see what floats." I caringly answered. "I appreciate that. I need him gone." Mia discretely whispered as she passed me. "Thanks man." Vic embarrassingly sighed as he plopped down into a chair. "Oh yeah, I'm pregnant." Tamia said nonchalantly as she threw me a wink, and sashayed out of the room.

"Alright Vic, I got some things to do before I head home. So, I'mma go 'head and bounce up outta here." I calmly said as I rose from the sofa. "Alright man." Victor sniveled after lifting his head from his hand. "I'll ask Jillian to check on that housing shit for you, as soon as I get back home." I said still feeling slightly sympathetic. "Thanks again, man." he said pitifully as he extended his hand for me to shake. "Don't worry about it. Everything's gonna be, alright." I reassured while grasping his extended hand. "You leaving, Haas?" Mia yelled from the kitchen before swiftly parading to meet me, at the front door. "Alright man." Victor said before leaving to distance himself from Tamia. "Alright." I said understanding, and accepting his departure. "Yeah, I got some things to do. And I still gotta go by, and check on mama Val." I said as Mia quickly advanced towards me. "Ok, babe. You be good. And tell Ms. Val, I said hi." she said as she approached. "I will and I'll do my best." I said opening my arms to embrace her. DOINK! "Mmmm. It's so weird seeing you without O." Mia said as she tightly wrapped her arms around me. "Everybody says that. But we're apart, more than y'all think." I casually affirmed, defending my individuality. I fastened my coat and checked my phone.

> ## {O}
> **If you make it pass Pagano's call me!**

"Yeah I can see that." Mia mockingly scoffed as she looked down to read my text as well. "I wasn't gonna ask but, if Vic can't have kids, who's the lucky guy?" I said as I jammed my phone back into my pocket. Mia reached around me and opened the door with a mammoth smile on her face. I stepped out the door and made my way down the stairs. "I'm sure he told you, we fucked again." Mia acknowledged as she held on to the door to lean out. "Yeah, he told me." I turned back to her and softly uttered with a hope that Vic was not within earshot. "Well this time, it took." Tamia confidently testified. "Bye, Haas." she melodiously voiced before closing the door. "Bye." I whispered dumbfounded by the possibility. 3-0-2-5-5-5-8-9-7-4.

CHAPTER 73

"Quentin"

My key loudly scratched and scraped across the doorknob as I nervously tried to insert it into the lock. I eventually got my key into the lock as the door forcefully jerked open snatching them with it. I suspiciously peeked into the apartment before slowly treading in. Once in, the door swiftly slammed closed causing Imani to reveal herself from behind it. I looked at Imani, who was soundlessly standing there with her fists balled, and her eyes swelled. I dropped my bag, in case she opted to mimic last week's occurrence. Slowly continuing into the apartment, I noticed Tasha sitting at the dining room table staring into her phone. "Good, you here. Now, I can disappear." Juice said bouncing out of his bedroom. "Yeah, I'm here. Thanks for keeping order, man. I'm sorry, you had to go through this shit." I replied solemnly. "It's all good. They were actually both, classy and composed. I'm guessing that's cause they saving all the drama, for you." he continued before suddenly, suspiciously looking beyond me. I promptly turned my head around to take notice of he was observing. There, now standing directly behind me was Imani.

I pivoted to address her, and before I was able to speak a word, she raised her fist and abruptly proceeded to punch me upon the jaw, rendering me to marginally stumble. "Bitch!" Tasha yelled as she dropped her phone, sprang from her seat and lunged toward Imani. Juice intuitively apprehended Tasha, before she could pass him for Imani. "Wha'chu leaping for, hoe? We both know, you don't got no sway this way." Imani animatedly cried out after recognizing Tasha was looming. I gathered quickly and stood between Imani and Juice, who was still holding Tasha. "Let me the fuck go, Juice. Juice, let me go!" Tasha yelped as she struggled in Juice's arms. "Let her go, Juice! Stop fucking touching me, Quentin!" Imani demanded while I barely guarded her paths around me. "Y'all need to calm, the fuck down. Y'all wasn't trippin' like this, before he got here. We not gonna let y'all, fight! So, erase that shit. Y'all both pregnant, could both catch charges. Serious charges!" Juice enlightened while reducing his bear hug embrace of Tasha, to just holding her arms. "Not to mention, affect the baby somehow." I sardonically reminded, turning back and forth to look at both women for some sensibility. "You right Juice, I'm calm. I just saw her hit my man, and I lost it. But I'm ok, now. Besides, don't want my little Q2 to have any problems, I caused by being reckless." Tasha mockingly announced while pulling herself from Juice's grasp. "You really are delusional, bitch." Imani replied, progressively decreasing her effort to get around me. "Watch your mouth, little girl. You're about, to have a baby. Bout time you start at least acting like your grown, sweety." Tasha derisively stated despite the fact that she had to peek around Juice's large frame. "I can't believe you fucked this, fake ass skank." Imani harshly stated while drilling her finger into my forehead. "Bitch, you were the side hoe. You, not claimed! You were just some pussy that he didn't have to work for, and that he only took 'cause I wasn't here! Ya bastard baby don't get to be called, *junior.*" she continued to viciously respond while peering from behind me. "Maybe, I should hang around a little while longer." Juice gallantly suggested after deducing the magnitude of my current situation. "Nah, man. Go do you. Like you said… I created this mess, right." I unconditionally insisted as I stepped aside to give him room to progress to the door. I quickly repositioned back between the ladies, to prevent them from taking advantage of Juice's absence. "You certainly did!" Imani scolded while looking up at me with a scowl. "I promise to have this taken care of, by the time you get back" I vowed to my closest friend and roommate, as he grabbed his coat from the coat rack. "Taken care of? You might wanna pack a bag, Juice. This not going away, that easy." Imani sarcastically uttered. "No need, Juice. She gotta leave soon. She gotta be back before her mom know she gone, or she'll get put on punishment. So, come home like you normally do, and I'll have all of our dinner ready, like I normally do." Tasha mocked as she gazed at Imani with a grin. "Bitch, you only had a home here, 'cause I wasn't fucking pressed for it. But if I ever decided I want it back, you'd no longer be called on, 'cause you'd be uncalled-for." Imani maliciously explained as she eyeballed Juice, then me and subsequently Juice again with a bearing of disappointment and disloyalty. "In that case, I'm outta here. Goodnight ladies. Til the next time, Ball." Juice mumbled before offering me his empathetic grimace. "Til the next time, Juice." I hopelessly uttered pretending to smile. "See you later, Juicebox." Tasha pleasantly said as Juice opened the door and exited. "Fake bitch!" Imani complained as the door closed. "Little girl, you don't know me. What makes you think, I'm fake?" Tasha appreciatively questioned as she backed away from me to marvel at herself. Being as Tasha was no longer in a threatening position, I rotated back to Imani. "I ain't gotta know you, I know fake when I see it. And you bitch, are fake as shit!" Imani declared as she too moved back a bit. "Why, because I am refined? Have class? No one ever taught you those things, sweety?" Tasha insultingly probed. "Class? Bitch, you was fucking somebody else man! You think, that's refined?!" Imani cynically barked. "Sweety, by the time I fucked him, he was already mine. Sorry, to tell you. But you were the one ultimately, fucking someone else's man." Tasha vindictively disclosed as she mischievously looked over my shoulder at Imani. "Wheww! You so fucking lucky, I'm pregnant." Imani grunted while unconvincingly charging toward Tasha via through me. "I bet, I am." Tasha casually responded as she unconcernedly turned away from Imani and I.

"Are y'all finished? Can we talk like adults, now?" I harshly challenged, no longer tolerating the spiteful conduct. "Fuck you, Quentin. You the one, that brought all this shit together. All you had to do was be a man, and keep ya dick in ya pants. Instead of pushin' it inside, the corny bitch on campus." Imani countered before aggressively pushing me, with her eyes rapidly starting to overflow with tears. "You like to make a lot of noise, don't you? Quentin never told me that you were such an, attention seeker. But I guess, it's true what they say. The dog with the littlest bite, barks the loudest." Tasha discourteously scoffed.

I glanced crossly at Tasha confident she would comprehend its meaning. "Ok, I'll stop." she conformed with a dissatisfied pout. "Thank you. Now, have a seat so we can all get this shit, over with." I indignantly demanded while pointing down onto the sofa. "Ok." Tasha reluctantly agreed before scurrying in the opposite direction. "Where you going?" I impatiently inquired watching her scamper over to the table. "To get my phone. I'm coming." she sharply retorted as she reached down to retrieve her phone.

"What're you still doing on the phone?" Tasha surprisingly yelped when seeing her friend's face still on the screen of her phone.

"GIRL, I HEARD ALL THAT YELLING AND I WASN'T HANGING UP UNTIL I KNEW YOU WERE OK. I WAS ABOUT TO CALL ERICA AND K'LYNNE TO SEE IF THEY KNEW WHAT WAS GOING ON."

"No baby, I'm fine. Just a little property dispute." Tasha confidently relieved.

"I HEARD IT ALL. SO, I KNOW WHAT PROPERTY YOU WERE DISPUTING ABOUT."

"I'm sure you did. I gotta go, try and resolve some things. I'll call you later?" Tasha shamefully disclosed attempting to quickly end the call.

"MAKE SURE THAT YOU DO. THAT WAY WE CAN DISCUSS YOU GETTING PREGNANT BY SOMEONE ELSE'S BOYFRIEND,"

"Bye girl." Tasha half-heartedly said before ending the call and jamming the phone into her pocket. "Will you c'mon." I severely demanded as Tasha lackadaisically traipsed her way to the sofa. "You too! Have a seat!" I barked to Imani, who was slowly pacing back and forth behind me. She sighed heavily before ultimately sauntering slowly to the sofa. "Why you trying to have us, sit down and talk about this. It's pointless." Imani huffily complained as she plopped down on the sofa. "No, it's really not. I'm taking accountability for what I did. I did, all this. I created this mess. I'm the common denominator. And there's nothing I can do, to make any of it go away. Which means, we gotta deal with it. We gotta find a way, to at least be civil. I'm not looking for y'all to be friends, but you can't be trying to kill each other, either. Your kids, will be siblings! We gotta think about, them." I candidly admitted as I sat on the back of the sofa behind them. "Oh, believe me I am. That's why I said, this is stupid. Ya side bitch, she can have you. I'm done!" Imani disclosed as she wiped away her tears with her hands. "Hoe, he's all yours. Enjoy!" she desolately pretended to support while ogling Tasha. "Me and mine, will be fine without y'all." she continued scoffing. "So, wha'chu saying? You're gonna keep my baby, from me?" I asked dumbfounded by even the thought. "No. What she's trying to do is convince us, and herself, that she doesn't need you. And she's willingly bestowing you to me, to prove that belief." Tasha assertively clarified. "But sweety, if you were really giving him away, you wouldn't have come here." Tasha continued to incisively convey. "Quentin, why is this bitch still talking?!" Imani seriously asked as she rose to her feet. "I said, you can have him! This's one time where the skank, actually won. You won! So, bitch appreciate it, and stop talking!" Imani sternly demanded before heading for the restroom. "Damn, y'all! Y'all can't stop, for ten fucking seconds?!" I hopelessly yelled before Imani closed the bathroom door. I looked over at Tasha, who was smiling intrepidly while writing something onto a small piece of paper she claimed from atop the end table.

"Imani, I'm just saying that, I'm the problem here. So, if you filled with animosity, and ill will, and wanna hit, hit me!" I confessed after Imani came stomping out of the restroom toward the door. "And, if you got something to say, or feel slighted or snubbed, say it to me." I leaned down slightly to encourage Tasha. "I better not find out she hit you again, Quentin. I'm not playing!" Tasha quietly warned before eyeballing Imani, who was retrieving her coat from the coat rack. "Whatever hoe!" Imani said as she swung her coat over her shoulders. "And fuck him and everything he talking about. Because when my baby drop, me and you definitely gonna get better acquainted." she continued to murmur to Tasha. "Good. Take this, so there are no excuses for us not to do that." Tasha happily agreed as she handed her the paper she'd jotted on.

CHAPTER 74

"Omar"

Hassan
302-555-1510

"Yo. I was giving you another half and before calling you, since you never got back about Pagano's." I calmly admitted while tediously scanning company emails. "Yeah. I, uh, I didn't make it over that way yet. But, I gotta talk to you about something." Hassan reluctantly confessed. "I knew you would. Every time you go up there, you come back with something. What's up?" I joked anticipating the usual hearty laugh. "Hold. It ain't moms, is it? She alright?!" I fretfully asked as I registered his tone. My jovial disposition came to an abrupt halt after recognizing where he was, and all news is not always good news. "I'm just on my way there, now. But we just saw her four days ago, I'm sure she's fine." he logically comforted. "You right. What's up then?" I asked relieved to know it wasn't a predicament involving mom. "Uh." he hesitantly sighed. "What's wrong, man?!" I anxiously asked after hearing his excessive apprehension. "I'm just gonna say it." Hassan ultimately announced as I closed the email page to give him my absolute attention. I picked the phone up from the desk and removed the speakerphone feature. "Ok." I approved slightly nervous that the most carefree individual I knew, was suddenly being coy. "I just came from Vic crib and… Mia think she might be, pregnant." he decreed after exhaling deeply. "That's cool. Her and Vic made up? Good shit." I said releasing my slight squirm in relief. "Uh, no. She still hate him, so she definitely not giving him no pussy. Even if she was, you know Vic can't have kids. But we do know someone who fucked her not too long ago, and he can." he dismally reminded. "Wait. Hold up. She seriously told you this?!" I probed as the possibility of the news progressively struck me. "Just now! But she's saying *she is*… not, *think she might be*." he continued to gravely testify.

I sat motionless except for a slight tremble, as beads of sweat rapidly formed on my face and neck. "O." I faintly heard Hassan say as my phone lay on my desk. "O!" Hassan yelled again to gather my attention. "How you wanna play it?" he tiresomely continued to ask completely loyal to whatever ruling I'd make. "Let me, call you back." I whispered as I stood up and closed my office door for fear that I may involuntarily explode. "Yeah, alright. Just don't do nothing, dumb." Haas shrewdly warned before ending the call. I slinked back over to my desk, grabbed my waste paper basket, and sat down as nausea began to overtake.

Buzz... "Mr. Gregory, Ms. Daranger is here for your one o'clock meeting."

"Give me a minute Toni." I struggled to mumble as I continued to violently heave into the trash. Knock. Knock. Knock! "Mr. Gregory, everything alright?" Toni said as she crept in before I could respond. "Oh damn. Eww!" she continued as she observed me with my head down projecting into the trash can. "You sounded like something was wrong, but I wasn't expecting all this." she said as she continued to watch while covering her nose. "I'll find an empty conference room to put her in, and then cancel the rest of your day." Toni reasonably itemized. I waved to her to show approval with my head still down. "Be right back." she disclosed as she stepped out of my office to implement her resolve tactics.

Knock. Knock. Knock! "Omar." Toni whispered as she appropriately entered my office. "You didn't give a chance to say, come in." I joked as she came in with an overabundance of paper towels and her shirt pulled up over her nose. "That's 'cause I thought, you might've died." she sarcastically replied as she closed the door. "You alright?" she asked as she dropped the towels on my desk and walked across the office to the window. "I'm alive." I said as I swiped across my face with my handkerchief. "Come stick your head out the window." Toni insisted as she lifted it open. "Why, so I can throw up on someone?" I asked while I clumsily rising to my feet. "No. So you can get a whiff, of fresh air." she confirmed as she made her way over to my desk. "Hello. Can you please send someone up to office D, in suite six? We had an accident, up here. Thank you." Toni pleasantly asked before gently placing the receiver back onto the phone. "So, you wanna tell me what that was about? You ate some bad coo...? Couscous. I was gonna say couscous." Toni apprehensively said as she grabbed some wet wipe packs from her pocket and a few of the towels that she'd brought in.

I pulled myself into the window and routinely stood in front of Toni with my hands to my sides. "What happened to, no changes? That's not what you were going to say!" I tried to ask as she opened a wet wipe packet and began to swab my nose and mouth. "I don't know. I almost did, but now I'm scared of who's listening. Who, knows? Scared, that everyone up here knows I want you." she quietly replied blushing at my effort to comfort her. "Don't want me Toni. I ain't shit. It's all, a façade." I uttered thinking of the dilemma I got myself into. "Don't say that. Why you say that?" Toni skeptically asked as she used the towels to brush across my chest and shoulders. "Speaking, truth." I said shamefully. "That's bullshit! When you come back, you'll tell me what happened that got you all messed up."

Toni asserted as she adjusted my tie to perfection. "Now, go be great at your meeting. You look, nice." she continued to strong-arm as she reached for the folder on my desk and pressed it into my chest.

"You gotta understand, this's Cricket. She was my first, and we was like eleven! So, fucking her is, was... *the norm*. It's what, I grew up doing. No matter who she was with, or who I was with, we did it. And we always bounced back, like nothing ever happened. I don't feel the slightest bit of guilt, when I'm fucking her. It's like, it's not cheating, it's supposed to happen. Put it like this, I feel more guilt looking at your *t and a*, than I did fucking her." I said in the closing of my recap to Toni. "So, you did run into some bad coochie!" Toni sarcastically scoffed in response to my predicament. "I really thought if you were going to make that mistake, it'd be with me." she said somberly as she rose her feet. She lifted her coat up from the sofa and tossed it over her arm. "Are you seriously going to make this, about you? I'm in a real fucked up place, right now." I reiterated as I looked up at Toni from the adjacent chair. "Yeah, you are! What're you going to do about it?" Toni asked blatantly unsuccessful in her endeavor at being callous. "Don't know. I wanna go home and confess to Tracey, and just hope she doesn't slit my throat. But Hassan doesn't think, that's a good idea. He thinks I should talk to Cricket, first." I replied as I sustained my spot on the chair as she slowly advanced towards the door to leave for the day. "Well, if I see you here tomorrow then I'll know, you didn't tell her." Toni declared as she bad-temperedly stamped out of the office. "Or she didn't hit the jugular." I fittingly jested as she closed the door.

The neighbor's dog barked and excitedly jumped on the fence as he always does if he's outside when I pull into the driveway. I slowly pulled up to the garage door, leaving enough room for Tracey to pull out if need be. "What the hell have I done?" I whispered as I put the truck in park. I turned off the engine and continued to remain stationary. "God, I thought you forgave me. I know I don't, come to you often. I know I'm quicker to ask of you, than I am to thank you for what you've provided. I know I'm not the model Christian, but I do believe and confess with my mouth what I believe in heart. I know that I'm just an actor in a script, that you have written. And even the freewill which you have granted me is concurrent with the plan, you have laid out. But I'm lost, with this one. So, God, if you could just send me a sign of what's to come." I prayed as I continued to linger in the truck while waiting to develop the courage to go inside. I looked up and waved back at Tracey, who was waving down at me from the kitchen window. I raised one finger to respond to her signaling, for me to come inside. I opened the door and tentatively extracted myself from the truck. "God you know my heart, I'm not a bad guy." I pleaded as I closed the door. I opened the trunk and collected my briefcase before going over to greet the neighbor's dog. I dropped my briefcase next to me and reached over the fence, to interact with the happily excited canine. "Hey Zeus. How ya doin', boy?" I asked as I spiritedly pet his head and neck. "Bye, boy. I gotta go face the music." I said before I tapped the gate and picked up my briefcase.

"Hey." I said as I slid the glass, patio door open, and meandered into the kitchen. "Hey. You alright? Is there something on your mind that I need to know, too?" Tracey asked before leaning in to kiss me. "No. Why you ask that?" I nervously asked. "Because, you only go over to say hi to Zeus when you're troubled. And the last time you lodged in the car for that long, you didn't know how to tell me that my father, had cancer. So, again I ask is everything, alright?" she reminded as she slipped on an oven mitt and pulled open the oven door. "It's nothing babe. I just got work shit on my mind, that's all." I stated as I patted her ass as I passed her and headed up to the stairs to my bedroom.

Hassan
302-555-1510

"Yo." I said as I answered Hassan's call while unfastening my shirt. "Yo. I'm just calling, to check up on you. You good?" Hassan inquired to determine the state of things. "No, you not. You calling to find out if I told, Tracey." I bluntly proclaimed as I snatched off my shirt and tie and tossed them onto the bed. "Not just, Tracey. If you told, anyone?" he asked worried that I'd let my guilt get in the way of logic. "I told Toni." I ineptly admitted while sitting down to remove my shoes and pants. "Fuck you tell her for?" he indignantly questioned. "I was real fucked up after you told me, that shit. I was hurling all over the place. And she walked in on it. Her seeing fucked up all in the face, and I didn't feel like, nor did I have the energy to lie, I told her." I honestly testified as I tossed the shoes across the room into the closet "Be careful with giving her full disclosure, on shit. If she still wanna fuck you, who knows what she'll do?" Hassan realistically advised as I reached to retrieve some sweat pants from my drawer. "Yeah I thought about that, too." I honestly agreed. "But honestly how much worst, could she make shit?" I unconvincingly asked as I rose to find my slippers. "A lot!" he harshly asserted. "Yeah, I get'chu!" I uttered surrendering to his logic. RING. RING!

Quentin
302-555-8975

"Hold up. That's Que, on the other line. I'mma hit you back." I said immediately after seeing the number. "Don't bother. Jillian just said, we're about to come over there." Hassan promptly divulged. "Alright. Be you." I said ending the call. "Be you, bro." he responded before I switched over to answer Quentin.

"Dad." Quentin voiced before I could even speak. "Yes, Quentin." I casually responded while scanning the area for my slippers. "You will never guess, what happened today." he said frantically. I found one slipper and promptly slid my foot into it. "The other must be under the bed." I considered instinctively. "What? They switched your position during practice, again? You a wide receiver now, or something?" I sarcastically asked as I laid across the floor to inspect under the bed. "No! Imani came up here today, to take on Tasha!" he passionately disclosed. "What?!" I asked astonished at the notion. I stopped my search for my second slipper to give Quentin my full attention. "Yeah!" he swore earnestly. "They didn't fight, did they?" I nervously probed in concern for the unborn children. "If not for me, and Juice they would've." he continued to proclaim. "Shit! That girl really got some balls, on her!" I mumbled, amazed by Imani's audacity. "What happened? Imani, just left?" I deeply investigated as I sat up from my stretched position. "She was here almost all day. But yeah, she left." he serenely uttered. "So, what happened?!" I enthusiastically asked as I put on the speakerphone mode, to continue looking for my slipper while listening.

"That girl, is off her rocker! She really coulda went to jail, for that shit. She lucked out with Tasha, not calling the cops." Hassan said from across the table after hearing my rendition of Quentin's day. "Yeah, we don't know that young lady, nor her tendencies. For Imani to travel there was just, stupid." Tracey voiced in agreement after placing her water-filled goblet back on the table. "I don't know y'all. I can't say that I don't empathize with her, and her situation. She was just betrayed, by the man she loves. That there, is some powerful pain. Some people, just don't have a tolerance for that kind of pain." Jillian casually preached as she stood to retrieve a second wine bottle. I pulled the corkscrew from the empty bottle and gestured for Jillian to give me the unopened one. "And, who's to say Imani was going up there, to fight? Maybe she just wanted, an explanation! I know, I do. I mean, would." Jillian continued as she handed me the unfamiliar bottle before eyeballing Hassan. "Regardless of why she went up there, her intentions were to somehow confront that girl." Tracey reminded while stabbing her fork back into her cake. "That was just her, asking for trouble." she continued to judgmentally insist. "Who cares? None of that matters! What matters is, Quentin now has two children on the way. That's twice as many baby moms, twice as many headaches... twice as many distractions! This could bulldoze the future he... we, have all worked for." I sternly reminded as I snatched the cork from the wine bottle. "I don't know, how to fix this." I mumbled quietly as I handed the bottle back to Jillian. "Omar, this is not something, you can fix. This was Quentin's doing, Quentin's decision making. Sorry baby, he's gonna just have to swallow this one." Jillian proclaimed as she poured her wine. "I can't concede to that. You mean to tell me, that one reckless decision defines his legacy?" I skeptically asked. "Yeah. It happens, all the time." Hassan firmly lectured as he stared at me intently. "But not in this case. His legacy is still, undetermined." he continued before raising his beer to his awaiting lips. "Now, what he does with this situation, yeah, that could define him." Jillian severely accompanied. "I just hope he gets the opportunity to continue on the path he chose." Tracey gloomily stated before rising from her chair. "I have no doubt, that he will. Neither of them seem dumb enough, to let that NFL money slip through their fingers." Hassan logically disclosed before finishing his beer. "I don't think it's all about, that money. Imani really does, love and want him." Jillian sincerely stated before rising to follow Tracey into the kitchen. "So does, Tasha." I responded desolately before downing my last bit of brandy. "Lucky him." Jillian jadedly murmured as she disappeared from sight. "If that's lucky, I don't want no parts." Hassan unenthusiastically responded after sitting back in his chair. "Me either." I quietly mumbled as I thought mournfully with respect to both Quentin and my, individual situations.

CHAPTER 75

"Quentin"

The front doorknob began to slightly shake, in conjunction with the sound of clanging keys. The door slowly opened, and Juice gradually crept into the apartment. "What the hell you doing?" I snickered at Juice's attempt to be covert. "You still alive?!" Juice sarcastically chuckled as he noticed me sitting on the couch. "Yeah. I'm good." I proudly admitted as I rose up to greet, my friend. "How the hell you get out of that, untouched?" he asked amazed, while surveying me for injuries. "I didn't say that. But it didn't get too bad, because of the babies." I confessed massaging my hand on the side of my face where Imani struck. "Look at your kids, already saving your ass." Juice savored as he stepped into his bedroom to unload his bag. "So, it's over? Everything's, all good?" he bewilderedly questioned as he returned with his coat in hand. "It'll never be, over. But for now, it's relaxed." I said before going into the kitchen to get a snack. "How?! They both just walked away? I mean, you had caucus downstairs, calling you the devil." Juice voiced in hilarity while hanging his coat on the rack near the door. I laughed at their comparison, of me and lucifer. "How many people, was down there? Do I know 'em?" I asked amazed that people were that involved in the particulars, of my life. "I don't know, you gotta ask Dee. She saw 'em, not me." he said coming to join me in the kitchen. "Oh." I uttered reluctant to come across any woman with knowledge, of my situation. I reached into the canister marked flour, for my hidden bag of pistachios. "You know how evil they gotta think you are, for someone to compare you to the devil?" he questioned in wonder with his head in the refrigerator. "Yeah." I answered just as shocked. "So, Satan. How'd you come out of it, still alive?" he sarcastically reiterated as he ultimately snatched a water, and closed the fridge door. "According to Verbal Kint... the greatest trick the devil ever pulled, was convincing the world he did not exist." I joked as I began cracking pistachio shells with my teeth. "But on the real, I just took accountability for it all. They calmed down, on their own. You're right, my kids saved my ass." I honestly admitted. "I think Imani, just wanted to see it all for herself. And Tasha, she just wanted to be recognized. They both got what they, wanted." I continued to disclose as I chomped on an unshelled pistachio.

"Yo, Ball!" Juice yelled from the other side of the bedroom door. "Yo." I grumbled as I lifted my head from the pillow. "Wake up, man. Dame and Will out here waiting for you." he continued to yell. "Open the door." I instructed as I tried to completely awaken. The door opened to Juice standing there, in his coat and hat. "Now, wha'chu say?" I questioned able to now hear him clearly. "I was saying Dame and Will out here waiting on you, and I'm about to roll out." Juice repeated. "Damn, I almost forgot about the meeting. Good looking out." I said looking over at the clock. "No problem. Where, Imani?" he probed while scanning the room. "Home, I guess. She didn't answer my calls, last night. So, I can only assume. Why you ask that?" I questioned bewildered by his inquiry. "Well, how she get there, if Miss Grier outside?" he continued to confusedly ask. "Fuck you mean, Miss Grier outside!" I animatedly asked as I vaulted from the bed and darted to the window. "Like I said, ya car is outside. Parked right where it was, yesterday." he reiterated with certainty. "No, this bitch didn't catch the train home." I said looking out of the window for my car. "Oh shit. You didn't know?" he asked bewildered. "Hell no!" I disclosed, increasingly becoming irate. "If she left the car, she had to leave the keys." Juice logically deduced. "I don't know. But she know she shouldn't be traveling like that, so late." I replied too upset to think about it. "That'd be fucked up, if she took 'em with her." Juice mockingly considered. "Wouldn't surprise me, if she did." I admitted as I raised from the window. "And they called you, evil. Damn! Til the next time, Ball." Juice pitied. "Til the next time, Juice." I said as he closed the door and left.

"You alright man? You ain't even look like you was trying to pay attention, during the meeting." Dame curiously asked as we walked across campus. "I'm good." I fabricated to keep from any further investigating. "Just got some things, on my mind." I honestly continued. "Well, you better get 'em off. Cause if I caught you lunchin', believe coach did too." he recapped absolutely.

3-0-2-5-5-5-8-9-7-4. "Hold on a second, Quentin." my dad insisted when answering the call. I opened the door to my apartment to see a figure swiftly scurry into my bedroom. I stealthily tiptoed across the apartment toward my bedroom. "Hey Quentin. Sorry about that. How are you? All is well?" my dad courteously asked directly into my ear via my earbuds. "Hold on dad. I think someone's here." I whispered as I reached my bedroom door. "What the hell you mean, you think someone's there?! If someone's in your place Quentin, get out!" "he yelled passionately. "Dad chill. Just hold on!" I sternly continued to whisper as I treaded softly into my room. "Damn Willow, you promised." Tasha disappointedly mumbled as she stood in front of my closest in her bra and pants on the floor still around her ankles. "Damn, Tasha! I ain't know what the hell was going on!" I harshly stated. "You said Tasha?" my dad repeated. "Yeah dad, it's Tasha." I answered as I raised my finger gesturing for Tasha to wait a minute. I stepped back out of the bedroom to remove my coat. "Y'all, and y'all games." my dad criticized as I tossed my coat onto the hook. "She was trying to surprise, me." I explained as I made my way to the dining room table. "I'm sure" he casually responded. "You know what really, surprised me? Coming out to find my car, still in the parking lot." I profoundly confessed as I dropped my phone onto the table and sat down. "What?!" my dad sharply retorted. "Yup" I casually answered while thinking about Imani's well-being. "She caught the train home?" he disturbingly probed. "I'm guessing so. She won't answer my calls, for me to find out." I hopelessly answered as I slid my phone, to and fro across the table. "Wow! That's the reason, she went up there." my dad rationally construed. "Hey. You never came, back." Tasha whispered, stepping out of the bedroom in my bathrobe. "Oh. Didn't know you were still on the phone, sorry." she whispered after seeing me sitting at the table playing with my phone. I raised my finger up to Tasha again to reiterate that I'd only be, one more minute. "Wait. I can do you one better, dad. She took the car keys, back with her!" I enthusiastically revealed while shaking my head. Tasha scoffed, before returning to the bedroom. "Damn Quentin, that's vicious! Kind of impressive though." my dad marveled. "I know this sounds like an inspiring life lesson to you, but you think you could send me the spare keys?" I asked "Not this time, Quentin. I'm not creditable enough, to condemn. But yeah, I'll overnight the keys to you. You should have them by tomorrow afternoon. Look at it this way, you got your car back." my dad sullenly said. "Nah, I'm gonna drive it home, and give it back to her. I'm just not sure when I can." I irrefutably answered as I stood to return to my bedroom.

CHAPTER 76

"Antoinette"

"That's good. That's exactly what you should do." Omar proudly said as I walked into his office. "Okay son, let me go. Toni just came in, to prep me for my meeting. And I'll give her the keys, so she can send them off." he continued as he gestured for me to sit down. I closed the door, turned the doorknob to lock, and sat down as requested. "Alright. Talk to you later, Quentin." he pronounced casually before ending the call. "Talk to you later? What happened to, you be you? Or my favorite, til the next time?" I worriedly asked as I prepped his meeting files. Omar looked at me, snickered, and furnished a fake smile. "I'm just not, me today." he solemnly said as his eyes closed and his head fell back onto his chair headrest. "Then who are you?" I said as I continued to scan through the folder. "I don't know" he muttered with a sigh. "Well, who do you feel like?" I asked curiously. "Don't know that, either." he wearily replied as he reopened his eyes and slowly erected himself. "Then there's no helping you." I said as I placed the file folder on his desk. "I know one way you can help. Can you gather the federal perspective on the aqueduct modifications, and add it to the those meeting files?" he openly inquired as he attempted to get himself together. "You already asked me to do that, earlier. It's right here!" I alluded to as I opened the folder, and pointed out the flash drive. "You really are, messed up!" I declared as I surveyed my broken boss.

"Here, let me try something." I insisted as I rose from my chair with a bending more than I had to, to tease a little. "No, he didn't just *not* look at me." I thought as I removed my blazer tossed it onto the chair before gradually stepping around his desk. "Sit back." I demanded as I stood behind his chair, placed my hands on his shoulders, and pulled him back. I gently walked my fingers up his neck and cheek to his temples. "How's this?" I faintly asked as I soothingly massaged. "Heaven Sent." he sighed as his head again tipped back and eyes closed. "So now, talk. What's on your mind?" I tenderly asked while I continued to massage. "Everything. This dumb shit, I got going with Cricket. Tracey. Quentin.

Work, bills. Hell, even you." Omar openly divulged while interlocking his fingers across his chest. "Me! What I do?" I enthusiastically grinned, shocked that he mentioned me. "C'mon Antionette. You really, wanna go there?" he temptingly asked. "You made it clear. We not going, where I wanna go. So, yeah. Let's go, wherever it is you're talking about." I sarcastically responded. "Nah. We're gonna let sleeping dogs lie, on that subject." he coyly stated with a subtle grin. "If it it's about me, I think I have the right to know." I perceptively uttered while reversing the massage rotation. "Knowledge, is sometimes dangerous. Some things are better left, unknown." he continued to tease with an even larger grin. "Is that right?" I lightheartedly questioned as I briskly removed my hands from his head, to wring and stretch them. "I'd like to think so." he calmly said. "Ok. You're entitled to your opinion." I responded while wildly shaking my hands in preparation to continue. "So, you're done?!" he nervously asked while opening his eyes to survey in all directions. "Not done, just relocating." I disclosed after positioning my hands onto his shoulders. "Wow. You are, tight! I could fix this, if I had my stones." I arrogantly divulged as I forcefully kneaded my thumbs into his shoulder blades. "What stones?" he asked turning to perplexedly look up at me. "I have special stones at home that I heat up and place on your body, when I give a massage. It relaxes your muscles, so I can get deeper into your muscular layers." I explained as I continued to knead into his upper back. "Deeper? Not sure if I could handle, deeper." he acknowledged with an understated moan. "It also takes away tension, muscle stiffness, and increases blood circulation." I continued to enlighten as my eyes too began to close. "Damn, look at you! This is what you do in your, spare time? Massages?" Omar probed enthralled by both the massage, and the knowledge behind it. "Not at all. I learned all of this so I can please, my ex." I admitted without hesitation, before reopening my eyes to see how he'd react. "Oh really?" he very attentively asked while flourishing a sizeable smile. "Yes, really. He used to come home tense, too. As his woman, it was my job to relieve his stress. All... of his stress!" I suggestively responded while ineffectively trying to restrain my grin. "So, I took some massage therapy classes, and learned some new tricks. Add them to the tricks I already knew, and..." I casually continued to inform as I slowly progressed my palms down his chest. "Well, you have an imagination." I encouragingly motivated while drawing my hands back up to his shoulders. "Hmph. Learn something new, every day. Antoinette Willmont, is not just a one trick pony, huh?" Omar snickered at his own awe of my unknown talents. "Pony? I'm a stallion, baby. The real-life,

Black Beauty." I conceitedly flaunted, lowering my lips to his ear, my breast resting on his shoulder. "Excuse me!" he melodiously crooned. "And the tricks I know, could be archived in a museum." I boldly admitted as I lifted my breasts from his shoulder. "You know what else the hot stones do? They expand blood vessels, so blood can flow freely throughout the body. The entire body!" I cunning revealed as I relocated my hands under his tie, bit by bit. "But I never really had a need, for that effect." I purposely let slip before clearing my throat to get his attention, to point out his remarkably evident erection.

"As sensational as this massage feels, you gotta stop." Omar required as he raised his head. "Why? Your meeting's not for another thirty-five minutes." I candidly asked while continuing to manipulate my hands up and down his chest. "Yeah but as you pointed out, I have additional blood flow." he said as he clutched my wrists halting my motion. "So, we have to stop, because of that? Grow up, Omar!" I harshly responded, rebelliously snatching away from his grasp. "Yes. We have to stop, because of that. I'll need time to settle down, and I can't do that with you still in here." he persuasively affirmed followed by a heavy exhalation. "So, you want me to stop? And leave?! Oh Omar, that hurts." I sarcastically mocked. "You know what hurts, Toni? When your shit is hard as a rock, and it's compacted in your pants." he scoffed while rotating his chair around to face me. "It's only like that, cause you're not completely relaxed, yet." I softly acknowledged looking down into his eyes. "Can't see how I could be any more relaxed than I am, now. That massage was epic and I swear, if I had your bonus, you'd get it right now." he confessed as he gently seized my hands. "Aww, thank you." I sincerely thanked while moderately turning my head to hide my red, blushing appearance. "No. Thank you. Your hands are unbelievable." he promptly stated while gently rubbing my hands in his. "Are you blushing, Toni. Wow, never seen you do that before." Omar professed sarcastically. "And you'll never see it, again." I said quickly re-establishing my firmness. "Why?" he debatably asked, seeming offended. "It shows, vulnerability." I strictly said in defense of my customary demeanor. With my hands still enclosed in his, he steadily pulled me down to where we were cheek to cheek. "Allow me to let you in on something, you are human. Sometimes our submissive side, shines through. Nothing we can do about it." he whispered before gently kissing my cheek. "I'm glad, you know that." I enlightened while confiscating my hands from his grip. I grabbed the arms of his chair and lowered myself down to my knees. "What are you doing?!" he nervously asked as I slowly reached for his belt buckle. I unsecured his belt, unfastened his pants, and began to gently tunnel my hand into his pants in pursuit of his dick. "Whoa, whoa, whoa. Wha-what the hell are you doing?" he devotedly questioned while promptly positioning his hands to impede my course into his pants. I pushed away his attempt to repel my hands and resumed with my endeavor. "I'm just, relocating again. Stop trying to stop me, you need this." I advised as I seized his dick and hauled it out from inside his pants. "Hmm." I passionately grunted, captivated by his impressive member as it magnificently emerged. "This, is too far Toni." he said as he attempted to remove my grip of his manhood while gazing intently at the doorknob. "Yes, it's locked. And we haven't gone far enough, if you ask me. Look at you, all nervous and fidgety. You're not completely relaxed yet. So, let me finish relaxing you!" I demanded as I used my free hand to aggressively shove him back. "Toni, if we had sex, I'd be combining my already reckless, with just foolish. You do remember the situation, I'm presently in?" Omar justly asked as he no longer exhibited any creditable effort, to stop my momentum. "That was because she was mad, and wanted some get back. Soon as the opportunity presented itself, she took it. Then she came across the opportunity to make it an even bigger punch to the gut, she's taking that one too. It ain't about you, or that baby." I instructed as I clenched his pride, gradually running my thumb up and down. "This here, this is about you. And who said anything, about us having sex... this time?" I continued before I commenced to vigorously tug and pull on his dick. "You have an answer for everything, don't you?" he scoffed before he unexpectedly began to comply with the inevitable.

"Not going the way, you planned?" he continued to laugh as my hand clung to the dry, tacky skin of his dick. "I'm truly thankful for your effort, but this won't work without lubricant. And I trashed that bottle of KY, weeks ago. Guess this is God intervening, to keep us honest." he mockingly suggested before pulling my hand from his member. I laughed at his teasing, but more so at his ignorance. "There are other things I can do, but I'll comply with you and God's wishes, and not resort to those." I quietly uttered, pretending to be grief-stricken. "Thank you!" he appreciatively uttered as he leaned forward to again bury his dick, behind his clothing. "Whoa wait. You still have that stress to get rid of, remember?" I reminded as I brushed his hand aside, foiling his attempts to put his dick away. I unfastened my pants and delicately slid my hand down them, navigating my fingers beneath my panties. I ran my hand across my inner thigh to collect some of the moisture dripping from my pussy. I followed that by patting the opening of my pussy before pushing my fingers partially inside.

I glazed the moisture across my hand and quickly drew it from my pants. I returned my now saturated hand to Omar's dick and repeated my previous exploits. "Told you baby, I got museum worthy tricks." I bragged as I slid my hand up and down his dick. "Shit!" he whined, expressing ultimate pleasure. "And as unbelievable as you think they are, my hands, aren't even close to being my finest resource." I bragged as I watched his eyes cross and head roll from side to side.

CHAPTER 77

"Omar"

Vic
302-555-7312

"Been waiting all day, for this call." I immediately stated when answering the call. "How you know it was me, and not Victor?" Cricket uncertainly inquired. "Because Victor, has no reason to call me." I sternly responded as I closed the file that consumed my attention before the call. "That's just wrong. But hi, Omar." Cricket ironically replied. "C'mon Tamia, we don't have time for this!" I continued to adamantly insist. "We don't have time, to be polite? And where did Tamia, come from?" she asked seemingly offended. "Cricket!" I yelled frustrated by the jokey demeanor. "Why are you yelling?" she sternly asked, promptly abandoning her jesting viewpoint. "Cause, I don't wanna play this game!" I seriously admitted while shutting down my computer for the day. "No game, Omar, I seriously wanted this one. But... always a God mom, never a mom." she solemnly professed. "So, you're not pregnant?!" I intuitively asked before erupting. "Nope." Cricket softly responded. "Not to be an asshole, but can you send me whatever verification you got? I just need to be sure." I unconsciously asked. "Proof?! You been giving me a wet ass for almost thirty years. I never once asked you for shit or did anything to fuck you over, and now you don't trust me?! Fuck you, Omar!" Cricket ferociously yelled. "You're right. I was sorry, as soon as I finished saying it. But you just don't know, how relieved I am." I regretfully avowed. "Oh, I know. That's why I made the call. I'm not going to tell your boy, though. And I don't want you or Hassan telling him, either. I want Vic to feel this, just like I felt his faggot ass." she cunningly specified. "I won't say shit, and you know Haas won't either. He like fucking with people." I thankfully agreed as I elatedly activated the speakerphone so I could freely rise to my feet, to celebrate. "Thanks, Cricket." I merrily praised while strutting from around my desk. "No problem, Omar." she half-heartedly expressed. "And Omar."

she bleakly continued. "Yeah." I calmly responded hearing her hopeless tone. "Don't let this stop you, from busting in me." she sarcastically continued. "Don't think I can, the way you fuck back." I earnestly replied, excessively grinning. "Bye, O." she softly said. "Bye babe, Love you." I genuinely uttered before ending the call.

I jogged back around my desk, snatched off my tie, grabbed my coat and danced out of the door. "Good night Toni. Yes, I'm leaving for the day." I said as I happily pranced my way over to her desk. "Damn, what happened to you?" Toni curiously asked, lifting her head from her monitor. "Cricket's not pregnant!" I enthusiastically whispered leaning over her work surface. "You lucked out, huh? I'm glad. I hated seeing you, like that." she confessed with a smile. "Guess now, you'll be more careful?" she shrewdly asked. "Yup. So careful, that I'll never do it again. Oh. Before I forget, can you overnight these to Que?" I unassumingly asked while reaching in my pocket for Quentin's spare car keys. "Sure. I was going to ask for those, when the mail carrier came." Toni instinctively replied extending her hand to accept the keys. "Thanks. Good night, Toni." I pronounced as I stepped away from her desk. "Good night, Mr. Wonder." she laughed as I made my way to the elevator.

3-0-2-5-5-5-1-5-1-0. "Lil brother!" I boisterously voiced as he answered the call. "I take it you talked to Cricket?" Hassan instinctively snickered. "Yeah, few minutes ago. How the hell do you always know everything, before me?" I intriguingly asked while slowly advancing passed the parking attendant's booth, onto the shockingly vacant road. "I ain't know shit until, just now." he honestly confessed. "I assumed, because she was supposed to go in today. And your voice is lifted." he intuitively acknowledged. "Oh. Well to confirm, she not pregnant!" I excitedly unveiled as I quickly weaved with Nascar ambitions, between the marginal number of cars. "I'm truly happy for you. You done fucking her, now?" he nonchalantly asked. "I think so." I honestly responded as I playfully thought about Toni as a replacement. "We out later, to celebrate?" he supportively asked. "Nah, I think I'm gonna play the crib, on this one." I answered as I slowed to turn into the supermarket parking lot.

CHAPTER 78

"Quentin"

"Gregs!" Coach Butters yelled, after loudly blowing his whistle into the locker room. "Yeah, Coach." I loudly responded while looking up from tying my boot laces. "HC wants to see you!" he strictly ordered. "Yes sir." I compliantly replied before hastily grabbing the rest of my things, and dashing to his office.

KNOCK. KNOCK. KNOCK! "You wanted to see me, Coach?" I uneasily inquired as I moderately opened the door, and peeked my head into his office. "Have a seat." Coach Franklin ordered from behind his desk. I quickly stepped into the office, and adhered to his demand. I sat quietly waiting for him to again, acknowledge my presence. "I want you to take a look at something." he casually said as he closed his book and stood. He walked around his desk to the monitor, mounted on the wall to my right. "Turn the chair, if you can't see." he benevolently insisted before retrieving the two remotes from the shelf, below the screen. He pointed the remote to the monitor, and the screen lit up. He then pointed the other remote at the overhead lights. The lights gradually dimmed, and he quickly returned his attention to the screen.

"Did you see where your assignment was flawed?" Coach sternly asked before he used the remote to again, illuminate the room. "Uhhh, yes sir." I nervously replied after observing his fixation of the game film. "Don't *uh* me, son. You see it, or no?!" he curiously probed as he walked to the conference table at the other end of the office. "Yes sir, I see it." I securely admitted as I ascended from my chair to follow him. "Good! Now. I'll admit, that was my fault. Luckily, it was an easy fix. An oversight that I've corrected and had Coach Butters explain, at this morning's meeting." he confidently confessed as he sat down. He reached for the marker in from of him and began to rapidly wave it in his fingers.

"Here, I want you to show me what he told you needed to be done, to fix it." he calmly requested as he offered me the marker and nodded his head toward the dry erase board, on the wall in front of him. I claimed the marker and slowly walked to the board. I stood incompetently, pretending to study the x's and o's already positioned on the board. "Sorry Coach, I can't." I shamefully confessed while turning to return the marker to him. "Why's that?" he inquisitively asked as he accepted the marker from me. "Because, I don't remember." I unwillingly disclosed. "It's not that you don't remember, son. Because you weren't paying attention... you never knew!" he sternly roared as he relentlessly slammed his palm onto the table in front of him. "I'm gonna make this clear... I plan on running this same play next game, with the adjustments. If you don't execute it to perfection, I promise the next time you touch a ball, will be in the damn shower. Do I make myself clear?!" Coach Franklin continued to bark as he rose to return to his desk. "Yes sir." I timidly responded while watching him saunter to his throne. He sat behind his desk, looked at me and pointed toward the door. I picked up my things and slowly advanced to the door. "For most of these guys, football is just something to do other than just sit and study. But for some of you, this is what you're planning to do sustain life. And you fit the few, who are good enough to see it through. Whatever else you got going at present, needs to be considered insignificant. Your ensuring your future Gregs, act like it!" he proclaimed as I gently turned the knob. "Now go get your rest, you have Chem lab in the morning." he compassionately said "Yes sir." I calmly said before opening and stepping through the door.

CHAPTER 79

"Antoinette"

"Remember the first night you came over here?" I asked while handing Omar the bowl of fruit I procured from the kitchen. "The night I came over so you could finish that first massage, with those stones?" he asked chomping down on a sliced apple. "Yeah. You fell asleep in my arms, for the first time that night." I disclosed while placing the small bowl of caramel dip on the nightstand. "I don't remember that. What I remember is, you being so horny that you were about to drug your son, just so you can get some." he cynically mocked as I climbed back into bed. "I was not gonna drug him! I was giving him some allergy medicine, 'cause he was itchy." I deceitfully replied. "Itchy? That's the lie you've been telling yourself?" he amusingly asked while slowly feeding me a chunk of pineapple. "It's not a lie. It's just not all the way true. But he does get itchy, sometimes." I misleadingly retorted after nibbling the fruit from his hand. "What made you think of that?" he curiously asked before gesturing for the caramel. "No reason." I modestly conceded, carefully passing him the bowl. "Nothing happens for *no reason*, Toni." he suspiciously responded accepting the bowl. "Well, no *real* reason. I was just thinking that it wasn't that long ago, that I was chasing you around that office. And now I'm getting visits like, twice a week." I happily disclosed before turning to lay on my stomach. I tucked my arms under the pillow and gently rested my head on it. "Aren't you glad, I let you catch me?" he sarcastically asked. "Let me?!" I offensively mumbled with my eyebrow raised. "Nigga, you ain't *let* me do shit. I skillfully conquered, this outcome." I vigorously continued, lifting my head from the pillow. "What?!" he curiously scoffed. "We went from my unbelievable hands, to a lunch break at the Hilton, in a week. You don't think, that was by design?" I arrogantly confessed before slamming my head back down. "Yeah, my design." he shadily proposed. "I guess that's the lie you been telling, *yourself*." I stated mockingly returning his scoff. "Yeah, I am glad you let me catch you." I cooperatively pretended to declare. "Thank you. That's all I wanted." he teasingly pretended to retort before he dipped a slice of pear into the caramel and held it to my lips. "And this, was all I wanted." I genuinely divulged before confiscating the saturated fruit with my teeth. "I mean the time, not the caramel fruit. You almost got it on my pillow. And, you can't get that out." I educated while munching on the fruit.

"You think anyone at the office knows about, this?" Omar inquisitively inquired as he casually tugged on the teddy covering my ass. "Why? You scared?" I sarcastically asked with my head pressed against the pillow. "No. I'm just wondering, how much I am thought about at the office." he continued to ask slowly raising my lingerie to expose my ass. "Don't worry, Omar. No one there worries about you, but me." I realistically answered, becoming discreetly curious about current Omar's intentions. "What?! You don't know what you're talking about, woman. I'm all the rage." he unconvincingly uttered, quickly erecting himself to become closer to my new found bareness. "Oh, I'm sure, you are. But they know, you're mine. They may not know I got you... but they damn sure know, I laid claim." I arrogantly voiced as I felt a gooey liquid stream slowly onto my naked ass. "But you don't chase like you used to, Toni. So, we can probably assume, they know you conquered." he sensibly responded attempting to divert my attention. I lifted slightly after spotting him place the empty bowl of caramel on the adjacent nightstand. "I doubt it. You work too hard to keep all this, a secret." I sarcastically uttered as he swiftly placed his hand on my back to force me immobile. "Hard to get out, remember?" Omar warned as he began to slowly rub to soothe my excessive movement. He finished his brief back rub and promptly reached into his bowl of fruit. He retrieved a piece of whatever was left, and proceeded to daub it into the puddle of caramel he poured on my ass. I listened, with a smile, at the crisp crunch of Omar behind me devouring his fruit. "I hide me from you... not you from me. You know that, right?" he uttered whilst slurping on whatever fruit he was now eating. "I don't even know what that means. Whatever it means, I don't need it. I know what this is." I realistically admitted. "You better get all that up. I can feel it running down, into my ass." I anxiously demanded after tranquilly closing my eyes. "I planned on it." Omar mumbled, seemingly focused on where to go from here. I smiled greatly, anticipating his tongue as he parted my ass in pursuit of additional caramel. "Ohh." I exhaled, quivering uncontrollably as he gently slid his finger, followed by his fruit and then ultimately his tongue inside my ass. "G-Good, I'm not trying to s-spend t-the whole night all sticky!" I stammered trying to gather enough composure to let him finish.

CHAPTER 80

"Omar"

DOINK. "Shit, why you let me fall asleep?!" I complained to a sleeping Antoinette as I scanned around for my phone.

{Hassan}
Yo leave wherever u r and get home now!

"Let me get my ass home." I whispered as I delicately slid out of the bed. "I'll never understand how she she's so grown and sexy during the day, but little girl adorable when she's asleep." I quietly laughed while I rapidly collected my things to creep out of her room. "It's eleven thirty now. I should be home about one. What can I say I did for that lost hour?" I asked myself as I stood in front of the toilet to urinate. I seized the washcloth of the folded linen Toni left for me, tossed it into the sink and turned on the water.

"Damn, how do I tell Toni that the money on the nightstand is for her ruined sheets and not her time? Think, O! Whatever you do you can't leave a note, or a text, or do anything to prove you were here." I mumbled as I drenched the cloth under the running water. "No evidence, Omar. That's not, what you do." I quietly expressed as I pressed the hot cloth against my face. I scrubbed diligently around my mouth to remove any trace of Toni, caramel or anything else out of the ordinary. "Women and their scented soaps." I mumbled as I considered using Antoinette's hand wash to scrub. I placed the bottle back on the soap dish and continued scrubbing my body with the soapless cloth. "Can't fuck up now, O. There's too much at stake." I logically whispered after calculating all scenarios and outcomes of my coming home smelling of fresh soap.

"I promise, when I find out who's been putting their raggedy ass car in my spot..." I said seeing the dried pool of oil as I pulled in front of the reserved parking sign with my name on it. "Hey Chris." I cordially greeted, noticing the young security guard as I extinguished the engine and slid out of the truck. "Hey Mr. G. Working late?" he admiringly uttered as he slowly wandered through the parking garage, smoking his cigarette. "Yeah, I was. I'm about to head out. Just gotta run back up, think I left my flash drive in the computer." I promptly responded as I slowly walked in the same direction, toward the fire exit door. "Not taking the elevator?" he asked realizing we were walking in the opposite direction as the elevator doors. "Nah, don't feel like waiting." I quickly replied, beginning to veer toward the fire stairway door. "Guess that way is, good exercise." he said as I approached the stairway door. "And this way, is closer to my truck." I reminded immediately before pointing back to my parking spot. "Ok. Well, you have a good night, sir." he said naively as he turned to continue his smoke. "You too, Chris." I said aloud before opening the stairway door. 3-0-2-5-5-5-8-9-7-2.

"HI! YOU'VE REACHED TRACEY'S PHONE, SHE'S UNABLE TO ANSWER RIGHT NOW BUT PLEASE FEEL FREE TO LEAVE HER A MESSAGE AND I'LL MAKE SURE SHE GETS IT" BEEP...

"Hey babe. Figured you two'd be sleep. Just calling, so you wouldn't worry. Just leaving, see you in a few." I said as I stood over my desk to use the landline.

"Good night, Mr. Gregory." the security guard pleasantly said as I pressed my thumb on the building's biometric sign out. "Good night, Ms. Gloria." I hospitably replied before turning to leave. "Night, Mr. G." Chris said as the elevator doors opened and he stepped into the lobby. "Night, Chris. I'm leaving for real this time." I grinned as I headed for the stairway door.

"Omee, you up?" I faintly heard Tracey ask as I slowly began to awake. I partially opened my eyes to her protruding belly advancing toward me. "Omee!" she eagerly whined positioning her belly directly over my head. I raised my hand and gently placed it on her belly. "What's wrong?" I said as I circularly massaged her belly. She placed her hand atop mine and moved closer to lessen my need to extend. "I'm hungry. Can you go to get me some pancakes, please?" she pleasingly asked. "Go get? Baby, I don't feel like going anywhere. Can't I just, make 'em?" I hopefully pleaded continuing to massage. "That's even better. I just didn't think you felt like cooking." she thankfully responded as she confined my hand's mobility to feel the baby's movement. "C'mon with that. I told you, you're carrying. Taking care of you is not a job, it's my privilege. I always feel like it, even when I don't feel like it." I sternly recapped. "I love you, Omee." Tracey said as she carefully tried to sit on the bed. "Aht aht! Don't even, try it. You know how hard it is for you to get back up. C'mon let's go downstairs, and sit together." I insisted as I slithered out of bed to follow Tracey.

"You sure you wanna sit here?" I worriedly asked as I slipped behind her to steady the stool as she sat down at the counter. "Yeah, I want to be near you." she smiled while rocking to establish comfort. "You slept late today. What time did you get in?" she continued as I pulled open the refrigerator door. "About quarter to one." I said as I surveyed the fridge for all of my needed ingredients. I gathered what I needed from the fridge, grabbed the mixing bowl from the cabinet and situated them on the counter next to the stove. "Is everything alright? Were you able to fix the problem?" Tracey asked while watching me prepare her meal. I turned on the griddle and began vigorously mixing the ingredients into a batter. "Yeah, I fixed it. Only took me about a half hour, to get it up and running. Then I spent the next three hours running diagnostics to figure out what caused the problem, in the first place." I said, spouting the fabrication I prearranged for just this inquisition. "And?" she continued to inquire as she grinned at the sight of me cooking. "It was an unwarranted variance in Carson's…" I uttered before realizing that she wouldn't understand my explanation. "Put it like this, Elliot Carson made another mess and I had to come clean it up." I continued proud of my detailed dedication to my falsehood. "Why does he even still have a job?" Tracey sternly asked as she wobbled to get down from the stool. "Your guess is as good as mine." I said aloud as she slowly trotted out of the room.

"You were the only one that had to go back in?" Tracey asked as she waddled up to the counter next to me. "What do you mean?" I asked as I poured the batter onto the hot griddle. "Carson didn't have to leave his family, to come back to work? What about, his assistant? What about, Toni? She didn't have to come in with you?" she continued to vastly probe as I gestured for her to pass the spatula to me. "Nope. They are just executive assistants, they're clueless to the ins and outs, of the job. And Carson, well let's just say I'm glad he didn't have to come back." I cleverly responded as I flipped the pancakes. "It was just me, and a few workhands." I continued to casually respond. "I wish I would've known all of this, before I asked for pancakes. Now, I feel self-centered." she declared as I began to place the pancakes on a plate to serve.

CHAPTER 81

"Emily"

RING. RING! "That's Mani. She's about to pull up." I intuitively said after hearing my phone ring. "That means, you gotta go?" my dad asked from across the table. "She got running 'round to do. Told her, I'd go with." I uttered as I stuffed the last morsel of pancake into my mouth. "She doesn't like being out, alone. She's worried she'll go into labor, and no one will be around to help." my mom explained before she opened her mouth so my father could insert the pancake filled fork, he had waiting to feed her.

HONK. HONK! "Just leave it. I'll get it, when we get up." my dad insisted as I hastily began to collect the empty dishes. "Thanks dad. Bye mom." I said as I quickly rose from the table. "Bye babe." my mom said as I scurried to get my jacket. "Be back at a decent hour." my dad demanded as I opened the door. "I will." I uttered before stepping out of the house.

"You gotta get a boyfriend. This running you around shit, is supposed to be his job." Imani bluntly voiced immediately after I closed the door. "Damn, I just got in the car. And you act like, I'm always askin' you to take me places. This like, the second time!" I passionately responded as we pulled out of the driveway. "You a whole lie! Where, London? Why you ain't ask her to take you to, Wilmington?" she selfishly questioned as we coasted past London's house. "She home. All boo'd up with her, no fuck boy." I callously laughed while checking the time on her radio against my phone for accuracy. "What's a, *no fuck boy*." Imani curiously questioned as she merged onto the highway. "London new dick piece. He like eating pussy, more than he like fucking." I mercilessly teased. "At least she getting some. My last nut, was your brother." she revealed chuckling at her own confession while effortlessly maneuvering through traffic, in my brother's car.

"Storm, what's in Wilmington? For real!" Imani probed, no longer able to endure ignorance to my intentions. "I just gotta pick something up, that's all." I partially admitted hoping she would just trust me, and leave it alone. "Something like what? You better not be getting me in no dumb shit, Storm! I heard about that shit, at your mom school." she sternly asserted. "No, it's nothing like that." I honestly disclosed as I admired the car adjacent to us. "Ohh, this my song!" Imani exploded as she turned up the volume on the radio.

"That body language, no discussion. The way she move is like she fucking." Imani melodiously sang, impressively well to the music. "This Jeremih shit, bang!" she admitted blissfully, gyrating slowly in her seat. RING. RING! "That's ya brother?!" Imani dynamically inquired while turning down the music volume.

Uncle Haas
302-555-1510

"No, it's Haas." I replied after observing the id screen. "Hey." I said after accepting the call. "Hey Em. You on your way?! If you not, let me know now, so I can head out!" my uncle doubtfully interrogated. "No need. I told you, I'd handle it." I arrogantly stated. "How're you getting there?" he continued to skeptically ask. "Mani, taking me." I openly admitted whilst appreciatively watching Imani. "I don't even wanna know, how you pulled off that one." he openly proclaimed. "I lied, that's how!" I inconspicuously admitted with the hopes that Imani didn't recognize I was still referring to her. "Hope that don't cost you, too much." Hassan cynically scoffed. "You know me. I'm not the one, to care." I earnestly reminded. "Bye, Em. I'll see you, when y'all get back." Hassan swiftly said before suddenly ending the call. "Bye." I quickly responded noticing his hurried conclusion.

"That was Hassan?" Imani asked after noticing I was no longer in conversation. "Yeah. He was making sure we left, on time." I disclosed as I dropped my phone in my lap. "I think, he fucked my mom." Imani unexpectedly divulged as we gradually pulled behind the jam of immobile vehicles. "He might have. I know I heard him talk about her ass, a few times." I honestly acknowledged, agreeing on the possibility. "You really think, he'd cheat on his wife?" she frowningly asked as we inched along the highway. "I wouldn't put it past him." I honestly answered as I continued to stare out of the window. "That's nasty, and a shame." she disapprovingly said with a disgusted grimace. "Speakin' of cheaters, you got real hype when you thought that was Que." I openly acknowledged. "I probably did. I ain't gonna lie, miss him. And, I'm hormonal." Imani candidly admitted. "You mean, horny?!" I jokingly asked. "Hell yeah, I'm definitely that." she openly admitted laughing at my remark. "You still love my brother?" I curiously ask as traffic slowly began to return to normalcy. "Of course. I got his name on my titties, and his daughter in my belly." she genuinely avowed as she looked impatiently for an advantage point in traffic to increase her speed. "I can't hide that I love him, I can't stop loving him. But I can't keep letting him play me, either." Imani level headedly justified as she happily observed her loophole through traffic.

"Make this next left." I insisted, reciting the directions I read on my phone. "What's down here?" Imani suspiciously asked after making the turn. "Just pull, in here." I requested pointing into the parking lot of a Dunkin Donuts. "Now what, Storm!" Imani sternly barked after slamming the car into park. "Nothing. We just gotta wait, for a few minutes. He coming!" I calmly answered looking into my phone, for some sort of update. "Who's coming?!" Imani indignantly snapped as she gazed out of the windows examining the area around the car. "I know that ain't the train station, across the street!" she intensely questioned scrutinizing the large building in our frontward view. "Yup." I nonchalantly replied while looking around at the other stores surrounding us. "Storm, I know you ain't have me drive up here, to pick up your brother!" Imani resentfully inquired after realizing the inevitable. "Yeah. He ain't have no other way back. You and the baby got his car, remember?" I casually replied with no concern for her opinion. "I ain't say I wouldn't pick him. I'd have picked him up. I pick him up from Aberdeen, any other time. I'm just saying I ain't trying to see him, right now." she single-mindedly expressed while dynamically rubbing her belly. "This some bullshit." she sourly sighed while opening the door to get out of the car. She closed the door behind her and immediately opened the door and climbed into the back seat.

"I wasn't trying to dupe you. But this was last minute, and he said y'all was arguing." I apologetically said as I captured an in-depth look at Imani's frown through the rearview mirror. "We was arguing cause he still messing with that, fake ass bitch." she hard-heartedly detailed as tears began to stream down her face. "He told you that? Cause he told us he wasn't fucking wit her, no more." I honestly assured. "No, he ain't tell me but I know." she sobbed as she used her fingers to catch her tears. "Even if he is, why you care?" I intriguingly inquired as I opened the glove compartment with hopes that my brother's collection of fast food napkins remained. "Why wouldn't I care? He mine. He fucking mine!" she cried out before noticing me slam the compartment shut and continue with my search. She wiped her face with her sleeve and reached for her clutch bag still located in the front seat. "I'll be back, I'm going to get some!" Imani said opening the door and exiting the car. I chuckled, watching her quickly waddle to the Dunkin Donuts. DOINK!

{Que}
Im here. R U?

"That his train, right there. I'm leaving the doors unlocked. B.R.B." I shouted to Imani just as she was opening the door to the eatery. She waved me away in disregard and proceeded inside.

"You hungry?" Que asked Imani as we passed the pizza shop, they used to frequent. "No." she whispered grimly as tears began to swell in her eyes again. "You ain't ask me, if I was hungry!" I mockingly pointed out. "That's because I heard, you ate four of dad's big ass pancakes this morning." Que confidently admitted as he and his car continued to reclaim their neighborhood. "Damn, mom tell everything! Drop me off at London's." I irritably requested.

"What made you cheat?" I unexpectedly asked Quentin, after physically feeling Imani's misery from the behind me. "You serious, right now?!" he sternly asked as he unbelievingly stared at me. "Yeah." I nonchalantly replied, refusing to turn away from his gaze. "Oh, I would love no know that, too." Imani sniffled as she quickly pressed herself to regain her poise. "I'm not doing this with y'all, right now." Quentin openly declared in an attempt to disregard. "Why not?" I quickly asked with a cynical grin. "Yeah Quentin, why not?!" Imani sternly shadowed. "Cause, I'm not!" he continued to bark. "You know why, niggas cheat?" I bluntly intervened confident in my theory. "Problem?" I asked Quentin while I stared at him aggressively. "You lucky you my sister, and I don't see you as a white girl." Quentin surrendered as he reluctantly continued to listen. "Please, go 'head and finish. Why do niggas cheat?!" Imani inquired preparing herself to intently take heed of my upcoming explanation. "It's not hard, when you think about it. Niggas always looking for, a come-up. So, when y'all think the grass greener on the other field, that's the field y'all wanna play on." I straightforwardly explained while continuing to stare at Quentin. "That's what you think?!" he calmly asked glancing over at me in disbelief. "Well, I gave you the chance to tell me, otherwise." I realistically retorted as I retrieved my phone to text London. "Yeah, that's what we think! You saw that grass was a little greener, and cut a little better, and was a lot easier to get to, and you jumped at the chance to go play on it. But then you found out it was fake, and now you too proud to be mad!" Imani gratefully agreed, now smugly smiling.

> **{Me}**
> **Be there in 5min**

"So, you think that shit too?!" Quentin aggressively asked Imani. RING. RING! "Again, she gave you a chance to tell us, *anything* else." she self-righteously answered before retrieving her phone from her bag. I looked back and smiled with Imani as she confidently wiped the dried tear streaks from her face. RING. RING! "Hey you!" Imani pleasantly spoke after answering her call. DOINK!

> **{London}**
> **K**

"I ain't know you risked everything, and jumped the fence to play on, astro-turf!" I sincerely declared smirking at Quentin's obsession with Imani's call. "Yup, he sure did!" Imani yelled, briefly snubbing her phone conversation to intercede.

"Hey." I said whispered while slapping Quentin in the chest. "What?!" he disgruntledly replied with his eyebrows raised and his head tipped back. I smiled at his transparent attempts to eavesdrop on Imani's phone exchange. "Stop!" I discreetly demanded. "Stop what?!" he irritably whispered returning his attention to the road. "So, you been mad all this time, 'cause you got caught playing, on *astro-turf*? I can't wait to meet this bitch!" I mockingly reiterated as we turned onto London's street. "Fuck you, get out." Quentin cynically replied as we pulled in front of London's house. "I love you too." I countered as I opened the door and exited the car. "Bye Storm." Imani gently said as she got out of the car to get into the front seat.

CHAPTER 82

"Quentin"

"Hold on." Imani charmingly requested into her phone. I need to drop you off. I didn't know I was coming to get you, and I got baby stuff to." Imani insisted after we pulled from in front of Storm's friend's house. "Yeah alright. If I gotta go somewhere, I can take my dad's truck." I accepted, doing my best to remain unconcerned with her phone companion. "I'm back." she gently disclosed into her phone. "I'm fine. I just had to deliver some disappointing info, to an old friend." she tenderly continued as she looked daggers at me. "Awww, that's sweet. But I promise, I'm fine. You don't have to do that." she warmly uttered, grinning softly at her acquaintance's remarks. DOINK! "Hold on one more time." she pleasantly once again requested of her suitor. "That's your baby mom?" she sternly asked transferring her attention to me, after hearing my phone chime. I scoffed while staring at her in disbelief before picking up my phone. "You can check it. Your shit don't bother me, no more." she harshly whispered before turning to return to her phone banter. "I see." I nonchalantly said before checking my phone.

> **{Storm}**
> **Thru u under bus 2 make her feel better.**
> **No hard feelings. ☺**

I smiled at my sister's admission of what I already knew. Imani noticed my smile and countered it with a hard scowl. "Okay. I'll call you when I'm on my way, sweety. Bye." Imani harmoniously divulged before ending her call. She looked at me with an outstanding smile as she jammed her phone back into her bag. "Everything alright wit'cha, boo?" she sarcastically questioned as we turned onto my street. "As far as I know." I calmly responded not allowing her to see me reacting to her attempts to goad me into getting angry. "How 'bout, you and yours?" I casually asked, continuing to play it cool. I pulled into the driveway behind my father's truck. "I don't have a boo! You the one that started a new family, not me. I was happy, when I used to eat your dad's pancakes!" Imani answered irritably as she opened the door and gave her best effort to storm out of the car. I grimaced bewilderedly as I opened the door and stepped out of the car. "You plan on bringing her up every time we speak, or see each other?" I calmly as she approached. "Probably! Why, is it a problem?!" she violently answered as I stepped aside for her to get into the car. "Nope. Can you hit the trunk, please?" I scoffed before she pulled the door closed.

I watched Pam Grier gradually carry Imani and my unborn baby girl out of the driveway, before carefully sneaking into the house. I gently placed my duffle bag on the sofa and resumed treading softly throughout. I slipped into the kitchen, then quietly trekked down into my father's den. "Where the hell they at?" I mumbled as I peeked into the garage to see if my mother's car was present. With both vehicles present and the house seeming abandoned, I crept upstairs to continue my search for, anyone. "Damn, they not here." I said after recognizing that the upstairs was as tranquil. "They probably out with Haas, and Aunt Jills. Ooh, I wonder if he took his truck keys with him?" I murmured as I headed toward my parent's bedroom to check. "He may even be in here, sleep." I thought as I pressed my ear to the door to listen for the possibility of my father in there. With no grumbling or growling sounds apparent, I carefully pushed the door open and peered inside.

My stomach knotted and I harshly dry heaved as I observed my mom. She was lying naked across the bed, covered partially by a blanket. Her eyes were closed, her legs were resting on my father's shoulders and her feet in the air. And my dad, with his knees on the floor, his arms wrapped around her thighs and his face pressed deep between her thighs. "Oh God. Oh God. Oh Omee!" she heavily exhaled as he vigorously moved his head in all directions. I slowly closed the door and hurriedly tiptoed downstairs to the guest bathroom for fear of my dry heaving becoming much more. "Shit! I hope they didn't hear that." I uncomfortably whispered after flushing the toilet.

"I need some air." I uttered after aimlessly skulking around looking for something to take my mind off of what I'd witnessed. "I'll just take her car." I whispered seeing my mother's keys hanging on the key hook in the kitchen. I scurried over to the key hook and seized my mother's keys. "Damn! I'd need to move his truck, to get out." I hopelessly mumbled, thrusting my head back in despair. "Yesss!" I hissed as I recognized my father's truck keys on her ring too. I grabbed a pen from the kitchen drawer, left a note on the refrigerator, and dashed out of the front door.

> {Me}
> Yo dad. borrowed your truck. be back in a few. call
> me if you need me sooner. left note on fridge.

"That'll work." I said after texting my father. I tossed my phone into the passenger seat and resumed journeying down the street.

[Method Man]
I came to bring the pain, hardcore from the brain
Let's go inside my astral plane

"Damn pop, we only seventeen years apart. Old school is cool sometimes, but this twenty-twenty." I uttered, bothered after initiating my father's playlist. I left the song on as to not alter any of his truck's settings. "This is my shit, though." I uttered recalling the greatness of the song. "Is it real, son? Is it really real, son?" I loudly sang while turning up the volume.

RING. RING! "What?! Damn!" I frustratedly yelled at my phone as it vibrated in the seat beside me. "Yeah!" I sternly voiced after turning down the music volume to hear the call. "Yooo. W'sup man!" a man's voice enthusiastically bellowed from the phone speakers. "Who this?" I bewileredly asked still frustrated about the interruption of the music. "It's James!" he animatedly explained. "I don't know, no James. I think you got the wrong number, Champ." I calmly stated anticipating returning the volume to its previous point. "C'mon Gregs. It's James! James Wesley." he continued to anxiously clarify. "James Wesley? James Wesley?" I mumbled to myself trying to decipher to whom I was speaking. "Who the fuck is James Wesley?" I frantically thought while continuing my aimless journey. "Oh shit. Wesley?!" I enthusiastically exclaimed after realizing that I was talking to a one-time teammate. "Yeah, man." he happily uttered once I discovered his identity. "Why you ain't just say, Wes? What's up, man?!" I warmly greeted. "Nothin' much. I just saw you ride by the gas station. Why you ain't tell nobody, you was in town?" he disappointedly asked. I looked around to see if I could see anyone else that I may know. "Just got here." I apologetically admitted. "Ok, ok. Well, we at the garage. If you can, come thru." he happily invited. "You going back there now?" I casually asked, anxious to possibly have a destination. "Yeah, walking in the door now." he said as a loud burst of music suddenly emerged behind him. "Yeah, alright. I'll stop through. I ain't doing, shit else." I openly admitted while looking for a parking lot to turn into, so I could turn back. "Cool, I'll let everybody know you coming." Wes yelled over the music before ending the call.

"Que! What's up?!" a man's voice melodiously hollered from across the room as I walked into the door. "Que! You came through!" Wesley yelled as he scurried over to the door to greet me. "Hey Que." a young lady's voice audibly pronounced from behind Wesley.

"Here comes the star!" Wesley voiced as he enthusiastically escorted me to his table adjacent to the billiards. "Que! W'sup brother!" Pence said with a pool stick in hand as he interrupted his game to approach me. "What's up, Pence?" I said as I embraced another of my former teammates. "Everything alright?" I continued to ask as I gestured for him to get back to his game. "Yeah, I'm good. Not as good as you, right now. With you about to go into the league, you got us all looking bad." he said, pointing to his opponent to resume the game. "W'sup?" I vaguely uttered addressing his game rival. "That's that the plan. Not to make y'all look bad, but to get to the league." I casually said re-addressing Pence. "You about to be a rich man!" he keenly said as he took his shot. "I guess. I know I'm about to have to work harder, than I ever have. And possibly be far away from everything, I know and love. Depending on where I go." I sullenly reminded as I surveyed the room for anyone else, I recognized. "Yeah, but think about all that money! You can buy, new love and knowledge." Wesley unashamedly verbalized from behind me. "Shut up, Wes! You sound stupid!" Pence aggressively stated before grabbing his beer from the counter behind him. "I be back." I calmly stated as I gradually began to walk away from the table. "Yo, Que. When you start getting that paper, come back and see me. I may have something, for us to collaborate on." Pence said raising his beer to me as I walked away. "I'll think about it." I audibly said as I progressively walked over to a familiar face. "Hey." Chaewon said as I approached her while she was emptying a trash can. "Hey." I casually responded before holding the can so that she can reline it with a bag. "I said hello when you first came in, but you were being attacked by all your fans." she sarcastically disclosed while collecting the bag to take to another can. "Cut that shit out." I uttered as I followed her across the room. "This the second time, I found you in here. You come all the way to Dover, to hang in the Garage? They don't got no chill spots, in Newark?" I genuinely asked as I again helped her with the trash. "As you can see, I'm not chillin', I'm working. This is my granddad's spot." she revealed as she knotted the bag. "Mr. Park is your grandfather?" I doubtfully questioned while contorting to get a better look at her ass as she bent over. "Yeah." she hesitantly acknowledged noticing me look at her. "Why you ain't tell me?" I curiously asked, trying to recall whether or not she actually did. "You never asked." she sensibly replied as she picked up her bag and advanced toward the opposite corner of the room. "Wait! Mr. Park is full on Korean and you, well, you look just straight up black. You don't look like you got any Korean in you, at all!" I declared still slightly skeptical. "Here, let me get that." I said confiscating the bag from her. "Besides the name, Chaewon?" she sarcastically asked, looking at me side-eyed. "Yeah, I know I don't look like it. My mom do, though. She got them eyes. I would kill to have them eyes." Chaewon divulged as I followed her to the rear door of the building. She pulled a set of keys from her pocket and unlocked the rear exit door. I stepped out of the building behind her and followed her over to a dumpster. "You gotta stay here?" I asked after getting a small taste of us alone together. "Yeah, at least until my uncle get here. Why?" she inhospitably probed as she opened the dumpster and indicated for me to toss the bag in. "Cause, it's loud in there. And, I was thinking about going somewhere, less busy." I misleadingly specified as she slammed the dumpster top closed. "And you wanted me to come, wit'chu?" she mockingly inquired as she held the door open for us to go back into the building. "Yeah, if that's good with you." I said as I undertook her hold of the door. "You know I fought your sister, right?" she said as she stared into my eyes while passing me. "Yeah, I know. That's between y'all. Besides, I know that to be over and done with." I said as I closed the door behind me. She reached around me and secured the door. "Between us? We was fighting, 'cause of you!" she harshly confirmed while leading me back into the focal point of the room. "Huh?" I uttered pretending not to hear her. "See, I can't really hear you. I told you, it's loud and busy in here." I sarcastically mocked as I continued to follow her. I laughed at her scoff while scrutinizing the lack of chaos, the other six people in the large room were creating. "C'mon." she sternly insisted as she changed direction and headed toward the small sitting area at the other end of the room. She walked over to the tall bookshelf in the corner, moved a few books aside, and reached her hand behind the remaining book on the shelf. "Wow. I never knew that was there!" I admitted, fascinated by the bookshelf swinging open, like a door. She stepped in through the concealed door. I followed behind Chaewon's signal for me to join her. "Mr. Park was on some 'ol, James Bond shit!" I said passionately impressed while stepping past her. She closed the door and quickly brushed past me, to lead.

"This is a lot better. Now I should be able to hear you." I said as she rested against some boxes placed on a table. "Less busy." Chaewon stated as looked at me with annoyance. "Let's get busy?" I jokingly asked, trying to get her to lighten her seemingly touchy mood. "Girl, cut that out. We ain't went there, in like forever." I continued to tease ineffectively. "Ain't nobody say nothing about getting busy with you. Don't even play like that." she scornfully demanded. "You only here talking to me, 'cause Imani don't want you no more! Congratulations on the baby, by the way." she continued to condescendingly proclaim. "Damn, I was joking!" I firmly defended. "And you the one that brought me to a secret room full of junk, with a dresser and bed in it. What am I supposed to think!" I maintained as I pointed out the objects throughout the room. "Why is this room, even back here?" I curiously queried while she stared at me indifferently. "I don't know, it's been here. My uncle Jae-jin stays here sometimes, that's why the bed's there." she nonchalantly confessed. "Oh yeah, I forgot all about his son, Jae." I enthusiastically stated. "He all Korean too, though. Mr. Park, ain't ya damn grandfather." I doubtfully assumed as she lifted herself from the boxes. "Why would I lie?" Chaewon sneeringly questioned while surveying the room. "Jae-jin, was from his first marriage. My mom, is from his second." she halfheartedly clarified as she attempted to get through to the other side of the cluttered room. She sucked in her stomach and began squeezing between me and the dresser. I backed up as much as possible to give her some legroom to maneuver. Our insufficient effort during her attempt to wedge past, caused her to knock a small box off of the dresser. "I got it." I offered before bending to collect the box and the mass of photographs that slid out of it.

"Oh shit! You are his granddaughter." I said after noticing a young picture of Chaewon while glancing at a few of the photos before stuffing them back into the box. "I already told you that." she irritably whispered while clearing a section on the bed big enough for her to sit down. "It's just... we been hanging in the Garage, since forever. And I never once saw you here, before. Except for last Thanksgiving." I embarrassing divulged while looking at the last photo before placing it in the box. "They said I wasn't old enough to come here, yet." I said leaning on the dresser to face Chaewon. "Oh ok." I agreeingly responded. "So, you wanted to get me alone. What'd you want?!" she harshly asked as she resumed her standoffish stare. "I just wanted, to talk." I uttered, transparently lying.

"Just talk, huh." Chaewon scoffed crossing her arms over her chest. "Yeah. Something wrong with, just talking?" I probed, defending my exposed fabrication. "Guess not, when you wanna talk. But when I wanted to talk, I got ghosted!" she callously announced providing evidence to her unsociable demeanor. "Now, cause you lonely, you changed your mind and I'm supposed to just give in?" she diligently questioned. "Nah, it's nothing like that. But, you're right. My bad, for even thinking it. Be good, Chae." I stated willfully relinquishing any hope of reconnection with Chaewon. I maneuvered through the cluttered storeroom and slowly opened the secret door. I stealthily stepped out and made my way over to Wes to greet him before I left.

"Alright Wes, I'm outta here." I said as I approached Wes, who was now playing pool, instead of watching. "You rolling out, already?" he said leaning his stick against the wall to address me. "Yeah. I'mma proceed back to headquarters." I said extending my hand for him to embrace. DOINK! "Alright. Don't be a stranger, man." Wes requested as he grasped my hand. "Alright man." I uttered as I stepped away from him while reaching in my pocket for my phone.

> {Newark High}
> **Ya bad for thinking what?**
> {Me}
> **You pretending to care? lol. it's a non-issue now**

I slowly advanced toward the door while waiting for a response from Chaewon. "Oh well." I thought as I pulled my hood up onto my head and treaded out of the door. I reached into my pocket, pressed the ignition button on the remote and hurried over to the running truck. DOINK! "She would respond now that I'm about to leave." I mumbled after pulling myself up into the truck. I left my legs to suspend outside of the truck as I retrieved my phone. DOINK!

> {Mani}
> **Bringing the car so u can get around. 6pm**
> {Me}
> **Not necessary. You got somewhere to go later, remember?**

I vindictively responded to Imani's text before continuing to check the other text that came through.

> {Newark High}
> Im pretending 2 care just like u pretended 2 just want 2 talk.
> {Me}
> I did want to talk. And apologize. You
> didn't give me the chance to.

Snickering at my false claim in response to Chaewon's text, I pulled my legs into the truck and closed the door. I cautiously drove across the rocky, dirt road desperately trying not to skip gravel onto my dad's truck's paint job. "Might as well get a pretzel before I leave the lot." I decided before quickly pulling into an empty parking spot at the gas station. DOINK!

> {Newark High}
> If all u really wanted 2 do is talk then call
> me. We can talk on the phone.

"Thanks." I said as I stepped in, crossing the path of the man holding the door for me. "How you doing?" I waved to the clerk as I advanced to the Icee machine at the far end of the store.

> {Me}
> Gimme a second. I'm up front at the gas station.

"Watch she ask me to come back, instead of call." I confidently muttered as I stood at the machine filling my cup. DOINK!

> {Mani}
> U eavesdropping now? don't worry about my plans. I'll
> leave the car & the keys at ur house if u not there.
> {Me}
> Yup

"Damn, it's that bad? You can see it all in your face." a man said behind me as I waited for the clerk to tally my snacks. "Five, thirty-four." the elder Korean man said after pushing keys on the cash register. "It's a female. It's always, that bad!" I contemptuously agreed as I turned to the other patron after surrendering my money to the clerk. "Thanks" I uttered as I collected my bag and change. "Have a nice day," I said to the stranger as I started toward the convenient store exit. "Wait! Quentin Gregory?" the gentleman animatedly yelled as I reached for the door handle. "Yeah." I reluctantly answered while turning back toward him. "Oh man! I remember watching you in high school. You were something to see!" he enthusiastically continued as he paid for his purchase. DOINK! "Thanks man. I appreciate you." I sincerely conceded before exiting.

> **{Newark High}**
> **Ok**

"Hear you may even be a second, or third round pick." the man said as I stood outside of the store, texting. "That's the plan." I acknowledged as I completed my text and paced to the truck. "Well congratulations. All of us back here in Dover, will be behind you on draft night." he continued to yell across the parking lot as I closed car door. "Thanks again. I'll do my best, to make you proud." I honestly yelled before backing out of the spot. DOINK!

> **{Dad}**
> **You can come home to take my truck, but not say hi?**

I smiled at my dad's text as I slowly pulled into the driveway. I looked up at the window to see if my mom was in the traditional spot she assumed, whenever my dad's truck pulled in. She looked at me smiling as my father stood behind her, with his hands on her shoulders.

"Hey Que-tee." my happily mom shouted immediately after I slid open the patio door. "Hey." I awkwardly replied, remembering her position the last time I saw her. "When'd you get here?" she enthusiastically continued while advancing to embrace me. "A few hours ago. Imani and Storm picked me up from the train station, in Wilmington." I disclosed as I carefully hugged my pregnant mother. "And that damn Emily, didn't even tell us." my father said to my mom as he re-entered the kitchen. "Hey son." he uttered with a large grin as he too came to embrace me. I continued holding my mother until my father was within reach. "I told her not to. Wanted to surprise y'all." I said as I embraced my father. "You surprised me alright. I got that text, and I ain't know what the hell was going on." he admitted as he turned to head back into the other room. "Yeah you should've seen him. He was all over the place. You hungry?" my mom asked before pushing her glass against the refrigerator door for ice. "I did see him." I quietly mumbled while uncomfortably cringing after hearing her use the phrases "all over the place" and "hungry". "What'd you say?" my mom curiously asked while holding her glass of ice. "No. I'm good, ma." I uttered before following my dad into the living room. "Yo dad," I stated as I tossed him his keys before sitting down, on the adjacent sofa. "Don't give 'em to me. Put 'em back, where you got 'em from." he demanded while tossing them back to me. I placed the keys on the table next to me with plans to put them back when I again stood. "Tell me, what kind of man takes his dad's truck, without even coming in to say hi?" he sarcastically asked as he stared at his tablet. "I did come in, to say hi. And I've been trying ever since to remove what I saw, when I came in to say hi." I ironically countered as my mom waddled into the room. "Oh God. You saw us?!" my mother shamefully asked sitting down next to my father. "I told you, I heard someone walking around the house." she continued repeatedly pinching my father upon his leg. "I'm sorry, baby." she self-consciously apologized while refusing to look up at me. "Sorry for what? I was with my wife, in my house, in the privacy of, my bedroom! Better learn to knock, next time." my father looked up from his tablet to sternly advised. I shook my head unbelievably at my dad before standing to go up to my room. "Where you headed?" my mother asked as I picked the truck keys up from the table. "To my room, to steal a nap." I yawned. "Ok. You want us to wake you, for dinner?" my mother graciously asked as I leaned down to kiss her cheek. "Please." I said thankfully.

3-0-2-5-5-5-1-0-0-1. "I ain't think you was gonna call." Chaewon offhandedly stated after answering the call. "I said, I would. I'm a man of my word." I confidently proclaimed as I placed the phone on speaker and tossed it onto the bed. "Heh. News to me!" she doubtfully scoffed. "You knew my situation, and I never once promised you anything." I stated as I pulled my shirt over my head. "You fucking me was your word, you didn't keep that." she coldly acknowledged. "Chae, we were partying, and drunk! I wouldn't count that as, a meaningful pledge." I reasonably reminded as I tossed my shirt into my hamper and fell spread-eagle down onto my bed. "I would, and so did your step-mom." she bluntly exposed. "You told my mom?!" I tensely queried, nervously rising to glance around the room. "Sure did, right after me and your sister fought! If I woulda known that was your sister, I woulda told her too." she continued to unwaveringly divulge. "Damn. You were going for the throat, huh?" I judgmentally asked relaxing slightly due to the length of time that has passed. "No. I think you got off, kinda easy. I mean, never told ya girl, right?" Chaewon asked believing herself to be considerate. "As far as I know, you didn't." I skeptically disclosed after learning that she's referenced this to my mother. "You know I didn't. If I did, you wouldn't be about to be a daddy." she logically stated. "Yeah, she probably wouldn't be carrying my child if she knew." I vacantly agreed as I lifelessly reclined. "By the way, what're y'all having a girl, or a boy?" she inquired giving the impression of being genuinely intrigued. "Uhh. A girl." I hesitantly answered after assessing which gender Imani was actually having. "Aww." she mockingly uttered. "Wonder what I'd be having if you busted in me, instead of on my ass?" Chaewon callously asked. "You don't want that headache." I acknowledged thinking about my current situation. "You don't know, what I want. You never tried to get to know me, to even find out." she firmly responded. I continued to lay there half-heartedly listening to her berate me.

Focusing more on my eyes progressively shutting than the conversation, I pondered ending the call. "Chaewon. Let me..." I lowly uttered. "Question... was you gonna bust on my ass again, earlier?!" she bluntly interrupted. "Huh?" I asked as my eyes widen attentively. "Was you planning on busting on my ass again? Or was you gonna try and do it in my mouth, this time?" she blatantly asked. "Told you, I wasn't trying to fuck." I deceivingly replied as I reached for my phone.

With the discussion going in the direction it was going, I removed the speaker function and rested the phone on the side of my face. "Oh yeah, that's right. You just wanted to talk." she mockingly voiced. "I don't know why, you find that so hard to believe." I fraudulently encouraged now enlivened by her talk of further sex between us. "Cause, I know you didn't just wanna talk! Just like, I didn't want to, *talk*." she disclosed, outwardly frustrated. "I pulled you in that room cause I wanted to fuck, just like you wanted to fuck. I just changed my mind, when I thought about how it worked out for me the last time we fucked." she openly continued to convey. "That's why you keep insisting, I wanted to fuck you?" I shockingly asked disappointed that I missed the opportunity. "I keep insisting that, cause I'm honest with it. Maybe if you were, I would've thought different about actually doing it." she bluntly disclosed.

"You want honest? Yeah, sex crossed my mind. I'm a guy, I don't know what to tell you. But I wasn't trying to fuck you, today. I just wanted to catch up, to do the talking we didn't do last time." I divulged, relentless with my deception. "Yeah ok." she suspiciously chuckled.

"So, when you coming back, so we can catch up?" she suggestively asked. "How long you gonna be down there?" I asked intrigued by the invitation. "I was about to leave. But if you coming, I'll hang around a little longer." she supportively encouraged. "Well right now, I'm waiting to get my car back. I'm about to lay down til they get here. Let's say seven, seven-thirty?" I eagerly asked, clearly anxious to get a second stab at sex with Chaewon. "Maybe. If I'm still here, and still in the mood to *talk*." she cleverly taunted. "Alright then. Text you when I'm about to head out?" I considerately asked implying to end the call now that we have a direction. "I guess." she remorsefully answered before ending the call.

"Damn, it's hot in here!" I whispered lifting my head from the pillow. I aggressively bounced out of the bed and reached up to pull the chain of the ceiling fan. I glanced over at the windows for validation that they were open. "That's why it's so hot in her." I uttered as I walked over to open, the closed windows. I scanned down at the street below as I raised the window pane. "She still got that, *it's alright if I'm late* shit going on." I whispered as I looked down at my watch, realizing it was a quarter to seven. Before I could turn to journey back over to my bed, Ms. Grier came slowly drifting up to a stop in front of the house. "There they are." I said referring to both Imani and the car. I smiled down at Imani behind the wheel as she mouthed words and laughed at whomever she was on her phone with. I watched her gradually disappear as she slowly raised the profoundly tinted windows. She awkwardly extracted herself from the car and slowly waddled up the walkway. I laughed quietly at her noticeably fighting her want to look up at my window as she'd always done.

I paid close attention to the happenings downstairs after hearing the doorbell's chime. I faintly heard Imani's greeting under the hindrance of the exceptional television volume. I heard my mother indistinctly speak, followed by the television volume lessening. Her ensuing eruption of laughter openly expressed her joy of seeing Imani. I remained in the window awaiting Imani's departure, concerned about the who and how she would be getting home. "Bye paw-paw." I heard Imani say before hearing the door slam close and the television volume immediately increase. "Damn. My baby, with my baby." I whispered while watching Imani walk as elegantly as she possibly could, down the walkway to the sidewalk. I quickly sidestepped behind the hanging curtain to camouflage, after seeing her turn back toward the house. "Who is she waiting for? Where is her ride?" I whispered as she turned back toward the street and continued to wait. "Alright, another five minutes, and I'll just take her home myself." I uttered while watching her stand there quickly pressing her fingers into her phone. DOINK! "That must be, Chaewon." I thought as I again looked down at my watch. "Fuck that, right now." I said as I watched Imani jam her phone into her purse and begin seductively sashaying into the street. She turned and began to smile greatly as a silver Nissan Altima slowly pulled up to a stop, in front of her. "Who the fuck is that?!" I eagerly asked as I watched her glance up at me, smile, and wave with poise, before opening the door. I dashed across the room, down the stairs, and out of the door in an attempt to catch her, before they could drive off. "Damn!" I shouted as I stood in the middle of the street staring at the distant brake lights, of that unfamiliar car. "What's wrong?!" my dad spiritedly asked as he trekked down the walkway toward me. "Nothing." I bitterly uttered as I marched past him, toward the house. "What's wrong?" my mom asked as I entered the house. "Nothing ma." I answered as my father stormed in the door, behind me. "What the hell, Que?" my dad barked as he pushed the door closed. "It's nothing y'all. I was just trying to catch Imani before she pulled off, that's all." I divulged looking at the unease in my father's face. "Yeah, alright. Your keys are on the hook." my dad skeptically asserted while returning to his chair to re-establish his comfort. "Thanks. It's cool, I promise." I disclosed before slowly walking back up the stairs. "What was that all about?" I overheard my mom ask as I crept up the steps. I stopped to hear my father's reply, thinking maybe he knew something. "I don't know. But I call bullshit, on the whole thing." he candidly responded.

I snatched my phone from the nightstand and immediately texted Chaewon.

> **{Me}**
> **About 2 b omw.**

"This bitch gonna make me kill her." I mumbled before tossing my phone down onto the bed. I plopped down onto the bed and began aggressively pushing my feet into my sneakers. "Who do I know, with a silver Altima?" I desperately pondered while tying my shoe laces. DOINK! "Damn, that was fast." I uttered stunned by Chaewon's hasty response.

"When the fuck, did she text me?" I questioned after picking up my phone and noticing an unseen text from Imani.

> {Mani}
> U better play peek a boo with ur daughter
> the same way u playn it with me. ☺
> {Newark High}
> U might wanna hurry. Not gonna wait 4ever.

"It was me that she was texting, when she was standing there in her phone!" I grasped while snatching my high school jersey from my closet. "She was on me, the whole fucking time. I wonder if she know I ran out there, after her?" I continued to question as I left the room. "Everything alright?" my dad asked as I reached the bottom of the stars. "I told you, I'm good." I deceitfully disclosed as I stepped around him to get to the key hook. "Cool. What do you want on your pizza?" he continued to ask while reaching in the drawer for a menu. "Pizza?" I asked puzzled by tonight's dinner. "Yeah. She fell asleep, and now she don't feel like cooking." he whispered trying to discreetly blame my mom. "As did you!" my mom yelled from the other room. I looked at my dad, who was shaking his head in disagreement. "I'm pregnant! What's your excuse?" my mom asked as we made our way into the living room. I couldn't help but imagine Imani and me in their shoes, as I laughed at my parents. "You leaving?" my mom asked as I grabbed my jacket from the rack next to the door. "Yeah, I'll be back shortly." I revealed as I stood at the door putting on my jacket. "Guess I ain't gotta worry about you, then." my dad said as he sat down next to my mother. "Just save me two slices of whatever kind y'all get, please." I solicited while grabbing the doorknob. "You got it. Please, be careful." my mom pleaded while seizing the food menu from my father's grasp. "Yes ma'am." I said as I proceeded out of the door.

"If it ain't Dover's own, GQ! What's up?" Kenny yelled as he walked down the steps of the Garage exit. "Nothing and everything, Kenny." I answered as I walked toward him. "How 'bout you?" I continued extending my hand to him. "I'm good man. About to head overseas, to play ball. My agent got some big things in the works for me, over there." he disclosed after releasing my hand from his tight grip. "Congrats man. I'm sure you'll do big things on the court over there." I sincerely praised. "I hope so." he anticipated while trying not to sound self-assured "Speaking of big things. I heard you declared for the draft. That's great man." he favorably acknowledged as we stepped aside to allow a car to move through the lot. "You still gonna finish school though, right?!" he passionately preferred. "That's the plan. Except, it'll be online classes and private tutors." I said hoping that he would tolerate that. "As long as you graduate, right?" he agreed as he pressed the button on his car remote. "Yes sir!" I respectfully matched as I turned to head towards the building entrance. "Alright GQ. I'm gonna go ahead home and get yelled at for losing more at poker, than I was allowed. You be good, alright? Don't let them guys in there, take you too." Kenny advised slowly progressing toward his van. "Alright Kenny. I'll keep my eyes open for you, on SportsCenter." I supportively stated as I slowly walked to the building steps. "And I, you." he replied while getting into his vehicle.

"Wha'chu doing down here?" Storm asked as I bumped into her and London exiting, as I entered. "Just seeing who down here, that's all." I dishonestly divulged. "What about you?" I asked subtly surveying the room. "Embarrassing these frauds." she confidently responded. "What's up, London?" I courteously inquired. "Hey, Que." London melodiously flirted. "That bitch Chaewon in here, somewhere. You want me to stay?" Storm genuinely asked as she began to unzip her jacket. "No, I'm good." I said resting my hand on hers to stop her. "Ok. Well then, I'll see you at home." she said fastening her jacket back up. "Yup." I said stepping aside to let them get to the door. "Real quick. Who in the circles, drive a silver Altima?" I inquired as she opened the door. "Uhhh, I don't know off hand. Let me think about it." she replied while holding the door so London could pass her. "Text me as soon as you know, Storm!" I insisted before turning to walk into the room. "Alright." she responded before letting the door close.

"Yo Que!" a voice yelled from beside me. I looked over at the small crowd of people playing darts and waved. I continued to walk over to the card table set up in the back room. "What's up Que?" Wes said as he looked up from the table. "Yo, you still here?!" I bewilderedly asked of Wesley while looking down into his hand. "Nah, man. I left and came back, just like you did. Just, not for the same reason." he grinned looking up at me cunningly. "Whatever, man." I uneasily responded. "No worries. I'm no judge, man. But it's over near the tv, if you're looking." he skillfully disclosed. I followed his depiction and glanced toward the area of the room, where the tv hung. "I be back." I said as I noticed Chaewon and her uncle looking at the monitor. "Yo, Jae-jin!" I heartily voiced to the proprietor's son as I came up behind him. "Quentin!" he improperly articulated as he opened his arms to hug me. "How are you? Still play football?" he mockingly queried while pointing my jersey. "Yeah. It's just, now I'm playing in college." I confidently responded. "Good, you going to college. Make family proud." he declared while continuing to adjust the television picture quality. "I'm trying, Jae." I honestly admitted scrutinizing Chaewon as she approached. "You know, Chaewon?" Jae naively asked as she appeared next to him. "Yeah, I know number twenty-four. Hey, Que." she revealed, smirking at me in my high school jersey. "Hey, Chae." I subtly replied while unnoticeably ogling her. "Jae-jin, I'm going to the back to finish up some homework." she exposed while discreetly throwing me a wink. "Ok." Jae-jin trustingly replied with no reason given to question otherwise. "It was nice seeing you, Que." Chaewon softly uttered while reaching into her pocket for her phone. "Nice to see you too, Chae." I declared before she enticingly walked away. "Well, I think I'm gonna to head on over to that card game, Jae. It's was good seeing you, again too." I avowed before turning to travel over to the card table. DOINK! "Good to see you, too." Jae said as he set out to do his rounds throughout the building.

I pulled out my phone to check my messages while leisurely roaming across the room.

> **{Newark High}**
> **Just pull door open and make sure u lock behind u.**

"Two pair, jacks high." the guy said sitting across from Wes said as I stood over the table for the third time. I continued to watch Jae-jin circle the room, waiting for the opportunity to get into the storage room undetected. DOINK!

> **{Newark High}**
> **U comin?**
> **{Me}**
> **Waiting for ur Uncle. He about to go out back.**

"You need help Jae?" I asked as I watched Jae-jin carry the large bag of trash toward the rear door. "No. Good exercise." he answered as he placed down the bag to unlock the door.

I watched Jae-jin go outside before walking over to the concealed door. I slowly pulled on the bookshelf and stepped into the room, locking the door behind me. "You always study with your shirt off?" I appreciatively inquired seeing Chaewon laying on the bed staring up at the ceiling. As she didn't respond, I waited in my position, continuing to merely watch and admire.

"You alright?" I asked after a slightly considerable amount of time had passed and Chaewon remained motionless. "I was just thinking. What if this time turns out, just like the last time?" she confessed as she solemnly erected herself. "I can't tell you, that it won't. I don't have those answers." I said while still standing and staring at her curved figure from across the room. "First honest thing you said to me, all day." she declared with a smile. "Come sit with me." Chaewon gently requested as she patted the spot next to her on the bed. I smiled back at her while shifting progressively around the boxes and clutter. "What're you smiling at? You think you about to get some?" she arrogantly provoked as I situated myself next to her. "No. I'm enjoying your company." I honestly professed, staring intently into her face to prevent the likelihood of me looking down her bra. "There you go, lying again." she disappointedly barked while vigorously sliding away from me. I shook my head unbelievably while observing her unnecessary grimace and cringe. "So, you think sex is all I think about? Is this some sort of psychological byproduct of how things, turned out before?" I sarcastically questioned. "Yes, I'm a man so I'm thinking about sex." I continued to tutor watching her begin to progressively release her disapproving demeanor. "Especially with you sitting here in your bra, trying to hold up them big ass titties." I openly admitted as I gestured toward her chest. "Whatever." she whispered trying to disguise her blushing by forcing herself to scowl. "I'll live, if we don't fuck. I may not be as happy, but I'll live. Hell, it'll honestly make me more righteous, if we didn't." I genuinely vowed as I crossed my arms in my lap to cover any sign of my erection. "More honesty? Wow!" Chaewon uttered impressed by my straightforward comments. "You can be righteous and true with her, but not with Imani? That's fucked up, Que." I thought as she began to gradually slither her way back over toward me. I smirked at her sudden return of sexual desire. "I wish I would've realized before today that you were, more than just some pussy. If I did, there wouldn't even have been a last time." I continued to genuinely admit realizing how cool she actually is. "Wow!" she smiled immensely before standing to slide her pants from around her waist. "I don't know if that was cap or not, but it got my pants off." Chaewon stated before gripping my jersey and lifting it over my head. She tossed my jersey aside, pushed me back onto the bed, and provocatively crawled up my body. I laid back with my hands at my sides trying to legitimately decide if I still wanted this. "You alright?" she gently whispered as she laid atop of me, pressing her soft, moist lips against my neck. "Yeah. Why?" I queried bewildered that Chaewon lobbied that question, at the moment. "Cause, you went limp on me." she candidly replied, sliding her hand down my chest. "He didn't, but you did." she continued as she slid down my pants zipper and grabbed a handful of my boxer covered dick. "My bad. I was just thinking about something. But, I'm good now." I falsely uttered while seriously trying to focus on the Chaewon I have, and not the Imani, I don't. "Thinking about some things? What else could you be thinking about, with all this in front of you?! And you better not say, Imani!" Chaewon arrogantly demanded as she removed her hand from my innermost.

I remained speechless, still thinking about Imani, the silver Altima, and even Tasha. I blankly watched Chaewon eyeball my body language, before angrily hoisting herself up from me. "I don't fucking believe this. Y'all not even together, and this bitch is still in the way." she indignantly murmured while commandeering her pants from the floor. "It's not really her, but more of how I did her dirty." I regretfully admitted as I erected myself. "And how I'm about to do Tasha dirty." I thought while still admiring Chaewon's figure. "Damn, if I can do that to them, what makes me think I won't do that to you. Or anyone, for that matter." I uttered before reluctantly following Chaewon's lead and claiming my jersey. "Cause, I fuck good enough to keep, what I wanna keep. You'd know that, if you woulda let me get my shit going." Chaewon acknowledged while jumping vigorously to pull up her pants. "You can go ahead, and disappear. I got homework to do." she sarcastically continued as she fastened her pants.

"You're back early." my mom stated as I closed the patio door behind me. "Yeah. I guess I don't know Dover, like I used to." I claimed as I tossed my keys on the hook and took off my jacket. "Well baby, you've grown beyond it. Here, help me with this." she said handing me the two wine glasses that she'd just retrieved from the dish rack. I trailed my mom into the other room. "Hey, Aunt Jill." I said as my aunt and an unfamiliar woman materialized into the room. "God Damn!" I mouthed at the woman shadowing my aunt. "Hey baby. How are you?" she replied while coming to embrace me. "I'm good, I guess. Where's Unc?" I queried as she confiscated the glasses from me. "Downstairs with your father." she replied turning to hand one of the glasses to the woman that followed her into the room. "Figures." I responded, observing my mom pulling a chair from the table. I turned to help my mom into her seat, as Aunt Jill and the mysterious woman sat at the table as well. I removed the wine bottle and corkscrew from my mother's grasp and opened the wine. "You allowed to have this?" I concernedly questioned as I poured my mother a minimal amount. "Yes baby, I'm fine." she whispered smiling and gesturing me to fill the other two glasses. "Thank you." Aunt Jillian stated as I filled her glass. "How you doing?" I uncertainly asked as I filled the glassed of the unknown guest. "Hi." she confidently responded as she picked up her wine flute. "Oh. Que-tee, I'm sorry. Quentin, this is Toni. Toni, this is my biggest baby, Quentin." my mom proudly acknowledged. "Dad's Toni?" I questioned as I recorked the bottle. I looked over at Toni, who had suddenly bean to choke on the large swig of wine she'd just taken. "You alright?" Aunt Jillian asked outwardly suspicious of Toni's outburst. "I'm fine." Toni responded in between coughs and efforts to clear her throat. "Uh, yeah. I'm your dad's assistant, at work. I can't say that I'm his, though. I belong to a six-year-old named, Andre. But it's nice to finally meet you, Que." she clarified while still trying to clear her throat. "I feel like I already know you, the way your family's always talking about you." she continued after ultimately collecting herself. "Same here." I agreed, doing my best to gaze at her, discreetly. "Well, I'm going to bed. I got a headache and I'm hoping that if I lay down, it won't get worse." I said as I leaned down to kiss my mom's cheek. "You okay, Que-tee?" my mother asked as I made my way toward the stairs. "Yeah mom, I'll be alright." I said confidently. "Tell Unc, I'll catch up with him tomorrow." I said addressing my Aunt Jill. "I sure will." she responded as she raised her glass in salutation. "Good night, y'all." I said as I turned back in the direction of the table of ladies. "Good night, baby." my mom said proudly. "It was nice meeting you." Toni said with a nod and a tip of her glass.

Knock. Knock. Knock! "Come in." I murmured raising my head from my pillow. The door gently opened and Imani peeked her head in. She quickly surveyed the room before opening the door completely. She stepped into the room, closed the door behind her, and waddled over to the edge of my bed. "Wha'chu doing here? What's wrong?!" I asked as I anxiously sat up preparing to run if it was baby-related. "Couldn't get it up, huh?" she cruelly mocked as she took a seat on the bed next to me. "I never remember you having that problem, before." she sarcastically continued while ashamedly shaking her head. "What are you talking about?" I asked renouncing any thoughts of dialog about her night. "You. Not, being able to fuck Chaewon Hargrove, tonight." she teasingly explained. "Huh?" I asked puzzled by how she knew who I was with, and what happened. "Don't act like you don't know, what I'm talking about!" she disapprovingly demanded. "I know. Everybody knows! She posted y'all business, on social media." she laughed as she looked down into her phone. "What?!" I skeptically asked hoping this was bullshit, and Chae wasn't that cynical. "Yeah. I got texted about it ten times, while I was out." she bragged as she raised her phone for proof. "Out with, who?!" I inquired seizing the opportunity to question her night. "That was killing you on the inside, wasn't it?" Imani continued to ironically question. "I saw you run outside in your drawers, trying to catch us pulling off." she laughingly disclosed while taking off her jacket and placing it on the bed behind her. "I didn't go out with him to spite you. But it did hurt, didn't it? Knowing that while I was supposed to be yours, I was sucking someone else. While I'm carrying your child, another nigga was caressing my belly. That shit is gunshot, not paper cut pain." she frankly admitted while trying to convince herself it wasn't retaliatory. "His name was Na'eer. Na'eer Young. And while you was out with Chaewon Hargrove, and I was out with Na'eer Young, this came through." she acknowledged while unlocking her phone so that she could show me tonight's texts.

> **{Nikki}**
> **Ur ex was with C.H. 2nite. Sending u her post.**

"Here let me read her post, out loud. You lucky I can't stand up, 'cause I would do this like a oral report." she eagerly joked while failing in her attempt to stand. "Just read it. Don't need all the extras." I harshly insisted. "Ok. All jokes aside… *Got fucked over again, by this nigga. He had me asshole naked with my pussy juicy and he couldn't fuck, 'cause he was thinking about some bitch name Imani. Had to finish it myself. Hashtag, this some bullshit. Hashtag, lame ass Quentin. Hashtag, fuck all bitches named Imani.*" Imani voiced as brazen as it was written. I laughed at Chaewon's brass while listening to Imani recite the note she penned to the world. "So, you came over to gloat? Get the car back? The keys are downstairs on the hook." I said observing Imani's enormous smile after reading Chaewon's post. "No. The car never crossed my mind. And neither did, gloating. I don't know why I came over here." Imani unclearly admitted while using her foot to push her shoe off of the other. "Yes, I do! I want to hear what happened, in detail, from your very own lips." she honestly requested.

"If you would've thought of me while you were at school, like you did tonight, we'd still be a happy family." she stated while moving my legs aside so that she could slink across the bed. I was perplexed watching her slide up next to me. And even more so when she confiscated one of the pillows from under my head. "What the hell she doing?" I thought as she continued to get settled. I watched her laying there, with her belly protruding high in the air and her arms at her sides. "That can't be comfortable." I asserted while readjusting my head, after losing a pillow. I immediately regretted proclaiming it, thinking about how often I've said that same to Tasha. "I'm used to it, now. It's this, or on my side. And that's not gonna work. So…" she acknowledged hopelessly. "I know you can't wait to sleep on your stomach, like you used to." I claimed cordially. "Nope." she giggled quietly. "Why can't you sleep on your side?" I naively inquired. "Because it'd be too painful to wake up looking at you, it'd bring back too many of my favorite memories. And turning my back to you, is probably how she got here." she scoffed. "Oh." I said bleakly looking down at the moonlight shine on the carpet.

I followed the moon beam's path to the moon itself and just stared at it. "Whoa!" Imani enthusiastically pronounced as she trembled slightly. "What?! What's wrong?" I queried redirecting my concentration back to Imani. "She must've heard me talking about her, cause she moving like crazy." she uttered while wincing significantly. Always fascinated by both of my kid's movements, I smiled intensely. I thoughtlessly extended my hand to place it on her belly to feel the movement for myself. "I'm sorry. I got enthused and almost touched you uninvited. May I?" I inquired after quickly pulling my hand back. "Uninvited?! You're always invited to feel for this little girl. It's almost a requirement. She's yours too, Quentin." she sternly answered while reaching between her legs to grasp the bottom of her dress. She pulled the front of her dress up and rested it on her breasts, exposing her belly and everything below it. "I don't know what all you trying to show me, but it's dark in here. Maybe I should turn on the light, so I can see better." I sarcastically joked. "For what?! That's not yours anymore. You threw that away for something you thought was better, remember?!" Imani harshly reminded. "This, is yours!" she continued as she grabbed my hand and placed it on her naked belly. "She's really moving around a lot, in there." I enthusiastically stated while she continually moved my hand to where the movement was most noticeable. "You really let some other nigga, rub on your belly?" I questioned downheartedly, knowing there wasn't anything I could do about it if she did. "No. I didn't suck nobody neither. I was just making a point." she solemnly confessed, removing her warm hand from atop of mine. "I couldn't, wouldn't, blame you if you did." I sincerely acknowledged, positively relieved that her still being untouched, was a real possibility. "Oh, I know! What I do, is my business now!" she severely reminded as I slowly pulled my hand off of her. "I know." I somberly uttered, trusting that the chances of us ever being welcoming again are doubtful. "Thanks Mani. Here, now you can turn on your side." I continued as I turned my body away from her so we both could rest more comfortably. "Goodnight." I stated quietly as I resumed my stare at the moon. "Goodnight Que." she gently responded as she turned on her side.

"Wha'chu doing?" I anxiously asked, staggered with awakening to Imani's hand rummaging through my boxers. I opened my eyes to the sight of Imani's hair and the back of her dress, which was pulled up to her waist. She eventually found and seized my dick. Her soft familiar hand, mixed with the sight of her uncovered ass, caused it to stiffen immediately. "Again, what're you doing?" I quietly asked as she pulled my dick out of my mysteriously unbuckled pants. "It doesn't seem possibly, that this can end well." I thought as she lifted her leg, resting it atop of mine, and backed her ass into my now rock-solid dick. "Inviting you to touch me!" she finally mocked while gradually guiding my dick inside her drooling pussy. She gently lifted and pushed herself back against me, driving me in and out of her. "Shiiittt." I whispered while placing my hand on her waist to push in deeper. "Ohhh. I missed this!" she whimpered before she began to progressively push back more aggressively.

I swung my legs off of the side of the bed to remove the pants that regardless of it all, I'd still had on. Slightly smiling at the possibilities that the situation had unveiled, I pushed my pants to the floor, stood, and walked over to the window. I watched as the feeble sunbeams shined gently from anywhere possible, as the house across the road blocked the majority of the sunrise. I pivoted my head from the spring morning view, to look at Imani, who was lying there, massaging her belly and blankly staring at the ceiling. "You okay?" I awkwardly asked, instinctively recognizing the sense of emptiness between us. "I don't know." she faintly whispered remaining vacantly frozen. "I was just a fuck, wasn't I." I quietly quizzed after turning to resume looking out of the window. "I don't know. I did, want you to be. But now, I really don't know." she whispered continuing to stare into her own private void. I walked around to the side of the bed where Imani was resting and dropped down onto my right knee. KNOCK. KNOCK. KNOCK! "Yeah." I yelled turning toward the door. "Hey, daddy said. Oh shit... Mani!" Storm stated while pushing into the room. "Girl, wha'chu doing here?!" she excitedly continued whispered as she quickly closed the door as gently as possible. "Hey, Em." Imani quietly whispered, scoffing at Storm's attempt at anonymity. "I said *yeah*, not *come in*." I irritably reiterated to Storm before raising up from my keeling position. "Whatever. Dad making pancakes. You want some?" she acknowledged as she crept over to Imani and me. "Yeah. What the fuck you sneaking around for?" I questioned as I motioned over to my dresser to grab some sweatpants from the drawer. "I was trying, to help you out. I don't know what the fuck you got going on, up here." Storm sternly answered as she stooped down to rub Imani's belly. "You want some too, Mani?" she asked while massaging circles across Imani's stomach. "No, I'm okay." Imani stated. "Tell him to make her some too." I insisted as snatched a pair of pants from my drawer. "I was. But I was going to, *ask* him. Let me see you go down there, and *tell* dad to do something!" she challenged after lifting her hand from Imani. "You know what I meant, Em!" I urged pulling my pants up to around my waist. "You can just take a plate with you, if you leaving." I gently acknowledged before opening another drawer to look for socks. I seized the socks from the drawer and then watched Storm make her way in the direction of the door. "Do this mean y'all back together?" Emily asked knowing if nothing else, Imani and I had sex last night. "No!" I quickly answered relieving Imani from the awkward position of even having to ponder that notion. "It means, we have things to talk about." Imani amended before Storm could open the door to leave.

CHAPTER 83

"Antoinette"

"Come on. We're going to be late." Tracey demanded as I continued to stuff my mouth with pancakes. "Hey baby." she continued as Quentin came trotting down the steps followed by one of his very pregnant young ladies. "Hey ma." he responded before turning to assist his former down the last few steps. "Hey Mani!" she enthusiastically stated as she appeared from behind Quentin. She followed her greeting of the young lady, with a partial embrace before returning her attention to me. "Toni, c'mon. You can finish that later." she said as she swiftly toddled past the table toward the kitchen. "I'm coming." I muttered indistinctly before swallowing my mouthful of food. "We still gotta wait for, Jillian." I snappily uttered, disapproving her attendance in our endeavors. "Hey Que." I said as he ultimately turned his attention toward me. "Hey." he nonchalantly responded before pulling out the chair across the table from me. He made sure that his baby's mom was sitting comfortably, before quickly heading to the kitchen. "How you doing?" she timidly asked while I was cutting my last pancake with the side of my fork. "I'm fine yourself?" I cordially responded stopping to look up at her. "I'm good, other than." she uttered gesturing to her pregnant condition. I smiled at how much she reminded me of me when I was young and obliviously pregnant. "Yeah, I see that. Congratulations." I said faking enthusiasm while continuing smile at her naïveté. "Since they wanna be rude, I'm Antoinette." I stated, gesturing toward my temporary inability to use my hands to greet her. "Imani." she said softly. "Ohhhh, ok." I said before placing the forkful of pancake on my tongue. "Yeah, I'm the girlfriend! Not to be mistaken for the side bi... chick!" she promptly clarified. "I know, that's right!" I applauded before hurriedly cramming the last of my food into my mouth. "Mm, that was good." I quietly murmured pushing my chair back to rise from the table. I picked up an unused napkin and used it to brush across the table. Pushing any crumbs, I created while eating, onto my emptied plate. "Nice meeting you. I'm sure I'll see you, again." I declared while standing to push in my chair. I stepped around the table and sashayed to the kitchen like a runway model, after noticing her admiringly ogling me. On top of walking with my normal, sexy strut, I fanned the slit in my dress to expose a little thigh as I paraded across the room. I could hear her scoff when my impressive show was forced to come to a halt as Omar came carelessly, crashing out of the kitchen. "Once again, it's on." he enthusiastically crooned while prancing into the room with a serving dish of stacked pancakes and bacon. "Here you go mama. Just like you like it." he said placing the dish of food in the center of the table. "Thank you, Paw-paw." she joyfully exclaimed, showing elation for her momentary homecoming. "Don't tell her that. She'll eat that whole thing by herself." Hassan sarcastically proclaimed as he poured out of the kitchen carrying a jug of milk and a bottle of syrup. "What's up, Toni." he nonchalantly mumbled as he passed by me. "Mom said, they're outside waiting for you." Quentin naively said as he trailed Hassan, with empty glasses and plates in his hand. "I'm leaving, now. Thank you." I warmly responded, procrastinating enough to catch Omar in his return to the kitchen, now that I know it was empty.

"Okaaaayyyy." I quietly sang, fascinated by how improved an absent roof makes Hassan's car look. "Wherever we going, I hope we not coming straight back. Not driving in that." I eagerly yelled from the patio, observing them down in the car impatiently waiting. "Nevermind, where we're going. Girl, what are you wearing?" Jillian sarcastically asked while smiling at my strut down the driveway. "This shit is sexy, ain't it?" I confidently queried while again taking an advantage of the opportunity to model how my titties and ass are featured in this form-fitting dress.

"Get yo sexy ass in this car, so we can go. We're going to be late." Jillian declared while leaning forward enough for her to pull the chair so I could slide in behind her. "You know she can't squeeze in through that little space, with all that talent." Tracey joked recognizing that Jillian's efforts weren't enough. "I see that." Jillian said as she let go of the chair. Seeing she was about to get out of the car I rested my hand on her shoulder to stop her. "I got this." I uttered before tossing my purse into the back seat. I leaned my ass against the car and then placed my hands on the car, at my sides. I pressed my hands down and jumped, propelling myself atop the car. I then placed my hand between my thighs to prevent any type of reveal before I fell backward, into the back seat. "You okay." Tracey asked as my legs waved wildly in the air. "I'm fine." I proclaimed, smiling as I looked up at my shoes glimmering in the sunlight. "In that case." Jillian said while quickly pulling from in front of the door. "You just gonna drive away, with my legs in the air?" I asked, amused by the gesture. "We all know this ain't the first time you had your legs in the air, in the back seat of a car. We've all been in that position before." she sarcastically retorted. "God knows, I have." Tracey chuckled while candidly agreeing. "Yeah, but not riding down the street. You showing my shit, to everybody." I lightheartedly uttered as I squirmed around trying to reposition myself to be able to pull my legs into the car and sit upright. "You'll be alright. You got panties on." Jillian ironically teased. "Toni, you do have on panties, right?" Tracey sincerely questioned with an expression of true concern on her face. "I think, I do." I playfully replied as I slid back enough to lower my legs. "You think? Well let me slow down so that they get a good, long look." Jillian mischievously stated as she jokingly began to slow the car down.

"Seriously girl, that dress is fierce. And you are working that split." Jillian sincerely admitted as she turned to watch me close the car door. "Why, thank you. Thank you." I responded smiling at the rare compliment from Jillian. "It's nice, but don't you think that, it's a bit much? We're only going to get a mani-pedi, and then hang out for a while?" Tracey questioned expressing her deviating opinion as we walked across the square to the salon. "Well, since I'm the only one of us three still on the market, I'm trying to make 'em take notice." I educated as I surveyed the area for anyone staring at me. "Yeah Tra, she has to put an obvious partition between those of us that are married, and those who're single." Jillian ironically explained to Tracey, pretending to agree with my underlying principle. "Damn y'all. I don't deserve no, dick I mean… man. Y'all got y'all, one to sleep next to. I'm not allowed to find happiness, too?" I genuinely inquired as I held the door open for the three of us. "By all means, find your happiness. I want that for you, more than anything. What I also want, is for you to know that it's about more than, just sex. We can all see, that you're sexy. What we want them to see, is that you're smart, you're funny, you're sweet, you're interesting. Advertise those things that onlookers can't see, with just a glance." Tracey lectured while we stood at the counter to notify the staff of our arrival.

"You gonna sit there and lie in our faces, and say you not getting none on the regular? You?!" Jillian blatantly asked while sitting across from me with her feet submerged in a foot scrub solution. "I didn't say that." I cunningly responded as the woman placed my feet into the basin at the foot of the pedicure chair. "I said I don't have nobody, to sleep next to. Well, to wake up next to." I reiterated while staring down at my feet and thinking about how I can't wait, for Omar to play with them. "Oh, so there is someone?" Tracey animatedly probed as she sat in the massage chair waiting for Jillian and me. "Something like that." I admitted, smirking deviously while watching bubbles appear around my wiggling toes. "Why am I just now learning this?" Tracey disappointedly asked, assuming that she'd known all of the comings and goings of my life. "Who cares why? You now, know!" Jillian promptly intervened as the stylist began working on her foot. "Now, we just need the details!" she continued before tilting her head back and closing her eyes. Unable to look over into Tracey's eyes, I relentlessly continued to stare into the foot basin. "Details, huh? Where do I start?" I coaxed myself before I began to tell my companions the details of my love life.

"Honestly? This man. This confident, successful, smart, sexy man just showed up at my house one night, wanting a massage." I earnestly confessed while I scrutinized the woman's progress on Jillian's foot. "You had sex, with a stranger?" Tracey asked astonished that I'd be so reckless. "Ewww, no. What do I look like? I'm look but don't touch, kinda girl." I replied just as amazed that she'd even suppose that notion. "Of course, I knew him. I knew everything about 'em. Only thing I didn't know at that point, was the one thing I wanted to know." I disclosed while waiting for someone to begin my treatment. "And, what was that?" Tracey asked as she too watched the woman work on Jillian. "If he fucked with his socks on, or not." I wittily responded. "So, when he came over that historic night, I stopped everything I was doing, to find out." I casually continued. "And?" Tracey curiously interrogated while now leaning toward me, focusing on my every word. "And what?" I questioned while reluctantly glancing over at Tracey. "Bitch, we said details. So, start gabbing." Jillian impatiently demanded. "Well, he originally came over cause I'd given him a shoulder massage beforehand, and he wanted me to finish." I said resuming my slightly uncomfortable reveal. "And you finished him off, right?" Jillian anxiously asked. "I couldn't, Andre was home. Not doing nothing, with my baby there. Even though he was sleep, he was still there. So, I just pulled out my hot stones and finished his *real* massage. But when Sonic came back, a few nights later... I hit him almost everything!" I admitted slightly leaning away from Tracey. "What's, almost everything?" Tracey urged, intensely intrigued by what my first night with my new flame entailed.

"As soon he walked through my door, I squatted down and threw him in my mouth. I tried to suck a whole generation, out his ass! I ain't even stop, when he put his hands in my hair. That's how dedicated I was." I said as I watched Tracey's mouth water with more chronicles about her husband and me. "Damn girl, a whole generation?" Jillian said, giving me a small relief from Tracey. Her interrupting questions gave me the chance to focus on her. I'd rather tell her about me and Omar than feel like I'm talking directly to Tracey. "Damn right, I tried to damage his psyche with that one." I boasted to Jillian leaning forward to concentrate on her. "And that's what you call, everything?" Tracey whispered from beside me apparently unimpressed by my narrative. "No, that was just the first let off. But it did, put him to sleep." I bragged attempting to achieve redemption of my sex goddess status. "You woke him back up?" Jillian scoffed gesturing to Tracey to back away from me, a little. Seeing Tracey lean back in her chair, I was able to lounge comfortably lounge, as well. "Damn right, you know how long I waited for this one? I wasn't nowhere near, done." I calmly confessed while watching the Asian woman shift to Jillian's other foot. "Omar goes right to sleep afterwards, too. Then, I'm left there awake, alone, and wanting more. It doesn't happen too often, but it does happen. Maybe I should start waking him back up, too." Tracey solemnly deliberated while going down her own personal tunnel. "Yeah, you do that, Tra." Jillian uttered disappointed in Tracey's mindset. "So, then what'd you do?" Jillian eagerly probed, predicting that I would say something spectacular. "I took him to my bedroom, and finished the job." I said nonchalantly before I turned to Tracey who was still in her own headspace. "Details bitch, details!" Jillian loudly whispered. "One of the things about being single, is that you can talk about things that we can't." Tracey explained after Jillian's requirement seemed to re-awaken her. "So, you took him to your bedroom and then..." Jillian continued, noticing Tracey's concentration reappearance. "Well, we didn't make it all the way to my bedroom, at first." I confessed, slightly ashamed to continue in present company. I glanced at the peculiar looks given between my companions, which preceded Jillian's impatient scowl at me. "Ok, we were going up the steps. And when I get near the top, I always run up the last few steps. Don't ask, I don't know why. But all the same, I didn't see a piece of chalk that Andre had laying there and I slipped and fell forward. But I caught myself, and landed on my hands and knees, on the top landing. When I tell you, this mutha-fucka dove straight for it, he dove straight for it! He pushed his head in and started eating my ass, like I was his last meal! And to this day I don't know how he did it, cause I had my little shorts on." I admitted while trying to focus more on Tracey just being a woman that I'm sharing my experiences with, than her being Omar's wife. "Wow! He stopped there?" Tracey uttered, eagerly wanting to know more. "Hell no. Girl, he waited until after he had his fill, and then he ripped them shorts right off my ass. And, that's when he went in for the kill. I mean, we went hard! Right there, at the top of the steps. And I was talking shit, and throwing shit back at him. But he whipped my ass, on them steps." I disclaimed gradually becoming more comfortable the more I spoke. "Shit, you got me wanting to go home to Hassan, right now! Maybe, if I fall up the steps, I can get it like that, too." Jillian joked as the woman completed the scrubbing of her feet. "Come on, Jills. Hassan, just like Omar, would've watched and laughed." Tracey reminded, disappointed by what she assumed would be her outcome. "Watch and laugh? Them dirty mo-fos, would've taken pictures and laughed about it again later." Jillian said, adding to Tracey's point.

"So, your night ended there?" Tracey asked as the salon's staff woman transferred over to begin the spa treatment on my feet. "Nope. I crawled to my room and we did it again." I swiftly answered while the woman slowly massaged my foot. "Crawled?" Tracey questioned, bewildered by my statement. "Why were you, crawling?" Jillian inquired in the interest of them both, while contently running her hand across her velvet soft foot. "Girl, I don't know if it was the four-month drought, or if it was him. But I couldn't move for almost twenty minutes, after that. Crawling, was all I could do." I honestly illuminated while trying to hold in my smile from the tickling of my foot. "He didn't try to help you up?" Jillian queried grimacing bewilderedly. "Yeah, he tried. I was just that weak. So, I just asked him to go in my room, and wait for me. He was in there half asleep by the time I finally made it in there." I explained laughing at the situation after re-thinking it. "How did you continue after that, if you were that exhausted?" Tracey sincerely questioned while leaning back intently, trying to learn. "Oh, a bitch got her second wind. I wasn't gonna let him just come to my house, and fuck the hell outta me! At that point... I had a point to prove." I sternly asserted as I smirked at my own boldness.

"I'm glad you found your one. Cause honestly, for a second I thought..." Jillian said reaching into her purse. "Let me guess, you thought she was eyeballing, your husband." Tracey abruptly interrupted. "Yeah, how'd you know?" Jillian astonishingly asked as she handed the cashier her credit card. "Jillian, do you realize that you think every woman, living and dead, has her eyes on Hassan?" Tracey acknowledged as she shook her head in disgust. "No, I didn't realize I always thought that. I say that, that often?" Jillian ignorantly asked while waiting for the card authorization. "I'm not even going to respond to that. Congratulations, Toni." she continued as she extended her arm to hug me. "What she said." Jillian added as she placed her arms around the opposite side of me as Tracey. "All that talking 'bout him made your coochie tingle, didn't it?" Jillian quietly asked. "Jillian!" Tracey cautioned as other customers began to surround the counter. "Girrrrl! I be at work and I sometimes have to change my panties, just thinking about him." I discreetly replied to avoid being scolded by Tracey.

"You have to one day invite your new beau, over to our house." Tracey insisted while looking out of the door glass, like a cat in a window. "Sonic is not really a, people person." I falsely indicated with the hope of an immediate defuse of the idea. "Have to change register ribbon." the young cashier disclosed as while reaching under the counter. "Ok." I replied, apparently being the only one who was paying attention. "Oh ok." Jillian tardily responded before glaring back at me peculiarly. "Did you just call him, Sonic?" Tracey inquired, confusedly returning her attention to Jillian and I. "Yeah." I nervously said hoping that we'd end this interrogation of Omar's information soon. "I thought you said Sonny, before!" Jillian asserted before confiscating a peppermint from the dish on the counter. "Toni, his name is Sonic? Like the food chain?" Tracey quizzed as I gestured for Jillian to gather a peppermint for me, too. "No, his name's not Sonic. That's just what I call him." I patronizingly answered placing the peppermint into my mouth. "Why?" Tracey curiously investigated. "I don't believe I'm telling y'all this. My son has a game called Sonic the Hedgehog." I embarrassingly began to fabricate. "Yeah, I remember that game." Tracey encouragingly intervened to raise my confidence. "Yeah, me too." Jillian confessed while signing the credit card receipt. "Well, on the game if you hit Sonic right, he explodes with his coins going everywhere, and then he dies til you ready to use him again. But just like my... friend, he blinks right back in the game, just as strong." I plainly explained as Jillian collected her card and receipt. "That's the dumbest, and coolest thing I ever heard." the customer awaiting behind me laughingly disclosed. I turned and laughed with her, while looking over at Jillian who had also remained behind to laugh with the stranger. "Exploding and getting right back up, huh?" the woman continued to laugh as I watched Tracey make her way out of the building. "Girl, I told her. All I can do is remember, those days." Jillian mentioned before we turned to press forward to catch up with Tracey. "Thank you." Jillian uttered to the cashier while opening the door to exit. "Remember?! You really saying these days, *always* have to go away?" I worriedly questioned as I stepped out past Jillian. "No. I'm saying, it hasn't been like that with me and Hassan, in years. I don't remember when it stopped, how it stopped, or even why it stopped. I just know, it stopped." Jillian said after releasing the door, to let it close. "At least you have the memory of those days, I've never had it like that with Omar." Tracey declared, silently walking up behind us.

"Don't get me wrong. He's good, really good." she continued as we walked down to their favorite after pampering bistro. "Yeah, we can tell." Jillian said brushing her hand across Tracey's belly. "You was saying, Tra." I asked irritably yearning to hear about Omar's so-called flaws. "My Omar is great. But, he's just always so... gentle. So, warm and loving." Tracey embarrassingly stated. "This bitch is not only spoiled, she's retarded." I thought as my face grimaced. "And... that's a bad thing?" Jillian confusedly asked. "Thank you!" I mouthed, relieved that I wasn't the only one questioning her perception. "No, not at all. But I'll ask you this. What woman is at work thinking about the way their man, *made love* to them, last night?" Tracey confidently asked as Jillian pulled opened the door to the eatery. We stepped in and Tracey immediately found an available table against the front window. "Here, I have to use the restroom." Tracey hurriedly uttered as she dropped her purse on the table and scurried off. "Soft? Omar?" I unbelievably inquired while sitting down. I placed Tracey's purse in the adjacent chair. "Yeah, I know. But then again, we gotta remember she's of a different breed." Jillian hesitantly reminded about her best friend. "But let's put a pin in that, for a second. I wanna know more about this beast, you're sleeping with." she continued as she leaned in for more privacy. "Sonic, the friend. Is that all you got planned for him?" she nosily asked suddenly seeming rather approachable. "I can't claim more, than that. His situation is, complicated." I disappointedly divulged while occasionally glancing out of the window at the people patronizing the shoppes. "Oh wow." she whispered while pondering how she should feel about my decision. I couldn't answer, I just stared at her remorsefully. "I'm assuming it's close to home. And that's why you made up that stupid ass, bullshit story about his nickname. You can't give up his real name, in case he ever comes up." she sullenly continued, disappointed by the confirmation of her previous assumptions. I could feel her approachable mindset, immediately lift from the table. "And that's not even the worst part." I mournfully professed looking up to see Tracey slowly approaching from the other end of the room. "Let me guess, you're falling in love with him." she smugly supposed before clutching the flower from the vase in the middle of the table. "Fell. Long before, we started fucking." I confessed as Tracey approached the table. "Figures." Jillian uttered disappointedly as she slammed the flower back into the vase.

"I'm sorry ladies. What were we talking about?" Tracey naively asked while pulling her chair out to sit. "You asked, what woman is at work thinking about the way their man, *made love* to her?" Jillian reminded, trying her best to change the subject to something other than my adulterous lifestyle choice. "Oh yeah." Tracey said obliviously. "I was just conveying that when you're thinking about your man sexually, it's about the *Animal* in him. Not the *Kermit.*" she continued to illuminate while waving to summon the waiter over to our table. "I liked Kermit, myself." Jillian courteously opposed. "Me too." I absolutely agreed. "But I get what you're saying. Sometimes you need that cold, ravaging, disrespectful shit." Jillian continued with a devious smile before looking up in anticipation at the emerging server. "Yeah. that's it exactly." Tracey gently asserted before pivoting to see the source of Jillian's interest. "It's the cold, ravaging, disrespectful ones, that don't hang around til morning." I solemnly murmured as the waiter arrived at the table. Seeing my melancholy demeanor in that last comment, Tracey forced a smile and comfortingly placed her hand atop mine.

"Good afternoon ladies." the flamboyant waiter magnificently expressed while distributing menus. "Hi Derrick." Tracey said softly while accepting her menu. "Hey Derrick. How are you today?" Jillian asked matching the waiter's energy. "I'm well, Ms. Worth. And you?" he cheerfully replied. "I'm good. Thanks." Jillian responded while reviewing her menu. "And Mrs. Gregory, you're glowing as usual. Baby girl is still being stubborn, huh?" Derrick informally inquired. "Yes, and I wish she would hurry up. I don't appreciate this limit to one, small glass of wine." Tracey declared before pointing to out Derrick what she wanted from her menu. "You changing it up today? Ok. Still keep it to half a glass though, right?" he thoughtlessly inquired as he jotted down her order. "Yes, Derrick. I'm still pregnant." Tracey sarcastically replied. Derrick ignored Tracey's comment, smiled, and turned his attention to me. "I'm sorry ma'am. Welcome to The Blue Cataleya. As you now know, my name is Derrick and I'll be doing my very best to serve you. Might I have your name? I don't think it'd be right, if I knew their names and not yours." the waiter socially stated while eagerly leaning down close to me. "Antoinette." I said following his line of sight, which went straight down into my cleavage. I looked up at Jillian, who was astonishingly evaluating our waiter. And then to Tracey who was grimacing spitefully. "You like that Derrick?" I encouragingly whispered, while arching to draw him to continue. "You like it more than you like this job?!" Jillian sternly interjected disrupting my performance from across the table. "Uh, no ma'am. Y-you said your name was, was Antoinette?" Derrick stammered after Jillian threatened his job. "Yes, and don't mind her, she was just playing." I kindly reassured after seeing the waiter nervously erect himself. "Weren't you Jill?" I asked to compound his certainty. "Derrick knows he was wrong for that. But no, I wouldn't get him in trouble for it." Jillian disclosed as I pointed down to what I wanted on the menu. "I would. Mine are just as big as hers, and you've never once looked down my shirt." Tracey harassed as the waiter walked behind her to get around to Jillian. "Aren't you married Ms. Gregory?" Jillian asked while laughing hysterically. "Yeah. But he doesn't know Toni marital status, and his unawareness didn't stop him, with her." Tracey stated while continuing to pretend to be offended. I tucked my hand under the table to hide my fingers, in case Derrick was actually trying to investigate. He leaned down next to Jillian as she made her meal selection. "You remember my usual drink?" Jillian cynically asked. "Yes ma'am." Derrick confidently replied. "Well Derrick, I'll have that and a king crab salad with vinaigrette. Thank you." she informed while folding her menu. "So that's the king crab salad with a vinaigrette dressing and a White Russian. The lemon pepper pork chops with the house vegetable and a half glass of white sangria. And the brandied scallops with rice pilaf and a pinot grigio blush." Derrick stated while pointing to each of us individually as he recapped. "You got it, Derrick. Thank you." Tracey said graciously while jokingly protruding her breasts. "Derrick, one more thing?" Jillian requested as the waiter began to retreat. "Yes, Ms. Worth." he politely said while turning to welcome her request. "Is Antoinette married?" Jillian inquired as I sat up straight and placed my hands in my lap trying to look as innocent as possible. "I would guess, she's not married." he embarrassingly replied before walking away red-faced. I giggled at both Jillian's bravado and the waiter's reaction to it. "That's that partition, I was talking about, Tra. It separates us, from them." Jillian tutored while pointing at herself, Tracey, and then me, respectively.

CHAPTER 84

"Quentin"

DOINK!

> {Tasha}
> I miss u!
> {Me}
> Miss u 2. Be back tomorrow tho. Other than that u ok?

"So, you never said what brought you home, this weekend." my dad stated while tossing his legs up onto the sofa. "Hassan sent me a ticket. He got his guy to do the inside lining of my suit, the way I want it. And! He said he can have it done, by draft night." I eagerly disclosed as I sat there skimming through my phone, waiting for Tasha to respond. "So, when're we going to get fitted?" he sensibly asked, assuming that being my reason for coming home. "He said as soon as he come back." I replied ignorant to any more information than that. DOINK!

> {Tasha}
> That seems so generic. U with HER?

"Then why'd he give up his car?" my dad asked as I read Tasha's response. "Damn. I can't win for losing." I quietly mumbled to myself as thought of a response to Tasha. "I don't know but Ms. Grier's out there so, we'll be alright." I said to my dad, successfully having two conversations simultaneously.

> **{Me}**
> **No. And even when I am, I'm wit the baby.**
> **Not her mother. Told u that already!**

"No, it's not. Imani and Em went shopping, remember?" my dad reminded while frolicking through channels in search of something to watch. "I thought they took the Volvo." I uncertainly retorted while staring into my phone. "Either way, it's fine. We'll take my truck. Let me go put some clothes on. I'm assuming, this was his plan anyway." my dad proposed before reluctantly turning off the television. He tossed the remote onto the sofa, and stood to get going up the stairs to change. DOINK! "I'm sure it was." I concurred before eyeing my phone for the rest of Tasha's conversation.

> **{Tasha}**
> **Hey. U still love me? B 4real!**
> **{Me}**
> **Ur caring my son. Why wouldn't I?**

"In fact. Come on up with me, so we can talk about this you and Imani situation." my dad insisted as his voice progressively faded from earshot. "Yeah, alright. Here I come." I sighed as I continued to wait for Tasha. DOINK!

"What's up old man?" I asked as I splashed down onto his side of the bed. "Roll over. You're on my clothes." he sternly informed while pointing to my mom's side of the bed. "Nah. I'm good. I know what y'all do on her side." I said while lifting up from atop his clothes. "Nothing more, than what you do in your bed." he claimed as he forcefully pulled his jeans up from under my leg and tossed them on the chair. "Speaking of that. That Toni, damn! That's a bad bi…" I halted after looking up at his expression. "My bad. But she's a beast and she know it." I apologized, before continuing to describe. "No wonder, mom and Jills always sweating bullets." I uttered as I reached into my pocket to read the text I received before coming upstairs. "She's just another female, son." he said before walking into his bathroom. "Yeah, I'd say that too if I wanted to keep her working for me." I said loud enough for him to hear from the bathroom.

> {Tasha}
> But like u say about u & Imani. You could
> just be with me 4 the baby's sake.
> {Me}
> If I was I wud tell u.

"There's wisdom beyond your years, between those ears." my dad said sticking his head out of the door with a great smile. "What're you smiling at?" I questioned smiling at my dad's high spirits. "You don't recognize where I got that from?" he enthusiastically asked after pulling his head back into the bathroom. "No. I don't think so." I admitted after deeply mulling it over. "Wait til your sister finds out, that I listen to her music closer than you do." he happily teased over the sound of water pouring from the sink's faucet. "I would've never guessed that was Storm." I honestly admitted, smiling at his arrogance.

DOINK! "You plan on telling me, or do I have to dig?" my dad inquired while walking out of the bathroom. "Tell you, what?" I questioned cluelessly. "Why last night was so much, like old times?" he mockingly asked standing at his armoire, continuing to groom. "Wha'chu mean?" I asked still oblivious to what he was referring to. "I mean. I saw Imani before I went to bed, and then this morning I'm feeding her pancakes. Only now, she's wearing the same clothes, as last night." he mentioned condescendingly while sitting down in the chair to finish dressing. "My bad, dad. We both fell asleep, and she never made it home. It won't happen, again." I apologetically confirmed before looking down into my phone.

> {Tasha}
> No. I don't think u wud.

"I'm fine. She's carrying my granddaughter. So, if she needs a place to comfortably stay, she has one. But that wasn't the case last night, was it? And before you answer, remember I got some wisdom between my ears too." he intuitively asked.

> {Me}
> U don't kno me like I thought u did.

"Dad, I don't know what happen. And that's a hundred percent. I was sleep, she came over and woke me up, we talked, and the next thing I know, she was screwing me." I genuinely revealed as I watched him lace his sneakers. DOINK!

"And what about that, right there? Where are you, with that?" he reasonably inquired while pointing to my phone. "I don't know. But I think, I'm about to find out." I confessed as I tried to think of what to send to Tasha, to discover what both my father and I wondered. "Yeah, you do that." he demanded as he rose from the chair. "I still gotta figure out what's in Mani's head, too." I mumbled disheartened by my shortage of crucial knowledge. "I don't know what she's thinking. But don't dwell too hard on last night, 'cause that wasn't about you." my dad advised as he nodded for us to leave the room. "It wasn't?" I asked while following him out of the room. "What do you mean it wasn't about me?" I asked chasing him both literally and physically for an answer. "It wasn't about you. In fact, you may not even have had to be, you. She is pregnant, which means she's very horny and very hormonal. You could've been, almost anybody." he tutored as I shadowed him down the stairs.

"Anybody?" I solemnly asked as I discontinued following him once reaching the bottom of the stairs. "Sorry, to put it that way. But yeah, anybody." he said before looking out of the window, to check for Hassan's arrival. "Wow." I uttered as I journeyed into the kitchen for a drink.

"Hey Dino. It's Hassan. Calling to let you know, we're on our way. See you in, twenty." Hassan informed before dropping his phone in the cupholder. "Who's this Dino, Haas? And how much is it going to cost me?" my dad asked while trying to find comfort in the passenger's seat of his own truck. "Yo. Why's everything with you, always about the damn cost?" Hassan harshly asked while looking for the switch to activate the windshield wipers. "Someone has to think about it, right?" my dad logically retorted. I pulled out my phone with the hopes that I'd find something on social media more entertaining than these two. "Oh damn." I thought, realizing I never checked my last text notification.

{Mani}
Wasn't lying about wanting to talk.
{Me}
I'm around.

"Mani said she wants to talk." I mentioned to my father craving any wisdom he'd have to share, as to why. "Mani? What about, the other one, uhh...Tasha? I thought, you was with her." Hassan interjected while turning back to look at me. "That didn't stop him when he was with Imani, did it?" my dad callously answered. DOINK!

"Hassan, what the fuck is this?" my dad realistically asked as we pulled into the driveway, of a house that looks owned by a little old lady. "You always bitchin'. I didn't ask you to find the dude, or pay for nothing. All I'm asking you to do, is get fitted and shut the hell up." Hassan insensitively barked before again retrieving his phone. I laughed at my uncle and dad's banter while glancing down at my phone at Imani's response.

> **{Mani}**
> **No matter wat u always hav ben.**

"Dino! We're outside." Hassan stated into his phone. The door to the house opened, and a tall man stuck his head out to wave us inside. "C'mon." Hassan insisted as he opened the car door. I peered over at my dad, chuckled, and then followed Hassan out of the truck. "Should I grab my pistol?" my dad sarcastically asked before closing his door. "Maybe." I suspiciously responded just as his door shut. We watched Hassan freely enter the door, that the man extended from. "You go first." my dad joked as he looked around his immediate area. "No, you got it." I mocked while pulling the door open for him.

I stepped into the unfamiliar house and was immediately greeted by the slender, freckle-faced, red-boned man standing next to Hassan. "So, you're the football player nephew, my brother says his boss is always raving about?" the strange man asked as he extended his hand for me to shake. "Yeah, that's me. Quentin." I answered suspiciously. "Hi Quentin, I'm Lucky." he said as he firmly grasped my hand. "Omar." my dad stated extending his hand as well. "Lucky" the man repeated while shaking my father's hand. "Well, I know y'all need these like tomorrow. So, c'mon with me. The faster I can get you measured, the faster I can get started... and finished." Lucky said as he led us through the house to his sewing room. I tapped my dad on the arm to point out some of the unique wigs and costumes hanging on the walls, doors, and racks throughout the house. "Wow." I whispered while observing piles upon piles of drawings and dress patterns on the tables and floors. "You take this seriously." I stated while scrutinizing this man and his eventful dwelling. "As serious, as you take football." he responded gesturing Hassan to remove his jacket.

"Thanks again." Hassan said as we slowly backed out of the driveway. "No problem." Lucky responded before going back into the house. "That was a good look, Haas." my dad praised while readjusting his truck to his preferences. "Yeah, Unc. Thanks." I appreciatively agreed before burrowing back into my phone for companionship.

"What time does your train leave tomorrow?" my dad questioned while watching me come down the stairs. "One pulls off at nine-fifteen, and the other at four-forty. But I didn't get a ticket for either one, yet. Haas said to just buy it when I get to the station." I openly informed. "What station you going to?" he promptly continued to ask, trying to get all of his questions in during the game's commercial break. "Those are for Aberdeen. Wilmington only has the one and that pulls off at seven." I said exploring the bar refrigerator, for a soda. "You don't like seven?" he asked as I stepped from behind the bar, with a soda in hand. "I don't mind it. I just didn't want to be inconsiderate and have someone take me that early. I'd have to leave out like five, five-thirty." I honestly asserted while sitting next to him on the sofa. "Well, I'm alright with, five. I can just go to work straight from there. In fact, can do the four-forty, too. I'll just leave work early. Whichever one." he said before turning his attention back to the television. "Thanks." I graciously uttered before doing the same.

"Hey. The lady of the house, needs y'all up here for a second." Toni said as she came partially down the steps. "Yeah, alright." my dad said while staring diligently at the television. I jumped up to oblige while laughing at my dad, who got up a lot less willingly. "Excuse me." I said to Toni, who was still on the staircase. "Excuse me." she softly responded as I swiftly brushed by her. I reached the top of the stairs and turned to look back down at Toni as she gazed at the television. "You sense it too?" Mani said as she quietly approached my side, to nosily glare down the stairs as well. "Sense what? And when did y'all, get back?" I quietly inquired before departing to learn what my mother needed. "Just now." she quietly admitted while putting her bags on the table. "Something about that Toni, sets off my radar." she whispered while following me to my mother.

CHAPTER 85

"Omar"

"You want me to tell her, you about to come?" Toni enticingly asked while standing on the stairs seductively leaning over the banister. "Come on, with that shit." I said rising from my chair to find out Tracey's need. "What?" Toni adorably said with a cunning smile. "You playing too much! Just go ahead upstairs." I quietly demanded as I pointed for her to go up the steps. "I was watching the tv. I got money on this game." she uttered pretending to be greatly disappointed. "You just want me to go up first, so you can look at my ass!" she softly hissed before turning to alluringly climb the stairs. I waited for her to reach the top of the stairs and then ran up behind her. "Excuse me." I uttered as I slid past her hurrying to Tracey.

"Baaaabe. This couldn't wait? It's the playoffs!" I whined while walking through my bedroom door. "What, did you two rehearse that? That was the same thing he said, when he walked in the room. The very same way." Tracey complained while sitting in the chair allowing Quentin to help her remover her shoes. "Then you know the severity of, the playoffs. What's wrong?" I hurriedly asked in an attempt to not miss much of the ball game. "Nothing's wrong? I can't want to see my men, for a second?" Tracey pleasantly inquired after sliding her feet into her house shoes. "Yes. But right now, there has to be a legit reason." I confirmed before pivoting to attempt to retreat back downstairs. "Well, like I was telling Quentin. I'm done with work and I have you, Jillian, and Hassan. I think he should take the Volvo back to school." she suggested while rising to her feet. I glanced over at Quentin, who was standing with his palms up and shoulders scrunched. "What? Why?" I disapprovingly asked quickly releasing the doorknob I had grabbed to leave. "Because if I or Imani go into labor, he's going to have to get here. If Tasha goes into labor, he's going to have to get there. And we can't wait around for trains, and train schedules. Right now, he *needs* a way to get around." she logically explained before walking passed me, out of the room. "He has a car. He was the one that thought it made sense, to give it away." I inconsistently stated as I followed her cautious stagger, down the stairs. "Omar! Don't pretend like you didn't feel like, that was the stand-up thing to do. You walked around here for days, saying how proud you were." Tracey sternly reminded. I turned to Quentin, who was following behind me, innocently awaiting an outcome to Tracey and my discord. "And! Omee, I haven't told you the best part. You're really going to like this part! If no one goes into labor before the next 3 weeks are out, you don't have to go up there and get him. He can drive himself and all of his things, back home." she mentioned continuing her efforts to influence while signaling to Quentin that it was okay for him to leave. "I was thinking about just flying him in, wherever he needed to be. But the whole bringing himself back home thing, kinda works for me." I whispered before kissing Tracey on the cheek and heading back to my den.

I could hear the cheers of Hassan and two female voices overpowering the television immediately after opening the door. "Don't care who it is but if someone is in my chair, get the hell up!" I loudly demanded before slowly trudging down the stairs. As I reached the halfway point of the stairs, I could see the feet of a woman scurrying away from my chair. I hurried down the rest of the way to try to catch the evacuating culprit.

"Please tell me the Sixers are still up." I requested as I plopped back down into my chair. "Yeah, but the Bucks just went nine unanswered, so it's only by six." Hassan replied solemnly while confiscating his beer from his wife's grasp. I reached down for the beer I'd placed on the table in front of me before going upstairs. "Who drank my shit?" I scathingly questioned while holding up my empty beer bottle. "Here paw-paw. I'll get you another one." Imani insisted while gesturing for the empty bottle from my hand. "Thank you, Mani." I stated relinquishing the bottle to my son's ex. "If I would've known you wanted it, I'd have got it for you." Toni sourly confessed while watching Imani assist me. "Or just not've drank from it in the first place, it wasn't yours. You don't touch things, that don't belong to you." Jillian candidly suggested from her seat in Hassan's lap. "Uh huh." Imani uttered aloud from behind the bar. I smiled while watching my best friend sit serenely with a beer in his hand and his wife in his lap. "Here." Imani said returning with a freshly opened bottle. "Thank you." I said graciously. "You welcome." she said before advancing toward Quentin who was sitting on the pool table with his feet dangling over the side. She backed in between his legs, rested her head back against his chest. I looked up at my son's serenity, as Imani pulled his arms around her to rest his hands on her belly. "Success." I mouthed while admiringly observing the peace throughout the room.

"Okay guys." Jillian yelled from atop the stairs. "Alright. It'll be over, in a sec." I audibly responded amid the closing seconds of the game. "It's over brother. Our boys, lost." Hassan sullenly admitted while ascending the steps to adhere to the call for dinner. "Yup." Quentin desolately agreed as he too stood to follow Hassan up the stairs. "Hey. You know why I'm calling. I'll be there in a few, to collect my bread." Toni enthusiastically laughed into her phone before ending the call. "Damn, pop. Did you know she wasn't a Sixers fan, when you hired her?" Quentin sarcastically asked while he climbed the stairs. I trailed behind Toni as she moved enticingly behind Quentin. "I like the Sixers. I just don't think they can beat Giannis, and them. Sometimes the one with the most *talent*, takes it all. That's just life." Toni ironically confessed before turning to wink at me. "And other times son, it's the system. It's the foundation, and how it's all molded together. Think Bill, not Brady." I sneeringly amended. "I don't know football, but I know who Brady is. Never heard of Bill. And that in itself, says a lot." Toni stated as we emerged into the dining room.

"Ok people. It's been real, but I gotta go." Toni announced while standing over the table, as we began to sit down. "You not staying, for dinner?" Tracey sincerely questioned while pulling out her chair to sit. "No. Not tonight, baby. I got a son to feed, and winnings to collect." she boastfully replied while smiling at the Sixers fans in the room. "But you know, I'll be back soon. Goodnight all." she continued before slowly strolling out of the room. "Goodnight, Toni." I unremarkably uttered. "Good night." Emily said as she bounced in from the kitchen. "Here, let me walk you out." Tracey said while attempting to re-ascend directly after sitting. "Stay there Tracey, I got it." Hassan volunteered while seizing the back of his chair to park himself. "No, you not! You and Omar can both stay right where you at, I'll do it." Jillian harshly commanded while hurriedly lifting from her chair to catch up with Antoinette. "See, your aunt thinks it's something dirty about Antoinette, too." Imani unsuccessfully tried to discreetly whisper, after pulling Quentin's ear down to her lips.

"Hey." Toni uttered as looked down at me from atop of the stairs wearing nothing but a sheer bathrobe. "Hey." I diplomatically responded stopping midway up. "Didn't think I'd see you, tonight." she disclosed while extending her hand for me to come and embrace her. "I didn't think I was coming." I said marching up to reach her hand. "Glad you changed your mind." she admitted as she gently pulled me into her bedroom. "Well, in order to speak what's on my mind, I figured I had to." I said as she slithered behind me to close the door. "Yeah, it was a long day. I hate being around you, and can't touch you, or kiss you." she professed while remaining behind me to remove my jacket. "It was a long night, too. You were the topic of conversation, for at least an hour after you left." I acknowledged while watching her seductively walk away with my jacket. "I'm used to being the topic of talk. That doesn't bother me." she nonchalantly disclosed while tossing my jacket on the bench under her window. She looked back at me with a smile and began preparing the room, as she'd done on all of my visits. She "That's funny cause you were the topic of our convo, too." she continued while moving from window to window, to close the blinds. "Me?" I asked concerned about any type of investigation. "Yeah. It was my turn to give details, about the dick I'm getting. You know, girl talk." she cynically divulged while turning away to smile. "Don't worry, I made up a name. Or rather, gave you a nickname." she wisely reassured as she sashayed from the window to the bed. "A nickname?" I said remaining by the door, with my eyes on my jacket. "Yup. Made up a whole story behind it, and everything." she laughed while stretching across to the other side of the bed purposely exposing her plump, ass cheek. I followed her outstretched hand to the television remote. "So, what was my nickname?" I curiously asked as I obtained the remote to assist her. "Thank you. Sonic." she giggled while pressing the remote's buttons to turn off the television. "Sonic?" I asked pretending to scoff. I slowly paced across the dark room contemplating whether to revisit Toni on the bed, or grab my jacket and head for the door. "Yeah, I know right." she naively chuckled as I stopped pace to decide.

CHAPTER 86

"Quentin"

"Good morning." I greeted while advancing through the kitchen toward Imani and my mother. "Good morning, baby." my mom said while pouring apple juice from the carafe into one of the glasses, on the counter. "Hey." Imani gently stated before opening the refrigerator door. "You're about to leave us?" my mom said raising the glass and extending it to me. "Not just yet. In a little bit." I said as I accepted the glass to drink. "You still wanna talk?" I questioned Imani while watching her pull the coffee creamer from the refrigerator. "I sure do." she firmly asserted while pouring creamer into the cup of tea, on the counter. She placed the creamer back into the refrigerator, and retrieved a spoon and large cutting knife from the drying rack, next to the sink. She dropped the spoon into the tea, and placed the knife on the counter. "Here you go, Ms. G." Imani sweetly stated to my mother, while carefully advancing toward her with the cup and saucer. "Thank you, dear." my mom pleasantly countered graciously accepting her tea. "You wanna talk, now? I kinda wanna get on the road before traffic get heavy." I urged while observing my mom and Imani's interaction. "It's uncanny, how you sound so much like your father." my mom alluded to as she cheerfully gawked at me. "Wish you lived like him! Then I wouldn't have to constantly fuss, about you one day being a good husband and father." Imani sarcastically added. "You know what, I take that back. For some reason, I think you gonna be a really good dad." Imani promptly modified while rummaging through her bag which rested on the counter. "I concur. Now, you two go and talk. I'll be in the living room, trying to stay awake during my webinar." my mother informed before exiting the room. "Ok." I said as she swiftly disappeared. "I'll come keep you company in a few, Ms. G." Imani announced loud enough for my mom to hear. "Take your time, dear." she countered from the other room.

"So, let's chat." I suggested as I lifted myself to sit up on the counter. "Not here." she insisted as she snatched her bag and proceeded in the direction of the stairs. "All of this up and down won't be, too much for you?" I plainly asked while hesitantly trailing behind her. "No, I'm good." she confidently asserted while trekking up the stairs. "Ok." I surrendered maintaining pace behind her.

"Question… I was just a fuck the other night, wasn't I?" I stubbornly parroted while extending my hand to catch her moderate stumble on the top step. "Why you keep asking me that?" she seriously solicited after stabilizing herself. "Cause, I never thought that'd be you and me." I sullenly said walking behind her into my bedroom. "We grew up together. We were friends." I continued before closing the door behind me. "You really wanna know?" she questioned while dropping her bag on the bed. "Yeah." I worriedly professed hoping my father was off the mark, in his assumption. "Yes. You were just a fuck, Saturday night." she claimed while turning to look me in the eyes. "So, you was just horny and I coulda been anybody?" I sullenly asked staring into the eyes that used to dance for me. "No! I'm not one of these lost thots, you see out in the street. I came here cause it's you, and this is your child. But yeah, I didn't want Quentin, that night. I wanted Quentin's dick." she nonchalantly answered while her eyes progressively lowered to the floor. "Oh." I solemnly uttered thinking of my father's wisdom. "That next morning was a different story, though." she strangely continued.

"You wanted to talk, let's talk." I frustratedly demanded now wanting to leave in haste. I remained with my back against the door and my hand on the doorknob in anticipation of my opportunity to depart. "All right. Let's talk, because I know you wanna hit the road, to get back *to school.*" she said turning back to the bed, to get her bag. I stood quietly waiting while she returned to the door with her bag on her shoulder. "Since I know how important school is, I'm going to let you go." she said as she advanced so close to me that neither of us could move. Her innocent eyes became full of intent, as her bag slid off of her shoulder, onto the floor. "But you are to go back… to school." she frigidly insisted as I looked down for any mess that may have spilled out of her bag. "Yes. where else would I…" I uttered quickly, before being interrupted but the shine of the knife blade she had adjacent to my front of my neck. "Good. Like I said, I know how important *school* is. And since that's what I wanna believe you're going back to, I'm not going to stop you. You'll go back to school, handle what you gotta handle, and then come back… home." Imani said gently brushing the knife blade against my Adam's apple. Her eyes began to swell with tears, as I held my breath to prevent any accidental cuts to my throat. Seeing my distress in breathing she slowly withdrew the blade from touching me, but kept it neighboring. I slowly raised my hand to wipe the tears forming in her left eye, and then soothingly caressed her shoulder. Moving progressively across her arm, I gently clinched her wrist, and pulled the knifed hand away from my neck. She aggressively snatched her wrist from my hold, and stepped back to collect her bag from the floor. I kept my eyes on her hand as she jammed my mother's large kitchen knife back into her bag. "Now, go ahead before traffic gets too bad. You got finals to get ready for. It's time to get it all, over and done with." she affirmed with a weak smile before grabbing my hand and removing it from the door knob. "Drive safe." she pleasantly stated before standing on her toes, to extend her lips up to kiss me. I pressed my lips against hers, then stepped aside so she could pull open the door. "I thought you wanted, to talk." I reminded while watching her step around me. "We just did." she whispered as she stepped out of the room. "God, I love you." I thought while observing her slowly sauntered down the hall. "I love you too. Always have." she turned and whispered with a wink before continuing on her course.

Reacquainted with her stubbornness and her outwardly intuitive awareness in me, I quickly raced down the hall to catch Imani. She turned toward me startled, upon my approach. I gazed piercingly into her eyes, before flinging my arms around her shoulders and passionately parting her lips with mine. She endorsed my actions with a slight moan, before driving her arms around my waist to pull me closer. "I love you." she quietly whispered between intervals of playful antics, with her tongue. "C'mon." I uttered as I released my hold of her to escort her back into my room. "Uh, uh." she said retaining her tight hold of my waist. "Right here." she demanded before pushing her tongue back into my mouth. I stepped forward backing her against the railing the ran throughout the hallway. She gently retracted her lips from mine before nudging me forward so she could turn her back to me. I surveyed over the railing, down the stairs, for any sign of my mother inadvertently coming to ruin Imani's impulsive pursuits. Imani lifted her hair to uncover her neck, inviting me to place my lips upon her. She whimpered aloud as I affectionately began to run my tongue all over the presumed area. "Here." she said before again pushing me back. This time to bend over just enough to reach down, and pull her dress up enough to uncover her perfectly shaped ass. I excitedly reached down into the front of my sweatpants and pulled out my dick. "Wait! I can't do this. I gotta problem with just fucking you, Mani." I sincerely announced after thinking about her weight in my world. I pushed my dick back into my pants and tried to reposition her dress so it would fall back toward the floor. Imani shoved away my clasp of her dress and caught it before it fell. "You gotta problem with fucking *ya girl*? Really?!" Imani mockingly responded while turning her head back to me with a smile.

CHAPTER 87

"Antoinette"

"Good morning." I said peeking my head into Omar's open office door. "Good morning." he bleakly responded lifting his head up from the computer screen. I turned and put my things down on my desk, before coming back to peek my head in again. "You alright?" I asked after lengthily watching him half-heartedly punch the keys on his keyboard. "I'm good. You?" he asked after pushing away his keyboard, to unwind. I stepped into the room, and closed the door behind me. "I'm ok." I falsely disclosed as I sat down across from him. "That's good." he calmly acknowledged while staring into my eyes. I cut my eyes down into my partially exposed cleavage, to see if his eyes would follow. "You're here, early." I uttered after looking up to see that they didn't. "Yeah. I've been neglecting the things that got me to where I am. I have to redirect my focus, to what's important." he sighed. "So that's why you left me lonely, last night? I'm now outta your circle?" I asked solemnly while slowly standing. "I'm sorry, for that. I had some things one my mind, and the cardinal flesh wasn't one of them." he said setting his sights out of the open window. "Cardinal flesh? You're back to sounding like, the old Omar. The one I fell in lust with, in the first place." I softly chuckled as I made my way towards the door. "Maybe I should take another look at what's floating around, on Indeed." I suggested as I slowly grabbed the doorknob. "That's not necessary. You, as my assistant, are one of the things that got me to where I am." he genuinely declared after pulling the keyboard back close to him. "I know. But it's not about you, Omar. You've made the decision that you feel would best suit the rest of your life. And, it's the right one. But, I gotta do the same. I'm in love with you, and I can't sacrifice my happiness and sanity by watching you go home every night. Knowing it'd never be me, you're coming home to." I sincerely admitted before opening the door. "If that's what you feel you have to do. But know, I'm not encouraging you to leave." he uttered while in agreement of my belief. "I know." I genuinely stated. "Can I tell you something?" he softly asked while moving the mouse to reactivate his screen. "What." I casually responded. 'I love you, too." he said before returning back to his work. "I know that, too." I arrogantly acknowledged before opening the door to leave.

CHAPTER 88

"Quentin"

"Hey." Tasha whispered as she materialized in my bedroom doorway. "Hey." I uttered while looking up from my textbook. "You didn't tell me, you were back." she mournfully attested as she gradually progressed toward my bed. "I'm sorry. I got caught up in studying. Besides, you didn't respond to my last text, I figured you were busy." I mentioned as I turned my book over, and placed it on my lap. "That was yesterday morning! You thought I was too busy, for a day and a half? You were the one that was with, her. Were you that busy that you couldn't shout me out?" she resentfully inquired while sitting at the bottom of my bed. "Any way I answer that, I'll look bad." I scoffed knowing that she was right in her assumption. "You shoulda just stuck with the studying excuse, instead of trying to start." she bluntly recommended. "I wasn't trying to start." I calmly clarified. "Again, were you *busy*?" she openly asked staring at me intensely. "Yeah." I remorsefully disclosed staring back into her eyes. "Gettin' busy?" she astutely questioned with a ruthless scowl. "Yeah, I was." I worriedly repeated. "I already knew you were. Was this before, or after you told me you missed me?" she intuitively queried as tears began to fall from her eyes. "I don't think, that matters." I said genuinely. "Yes, it does." she heartbrokenly stated before turning her face away from me. I rose from the bed and grabbed the box of tissue, from the dresser. "No, it doesn't. If it was before, I shouldn't have told you I missed you. If it was after, I shouldn't have fucked her. Either way…" I lectured while offering her the tissue. "Is that what you did? You *fucked* her?" Tasha skeptically probed while tearing the tissue from my hand. She brushed her eyes with the tissue, smearing her make-up across her face. "No. Feelings were absolutely involved." I sorrowfully admitted while sitting back down on my bed. She stood up quickly and began to hysterically laugh. "You're not upset?" I surprisingly questioned. "Oh, I'm upset, but I expected it. Imani had karma on her side. And if there's anyone out there who would be able to take you from me, it's them two." Tasha recognized while tossing her used tissue onto my bed. "Be that as it may, I'm not okay with it. You and I are tied together, for life" she continued while rubbing her belly to remind of her current state. "So, somewhere down the line, no matter who you're with or who I'm with, we're going to give another go. And we both know it." she logically explained while sliding open the closet door. She reached into the closet and began flinging out sneaker boxes. "What are you doing?" I curiously questioned as boxes wildly landed on the bed around me. "The inevitable." she answered while running her finger down the boxes to read the labels. "What's that mean?" I asked with the hope that she meant what I think she meant. She looked at me with a condescending glare, released a pouting huff, and then turned to continue her course of action. "So, you're ending it?" I sullenly continued, curious for an explanation. "For now. Perfect timing, huh?" she intuitively asked while continuing to dig through my closet. "So, your plan was to come over here, and end us?" I asked with an uncontainable hint of gratification. "No. My intentions were to come over, make my man his dinner, rub his shoulders, and then drain him! But seeing as though that already happened, I'll just take the hint and go. I'm not needed, like she said." she blatantly clarified as she arose from inside of the closet. "But don't stress yourself about it, it wasn't you that ended us. Life, ended us." she continued nonchalantly. "Life?! Life is nothing more than a collection of decisions made, and actions taken. Your words, not mine." I reminded bluntly while watching her open the dresser drawer that she delegated to herself. "You like quoting me, don't you?" she snickered while tossing her things from inside the drawer, onto the bed. "Let's pretend to be true-to-life for a second, Quentin. All fantasies aside. My last final is in a week. A week!" Tasha proudly reminded while looking on the dresser for any of her personal belongings. "Then it's back home to Harleysville, to try and figure out what I'm going to do. I can't come back in the fall, because I'll be about to have a baby." she continued bluntly as she turned to look for an empty spot on the bed to sit in. "And you'll be, who knows where, after you're drafted." she continued pleasantly after pushing boxes away to create a spot. "We might as well just end this now, and go our separate ways, to avoid the bullshit." Tasha sternly said in an attempt to be hard-hearted about the situation. I sat speechless while focusing on her, in unbelieving wonderment. "Besides, she's where your heart is. She's where it's always been." she nonchalantly continued while sorting through the pile she gathered on the bed.

"You finished?!" I harshly asked irritated by her incoherent babbling. "Yeah. What else is there to say?" she softly asked while dumping the contents of the boxes onto the bed. "I don't know? You've been doing a great job of listening to yourself, for the last ten minutes!" I sternly divulged with my head tipped back and my palm running slowly down my face in frustration. "First, and most important... you're carrying my son." I calmly reminded her while trying desperately to maintain my serenity. "That's my legacy! My other reason for living! Why the fuck would you think, you'd not know where am? Or, how to reach me?" I barked as I watched her sort through her things. "I didn't say that. I'm saying *at this point*, we don't know where you'll end up." she softly retorted after looking up at me woefully. "And all of this shit about you not finishing school, that's bullshit. So, let's not go there, either." I sternly said ignoring her wretched expression. "You can't say somewhere down the line, we both know, that we're going to give it another go. And then follow it up with this whole, I'll never see you again vibe! You sound foolish." I continued to snap after recollecting her contradicting statements. "I'll be there. And when I say *there*, I mean in the hospital. In your face. From the day he's born, til the day I die. I'll be there!!" I firmly assured. "Excuse me." I cordially requested as I pulled my legs around her to stand. "Now, if you and I are over, fine. Let's just rip it off like a band aid, and keep it moving." I said while slowly marching to the closet to retrieve the gym bag that Imani bought my last year. "How can you be so nonchalant about this?" Tasha questioned before quickly searching for the tissue she threw onto the bed. "Cause right now, it's a front. I'm going to spend the night in tears, just as you probably will." I openly admitted while leaping over to the dresser to grab her another tissue. "But that's life. That's the decision we made and now, we gotta live with repercussions." I continued while handing her both tissue and the gym bag. "You were able to admit that you were frontin'. You're one up on me." she confessed while wiping the make-up polluted tears that began to stream down her face. "That little speech you gave, was a front. Just wasn't a good one." I acknowledged while watching her begin to pack her things.

"I'm gonna miss you." she said after she finished stuffing her life with me, into a gym bag. "Remind me of that tomorrow, or the next day, and/or the day after that. Or when I see you at the hospital. Or send for my son. Or even visit him, in Harleysville." I realistically said. "That's something else we need to discuss. My son, living in Harleysville. Who the hell lives in Harleysville?" I playfully asked while confiscating the bag from her. "People who move out of, Dover." she replied sarcastically extending her hand for me to usher her rise from the bed.

"Can I take you home?" I asked while continuing to hold her hand well after helping her up. "No. I wanna walk. And, I wanna do that by myself. I got some things to think about, you know." she replied starting to head for the bedroom door. "Yeah, I know." I uttered quietly. "Can I at least walk you, to the door?" I desperately pleaded while following her out of the room. "There's no way I'd let you get away with, not walking me to the door." she said as she increased her pace through the apartment towards the door. I admiringly looked at Tasha slowly stroll through the room. She smiled while stopping to stare at Juice and Dee who were kissing, and had no clue we were even in the room. "Good night, baby" she whispered as we approached the door. "Good night, Tasha." I whispered as tears began to fall from my eye. "C'mere." she demanded. I stepped up as close to her as I could, flinching slightly as she extended her hand to wipe my tear. "Kiss me, like you'll miss me." she insisted as tears again to pour from her eyes. "I miss you already." I confessed as I gently placed her bag at our feet. She stretched her hands around to the back of my head and pulled me in closer. "I love you." she mouthed as her excessively flowing tears, began to trickle onto her shirt. "I love you, too." I said before she violently pushed her tongue into my mouth. I gently sucked on her lips while playfully pursuing her tongue with mine. I felt her grip of me progressively tighten the longer we kissed. "Awwee" Diyonte quietly crooned as we continued to extract our goodbyes. She maintained tightly pulling me in, as I attempted to retract to end prolonged our kiss. "Damn, y'all!" Juice said realizing that our goodnight kiss was a bit extended. Unperturbed by Juice's nosiness Tasha persisted in her kissing endeavors.

"Wow!" I said when she finally released her hold of me. "Sorry, but I'm really gonna miss you. And I had to keep kissing you until taking that bag back in the room, and fucking you, left my thoughts." Tasha enlightened while wiping the tears from her face. "Uh umm." Dee grunted with an enormous smile. "I'm sorry, y'all. I missed my baby." Tasha uttered expressing her misleading regret. I picked up the bag and gently placed it on Tasha's shoulder. "You leaving?" Dee moaned as she kneeled into the sofa to turn to face us. "Yeah. It's about time I get gone." Tasha uttered as she sorrowfully looked into my eyes. "Oh girl. Let me walk you, downstairs." Diyonte requested as she jumped from the chair. "Goodbye, y'all." Tasha solemnly said as she opened the door. "I love you." she quietly whispered again before gently kissing my cheek. I looked down at Juice as he subtly shook his head. "Be right back. Don't lock the door." Dee mumbled while swiftly floating pass me to catch Imani.

"So, that's it? All is right with the world, again?" Juice calmly asked after I gently pushed the door closed. "I don't know if that's it. But yeah, this feels right." I responded with a smirk, while calmly sauntering back to my room.

I pushed the pile of empty shoeboxes onto the floor and stretched out across the bed. "Two kids." I whispered before reaching under my pillow for my phone.

> {Me}
> Hey.

"Professor Mariston's final is gonna whoop my ass." I complained wile frustratedly rubbing my hand across my face. Doink!

> {Mani}
> Didn't kno how much I missed gettin these. Til jus now.
> {Me}
> Missed sending them.
> {Me}
> Just wanted to put all cards on the table.

"How the hell do I tell her this?" I asked myself while struggling to stretch from my bed to my desk to acquire my laptop. RING. RING!
"Hey!" I eagerly pronounced as I answered the call. "What cards?! What'd you do now, Quentin?" Imani harshly asked. "I gave away the bag you bought me." I carefully confessed with a moderate cringe. "What bag?" she curiously questioned. "That big gym bag, the one you bought the last Christmas that we were together." I clarified anxiously. "Who'd you give it to?" Imani firmly interrogated. "All of Tasha's things, were just packed in it. And it was given to her." I nervously continued to confess. "All of her things?!" she sternly probed. "Yes." I tensely answered. "She has nothing else over there?" Imani asked. "Nope." I calmly replied beginning to regret being honest. "No reason to come back?" she skeptically continued to interview. "No." I openly responded. "Good. Let her keep the bag. She can give it to y'all son." Imani cordially suggested. "You ain't mad? I really thought you'd be mad?" I asked hoping to get it out of the way now, so I'm not blindsided later. "And that's our problem, you can be real careless and selfish, sometimes. If you thought it'd make me mad, why would you even do it?" she logically asked. "Damn, I fucked that one up too." I

gloomily stated, disappointed in myself for trying to do, what I thought was the right thing. "I should've just waited for her to bring it up and then just lied about Tasha and the bag." I thought while lifting my laptop open. "No, you just gotta start thinking before you say and do. Your about to be a dad." Imani tutored.

CHAPTER 89

"Tiffany"

"Good morning all" I said cheerfully walking onto the office floor. "Good morning, Tiff." Alicia jubilantly responded as I happily danced past her desk. "You're in a good mood." Eric stated as he entered the office behind me, still carrying his bicycle. "Where you been? Tiff's been this walking on sunshine, for a while. And the closer that football draft gets, the more overjoyed she gets." Alicia answered proudly while looking up at me with a boisterous smile. "Oh, that's right. Your son's about to play professional football." Eric conjured while lowering his bike from his shoulder to push to his cubicle. "God bless him." Tanae complemented as she emerged from inside of Missy's office. "Good morning, extended family." she warmly continued as she quickly approached. RING. RING! "Hey Nae." I courteously expressed before pausing to listen out, for what I thought was my desk phone ringing. "Excuse me y'all." I quickly stated as I hurried to my workspace to catch the call. RING. RING! I scurried through the maze of partitions to my desk. "Hello!" I breathlessly uttered into the phone. "Guess not." I mumbled after recognizing that I had missed the call. "They'll call back." Missy chuckled while resting her arms on the barriers that concealed my workstation.

"Hey Missy." I said after turning to acknowledge her presence. "Hey Tiffany. How was your weekend?" she insincerely inquired reaching down onto my desk to procure one of the picture frames. "Weekend? It's Tuesday, Missy. We were both here yesterday." I confidently informed, contradicting her pathetic inquisition. "It is, isn't it? We were both just so busy yesterday, it must've just gotten away from me." she uttered while pretending to stare at the picture of Quentin. "You know things like that happen, when you start getting old." I mocked while extending my hand to gesture the return of my photograph. "I'm not as old as you think." Missy acknowledged as I physically confiscated the picture to reinstate it back onto my desk. "Such a handsome, and talented young man." she mentioned as I placed it back in its original position. "Thank you." I calmly stated while waiting for her to verbalize the reason she was here. "I don't mean to sound rude. But I have to get ready for your conference call. Is there something, I can help you with?" I politely asked after her stay exceeded the normal amount of time she claimed for her daily annoyance. "Yeah, about that conference call. Some of my bosses, were approached by their bosses, and umm…" she apprehensively uttered "You want access to Quentin?" I sternly asked interrupting her pitiful plea. "Not me personally. The paper does. They want to know if you'd talk to him about giving them, exclusives?" she embarrassingly admitted as she stood straight, relinquishing her laidback stance. "Exclusives? Exclusives, to what?!" I aggressively asked while hanging my jacket on the back of my chair. "Nothing specific. They just want the jump on everyone else in regards to… him, basically." she hesitantly confessed. "That's what this whole conference call is about?" I suspiciously asked as I logged on to my terminal. "I'm not sure. But yeah, probably." she tentatively disclosed. "I knew it was something." I scoffed witnessing Missy's uncomfortable demeanor. "I'll just tell them you can't do it. That your relationship with him is…" she quietly mumbled with the notion of trying to liberate me from any complications. "None of their damn business!" I crossly exclaimed. "Thank you. But I don't need you to tell them anything. I'll tell them myself." I calmly stated to Missy. RING. RING! "Excuse me Missy. I have to take this." I said after looking at my cell phone. "Ok. I'll be in my office if you need me." Missy amiably acknowledged.

RING. RING! "Hello." I anxiously said after seeing Tasha's name on phone ID screen. "Hey Miss. Bromwell." Tasha softly articulated. "Miss. Bromwell? What happened to Grandma T?" I surprisingly asked while watching Missy maneuver her way through the assemblage of workspaces to her office. "I didn't know that was still allowed." she gently stated followed by a faint snivel. "Why wouldn't it…? Oh. I guess he said no to staying with you, until whenever his camp starts?" I intuitively inquired from her sounds surrounding her soft words. "I never got to ask. He went back to Imani." she mournfully uttered. "Oh baby, I'm sorry. But I wouldn't worry about that too much. You found him once, you'll find each other again." I promptly bared to attempt to restore hope. "I really want to believe that." she dreadfully yearned. "You should, it's the truth. He's your Waldo." I desperately said void of anything else to say. "Waldo?" Tasha blankly questioned blatantly showing her age. "I guess you're too young to remember *Where's Waldo*, huh?" I said regretfully, realizing I'd have to explain. "I guess, I am." she uttered now curious of the justification for my reference. "It was a, I don't even know how to describe it. They used to be books, and posters, and pictures. But to make a long story short, he was very unique looking, and almost impossible to find little, cartoon man. And your job was to find him among of hundreds of other cartoon people and chaos. Now, there was only one Waldo on the whole page, of all of these people and things. You just had to work hard to recognize him. But the good thing was, once you found him, you could always find him again." I consoled trying my best to encourage on the fly.

"Thank you for trying, Miss. Bromwell." Tasha stated recognizing my reach to console her melancholy disposition. "That's, Grandma T." I disclosed continuing my effort to pacify. "Thank you, Grandma T." she sincerely amended. "No problem, baby. Just do me a favor and give me prior notice, next time. I need time to prepare a great lecture." I playfully joked. "Ok." Tasha said with a quiet chuckle. "Well, I have to prepare for a meeting that may just cost me, my job. So, I'll call you later?" I earnestly acknowledged as I re-opened the memo informing of the conference call. "You okay?" Tasha genuinely questioned. "I've never felt better in my life, Tasha." I honestly responded while staring at the monitor. "Ok." Tasha stated with conviction. "Bye-bye, Tasha. Wait… have you even thought of a name for him, yet?" I curiously asked wavering my focus between my grandson's mother, and my wording to inform my bosses of the bad news. "Yeah. Quentin Hassan Gregory, Junior. He was conceived by real love. So why would I name him anything, but that?" Tasha proudly and passionately divulged. "I like that name, Tasha. I really do!" I candidly conceded. "Bye-bye Lil Que." I melodiously asserted while smiling uncontrollably. "Bye grandma." Tasha responded happily.

CHAPTER 90

"Hassan"

"It's on my desk, Chloe! You and Justin need to find it, and fix it. Before I get in there, tomorrow!" I callously barked while slicing a strawberry for Jillian's mimosa. "We will, Mr. Worth." she fearfully responded. "See you, tomorrow." I sternly stated before ending the call. I stuffed my phone into the pocket of my robe, placed Jillian's drink atop the tray and carefully carried it upstairs.

"Babe. You gotta do something about this girl, you had me hire. She can't do shit, by herself." I pleaded as I backed into the bedroom door to open it. "I didn't have you hire her. I had you fired that other one, the hoe." Jillian aggressively confirmed before opening her eyes and lifting her head from her pillow. "Aww, thank you!" she pleasantly said after noticing me carrying her breakfast. "What'd you do?" she skeptically asked while sitting up to accept the tray of food. "Is that you first thought? That I did, something? I'm offended." I said before pretending to take back the tray. RING. RING! I sighed while reaching into my pocket to silence my phone. "Damn." I frustratedly exhaled while looking down at the phone ID screen. RING. RING! "Who is it?" Jillian asked noticing my frustration.

> **Worthwhile Architecture**
> **302-555-8448**

I uttered while lifting the phone to flaunt the screen. RING. RING! "Here, give it to me?" she sternly requested while gesturing for me to give her the phone.

"Hello." Jillian said pleasantly while trying to discreetly chew her food. "Ah hah." I teased while pulling back the cover to climb back into bed next to my wife. "Chloe, I'm assuming he left you with the tools and information needed. And if not, Justin is there to assist you. So, what's the problem?" Jillian reminded while taking another bite of her English muffin. I smirked at Jillian trying to handle the incompetence of my new staff, while continuing to peacefully eat her breakfast.

"C'mon Chloe. You and Justin really gotta learn how to function when he's not there! You can't always call him, for every little thing." Jillian sternly advised while using her fork to slice into her omelet. "I wanna see you succeed with him. But his assessments of you right now aren't looking too good, girl." Jillian openly communicated to my incapable assistant.

"Hey. Wake up?" Jills faintly said. I opened my eyes to Jillian's face very close to mine. "Hi." she whispered after noticing my eyes open. She gently shook her head, brushing her nose against mine. "Eskimo kisses." she said with a smile as continued to play.

"C'mon. You gotta wake up." Jillian insisted after receding her face from mine. "No. Why?" I jokingly grumbled while crossing my arms across my face. "Cause, you promised me a day together." she reminded as she grabbed my wrists. "And I'm taking this one, and we're not spending it in bed. So, c'mon!" she exclaimed while tugging my wrists to sit me up. "What's wrong with staying in the bed, all day?" I pouted as she stood looking down on me. "Cause, we stayed in bed all night. Now, get up." she demanded while putting on her bathrobe. I watched intently at my wife, as she aimed her back to me to remove bra. "Why do you do that?" I asked as she bent to push her shorts to the floor. "Do what?" she ignorantly questioned while picking up her attire. "Hide your body, when you taking off your clothes. Like I'm a stranger, or something." I asked genuinely before making my way toward her. "I-I don't know. I think about that, myself." she stammered, startled by my creeping up behind her. I placed my hands on her shoulders and adamantly slipped off her robe. I ushered her robe to the floor and brushed it aside with my foot. "There you go!" I passionately said after stepping back to appreciate the backside of her almost naked body. "Now turn around!" I demanded while continuing to ogle her. She began to somewhat tremble as she turned slowly toward me. "What the fuck?" I whispered watching her struggle transparently to keep her hands from covering the exposed parts of her body. "What's wrong?" I asked sincerely worried about the woman I've been married to for almost two decades. "Told you, I don't know." she softly replied before looking down at her robe. "You weren't like this before. You used to flaunt this body, like it was diamond coated." I assertively divulged while using my finger to push her face back towards me. "Yeah, I know. But I'm older now. Everything's not as firm as it used to be." Jillian apprehensively admitted before returning her attention to the discarded bathrobe. "Are you serious?!" I asked becoming slightly frustrated by her opinion of the woman I said I do to. I tucked my head down into the line of sight between her and the robe and the gestured for her to concentrate on me. "I don't look like I did ten, fifteen years ago, Hassan. And with these thirsty, little, young girls out here looking the way they do. Causing your eyes, and who knows what else, to wander. Yeah! I'm serious. And I really believe, have reason to be." Jillian uneasily asserted while finally staring me in the face. "C'mere." I said seizing her at the waist. "What the fuck makes you think I don't still consider you, sexy?! You're fucking beast!" I sincerely confessed while pulling her closer to me. "News to me. Cause if I was a *fucking beast*, I wouldn't have the feeling in my gut that you're constantly cheating on me." she mournfully disclosed while unwaveringly gazing into my eyes. "You really think, I'm cheating on you?" I solemnly inquired as I slowly released my grasp of her waist. "Yeah, I do." she softly said before dashing to get her robe. "Wow." I astonishingly exclaimed while falling back onto the bed. Even after all of the cheating I've done, I never once felt any remorse about it until just now. "So, if you thought that, why stay around?" I sincerely asked as I watched my beautiful wife put her robe back on. "You don't already know?" she solemnly asked while searching around for her robe belt, to tie it closed. "Not for the life of me." I honestly responded while sitting stock-still. "Cause I really do, love you. And I don't want to believe, that my gut is right." she reasonably admitted while tying her robe's belt. "What if you gut was right?" I asked curious of the consequences. "Are you saying that you cheat, on me?!" Jillian interrogated before she drifted swiftly over to her dresser. "No! I'm just saying anything's possible. And sometimes your gut gives you notions, for a reason. Reasons that your heart tends to block to protect itself." I stated continued to delve into what consequences I may be in for. She reached down to her bottom drawer, opened it, and pulled out a rolled towel. She placed the towel on the dresser and gently began to unroll it. "Well, if my gut was right, I don't know what I'd do. I mean, we've been together through it, this long. I'd probably make my way pass the past. And then promise to kill you slow, if you ever do it again." Jillian said as she picked up one of the two guns that were revealed when the towel was spread. She capably pushed the clip into the gun and drew back the chamber. "What the fuck you doing with those?" I nervously asked while quickly rising from the bed. I stood guardedly observant as Jillian placed the gun back onto the towel, before picking up the other one. "I got these back when my gut first started revealing to me, your foolish tendencies. So, I've had them for a while now." Jillian admitted as she raised the gun and focused precisely through its sights at a spot on the wall. "But since your telling me my gut was wrong, we don't need to even think about it." she said while placing the gun back onto the towel. "Even though your gut was way off, on this one. I'll make the promise anyway, just to cleanse the soul, and reassure the uncertain. From this day forward, I promise to never take *any* part of this marriage for granted." I wholeheartedly assured as I watched her roll the pistols back up into the towel. I gently walked across the room toward her while intently watching her place the rolled towel back into the bottom drawer. "I don't know why, but I believe you." she said as I slithered up toward her and began untying her robe belt. "Good." I mumbled while I pressed my body against hers and slowly kissed her neck. "Oh no, no, no! If I let you stay on this route, we're going to end up back in that bed. And I told you, I want us to go out." she sternly insisted while marginally shoving me backward. "Aww. C'mon, babe!" I pleaded wanting to end our emotional rollercoaster on a high note. "Nope. Besides, we got all night for that." Jillian disclosed as she slipped from between my body, and the dresser, and advanced towards the door. "I guess you do still think I'm sexy." she advocated as she gestured toward the tent that I was pitching in my lounge pants. I looked down at what she was referring to and then looked back up at her with a smile. She threw me a wink, brushed the robe from her shoulders so it would fall to the floor and seductively continued out of the room in just her panties.

CHAPTER 91

"Quentin"

"You miss me, already? I just left you three days ago." I sarcastically teased after answering Juice's call. I slowed my pace down to an effortless jog, to carry on with the conversation. "Yeah. I miss you, 'cause Dee been here since you left! And this shit is driving me crazy. I go to sleep to her, I wake up to her, this shit is too much!" Juice hysterically complained. "Wha'chu talking about? You spend the night with her, all the time." I calmly reminded while trying to hold in my laughter. "A night! At her place! Then I get up, and take my ass home. Now, there's nowhere for me go." he continued to desperately bark. "It can't be that bad. You put up with Tasha, being there." I casually mentioned while looking down at the monitor on the treadmill, for my remaining time. "Tasha could cook! And, she spent her time attached to you, not me! And, when you weren't here, Tasha watched tv, in your room! I didn't come in every night, to housewives of the rich and famous. Or whatever that dumbass shit, is called!" Juice viciously griped. "That's right. The big tv ain't in the front room, no more." I calmly recollected while continuing my now easygoing workout. "No, it it's not!" he harshly declared. "Well, that's on you. Cause I told you to keep it, when I was packing up. You the one that let your pride fuck you over." I harshly reminded. "Whatever man!" he sternly disregarded. "That's what you called me for, to bitch about Dee?" I said with a desire to elevate my workout to the degree I was at before he called. "Man, she using my deodorant!" he desperately exclaimed. I quietly chuckled at Juice's desperate cry for support. "But I called to tell you that you left your leather jacket, and watch here." he continued beginning to re-establish his normal composure. "What watch?" I promptly asked as the treadmill began to beep, notifying me of my remaining three minutes. "The Tag Heuer, with the green face." he straightforwardly replied. "Oh shit! How I leave that? I cleared my whole room." I questioned, confused at how I could leave something so significant. "Cause, it was in the pocket of the jacket, and the jacket was in *my* closet. It's been there so long, we forgot about it." he bluntly explained. "I swore I got everything. Damn!" I said amazed that I'd forgotten anything, as meticulously as I searched while packing. "Yeah, I know. If you want me to send it to you, you gonna have to front me the coins. I'm tapped out." Juice candidly professed followed by a slight chuckle. "Nah, that's cool. I'll be back for a few days next week, for finals. I'll just grip up the jacket then. But the watch, I want you to have that. That's yours." I firmly informed, slightly disappointed by the workout time lost. "I gotta get the most of these last few minutes." I quietly mumbled while altering the machine speed. "Man, I don't want your charity! This is, your watch." Juice proudly exclaimed. "Charity?! I'm giving my brother, my watch. Ain't no charity! You're not some stranger, that I pity. You're my brother, and I'll call you that, the rest of my life! What the fuck you mean, charity?!" I harshly clarified while back to productively training. "Whatever man. I'll just see you next week, we'll hash it out then." Juice nonchalantly stated. "Cool. Tell Dee, I said hi." I sarcastically requested before chuckling loudly. "You laughing at my life?" Juice laughed submitting to his current circumstances. "You laughed at mine." I happily reminded as the treadmill beeped again, signaling the last thirty seconds. "That's cause your shit, was funny. But ok. Payback is a bitch, and I'll see you next week. Good luck in the draft. I'll be watching them, not call your name." Juice playfully threatened. "Til the next time." he continued sincerely. "Til the next time, bro." I said as the treadmill began to reduce speed automatically. I ended the call and walked out the remainder of my time on the machine.

"Hey all." I mumbled while stepping through the door. "Hey baby." my mom pleasantly greeted as I closed the door behind me. "I hope you left gas in the tank. Your mom has a doctor's appointment in the morning." my dad sternly disclosed before standing to approach me. "Speaking of tomorrow's appointment, do you think you can take me?" my mom nervously inquired as I hung my jacket on the coat rack. "Yeah, just wake me up before its time to go." I solemnly requested before proceeding toward the kitchen. "Hey young'n." Hassan said as he rapidly emerged from the kitchen. "Hey Unc." I responded while maneuvering to avoid a collision. "Whoa. Where you going?" he inquired while stopping to turn and catch me. "To get some water, and then I'm getting in the shower. Why? What's wrong?" I questioned as I started to resume my route to the kitchen. "Nothing's wrong. But come check this out first." Hassan replied with a confident smile. "Alight here I come." I said scurrying to the refrigerator to grab a water.

"I don't believe I agreed to this." my dad said as I entered the room. I slowly advanced watching the three of them stand suspiciously around the dining room table. "I do. It's for Que, and you'll do anything for your family. That's why, we love you." my mom said before reaching up to kiss my dad's cheek. "Aww." Hassan sarcastically uttered. "Nigga, get a life." my dad retorted. "What's up?" I said approaching from behind Hassan. "Here." Hassan said exhibiting the stack of garment bags on the table. He lifted the top one, peeked into the zipper, and then passed it to me. They remained fixed watching me, as I put my water down and slowly unzipped the bag. "Oh wow. This is nice!" I energetically exclaimed after unveiling the suit. "Ya boy, did his thing." I continued to happily compliment. "That is, nice!" my mom cheerfully agreed while lifting her phone to take a picture. "Let me see yours, dad." I asked eager to see what my dad will look like next to me. I resumed admiring my suit as my dad reached down and grabbed the garment bag still on the table. "Haas, you got one too?" I queried finally looking at a third garment bag. "Yeah. Go 'head and try it on." Hassan requested as I pivoted the suit to see it from all viewpoints. "Yeah baby, put it on. Let us see your swagger." my mom insisted while continuing to take pictures. "Can't. I just came from the gym, and I stink. I'll throw it on once I get out the shower." I openly admitted before grabbing the bag to put back around the suit. "Alright. Then I'll wait for you, to try mine on." my dad promptly disclosed as he unzipped to revealed is attire. "Ooh baby, yours is nice too." my mom enthusiastically alleged while turning her phone toward my dad. "Damn dad, that is nice." I happily agreed proud to have my dad with me for this life-changing experience. "Yeah, it is!" Hassan willingly declared while smiling at his accomplishment. "It compliments Quentin's suit, nicely." my mom continued said confiscating the suit from my father. RING. RING! "Yeah, it does. And, it stands out, but subtly, like me." my dad declared as my mom aligned the suit up against his chest. "Let's see yours, Haas." my dad requested as my mom raised his arm to extend the suit sleeve against it. "Yeah Haas. Come on, hurry up! I wanna get in the shower, so I can come back and try this on." I said while gently placing the garment bag back across the table. RING. RING! "Well go 'head and get in the shower, and I'll show it to you when you get out." Haas promptly countered as he reached into his pocket to retrieve his phone. "Yeah, hurry up and get in the shower, babe. I want to see you, try it on." my mom insisted while giving the suit back to my dad. "Alright. I'll be right back. And mom, don't post those pics. I don't want nobody to see the suit, until draft night." I requested before dashing up the stairs.

"Uh oh. Look at old school!" I stood on the steps and enthusiastically yelled after spotting my father and uncle parading through the living room. "Come on down, Que. Wha'chu waiting on?!" my aunt Jillian insisted from across the room. "Yeah baby, come on. I'm dying to see you in your suit, too." my mom pleasantly admitted while waving her camera. I sauntered down the remaining steps to join the on-going fashion show. "The pants fit nice." Imani said as she strolled out of the kitchen carrying a bowl of ice-cream. "Hey. How long you been here?" I happily asked after pivoting to greet Imani. "For a while. You were in the shower when I came in." she said before lifting to kiss me. "C'mon. That's how y'all got pregnant, in the first place." Jillian sarcastically affirmed while pulling me away from Imani. I licked my lips to remove the residue of the sweet strawberry ice-cream she'd left with her kiss. "Tuck in your shirt and where's your jacket?!" Jillian sternly asked as she shoved me towards the other room. "And your shoes?" my mom added before she began digging into bags for my box of shoes.

"Here he comes. GQ's man of the year, Quentin Hassan Gregory!" my mom announced as I stepped into the living room, in my suit. "Look at my boy!" my dad eagerly said as he enthusiastically approached my side. "Yo. Your weird ass homie, put in work. This shit is lovely!" my dad announced as he stood with his arm around me, posing for my mom. "Yeah, Haas. He really did do an outstanding job." my mom said while taking photographs of my father and me. "Yeah, this shit did come out first-rate, didn't it?" Hassan concurred while admiring himself in the mirror. "Babe, he did a real nice job. It's durable. No exposed stitching. And that lining, trim arrangement is savage." my aunt Jillian expressed as she stood behind my uncle tugging on his jacket, looking for weak seams. "Wait a minute, now. I told him, how to do the lining. And it is quite adorable, isn't it?" I arrogantly asked as Imani stepped in to take a picture with me and my father.

"Actually, it was my idea to use both baby's sonograms pictures, as lining!" Imani promptly corrected as she pulled my arms around her chest to pose for the picture. "And yes baby, it is *lotion*." she seductively whispered. "Lotion?" my mom asked aloud after overhearing Imani's comment. "It's a young person thing, mom. You wouldn't understand." I quickly clarified as my dad laughed heartily before stepping out of the frame for the next few pictures. "Oh." my mom said on impulse while continuing to take photographs. "Why don't you have the trim on yours?" Imani perceptively asked my uncle. "I let them have that. I just got the same suit, in the solid navy, plain black trim." he nonchalantly explained while still changing poses in the mirror. "It's still sexy though, babe." Jillian encouraged while coming over to get in a picture, with me. "Unc, this was the best look out ever! Thanks." I genuinely praised as my mom handed Imani her phone so that she could get into the picture with aunt Jillian and me. "Yeah. Seriously Haas, good looking out. What I owe him?" my dad again inquired after stripping off his jacket. "I told you about that money shit before, man. You ain't the only one with capital. This is for my nephew. I'm just as proud of him, as you are." my uncle Hassan sternly answered. "You're right. And thanks." my dad retorted before heading to the dining room to remove the rest of his suit. My mom promptly followed, in case my dad needed help of any kind. "Alright. Now that they're outta the room, what the fuck is lotion?" my uncle asked while removing his jacket. I looked down at Imani and then uneasily at my aunt Jillian. "Don't look at her. Nigga you grown! And we obviously can see you fucking, so…" Hassan blatantly affirmed. "Don't look at me, I was trying to figure out what it meant too." Jillian warmly agreed. "What does lotion do? It moisturizes. So, if something is sexy enough to keep her moist, it's called lotion." I nervously explained while scrutinizing my aunt's facial expression for an indication of her mood. "I like that!" Hassan excitedly confessed as he stood in the mirror mouthing the word. "You would! And it's not about him being grown or having sex. We raised that boy to have respect, and he was showing it! Now, go take that suit off, so that we can get going." Jillian sternly stated before grasping my uncle's original attire.

"Hey Grammy!" I exclaimed with my mouth muffled by a bunch of lettuce. "Hi baby. How are you?" Grammy energetically questioned, the same way she always does. "I'm fine. Did you get the pics, that I sent you?" I eagerly queried after swallowing my salad. "Yeah baby, I got'em. You look so nice, in your suit. And I love that you got the babies with you. Where are you guys going, looking all sharp to the tee?" she asked merrily. "Those are the suits for Friday night. We were just making sure they fit right. So, Hassan's friend could fix'em, if they didn't. But wait til you see me with the shirt and tie on, with it! I'mma kill'em, Grammy." I excitedly interpreted. "I'm gonna ask you the same thing I asked your father. Are you prepared for the possibility of you going… on Thursday?" my grandmother seriously asked. "Nah. They only do the first round, on Thursday night." I willingly communicated. "I know!" she immediately admitted. "I'm good, but the masses don't see me as good enough to be, first round material. Not with the Alabama's and Ohio State's and all those other cats, out there. I'm going to have to work my way up through the league ranks. And that's exactly what I'll do. I'm gonna Tom Brady the sh-, *the mess*, outta that league!" I passionately explained to my grandmother. "You coming down, on Friday?" I spiritedly asked, eager to see my grandmother. "No baby. I wanna see this on tv! If I'm there with you, I'm your Grammy. But, if I'm watching it on tv, all excited, jumping up and down, and yelling at the screen... I'm a fan. And if I was coming to see them draft you, I'd come on Thursday!" my grandmother vivaciously explained. "At least I know I got one fan out there, rooting for me." I sincerely proclaimed before stuffing the fork of food back into my mouth. "Baby, I've been your fan since the day you were born!" she quickly clarified. "I wish Pop-pop was her here, with me." I solemnly announced. "He is baby. He really is." she devotedly countered. "Alright Grammy. I love you but I gotta salad, to finish. So, I'll talk to you, later." I requested authentically. "Yeah, and I got fish to fry. I love you, baby." she pleasantly replied. "I love you too, Grammy. Bye." I said tenderly to my grandmother. "Bye-bye, baby." she quietly said before ending the call.

CHAPTER 92

"Omar"

"Just think, in two days, I'll know what team defense I'll be picking in my fantasy league." Hassan stated while reaching for a pool stick. "Yeah. I know. I never thought we'd be in a position like this. I just wanted the boy to grow up to be something. Never expected, all this." I honestly admitted while collecting the balls into the triangle. "I did, I ain't gonna lie. Ever since that first church league football game." he divulged before taking a drink from his glass. "Yeah. I am pissed, I missed that game. Especially since, I don't even remember why. I just know it had something to do with, work." I shamefully disclosed. "Pop saw something special in that boy, and signed him up as soon as he was old enough." I sullenly continued. "He wasn't wrong, he caught three touchdown passes in that game. Me and pop was in that crowd going crazy." Hassan proudly disclosed. "I know. They called me, as soon as they got home." I revealed while looking around the room for my drink. "Yeah. Pops was proud. He kept saying, he move like Quincy, that boy run just like Quincy did." Hassan exposed as he set to take his shot. "Can you imagine if he was still here?" I bleakly questioned while watching the balls glide quickly across the table. "Well I guess you can't, being married to his girl, and all." I sarcastically mocked as I continued to survey the room. "You got jokes. That's why I'm not gonna tell you, where you put your drink." Hassan responded while circling the table for his next shot. "I told you even before they met, that she was gonna be mine. So, if I was to be accurate with it… he was messing with, my girl. And it ain't like I smutted her, I married her." Hassan said, firmly defending his relationship with his wife. "I know you love Jill, man. I was just fucking with you." I laughingly apologized as I spotted my drink across the room.

"What if I told you I stopped doing Jills dirty? What would say?" Hassan asked while slowly raising the television volume. "Honestly. I would say I heard this shit from you, before." I candidly admitted before taking a gulp of my drink. "See! That's what I said, when I said it to myself." Hassan sincerely professed. "Why're you trying to stop, this time?" I realistically asked based on Hassan's history. "I know. There always a reason, right? But this time, I promised her that I would." Hassan passionately confessed while gesturing for me to take my shot. "Oh shit! You never did that, before." I said staring in amazement. "Yeah, I know." he uttered as I prepared to take my shot. "You know what else, I never did? Broke a promise to her. I fucked up my vows and promises to God, but never once to her." Hassan perplexedly admitted before going to refill his drink. "Wow. That's deep. Guess you gotta stop, can't turn back now." I sincerely said as I continued to shoot.

"What if told you I did Tra dirty?" I asked while signaling for him to take his turn. "I wouldn't believe it. Not because you wouldn't do it, but because you can't hide nothing from me." Hassan arrogantly replied while bending to shoot. "Well, I did." I honestly admitted. "You mean that shit with, Cricket? That shit, don't count. That was, Cricket! That's shit is like, once every ten years." Hassan profoundly overruled. I scanned up the stairs to be sure that we were still home alone. "For the last three plus months, I've been fucking, Toni." I quietly disclosed after pondering intently. "What?!" Hassan excitedly exclaimed. "Yup. I was bustin' her ass, at the least, twice a week." I smugly confessed before finishing off the last gulp of my glass. "When the fu-? How the fu-? You bullshittin'." Hassan skeptically muttered as he slammed down his last swig and passed his glass to me to refill, as well. "Look at my face. Do I look like, I'm bullshittin'?" I said staring him in the eyes before accepting his glass. "When the fuck you start that?!" he enthusiastically asked forfeiting the game by tossing his pool stick on the table. "Right after, Cricket. I was real fucked in the head, about that baby shit. And she was the only one listening. The only one, I could talk to. And shit just jumped off from there." I confessed while filling the two glasses with brandy. "She knew what, she was doing." Hassan quickly recognized as he approached the bar to sit. "Yeah. She had that whole shit, planned." I drearily said recalling the moment it all went amiss. "How the fuck you get away with that, without me knowing?!" Hassan arrogantly questioned. "You don't know everything, man. Some shit I keep to myself. That way if I go down, you don't go down too." I earnestly confessed as I came from behind the bar, to sit down next to him. "Nigga we going down, together! Blood or not, we all we got!" Hassan sternly reminded while raising his glass to toast. I raised my glass and gently crashed it against his. "That's why she put in her notice?" he calmly queried. "Yup. She put it in, the moment I ended it." I serenely divulged. "So, how was she?" he curiously questioned. "Exactly how, she looks like she would be." I honestly admitted while trying to be discreet with my stupidity.

"So, tell me about this promise to Jills. What brought it about? Cause you been doing dirt, since day one. Just keeping it authentic." I curiously probed after I pushed down another gulp. "She said her gut told her, that I was cheating." he mumbled before taking another sip. "Her gut? Well, her gut is seventeen years too late with it." I ironically stated. "Her gut also told her to go out and buy two pink handle, thirty-eight revolvers." he candidly disclosed. "Oh shit!" I quietly exclaimed. "Yeah!" he coincided. "So, you promised her, to keep her from shooting your ass." I intuitively inquired after taking my last gulp. "Nope. I was already in the clear. You know me, I give speeches. I speak until I'm believed and then, it's back to my bullshit." Hassan candidly acknowledged while watching me slam my glass down upside down. "Yeah. That's you. So, why'd you promise her?" I curiously asked as Hassan turned his glass upside down as well. "Because, it's time. Ya know?" Hassan genuinely asserted. "Yeah, yeah, I do." I honestly agreed.

2-1-5-5-5-5-9-7-1-1. "Hi Omar! I'm so happy that you called! I'm so excited!" Tiffany animatedly exclaimed after answering the call. "Hello Tiffany." I calmly responded before blowing to cool my coffee. "Hi Tiff!" Tracey enthusiastically yelled from across the kitchen. "Hey Tracey. How you doing?! You ready?!" Tiffany shouted back. "She said hi, babe." I casually informed before grasping my mug and leaving the room. "I don't know why I thought I had to call, and remind you." I said as I carefully carried my cup into the living room, with Tracey trailing with her watering can. "I don't know either. I'm partying all three nights. Even though I really think he's gonna go, tonight." Tiffany enthusiastically divulged. "You think so?" I asked while watching Tracey maneuver to water the plants. "Yeah. It may be later tonight, but I think it'll be tonight. I like either Green Bay at twenty-two or Seattle at twenty-eight." Tiffany instinctively proclaimed. "Wow. You've been doing your homework." I said impressed by her knowledge. "Babe, she having a party tonight, tomorrow and Saturday!" I disclosed as Tracey approached to water the rubber tree plants potted, near me. I gestured for her to give me the can and rose to accept it. "Maybe we should go to Philly, for a while?" Tracey joked while watching me water my favorite plants. "Well, I'm just calling around, to remind everybody." I said to Tiffany while smiling at Tracey's joke. "Wait! Has he called you?" I curiously asked while continuing to water my last plant. "I spoke to him twice, last week. He called to tell me that he and Imani were back together.

And then, to wish me Happy Birthday. At least one person remembered." she sarcastically criticized as I returned the can to Tracey. "Yeah me, who you think told him to call!" I firmly acknowledged as I sat back down to my coffee. "I'm just messing with you, Omar." she quickly confessed. "I know the husband rules. With that being said, you only have about thirty more seconds, on this call." she realistically disclosed before laughing cynically. "Well I'm glad you know." I thankfully responded. "Until tonight, then." I calmly continued. "Bye Omar." she gracefully said. "Good day, Tiffany." I charmingly responded after watching Tracey return to the kitchen to refill her can. "It damn sure is!" she passionately whispered before ending the call.

"God damn!" Hassan astonishingly yelled as he stepped into the house. "Yeah, I know. They done turned my damn house into a fucking, movie studio." I agreed as I approached to greet him. "I see." he continued forcefully. "Your son is about to join the elite, and your complaining about a few cameras?" Tracey said as she came to welcome Hassan. "Hey Haas." she softly continued. "Hey Teach." he said bending slightly to kiss my wife's cheek. "Where's Jills?" she asked rubbernecking at the door behind him. "Still at the hairdresser." he disclosed as he surveyed all of the equipment. "This shit is wild, man." he continued after assessing everything. "Tell me about it! It's like fourteen cameras, ten microphones, a partridge, and a pear tree, in here." I grumbled while heading into the dining room. "They need all of that?" Hassan inquired while following me into the room. "This is the set-up that the guys from network came, and put together. Why are y'all complaining? It's for, Quentin!" Tracey pleasantly inquired while sitting down at the table. "Because, when you watch the shit on tv, it's eleven seconds of air time, from one outta focus angle and I don't ever remember, hearing them. At least not clearly." I distinctly described while pulling out a chair to sit. "He's not wrong, Teach." Hassan uttered from across the table. "Dad, you still complaining?" Emily said as she skipped down the stairs. "Hey Unc." Emily said as she maneuvered around the table to embrace Hassan. "Hey baby girl." Hassan pronounced while raising his arms to hug Emily. "Oh, I didn't tell you, that one of them ESPN niggas try to seize my daughter, in my fucking house!" I announced after seeing Emily sparked the thought. Emily began to laugh at my fury, which caused Hassan laughed the entire situation. "That shit is funny?" I asked irritated at the disrespect. "Yeah!" Hassan openly replied. "Was he cute." he continued to interrogate Emily. "Unc. I'm try'na tell you. And, he works for ESPN. What?!" Emily excitedly responded before slowly walking around the table toward me. I looked over at Tracey, who was shaking her head, and smiling. "Em, get away from me." I said as she lowered to kiss my cheek.

"Where's the golden boy?" Hassan said as he came back to the table eating a bag of microwave popcorn. "I don't know. That last time I saw him, was this morning. When he was leaving with you two, to get your haircuts." Tracey admitted gesturing for some of Hassan's snack. "He went to find something to wear." I disclosed now mulling over what I'd like to snack on. "Didn't he just do that?!" Hassan sternly queried. "Apparently, that's for tonight." I calmly divulged. "Now, he's thinking he needs something for Saturday night." I bewilderedly continued. "They don't even film the player on Saturday night!" Hassan promptly affirmed. "I tried to tell him." I disclosed as Emily came back down the stairs. "Speaking of stupid." Emily said as Tracey's car pulled into the driveway with the music piercingly blaring. "Omar, I'm going to need him to stop playing my radio that loud. He may bust one of my speakers." Tracey pleasantly requested while stretching to glance out of the window. "Then tell him, babe!" I sternly demanded before rising to go into the kitchen.

"Hey, pop." Quentin muttered as I reached into the cabinet for my cookies. "Hey, Que." I said pulling down my hidden box of vanilla wafers. "Save me some." he requested while walking past me with a handful of bags. I followed him out of the kitchen, and into the dining room. "Nigga, cut it out with the radio, before you bust her speakers." Hassan cried out as we entered the room. "That, was easy. Y'all make things, so complicated." he arrogantly continued while munching on popcorn. "Ohhh kay. What did I walk in on?" Quentin unsurely queried. "Nothing baby." Tracey swiftly assured before gesturing for my box of cookies. "Here." Quentin said to Emily while extending one of the bags he was carrying toward her. She lifted her face from her phone and came over to accept the bag. "Why y'all in here?" Quentin suspiciously inquired as he placed his bags on the table. "I don't know about them, but I'm scared to go in there. I don't wanna fuck up, that arrangement." Hassan sarcastically mocked while licking the salted popcorn butter from his fingers. "What arrangement?" Quentin curiously asked as he tried peeked into the living room. "What's this for?" Emily asked Quentin as she displayed the contents of the bag. "I don't want you making me, look bad." he answered while advancing towards the living room. "Look bad? My daughter hasn't look bad a day in her life!" I asserted while confiscating my box of cookies from Tracey's clutch. I continued to follow Quentin, into the living room. "Damn." Quentin calmly said after observing all of the gadgets that were geared up to broadcast, his big night.

"How come nobody told me, we were wearing our Penn State gear?" Jillian complained as I moseyed down the steps. "Because tonight's really not that big of a deal. It's tomorrow night, that we'll show our asses." I informed as I approached her at the table. "How you know?" Hassan skeptically questioned while dancing his way in from the living room. "They got him going early, to mid second round. Them experts and analysts don't usually be that far off, when it comes to shit like this." I communicated as I snatched a baby carrot from the table. "We'll see." Hassan retorted before he began singing to the music that Emily was playing in the living room. "She wanna fuck, and I say church…" he sang before following my lead of stealing from the veggie tray. "Where the words?" I curiously asked after freezing to intensely analyze the music. "Em, I mean Storm, is in there performing for the cameras. "What?" I perplexedly asked while crunching on my second carrot. "Look!" Hassan demanded while pointing into the living room. "I'm photo shoot ready, looking like sexy. Calling paparazzi to tell'em where they can catch me." Emily melodiously barked into the cameras, positioned for the upcoming announcement. We stood in threshold between the living and dining rooms, and watched Emily continue performing. "You heard the rumors, now you wanna test the skills? I'm not hard, cause I'm dressed to kill? With my soldiers. Yes we all car-essing steel, and stay ballin' like tes-ticles? You stressed for real!" Emily harshly delivered in conjunction with the scene setting music. "Not bad." Hassan uttered impressed by Emily's routine. "I told you, she was nice." I recapped to Hassan before turning to check on Tracey in the kitchen.

"You alright, in here?" I asked after entering the kitchen. "I'm fine, babe. Has Quentin come down yet?" she pleasantly inquired while finalizing her fruit tray. "No, not yet." I answered before opening the refrigerator for something to eat. "What're you looking for?!" Tracey sternly asked. "Something to eat!" I despairingly answered while rummaging around inside the fridge. "Get out of there!" Tracey demanded while pushing the refrigerator door closed. "Carry this into dining room for me, please?" she requested while gesturing toward the fruit tray. "Babe, I'm hungry!" I complained as I grabbed the tray. "Here munch on this." she insisted jamming a pizza roll into my mouth before leading me out of the kitchen. "Pizza rolls?" I inaudibly queried while chewing vigorously. "His favorite food!" Tracey enthusiastically reminded while pointing for me to put the tray upon the table.

"It's starting!" Hassan yelled before turning up the volume on the tv. "Where's Que?!" I excitedly questioned before darting up the stairs. I peeked my head into the kitchen and then scurried into the living room. "Calm down Omar. He's up in his bedroom. He'll be down shortly." Tracey pledged as I frantically passed her for the second time. "You do know he can't come down there, with you guys. He has to be up here, in front of the cameras, just in case." she endured "I keep telling y'all they're not showing the second round, until tomorrow." I echoed before turning to head back down into the den. "We can't be down here. The cameras are up there!" Hassan inadvertently repeated as he came barreling up the stairs followed by Jillian and then Emily. "That's what I was just telling Tracey." I joked before kissing her cheek.

"Wheeewwww! Look at you!" Tracey bellowed after being the first one to spot Quentin, come down the stairs. "Aww shit, now!" Jillian followed after standing to applaud. I confusedly looked at Quentin, then Hassan, then Emily and then finally back at Quentin. "What y'all cheering for? He ain't impressing nothing, yet. He's still a college drop-out, in a Penn State sweat suit. Can we wait til it's over?" Emily sarcastically asserted what both Hassan and I were thinking. "Don't mind your sister. That's her way of saying, she loves you." Tracey disclosed as she followed Quentin into the living room. "I'm not paying her, no mind." he nonchalantly responded as he entered the room. "Where's Imani?" he said pivoting to survey the house. "She hasn't gotten here yet. You haven't talked to her?" Jillian said before sitting down on the arm of the sofa. "No! She shoulda, been here!" Quentin anxiously answered before pulling out his phone. "They're about to call the first pick, so she better, hurry up." Hassan uttered as he turned his focus onto the television.

"The biggest night of my life, and I can't find my girl." Quentin said pacing across the living room. "You know they watching you do this shit on camera, right?" Hassan sternly mentioned. "Sit down. Chill. I'm sure she's fine." I reassured Quentin while rising to escort him back into his seat. "It's fine. They'll just think, he's anxious to get drafted." Tracey comforted as she extended her hand for him to hold. "I ain't worried about what these people think. I'm thinking about, my daughter!" Quentin rationally revealed before looming to stand again.

[Roger Goodell]
With the sixth pick in the 2020 NFL draft...
the Detroit Lions select, Brian Leithler the third, Safety, Penn State

"Damn, he went six!" Quentin uttered with a respecting smile. "One of your teammates, Que-tee." Tracey excitedly touched upon as we all stared at the television. "That was her der dude, wasn't it?" I intuitively asked assessing all of the information Quentin has given over the last few months. "Yup." he casually stated with his head in his hands. "Who's dude?" Jillian quietly asked after tapping my arm. "That was Tasha's boyfriend, before her and Quentin started their thing." I coolly answered.

"It didn't happen yet, did it?!" Imani zealously solicited as she came crashing through the front door. She ran over to Quentin, who stood to give her the leeway to jump into his arms. "Where you been?" Quentin anxiously asked as he quickly released her concerned by her pregnancy. "Did they call you, yet?" she restlessly inquired with her arms still around Quentin. "Too many questions. Too many questions! No, to you. And you'll find out later." Haas firmly stated to Imani and Quentin respectively as he stood to push them both onto the sofa.

"J.T. went sixth." Quentin quietly informed Imani as he happily massaged his hand across her belly. "The crazy white boy? Tasha's boyfriend." Imani probed taken aback. "Yup." Quentin answered relieved by her presence. "Wow. But you said he was good, so I'm not that surprised. What number are they on now?" she keenly inquired while tossing her leg atop his. "Nine. So, what happened? Why you get here so late?" Quentin softly questioned while maintaining her belly rub. "I had to get a ride to get Ms. Grier, from the shop." she softly responded. "Why was the car in the shop?!" I asked acutely, harshly interrupting their little question and answer session. "It was cutting off on me." she timidly admitted. "Why didn't you say, anything?" I promptly asked. "Dad, I got this." Quentin strictly notified. "Why didn't you tell me?" Quentin tenderly asked. "Cause, y'all had so much going on, I didn't want to add anything more on your plate." Imani openly admitted looking at Quentin and then me. "That's my little girl. There will never so much on my plate, that I can't take care of her." Quentin said gesturing down to Imani's belly. I nodded my head, as my son looked up at me for approval. "So, what did they say was wrong with the car?" I concernedly asked leaning in to quietly speak. "It wouldn't stop talking, during the draft!" Hassan sarcastically emphasized. "Don't mind him." I laughingly ordered while snubbing off Hassan. "The first the guy, said it was the ignition relay. And then the second mechanic came in, and said it was dirty spark plugs. He cleaned them and then said I needed to get new... inner tank seals? So, it wouldn't happen again." she explicitly clarified "So, he replaced the intake valves and seals?" I curiously asked.

"Yeah, that's it. Intake valve seals." Imani confidently confirmed. "Did he ever re-check the, ignition relay?" I seriously asked, concerned with her mechanic's knowledge. "I think they did, I'm not sure. But it didn't act up on me, coming back from the shop." Imani confidently affirmed.

[Roger Goodell]
With the thirteenth pick in the 2020 NFL draft…
the San Francisco Forty-Niners select, Deshlen
Hex, Wide Receiver, Ohio State

"We're getting closer. How did they say this whole thing works?" Jillian sensibly asked while returning with a small plate of vegetables. "I'll get a call from the head coach of the team, that wants to draft me. While I'm on the phone, they cut on the cameras and microphones and stuff. Then they announce it and show us on tv." Quentin acknowledged while staring closely at the television. "Here babe." Imani said as she approached him holding a large plate of pizza rolls and two bottles of water. "Is this enough?" Tracey compassionately asked while moving towards me, exhibiting a plate of food. "Yeah. Why are you up, getting my food? I can get my own food. You sit, and rest." I cordially demanded while accepting the plate. "Ok. Next time, I'll sit and rest." Tracey sarcastically retorted before stealing a broccoli stalk from my plate and returning to the other end of the room. RING. RING!

Smiles erupted through the room and everyone's eyes widened before intently focusing on the glow of Quentin's phone screen. "The Eagles are up, next! Please God, let that be Dougie Pete." Hassan excitedly prayed before Quentin could lean in and legibly read the screen. RING. RING! "False alarm! It's the mistress." Imani indignantly conveyed after looking down at the phone screen alongside Quentin.

"What do she want?" Quentin mumbled before answering the call. "Hello." he grumbled into the phone as we all converged on him and his call. "Huh?" he uttered perplexedly. "Yes ma'am." he said uncertainly. "No ma'am, I was not aware." he inexplicably continued. "Ask him, what's wrong?" I nervously whispered after leaning to tap Imani. Quentin raised his finger to signify one minute, and then rose to leave the room. "What the hell is going on, with this broad?" Hassan asked harshly as Quentin left the room. "I knew she was going try to somehow interfere in his day." Imani sullenly whispered while glowering at Quentin, pacing in the other room. "Just scandalous." Jillian sternly proclaimed. "Ok everybody. Let's find out if she's okay, before we start with the name calling." Tracey gently insisted.

"Tasha's in an ambulance on her way, to the hospital. She's bleeding like crazy, and they don't know why. Tiffany's on her way there, to meet her." Quentin solemnly explained while being followed back into the room by Emily. "Damn." he sighed as he fell back down onto the sofa. "What're you going to do?" Hassan asked before I could. "I don't know." Quentin hopelessly disclosed while resting his head on the back of the sofa. "I'm sorry, baby." Tracey quietly stated while running her arm across the back of the chair to massage atop his head. "Yeah, me too. I wouldn't wish this on anyone." Jillian somberly endorsed. "Son, if you wanna go to Philly, to check up on things? Go! This is your child, we're talking about." I genuinely advised. "For real! The NFL ain't going, nowhere!" Hassan stated in accord. I watched powerlessly, as tears began to pour from my son's eyes, on what was supposed to be the happiest day of his life. "Quentin... go! Everything else will take care of, itself." I seriously insisted. "I wouldn't hate you, if you wanted to go to Philly?" Imani gently declared before laying her head on Quentin's chest. "You wouldn't?" Quentin quietly asked after apparently making up his mind to go. "No. It's for your son. I already thought through these things, before I took you back." Imani whispered gallantly. "You want me to go, with you?" I devotedly inquired after rising to prepare myself to leave. "Nah, you stay here, in case mom goes into labor. You can't be that far away from her" Quentin logically advised after kissing Imani's forehead and nudging her to rise so that he could stand. "You want me to take, you?" Hassan nobly queried looking up at Quentin and I, from his favorite chair in my house. "Nah. I'm good, Unc. Y'all stay here, and finish watching the draft. I'll need everything to look good on the camera, for me." Quentin dismally jested before leaving the room. "Shit, we forgot about the draft." Jillian said spiritedly while gesturing for Imani to pass her Quentin's plate of pizza rolls. "No, *we* didn't." Quentin promptly announced while re-entering the room. "What if they call to draft you, while you gone?" Emily sensibly asked before sitting in my chair. "I wasn't pegged to go tonight, but even if by some chance that I do, I got my phone." Quentin said as he stood over Imani to usher her up from the couch. "I'll be back." he said quietly before pulling her in to hug her. "I know you'll be back, be good." she responded in an excessive clinch. "I'll be better than good, I'll be yours." Quentin uttered before leaning down to kiss a mother of his unborn child. "C'mon man. Go ahead so you can get back." I said while advancing to the door to escort him out. "I'll be back, mom." Quentin murmured while leaning down to kiss Tracey's cheek. "Alright aunt Jills. Unc. Headache. I'll see y'all when I get back." he expressed while waving to everyone else in the room. "I've been waiting for what seems like my whole life to get here. Am I now, walking away from it?" he pessimistically questioned as he approached me, at the door. "Don't worry, I'll have them wait for you." I encouragingly joked as I opened the door.

[Roger Goodell]
With the twenty-second pick in the 2020 NFL draft…
the Green Bay Packers select, Michael
Arin, Offensive Tackle, Oregon

"There goes Tiffany's guess." I mumbled as I diligently continued to watch the draft. "I'd have thought, he'd have called by now. Call him Omee." Tracey solemnly requested while sliding her fingers across the game on her phone. "Babe, you have your phone, in your hand." I calmly asserted. "Tiffany thought he was going to be drafted, by the Packers?" Jillian questioned obliviously. "Either the Packers at twenty-two or the Seahawks at twenty-eight." I detailed while opening my bottle of beer. "Good picks. They both need help at linebacker." Hassan uttered while gesturing for my bottle opener. "Yeah, I know." I agreed as I tossed him the opener. "She said, twenty-eight? So, he still has a chance, right?" Jillian purposefully asked determined to gain detailed knowledge of what's going on. "I hope he doesn't get drafted tonight. I want him to hear his name called." Imani said lying curled on the couch. "Me too. And I would like to see him in his suit, when they call it." Tracey avidly added. "Didn't he say, Tiffany was going to the hospital?" Hassan observantly questioned while bowling the bottle opener back across the carpet, to me. "He did, didn't he? Call Tiffany, Omar! Let's see what she knows, about all of this." Tracey demanded staring at me intensely. I glanced over at Hassan, who was snickering at me sigh, as I pulled my phone out of my pocket.

2-1-5-5-5-5-9-7-1-1. "Hello Omar. I was just about to call you." Tiffany pleasantly stated. "So, what's going on?" I impatiently asked as Emily raised the remote to lower the television volume. "They believe it's a mild placenta abruption. But she's about to be examined, so they know for sure." Tiffany openly illuminated. "The word mild sounds soothing, but the rest of that shit sounds serious." I fearfully admitted while stressfully lowering my head and pinching the bridge of my nose. "What is it, Omar?" Tracey nervously inquired after coming to stand over me. I glanced up as Jillian and Hassan rose from their seats, as well. "A mild placenter abruption." I naively replied standing to join them. "Should we be worried?" I openly probed as everyone readied to leave, if necessary. "Not until one of us calls you back. Oh yeah, ummm, I did just speak to Que. And he said, he's about thirty minutes away. We should know something, by then. Until then, stay calm and watch the draft for me." Tiffany sincerely requested. "Ok. We'll wait for your call." I said gesturing for everyone to relax. "Ok." Tiffany gently responded. "Thanks for your help, Tiffany." I gratefully stated. "Just trying to catch up to you, O." she answered before ending the call.

RING. RING!

{Tiffany Lane}
215-555-9711

"Hey Tiff. What's the word?" I nervously asked after answering the call. "They were right, it's a mild placenta abruption." she calmly reported. "Ok. So, what're they going to do?" I curiously asked before pressing to activate the speakerphone. "Since she's not too far from being full term, they're going to keep her here in the hospital. They just wanna make sure that she doesn't start bleeding again, and that the baby's getting enough oxygen and nutrients. But as of right now, the baby's fine. He's stable, and his heart rate is normal." Tiffany gladly bared for all to hear. "That's so great." Tracey merrily stated. "God is good!" Jillian graciously said. "All the time!" Tiffany automatically responded. "How's Quentin dealing with it all?" I asked in regards to my son's mental well-being. "He doesn't know, as of yet. He hasn't gotten here for me to tell him, nor is he answering his phone. That's why I thought, to call you. In case, you've spoken to him." Tiffany calmly disclosed. "Why hasn't he gotten there yet, Omar?" Tracey yelped as Imani hurriedly extracted her phone to call him. "I don't know. But let me call around to find out, what I can find out." I self-confidently requested. "He's not answering." Imani worriedly said before searching her phone for any texts or social media posts. "Tiffany, I'll call you back." I sharply stated. "Alright. I'll have him call y'all, as soon as he shows up. If, you don't get a hold of him beforehand." she promptly countered. "Ok." I immediately uttered. "Omar, wait! If he's not answering his phone, what happens if the league calls to draft him?" Tiffany realistically asked. "Oh, don't worry about that. That phone call, video from home arrangement, is just something for the fans. If a team wants him, they're drafting him. Phone call, or not!" Hassan confidently answered before picking up his phone to join in the search. "I just don't want him, to forego his dream." Tiffany sullenly said. "None of us do." I said before ending the call.

"Hey mama." Hassan said prior to leaving the room. "I just hung up with her." Emily said while passing Hassan to re-enter the room. "I'm starting to get scared." Imani said while frantically resuming her calls to his phone.

2-1-5-5-5-5-9-7-1-1. "Hello. O..." Tiffany started casually. "When was the last time you heard from Quentin?" I abruptly interrupted. "When I told you he said, he was about thirty minutes out. That was... wow, an hour and a half ago." Tiffany divulged oblivious to what was going on outside of the hospital. "Where was he, when you spoke to him?" I calmly asked, especially trying to maintain my composure. "He was about to merge onto four seventy-six." Tiffany responded slightly more agitated. "He shoulda been there, a looong time ago." I severely notified. "The last time she heard from him was an hour and a half ago, and he was just getting on four, seventy-six." I echoed to everyone as they stared at me for information. "I'm about to head up there." Hassan feverishly asserted before forcefully standing to leave. "Wait. Before you guys do anything, I'll go. I'll backtrack four, seventy-six and a part of two, oh, two, and see if I can find him. It'll be a whole lot faster, than you guys coming up here. I'll call you from the road!" Tiffany said before sprinting out of the call. "She's going to ride along his route, to see if she can find him." I disclosed to before sitting on the sofa between Tracey and Imani. "Maybe the car cut off on him." Jillian proposed as she sat on the arm of the chair next to Imani to massage her shoulders. "I hope not." Imani somberly whimpered before resting her head in Jillian's lap.

RING. RING!

{Tiffany Lane}
215-555-9711

"Hold up! Shhh! This is, Tiffany!" I said quieting the abundance of ill-fated speculations. "Hello." I calmly said. "What's all the noise?" I promptly asked unable to clearly hear Tiffany because of the noises behind her. "Is that someone screaming? Tiffany! What's that noise?" I said becoming impatiently frustrated. I rose from the couch to give myself more room to move with my agitation. "Screaming?" Hassan fretfully asked before rising to approach me. "Who's screaming, O?! Is it, Quentin?" Hassan harshly questioned as he began to get flustered. "Tiffany! What's going on?" I tensely inquired as Imani rose to take my side. "Tiffany! Where are you?!" I desperately questioned as Tracey materialized to comfort my other side. "Omar!" Tiffany hysterically cried out. "What?!" I frantically snapped as I began to really think the worst. "What is it?! Say something!" I firmly demanded before raising my foot to push the coffee table from in front of me to alleviate the feeling of confinement. "Tiffany!" I desperately yelled as Hassan attempted to take my phone.

"Hello." a male's voice timidly pronounced. "Hello! Who this?!" I neurotically shouted at the unknown man. "Hey guy. Listen, she just dropped her phone. She's losing her shit, right now. Her son was just in a car wreck, and we think he may have died." the man sullenly disclosed. "Omar! Omar, our baby!" I could hear Tiffany passionately yell as I dropped my phone and fell to the floor.

[Roger Goodell]
With the thirty-second pick in the 2020 NFL
draft… the Miami Dolphins select,
Quentin Gregory, Linebacker, Penn State University

CPSIA information can be obtained
at www.ICGtesting.com
Printed in the USA
BVHW072258120121
597682BV00001B/3